# SPIRALCHAIN

## Book 3: Metalbreaker

JEREMIAH L. SCHWENNEN

Spiralchain: Metalbreaker


ISBN 978-1-542-51395-1

For Tom, who never gives up on me. I will always return that favor.

Also,
For Tasha and Jeremy, who have brought good energy into my life.
For Tyson, who makes me laugh so hard it hurts.
For Andrew, who rises to every challenge I conceive.
For my colleagues, who make bad days better and good days grand.

And for the readers of Mindshaper, who have had the courage to take this next step on the journey with me.

**Novels of the Spiralchain**

*Gatemaker*
*Mindshaper*
*Metalbreaker*
*Fatewaker (Forthcoming)*

# 1
## Core

*The Lewis High Alumni Choir sounded amazing.* Graduates from twenty-two classes gathered together in their ivory and green robes and sang a rousing medley of time-honored favorites. The auditorium was packed to capacity, with family and friends all crammed into tight seats waiting to see this momentous event.

Becky was tragically uncomfortable in her own robes. The ugly square cap fit poorly on her head, and the tassel, dangling in her peripheral vision, annoyed her. She scanned the crowd and saw to her utter dismay that JC was sitting with her parents. He had one hand in his pocket, and she knew what he was hiding there—in spite of her stern warnings.

No one else was here to see her, and that suited her just fine. As much as Becky enjoyed being the center of attention, this was a day about much more than just her stumbling across the stage in a too-long robe to pick up a diploma. Today was, as the graduation speaker had so eloquently explained, a day of transitions.

As the choir wrapped up their final number, Becky looked over the three hundred young men and women that comprised her graduating class. There were mortal enemies there, to be certain, but also people she could almost call friends. Adam was there—two rows in front of her, alphabetically—and somewhere in the back she knew Todd was present as well.

It was almost impossible to believe they were really graduating. After thirteen years of school, this chapter of their lives was about to close. The future was big and scary and almost limitlessly possible, but for right now it took everything she had to keep focused on not crying.

Why was she so weepy? She never really liked this place, or the vast majority of these people, and yet here she was, teary-eyed and lips quivering.

She closed her eyes as the principal stood at the podium, enumerating the advantages of a first class Lewis High education. She'd heard the speech before, at dress rehearsal, and it had almost made her cry then too. Cautiously, she sent her thoughts out, riding the gentle, subtle magic of mindshaping that she had inherited from Tatyana last summer. She felt Adam's familiar mind and tapped softly on its periphery.

"I'm trying to listen, Becky," Adam replied tersely.

"Tough. If I listen to this one more time, I'm going to sob and that is not how I want to end my career here. So I need you to tell me a story." Becky smiled. She loved this secret channel of communication and the closeness that it had brought between her and Adam and between her and JC. She was always careful not to push it too far—wary of the permanent, always-open connections that could form if she was reckless.

"About what?" Adam asked.

"About what comes next. After we cross that stage."

Adam was silent for a moment. The band started to play, and the students in the first row—those with the brilliant gold honor chords draped around their necks, proceeded to the stage. Adam replied, "It's going to be fine."

"Tell me, please," Becky said. "I said please. You know how rare that is."

"Tonight we'll have an amazing graduation party. People we barely ever talked to will show up and act like we were best friends for years. Our family members will give us silly gifts, and cash, and then we will spend the summer living like kings." Adam's voice was warm and encouraging in Becky's mind.

"Then? What after that?"

"Then we'll go to college. You'll go be a brilliant architect in Ames, and I'll go be a modestly successful mathematician in Michigan. Then we'll graduate and get married to the loves of our lives and live happily ever after." Adam paused for a second as the next row of students proceeded towards the stage. Names were read one by one as they crossed, and the crowd erupted into cheers each and every time—even though the teachers and administrators had stressed, adamantly, that applause be held for the end.

"Why aren't we going to school together?" Becky asked for what felt like the hundredth time. College was a big deal, and she struggled with the idea of trying to do it alone. She hadn't done much without Adam by her side in years, and she worried about standing on her own. It made her sick to her stomach, and nothing made it better.

"Scholarships, Becky. Money rules the world. But I don't understand why you are so worried. I'll be there with you all the time! I've got the power to bend space, for God's sakes!" Adam's row stood. "You're stuck with me. Don't worry."

He sent back no further thoughts as his row climbed the stairs at the side of the stage, and Becky watched with pride. There had never been any doubt in her mind that she and Adam, and even Todd, would graduate high school. When Adam's destiny as a Gatemaker had been revealed, everything had grown harder, but still she believed. They had barely made up the credits missed when they were drawn to the worlds of Murrod and Onus as a result of that discovery—Becky's grade point average never truly recovered from the absence. Then last summer they had endured so much on the futuristic world of Rettik but also here at home. Her father still carried many scars from that summer, and all of them carried the weight of Jonas and Tatyana's deaths in their hearts.

Last summer changed everything, and now today would complete the metamorphosis. Today they would leave behind them childish things and become, in the eyes of the law, their parents, and perhaps even each other, adults.

The names were read. The students marched across the stage. Row by row, Becky drew nearer the moment of transition. She looked back over her shoulder and saw Todd, solemn as always, talking to no one. After today, only JC would be left here, trapped for one last year as a student in these halls. She would go away to school, only an hour away, but away nonetheless, and life would go on. There would be no more adventures on other worlds—that was all behind them.

Tatyana was dead. The Obliviates were defeated. Jonas was dead. Peace had been restored to Onus. Whatever destiny the Wyr had written for the Children of the Line, it was at an end.

The time had come to become something new.

Becky's row of students stood, and they shuffled slowly towards the stage. She winced as the name of a classmate was grossly mispronounced and then, as though time were skipping whole beats before her, she was standing at the foot of the steps. She climbed them, one by one. She walked across the stage, one foot in front of the other, and shook hands with the principal as her name was read. She took her diploma in one hand and looked back, quickly, at the crowd. As she scanned out, she saw Steven first.

He was in uniform, assisting with security at the event, and he was handsome as ever. He'd been hitting the gym hard the past few months, and though Becky had never seen him in that light before, she had recently been forced to admit how much she cared for him. Part of that, she was sure, was the legacy of Tatyana wiggling around in her mind, but she was happy he was there. He smiled at her and nodded his head, and she continued her scan of the crowd. She saw her parents again, standing, clapping, and then she saw JC stand, hollering at the top of his lungs, and pull his hand from his pocket.

Clutched tightly in his fist was an air horn. He squeezed the trigger and a massive roaring sound issued forth, shaking Becky to the core. She wanted to wince, or cry, or shake her head in embarrassment, but instead, to everyone's shock but no one's greater than her own, she laughed.

¤~¤~¤

Steven Mollison sat across the desk from his boss and said, very calmly, "I quit."

The chief of police leaned forward and said, "Bullshit."

Steven shook his head. "I've been thinking about this for months, sir. I just don't think this is the right place for me anymore."

The chief whispered conspiratorially, "This isn't about those sexual assault charges, is it? Those were dropped, Steven—expunged."

Steven smiled. "It isn't that sir. I wish it was that easy to explain, actually. My heart just isn't in it anymore. It's been a hard year, and I need to try my hand at something new."

The chief was silent for a while before asking, "Does this have anything to do with the reference call I got last week?"

"Could, sir. I need a change." Steven stood up and placed his badge and his pistol on the desk. "I hope we can end on good terms."

The chief reached out and slid the badge and pistol towards him, dropping them down into a desk drawer. "You were a fine officer, Mollison. I hope that this new outfit knows what it's getting."

"They know, sir. And thank you, for everything." Steven stood up and extended his hand, which the chief shook vigorously. A few moments later, Steven was standing outside, enjoying the late May weather and wondering if he was making the right choice.

He walked home—he had driven his patrol car to the station, after all, and as he passed the Veil Building he couldn't help but look up. More than forty floors above street level, that building was the place where she had died. There wasn't a day that went by when he didn't think about Tatyana, about her sacrifice and the events of that night, but those memories no longer wore at him as they once had. Over the past ten months, his memories, his love, of Tatyana had grown no weaker. She did not fade, and while that was a blessing it was also a curse. Every day the pain of her loss was fresh, but so too was the memory of her presence in his life. He struggled to cope with it.

His phone rang, and he answered absent-mindedly.

"So is it done?" Nathaniel Candor's wheezy voice asked pointedly.

Steven grunted. "I'm all yours."

"This is a big deal, Steven. Without you on board, I would never have dared to try it. Someone has to be in charge of security, and the right man for the job was Jonas. Without him, I had given up on the plan altogether until you mentioned you were thinking about leaving the force." Nathaniel explained. "I think this is for the best though. I think it'll be good for you."

"I hope so, Nathaniel. Is everything taken care of on your end?" Steven asked, hoping to change the subject. Everyone in his life was worried about what was 'good for him.' His mother was constantly nagging at him, his next-door neighbor was on his case—everyone wanted to fix him. They didn't understand what he was going through. There was no moving on, there was only acceptance. In ten months, that acceptance hadn't yet come... and he wasn't certain it ever would.

"My sources tell me the formal acceptance of the bid, and resultant transfer, will be official July 1. The funding is all in line. We'll be able to stay in operation for a good fifteen years with the endowment that you and Becky arranged. My lawyers have assured me that everything is legal, although I'm still pretty sure I don't want to know how you did it." Candor coughed. "It is legal, right?"

"Legal enough. You're right, Nathaniel, you do not want to know the details." Steven smiled. "Suffice it to say, I'm very happy to be the new head of security for the Alders Project."

"And we're happy to have someone with your unique talents, Mr. Mollison," Nathaniel said. "Enjoy your week off, Steven. We've got a lot of work to do if we're going to pull this off."

Steven ended the call and slipped his phone back in his pocket. These were interesting times, and in a way he was glad to be a part of them. But he wished he wasn't a part of them alone.

He looked around to ensure that no one was watching and then stepped off the sidewalk and knelt down next to a large potted tree in the plaza that surrounded the Veil Building. Once out of sight, he flexed the muscles of his mind that commanded his own brand of magic, shadowbending, and allowed the shadows to carry him home.

¤~¤~¤

"We have to talk," JC said calmly as Becky lifted her bedroom window. He stood outside her window in a pair of blue jeans and a white sleeveless t-shirt, barefoot. His left hand rested on the windowsill while his right was tugging absently at the red metal chain that encircled his neck.

Becky sighed. She was still dressed, in spite of the near-midnight hour, and she took a step back from the window and gestured for JC to climb inside.

"Is there some reason this couldn't wait until morning?" Becky asked. "Our late night window conferences have not, historically, been our finest hours."

"I've been doing a lot of thinking since your graduation party," JC said carefully. He climbed through the window and landed, soundlessly, on the carpeting of Becky's floor. He looked around at her room and saw that she had been making progress on packing.

"And what have you been thinking about?" Becky asked.

"You seem to be in a hurry to leave," JC said, gesturing to the boxes in the corner. "And there's a promise you made that I want to see kept."

Becky arched an eyebrow. "What promise would that be?"

"I want to go back to Onus," JC said. He grabbed hold of his collar and said, "It's time to get this thing off."

"Are you sure?" Becky said. "When we talked about it, things were really intense, and I didn't know if you really meant it."

JC sat down on Becky's bed and grabbed her hand, pulling her down beside him. "Do you know what I've learned about fear, Becky?" He closed his eyes and squeezed her hand tight. "I learned that fear is bigger than we think. For the year and a half that I've had this thing around my neck, I haven't been afraid. But I didn't know what else I was giving up."

"I don't quite understand," Becky said, squeezing his hand back.

"Fear is complicated. It's worry, and anxiety, and..." JC trailed off. For many beats of his heart, they sat in silence. Then, in a voice like a whisper, he said, "And grief. We've lost people, and I haven't cared, Becky. Jonas died in the hospital, and we went to his funeral and everything, and I just didn't care. I didn't cry."

"Not everyone cries, Joe. That isn't the result of magic metal. That's just who some people are." Becky leaned over and rested her head on his shoulder. She inhaled the scent of him and sighed softly. She wasn't always sure what the future held for them as a couple, but she was, as always, glad that they were together now.

"I do. I did. I mean, I used to. Cry. I used to do a lot of things that I don't do anymore. We helped the Metalbreakers escape from Murrod, Becky. They live on Onus now, with Jara and Duke Rega and all of the people who think we're superheroes or whatever. I want to ask them to take it off."

Becky whispered softly, "Adam won't go for it."

JC nearly shouted, "What does that even mean? He's the damn Gatemaker—it's his job!"

"He's reluctant to leave home again, Joe. You know that. Ever since we beat the Obliviates, he's been nervous about opening the gate again. Since Mathias left, he hasn't even considered it. Things got so bad for his family in Ashfield after the last time... I don't think he'd do it just for you." Becky sighed. "But we can ask."

"Then maybe he doesn't have to do it just for me," JC said. He put a hand on Becky's knee. "Maybe he can do it for *everyone*."

"What are you thinking?"

JC held up his right hand with three fingers displayed. "Tatyana, Adam, Steven. Three Children of the Line. There are three more, right?"

Becky nodded. "That's what the records of the Wyr on Onus said."

"So we need to find the others. You are all so gung-ho to move on from Des Moines and go be grown-ups, but that's a pretty big chunk of unfinished business. Jonas is gone, but we can finish his job. We can find the others." JC smiled. "He can't say no to that. It's his destiny!"

Becky said, "It might work. He might go for that."

JC stood up and turned to face Becky. Then he dropped to one knee and grabbed her hand, holding it tight in both of his. "I want to ask you to marry me, Becky Hanson. But I'm not going to. I won't do that until I can overcome my fear, my nerves, on my own. Help get me to Onus, and let's find out what kind of man I am without this red crutch around my neck."

Becky, eyes wide and just a bit bleary with sudden, unshed tears, said, "Then let's go to Onus."

JC stood up and leaned forward, kissing Becky and pressing her back down on to her back on the bed. They didn't say anything more that night, but it was quite some time before Joe climbed back out of the window.

¤~¤~¤

"I don't feel great about this," Adam said quietly. No one was particularly listening to him, of course—this entire trip was being made with virtually no consideration for Adam's feelings on the matter.

He sat in the rolling chair behind the control desk in the Artifact Chamber—the over-sized sub-basement room of the Army Post Road installation where the massive Spiralgate was kept hidden away from the world. Three spotlights illuminated the metal bands that comprised the device—circles of dark gray Bindmetal that ran vertically, pinned together at an invisible pole like lines of longitude on a globe. Only Adam could bring the gate to life and connect the glowing portal that would form to other worlds. He was being asked to do so now, and he had agreed—reluctantly.

"You promised," Becky said. She was standing nearest the device, one hand carrying a large red suitcase and the other holding tightly to JC's hand.

"That was a long time ago. Things have changed since then—life here isn't as awful as it used to be. When we all decided we would leave again if you asked, that was because we wanted to run away from life here. I don't feel that way anymore." Adam put his feet up on the control desk. "Besides, things have just finally calmed down for my family. You weren't the ones getting called in for questioning by weird-ass government people for six months of your life, or having your parents accused of terrorism, or watching your whole life teeter on the brink of ruin. The last time I opened this door for us, I was stupid, and it almost cost me, and my family, everything. I don't understand exactly why the feds dropped the investigation, but they did—and now you're asking me to put the peace we've finally known at risk again. It's not... it's not wise."

JC turned away from the Spiralgate and said, "Dude, I get that. Your life may be all sunshine and whatever-the-hell now, and I'm glad, but I need this. I have asked you for like one thing, ever. This isn't like last time. We're being smarter. Safer. We've got good cover stories with our families and no witnesses to rat us out. Why are you bitching about this so much?"

"Mostly, he's bitter that I can't go with," came a voice from the corridor outside the room.

Adam smiled and put his feet down, standing and rushing to the door to greet Todd. Todd was wearing a white t-shirt and a pair of blue basketball shorts, and unlike Adam, Becky, and JC, he didn't have anything else with him. No bag or suitcase or anything. Adam's heart fell.

"I thought maybe you changed your mind," Adam said, giving Todd a quick peck on the cheek.

"Sorry. I have some things here I have to take care of, and I wasn't really that big of a fan of Onus in the first place. You guys will be fine. And if things get really rough, you can pop back here and grab me. No big deal." Todd nodded his head towards Becky and Joe. "You two look ready."

"I was ready three days ago," JC grumbled.

Becky let go of JC's hand and took a few steps towards Adam and Todd. "You didn't see any of the others on your way in, did you?"

Todd shook his head. "Sorry."

Becky shrugged. "He'll be here. I'm sure of it. I'm just glad we actually know what we're getting into when we go through the gate for once. It seems like every time we've ever gone through, we've been running ragged. This time is different. And it might even be fun," Becky glared at Adam, "if someone pulls the stick out of his ass."

JC choked back a laugh from across the room.

Adam rolled his eyes. "Yeah, I can't wait to get this trip started," he mentioned. Sarcasm dripped from his words.

A moment later, three more people entered the room. Nathaniel Candor lead the trio, his hairline even more receded than when last Adam had seen him. It had been several months since they had last all gathered at Candor's house, and time was certainly wearing heavily on the Director. Of all of them, he had taken Jonas' death the hardest.

Close behind Candor were two other familiar faces. Ervin Jaske, wearing his plain white lab coat as always, entered the room and immediately went to the control desk, not bothering with any pleasantries. Ervin wasn't the most social of the rare few individuals that knew the truth of the gate, but he was brilliant. He kept things running smoothly here, and he would do so again today when Adam opened the portal. Without Ervin monitoring the Obliviator to ensure that it was operating as required, each opened gateway ran the risk of allowing more of the demonic Obliviates back into the world. That was a risk Adam was not willing to take—and it was why it bothered him so much that no one was hesitant to jaunt off to another world again.

The last new arrival was the one they had been waiting for—Steven. Steven wore tan cargo pants and a black t-shirt, and he carried no gun or badge. It was strange for Adam to imagine that Steven wasn't a cop anymore. That was the defining characteristic of the tall Shadowbender, at least as far as Adam was concerned. Steven was a few years older than Adam, and his freshly shaven face was slightly angular. He looked angry, even when he was not. They had never been particularly close. It was possible that Steven's presence was another reason Adam was so reluctant to take the plunge and head back to Onus.

"I didn't exactly know what to pack," Steven said, lifting up the duffle bag he was carrying. "I've never gone through this thing before."

"I'm sure you'll be fine," Becky said, smiling. "No beard?"

Steven blushed slightly. "Trying something new."

"It looks good. I mean, I like it," Becky said. She looked away from him uncomfortably and adjusted the loose-fitting red t-shirt she was wearing.

"Less flirting, more traveling to other worlds, people," JC said impatiently. He still stood at the base of the Spiralgate. He had a simple backpack with him, by far the smallest luggage of any of them, but he made up for it with the pair of energy rifles that he carried slung over his shoulders. The straps of the rifles crisscrossed over the threadbare gray sleeveless t-shirt he was wearing.

Adam whispered in his mind to Becky, "Is there something I should know about?"

Her response came quickly and, he thought, nervously. "No. Why?"

"Never mind," Adam said. He felt Becky close the connection—which was, in and of itself, unusual—and he turned to Todd.

"I'm going to miss you like crazy. I don't know how long we'll be gone, but it should only be for a few days. Just long enough to find a Metalbreaker to help Joe and to find Jara to help us figure out who the other Children of the Line are." Adam leaned in and rested his forehead against Todd's. "I don't want to leave you," he whispered.

"Tough. I'll be here when you get back. I just can't go running off to Onus right now. Maybe we'll sneak off to some other world later this summer. I don't know." Todd took Adam's chin with one hand and brought him in for a deep kiss. "I'll see you soon."

Adam forced a smile and turned back towards the Spiralgate and the others.

"It's bad timing, Steven," Director Candor said to Steven as Adam walked past. "Things are very sensitive right now. Are you sure this is necessary?"

Steven nodded. "We'll never make this world completely safe until we know who the rest of the Children of the Line are. Adam and I and these three people we haven't found yet have some kind of purpose, allegedly, and I'd rather get that done with once and for all so we can all get back to living our lives."

Candor said nothing more, and Steven stepped up beside Adam. Immediately to Adam's left was Becky, and beside her Joe. They all stood, watching the dormant Spiralgate and waiting. Adam looked back over his shoulder and asked Ervin, "Is everything running right?"

Becky nodded, but Adam didn't understand why.

Ervin replied, "The Obliviator is running within the parameters we established. You are free to activate the artifact."

Adam closed his eyes and willed the glowing symbols of his magic to appear. Dozens of complex shapes manifested in his imagination and, he knew, in the air around him for all to see. He strung the shapes together, transposing and arranging them in ways that allowed them to form the all-important geometric keys that unlocked the Spiralgates of all the worlds. There were 49 remaining gates in the Spiral of Worlds, and Adam knew the coordinates to them all. The first key he built unlocked the single Spiralgate on his own world, a place the other worlds called Core, and as he did so, he opened his eyes to see the wonder before him.

The Spiralgate started to spin. The bands contracted slightly, warping and shifting in such a way that they could all spin around their invisible axis without touching. As they built speed, a humming sound issued from the gate itself—the sound of the Obliviator, installed in the ceiling of the room and channeling its technological magic down into the gate. The bands moved faster and faster, beginning to glow first blue and then white. Once they reached their peak speed, their individual shapes were indistinguishable from the dome of radiance. Then the dome began to lift, elevating inch by inch until three-quarters of a sphere of white light burned before them all. The spotlights in the room failed—as all the power would, for a few moments—and Adam said to everyone, "It's open."

They filed in one at a time, Joe first. Adam crossed the threshold into the sphere of light behind Becky, with Steven close behind him.

Inside, the sphere of light revealed itself to be a tunnel, a snaking corridor of blue and white energy, solid to the touch but disorienting to the senses. It curved away from Earth, from Core, and tunneled through the universe, seeking the initial location Adam had signaled—Onus. Of the seven gates on Onus, Adam was most familiar with the Weigar, the gate nearest to Rega Holc, the seat of the Council government and, he hoped, a good place to start the search for both Jara and the Metalbreakers.

As they walked quietly forward, Adam saw Steven come up beside him, a look of wonder on his face. Adam asked softly, "It's pretty neat, isn't it?"

Steven whispered, "Oh yeah. I remember, a little, what Tatyana felt when she did this. I could feel her awe, through our link. But it isn't the same as actually being here. How long does it take to get to the other side?"

Adam held out his hand and wobbled it from side to side. "It varies. It varies a lot. It feels like about an hour, usually—but you can make it much longer. In fact, you can make it last forever." Adam thought back to his last time in Rega Holc and the horrible battle, within a portal, against Lyda. He'd left her there, in an endless transit corridor. His stomach churned. Maybe his reasons for not wanting to return to Onus were less noble than he had claimed...

A voice from behind them said, "But it goes much faster with good company."

Adam spun around to see Todd standing there. He had nothing in his hands, but his dark skin gleamed with sweat.

"What are you doing here?" Adam shouted, turning and grinning.

Todd pointed one thumb back over his shoulder. "Changed my mind. Almost too late though—that door slammed shut pretty quick."

"The gang's all here then," Becky said from up ahead. "Maybe now we can all put our heads together and make a plan? Once we get to Rega Holc, we'll have to connect with the Duke. He might know where Jara and her grandfather are."

"No need," Joe said, stopping to turn and face the others. He held one hand out, closed, and Adam quickened his pace to see what was in the hand. As Adam drew nearer, Joe opened his hand to reveal a small metal and glass compass resting on his palm.

"I didn't know you still had that," Adam said, impressed.

Joe smiled. "Some of us don't need magic powers to be badass." Then he scratched absently at the chain around his neck and added, "And it's time I prove it too."

¤~¤~¤

As the light of the Spiralgate faded from Nathaniel's vision, and the power in the Artifact Chamber slowly came back on, The Director leaned heavily on the control desk.

"What's the matter, sir?" Ervin asked as he stifled a yawn.

"It's damn bad timing, Ervin. Damn bad. With the proposal review coming up, we really needed all hands on deck." Nathaniel sighed and rubbed at his eyes with one pudgy hand. "I'm nervous."

Ervin nodded and stood slowly. He gestured upwards, to the ceiling or, Nathaniel supposed, the installation above them. "I'm not certain this is even necessary, Nathaniel. Why couldn't we just leave things the way they were?"

"Because the Fourth of July changed everything, Ervin. I burned off every bit of political capital I could get my hands on to bury our involvement in the Obliviate fiasco—but people noticed. Powerful people. We have to get the Spiralgate out of government control before those people put two and two together and realize it's here. Top secret just doesn't mean what it used to."

"I'm surprised you convinced the brass to release this place," Ervin commented. "They used to care about it an awful lot."

Nathaniel said simply, "That was before Lorenz went bad. Your own reports verified that no useful intelligence has come out of this place in years, and General Horton struck the Embrew event from the records. As far as anyone outside this room and the General's immediate staff know, this machine hasn't even come on since they built the installation around it. Horton was happy to recommend the decommissioning."

Ervin sighed. "I'll miss the pension, sir."

"You and me both. Sacrifices for the greater good, Ervin. It took me too long to realize that what we're talking about *is* the greater good. In four weeks the APR installation will go to public auction. We'll spend a very pretty penny of the Alders estate money that Steven and Becky acquired for us, and we'll buy this place lock, stock, and barrel." Nathaniel joined Ervin in walking out of the Artifact Chamber.

"Is it strange that doing the right thing required doing the wrong thing first?" Ervin asked.

Nathaniel shrugged. "I've discovered that having your daughter possessed by a shadow monster broadens your tolerance for gray areas considerably."

# 2
## Onus

*They emerged from the Spiralgate on the sandy beach of Onus' northern coast.* As far as JC had been able to determine during their last visit, Onus was really just two continents, with the incredibly unimaginative labels of 'the northern continent' and 'the southern continent,' and that meant they were, essentially, at the top of the world.

"Rega Holc is that way," JC said, pointing off to the west and a path that was familiar to most of them. "But the compass says we need to go that way," he pointed to the southeast, towards the great range of mountains that loomed across the horizon.

"Is it pointing to Jara or to the Metalbreakers?" Adam asked. "I kind of feel like Jara is the higher priority right now."

"Interestingly enough, it's my compass, so I'm the one calling the shots this time," JC said sternly. "Metalbreakers first. I've waited too long to get this thing off."

Becky grabbed JC's hand. "Both things are important. Can you tell which of them is closer? Maybe we can make up our minds that way?"

Adam slung his bag of clothes over his shoulder, hooking his thumb through the strap, and said, "It doesn't really matter. We can do it your way, Joe. We'll walk for a while so I can get my bearings, then I'll try to crossgate us to your Metalbreakers." Adam, Todd, and Steven started trudging through the sand towards the pebble-strewn plain that swept away towards the south.

"I'm proud of you, Joe," Becky said as she and Joe followed in their footsteps. "But try not to bite everyone's head off. That's my thing, not yours. We're on Onus now—it's only a matter of time before we all get what we wanted."

JC didn't say anything. He looked up at the mid-day sky and tasted the sea-salt in the air. Growing up in land-locked Iowa, he'd had very little opportunity to experience the ocean, and he found he liked it. Of course there was lots to like about Onus. It was a medieval world, a place of farmers and villagers, of swords and spears, of castles and keeps. The complexity of life back home was absent here, and he loved that. It was exchanged for a curious blend of savagery and civility, but it was a combination that suited him quite well.

As they walked, JC reached into his pocket and pulled out his cellphone. A tiny light flashed in the corner to indicate that it was receiving no signal, and he smiled. "You know how we're on these things all the time back home? It feels like the world would stop spinning if I didn't have my phone on me.

But the minute, the first damn second we step foot in another world, I let it go. It's like the habit just vanishes. Why is that, do you think?"

Becky shrugged. "I've never really thought about it all that much."

"It's a crutch, I think. I think the phone is a crutch we use to make ourselves feel important or connected or whatever. But here, or Rettik, or wherever we end up next, I don't need a crutch to hold me up and make me feel special. When we walk through Adam's lightshow, all of the sudden we're all special." He stopped walking and turned back towards the Spiralgate. The great machine was now idle, sitting dormant and still. Beyond it, gulls flew low over the sea. With a heave, JC hurled his phone through the air, far from where they stood. It landed with a puff of sand somewhere quite a ways down the beach, and Becky elbowed him.

"What happens if someone finds it, Joe? What will they think? This world doesn't have anything like a smartphone!" Becky took a step towards where JC had thrown the phone, but he caught her firmly with one hand.

"They'll think, 'Hey, this piece of junk sure is useless!' and you know what? They'll be right." JC turned back towards the mountains. "Let's get moving. I've got to talk to a man about a pair of magic bolt cutters."

¤~¤~¤

Igar Holc was not an ugly city, but its appeal had been fading of late. Jara walked down the Avenue of Glass, munching on an apple. She wore a plain brown tunic and breeches—boy's clothes, as her mother and grandfather had both glumly pointed out—and her hair, grown long to the waist, was an unkempt mess. Glassworkers sat on stools outside the doors of their shops, blowing and shaping their wares as Jara strolled idly past.

The Avenue of Glass was Jara's favorite part of the so-called "Bridge City," and even this amiable, sometimes miraculous stretch of cobbled stones and brilliant, glittering glassworks had grown old. Jara lived in Igar Holc with her grandfather, the scribe Moultus, and her mother, Hessa, in a small, private estate provided by what Duke Igar called "the largess of the Wyr." It was a singularly boring existence for a girl who had come to revel in the daring excitement of life on other worlds and mortal danger. It seemed though that those days were behind her.

Yors had returned to the North, to his people, and once he left more than six months ago, life had begun its steady decline into lethargy. The visions that were Jara's birthright as a Wyr—a Fatewaker—were few and far between, and peace had settled across Igar Holc and the northern continent beyond its walls like a comfortable, well-worn blanket. There was no adventure to be had anywhere here, and the very notion of that left Jara feeling ill.

"Are you back again, girl?" Jort asked with a broad smile. He was perhaps the worst glassblower on the Avenue, but he was Jara's favorite. He was a scrawny man with burns running all along his dark-skinned arms. His hair was grown long and woven into a braid that he coiled around his neck in a fashion that he swore was common among the Dwellers in the Sands, his people. He always remembered Jara, and when he was feeling generous, which seemed to be his natural state, he would slip her one of his 'masterpieces.'

Jara nodded and stopped in front of Jort's shop. She looked at the small shelf where he displayed his recently finished pieces as they cooled, and she made a wry face. "Not going so well today, I see?"

Jort flicked his tongue out of his mouth in a mocking expression and replied, "Are you taller than you were yesterday?"

Jara blushed and turned away, raking the fingers of one hand through her hair. Jort knew how self-conscious she was about her height. Since coming to live here, after rescuing her mother from the dungeons of Hyrak Arn, back when she was an adventurer instead of a city girl, she had grown nearly six inches. None of the rest of her features, aside from her hair, had bothered to even attempt to keep up with her height, and she hated how she looked.

Jort put down the tongs he was holding and stepped from behind his counter to put a well-worn hand on Jara's shoulder. "I only tease because you tease so easily, Jara. I mean no offense."

She nodded and smiled. "I only tease so easily because I respect your artistry, Jort," she said as she pointed to the shelf. "Who else in Igar Holc could craft such wonderful... whatever those are?"

Jort could not restrain a great, cackling laugh. "They are Amryw. Dream shapes. You northern folk have no culture!" He picked up one lump of glass, vaguely shaped like a five-pointed star, and handed it to Jara. "My people see truth in our dreams, and we make that truth in whatever shape the Purpose places in our hands. I work glass, so my Amryw are glass. I dreamed of a shaking of the very world last night, and the pictures that lingered behind my eyes demanded to be made."

Jara turned the glass figure over in her hands and looked from it to the others on the shelf. There were five of them in total, mostly star-shaped and standing upright upon the bottom two points of the star. One was of dark, smoky glass, while the one in her hand was clear but flecked with blue swirls. One was quite short and crafted of somewhat lumpy violet glass, another elongated and glazed in sleek black glass that rolled down the top half and faded to droplets as it neared the base. The last was crystal clear save for a ringlet of red glass that circled the base of the top point of the star.

"I didn't know your people were so spiritual," Jara said.

Jort sighed. "We are so few, most know next to nothing about us. But I came to the mighty city of Igar to spread truth as much as to sell glass."

"I hope you are more successful at spreading truth than you are at selling glass," Jara said with another smile. "I don't think I have ever seen anyone buy anything at your shop."

"When a man makes Amryw, he grows accustomed to a certain degree of poverty," Jort confessed. "An Amryw speaks only to those who it is meant to speak to, and who is to say that person lives in Igar Holc? But I survive. It is the birthright of the Dwellers, they say."

Jara handed the figurine back to Jort and said, "I hope you find the one that these speak to."

Jort said nothing as he took the figure and placed it back on the shelf. Jara looked one last time at the figures sitting there then bowed politely at Jort and turned to resume her wandering. No one would be expecting her back at the house for a few hours yet, and she would enjoy the chance to stretch her legs and avoid the studies that her family insisted on inflicting upon her.

She took no more than a few steps away from Jort's shop when a powerful tugging drew her to a halt. She turned back and felt herself drawn to the shelf, to the figures. She walked back up next to them and picked up one of them—the clear one with the red circle. She looked at it carefully, and Jort said nothing, merely watching her.

"Joe?" she said softly. She placed the figure back down on the shelf and then picked up another—this time the violet figure. "Becky?"

Jara looked up at Jort and said, simply, "I think these are for me."

"Then they are yours," Jort said. His face was heavy, wrinkles creasing his usually smooth brow.

"What do I owe you?" Jara asked.

Jort shook his head. "Amryw are not purchased. They are given."

"Seems a silly way to run a business," Jara mumbled.

Jort did not reply, but quietly and carefully wrapped the figures in a length of fabric and bound them with a leather strip. Jara took the parcel and thanked the glassblower once more for his help.

"What do they tell you, if I may ask? I always wonder what whispers the shapes have for those they seek." Jort's eyes were wide.

"Two things, actually. They tell me that my friends are here, or are coming." Jara tucked the package up under one spindly arm.

"And the other?" Jort asked.

"That my mother's been doing something very bad. Again."

¤~¤~¤

"So do you just tell it to find a Metalbreaker? Because if that works, why the hell aren't we just sitting in Des Moines telling it to find Children of the Line?" Todd asked as they continued their trek into the Borrik Mountains. Adam had crossgated the group much closer to the mountains, but now that the peaks were upon them, he claimed it was much harder to safely open portals.

Becky was not a fan of the outdoors, but even she had to admit that the mountains were beautiful in the dusk light. Everything was purer, more majestic, on Onus. The smog and the soot and the industry and the commercialism of her own world was absent here, and that absence was something she could get behind. Like JC had said, maybe things were better here. She had certainly thought that when last they stood on the soil of Onus—back then she hadn't wanted to go home. Now, she was less certain what she wanted. Home was safe and predictable, but Onus was something bigger. She wasn't sure.

JC replied flippantly, "Gee, why didn't I think of that?"

"So what are you doing then?" Todd asked again, impatiently. Beside him, Adam kept looking around nervously. Becky almost darted into his mind to see what he was up to, but she decided against it. She was trying to respect everyone's privacy, but the better she got with these powers, the harder that became.

"There were a bunch of Metalbreakers that came to help in the siege of Rega Holc. One of them was a guy named Ambrek. That's who I am searching for. He helped when so many of the others blew us off, and that makes me think he might be interested in helping me now." JC checked the compass and then slid it back into his pocket. "I have actually thought this out."

"I'm not accusing you of anything," Todd said. "I'm making conversation."

"While all of you are conversing," Steven called from behind them, where he had fallen several yards back as he looked at every peak and hill like it was the discovery of the pyramids in Egypt, "Has anyone noticed that this place has two moons?"

Becky smiled. "That's nothing. One world we went to has three suns!" She looked to where Steven was looking, spotting the two moons of Onus hanging near one another, growing quite large and full, in the oncoming night.

Steven shook his head in disbelief. "I'm pretty certain I'll never get used to this."

Adam held up one hand suddenly. Everyone stopped, and Becky watched Todd's entire body tense and crouch into a kind of compacted, compressed posture—ready to pounce. JC quietly drew one of the energy rifles, the devices he affectionately called his Booms, up to his eye. He sighted slowly down the barrel as he pivoted, searching for whatever Adam had seen.

It had been nearly a year since their journey to Rettik, but their time in that war-ravaged place had not been forgotten. It almost chilled Becky to see the hardness that it had left in them all.

"There's something hidden up ahead. I can feel it, the space of it, but I can't see it. I've been feeling it for the last mile," Adam whispered, "But now I can feel movement. Becky?"

Becky nodded and closed her eyes, drawing the magic of the Kem into her mind and shaping it into a working that she cast out like a net, skimming the world around her. She swept her thoughts around, trying to catch any other, unfamiliar, minds—and she did.

She held up two fingers as she opened her eyes and pointed ahead, to their right.

The path they were following through the mountains was well traveled and well worn. They had crossed through the Underpass about an hour ago, and now they were in the narrow valley between two tall mountains. The place where she sensed the thoughts appeared to be the face of the mountain to their right, but something was not right there.

"You have about three seconds to show yourself before I laser your mountain in half," Joe shouted loudly.

Becky groaned softly.

"That not real word," grunted a deep voice from what appeared to be the solid face of the mountain.

"I'll show you a real word," JC said, aiming the weapon high—much higher than the source of the mysterious voice—and pulling the trigger.

The muzzle of the rifle blazed brilliantly in the slowly fading daylight, and a loud roaring sound rang in Becky's ears as it carved a dark line of slagged stone in the mountain.

When Becky looked back around, she noticed that Steven was missing.

"That is lasering," Joe said smugly, "and there's a whole lot more where that came from."

Without warning, the wall of stone shimmered, revealing an encampment honeycombed in the side of the mountain. A half dozen caves opened at various low elevations, and in the mouth of the lowest a massive man, easily the largest human Becky had ever seen, stood with a horrifyingly large crossbow pointed at them. His black beard and hair were a great tangle, but his deep-set eyes were bright and, she thought, wiser than his words would lead one to believe.

A moment later, a bolt from his crossbow sank into the ground a fraction of an inch from Joe's foot.

"That *crossbowing*, and much closer to hitting big mouth than lasering was to Yors," the big man said simply.

With a faint hissing sound, the shadows of the cave around the large crossbowman seemed to elongate and disgorge a new shape—Steven. His long, lanky limbs came up from behind the man and he brought one arm around the giant's throat while the other grabbed and dislodged the crossbow.

"It would be best if we both stopped shooting at one another," Steven said calmly. "I don't want to do anything unpleasant."

The large man—Becky imagined his name was Yors, because otherwise his last sentence made virtually no sense—grunted once, stopped struggling, and said softly, "Yors hate Rak."

"Yors needs a bath," Steven replied. "Tell your friends to stand down."

Yors stammered a bit, but Steven constricted his hold on the man's neck. The large man shouted out a single word, "Hob!"

From several of the tunnels, brief glimmers of light could be seen, and Becky saw Adam suddenly grab at his stomach as though seasick.

"They're flashing—short-range teleporting. A whole bunch of them. It's really screwing with the spatial field here," Adam muttered. "Why is it that everyone and their damn mother can do that but me?"

Todd, relaxing slightly, offered, "Get over it. You open doors between worlds. You win."

There appeared to be a stalemate for nearly a minute, but then, from the highest cave opening, nearly fifteen feet above where Steven held Yors, a soft voice called out, "I am the only one left. I won't fight you. Please let Yors go, and take what you came for. We have little to offer."

A man, tall, bearded, and fair of hair, emerged. While he looked only vaguely familiar to Becky, JC clearly recognized him. "Ambrek!" JC shouted. "Ambrek, it's me, JC! Do you remember me?"

The smith, looking worn and much older than when they had last seen him, climbed out of the cave cautiously. "Is it true? Are these really the Saviors of Rega Holc before me? And the Gatemaker who freed us all from the bondage of Murrod?"

Becky answered, "Of course it is. Do we look like we are from around here?"

Ambrek smiled nervously and replied, "No, indeed you do not. Yors—these are good people. Friends to us all."

"Yors not sure this how friends act," Yors replied, squirming in Steven's grip.

Steven looked to Adam, his expression seeking agreement, and Adam nodded. Steven released Yors and took a few careful steps back, hands outstretched. "Sorry. I was just trying to keep everyone from shooting everyone else full of holes."

"A respectable plan," Ambrek said, making his way down a narrow path along the face of the mountain from his cave to the cave at the path-level where Steven and Yors were. "Sadly, that is not how the people of these mountains tend to behave."

"Are you at war or something?" Adam asked. He pointed to the caves. "Those don't exactly look like the deluxe accommodations I would have expected from the greatest makers of stuff this world ever produced."

"We are, in fact, at war. War that has kept us from being able to put down roots and to start the lives here that we all so richly deserve. Perhaps your coming might aid us in that endeavor?" Ambrek extended a hand to Steven, who clasped it cautiously. "I am Ambrek, leader of the Free Smiths of Onus."

"And who exactly are you at war with?" Steven asked.

"The Jovs," Ambrek said sadly. "Our fellow Metalbreakers have turned against us. Not far from here, a new Jov Nought is nearly built, but instead of a place of learning and training, it is a fortress from which our new leaders issue demands and mete out punishment."

"You are actually fighting with the others?" Becky asked. "There are so few of you."

"That is the tragedy, young savior." Ambrek sighed. "After all we have been through, still all comes down to one simple truth—the same truth that damned us to Murrod thirty years ago. We Metalbreakers are ever at the mercy of the supply of Bindmetal, and the others will do anything to eliminate those of us who oppose their plan to reclaim all that was ever forged by Jov hands."

"Wonderful," JC said, stepping closer to Ambrek. "I've got some Bindmetal right here that they can have without any fight at all."

¤~¤~¤

The sea breeze was cool and carried the scent of dead fish—the legacy of the plague birds that had been sighted off the coast of Emer's Hope, most likely. Of all the scents of the sea, things to which Grell was quite accustomed, none was more repugnant to his senses than dead fish.

Grell Dorukast stood on the promontory cliff, the single vantage point of value on this rat-shit island, and peered out at the glimmering Endless Sea. The moons were bright and full tonight, and he watched their reflections dance upon the waves. In another life, perhaps, Grell had been a poet. He was not built with the parts of a poet, though—his square features and broad shoulders marked him a laborer from the moment he had been cut from his mother's dying womb. Wind whipped his long, pale hair and he closed his eyes, reveling in the moment.

It was finally finished. After ten years of careful work, of saving and of stealing, of crafting and of experimenting, he and his crew—bastards and brigands all—would set sail with the rising of the morning sun. He would leave Reef Circle behind him, quit once and for all of its petty potentates and its paltry bounty.

He shifted his focus from the distant sea to the single dock on the island. While most of the Starlight Islands were thriving hubs of travelers and wanderers, he had chosen Reef Circle as his shipyard precisely because no one came here. Here he and his covenant could build in peace.

On a typical day, back when Grell had first arrived here, back when he was a man of twenty summers and just learning about the burden his parents had left on his shoulders, three great ships and a half dozen darting vessels were tethered to the long, sturdy dock. Today, only one ship floated in the sheltered harbor. All others were gone—just as all other inhabitants of Reef Circle had been driven away or put to death. The work here could have no witnesses, save those sworn to Grell, and so he was the mayor of an abandoned island. In a few short hours though, he would set aside that empty title and instead claim the honor he was born to wield—that of captain.

The Razormaw was a great ship, long and large, but it was unlike any other ship that plied the Endless Sea. It had three decks: fore, main, and aft. It was carved of dark wood, with three masts thicker than any Grell had ever seen. Its hull was lined with smooth discs of polished metal, causing the ship to sparkle in even the feeblest of light, and at its front, where custom dictated a figurehead, there was a carving of a great, toothy mouth, wide open and ready to swallow all that came before it.

A crew of forty would be required to keep the Razormaw in fighting shape, and her six holds were wide and deep. Her sails, furled for now, were a rich night-blue in color, and when his prey saw that mighty ship plowing towards it, skimming the waves at his command, there were few that would dare stand against her.

The Starlight Islands were famed for the quality and quantity of pirates that called them home, but there was no pirate that could ever hold a candle to Grell. He was about to set sail not for ransom or for glory, but for a kind of vengeance that he could feel in his bones. The Razormaw would pass the seven arms of the Starlight Islands, of course—and he would take all he required from any he encountered—but their goal was far grander. The mainland—a place of mythological significance to so many of the superstitious men and women of the Islands—was his target.

He would claim the vengeance denied his father for the death of his mother. All those responsible would pay, and in the doing, the name Grell Dorukast would become legend.

"Dreaming?" asked a mocking voice. Grell did not turn—he had no need to look to know that his companion was Vediri. She came up beside him and put one bronze-colored hand on his shoulder. Rings adorned each of her fingers, and Grell swatted her hand away as soon as it touched him.

"It is important to remember the things we leave behind," Grell said gruffly. "After tomorrow, Reef Circle will be just another place beyond the horizon."

"Will you miss it?" Vediri asked. "Because I will not."

Grell shrugged his wide shoulders. He acknowledged his first mate, in more ways than one, by eying her carefully. She wore clothes he had not seen before—loose fitting garments of dark silk belted tightly at the waist with a sash of heavier red fabric. She was taller than Grell, which was saying something, but she was not a willow-thin woman like so many of the other females he had taken into the covenant. Vediri was a solid woman, a brawler and a biter, and her dark hair was short and drawn into tight braids that protruded from her head like spines on a puffer-fish.

"I wondered, at times, if you would see this through." Vediri asked softly. "We spent so long as shipwrights, is the fire for what must be done still burning?"

"Has my fire ever been unequal to the tasks that the damnable Purpose has placed before me?" Grell balled his hands into fists. "Have I ever failed at what I set my mind to?"

She said nothing. They had been together for so long, they rarely needed words. Most of the time that they spoke, Grell suspected, Vediri simply wanted to hear the sound of her own voice. It had been many years since they had last been lovers, but she was closer to Grell than anyone had ever been.

They stood watching the moons and the sea. Without words, Grell conveyed his resolve and Vediri accepted it. Tomorrow, the Razormaw would set sail, and the journey to destroy the ten Dukes of Onus would begin.

¤~¤~¤

"You're over-reacting," Jara's mother said calmly. They stood in the kitchen of the manor house that Duke Distat had provided for Jara, Hessa, and Moultus' use, and Jara's mother wore a long apron as she busied herself about the kitchen.

Jara, of course, disagreed with her mother's assessment. "I can't believe you did this to me!" Jara shouted. The noise would surely draw her grandfather out of his study, but she didn't care. Maybe Moultus would take her side—stranger things had happened.

"You deserve the chance at a normal childhood, Jara. I gave it to you." Hessa rubbed absently at the leather band that encircled her arm, and Jara considered, in a fit of anger, reaching out and plucking the band from her. Without the magic coin contained in that strap, her mother was... not well. No matter how angry Jara was, that was a line she would not cross.

"I'm not a child anymore, mother. I'm fourteen summers old!" Jara stomped once on the cold stone floor then realized that this particular behavior wasn't proving her point very well.

Hessa took a seat on one of the two wooden stools near the stove and folded her hands in her lap, kneading the stiff fabric of the apron nervously. Jara remembered that gesture well—it brought to mind watching her mother cook in the kitchens of Gar Nought. That felt like a lifetime ago.

"I wish you understood how hard this is for me," Hessa whispered. Her voice grew louder as she continued on. "I watched those visions, that magic, eat at my mother. There were days that she was barely herself at all. The magic of the Wyr will consume you, Jara. I don't want that for you."

"But," Moultus' voice, creaking but firm, came from the doorway of the kitchen, "that isn't your choice."

Jara's grandfather wore a simple gray robe, and his short stature and wrinkled flesh were capped off by a wild tuft of thin white hair. His eyes were sad, as they always were when anyone spoke of Jara's late grandmother.

"Give me back my power, mother," Jara said simply. "Things are happening, and I have to know about them."

Moultus entered the kitchen properly and stood between Jara and her mother. "How do you know this?"

Jara laid the parcel from the Avenue of Glass on the table and unknotted the leather strip, rolling the cloth out and revealing the small glass figures. "The Purpose was speaking to me through glassware," she said. She could not help but smile.

Moultus, eyes wide, leaned in to look at the figures. "What do they mean?"

"Adam is here, grandfather. The Gatemaker. Or he's coming. And the others. If a Child of the Line is coming back to Onus, something very important is about to happen." Jara looked to her mother pointedly.

"Very well," Hessa said sullenly. She lifted her hands from her lap and rubbed them together vigorously. After a few moments, a bright pink glow began to flicker and flash around her hands. A second later, the light vanished. "It is done."

Jara knew nothing else after the light vanished, as her mind was swallowed by an onslaught of vision and prophecy.

# 3
## Onus

*Steven ran his fingers across the smooth ring of white metal next to the cave entrance.* It was warm to the touch, unlike the cool stone of the mountainside. The sun had fallen well below the horizon, and the twin moons of Onus were bright and large high overhead. Steven tasted the night air and rubbed his hand absently at his chin. It had been several years since he last went clean-shaven, and he found that his face itched ferociously.

"What are you thinking?" Adam asked quietly as he emerged from the cave.

"It's too tight in there for me," Steven said. "And nerve-wracking. They don't need my help to stare at Joe's neck."

Adam nodded. "Checking out the scenery?"

Steven tapped the metal ring. It was a hand-length across and embedded flush with the stone. It made a deep ringing sound as he tapped it. "I know how Joe's collar works, erasing fear, and I know how the Spiralgate works, connecting worlds, but what else can this Bindmetal stuff do?"

"All that a Metalbreaker can imagine," an old voice croaked from above them. Steven looked up to see one of Ambrek's fellow Jovs hobbling down the narrow path. He was quite old and walked with a pronounced stoop. His head was bald and his clothes, like so many of the Jovs, were thick leather adorned with scorch marks and soot. "I am Houg, and I don't believe I've had the honor."

Houg finished his descent and extended a hand towards Steven. Steven took his hand and shook it firmly, surprised at the strength in the old man's grip. "Steven Mollison," he said as introduction.

"Rak?" the old man inquired, squinting his eyes. "And a strong one, I'd say."

Steven felt himself blush. This part of everything—the casual familiarity these people had with magic—was hardest for him to take. For too long he had looked upon his gift as a curse, as a promise of an early death. But now, since the destruction of the final Obliviate last year, he knew that this old man was right—he really was strong. But strength was not confidence. Not yet.

"And I'm Adam," Adam extended a hand towards Houg. The old man did not look away from Steven, but said pointedly, "I know who you are, Gar. I can smell a Gatemaker anywhere. And while I am thankful you rescued my people from our prison, I have no forgiveness or use in me for your kind."

Adam dropped his hand, and Steven could see the shock in his eyes. He attempted to change the subject, asking, "So Bindmetal can do anything you imagine, you said?"

"Aye," Houg gestured towards the ring of white metal. "Those pieces there are prepared to make a thing unseen. Other bits and scraps have been purposed in other ways. A Jov of a certain skill can fold any kind of magic, any kind of imagination, into the crafting of a piece of Bindmetal and the metal will hold that magic forever."

"It seems like, with power like that, you could build yourself better accommodations," Steven said. "These caves are rough living by any standard."

"Indeed they are. Would you care to see what is possible, for a Jov in his prime?" Houg asked in a low voice. "I would show you with your own eyes what Ambrek only dances around with words."

Steven looked to Adam inquisitively, and Adam shrugged his shoulders. "Sure," Steven said. "Will it take long? I don't want the others to worry."

"If the Gar," Houg said, still not looking directly at Adam, "can open a portal to a place I describe, it will take almost no time at all."

Adam replied, "Does that mean I get to go along?"

Houg snorted and stepped past Steven. He rested his hand on the white Bindmetal ring beside the cave entrance and hummed softly. A moment later, with a sharp popping sound, the metal leapt free of the stone and he snatched it up, squeezing it tightly in his hand. "We will be unseen. Still your tongues, though—this particular working masks nothing of sound."

A few minutes later, still without eye contact, Houg had described a location several miles deeper into the heart of the mountains. Steven watched as Adam drew the crossgate into existence, and he and Adam both followed Houg's shambling gait as they entered the disk of green light and emerged in the shadows of Jov Nought.

The academy of the Metalbreakers was new. It gleamed in the moonlight with the polish of a showroom-new car, and Steven was first taken by its beauty.

The structures themselves were low and cut of stone, organized around a central courtyard that they could easily see from their vantage point atop a cliff outside the academy. They were all encircled by a smooth and perfect circle of metal that was embedded in the stone of the ground around their home. This metal ring was far more complex than the ring of white metal Houg now carried. It was five rings inside of one another, the outermost white, then red, then violet, then green, then blue.

Inside the academy, within that ring but moving around freely from building to building in spite of the late hour, were dozens of Jovs. Most were men, all older than Steven, but once in a while he caught a glimpse of a woman, and these were of varying ages. They laughed and they joked, and they looked well fed. Everywhere there were glints and sparkles of metal, of Bindmetal, and it finally occurred to Steven that they were all making their way to the central square of their academy.

"What is happening?" Adam whispered.

"The Forge is in the square," Houg whispered back. "Every night, a new working is revealed. They gather to share in the wonder and the beauty of each other's work. It is the Jov way."

"But," Adam inquired, "I thought there was no Bindmetal on Onus. Wasn't that why your people were trapped on Murrod in the first place, in exchange for Bindmetal?"

Houg nodded.

"Then what are they crafting the new workings from?" Adam asked.

"Old ones," Houg said sadly. "As I am sure Ambrek told you, our brothers have fallen to pillaging and looting. They strip all those they come across for the treasures of the past and melt them down to create an illusion of the future."

"Is there that much Bindmetal just roaming around the world?" Steven asked.

"This isn't random stuff," Adam said suddenly. "Look at those rings in the ground—those must use pounds of material. Only the Council has this much Bindmetal. The Dukes and Duchesses of the great cities."

"Aye," Houg nodded. "Distat Holc fell to the armies of Hyrak, and it is not so very far from here. Brennid led the Jovs in a raid on the place most of a year ago, and cleaned it out. He took something noble and tainted it with selfish greed."

"I'm a little less familiar with everything, but can you tell me something else?" Steven asked. "Why are all of the Metalbreakers older? And why are there so few women?"

Houg said nothing. He looked up at Adam, finally, and said simply, "Take us back."

And so Adam did.

¤~¤~¤

Time was a river, always rushing onward. It was equal parts destiny and chance, but the two floated with different weight. Destiny was oil upon the top of the water, slippery and difficult to hold, but beautiful and cloying. Chance was the water itself, heavy and unpredictable. Together, churning and frothing, they rushed from the source, from the Purpose, to the mouth, the Rot. Time began and it ended, and it traveled in set courses, but its swirls and eddies were not always able to be known, even to those best accustomed to reading the river.

But like any river, it could be dammed. To stop the flow of water was unthinkable, unconscionable, but it could be done, with enough effort, with enough power. Time could be held back, or at least its components—fate and chance—could be kept at bay. But no dam extended ever upward and ever outward, and eventually the surging, crushing weight of the water would be too much.

Jara's mother possessed a power Jara knew little about. She could dam the tide—she could wake, or still, the connection any being felt to the Purpose. She could stir dormant potential to full talent, turning ordinary men and women into magicians of any order, but she could just as easily sever the bonds of destiny in one's life, ending the magic and maybe even more.

Jara did not know if this power was unique to her mother, unique to her mother's trauma at the hands of Hyrak, Lyda, and the others that answered to the black and red banner of their uprising, but she did know that it was a gift she herself did not possess.

But like the oil atop the water, destiny had floated to the peak of the dam and trickled over, sliding down the side of that dam in a shimmering cascade of multi-colored magic. It had found her in the form of glass lumps, but it had found her nonetheless. Jara was, like her mother and her mother's mother, of the Wyr, and destiny was her blood.

When her mother cracked open the dam she had built and allowed the natural order of the universe, of the Purpose, to resume its flow through Jara, all that the magic had wished for Jara to know in the months since her mother had surreptitiously stripped Jara of her gifts came back upon her in a hammering torrent of vision.

None of the images made sense. They were too many, too grand in scope, to separate. She saw so many familiar faces, and so many new ones, all bound up in anger and pain and rage and suffering. She saw suns blotted to darkness and cities shattered. She saw great hairy beasts speak in the tongues of men and she saw a writhing tangle of dragons, black and white and gold, hissing and biting at one another as they tumbled into an inky black abyss. She saw a helmet of heavy black metal, pointed and layered and revealing nothing of the one who wore it. She saw tears streaking the faces of her closest friends. She saw snow and ice and shelves of books. She saw open wounds burst into violent flame. She saw all of this and so much more. She saw six figures standing in a line. She saw a world slip free of its place in the universe and float, adrift and lost, towards something dark and terrible beyond her sight. She saw a bolt of blue light that neary blinded her.

Jara awoke on the floor of her mother's kitchen. Sweat soaked her skin and all of her clothes, and she found her head resting in her grandfather's lap. Her mother, with eyes heavy and sad, looked down at her and whispered, "I only wanted to spare you."

Throat dry—she believed she had been screaming, perhaps—Jara replied, "Something has happened. Something is wrong. Evil is at work in the worlds."

She looked up at Moultus and said, "I have friends coming. We need to get ready for them."

¤~¤~¤

Narred was a different man than he had been when Shayra first met him. For the year they had spent living in Kem Nought, he had grown warmer, gentler, and softer. While at first she had welcomed these changes in him, they no longer filled her with joy. She'd not realized it at first, but it was the hard edge of the man that had drawn her to him, in the beginning. This newness, this softness, worried her.

"How can you continue with this madness?" Narred shouted. He stood across the common room of the Flesh, the residential tower of the great crystal city of the Mindshapers, and he shouted in spite of her many protestations that he cease. In Kem Nought, there were few who ever had need of using their voice, for all save Narred could speak with their minds. And even he could communicate with her in such a way, through the link they shared, but when he was angry, he resorted to crass verbalizations.

"It is what must be done. I have forgiven you for the black deeds of your past, why can you not do the same for me?" Shayra implored. Above them, in the private levels of the tower, the eleven children that comprised the rest of the living Kem were sleeping, and she hoped they would continue to do so. All were now invested with the mind of an elder Mindshaper, so they would not grow frightened or fearful of the noise, but it was the content of his angry words that worried her more. If the others suspected how Narred felt about the work they were doing, they would surely demand he be sent away.

No matter how he wore at her nerves with his needling and fuming, she did not want him gone. She loved him, and he was a part of her even as she was a part of him. To be separated by distance would be too great a burden to bear. And so they quarreled.

"What I have done is actually *in* the past, my love," Narred folded his arms across his chest, "while you continue to carry out your sins."

"There can be no more talk of this," Shayra said sharply. "We will travel into the world again tomorrow morning and we will collect another child. They are out there—they always have been. When all of the lost are found, we will be free. Is that not what you want?"

Narred crossed the space between them and took Shayra's hands in his own. She looked into his dark eyes, and she saw past his crooked features. She saw his love for her, and his desire to atone for the darkness in his past. "Why can we not go now? Let the Kem name one of the others Collectress and wash your hands of this ghoulish work."

"I carry them with me," Shayra replied with a sigh. No matter how often she explained this, it never seemed to stick with Narred. "I cannot cast aside this duty any more than you could resist your master's command that day in the Source."

Narred released her hands, and Shayra felt icy walls of resentment slide into place in his mind. For one of her power it would be no challenge to melt past them, but she would not—she knew already what lurked behind them.

Narred was a creature of manipulation and advantage by nature—it was in fact one of the qualities she most enjoyed about him. He did not, however, like being the subject of such manipulation. When his master, the warlord Hyrak, had been defeated, he left a command, somehow born of Mindshaper magic, in Narred's mind to seek a way to make contact with him. Narred had done so—and in the doing, betrayed the trust of Shayra—to no avail. The call had gone out, but Hyrak had not shown his face anywhere in Onus in the long months since. The scar of that act, of Narred's trespass into the most sacred of places of the Kem, would never heal in either of their hearts. Perhaps Shayra was cruel to have brought it up—she knew that Narred was thinking worse of her, behind those icy walls.

"Then why wait for morning?" Narred said. "I can have the wagon packed in an hour. I would prefer to leave this place behind sooner rather than later. And I will help you to find another child to murder in the name of your people. And you can continue to believe that someday you will find enough that the others will release you from their service, but answer me truly, beloved—can that ever be possible? What number of resurrections must you perform before the last of the memories in your towers are satisfied?"

Narred stomped up the crystal stairs, leaving Shayra alone. She sat down at the table, crafted of glass, as all was in this beautiful academy, and wondered at his words.

"It is not murder," she whispered aloud. When the mind of a Kem, stored in the crystal well of the Soul tower, was invested into the body of a person, often a young child, with Mindshaper potential, the child did not die. But who the child was before the investiture was lost—of that matter there was no conjecture, no reversal. Was Narred right? Was it murder?

She was not certain. She was, however, certain that his last point had been well-struck. Hundreds of Kems' minds existed in the Soul, and others—far older—dwelled in the Source. Was it her task as Collectress to restore them *all* to bodies? Would it ever end?

She closed her eyes and placed these thoughts, these doubts, behind her mental shield. They joined other doubts and other worries, tucked safely away where her people could not see them. The private place of thought behind that protective barrier had grown quite crowded.

Shayra was a collector of children and of minds, of talent and of promise. Now, she was also a collector of doubts. Of fears.

¤~¤~¤

"This is bullshit," JC said, throwing his bag down on the cave floor. Torchlight filled the room with a warm glow in the early morning, and as Becky woke she saw that Todd, Adam, and Steven, also sleeping on mats upon the floor, were similarly roused by JC's shouting.

"I am sorry," Ambrek said softly. "I have consulted with my best men, and none of us have the talent required. Your necklace was the work of Jarrek, and his skill was significantly greater than any of ours. It will take someone of equal skill in the working of red Bindmetal to put an end to this working safely. We could destroy the metal, but to do so would have disastrous effects upon your mind."

"You probably knew that when we got here, didn't you?" JC shouted. "You just kept us busy so your old dude could try to sucker Adam and Steven into getting involved in your little civil war, is that it?"

Becky stood up and grabbed his arm. "Calm down, right now."

He glared at her, eyes wide and lip quivering with anger, but he said nothing. Becky continued to hold his forearm and looked away, towards Ambrek, to say, "That's not how it was, right Ambrek?"

"Of course not," the middle-aged smith replied. "I did not even know Houg took your friends to Jov Nought until an hour ago. We have no need of anyone else fighting our battles." Ambrek's words appeared directed past Becky and Joe, and she chanced a quick look behind them, where sure enough, the older Metalbreaker that Adam had told her about was standing.

"But where am I supposed to find someone who can take it off?" Joe asked. "Jov Nought? If we go there, will they do it?"

"If they got to keep the metal they might," Steven said. "That seems to be what everything is about with them."

Todd shook his head and stood up, extending a hand to help Adam do the same. "Risky."

"Why?" Steven challenged. "I believe what Houg told us. That was a town full of people who'd do anything to get their hands on more Bindmetal."

"And that's the problem," Becky said quietly. "Todd's right. It's too risky. Maybe someone there can break the chain and we give them the metal as payment and everything works out great. But maybe there isn't anyone that can, and they decide to take the chain by other means."

"I'm pretty attached to my head," JC muttered. "And I'd like to stay that way."

"But if we can't go to Jov Nought to find a Metalbreaker strong enough to do it, where can we find one? There aren't exactly Metalbreakers popping out of the woodwork anywhere else." Adam said.

Ambrek sighed. "Indeed. I fear that there may be no options for you, Savior Joseph."

"Or we've got to go to plan B," Becky said.

JC looked at her and said, "We have a plan B? When did we get that?"

"We had it all along, Joe," Becky chided. "I'd say our list of questions for Jara just got one longer."

A loud voice boomed from the back of the cave—beyond the light of the torches. "Jara?" it asked. Yors stepped forward into the light, larger than life and bleary-eyed. He had twigs and leaves tangled in his unruly beard, but his dark eyes were wide. "Yors want to see Jara again!"

"I don't know," Adam said hesitantly. "We try to travel pretty light."

"Yors help," the massive man said, pleading. He extended a hand, stout fingers stretched wide, towards Joe. A moment later, Becky heard a ringing sound issue forth from one of the links of chain around Joe's neck.

Yors dropped his hand, and sweat poured down his forehead and nose. Becky looked more closely at Joe's collar and whispered, "Do you feel any different?"

Joe shrugged. "Not really. Why?"

Becky reached out to touch the chain around his neck. It was made up of forty links of red Bindmetal, and they were usually warm to the touch, growing hotter as they worked harder to block fear from Joe's mind. One link though—the one from which she had heard the sound—looked different. It was slightly misshapen, stretched a bit thinner, perhaps even a bit brittle. But it was also, as she slid it around in her hand, cool to the touch.

"One of them is dead," she said.

Yors nodded and grunted in agreement. "Yors strong enough. Take long time, but Yors turn magic off."

"But Yors," Ambrek said. "You must be careful. The price..."

Yors nodded, whispering, "Yors know."

"Then Yors is sure as hell going with us," JC said, grinning. He gave Becky a quick kiss and then walked over to Yors and held up one fist.

Yors stared at his hand blankly.

"Don't leave me hanging, dude," JC said. With his other hand, he took Yors' giant hand and balled the fingers into a loose fist, lifting it up and bumping it against his own.

Yors smiled sheepishly.

Becky rolled her eyes and turned to face the others. "Are we ready to go then? Joe fires up the compass and we go find Jara?"

"No compass," Yors said, smiling. "Yors know where Jara lives."

"Dude, I could kiss you. I'm not gonna or anything, but I could," JC said.

An hour later, they had eaten a small meal with the Metalbreakers of Ambrek's faction and made promises to keep the camp's location secret. Ambrek apologized again for being of little help, and Becky and Adam consulted with him on matters of geography as Yors explained the location of Jara's new home. Igar Holc was far from any of the places they had visited on their last trip to Onus, and farther than any single crossgate that Adam had ever before built.

"I could do it as a string of gates, that might be safer," Adam offered. "Traversing a whole continent in one portal is a pretty big job. Lots can go wrong that way."

Becky acquiesced and together with a rough map that Ambrek sketched out for them, they plotted three portals. Adam would layer them one atop the other so that they never had to truly exit into the unknown countryside of Onus, and once he was comfortable and Becky was confident that he knew what he was doing, she left him to make his final mental preparations and went outside of the cave to see the others.

Todd was leaning back against the stone entranceway as Becky emerged, and he asked her, "Why is it so important to you?"

"Why is what?" she asked.

"Finding the rest of the Children of the Line. That's how you sold Adam on this whole trip, but I don't understand why *you* give a rip. The Obliviates are dead. That's the end of the story," Todd said.

"If you believe that, you're an idiot," Becky replied. "We have a destiny, and I'm pretty sure it hasn't happened yet."

"There is no 'we,' Becky. Adam has a destiny. Steven has one. The three names we came here to learn, they have one. But not *we*—not *you*." Todd narrowed his eyes at her. "Which is why you should have left well enough alone."

"Tatyana died," Becky said, her voice growing louder in spite of her best efforts to rein it in, "and she left her powers to me. So maybe I do have a part in all of this, Todd. More than you have, that's for damn sure."

Todd smiled. "One day, you are going to get exactly what you deserve, Rebecca."

"Is that a threat?" Becky asked.

Todd said nothing.

Becky couldn't resist. With a burst of power, she dove into Todd's mind, leaping into the black non-space of mental communication and summoning Todd to stand before her. He appeared in the formless blackness, faintly glowing with his own inner light, as Becky was, and he folded his arms across his chest.

"I wondered how long it would take you to do this," Todd said.

"Ever since the Fourth of July, you've been different, Todd. Encouraging Adam to apply to school in Michigan, pissing me off every chance you get—I'm sick of this mystery act you have going on. What's your deal?" Becky scowled and flexed her power, readying to force her way past Todd and deeper into his mind if necessary.

Todd, however, surprised her. He stepped aside and unfolded his arms, gesturing past him, towards the darkness beyond—towards his private thoughts. "I don't have a deal, Becky. I want what's best for Adam, and for all of you. If you really believe in his destiny—in yours, if you think you are going to be playing Tatyana's part—you'll let it come when it wants to come. All of this, coming here, trying to find the other Children, is meddling. Why can't Adam live his life like a normal person until he has no other choice? Why can't you just let that happen?"

Becky was uncharacteristically at a loss for words.

"I don't have a big secret agenda, Becky. I just know that the Purpose doesn't need us to tell it what to do." Todd closed his eyes. "Go ahead and look if you have to. I won't stop you."

Becky sighed and turned away from him. "No. You... you're right. I'm pushing things."

With a dismissive wave, Becky ended the mindshaping working and both she and Todd were back once more in their bodies, in the real world—and no time had passed. She sighed aloud and turned from Todd, muttering, "Adam will be ready to gate in a second."

Todd said nothing more either, and he walked beside Becky down the short trail that led to the space Ambrek's men had chosen for Adam's crossgate. It was concealed and well off the main path through the mountains, and Steven, JC, and Yors were already there. Yors was carrying everyone's bags, and still he had strength enough for a large sack of his own, which he had slung over his shoulder. He struck Becky as slightly Santa Claus-like, except his beard was ink-black rather than snow-white. There was jolliness in him that seemed out of place, though, and she found it almost infectious. Almost. She wouldn't be bursting into song anytime soon, of course.

Adam followed them a few minutes later, with Ambrek at his side. Without a word, he walked to the center of the clearing and began to spin the crossgate to life. It was large and golden in color, and Ambrek leaned over and whispered in Becky's ear as they watched, "It is truly a wonder to behold a Gatemaker at work. For so long, we saw only the evil that was done to us by the Gars that left us on Murrod. It took decades before I could see the beauty in their work again. Inner peace comes slowly to a Jov."

Becky nodded. "What happened to your people wasn't right."

"But that did not stop it from being done," Ambrek sighed. "The exile was hard enough, but the slaughter..."

Steven, standing nearby, asked, "What slaughter?"

Becky closed her eyes. She knew the story—enough of it, at least. She'd read of it at the Council Tower, and she'd heard pieces from other perspectives—from Mathias, and from what Adam remembered of what Embrew had said. She didn't care to know more.

"Our wives and our daughters were killed by the lords of Greendeep, the land where we were to be slaves," Ambrek said sadly. "Those of our kind that were women, the female Jovs, were allowed to live for a time, but by the end of the first year they too were put to the knife. Sisters and wives, daughters and mothers, killed before our eyes."

"Why?" Steven asked.

"Because Murrod is a savage place," Becky replied. "And because if you pour enough fear into anyone, they can become a monster."

The portal was finished—glowing brilliantly and casting a golden light over everything. Becky hugged Ambrek—a gesture that was almost as unfamiliar to him as it was to her—and whispered again, "It wasn't right."

In silence, Adam led them through the portal, Yors now among their number. Becky wished there was something more to say to Ambrek as they left, but no words came to her. Steven walked beside her as they passed from a short tunnel of golden light into one of green, then another of orange.

When they emerged, perhaps one hundred paces in total, from the final portal, they appeared in the middle of a loud, crowded street. The sun was shining high overhead, and Adam immediately looked around, panicked, as he closed the portal.

"What is it?" Becky asked.

"The last time I gated into an unfamiliar city, I opened the gate on top of someone. I killed him." Adam said. "I... I don't think anyone's hurt."

"Of course not," came a small, mirthful voice. "I cleared a space for you, but what in all the worlds took you so long?"

Becky looked around them, and then she saw her—Jara. She was much taller than when last they had met, nearly the same height as Becky now. Her hair was very long and a bit darker than it had been before, and her features were sharper, leaner. But there was no mistaking her.

With a squeal, Jara threw herself at them all, attempting to somehow hug them all at once. From the tangled knot of travelers, Jara said, laughing, "I can't wait for you to meet my mother."

¤~¤~¤

Mandor Arn jutted up from the plains like a tooth, pale gray in color and six smooth stories in height. It was surrounded by a defensive wall and, beyond that, a nearly impassible field of spikes and trenches. It was a military fortress, one of the four great fortresses still standing in the once disparate South.

When the Council formed, most of the warlords were defeated. Shanner and Horrix were broken completely, their fortresses dismantled and their legacies forever wiped from Onus. Quora was slain and her fortress abandoned, becoming many years later the home of Warlord Hyrak. Some of the warlords did not die fighting, but instead united with the Council, forming alliances where once there had been bloodshed. Mandor, Gollus, and Jerrit swore fealty to the Council, and in return they protected the contentious Southwest.

Nearly three hundred people called Mandor Arn home, including Priya, fifth Warlord of Mandor Arn. When Priya's father died and she assumed the mantle, it had been a time of peace. Warlord was a title that meant little more than judge and administrator these days, and she spent most of her time doing two things that she loved best—quelling disputes among cattlemen in the villages under her protection and having babies.

Some women were born to don armor and swing broadswords, but Priya was not such a woman. She was a warlord that craved peace, and in the times of peace she was happy. With her husband at her side, she gave birth to seven magnificent children, assuring that the line of Mandor would extend safely into the next generation.

When Hyrak came, bringing open war to the South, Warlord Priya lost much. Her eldest three children died fighting Hyrak, as did her husband. Villages that had looked to her for advice and wisdom were razed by Hyrak and his men, or by his monstrous Gatemaker consort, Lyda, and there were some that said Priya never recovered from her grief.

As Hyrak's army faded—broken at Rega Holc and scattered without true leadership across much of the world—many thought peace would return. Had they but asked Priya, they would have known better. Priya knew that peace could not come again to the South—that the South would never again know peace. After generations of servile obedience to the Council, to the idea that the strong would protect the weak, all those hard-fought truths had been revealed as lies.

But no one had asked Priya. She stood at the single gate to Mandor Arn, the reins of a horse in her hand. She was an old woman now, nearly fifty and past the time of bringing new life into the world. Her four remaining children were inside, the oldest caring for the youngest and none of them yet adults. Every man and woman that still swore loyalty to her was out there, in the fields surrounding the fortress-tower, lurking in ditches and beneath cover, waiting to spring up and strike at her enemies.

Priya would draw their foe into confrontation, and her people would bring this skirmish to an end. They had done it before, and would do it again—this was what life would be in the South. Hyrak had made it so, and there were none alive who could make it otherwise, in her opinion.

Priya mounted her old, familiar horse—a beast she loved more than almost anything. It had been her husband's gift to her for their wedding, brought at great expense from the horsemen of Stes. As Priya sat high in the saddle, she drew the banner flag from its holder at the stirrup and unfurled the great sigil of Mandor Arn, the upraised shield emblazoned with a shooting star, and called out, "Mandor Stands!"

Her enemies could hear her.

The lands surrounding Mandor Arn were plains, although they were less than a day's hard travel from the first stepping-stones, the great elevated plateaus of rock that peppered the landscape between her domain and the southern coast. In spite of the unimpeded vantage point of the watch post atop the tower, still her enemies had drawn much closer than should have been possible. They carried colors, in the glimpses that her lookouts had been able to catch, but they were colors unfamiliar to her—upstarts or renegades, marshaling under a banner that did not matter in the great book of history.

They were close enough to hear her, and that was all she cared to know.

They charged from concealment, and in that instant, Priya knew better what they had done. They emerged from the earth, overturning great sheets of sod as they disgorged from tunnels she had never before seen. Hundreds of men and women, armored lightly and armed heavily, surged out into the open plains. They carried mauls and axes, picks and swords, and as they rushed forward, charging what appeared to be vulnerable defenses, Priya sprung her trap.

She dropped the banner to the ground and shouted anew, "Mandor Rises!"

The soldiers of Mandor Arn leapt from trenches and ditches, spears at the ready and gouging deep into the enemy. Blood splattered and sprayed across the open field of battle, and every blow struck carried the possibility of knocking the foe down and back, tumbling them down upon the sharpened stakes that littered the field beyond each trench.

For a time, the battle leaned in the favor of the defenders, and Priya could but watch in satisfaction. But then she saw, at the extreme edge of the battle, her true foe. Climbing with great care from the tunnels, for he was far too old to move spryly, Priya saw her neighbor—Gollus Golluson, third Warlord of Gollus Arn. She would know his fat old body anywhere, but he wore his ceremonial armor, hammered out to allow for his ever-expanding gut. He was draped in the green and gray of his house colors, and though she could not see his face from where she sat upon her horse, she knew the bastard would be looking smugly upon the struggles between them.

She turned back over her shoulder. One woman stood there, held in reserve—a symbol of alliance that Priya had promised to keep, even when others had forsaken honor and peace. Cambria, of the Vols, asked simply, "Now?"

Priya nodded sharply. "Save the future of my people. Save my children."

Cambria said nothing more, but extended one hand out and up, forefinger and thumb spread wide. Priya knew enough of the Boltsenders to know of their communication techniques, and she hoped that Cambria's signal would summon aid in time.

"The word is sent," Cambria said. "I am sorry that our fears came true, Warlord. Were these just brigands, or vestiges of Hyrak's legions, we would have all been happier."

"Not me," Priya grumbled. "I don't care who crashes against my walls. I have played enough of your politics."

Cambria nodded and stepped past Priya and her magnificent white horse. "I would be happy to add my lightning to your people's efforts," she stated.

With a crash, another long strip of sod, supported on great wooden planks, was overturned, this time on the western front. More soldiers spilled forth, charging to join the fray. Priya had no more tricks, and her people were growing steadily outnumbered.

"Gollus is not the only one that knows how to build a tunnel," Priya said quietly. "Your lightning will do no good here. Take my children to safety.

There is an exit tunnel, built into the cook's cellar. It will take you far from here—near the Vale of Steam. Protect my children, Cambria, and whatever remains of the legacy of Mandor Arn will remain allied with your precious Council."

Cambria bowed sharply. "I am sorry we could not do more, Priya."

"You have done too much," Priya said, acid dripping in her words. "Where once we were wolves, you made us believe we could be sheep. Now, someone else has come to sheer our wool and you wonder why we can bare no teeth in our defense. Who is the greater fool?"

# 4
## Murrod

*Mathias had callouses on his hands and his shoulders were constantly sunburned.* His red-gold hair was paler than ever before, and his back hurt. He wore loose-fitting trousers covered with pockets, and rarely much else—he went barefoot each day into the fields and felt the soil churn beneath his toes. His chest and arms were both broader than ever, but he was still a bit shorter and a bit smaller than his many co-workers.

He was among the youngest of the men of Greendeep that had fallen upon hard times and resorted to manual labor in the fields, but he enjoyed their company. As the three brilliant suns of Murrod looked down on their work, Mathias believed that the work was worth doing and the company worth keeping. These were good men that had simply been misused by the system of government and reincarnation that controlled all aspects of life in the Prince Cities of Greendeep.

As Mathias crawled on his knees, plucking deep-set root vegetables from the field, he shared in idle conversation with Norrun, perhaps his best friend in the labor fields. Norrun was quite old—nearing the end of his incarnation at a robust forty years of age—and he had been in these fields longer than anyone. His head was bald and his eyes surrounded by many tiny wrinkles, but Norrun was still strong and tall, his skin bronzed deeply by more than a decade toiling in the sun.

"I remember when I was about the only one here," Norrun said as he struggled with a twisted gnarlroot. The pungent aroma of the freshly pulled vegetables made Mathias' eyes water a bit. "Back when most everything was still done by the Ellir."

Mathias grunted and pulled a pair of the pale green roots, snipping their leafy tops off with a pair of shears produced from one of his many pockets. "I imagine they were much better at this than we are," Mathias said softly. "What with the four arms and all."

"That they were!" Norrun laughed. "It was a sight to see. But a few years back, when the uprisings started, it got too risky to keep them so far from the boxes, so men got involved in the work of working again."

Mathias said nothing. In many men, there was deep resentment about the Ellir uprisings, and that had not grown softer during the time Mathias spent away from this world. In fact, it had grown quite worse. When Mathias left, so too had the Metalbreakers responsible for building and maintaining the sunboxes that kept the Ellir docile and the people of Murrod safe. When he had returned, the better part of a year ago, he had discovered a world where the Ellir no longer toiled in service to the men of Greendeep. Manual labor had returned to men accustomed only to bureaucracy and the work of the mind, and as much as Mathias thought this was a change for the better, there were other hardships to consider. There were still stories almost every day of Ellir attacks—in the night, of course—on innocent men.

"So, Mathias, what plans are you keeping for this nightfall?" Norrun asked with a coy smile. "Because I have laid hands on a fine bottle of wine if you'd care to help me drink it."

Mathias shook his head. "We've been through this before, Norrun. I'm happy to drink with you, if you like, but that is all that will happen."

With a frustrated growl, Norrun ripped a pair of gnarlroots out with a single grasp-and-pull, throwing them hard into the wooden bucket at his side. "What is your problem, boy? You're a field worker—you can't possibly be worried that you'll reincarnate any lower than this!"

"It isn't about that," Mathias apologized.

"I'm that ugly? You know, before I came here, before I fell to this, I had prospects. But once you get the dirt between your toes, your prospects turn to dust. And it's better to be with *someone* than to be with no one." Norrun sighed. "I have affection for you, Mathias. No one else listens to my stories like you do."

Mathias stood up, wiping his hands on his trousers. "You are my friend, Norrun. A good one, too. But I cannot couple with you. It would not be fair to either of us. My heart is not mine to give, and your life is worth more than the value I would add to it."

"What in Chron's name is that supposed to mean?" Norrun asked, also standing.

"I have no records," Mathias said quietly, stepping in close to Norrun so that none of the others could overhear. "My incarnation documents were ordered destroyed by Chaplain Reid more than a year ago."

"Why would he do such a thing?" Norrun asked, eyes wide.

Mathias whispered, "It's complicated."

"Then what happens when you die?" Norrun looked around nervously. Mathias was certain that the field hand had never before met an undocumented man—as far as Mathias knew, he was the only one of his kind.

"I have no idea," Mathias said softly. "But I don't want to drag anyone else down with me. That's why I'm here, in the fields as far from Imperia as I could make it."

Norrun extended a hand and said, "Well, your secret is safe with me, boy. I just have one more question, then I'll leave your mysteries be."

"That's a fair proposal," Mathias said.

"Where were you, between your falling out with the Chaplain and your arrival here? Where does a man that has no standing in the world hide?"

"If you don't mind, Norrun, I would like to share that wine with you tonight. And while we drink, perhaps it is high time I told you about Spiralgates and my travels to other worlds. In return, maybe you can tell me a story too." Mathias smiled and returned to the ground and the work that kept him out of trouble and invisible to those who would hunt him.

"Sounds like the story you have to tell is better than any of mine," Norrun said, still staring at Mathias. "What do you want to hear about?"

"I want to hear whatever else you know about the man that they say rallied the Ellir revolt," Mathias said grimly.

He'd come home to Murrod to find the truth about himself, but he'd also stumbled upon something far bigger than that. The day would come when he found out who he was, who he had been in the lives before this one. But first he had to find out if the stories of Norrun and the others were true—was Hyrak, Warlord of Onus, alive and well on the world of Murrod?

¤~¤~¤

It was a serviceable place to sleep, but the coastal caverns of Bluetide were a pale shadow of the majesty of Hyrak Arn. The cavern where he now lived was dry, built up on a hill along the coast and just high enough that the rising tide never encroached upon the sandy floors within. The cavern had essentially three rooms, one of which was deep within and well insulated from the constant chill of the region. One of the two chambers nearer the mighty sea was less pleasant, and it was there that he kept his prisoners. What was a warlord without spoils of war, and for he who had once brought the lands of Onus within inches of total subjugation, Hyrak felt that the beginnings of his spoils were merely... satisfactory.

Not far from here, in a cavern that was below the water as often as it was above, the dragon slept. Hyrak and the dragon had come to an agreement more than a year ago, when he was still new to this place, unburdened with knowledge of his purpose and destiny. When all of that came back to him in a sudden burst of clarity, ten months ago, the simple arrangement he had made with Ehbor became all the more valuable.

"Is there anything else I can do for you, Lord Hyrak?" asked the Ellir that knelt before him. Hyrak sat in the closest thing he could scavenge to a throne. The tall, four-armed creature, its dark blue skin making it nearly invisible in the feeble light of the single torch that burned in the cavern, was but one of the score that answered to his call day and night.

In this land, the Ellir were creatures of subservience by day and savage ferocity by night, but even amnesiac, Hyrak had seen to the truth of the matter. The light of the three suns weakened the telepathic connection between the Ellir and their mighty dragon-god, Ehbor, and left them purposeless and servile. But in the darkness, that bond grew strong. The will of the dragon was carried out by the hive mind of Ellir brutality—except for those that Ehbor had given to Hyrak. It was a simple matter to insert himself into the connection between them and their master, at least for the handful that he required, using his own abilities.

Hyrak was a son of the world Rettik, where science, built at the expense of dragons like Ehbor, replicated nearly all forms of magic. An accident had left him far from home and utterly changed, and he took advantage of his circumstances, as always, to begin his conquest of the world Onus. Along the way, he had acquired power of his own—magical talents imparted to him by the touch of a damaged and broken Fatewaker that he had tortured until she poured the power of mindshaping into his soul.

Then he had been betrayed. Betrayed by the one person he had dared to allow into his affections—a woman he had known better than to trust. Hyrak was no longer capable of love, but he had been soft on Lyda, and that softness had bred in her contempt. In a glowing corridor between worlds, she tried her best to murder him—only because of his unique characteristics did he survive.

He was a changed man here on Murrod. Scars covered his body from head to toe; molten metal and the lambent energy of the Spiral of Worlds had racked his body and left him hairless and hideous. His eyes were bled of color, milky white but still capable of seeing. His beautiful armor was no more—its slagged remnants responsible for so much of his disfigurement. He was starting over, with little more at his disposal than twenty Ellir, the two prisoners in the front chambers, the power and knowledge he carried from his visits to five worlds, and a need to command all that fell within his gaze.

"You are dismissed. Return when the sun rises." Hyrak gestured towards the cavern entrance.

The Ellir said nothing and stood slowly, backing steadily out of the cave and disappearing into the night.

Hyrak listened to the sounds of the sea and the cawing of the birds that swarmed whenever Ehbor slept. He imagined himself back on Onus. That was where his destiny was—he knew this with conviction stronger than any force in all the worlds. But he had no way to return—not yet. He had plans and schemes, but none of them mattered if he could not return to that world a conqueror.

Resistance had blossomed in his wake, as it always would. Human nature demanded rebellion against dominion, even when dominion was what humanity most required. It was that nature that Hyrak depended upon. The message he received from his minion, Narred, had indicated that his armies were broken and scattered. The Council of Onus had drawn itself together at last and repelled his forces, and so when he finally did return, he would face stronger opposition than ever before. There was nothing to be done for it—he had to deal with the problem as he always had: one calculated step at a time.

Hyrak stood slowly and walked out to the front cavern, smiling grimly at the captives who had been his constant companions since his arrival. One was a bear of a man, barrel chested and large-armed. He was sleeping, heavy snores echoing in the chamber, and Hyrak chose to let him rest. He was a maker of grand things, and his talents would be required if ever Hyrak's schemes were to come to fruition. He was a prisoner in the sense that he could not leave, but he was a cooperative captive, and in some small way Hyrak almost counted him an ally.

Next to him, huddled in the corner of the cave, wet and miserable, was the true prize. Long gray hair, tangled and knotted, fell before the man's face. His body was frail, wrapped in tattered and soiled robes. Hyrak crouched down and pushed the filthy hair out of the man's face, revealing the smooth scar tissue that covered where, once upon a time, he had possessed eyes.

"Is today the day I die?" the prisoner asked sullenly.

"No," Hyrak responded sternly, "I am not yet done with you, Embrew."

¤~¤~¤

Chaplain Reid was dying. This was not a surprise—he was forty years old, and like clockwork the end of his life was upon him. He held on, held out, longer than most, because there was so much left to do. Reincarnation was all well and good, but it came at a bad time for him and for his nation. The Prince Cities of Greendeep were in terrible tumult, and they required strong leadership. The Minister of Security was a vital role, and the time it would take to find and train a successor to Reid was not time that any man of Greendeep could afford to waste.

Theirs was a society built on the absence of labor, forced now to labor for the first time in generations. The Ellir were no longer well controlled, the sunboxes that bound them in the night malfunctioning and dismantled, and everything was different.

Reid worried about more than the cultural revolution that was upon his people, of course, but it was the need for a labor class that haunted these final days. In the night, when he dreamed, he feared for reincarnation—he feared for what the next life would hold. He had not gained status in this one—he had not bound his destiny to those necessary to improve his station. His only bindmate was dead, killed by invaders from another world on a rampage through Murrod more than a year ago. So he would come back lower— of this there was grim certainty. But as each of his final days ticked by, and as he made final preparations to arrange for the construction of a true working class among the men of Greendeep, he feared that he might, in a turn of irony inflicted by the dragon-god Chron, find himself reborn in the very base class he was striving now to create.

"It is not the future I imagined for myself," Reid said idly to the runner that stood in his doorway. "But it must be risked. All must be risked, if we are to survive. Monsters plague us in the night, and the women strike time and again in the light of the suns. We are besieged."

"Yes, sir," the runner said, humbly. He was young—barely released from the nursery, Reid imagined. He was fit and firm-bodied, with long, dark hair and dimpled cheeks. He would be a fine catch for someone—a massive step up in the social hierarchy for craftsmen, merchants, and such—but when all was done, when the last signatures were signed today, even a lowly runner would be unreachable for the new worker class.

He and the other chaplains were consigning a quarter of the population to perpetual reincarnation as laborers, and as much as he worried about that, his worries would not stay his hand. It had to be done. Food had to be grown, buildings had to be constructed—civilization had to go on. For the past year, things had been slowly falling apart, and that could happen no longer. The handful of Metalbreakers that had not escaped with the traitorous Mathias would be busy until they drew their last breaths securing the perimeters of the Prince Cities—the true work of keeping the society of Greendeep moving forward would have to be done by the men who had always called it home.

"How old are you, boy?" Reid asked the runner.

"Twenty-two, sir," the runner replied, blushing. "Is that suitable?"

Reid said nothing. He didn't know what was suitable anymore. Old age had robbed him of much of his fire and passion—reality had stolen the rest. "It is fine," he said at last. "I knew another runner once, about the same age as you. He was a good messenger."

"And what happened to him, sir?" the runner asked.

"I tortured him and then he ran away past where I could follow," Reid said simply. "He was a traitor to our entire race."

"What, sir, brings that to mind?" the runner asked, his nervousness evident in his stance.

"Runners cannot be trusted," Reid said. He reached down, into a long tube affixed to the side of his desk, and produced a long saber of blue Bindmetal. It had once belonged to his bindmate, Herracis. Its stroke was sure. With precise skill, he launched himself across the room, stabbing the runner in the chest. The magic of the blade continued its timeless duty and stripped the boy of life, sending his soul to the nursery to be born anew.

Reid withdrew his weapon from the boy's body and said softly, "I do you a kindness, boy. This is not a world in which you wish to live."

¤~¤~¤

They stared at each other from across the line. If one was to go back even a year, there would have been no line burned into the jungle terrain surrounding Greendeep, but now there was, and Tyrick was not confident that it was worth the metal it was lined with.

He was leading the maintenance crew today, and they had been tasked with investigating four potential breaches to the Hineros Perimeter. His crew included four executive knights from the Ministry of Security, all better with a blade than Tyrick ever would be. He was here as a surveyor, brought in to supervise the smith and coordinate the work.

Their group moved slowly from breach to breach, for the warriors pulled with them a large two-wheeled cart, made of wood and shaped like a box with two rods protruding as handles. In simpler times, Ellir would have been yoked to the cart and hauled it and its contents to the work site, but these times were not simple. The cart was off to the side of the site now. This was their last stop of the day, and the three suns were slipping lower in the sky. He rubbed absently at the thin line of beard that traced his jawline as he studied the situation.

On the other side of the three-inch wide scorched line was a single Ellir. It stood, staring blankly at Tyrick and the warriors. It wore rags across its dark blue shoulders, with another rag tied around its waist protecting what passed for the modesty of such creatures. Its four arms were well muscled and long, but it carried no weapons. Of course, Tyrick had to remind himself, an Ellir needed no weapons to end a man's life.

The creature could not pass the boundary—this was the purpose of the perimeter. A line of Bindmetal scraps and filings prepared by the last of the Jovs still in service to the sons of Chron was all that stood between the Ellir and killing every denizen of the Prince Cities in their sleep. Tyrick, as one of the few members of the newly formed Surveyor's Guild, was responsible for keeping the feeble perimeter from falling into decay. All three Prince Cities lacked the Metalbreakers to properly enchant a more permanent solution.

"If we give it an order, it has to obey," one of the knights said quietly. Tyrick shook his head and whispered back, "Too risky. The suns set even now. Once the last of the light is gone, it is free to slaughter us. We are better off leaving it be and getting to our work. The perimeter is soft here—we must get it fixed before nightfall." Tyrick gestured towards the Ellir and said to the men, "Watch it. Do not cross the line. I will start the repairs."

Tyrick cautiously turned, afraid to take his eyes off the Ellir but knowing he had no choice, and approached the rear of the cart. The heat of the early evening was still quite intense, and he swatted at insects that buzzed around him. He set to work on the intricate lock at the back of the cart, sliding the four-part mechanism in the right pattern to spring the clasp. He made soft sounds, trying to quiet the cargo as he opened the door.

The work of surveying and repairing the perimeter was good, honest work—the type of work that would see him well placed in his next incarnation. He kept this thought firmly in mind as he climbed into the cart, because everything that came next he found repugnant.

He did not know the name of the smith that was held prisoner inside the cart. He was young—younger even than Tyrick's twenty-four years, if he was any judge of age. The smith wore thick leggings with stout chain binding his ankles close to one another. He wore no shirt, and Tyrick could see the doughy muscles in the young man's pale torso twitching. His hands were also chained together at the wrists, but extended before him rather than behind as prisoners often were. The chains themselves were fascinating constructions, made of a specially treated wood rather than metal. They rattled dully as the smith crawled towards the sound of Tyrick's voice.

The smith's head was unseen, obscured inside a box of the same solid wood, fitted about the smith's neck in such a way that it gripped snugly. A tiny door in the lower part of the box, near the chin of the smith, allowed the keepers to feed the poor captive. As it was told to Tyrick, these last smiths, the ones who had not fled from the Prince Cities more than a year ago when the Ellir uprisings intensified, had never seen the light of the suns and never seen another living face. They were treated as little more than beasts.

Such things were necessary for the defense of Greendeep, he was assured.

With as much gentleness as he could muster without appearing weak in front of the knights, who he was most certain had been instructed to watch him closely, Tyrick helped the nameless smith out of the cart. He led him, slowly and carefully, towards the perimeter.

If the Ellir knew what the smith was, it made no visible sign of such knowledge. It merely watched events unfold as it had the past few minutes, standing passively and observing.

Tyrick helped the smith kneel down at the perimeter, careful to keep him on this side of the line, and pushed the smith's hands down into the soft metallic soot of the perimeter line. He thought encouraging thoughts to the smith, and wished that the smith had a name, so that he might speak it and comfort him in some way. But none of these things were possible.

The smith was well trained, even if his misery was evident. His fingers plunged into the Bindmetal-enriched soot, working the magic of the Jovs through the material and strengthening the enchantment that would keep the Ellir on the outside of the line through the night. Five minutes later, the work was done—and the last of the daylight was nearly spent. Tyrick leaned down to pull the smith's hands from the soot at the perimeter, and as he did so, the smith pulled back suddenly, wrapping his hands around Tyrick's instead of the other way around. He squeezed, not with the strength at his command, but with a soft, steady pressure. It was not a threat; it was a plea. Before Tyrick could do or say anything, one of the knights grunted.

"That was too close," the man said pointedly. "Get it back in the cart so we can be on our way."

Tyrick nodded and helped the smith up, but no sooner did he do so than a ghastly howl caused him to start, spinning back towards the perimeter.

The suns were truly set, and the Ellir raged and wailed against the invisible shield of the perimeter. It pounded its four mighty fists against a wall that existed only to its kind, and foam flecked at its yellow teeth as it howled and screamed in a language that Tyrick did not speak.

One of the men drew his sword, but he knew better than to attack—if he crossed the threshold, he would make it possible for the Ellir to do the same.

Then, as quickly as it had begun, the Ellir ceased its mindless assault and vanished into the jungle. All was still and quiet as the men helped Tyrick load the smith back into the cart and secure the lock once more. Then the knights lifted the cart handles and began the steady march back towards the city, leaving Tyrick to follow behind, wondering many things.

¤~¤~¤

"It is a savage plan. Unworthy of your brilliance, but undeniable in its effectiveness," the Ellir said. It spoke with the voice of the dragon-god of the Ellir, Ehbor, and Hyrak knew that everything the creature heard was heard, in turn, by its master.

He stood on the coast of the cold sea, not far from the den where Ehbor slumbered his eternal life away. All around him, Hyrak had gathered his Ellir, the twenty such creatures that answered to his wishes instead of the dragon's. The singular Ellir that he spoke with, the mouthpiece of Ehbor, was silent, indicating that it had said all its god commanded it to say.

"Your endless squabbles with your brother and sister must end. My plan will resolve who amongst you is the greater once and for all." Hyrak smiled. While he had little experience in dealing directly with dragons before his arrival on Murrod, it had taken him no time at all to come to grips with how this one thought.

"In the distant past, we preferred direct confrontation," Ehbor replied through the mouth of the Ellir. "We tried it once more not long ago, and that last battle left me gravely wounded. My sister is perhaps the stronger of us, physically, but her forces are inferior to mine in every way."

"Which is why the old ways of direct confrontation are no longer worthy of you," Hyrak said carefully. "You are too great a being to cling to laws that would declare you defeated. Join me in rewriting the rules and proving once and for all that you are the champion."

"You would have me break the truce of pawns. My Ellir and Ahmur's daughters do not currently war—thus I allow my children to focus their efforts on those who enslaved them. And in doing so, they weaken my brother, who is the mightiest by far of the three of us in terms of sorcery." The Ellir speaking Ehbor's words shifted uncomfortably.

"I agree. That is why Ahmur's daughters in Goldvast must fall before we have any hope of taking Chron in Greendeep—you must claim her forces for yourself, adding them to your own army. That is all there is to it. If you wish to continue this endless stalemate and these foolish games, so be it. I offer you definitive victory for the first time in your ageless existence, but if you are too cowardly to seize it..." Hyrak turned away from the Ellir and drew in a breath. This was the moment he could not plan for. Perhaps Ehbor could be manipulated as men could be manipulated, and perhaps not. After this, he would know.

The Ellir mouthpiece said nothing for a time. When it spoke again, its body shook with the rage of the dragon.

"I am not a pawn to your ambition, Hyrak! Tell me why you wish this, what is in this for you?"

Hyrak turned back and smiled. "I have been watching and listening since the day I woke up on this benighted world. I need an army in order to return to my own world victorious, and I will take my army as the spoils of your war. You can vanquish Ahmur, and then Chron, and claim all of Murrod for yourself and your children. I will then take the daughters of Ahmur and the sons of Chron for myself. They are of no use to you. They will be *my* army."

That was when he felt it—as he expected. The dragon's mind lashed out and struck against his own, probing into his thoughts to determine the truth of his words. But Hyrak was a Mindshaper, by decree if not by birth, and he had been practicing his arts with rabid intensity since Narred's message had brought him back to his senses. His shields were strong and subtle, nearly as impenetrable as they were invisible. He fell back in his mind, deliberately, in a carefully structured feint designed to reveal to Ehbor only what he wished to reveal. The dragon collected impressions, thoughts of Hyrak's nervous fear of the dragon and his ardent desire to leave Murrod with the men and women of Murrod at his back as soldiers and conscripts. The truth, the depth of Hyrak's ambition and the complexities of his true plans, remained hidden from even the dragon's immense power.

The dragon pulled out, believing he had bludgeoned past Hyrak's defenses, and Hyrak guarded his expression carefully, striving to give the dragon no indication that he even knew the invasion had occurred.

"Then it shall be done. I have given the order. One hundred Ellir gather even now at the borders of Goldvast, waiting your command. Use them wisely, warlord... or I shall visit endless suffering upon you," Ehbor said.

"Of course, my lord," Hyrak said, bowing deeply. "I am but your humble servant."

# 5
## Onus

*Small things add up into big things.* My mother doesn't believe in small things at all, actually—she thinks everything is important and significant. She says all we are is the collection of all the small things we have ever been. When I was little, getting stuffed in closets by my older brothers, I took comfort in that, because I was a small thing and I wanted more than anything to add up to something big.

As much as I love my mom, my whole family, it's hard to see eye to eye with them anymore. I'm not so little, but they're all still bigger, older, and wiser than me—at least they think so. To them I'm just Joey, the runt. Yes, they call me Joey, and no, you can't. Nobody can. Not even Becky. It's JC these days anyway—that's the me I want to be, the me that I decided on, and even if my mom can't get past her little Joey, I'll be damned if anyone else gets to make me feel small or unimportant anymore.

Growing up with two older brothers—notably older, by the way—can do a real number on a guy. They were both big football rock stars. So was my dad, which meant they were the kinds of kids he could relate to. By the time I was old enough to start playing football for real, in middle school, it was pretty obvious that I was more like my mom, wiry, than like my dad. I thought maybe that meant I was a little more quarterback and a little less linebacker, which would make me even cooler than my brothers, but that wasn't to be.

JC Stein is a bit of a screw up, you see. Always has been. The first time my mother ever told me that small things add up into big things, she wasn't trying to make me feel better about being the youngest and the smallest—she was trying to lay on the guilt because I'd just done a fair number of small but bad things. I was always in trouble at school, always in trouble at home—trouble might as well have been my middle name. And my mother sat me down on the peach-colored sofa in our living room and told me, "Joey, all these little things, these little problems, they may not seem so bad to you, but they don't stay little forever. Little things add up into big things, and if you aren't careful, they get too big for you to handle. And your father and I won't always be there to bail you out of trouble."

I kinda smile about that now, you know? I can't think of a time in the last few years where they really *were* there to bail me out at all. These days, I do most of the bailing out for people. I saved everyone's lives on Rettik. I saved Becky on Murrod *and* Onus. I'm a frickin' superhero—but no one at home knows that.

My brothers still run their big meaty hands over the top of my buzzed head like I'm a dog or something. My dad still lectures me about responsibility and taking life seriously and growing up, when the most serious thing he's ever had to do was get a damn vasectomy so that he wouldn't accidently bring any more disappointments into the world after me. And my mom... she means well, but she doesn't know. She doesn't see who I am, who I have had to become.

And as long as this collar is around my neck, no one ever will. Not because I'm afraid to show them, to tell them—that's obviously not the problem. It's because I don't know who I am or what I am either. I am not JC the fearless, champion of Rega Holc and savior of Onus. That... that is the collar. It didn't bother me at first, because it helped me get past the one thing I could never figure out how to do myself, back in my old life, before we traveled through that first Spiralgate. I could never get past the fear that I wasn't good enough, or not as good as everyone else. The collar was supposed to answer that question, and it did, but it just left me with more questions.

It only helped in little ways, it only changed me a little. But like my mom always says, little things add up into big things, and now I'm not sure how much of me is still me and how much of me is something else entirely.

I have to get this goddamned thing off while there's still a little of me left in here. I don't know how much longer I can hold out.

¤~¤~¤

Jara introduced her friends, one by one, to her mother. Her voice was unsteady and her eyes just a bit wet as she did so. This was, after all, the first time she had ever introduced her mother to her friends. It was actually the first time she had ever, truly, *had* friends. Now here they were before her, and here she was, at long last, with a family. For the first time since the sacking of Gar Nought, her life felt complete.

"And this," Jara said as she came to the last denizen of Core now standing in her mother's warm and well-lit kitchen, "Is Steven." Jara smiled broadly. "He was my first friend on Core."

Hessa Moultuson inclined her head slightly with a thin smile. Jara could see discomfort in her mother's eyes, but she did not care—there was a rightness in being reunited with the Children of the Line, and that rightness warmed her on the inside. Her mother would have to grow accustomed to Jara's importance in the universe eventually.

"It's nice to meet you, ma'am. Your daughter changed all of our lives two winters ago," Steven put one hand on Jara's shoulder and she beamed. "It's very good to see her doing so well."

"If you can call it that," Jara said with an overly dramatic sigh. "Igar Holc is a dreadfully boring place. We've been here for months, and nothing exciting has happened at all. But then I realized you were coming, all of you, and I knew that would change. Thank the Purpose you didn't take any longer! I'd have gone mad!"

Yors, standing in the doorway in an effort to be out of the way in the cramped quarters of the kitchen, slid out of the frame just enough to allow the tiny form of Moultus to slip into the room. "Yors sorry. Big."

"Oh yes, yes, I haven't forgotten you, my boy," Moultus said absently. He squeezed past JC and Becky to reach the central table in the kitchen and produced, from inside his robe, a folded piece of parchment.

"It appears that you have come at a most opportune time, friends," Moultus spread the yellowed sheet out on the table, revealing a message written in flowing script. "It seems big things are afoot in the South."

"We might have known about them earlier if someone hadn't meddled," Jara muttered.

Her mother said nothing. She looked away and rubbed absently at her armband, and Jara felt a bit sorry for the scorn she had shown her mother since last night. So much had changed between them, during the time her mother was held captive and Jara had been off on other worlds, that it seemed like they might never understand one another again. But Hessa was her mother, and that meant she deserved to be treated better than Jara had been treating her.

Adam and Becky both leaned in to read along with the letter as Moultus read it aloud.

"The Council summons Moultus the Scribe and Jara Wyr-Born to a gathering of members to be held on the day of Summer's Twins at the grand hall of Ain Holc. Matters of grave import to the security of all Council lands demand your presence."

Moultus sighed. "It is signed by Duke Igar himself. I'm afraid refusal is quite out of the question."

"Why would you refuse?" Adam asked. "It must be a great honor to be held in such regard."

Hessa shook her head. "It is not an honor we wish for our family any more. We have been trying to stay out of the affairs of Dukes and Warlords, but it seems that we have not yet won free of them."

"What's Summer's Twins?" JC asked. "It sounds like a party. I'm not against parties or anything, but we kind of have our hands full with important business."

"Every season there is one night when both moons are full. Those are the days of the Twins. Summer's Twins is seven days from now." Jara smiled. "And Ain Holc is about 5 days from here if we can convince Duke Igar to spare us horses."

"I can just crossgate you there, Jara," Adam said. "Seems silly to waste all that time on the road."

"Not a good idea, Gatemaker," Moultus said sharply. "These lands are not the North. I wouldn't be surprised if you stepped out of a crossgate with an arrow in the chest anywhere south of Igar Holc. The southern continent was laid waste by Hyrak's forces riding on the back of Lyda's crossgates. The war may be over, but some things will not be forgotten for generations."

"Well why do we have to go to this meeting?" Todd asked. "The invitation is for you two. We can just get the answers we came for and let you be on your way."

Jara looked as if struck. "You... you aren't staying?"

Adam shook his head. "We just came for some help, Jara. We can't stay."

Jara drew in one sharp, trembling breath and then bolted out of the kitchen, shoving her way past JC, Steven, and Yors. She ran up the short flight of stairs that led up to the sleeping chambers and slammed the door to her room shut behind her. She threw herself onto her bed and pressed her face down into the pillow, hoping that none of them would hear her crying.

¤~¤~¤

For the first time since the ship had been built, she was within sight of no land mass. The Razormaw was a special ship, to be sure, and Grell had great confidence in the craftsmanship that had brought her to life, but still, it was an odd feeling to be away from all signs of land.

In the Starlight Islands, there was always land nearby. The six-dozen islands that made up the chain were spread far and wide, but always one was within sight, unless a particularly heavy fog lay upon the water. But they had sailed out from Reef Circle, itself one of the northernmost islands, and headed due east. Now, eighteen hours from departure, the last signs of their old lives were behind them.

Grell stood at the helm, his hand at the wheel and his eyes at the horizon. The sun was setting behind them, throwing the shadow of the ship's dark blue sails out on the water before him. He had no qualms about sailing at night—they had strung great lanterns from the prow of the ship and his chief watchman, Fendris, had the keenest eyes of any man he had ever known. Furthermore, there was little to fear in these waters. The pirate clans of the Starlight Islands had no reason to push this far east, and the meager ships of the mainland were no match for the tumult of the Endless Sea.

They would push on without stop, directly, for their first target. The men who worked the lines of the sails did so quietly, their boisterous song and raucous laughter of the daytime subdued. He knew that his lack of fear for this journey was not shared by all forty souls aboard his vessel—but they were loyal. Each and every one of them had reason to hate the mainland and the Council that governed it. It was a world unto itself, but a place that almost every man and woman of the Starlights could trace their lineage back to. All of them had fled something, once upon a time, but soon Grell would balance those scales. All the wrongs done to the poor and the weak, the strange and the broken, would be made right when he had crushed the ten thrones that ruled as one.

"I brought you a cloak," Vediri said as she approached him from behind. "But I suspect vengeance provides you warmth enough this night."

"Every night." Grell said simply.

"She makes good time, Grell," Vediri said as she stepped to her captain's side. She did indeed have a cloak draped over one heavy arm, but she said nothing more about it. She instead looked out into the distance. High overhead, the two moons, nearing fullness but not yet plump with light, were largely shrouded by black clouds. "If we avoid storms, we will be within sight of the watchtowers in five days' time, by Fendris' reckoning."

"We won't be avoiding storms," Grell said, pointing towards the moons. "Those clouds are ripe with anger. Tomorrow night at the latest, they will sow it upon us." He smiled. "Which is good. We will need the storm, and every other we can find, if we are to win the first and most important victory."

Vediri smiled. "If? What happened to the legendary confidence of my captain?"

"Your captain is not a fool. If what we seek to do was easily done, it would have been done before us." Grell closed his eyes. "The Purpose is on our side. What I would have us do *must* be done. But I am not fool enough to think it easy."

"Of course not," his first mate replied. "I would ask one last thing of you though, before I turn in for the night. Some of the men used to ply the fishing trade, as you know, in Distat waters. A few of them tell tales of the Sea Dragon, Candara, who prowls Asira's Belt. You are aware that we shall track quite near that range before we reach landfall, I assume. So what is your plan for taming the beast, should we run afoul of her?"

Grell's lips curled back in a broad, hungry grin. "I have no fear for legends of the leviathan. Should the plan come together as I hope, you may even learn why."

"Keeping secrets from me, my captain?" Vediri asked with a gleam in her eye. "How daring. You know how I enjoy the challenge of ferreting out secrets."

"Sleep, you snake. I will have need of your talents soon enough. You shall take the helm with the sunrise. Perhaps by then I will have calmed enough to sleep. I know Fendris marks the time as five days, but I think it more likely to be six before the first of the Holcs is sighted. We have many preparations to make before then."

In the sky, the clouds draped before the first moon flashed with lightning. In his hands, the great wheel of the ship thrummed as the magic woven into her every beam and timber slowly stirred to life.

¤~¤~¤

"Jara, can I come in?" Steven stood at the door to Jara's room. The home that the Duke of Igar had provided for Jara's family was nice enough, for a world without plumbing or electricity. Steven wondered how the others adapted to this all so easily—it was awkward as hell for him. While they had been in the mountains it had been different—a bit like camping, really. But now to be in the heart of a city—one of the world's largest, by all accounts, the differences between Onus and Earth were difficult to handle.

But on the other side of this door was a hurt little girl, and that much he understood. Downstairs, serious and heated debate was going on about whether they would travel with Jara and Moultus to this meeting of the Council. Steven had excused himself because he simply didn't care. This wasn't his home, but Jara was his friend. Jara had made it possible for him to wake up and stop being the pawn of the creature he had known as Jamison Alders. Because of Jara, he was able to start living his own life, free of manufactured guilt placed in his mind by a sociopathic shadow-thing. The fact that he lived a life where those sentences even made sense was a bit troubling.

"Why?" Jara called from inside. "So you can ask me whatever you came to ask and then run back to your stupid world with its stupid cars and guns and televisions?"

"I'm not here to ask you for anything, actually," Steven said. "I do have something for you though. A present from an old friend."

A few moments later, Jara opened the door slowly, cautiously, and Steven stepped into her room. It was small and little more than a place to sleep, but Steven could see in it a charm that was hard to describe. On a small shelf beside the bed there were a few books, large and heavy leather-bound affairs with yellowed parchment pages.

"I don't have any old friends," Jara said, sitting back down on her bed. Her hair was even more of a mess than it had been when Steven had first laid eyes on her upon emerging from Adam's crossgate, and her eyes were puffy and red from crying.

Steven sat down on the bed beside her and placed his duffel bag on the floor at his feet. He lifted Jara's chin with the gentle touch of a forefinger and said, "That is not true. All of us care about you, Jara. Just because we are not here with you doesn't mean that isn't true."

Jara stared at him, blinking a few stray tears from her eyes, and sighed. "I'm acting very silly, aren't I?"

"Not silly at all. I know how hard it is to feel alone." Steven said softly. "It makes us a little crazy, I think."

Jara stared at him, and Steven saw something happen in her eyes—they seemed to lose focus for a second, then snap back, and he saw something different, something serious and heavy, lurking within her.

"Did you just ruin the surprise?" He asked, half-joking. He didn't clearly understand what Jara's abilities could and could not do.

"You lost one of the Children of the Line," Jara said in a low, steady voice. "Why didn't any of you tell me?"

Steven felt his heart skip a beat, felt his stomach lurch. This wasn't what he wanted to talk about. This wasn't what he came here to do. "Don't... Don't say anything else about it," he whispered.

Jara's eyes glazed over, a milky pink color suffusing them as she spoke in a stiff, archaic tone. The words issued forth with a kind of echoing vibration that chilled Steven.

"The hope of Wyr and all mankind is hidden in those of the Line. Guarded well hidden far from sight, these six alone can put all right. Each must do what others cannot, if ever light shall vanquish Rot. Should one child slip free from this plane, so goes all fate and breaks the chain."

Steven's blood turned cold, but not from grief—from fear. The words sank into him, their meaning clear, and he realized that perhaps all of this, all of everything, was for nothing. Where once there were six Children of the Line, now there would be only five.

Jara's eyes cleared and she looked up at Steven and said, "I'm sorry. I didn't know her, except for a dream, once. I can feel how much she meant to you though."

Steven looked at Jara carefully. She seemed unaware of what she had said, unaware of the snippet of prophecy that had slipped from her lips in that strange trance-like state. He thought of saying something to her, but he did not. He wasn't sure that he would say something to any of them. Hope was too precious a thing to kill so casually.

Steven bent down and unzipped his duffel bag, pulling forth a small paper bag. He handed the bag to Jara and said, "Someone wanted you to have this."

Jara unfolded the bag and pulled out a lumpy round cookie. Her eyes grew wide and a large smile lit up her face as she lifted the precious treat to her mouth and took one over-large bite from it, causing moist crumbs to spill down her chin and into her lap.

Steven watched her devour the cookie. She chewed mightily at the candied orange slices, the baker's secret ingredient, and sighed indulgently as the last bite passed through her lips.

"Eleanor says hello," Steven said with a smile. "I wanted to let her know you were OK, after you just vanished from her life that night at the police station, and she insisted I bring you one of her orange slice cookies. I have to admit, it was awfully hard to resist the temptation to eat that myself."

Jara leaned her head on Steven's shoulder. "Thank you. Thank you for coming, and for coming up to talk to me... and for bringing the cookie."

"Every kid deserves a sugar rush once in a while," Steven said simply.

"It isn't about—"Jara started.

Steven interrupted her, putting his arm around her shoulders and giving her a squeeze. "I know. So... you up for a road trip?"

¤~¤~¤

The first three days of travel were horrible. Yors rode not upon a horse but upon a great, stubborn mule. Duke Igar, himself a large man, had few horses in his stables capable of handling someone of Yors' size, and the best of those the Duke reserved for himself. The Duke's party traveled alongside Moultus, Jara, and their entourage, so the group, in total more than twenty people, made poor time as they sauntered on horseback, or mule back, down the well-traveled Great Road of the South.

Yors brought up the rear of the party, as he often did. Every few hours, Jara rode back to talk to him, and if it wasn't for her visits he would have turned around and started the long journey back to the Borrik Mountains already.

Things were hard for Yors. He couldn't express himself in words, not the way everyone else could—but his mind was sharp, if slow. He was observant and experienced in many things, but he was always treated as though he was an oaf or an idiot. Most of the time it didn't bother him much, but after three days on the road with only Jara's occasional, if wonderful, conversation, he wondered if he hadn't made a mistake. At least with Ambrek and the others he was valued. If he were still able to draw Toren forth, his other, artificial personality, he would fit in better. He missed his other self, the one he had sacrificed to heal Jara's mother of her insanity. Toren had been more than a mask or a disguise to Yors, he had been a chance to live a different life and to leave the worst parts of his own behind. But now he was gone, and Yors had no choice but to be Yors. And clearly Yors was the last thing these people needed.

The entourage pulled off the side of the great road as nightfall crept upon them the third night, and the Duke's men set about erecting tents and preparing the evening meal. A tent was raised for Moultus, Hessa, and Jara, another for Jara's friends from Core, and then a large number for the Duke and his advisors. No one offered Yors a tent. The Duke's men took the early watch shifts, and Yors watched them keeping watch long after everyone had gone to sleep. Yors himself slept little, most nights—sleep was the time he found himself most likely to remember his baby girl and his wife, and he did not care to put himself through that more than he had to.

The moons, growing larger every night, were shrouded with pale clouds this night as the hour ticked past midnight by Yors' reckoning. They were empty clouds that once carried storm winds, if Yors was any judge, but as so often happened, they had shed their load of trouble over the sea.

Yors could hear no other sounds from the camp and suspected that, like last night, the Duke's watchmen had fallen asleep at their posts. Yors kept his crossbow loaded and sitting comfortably in his lap as he took up the slack for these pampered men more used to standing at ceremonial posts than out upon the fields of battle.

A soft rustle from behind him caused Yors to tense up, and he slipped his finger carefully across the trigger of his crossbow. A moment later a person flopped down on the trampled grass next to him, a meaty rib bone in his mouth. It was the Core-born child with the Bindmetal chain—the one called JC.

"Yors on duty." Yors said directly.

"Noted," JC said, devouring his pilfered food. "Thought you could use some company."

Yors grunted dismissively.

"I wanted to apologize for that whole 'lasering your face off' misunderstanding, back in the mountain camp." JC said. "I'm not really a very good apologizer though, so that was pretty much it. We cool?"

Yors squinted at JC. "Yors not understand half things JC say."

"You and my folks would get along great then," JC said, smiling. "I'm just hoping we don't have any bad feelings between us. I mean, you helped me with my problem," JC plucked at the one link of the chain at his throat that Yors had successfully stripped of its enchantment, "and I want you to know I owe you in a massive way."

Yors nodded. "Yors like to help. Yors helpful."

"I'm thinking that there has to be a way I can pay you back, my man. Especially if you are going to keep working at it. You are going to keep working at getting it off, right?" JC asked hopefully.

Yors nodded sharply. There was no reason for him not to help the young man—a good Jov was a friend to all who needed his services. That had been the teachings of the smiths at Jov Nought when Yors was a boy, so long ago, and even if everyone else had forgotten those teachings, he had not. If he was careful and judicious in his use of the magic, he could solve the boy's problem.

When Yors talked to this young man, it reminded him how very old he was. Yors had seen perhaps fifty summers, and this boy had seen so few.

"So I know what I'm gonna do to help you out. I'm gonna teach you about pronouns." JC smiled broadly.

Yors arched one heavy eyebrow at the boy. "Yors not know this word."

"Obviously," JC said. "It's like this—and stop me if this gets confusing because on my best day I only half pay attention in English class—but there are all these parts of speech, these kinds of words, and pronouns—"

Yors tensed and swung his free hand up to muffle JC's words. The boy tensed as well, sensing the same thing that Yors had sensed—intruders.

They both stood carefully, Yors with his crossbow at the ready and JC brandishing a burning stick plucked from the campfire. The boy's usual weapons were out of sight—back in the tent, Yors presumed.

They stalked as quietly as they could away from the camp for a few yards, trying to catch sight of whatever it was that they had sensed. A moment later, the horses, staked and grazing a hundred yards from the camp in a small copse of trees, suddenly screamed. The noise of them started to stir the camp, but Yors did not wait, rushing towards the trees with JC close behind.

As they burst into the clearing, the scene before them was one of carnage. The men stationed to watch over the horses were dead—all three of them laying upon the grass, their bodies contorted in agony and their faces a frozen picture of horror. Their eyes were gone, each of them plucked out by the thing that stood at the center of the clearing now.

It looked like a man, but Yors reserved that word for things far nobler than this. The thing wore black metal armor with a bright red rune painted upon its breastplate, and swirling around it, floating in the air and clawing at the horses that had not already torn free of their stakes, were four wraiths.

"What the hell is that thing?" JC asked, pointing his torch-club at the armored creature at the center of the carnage.

"Necromancer," Yors spat. "Spirit Slaver."

The necromancer took little notice of Yors and JC, instead concentrating on communing with whatever dark forces it worshipped. In its gauntleted hand, Yors could see the eyes of the fallen soldiers, and a righteous fury welled up in the Metalbreaker's heart. He lifted his crossbow to his eye line, sighted quickly, and fired the first bolt. It struck sure and true, passing through one of the phantasmal wraiths that flickered about the necromancer and punching through the sorcerer's breastplate, resulting in a fountain of dark red blood.

The necromancer cackled, taking the hand that did not grip the organs of the fallen men and smearing it up through the rushing blood, bringing his metal-wrapped fingers to his mouth and suckling on the hot fluid.

"Rend them and their hearts are yours," the necromancer muttered.

The wraiths took note of Yors and JC then, rushing forward. They were human-like, lacking lower limbs but instead trailing off in tattered rags. They glowed faintly red, and Yors knew that the boy likely had no idea how to fight such creatures. Were it a specter, perhaps he'd have had a chance, but wraiths... even Yors was uncertain if he was equal to the task.

JC swung his torch at the first wraith with a mighty grunt, and the burning log passed harmlessly through the wraith, flickering and sputtering. The wraith itself slowed momentarily. Yors recalled hearing, as a boy, that creatures of the Pit did not always know they were dead, and that such confusion was sometimes the only hope the living had of escaping an encounter with them. Yors fumbled in the quiver of bolts at his thigh, looking for the black-tipped Bindmetal bolt that he had forged for himself on the long walk back to the Borrik Mountains when he had first left Jara. His fingers landed upon the short metal shaft and he fitted it to the crossbow as another wraith joined in the assault.

The first clawed at JC. Its phantom fingers, tipped in very real barbs, tore at the flesh of the boy's upraised arms. JC cried out and dropped the torch, which sputtered and flickered on the grass. In a few moments, the grass would catch fire and they would have other problems on their hands.

The second wraith angled for Yors, and it flew directly towards his crossbow as he lifted it. He used no lever or crank to pull the firing mechanism—he used only the main strength of his mighty limbs. The crossbow cocked, and he fired it as the wraith descended upon him. The bolt tore into and through the wraith, shredding its spirit form as it flew and then slamming into a tree trunk two-dozen yards away. Yors could call it back to his hand with a moment's effort, but he had no moment to spare. The other two wraiths fell upon him now, and as they did so, the necromancer ceased to pay them any heed. The wound in its chest seemed to be no more than an inconvenience to the sorcerer, and it returned to the business of harvesting organs from the horses that the wraiths had felled.

If something didn't change shortly, the necromancer would soon be harvesting the organs of Yors and JC as well.

"Joe!" came a deep voice from behind. Yors could not turn to see it, but somehow JC managed to, and then with a thump and a high-pitched whine, the clearing was ablaze with light. JC, blood running freely from great gashes all along the length of his arms, had stood once more, one of the strange foreign weapons he usually carried in his hands. He pulled the trigger again, and again the clearing lit with the blazing beam of the weapon as it issued forth, slicing the wraith that had beset JC to ribbons of fading red light.

A second beam came from the other side of Yors, and there was the dark-skinned boy, Todd, the other of JC's weapons in his hand. His weapon he trained on one of the two wraiths attacking Yors, and as the weapon flared once more that wraith fell to pieces as well.

The last of the wraiths retreated a bit, swirling rapidly in the air, dodging as both JC and Todd took shots at it.

"Don't cross the streams!" JC shouted to Todd, a savage grin on his face.

"What?" Todd asked.

"Don't tell me you've never seen it? Seriously? Were you raised in a barn or something?" JC said, shaking his head.

While the boys attempted to box the wraith into one of their lines of fire, Yors took a breath, centered his mind, and called the bolt back to his hand, tearing it free from the trunk of the tree with his Metalbreaker magic. As it leapt to his hand he fitted it once more to his crossbow. He looked up, ready to aim at the necromancer... but the creature that was once a man was gone.

"Gotcha!" JC shouted as he fired and then pumped his fist in the air exuberantly.

Yors looked around. Three men were dead. Four horses were dead, the rest run off. The wraiths were scattered, banished back to the Pit until they could pull themselves back together. The necromancer though, the true author of their misery, was nowhere to be seen.

"Want to tell me what the hell that was all about?" JC asked as several of the Duke's men finally entered the clearing, swords at the ready.

"Yors already said. Necromancer." The smith shook his head. So much death. Always so much death.

"Well... we kicked his ass. And that was just what I needed. Got the juices flowing, you know?" JC smiled and patted Yors on the shoulder.

Yors continued to shake his head and raised one hand to JC's neck, grabbing the collar and squeezing it tightly.

"Dude—can't breathe..." JC struggled. The collar was so tight that there was not room for Yors' hand inside of it, at least not while also allowing JC the opportunity to breathe.

With a resonant chime and a puff of smoke and sparks from between Yors' weathered fingers, another link on the chain cracked, just slightly, releasing its magic into the world around it.

JC's eyes went wide, and for a moment—just a moment—Yors could see in those eyes terror, and sorrow... and then both were gone, carried away by the brilliant craftsmanship of the Jov.

"Thirty-eight," Yors said solemnly.

JC said nothing. Todd watched them both with an expression that Yors could not read. All around them, Duke Igar's men made preparations to burn the dead.

## 6
### Onus

*Ain Holc was nothing like Igar Holc or Rega Holc.* JC had begun to believe that all the cities of Onus had a certain feel to them, with their walls and their broad roads and their various districts neatly aligned along avenues and streets. But when they finally reached Ain Holc, the northernmost city of the South, he couldn't help but feel fortunate that their travels had never before brought them to these places.

It was easy to see that Ain Holc had once been a jewel of a city, but there was little left of it. The original outer walls, crafted of stone and wood, were long gone. The tumbled and scorched remains of the walls still littered the grassy fields surrounding the city, and only the main roads appeared to have been cleared. New walls, sturdy if ugly affairs of blocky sandstone, had been erected, but they offered only the barest illusion of security compared to the thick and ancient walls of Rega Holc or Igar Holc.

"She was the first city to fall to Hyrak's march," Moultus said from behind him, pontificating to no one in particular. "Once she was prized for her silk and spice trades, but neither has yet truly recovered from the occupation."

JC shook his head as they walked through the scavenged double gates of the city. They looked so much like those of Rega Holc—the gates he had nearly died defending—except these had not withstood the attack of Hyrak's army. They had been pieced together with wooden planks, the carved sigil of the House of Ain shattered but visible, barely, through those wooden patches.

Their party was ragged and mostly without horses—the stout Duke Igar had of course claimed the one horse that had not run away for himself—but they had survived the remainder of the journey without incident.

While much of the city inside the new walls was in ruins, there was no shortage of life. Bright sheets of cloth covered holes in walls and served as drapes and doors for those who no longer had such luxuries, and within the city boundaries there were people everywhere, shouting and calling to one another, selling goods and plying their various trades. The stone of the city was the same sandy color as the walls, and everywhere they went the air carried a strange mix of smells ranging from refuse to flowers.

The people had a slightly sallow skin tone, almost like Becky's Asian features, except that they lacked the distinctive shape of the eyes. As city watchmen led their party towards the palace, JC tried to remember if he had seen any other people from this region before, and he couldn't place a one. By the time he had become involved in the war, most of the South had already fallen. Aside from a band of soldiers that the Rak had spirited up from Stes Holc, which he understood to be even further away, no other southerners had really been in a position to participate in that final battle at the top of the world.

The sky was bright and unmarred by clouds. A portly man with thick, dark hair stood at the gate of the palace compound as they approached it. His hair stuck out in unkempt tufts from beneath the conical helmet he wore. He held, clutched in his short fingers, a horn. As Duke Igar approached, the herald put the horn to his lips and belted out three piercing, obnoxious notes. JC felt his teeth stand on edge, and as he looked around he saw he was not alone. Adam winced and Becky, who had been talking with Jara, looked up and shot a withering glare at the small man.

"Perhaps it's best these people haven't discovered the radio yet." JC muttered.

A moment later, they were escorted by household staff to chambers prepared for them in Duchess Ain's guest house. This building appeared to have weathered the war better than most others, but even here there were scorch marks on the walls and gaping cracks in the foundation stones. The group was split by the servants, Duke Igar and his people led in one direction while Jara's party, as they were called, were directed in another. JC filed into a room with Becky, taking note as Todd and Adam took another, Moultus, Jara and her mother a third, and Steven and Yors claimed the last room in the hall.

"Oh I bet that'll be a blast for Steven," JC said as he closed the door and collapsed on the feather-stuffed bed. It was not nearly as comfortable as his mattress back home, but it beat the heck out of sleeping on the ground the past five nights.

"I'm a little nervous," Becky said carefully as she sat down on the bed near JC. She didn't lean back, and he could see her rubbing her hands together anxiously.

JC sat upright. "It's a Council meeting. You've been to one before."

"It isn't that. Well, it is a little. I hate that no one knows why the Council was summoned. Moultus says they almost never convene outside of the Council Tower, either the old tower on the northern coast or the new one in Rega. So that's weird. But more than that, there's something up with Jara. We talked a lot on the way here, but anytime I tried to get to the point, the big questions, she changed the subject. "

"It'll be fine. All of it. We're having a little adventure—just a small one, I promise—before we get down to business and get you and Adam back home so you can pack up and leave us all behind." JC sighed. "And I got to bust some ghosts. I think I need to make a bucket list so I can cross that right off, you know?"

Becky laughed and kissed him, and JC marveled at the ease with which she did that now. She was more comfortable with who she was, and with her body, these days. If he hadn't already loved her, he would have started right there, in that moment.

Which was of course why the moment couldn't last. Happy times were always too short.

A sharp knock on the door caused them to disentangle from one another, and JC hopped off the bed and slipped the door open, revealing Jara. Unlike JC or Becky, she had changed when she'd had a few moments behind a closed door, and the ivory-colored dress she wore was actually quite nice. Her hair was combed, if still a bit wild, and hung down her back, secured by a bright gold pin. On her face was an expression JC knew all too well—disgust.

"You do dresses now?" JC asked, smiling.

"I make my mother happy. Even when it makes me miserable," Jara sighed. "We have to go. The meeting is starting, and we don't want to be late."

JC ran a hand through his nearly non-existent buzzed hair, as though that somehow made him more presentable, and turned to offer his arm to Becky. She took it, and they joined Jara in the hall, as did the others. They were an interesting crew. Most of them still wore their clothes from home, and they all stood out quite a bit.

"Is your mom coming?" Adam asked from the rear of the group, where he half-walked and half-stumbled as he tried to tie his shoe in motion.

Jara shook her head. "She doesn't like things like this. The invitation was for grandfather and me anyway, so... I'm probably pushing how many guests I am allowed to bring already." She smiled and they turned a corner to see the polished wooden doors of the great hall. A guard opened the door soundlessly, and the seven of them entered in similar silence.

JC resisted the urge to comment upon the décor, which was lacking, and the smell, which was certainly not lacking, thanks in part to the incredibly tight, vice-like grip that Becky had placed upon his arm.

"Not one word. Not. One." Becky projected into his mind.

JC smiled and sent back no smart-mouthed reply. For some reason he didn't care for being a smartass via telepathy. It simply didn't have the same gravitas that his verbal ramblings possessed.

"Gravitas? Seriously? Where did you learn that word?" Becky questioned silently in his mind. As she did so, they each took seats along the vast rectangular meeting table that dominated the hall. Torchlight flickered on all the walls and columns, and the sunlight from outside brightened the upper reaches of the hall through stained glass windows—most of which were patched with silk at the moment.

JC replied solemnly, "I read stuff sometimes. I like that word. It sounds like a super-hero name. I looked it up and realized it would be a pretty dopey super-hero name, but it's a kickass word for sounding like I belong with a crazy smart girl."

Becky sighed and shook her head, then the mental communication fell silent as the remaining guests of the Council filed in through other doors, occupying every seat at the table, save four.

At the head of the table, JC saw a familiar face. Duke Rega was a large, strong man with dark hair and a thick but neatly trimmed beard. He wore simple traveling clothes, as did most of the people around the table. He carried himself with an air of formality as always, but JC could see there was something different about him from when last they had been in such a position. Duke Rega was not afraid. He was not speaking from a place of desperation or of panic. It was nice to see.

"Council and honored guests. We have convened here, in the Protectorate of Ain, to share intelligence and gather wisdom from our peers on the safety and security of the southern continent. As these are matters in which I am poorly versed, I shall cede the right to lead these proceedings to our host, the Duchess Ain." With an elaborate bow, Duke Rega stepped aside and joined his own advisor not far from the head of the table.

Duchess Ain stood, and the moment she did, JC remembered her. He remembered unkind words about her, mostly, but her severe expression, her dark hair pulled back so tightly that it simply had to hurt, and her upturned nose brought back clear images of the Council at Rega a year and a half ago.

"Normally, we would wait for all ten thrones to gather before we entered upon our business," the Duchess said as she stepped to the head of the table, "but Duke Stes and Duke Weldaf will not be joining us. Events in their regions keep them too busy to slip away now, and this is for the best. In truth, this session was called more for the benefit of the North than the South, for you have much to learn."

Not far from where JC sat, one of the other Dukes muttered something unflattering under his breath. JC tried to suppress a smirk, but he felt like he failed. He didn't want to put his hands on his face to check.

"Leave your indignation at the door, Duke Mendul. Of all of us, you know least what it is to struggle with the consequences of war. While my people died by the hundreds, while my husband was roasted like a spitted pig before the eyes of his people, you cowered in your hiding hole." The Duchess glared with naked hate at Duke Mendul.

"Perhaps you could reach the point then, Salla?" asked Duke Distat. JC remembered the friendly blonde man, more ranger than bureaucrat, and recalled having liked him. He seemed older, and far more tired, than when last they had seen him, but still there was a warmth in him that so many of these other royal-types lacked.

The Duchess turned her glare to Distat, but she softened when she realized who had spoken.

"Formality, your grace," Ain chided him softly, her temper almost instantly reigned in.

"Of course. A foolish mistake on my part, your grace," Distat replied, smiling warmly.

Duchess Ain took a moment to compose herself, then resumed, "I know most of you traveled by horse or by foot, so you have seen the devastation for yourself. Those of you carried by the Rak have surely, at the very least, seen the damage done to my city, to my people. We are in dire straits, your graces—and Ain is not alone in this."

Beside Duke Distat an unfamiliar figure stood, thin and stooped by age. "Rura Holc is only two days' light travel from Ain. As you all know, no two cities in all of Onus are as near as we two, and for a time we were able to lean upon one another, but that time has fallen away. We have barely enough food to feed our people, and repairs go so very slowly on our defenses. Our garrisons will not be at full strength again for years."

"Have you not been reinforced by the Orders?" asked another unfamiliar face.

In his mind, JC heard Becky whisper, "Duke Norwin."

Duke Rura sighed. "The Surs have offered us as much aid as they can manage, but there is only so much the Bloodmenders can do to stave off starvation, and few of them are any good at all with a hammer and saw."

"And the Vols," Duchess Ain added, "are quite busy with their own problems. The Stepping Stones are a disaster of strife and infighting. Word from Stes Holc and Weldaf Holc is slow in coming, when it comes at all, but it seems they too struggle with the same problems that plague the rest of the southlands."

"What are those problems? We broke the back of Hyrak's army more than a year ago—closer to two! The repairs in the North have gone far faster. Even in Herin Holc we have nearly completed rebuilding our walls after Lyda sank them. What is it that prevents you from making such headway for yourselves? Surely you have not called us here to beg for coin and grain," another unknown Duke said. JC surmised he was Duke Herin, but at this point, he didn't particularly care. While this was all very important, it was also very boring. He hadn't crossed into this world to debate trade agreements and loans, after all.

"The arrogance of the North is never more proudly on display than when the six of you are in a room together," Duchess Ain nearly spat.

"Now hold your tongue, Duchess! Igar Holc has always stood with the South, and this is no exception. We have sent countless wagons of supplies to you in the past few months, with never a glimmer of thanks. Don't lump me in with the rest of the North!" Duke Igar shouted, slamming his heavy hand on the table.

"Yors confused!" Yors said, standing from his place beside Steven. The big Metalbreaker didn't pound on the table, but he did not have to. As he stood all eyes in the room were upon him.

JC put his head in his hands. "This is something I would do. He's totally stealing my act."

Duke Rega lifted his hands in a calming gesture and said to Yors, "We get a bit hot-tempered is all, my friend. I'm sure we will get to the bottom of what has everyone's tunic in a twist before much longer."

Yors nodded sharply at Duke Rega then said sheepishly, "Oh. Yors sorry." With a deep blush rising in his barely-seen cheeks, Yors sat back down.

"Perhaps we can be a bit more direct, for the benefit of our overlarge friend here?" Duke Distat asked.

"As was said, it has been well over a year since the back of Hyrak's army was broken, but that was not the end of the war," Duke Rura said. "Duchess Ain, if you would explain, please. I'm not as clear on all the details of our neighbors as you are, you know."

Ain cleared her throat and began to speak, gesturing expansively for emphasis and pacing the length of the table as she did so. "Hyrak left forces behind him each time he conquered a city. As he marched first south then north, he gathered new men and women to his banners from the disaffected and angry, those who had long felt that the policies of the Council kept them from what was rightly theirs. There is no shortage of such thinkers in the South, and as Hyrak occupied first Ain Holc then Rura Holc, he left hundreds of soldiers and key commanders behind to secure the territories. But his army did not grow noticeably smaller. His next march carried him to the Stepping Stones, through the three Arns that govern there. They negotiated with him, much to the chagrin of all ten members of the Council, but what's done was done. He circled around the Fdar Sands and choked out Duke Weldaf, this time gaining followers and conscripts from the nomadic encampments at Polus. He marched on Stes, again recruiting from the villages and camps in order to bring low the cities, and Stes Holc fell, though not as completely as he imagined.

"It took Hyrak years to do it, but he subjugated the entire Southern Continent and saturated the lands with soldiers loyal to him. Then he turned his attention northward, through Igar Holc and the Green Reaches, and the rest is well known to you all. In the North he moved faster, and with each conquest his army lessened, because in your lands people cling to the great cities for protection. Banditry and revolution was not the way of life among the free peoples of the northern continent, and in many ways, it was this that let you win."

The Duchess sat back down in her seat at the head of the table. "I have summoned the scribe of the Council, Moultus, to verify this accounting. Scribe, is this the truth of the thing?" she asked Moultus pointedly.

Moultus coughed a few times, clearing what sounded to JC to be a particularly gruesome lump of phlegm from his throat, and answered simply, "Close enough, your graces. There is some question of record on the sequence of events in the Fdar Sands before Weldaf Holc was taken, including a fascinating account from the Dwellers that seems to indicate that Hyrak's men actually took Weldaf using— "

Duke Rega raised his hand in a signal for silence, and Moultus complied quickly. "So you invited us here for a history lesson?" he asked the Duchess Ain.

"You need to understand the difference of culture in order to understand what we are telling you, Rega. The war has not ended here, it has merely changed its face and colors. Each of Hyrak's commanders has established himself as a despot under his own banner, so we have a dozen armies prancing about claiming to be the true successors to the legacy of the Warlord. Perhaps if any of you had been able to bring Hyrak's chief lieutenant, Narred, into custody, we might have been able to learn more about these men and their operations, but as it stands now, they elude us. They strike in the night, in the day—whenever they wish. Igar, you mentioned supplies you have sent to us these past few months? Not once has such a caravan reached us. Always they are waylaid on the road, their goods stolen and, often, their throats cut. And it is worse the farther South you go. There are rumors that the Arns war with one another, and that Stes Holc can do little more than fight delaying actions against a horde of savages still bent upon bringing the city down in Hyrak's name."

The Duchess closed her eyes. "We need more than money and food, your graces. We need your soldiers. We must bring the South back under Council control before there is no South left to claim."

¤~¤~¤

"Both of them?" Narred asked incredulously. He was sitting on the front bench of the wagon with Shayra at his side, and his wife had just spotted a pair of young farm boys, twins, in the village square of the tiny mountain hamlet of Founderstone.

Shayra nodded. "They both are touched by the magic, though neither has woken to it yet."

"They look quite well fed, my dear," Narred said, urging the mule to action once more. The great stubborn beast started forward, and Narred was careful to look no more at the two boys as they wrestled with unloading a great sheaf of grain, taller by a head than either of the two boys, from their father's wagon. "They are not orphans. They will be missed if we take them."

"I know that," Shayra said softly. "But two in one place is a sign. The Purpose wants them to come with us."

"We excuse many horrible things by telling ourselves that, Shayra," Narred replied curtly. "Let us tend to our actual business here, and give me a chance to think."

"Of a way to talk me out of this, or of a way to get it done?" Shayra asked.

"Neither. Both. I don't know. We need to get the vegetables for the children back at Kem Nought. Honest work." Narred hopped down out of the wagon and tied the mule to an anchored post outside the Founderstone market. They had been here before—he actually preferred coming here for their food because the place was so small and so remote that he didn't need to hide his recognizable face.

"I love that you have turned over this new leaf, beloved," Shayra said as she eased herself down from the wagon, "but sometimes I wish that you were a bit more of the man you were when we met. That man did what needed to be done."

Narred turned to face her in her silken robes. Her hairless head did not lessen her beauty, and even angry with her he could not help but wonder at how she took his breath away. "And you have become a different person as well, Collectress. When first we met, I was the monster and you the maiden. If I am turning too soft, it is because you have turned too hard."

Shayra nodded. "You still speak such words as though I have not heard them echoing in your mind a thousand times. I will collect the boys. Tend to the food. We are done here."

Shayra turned away from him, and Narred, fists balled tight, pushed through the swinging door of the Founderstone market. The merchants here, led by a thick bellied old man named Berrin, had become friends these past few months, but Shayra was right. They were done here now. There would be no coming back after they stole those two little boys from their family. They were six summers old, and they would soon never again be who they were meant to be, their souls overwritten by old, dead Mindshapers in the crystal halls of Kem Nought.

What made the Purpose of those Kem greater than the Purpose of those boys? Narred remembered his anguish standing at the side of Hyrak, asking that same question—what made the Purpose he served more important than the Purpose destined for all the men and women and children that died in his war? Back then, Narred had justified it with fear—Hyrak was immortal, unkillable, and thus the only way to survive him was to side with him. But now, what was his justification for allowing such darkness in Shayra and the Kem?

Did the fact he followed out of love instead of fear make him less complicit, or more?

¤~¤~¤

"Tower sighted!" Fendris shouted from the crow's nest. He'd been on watch most of the voyage, save for the night of the fierce storms, and this was the first thing he'd seen at all. No sea dragon off Monk's Gap, no trading vessels trying to skirt paying Council duties by swinging wide of the watchtowers—nothing.

Fendris slipped up and over the short wall that kept him from tumbling out of the nest when he dozed and scaled down the center mast, his nimble feet gripping the heavy metal staples in the smooth wood as ably as another man's hands. He was wiry and fast, and before much commotion had truly been raised on the deck, he was off the mast and racing to his captain's side.

"Bearings say this should be the mid-guard, yes?" Captain Grell asked without looking away from the spyglass he held to his eye.

Fendris grunted, "Aye. Not quite sure why this is the one you want though. Heard from a sailor used to run with Brotti on the Glory that the high-guard is easy to bribe."

"We aren't going to slip past the watchtower, Fendris," the captain stated, lowering the spyglass and sliding it into a small nook made just for it in the mounting of the ship's wheel. "We're going to bring it down."

Fendris barely stopped himself from letting his jaw flop open. "With what, sir? My good looks and your pretty blonde hair?"

"This is a voyage of lessons, my friend. And the first lesson is for Duke Igar. The sea is free, as all men should be, and we will make sure this lesson is well learned." Grell turned from Fendris and shouted towards the rear of the ship, "Vediri! Ready the lancers!"

Fendris sidled out of the way as the captain spun the wheel to correct his course—angling the ship directly towards the tower. The tall stone structure, round and ominous, was now visible to all the crew, not just those blessed with Fendris' keen eyesight.

Below them, a creaking sound could be heard, and Fendris darted to the railing at the forecastle to see the paneling in the great carved mouth of the ship pulling back, retracting on rails as men below deck worked at clever winches of the captain's design. He could hear Vediri barking orders down there, and at least twice he heard the cracking of her whip—a sign that she felt the men required better motivation. Slowly, but steadily, he watched as a large metal object, triangular and easily twice the size of a man, protruded from the open panel above the waterline, like a barbed tongue hanging from the Razormaw's gaping jaw.

A pair of bright red lights—old Bindmetal beacons, if stories were to be believed—began to flare atop the watch tower, and Fendris pulled back from the railing.

"I'm sure you aim to fork anyone that gets near well and good with that pig sticker on the bow, sir, but what will you do when they start with the arrows? We don't look friendly enough that they'll let us sail within pilot range before they light our sails with fire arrows and whatever other unpleasantness their graces have dreamed up for collecting sea taxes." Fendris squatted down, hoping to minimize his already small profile. He loved his head quite dearly and couldn't grow accustomed to the idea of an arrow sticking out of it. Many of his closest friends cut a stylish figure with an eye patch, but Fendris didn't think the look would suit him.

"What did I tell you, when I asked you to join this crew, Fendris?" Grell asked softly. "That night, in Gastrig's place?"

"That there would be lots of women, sir." Fendris replied solemnly. "Large-breasted ones."

"After that." Grell made a minimal correction to the wheel and then closed his eyes. Fendris wasn't quite sure, but it seemed the captain was humming.

"Trust you, you said," Fendris answered. "And I do, sir. With my life, obviously."

"Good," Grell said, opening his eyes. "Because you shall see something to tell the children those large-breasted women will bear you, now!"

Captain Grell pointed forward, and at first, Fendris saw nothing of note. The sea churned. The watchtower, painted a slick black and now peppered with additional sources of light—bowmen with burning arrows, just waiting for the ship to come into range—gleamed. The ship pushed forward. Then the small-statured pirate noticed that rising from the sea around the ship, clinging to its metal-studded hull, was a thick, billowing mist. The sheet of fog whipped up and around them, swirling and spreading like a creature possessed.

"I'm not rightly sure I know what I'm seeing, sir," Fendris whispered.

The order was given at the watchtower, prematurely and likely in response to the strange fog cover, and a volley of burning arrows arched through the sky, high overhead, intent on raining down upon the Razormaw. They had no such opportunity, though, as winds rose up, seemingly from the ship itself, and buffeted the arrows about, knocking them far off course to plop and fizzle in the water far to port of the ship.

The fog continued to grow, and the wind continued to howl. More arrows were fired—three volleys in rapid succession—but none struck their mark. The watchtower grew larger and larger before them, until they were nearly within spitting distance.

"Your bewitched winds are not likely to keep boarders at bay, sir," Fendris exclaimed as men with grappling hooks and ropes began filing out of the tower and onto the rocky beach at its foot.

"Fendris!" the captain chided.

"I know, I know. Trust you, sir."

From below, Fendris heard Vediri issue a single command—the first sound he had heard from below decks since the fog and the winds had started. With an immense twanging sound, the barbed point at the front of the ship launched out, a harpoon propelled by what had to be a most ludicrously large arbalest.

The projectile, trailing a light chain of brightly shining metal, struck the tower, piercing its lacquered surface and digging into the beams and stones that held it all of nine stories tall.

"Burn!" Grell shouted.

Fendris fell back, shielding his eyes, as an endless stream of lightning poured out of the ship, riding the chain up to the harpoon and then lancing out to crackle and burst upon the watchtower. For an achingly long count of twenty beats of the heart, the lightning raged out of the Razormaw and into the watchtower. Then it stopped and tentatively, fearing the brightness might render him blind, Fendris chanced a look at the watchtower.

There was nothing left of the mighty structure. Nor the men who had occupied it. Save for a heaping pile of ash, a few large blocks of stone, and a thick, stinking smoke in the air, the mid-guard watchtower of Igar Holc's coastal reaches was gone.

"How?" Fendris stammered out.

"The Razormaw is unlike any ship ever built, Fendris. She eats storms and spits them back at her enemies. And she will do so much more than that, by the time we are done with her. Vediri," he shouted below, "gather the men and get out onto that island. I want everything that didn't burn to ash brought back on this ship in the next hour!"

"What are they fetching?" Fendris asked.

"Bindmetal," the captain replied. "The ship isn't quite finished, but with only a bit more Bindmetal, she'll be all that I have planned for her."

"But what are you needing with Bindmetal, sir? It isn't like you can work it—only a..." Fendris gulped hard, catching a mouth full of the acrid smoke in the process.

"I'm a Metalbreaker, Fendris. Didn't I mention that to you when I hired you?"

"No sir. I'd be likely to recall such a thing." Fendris shook his head. A Metalbreaker pirate. That was something you didn't see every day.

¤~¤~¤

Gendric Tharsicast should not have been the leader of the Vols. His deceased mother had been their leader, but such a title was certainly not hereditary—they were a militant order, and by all rights the leadership should have fallen to the best warrior, or the keenest strategist, or something along those lines. Gendric was neither of those things, though he was far from inept. And yet here he was, riding away on horseback while a veritable flock of angry mercenaries tried to perforate him with crossbow bolts, in an effort to get back to the rally point and tell his brother and sister Boltsenders to do as they were told and hold the line at Jerrit Arn.

Bolts whizzed past his head as he hunkered down lower, as flat against the racing animal's back as he could make himself. His armor chafed uncomfortably and he knew the horse had already been pushed too hard today, but he had little choice. If he didn't pull this squad together, the brigands that Gollus Golluson had hired out of the desert would approach Jerrit Arn from its least defended side and countless lives would be lost.

He seemed to be gaining enough distance on his pursuers that he could ease up on the horse a bit, and Gendric chanced a transmission. He threw one hand into the air, thumb and forefinger extended, and cast about with his Boltsender magic, searching for a signal from one of the half dozen Vols he had brought with him on this supposedly easy duty.

None of them were transmitting right now. That might mean they were dead, but it could also mean they were not following protocol. These were young men and women, recruits from since the end of the war and the opening of the academies, and if their training was inadequate that, like all else regarding the Vols, was on his head.

Gendric pulsed out a simple message, instructing them to regroup at the marked Stone. He tried to send a picture of the low stone pillar that he had scored with his sword this morning along with the words, but it was virtually unthinkable that any of these recruits yet had the talent to read a visual transmission.

He heard the rising voices of his pursuers and feared they had gained a second wind. He had no such luck—there were no second winds and no chances to rest. The hundreds of square miles out here in the Stepping Stones were perfect for traps and ambushes, and the civil war between Gollus Arn's power-mad geriatric dictator and the others was keeping the Vols running ragged. If help was coming, Gendric didn't know about it. Nenasha was thousands of miles away at Rak Nought, and even his best friends among the Vols were far from him on dangerous assignments.

Getting no answer from the recruits, Gendric took a moment—the only one he had to spare—to fire off one more transmission, this one coded for Cambria. She was one old friend that had never let him down, but even she had gone silent these past few weeks.

He had no time to wait for a reply. The people of Jerrit Arn were counting on the Vols to save them, and at the moment, that meant they were counting on Gendric.

¤~¤~¤

"Shhh! Quiet!" Cambria shouted at the children in her charge. She had both hands in the air, working at her magic as carefully as she could, but the Vale of Steam was wreaking havoc on what few signals she could get hold of.

All around her were children. She had two dozen children, the oldest among them ten summers at the most, that she had smuggled out of Mandor Arn as Gollus' forces had crushed past the last of the fortress' defenses. Now she was all that stood between this band of children and the horde of mercenaries and cutthroats answering to Gollus' coin out there.

The Vale of Steam was tropical, blisteringly hot and humid. The children were exhausted and cranky, and Cambria wasn't much better. She was soaked through but unwilling to shed her Vol armor. Her copper-threaded sword had been left behind in the chaos of herding twenty-four children down an unlit tunnel for the better part of three days.

"Are we going to eat soon?" asked a small girl—one of the last children of the old bloodline of Mandor. Cambria hated that she didn't know the girl's name, but she hated many things about this assignment.

"Soon, yes. I just have to find us something worth eating," Cambria muttered. "Help keep the others quiet, please. We're scaring away the game."

She wasn't sure how much game there even was in this sweltering stink-hole, but they could hear creatures croaking and skittering about at night, when they tried to sleep, so there had to be something to eat besides the occasional fruit that they had been living off of since they arrived.

Cambria detached from the children, pushing away from them once it appeared that a few of the older ones were wrangling the younger ones properly. She summoned as much of her power as she dared, calling a small flickering bolt of flame to dance about her fingers, ready to project at the first edible creature she came across. Lightning was easier for a Vol, but fire was more suited to hunting.

She spotted a trail, quite wide and well-traveled, showing markings of a large number of creatures passing through in recent days. She followed it, marking her bearings as best she could so she would be able to find her way back to the children, and the trail twisted and wound deeper and deeper into the heart of the Vale. It would take a person days to cross the Vale of Steam on foot, so Cambria had no idea where she was in relation to anything else, but when she turned one last time upon the trail, she saw something magnificent.

She stood in a large round clearing. It was perfectly circular, and perfectly smooth, easily five hundred yards across. The ground here was a kind of dark stone she had never seen before, peppered with flecks of crystal and veins of rich metal but smooth and cool to the touch. At the very center there was an indentation, a pool, perhaps a hundred yards across, and in that dip was clear, sparkling water. She knew that water might well be a mirage brought about by the heat, but she was willing to chance it. It was a place protected from the heat of the jungle, somehow, and that was what the children needed.

What in the name of the Purpose had created such a place she had no idea, but nor did she care. It was as good a place as any she would find to set up some form of camp. She had no idea what she was going to do next, but at least now she had a place to start.

# 7
## Onus

*For as long as anyone on Onus could remember, there had been one infallible truth at the heart of the world:* The Wyr knew what to do. But the Wyr were fading away, and had been since long before Jara was born. In fact, she was the only practicing Fatewaker that any of the Council even knew of, since Jara's grandfather had made it a point to keep Jara's mother's abilities a secret.

So all of the curiosity, fear, and worry of these seven men and one woman, an assemblage of the most politically powerful people in the entire world, was placed upon the frail shoulders of a fourteen year old girl who had never met another trained Wyr in her entire life.

"We summoned you here to help us plot a course of action, Jara Abison," Duke Rega explained, as though Jara did not already know what he wanted—what they all wanted. They wanted someone to tell them what to do so that if things went poorly, they could blame the Wyr. That much Jara knew well, and it didn't take special insight or magic to see it. Like everyone else on this or any world, they wanted someone else to make the hard choices for them.

"Of course," Jara said hesitantly. She thought many things—dangerously heretical things, actually—but she kept those notions bottled up. Moultus had insisted she behave appropriately at this meeting, and she would play the part of advisor as best she could. It was a part her grandmother had played, long ago, so she knew somewhere, deep down, she had it in her. And she was wearing the silly white dress her mother liked so much, so she imagined she at least looked the part of timid prophetess.

"What is the proper course of action in the South?" Duke Herin asked. "Should we bring men, soldiers, into the fields of battle again so soon?"

Jara closed her eyes. She tried to rouse the magic, to stir it to action, but that had never been the way it interacted with her. The magic of the Wyr did as it wished, and Jara was more often its pawn than its master. If she ever met a true Wyr, one versed in their secrets, the first thing she would ask that person was, quite obviously, why the magic refused to do as it was bid. But these people expected an answer, so an answer she would give them.

"Turmoil in the South can only bear fruit of ruin for the North," Jara said carefully. Images began to flicker in her mind, images of fire and smoke, of bodies strewn about unharvested fields, and more. But they were hazy and indistinct, always awash in the background with a bright blue light, creeping in from the periphery of her visions. The light flickered, dampening from time to time as though something passed between her and it. The images would not resolve, no matter how she prodded them with her magic. She looked up, across the ruined fields, and saw banners flapping in the wind—the colors of each of the great cities were there, scorched and stained, many hanging in tatters from shattered poles.

"There is chaos in the air," Jara muttered. "I see the Council torn. There are few soldiers upon the field of battle—but many dead."

"What does that mean? That we are indecisive? That takes no special gift to see!" Duke Mendul snapped irritably. "I never put all that much stock in these fortune tellers myself. I should have brought the Collectress of the Kem with me. She calls me patron, as you all know..."

"Yes, we know, your grace," Moultus interrupted the balding Duke. "But that has no bearing. Allow my granddaughter to plumb the depths of the Purpose a bit longer before you write her off and seek to replace her with a woman whose talents are in no way appropriate to the task at hand."

Jara opened her eyes for just a moment to catch a glimpse of the chagrin on Duke Mendul's face, then, smiling inwardly, she squinted them closed once more and tried to do as her grandfather had asked—she tried to dig deeper into the images.

The blue light at the edges of her vision continued, flickering as shadows passed by. Away from her, north of her, she thought she felt a trembling. To the south, she heard a ringing sound, and she saw herself standing in a temple without walls, a temple of memory, and weeping as darkness poured into her. The images shifted then, to show her friends, Joe and Steven and Becky and the others, with Yors as well, trudging through snow towards a mighty glass castle. The snow melted and the image shifted again, this time back to the field and the corpses. She picked up an ear of corn in the field, peeling back its husk to reveal rotting kernels, their bright golden skin shot through with streamers and spirals of black corruption. Then the blue light all around her grew brighter still, and one of the flickering shadows felt as though it were right behind her. She spun and caught the author of that shadow in one outstretched hand.

He wore black plate mail armor, the details of which she could not make out. He had a heavy helm upon his head, which Jara reached up and removed with one hand, granted strength by conviction. Beneath the helm, the armor was empty... but not forever. Only for now.

"Jara, my dear? Do you have anything more you can share with the Council?" Moultus asked gently.

Jara nodded as she opened her eyes. "Something very bad will happen soon at Igar Holc. Very soon. We may yet survive if we all come together, all the Council as one, but it will be a hard-fought battle. The casualties will be severe. And there is something more, just out of sight, that I cannot yet see the shape of. Send for the soldiers, your graces. If the Purpose wills it, they will be here before this last piece of the puzzle reveals itself."

"Hardly definitive proof of need for a full scale mobilization," Duke Norwin mulled softly. "We do have brigands and bandits in the north as well."

"The troubles here, now—they are the kind of victory that can be won, Duke," Jara said flatly, emotion restrained as best she could. A few more images danced in her mind, and the intuition of her magic was assembling them into understandings, none of which she liked. "But if we do not win this victory, on this field, that which comes for us next will not be stopped. This is the certainty of the Wyr. All else is conjecture, but this is fact: If you do not tame the South now, in spite of the price that we will surely be called upon to pay, you will lose all of Onus later."

The room was silent. It took Jara a moment to realize precisely why she had gained the full and undivided attention of everyone in the room... even Joseph, who was staring at her slack-jawed.

Jara looked down to see that she was, ever so faintly, glowing. She was also floating three inches out of her chair, but that was somehow less strange to her.

¤~¤~¤

The general atmosphere of the Council meeting grew rather grim after Jara's prophetic lightshow, and many of the non-royal guests were excused from the following discussions of troop distributions and logistics. Adam was fine with that, as it gave Todd and him a chance to retire to their room and talk with a degree of privacy they had not had since well before entering the Spiralgate to come to Onus.

"I'm surprised you aren't in there volunteering to ferry soldiers halfway around the world," Todd said as he closed the door behind him.

The room was fairly small and unadorned compared to the rest of the royal chambers of Ain Holc. There were silk-draped ceilings and a large but simple bed, but little else. Adam paced in a small circle beside the bed, near a tall glass pitcher of water that carried a distinctively floral scent that made it unappetizing.

"This has gone on way too long already. I talked to Becky, and she's going to pump Jara for the answers to our questions tonight so we can be on our way home tomorrow. We are not getting mixed up in another war on this world." Adam sighed and rubbed his hands together. "I know I sound like a broken record, but I really thought we were coming up on being able to put all of this behind us."

"You're the only person in the known universe that can open the Spiralgates, Adam. I don't know if all of this will ever really be behind you." Todd sat down on the bed and motioned for Adam to join him, but Adam shook his head.

"But why? Seriously, why? How much more does the Purpose or the prophecy or whatever the hell is calling the shots for the Children of the Line want with me? I helped save Onus once already—how many times does one world need saving?"

"As many as it takes to keep it saved, I suppose," Todd said quietly.

"But we gave enough! We've seen enough that no one our age should have to see. Every time we travel through that tunnel of light we find a world even more screwed up than ours. Maybe the work we are supposed to do is back home. Do any of the others think about that? What if right now there is something happening on Earth that requires us to save the day, and we aren't there because we are here screwing around while the people of Onus kill each other. Again."

Adam was agitated. Once upon a time, Todd had been the one, even more than Becky, that could bring him down from a place like this—but things hadn't been quite the same with them since the Fourth of July. In some ways, Adam feared that they were growing apart. In other ways, he wondered if his mother meeting Todd at long last had put some new strain on their relationship. He wasn't sure the cause or the extent, but their senior year of high school had clearly shown him that things were different. Todd was more guarded with him, and he somehow seemed to have lost the gift he once had to always bring Adam back to center.

"I'm sure you don't want to know what I think," Todd said, standing up to look Adam in the eyes, "but I will tell you anyway. I was against this trip too—don't forget that. But now that we are here, maybe this is a chance to get everything out in the open. To find out who the other Children of the Line are and to find out what exactly you are all supposed to do that is so damn important. So maybe you should focus on getting things squared away instead of the pity party?"

Adam stared back at Todd. "It isn't a pity party. I just don't understand why I have to keep being destiny's whipping boy."

"Get used to it," Todd said simply, looking away. He paced over near the door and put a hand on the handle, still facing away from Adam. "I'm sorry. I shouldn't have come. I was right to try and stay behind. I wasn't ready to come back here and see all of this again."

He turned the door handle, but Adam stopped him, dropping an intercession of Gatemaker magic upon the door that kept it from moving. "What does that mean? Will you please, please, just tell me what's going on with you?"

Todd turned back, and Adam could see that there was something in his eyes that he had not seen there before—guilt, perhaps. Or shame?

"I can't. Not yet. I'm not ready. It would change how you feel about me."

Adam nodded and released the intercession. "OK. Um... you can leave, if you want. I don't want you to, but I won't make you stay."

Todd sighed and moved away from the door. "I don't have anywhere to go anyway. I thought I needed space. Or that you did. But here we are, with a door and a bed and no mother of yours knocking every ten minutes to make sure we are still alive."

"So maybe there are some upsides to this trip?" Adam asked.

"Just one or two," Todd said, smiling. Whatever turmoil had been there, in those deep brown eyes, was gone, replaced once more by the cool confidence that had captivated Adam from the moment they met. A tiny part of Adam's mind wondered what he had almost learned today, but that part was easily drowned out by the parts of him that were just happy to be close to Todd.

It was hard to imagine that anything Todd might say would ever make him feel anything but love for this amazing, gorgeous young man.

¤~¤~¤

The ruins of the third and final watchtower were still smoldering as Grell bound his long blond hair back out of his eyes and began his work. The men were out scavenging what Bindmetal had survived the attack even now, while he started to smith the metal collected from the other two towers.

For ages, Bindmetal forged with enchantments big and small had been an uncommon but vital part of Onus. It wasn't until thirty years ago, when the Jovs had been traded to the alien world of Murrod, that the flow had peaked and then slowed. Then when the Gars ceased to ferry people between worlds, somewhere near twenty years ago, new Bindmetal ceased entering into circulation. The watchtowers were old relics of the pirate wars, in a time before any still living drew breath. They were outfitted with beacons, spyglasses, and defenses of the precious metal. It was in the combination of the scraps of what remained that Grell would fit his ship with the last of her gifts.

The lowest hold, at the rear of the ship, had been built to his exacting specifications. It was a well-stocked forge. Every surface of wood was lacquered with a thick resin made from the stunted trees of Garoo Island. Grell had lost a dozen men each of the three times he had raided that island and stolen the sap of those ugly, twisted trees, but it was worth it. Thanks to the Garoo laquer, he had a forge aboard ship that did not run the risk of burning the ship to cinders at its every firing.

He had shoveled the Bindmetal items into a long trough and set to heating the trough thoroughly, melting down the blacks and the reds, the blues and the whites, the greens and the yellows, the oranges and the violets. The eight colors of Bindmetal were of little consequence to him—he had never learned the secrets of drawing specific magic out of specific types of the stuff. Grell was a Metalbreaker, but he was no Jov—the secrets of that order were lost to him as they were lost to this world when the Council sold them into slavery. It was the greatest wrong done by an organization bent upon doing wrong, and it was but one of the things for which Grell would make the aristocracy of Onus pay.

The molten metal sang to him with a tone and rhythm that he alone on the ship could hear. It was only through his coaxing and his chanting that the heat could even melt the metal—only a Metalbreaker could change the shape of Bindmetal in any way. The amalgamation of types of metal before him would suit his needs, and he set about the true work of shaping it.

With a pair of pincer-like tongs he plucked a large glob of molten Bindmetal from the trough and set it to anvil. He hammered upon it as he sang a song taught to him by his father when Grell had been but a small boy longing for his mother. It was a song of the sea, and it soothed him.

The metal slowly took shape at the song's direction and the hammer's insistence. It thinned into a sheet, vaguely circular, that was much like the disks that studded the hull of the Razormaw, save it was far thinner. The ovular sheet was large, and grew only larger as he pounded it flatter and flatter, applying the arts of smithing as much as the arts of metalbreaking to render it supple and vast. When finished, it was nearly as broad and long as a full-grown man, and it was but the first of six he had to make.

He set the polished sheet of dark metal, swirls of color evident in its sheen, on a pair of sawhorses to rest. As he did this, the heavy door to the forge creaked open to reveal Vediri, a grin on her plain features and soot streaking her spikey hair.

"I begin to believe that this voyage *is* fated, you old crook," she said.

"Did I not tell you that we had the Purpose on our side?" Grell asked, wiping sweat from his forehead with the back of his hand. The room was blisteringly hot, and the waft of cool air that had followed Vediri's opening of the door merely called attention to it.

She laughed. "You've told me many things that were not true, Captain. But this one I begin to believe. We found the metal you were looking for—more than enough for the blades and in that bright blue color that I like so much."

"The inventory of the northern watch tower was not a mystery, Vediri. It's good planning, not good fortune, that you celebrate."

"Let me finish then," the first mate insisted. "The last of the storm reserves were spent here—as we expected. The Bindmetal batteries in the fore hold are dry. But here is the good fortune I spoke of: there is a storm brewing not far north of here. Fendris can smell it, and the gulls fly wide to avoid it—a sure sign of its fury. We may be able to resupply the storm batteries before we close with the mainland."

"North of here is Asira's Belt," Grell said simply. "There are no storms in Asira's Belt."

"Hence the providence of our journey," Vediri said, renewing her grin. "You needed a storm, and a storm appeared where one ought not to be."

"Interesting." Grell pushed past Vediri, extinguishing the fires of the forge with a wave of his hand as his magic slammed shut heavy metal caps that cut of the supply of air to the fire.

Vediri followed the captain close at his heels. As the two of them climbed the rough-hewn stairs to the deck, each step creaked and moaned. The entire ship whispered at Grell's passing, telling him of its ills and complaints. Metal nails spoke their protestations as he emerged into the smoky air.

"Fendris!" Grell called. In no time at all the scrawny watchman was at his side. "Where is this storm?"

"There, sir," Fendris pointed, rushing to the railing of the ship. "A mighty one, by the smell of it."

Impatiently, Grell grunted, summoning his spyglass from its compartment at the ship's wheel and causing it to launch through the air, tumbling end over end as it landed in his outstretched hand. He lifted the polished metal tube to his eye and sighted through the lenses. There was indeed a storm brewing, but through the glass he could see that it was no product of wind and cloud. The storm was rising up, out of the water, boiling into existence at the behest of the mighty creature that floated in the water beside the towering column of storm—the sea dragon Candara. Her great tentacles, sprouting from powerful shoulders, worked in intricate patterns in the air and her baleful eyes glowed, though Grell was surprised to see that one of the creature's three eyes was dead—somehow struck from its massive skull. The dragon's serpentine head turned away from the storm it was crafting and looked directly at Grell. He knew then that the creature saw him, or felt him, and knew him for who he was.

"Bring the men back from the island." Grell lowered his spyglass. "I don't understand what she is doing."

"Who?" Fendris asked, confused.

"Candara. The old sea witch herself is making that storm, though who can say why. She is not known for her benevolence." Grell turned away from the railing. "Give the order, Vediri. We will bleed off as much as we can... but we won't be chasing it into the Belt today."

Behind him, Grell could hear Fendris whispering to the first mate.

"We have bargains with the sea dragon?" Fendris asked fearfully.

Vediri said nothing, but began shouting orders to make ready for sail.

Grell walked back to the wheel and slid the spyglass into its slot. He had smithing to do before they reached port, and the likelihood of trouble between now and then was high. They needed the power of that storm, and he imagined that she knew it. He couldn't risk getting too near her though. He couldn't explain to these men the nature of their relationship, not now, and he needed them as much or more than he needed the storm—for now.

¤~¤~¤

There was a small stool in the corner of the room that Steven was to share with Yors, and so he sat on it. Light breezes outside caused the fabric-draped windows to flutter, and he caught stray scents wafting in from outside. The smells were perfumed and cloying, but the sweet smells were obviously layered over top of deeper, thicker stenches. He had encountered similar smells during his brief time overseas, back on Earth—a time of war that he did not often think back to. Aside from his tangles with the Obliviates, he had dedicated his life since returning home from that far away desert country to bringing peace.

But here war was at the center of everything again. The conversations of the Dukes were about deployments and rations as much as they were about diplomacy and politics, and the idea of it all made him queasy. Steven had tuned out as much of it as he could, focusing instead on the simpler things. The architecture was not as different from back home as he might have expected, except for the obvious medieval period of it all. The people looked human enough—were human, as best he could tell—and even the smells and the sounds were similar enough to being home that he didn't truly feel the distance that stretched between him and his own bed back in Des Moines.

But then, when he started to forget how strange this all was, he would see the two moons, or he would see Jara floating above her chair, and it would all come crashing back to him. He wondered what Tatyana would have thought of this place, and he considered retreating for a moment into that quiet place in his heart where he still felt her, but he resisted the urge. It was agony, every time he did so—yet again and again he did.

Yors entered the room after Steven had spent quite some time daydreaming. The big smith nodded his head cordially and made a somewhat polite grunt, then took a seat on the bed, pouring cool water from the pitcher beside the bed into a large cup.

"Yors bothered by something," he said plainly as he tilted the cup back. Much of the water somehow missed his lips, and when he lowered the cup his dark beard was soaked through at the edges of his mouth.

Steven asked, "What is it?"

"Yors feel Metalbreaker magic, steady and strong, coming closer." The Jov returned the cup to the tray beside the pitcher and stood, crossing to the window and pulling back the bright orange fabric to look out at the neatly-sculpted garden. A wall separated the view from the city of Ain Holc itself, and Steven could not imagine that what lay on the other side of that wall was at all as appealing as the garden.

"Are there many of your people this far south?" Steven asked conversationally. He knew very little about the Metalbreakers, aside from the insights provided by Yors' campmates after he and Adam had snuck off to see the burgeoning Jov Nought encampment.

Yors shook his head. "There not many of Yors' people *anywhere*. None south. All Jovs taken to Murrod when Yors young—right after Yors' baby girl born." The big man closed his eyes, and for a moment, Steven thought he would not go on. Then, with a shuddering release of held breath, Yors continued, "Thirty summers and more since then. When Gatemaker brought Jovs home, all Jovs come together, except ones left behind on Murrod. Even when split up into two groups, Jovs stay together. All near Borrik Mountains. No Jovs down here."

Steven stood from the stool and joined Yors at the window. "Maybe I could go look around? I'm not much use here at all, and with my powers, I can sneak pretty well. If I ride the shadows in the direction you feel this person, I might be able to figure it out."

Yors looked excited. "Yors go with?"

Steven replied, "I'm afraid not. I'm not very good at moving other people with me yet, and you... well, you're really big."

Yors sighed again and let his shoulders slump. He was the very definition of the word crestfallen, and Steven considered his options.

"Maybe—maybe I can. I haven't tried it in a while, and the magic does seem to flow a little easier here on this world. Let me see if I can carry you." Steven moved to the relatively open space near the door, away from the light of the window. The shadows here were feeble, thanks in large part to the large square cutouts in the ceiling that allowed filtered sunlight to stream in, but there was enough to work with as he concentrated.

He drew in several deep breaths and then exhaled them all at once, willing the shadows to gather about him, transitioning his body out of flesh and into the ephemeral substance of night. Once he shifted, he would try to shift Yors as well. Travel in this form was fast, and they could surely investigate Yors' miniature mystery and be back before any of the others had a chance to even worry about them.

As the last of him merged with the shadow, Steven suddenly felt his body constrict and contort, his limbs bending in upon themselves in a way that would have been utterly painful had he been solid.

A pair of hands, thin and feminine and ending in wickedly sharp fingernails, emerged from his chest, flowing into, out of, and through him as a seamless extension of his shadowform. The hands slowly extended, resisting his efforts to banish them, and when they reached the crook of their elbows, they twisted, turning around and reaching up to wrap around his shadowform throat.

Steven gripped at the slender stranglers, straining with all of his physical might, but his body was not the muscle that mattered in this. He tried to tap into the magic, to shred the shadow or to slip away from it, but whatever was happening, whoever was doing this, was stronger than he was—or at least better at this.

In the back of his mind, nightmare-fueled images of Alders leapt to life, and he began to panic. Even though he was not certain he even needed to breathe while in his shadowform, he gasped for air as the hands choked the life from him.

He felt his shadowform failing, retreating, as he transformed back to flesh and blood, but the shadow flowed inward, towards his center of gravity, meaning that his head and throat became flesh before his chest, and the shadowlimbs still extended from his chest and doubled back upon him, now truly strangling him to death.

Yors swung his meaty fists at the shadow limbs, but while solid enough to do grievous harm to Steven, they yielded easily and insubstantially to Yors, and the big man called out for help.

Steven heard a faint whisper in his ear, coming from the shadows of the room and the shadows still cloaked about him. "None may touch the shadow save the Rak. Tell your masters we are watching!"

Then, as quickly as they appeared, the hands of darkness vanished, and Steven collapsed to the ground, wheezing for air.

"What the hell was that?" he managed to choke out between gasps.

¤~¤~¤

Jara sat at the foot of the bed. Steven lay in the bed, sweating profusely. He had stripped his shirt, but still he was warm, and the setting of the sun had not appreciably cooled the warmth of the guest chambers.

It also did not help, as far as Jara was concerned, that there were so many people crammed into this room. Yors guarded the door, while Adam and Becky, Todd and JC all crowded around the bed. Jara had assured them that he would be alright, even going so far as to use her "I really mean it, I saw it in a vision" voice, but still they would not leave.

"But what happened?" Adam asked, worriedly. "Is it some kind of trap? Is this what would happen if I open a gate or if Becky tried to mindshape?"

"You've already used your powers since we got here," Todd pointed out.

"And Becky never stops mindshaping," JC added. "I don't even think she knows she's doing it half the time."

Adam looked about in frustration. "Well that's all I have for useful theories."

"It's probably much simpler than all of that," Jara said at last. "It's a little complicated, really, but I suppose if we are all going to sit about watching Steven recover, I can try to explain it. Let's go outside."

She hopped down from the bed, and as she did, Steven reached out and caught her hand. "I'm not asleep. Don't take them anywhere—I want to know too."

Jara wrapped her free hand around Steven's, feeling the sticky heat in it, and she nodded slightly. He needed to rest and rebuild his strength, but he wouldn't listen—she was suddenly overcome with the sad realization that this was how she probably made her own mother feel most of the time.

Her mother, of course, was at the heart of this whole affair.

"I am a Fatewaker because it was passed down to me, mother to daughter, as the magic of the Wyr has always been. It was thought that the magic faded in our family after my grandmother, but as it turns out it lived on in me. Except it doesn't work that way—it doesn't skip generations or anything like that," Jara explained slowly, keeping her voice low. The things she was about to say were delicate things—things about which the Council did not need to know the full extent.

"So my mother had the magic as well, but she never knew it—it just didn't stir in her like it did in me. She might have lived her whole life without ever working a single aspect of the arts, except that somehow she caught Lyda's eye. Lyda hauled her to Hyrak, and Hyrak... he tortured her. For days, or weeks—we don't know. The torture woke up her powers, but it woke them up different. She doesn't see fate, or the Purpose, not like I do. She actually *makes* fate—she changes people's destiny. With a touch, my mother can stir even the faintest glimmer of magic in someone to life, or still even a raging power to quiet." Jara looked at the door, and Yors nodded sternly. In this, as in so many things, she knew she could count on her Metalbreaker friend to protect her, her mother, and their secrets.

"Before we rescued her, they forced her to use her talent on many men and women. We don't even know how many. The Lightning Legion that Narred attacked Rega Holc with? Those were Boltsenders woken by my mother. The necromancer that attacked us on the road south from Igar Holc? A Wraithtender woken by my mother. Even..." Jara stopped. The next words were stuck in her, and no amount of conviction or will would cause them to slip from her lips.

"Hyrak." Becky said softly. Jara could feel the tickling presence of Becky in her mind, skimming the surface of her thoughts. In another time or circumstance, she would have been outraged at the invasion of privacy, but here and now, she was happy to simply have it in the room.

Jara nodded and added, "Even Hyrak. He forced her to wake powers in him as well, though I can't say I know what they were, or why it matters since he's gone. But she did it. Against her will, driven mad with pain and torment, my mother made scores of bad men and women powerful."

"So I was attacked by some kind of rogue Shadowbender?" Steven asked weakly, his voice still hoarse.

Jara sighed. "Probably not. The Orders know that somehow these mercenary magicians are out there, and they have been trying to bring them to justice. The Rak took it very personally for some reason, so I imagine that you were on the receiving end of a Rak ambush laid for untrained Shadowbenders. Because they've never met you, they mistook you for their enemy instead of their savior."

Steven closed his eyes and leaned his head back onto the feather pillow. "I am no one's savior."

"You are a Child of the Line, which makes you that and more," Jara said. "And I suppose that brings us to the specter in the room."

JC looked around in a hurry, his eyes wide and his hands balling into fists. "Specter? Now?"

"An expression, Joseph. The thing in the room about which everyone knows but no one wishes to speak." Jara slid down to sit on the floor with her back to Steven's bedside.

"We call that an elephant," JC said.

Jara replied, "You did come here to ask me about the Children of the Line, right? It seems to be the only thing that makes sense. The one piece of unfinished business between us before you all go back to your world and leave me to all of this splendor." She tried to mask the sarcasm in her voice. She failed.

"We know you can't really tell us what we are supposed to do," Adam said tentatively, "but we were hoping you could help us in another way. It seems like the work of the Children of the Line will require all of them, and we only know three. Assuming Becky stands in for Tatyana now..."

Jara nodded. "The Purpose usually finds a way to get what it wants."

"So who are the other three?" Becky asked impatiently. "What can you tell us about them? We want to find them, to gather the Children, and do what we are all meant to do."

Jara closed her eyes. "I will try to find an answer for you."

She tried to plunge into the rushing waters of destiny, to draw forth images and impressions like she had many times before, but—also like many times before—the waters resisted her. She pushed ahead, not wanting to let the others down, and then, abruptly, her eyes snapped open, images and words fixed vibrantly in her mind.

"I can't answer the question," she said directly, the words nearly tumbling from her mouth. "It's not here. The Wyr, somehow, they struck the truth of the Children of the Line from the world. It's blank, unreadable. I've only ever once seen something like it." She avoided looking at Todd. Ever since her first attempt to read Todd's fate, Adam's boyfriend made her uncomfortable. But she finally knew something about him she had not known before—the lack of vision she experienced in regards to him was not a quirk of fate or an accident of failed training—it was somehow deliberate.

A theory began to form in her mind, a guess built on conjecture and nothing more. Now wasn't quite the time.

"We know that there are six Children of the Line. Becky and I read more about them as well—we know that Onus sent thirteen members of the orders to Core to watch over the bloodlines that would yield the children and ensure that no evil befell them. But the names, the identities, of those bloodlines are hidden from me." Jara smiled.

"That's completely unhelpful," Joe muttered. "I'm only five percent de-collared, and we are oh-for-three on names of Children of the Line. Adam, I'm sorry I made you bring us here."

"Hidden from me," Jara said, her smile becoming a grin, "doesn't mean hidden from *you*. There is a place that I have seen in visions from time to time, even, I think, today with the Council. On the world of Arctos, the Archive resides. All things that have ever been known on any world, at least until the shuttering of Gar Nought, are recorded there. I know, without question, that the secrets the Wyr buried will be found in the halls of the Archive." Jara made a point to fix her eyes on Todd now. "And I can't wait to dig them up."

# 8
## Murrod

*For more than a week, the fields of Goldvast burned.* The Ellir had ceased to use fire two nights ago, but the damage was already done. The outer villages were razed, and most of the women had fallen back to the inner communes. A small but dedicated group of the warrior-defenders of the female nation had retreated to the temple though, and it was there that Plyssa found herself.

When in battle, she wore the mask of her spirit totem, the snake, but the suns were high overhead right now, so there was no need for the mask. Her auburn hair was short-cropped and caked in soot and mud from the campaign in the east, and she waited now, as most of her squad did, in the shade of the idol.

The Temple of Ahmur was the spiritual center of Goldvast and the home of their mighty dragon-god. It was here that the mother of all women collected her precious hoard and meted out her justice and wisdom, but during the campaign of terror that the Ellir had rained down upon Goldvast, the goddess had not once emerged from her subterranean chamber. It was not like her, and it had placed many of the women ill at ease.

"Why start this now?" asked one of the other women. She wore the mask of the bat, a great ugly affair of black with sprawling upswept wings at the side and bright red stonework eyes placed just above the mask's eye slits. Some of the women wore their masks almost always—mostly women from the western villages, nearer the frequent clashes with the men of Greendeep's frontier city of Hineros. Plyssa, raised in the mostly conflictless central regions near the communes, never could feel comfortable with the mask on outside of battle.

"The Ellir no longer serve the Princes," a third woman, with a wolf mask, said in a high voice. "Perhaps they simply seek a homeland of their own? Nothing grows in Bluetide, and the men have worked that strange circle that bars the Ellir from entering their lands—we offer the best chance the Ellir have of feeding themselves. Even the blue skins must have heard tales of the bounty of our fields."

Plyssa coughed. "Were you not the one telling stories a few days ago about Ellir eating babies? If that is the substance of their diet, they have come to the wrong place. Our babies are all too few and far too distant from the points of incursion. It seems to me that their efforts are targeted, it is just hard to say at what they point. Perhaps they do want a new, more habitable homeland, but why now?"

A pushing sensation, growing steadily more overwhelming, flared into Plyssa's mind. From the gasps and body language of the handful of women around her, it appeared she was not alone in the experience.

"Attend me," said the voice of Ahmur, resonant and firm, in the minds of her subjects.

They nearly stumbled over one another as they raced past the great stone idol, carved in the likeness of Ahmur as tribute to her stunning victory over her brother, the dragon-god of the Ellir, nearly two years ago. Beyond the statue was the great cavern that opened into the ground, and Plyssa found herself at the front edge of the party of seven as they passed the tributes of gems and metals, rushing deeper until they reached the enormous cavern where the dragon-goddess dwelled.

Ahmur was magnificent, as always. She was white in color, massive and majestic and flawless in every way. She was coiled in a pile of gemstones, her head facing the tunnel from which they emerged, resting upon her folded forelimbs.

"Your speculation stirs curiosity in me," Ahmur murmured in their minds. "Why is it that you see pattern in this? Never before have the Ellir struck in such a way."

"Perhaps their god seeks vengeance upon you for his defeat at your talons?" wolf-mask asked. Her voice was not so high now, Plyssa noted.

"This is pointless vengeance if it is that. I could lay waste to the Ellir anytime I wanted, while the suns burned high in the sky and their will is weak and empty. My brother is not fool enough to rouse my wrath in such a way." Ahmur opened her three eyes wide and fixed them upon Plyssa. "What do you think, child?"

"My opinion is not worthy of note, goddess," Plyssa responded, prostrating herself upon the ground. In her mind, she felt a sense of something strange and thought, perhaps, it was the draconic equivalent of satisfaction.

"It is if I note it. Above, you spoke of purpose. Ellaborate on of this." Ahmur instructed.

"I merely observe patterns, mighty Ahmur. The burning of the fields was systematic, predictable, yet we could do little to stop it. We withdrew in likewise predictable ways, and brought more warriors to the fore, and now the burning has stopped, but calculated strikes begin in its place. The Ellir push us every night, driving a straight line towards the communes, where our defenses are strongest. We have adjusted accordingly." Plyssa lifted herself up off the floor of the cavern. "These are tactless tactics. Their aim would seem to be our destruction, but they are so easily predicted that we will surely avoid serious loss of anything but land, which we will in turn retake each day when the suns rise."

"What do these patterns suggest to you then? What motive drives our four-armed foes?" Ahmur mused.

"Perhaps this is an elaborate scheme to gain something else instead?" bat-mask asked. "What is it that Ellir want?"

"They don't want anything," Plyssa said, "but what their master wants. And you don't believe they do this at the direction of their master, goddess?" Plyssa queried.

"Ehbor has never embraced his role as god of the Ellir as I have mine. So often, he leaves them to their own devices." Ahmur lifted her head, shifting her body and causing a cascade of gemstones to spill out all around her on the cold stone cavern floor.

"If Ellir want nothing, and Ehbor wants nothing, than none of this makes any sense." Plyssa sighed. "I have failed to provide an answer, Great Ahmur." Plyssa feared the response of her goddess, but the great one's attention was suddenly pulled elsewhere.

"We are not alone," the dragon shouted aloud, her eyes flaring brilliantly.

"What? Who is here?" bat-mask shouted. All around Plyssa, warriors drew spears and daggers, readying themselves and backing up against Ahmur, forming a protective circle against their goddess.

"The true master of these Ellir attacks is above us, my children," Ahmur whispered in their minds. "And it is not my lazy brother."

¤~¤~¤

Hyrak had never left them alone this long. A single Ellir checked on them during the daylight hours, bringing food and fresh water, but otherwise there had been no contact with anyone for more than a week.

Embrew pushed his dirty, stinking hair out of his face, feeling the cold, clammy dampness of it. Everything was clammy and damp in this cave-prison, and he wished more than anything to die. He thought he would, at the beginning, when Jarrek's knife had ripped open his belly and the Spiralgate had closed before him, carrying Jara and Adam and the others away. Leaving him behind with the man who had nearly murdered him. But even though guilt was the blood that truly flowed through the old, blind Gatemaker's veins, he had not been willing to die in that moment. He'd summoned all his strength, pushing past the violet Bindmetal bracelets at his wrists that handicapped his powers, and sealed the wound with the force of his arts.

Jarrek took him prisoner then, in this very cave, and tormented him for many days. Each day, Embrew had a choice—to die or to live. He could continue the working that held his stomach together, sealing the flow of blood and allowing the possibility that his old and tired body could heal the wound naturally. Or he could release the working and bleed out. In spite of the horrible things Jarrek did and said to him, each and every one of those days, Embrew chose to live.

His powers, strained as they were through the manacles that marked him a traitor to the Gars for indiscretions both unforgivable and long-past, could do no more than keep him alive. He was a prisoner to Jarrek, unable to fashion even a simple crossgate to spirit himself away while he spent precious energy keeping his insides inside of him.

Then Hyrak had come. Embrew knew him by the sound of his voice, and though Jarrek did not, he would not listen to Embrew's pleas. Jarrek took Hyrak in, and before either of them knew it, Hyrak had made Jarrek as much a prisoner as Embrew. They persisted in that state, both prisoners of the man, for months... and then, one day, Hyrak remembered who he was. Then Embrew became truly afraid and the torment resumed.

"Do you suppose he abandoned us?" Jarrek asked.

Embrew could not see him—he could not bring himself to waste what little strength he possessed to sense the space of the cell around him. Why bother? He knew the cell like the back of his hand, for he had not left it in more than a year. It was a jail cell without bars or chains, but instead a far simpler lock—Hyrak was in their minds. Even with him not standing here, he would know if they tried to escape. Thus there was no escape. No hope.

"You know," Jarrek muttered from the pile of wet straw where he was surely laying, "this reminds me of the way you Gar bastards abandoned my people on this freakish world."

Embrew had not the strength to fight with the chief of the Jovs, and so he said nothing.

"When I heard your name on the beach, with the promise of Onus just on the other side of the Spiralgate, I knew that this was worth giving up my return home. The great Embrew, one of Corudain's favorite lapdogs, within striking distance. I dreamed of that for years, you know."

"You truly do have nothing new to say, do you, Jarrek? After all these months together, you still seek something I cannot give you." Embrew leaned down, resting his weary head upon his knees. "I did not give the order, nor did I agree. And to think of myself as a favored student of Corudain is laughable, for much befell our order after the Jovs left Onus."

"Were exiled! We did not *leave*, you old fool, we were cast off, bartered away like an unwanted saw or a rusty hammer." Jarrek spat towards Embrew. Embrew did not mind. It was all the same to him by this point—damp.

"He has a plan for us," Embrew said softly. "He has not abandoned us, because he wants us to do something. Jarrek, I beg of you—do not give him what he wants."

"If it will bring you pain, I will pluck out my own eye and let the man eat it like a grape," Jarrek grunted, laughing at what passed for a joke in his twisted, hate-filled mind. "What do I care for anything he might do? My people escaped. This world deserves whatever torment Hyrak wishes to visit upon it."

"I will not do what he wants," Embrew said simply. "And he cannot compel me. And it shall be known that the iron will of the Metalbreaker was broken, even as the lowly Gatemaker stood strong in his resolve."

"I do not care. Do you know why?" Jarrek's voice grew low and conspiratorial. Embrew knew better than to get his hopes up.

After allowing silence to stretch for a moment, Jarrek answered his own question. "Because I already know what he wants, old man. And as payment for my services, he is going to finally, after all this time, let me do what I have been trying to do since I learned who you were. All I have to do is make a few little trinkets for Hyrak and he's going to let me kill you, you traitorous son of a bitch."

¤~¤~¤

"There are better ways to die," Norrun said with a shake of his clean-shaven head. "Ripped to shreds by a wild Ellir. Sour fever. Ground to paste by the dragon-god's magnificent tail. All of these seem less horrible than this."

Mathias smiled. "What's life without a little risk?"

The pair approached the gates of Imperia, each pulling a wagon of gnarlroot vegetables. Normally these deliveries were handled by other men from the fields, but Mathias had bribed them with a bottle of the wine that Norrun never seemed to have any difficulty getting hold of. While Norrun looked much like he always did, Mathias wore a short grey smock with a hood, and he kept the hood up to conceal his face. Many men wore head coverings during the day to keep the harsh light of the three suns at bay, so he hoped he would not stick out too much, but it was hard to say.

"Longer. Life without a little risk is almost always *longer*," Norrun replied. "Although I'm not sure I have any right to complain. I've not long left for this world anyway, in this life. I was thinking that perhaps if I get involved in a bit of your heroics, I might come out a few rungs higher on the ladder in the next go round. Maybe a craftsman. Or a bathhouse attendant." Norrun grinned. "I really like that last idea."

Mathias could not help but laugh. In spite of the danger of being recognized by any of Chaplain Reid's men in Imperia, Mathias had enjoyed their two day trek to the city. Norrun was, he hated to admit it, growing on him. He didn't love him, but he could see the appeal of the older man. He was warm and funny, wise and, in many ways, the closest thing to a friend Mathias had on this entire world. The friends he had possessed before leaving Murrod all surely thought him dead now, or, at the very least, an enemy of Greendeep. He wondered what precisely the Chaplain had told people about him. The truth would not have suited the Ministry of Security well at all, so the lie was probably most impressive.

"If I would have known all it took to get you in a better mood was to tell a few stories and to risk my hide for you, I would have done it a year ago," Norrun continued.

"I have to know more about what's happening, Norrun. Your stories of the stranger Hyrak that brought the Ellir together—they fascinate me. If this Hyrak is the same Hyrak I know of, things get very complicated. For all of us." Mathias, head low, bobbed his head in acknowledgement as the admissions knights motioned for the pair to continue on into the city with their carts.

"Man wants to spend his life organizing Ellir, he's going to end up dead, one way or another. For all I know, the man's just a legend. Been hearing stories of him for more than a year, and if the Ellir are all organized now, I certainly haven't seen proof. Haven't seen a one of them in months, truly, aside from the handful that are still kept in the few sunboxes what still work." Norrun waved at a young man painting a sign outside of a dining hall. The young man looked away, embarrassed, and Norrun grinned.

"I love people. The way they look down at you and me like we did something wrong to end up where we are. Like it couldn't happen to them any second from now. Forty years is not all that long to live a life, you know. Plenty of time to screw it up, not nearly enough time to make it right." Norrun gestured to a side street up ahead. "That's where these go, if you want to actually take care of business before we sneak off on your suicide mission."

Mathias followed Norrun's lead as they pulled the two-wheeled carts down the side street and towards the vegetable vendor that owned the fields where they worked. The number of people milling about in the streets at this hour, in the center of the day, astonished him. He had spent so long out in the fields that Mathias had forgotten what the Prince Cities were like.

So many of the men were beautiful. Not all, of course, but many. Young and vibrant and full of potential. Theirs was a society built to keep its members perpetually in their prime. The thriving variety of people, not just of age and of physical appearance, but of gender, on Core was sorely lacking here. He missed that world a great deal, sometimes—at least parts of it. He wondered though if any part of that world missed him.

"You! Drop those in the back there, yes!" shouted one of the salesmen at the vendor's lot. Mathias parked his cart and helped Norrun do the same, partly lifting the heavy wooden contraption to skip it over several deep-cut ruts in the street.

"We'll be back for empties in a few hours," Norrun said.

"Don't expect to get much done in the city today," the salesman said crossly. "Joint Ministries are making an announcement today and they've ordered curfew afterwards. That should be happening here in an hour or so. I'll have one of the stewards make up some cots for you in the warehouse."

"Much obliged," Mathias said, and then he and Norrun left the vendor's lot and pushed back through the crowded streets.

"What do you think the big announcement is?" Norrun asked.

"Hard to say. Let's get done what needs doing so we can be back in one of the squares to hear for ourselves." Mathias led the way, the rhythm of the city coming back to him, as natural as his own heartbeat. When he was a courier here, he knew routes to and from nearly everywhere, and much of that knowledge continued to hold true. They took an intricate series of turns and twists, Norrun often struggling to keep up, before they reached the place Mathias wished—the courier hub.

"That is an ugly building, lad." Norrun said grimly.

The courier hub was a square building, situated near the center of Imperia. It was precisely in the center of the various Ministry offices that peppered the city core, making it the perfect routing center for the various runners that did the important work of facilitating bureaucracy in this, the "most civilized" of the Prince Cities. Before fleeing Murrod, this had been Mathias' place of employment, and he knew that if there was anything worth knowing in Greendeep, someone in that building had carried a message about it.

"It doesn't need to be pretty. It gets the job done." Mathias stopped just short of the simple black front door of the building.

"Nervous?" Norrun asked.

"Petrified." Mathias rubbed his sweaty palms on his trouser legs. "There was a dispatcher who was really, really fond of me. He's my best bet for getting the answers I want, but... it's hard to say. Maybe he'll sell me out and summon the judiciary knights the moment I walk in the door, maybe he won't."

"Then if you don't mind, I think maybe the best place for me is right out here," Norrun said hesitantly. "You'll blend in better without me anyway."

Mathias didn't argue with the field hand. He gestured towards a small bench not far away, sheltered in the shade of a well-groomed clusterfruit tree. "Give me ten minutes. If I don't meet you there in ten minutes, you should go far and fast."

Norrun nodded. "Be safe," he said, touching Mathias on the cheek. "I ain't finished trying to win you over yet."

Mathias smiled and turned away, pushing through the black door of the hub and into a world he had thought he'd left behind forever.

Inside, the building was chaos incarnate. Young men ran everywhere, scroll cases strapped across their backs or around their waists, bodies gleaming with sweat as they raced out of dozens of different doors at two different elevations. Some of the more important buildings were connected to the hub by tunnels, and many of the runners were using those tunnels to get around the intense street congestion outside.

No one questioned Mathias, for there was virtually no reason anyone would want to break into the hub. Careful to stay out of the lanes of traffic as men dashed through, shouting and laughing at one another when they had breath to spare, Mathias worked his way towards the inner chambers of the building, seeking the dispatch offices.

Glass walls separated the dispatchers from the cacophony of the transfer floor, and Mathias passed the first glass wall to see the scroll room had not changed at all. Great chutes and rows of boxes and shelves held the messages that were awaiting transfer at the hub. While the most important messages were delivered by a single courier from point A to point B, many others, and those most inexpensively delivered, traded hands several times as dispatchers consolidated and coordinated runners to maximize deliveries per courier. It was complex, intricate work, and considered by many to be virtually ministry-level work in terms of prestige for reincarnation purposes.

It was that prestige that made short-lived affairs between runners and dispatchers so commonplace at the hub. Rarely did a bondmating occur between such people, for dispatchers considered themselves above linking their prospects to a lowly courier, but always there were empty promises. Mathias sighed as he walked the narrow corridors between dispatch offices, looking for Kemer. Kemer was like the others, of course—a letch of the highest order that lured twenty year-old young men fresh from the nursery into his bed with promises of social promotion—but he had never tried such things with Mathias. He'd been a mentor to Mathias, but also the man that taught him to yearn for the best life possible.

Mathias found Kemer where he expected to, in the farthest office from the main floor. Kemer hated noise—he claimed to have been the one that installed the glass walls in the first place—and that had not changed. In fact, very little had changed, as Mathias pushed through the thin wooden door of Kemer's office to find him doing his best to seduce a courier. The courier was quite average, as far as Mathias could tell, but obviously young. While Mathias was only truly twenty-four, a mere four years older than this boy, those four years had brought with them a degree of worldly experience that most of these couriers would never know.

"I need to speak with you, Kemer," Mathias said, keeping his hood pulled over his head as best he could.

"I'm a bit busy here," the dispatcher replied. "Try me in another hour, boy."

"If it takes you an hour to talk that boy into going home with you, I'm vastly disappointed," Mathias replied, taking down his hood. "I need to talk now."

Kemer's eyes grew wide, and he dismissed the courier without a word. The courier, clearly confused and hurt, ran past Mathias, head hanging low.

"What in Chron's name are you doing here? Do you know there's a lifetime kill order in your name?" Kemer asked, pulling Mathias all the way into the office and locking the door behind him.

"I imagined as much." Mathias looked at the small trinkets on Kemer's desk. One of them was a pair of intricate metal rings—the symbol of union in Greendeep culture. "I see you haven't found the one yet."

"No such thing. It's all a hoax anyway," Kemer muttered by reflex. "Why should I spend this life worrying about what the next one is going to look like? I won't remember it anyway."

"Spoken like a true heretic. I need your help, and I know I probably don't have a lot of right to ask for it." Mathias sighed. "You were the only person I thought might still talk to me without putting a sword through my chest."

"Guilty as charged," Kemer replied, settling into his chair. "How can I help?"

"That was surprisingly easy," Mathias observed.

"Chaplain Reid hates your guts. He's also killed three perfectly excellent couriers in the past month for fear of his memorized messages being exposed. Helping you is as close to slicing that bastard's throat as I will get. So go on, tell me what you risked that pretty head of yours over."

"What do you know about the man that they say is organizing the Ellir?" Mathias asked.

"Lies told to keep folks in at night. The boogeyman they call Hyrak that commands the endless hordes of the Ellir to do his every whim. Nonsense." Kemer shook his head. "You came all this way for nursery stories?"

"What does Reid know about him?" Mathias asked, leaning in.

"Are you deaf? I just told you, the Chaplain has killed three of my best men to keep us from knowing what he knows." Kemer looked down at the floor.

"And you wouldn't be you if you didn't know anyway," Mathias coaxed. "I need to know. It's important."

Kemer sighed. "Fine. The Ministry of Security is in an uproar about it, among other things. The loss of the Ellir turned everything upside-down, and that's not getting any better. But this Hyrak fellow, when he appeared, he made them take note. They invested a fortune in defenses to keep the Ellir out. Reid... I think Reid believes in this Hyrak. Something's happening outside of Greendeep that has him very nervous."

"When was the last assault from Goldvast?" Mathias asked.

"There hasn't been one in months. Officially, the women have been focusing their efforts on Hineros, but that's smoke. I know for a fact the women haven't touched foot in Greendeep, our side or Hineros', for at least four months. But the way we are funneling money to Hineros, you'd think they were trying to rebuild from a war. They say that even Monarka is dumping money into Ministry of Security holdings in Hineros." Kemer tapped his finger idly on his desk. "World's gone a bit crazy when the Princes start sharing their pocketbooks with one another."

Mathias nodded. "So I think that's where the next piece of the puzzle is. And at least no one in Hineros wants to kill me on sight."

"I wouldn't be so sure. Chaplain Reid had a lovely drawing of you circulated a ways back—a fair likeness, by my estimation. I wouldn't take too many foolish risks." The old dispatcher stopped his tapping. "And you can't come back here."

"I shouldn't need to, Kemer. But why not?" Mathias stood slowly, suspecting that he had already stayed long enough that Norrun was likely to be panicking outside.

"My number's been called. End of next week, I'll be forty. Some folks say Chaplain Reid's pushing forty-two, but us normal men don't have many days in us past forty. I'll be starting a new life next time you come to this office, and my predecessor won't have my charming disposition. Or a soft spot for your dimples." Kemer stood and extended a hand towards Mathias.

Mathias took his hand in his and squeezed. It was the closest that Murrod had to a handshake, like on Core, and it was a gesture of extreme respect. "You were always better to me than I deserved."

Kemer nodded. "Damn right I was."

Mathias turned and unlocked the door behind him, slipping out of Kemer's office and through the tumult of the hub. No one stopped him, and he did not look back.

Outside, Norrun was waiting right where he should have been, and Mathias joined him on the bench for a moment.

"Did you get what you needed?" the old field hand asked.

"How do you feel about a trip to Hineros?" Mathias asked in reply.

Norrun sighed.

Before Mathias could say anymore, a loud, clear note rang out—a brassy sound, clearly carried by a horn of some kind. On every street corner that Mathias could see, and the avenue was long and broad, so he could see many, a courier was standing. A city-wide announcement would take many couriers indeed, and the expense was extreme. Mathias himself had never been a part of such an announcement in the years he had worked in the hub.

"Men of Greendeep, young and old. The Princes, by the blessing of Chron, and acting in the agency of Chaplains Reid, Voss, Emorran, Callisar, and Roakus, hereby declare for now and all time, that the Ministry of Incarnation shall draw forth a line of demarcation in thirty-three days' time. Thirty-three days hence, a census shall be taken of all men living, from nursery to final nights, and in that moment, each soul shall be declared above or below this line. Those above shall know no change in circumstance from the lives we have always known, carried out again and again in the time-honored process of reincarnation. Those below the line, however, shall be stricken from the records of the Ministry of Incarnation and instead transferred to a new ministry, the Ministry of Labor. From that day on, in perpetuity, those souls below the line shall incarnate again solely in the purview of this new ministry, serving henceforth as the labor class."

A murmur of shock ran through the crowded streets. Those occupants of the hub not frantically engaged in other tasks had piled outside to hear the announcement, and in many of them Mathias could see wide, fearful eyes.

Courier was a noble position, a fine start to a life—but was it noble enough to avoid this line of demarcation? Who was to say how high the line would be, what portion of the population it would affect?

"It is definitely time to get out of this town," Norrun said, his eyes dark.

"Guess we know where people like you and I will be on the next spin of the wheel, my friend." Mathias put a hand on Norrun's shoulder in comfort—but also in shock.

There was no chance of promotion for either of them. Laborers were the lowest of the low—no matter where the line was drawn, they would be below it. Mathias was not personally affected—he would not reincarnate at all—but the implications of this change were massive.

"Unless," Mathias mused aloud.

"You are thinking the same thing every other damn fool is thinking. That's why we have to get out of here right now." Norrun quickened his pace, and now it was Mathias who had to struggle to keep up. "They have a little more than a month to slip a ring on the finger of the highest-stationed man they can find," Norrun growled. "These sun-bleached idiots are going to start killing each other over prime husbands."

¤~¤~¤

Hyrak wore a suit of leather armor, crafted from the tanned hides of large jungle beasts that were relatively common in the triangular area of jungle where Greendeep, Goldvast, and Bluetide all abutted. It was not the heavy plate mail he preferred, but given his unique attributes, armor was largely a matter of taste instead of function. He would have a new suit of plate mail soon enough. For today, the leather would suffice.

He carried a large sword, made to exacting specifications by Jarrek, in one hand and a broad, square-shaped shield in his other. He wore no helm, again in violation of his usual style, but this was quite deliberate. The female warriors of Goldvast were impressive—he believed any one of them a match for all but the finest of his own mercenaries back on Onus—but he found their ridiculous animal masks distasteful. When they knelt to him, the masks would be the first things to go.

It didn't hurt that his own face, marred as it was by massive seams of scar tissue, was more gruesome than any mask. Even his old helmet would not instill as much terror as his new face and his brilliantly white eyes.

A small rush of warriors poured out of the tunnel that led to the dragon's lair. Hyrak had sent Ellir to spy upon the temple each of the past three nights. As the bulk of his forces pushed straight past the temple and towards the heart of Goldvast, Hyrak himself had brought this small scouting party off to greet and deal with the greatest threat in all of Goldvast, their dragon-goddess.

Two of the warriors charged at him, spears at hand. One wore a mask shaped like a bat, another a wolf. They were both quite a bit smaller than Hyrak, but their size gave them a quickness that he, even for all his skill and prowess, could not match. They danced around him in a flurry of movement, stabbing and slashing at him. The armor and his deft use of the shield deflected many of the strikes, but some bit into his flesh, particularly at the sword arm and in the less-protected midsection.

With a steady calm, Hyrak whirled himself around, sword cleaving in a powerful diagonal. The bat-masked woman ducked, but not low enough, and his blade bit into her across the back, eliciting a scream and a spray of blood. As the bat went down, the wolf roared forward again, lunging with spear extended. Hyrak parried the spear tip with the crossbar of his sword and then closed the distance between them, rendering the spear all but useless. The wolf surprised him though, dropping her spear and drawing a pair of daggers from concealment beneath her leather armor. She scissored with the blades, catching Hyrak up close and severing one of the straps on his own leather breastplate even as she tore a gash in his side.

"You are not worthy of the gift you are about to receive," the wolf-masked woman growled in his ear.

"Pity," Hyrak grunted, dropping his shield and punching the wolf mask directly in its center. The painted wood shattered, but his fist did not slow, driving chunks of jagged wood directly into the woman's face and causing her to go down shrieking. "I brought no gifts in exchange."

More warriors charged at him, but they were less sure of themselves in the wake of their sisters' defeat, and Hyrak easily repelled them. He did little harm, avoiding dealing any killing blows, for he knew what he wanted, and these small fish were not it. One woman did intrigue him, in the whirl of battle—a sturdily-built warrior with a mask painted like a snake. She hurled a blade at him, which he swatted out of the air with his sword, but otherwise did not close with him. She alone amongst the dragon's honor guard showed any sense at all.

"You are the one they call Hyrak," whispered a voice in his mind. Hyrak smiled grimly as he pushed away the last combatant. She fell into the churned up soil at their feet, and Hyrak kicked her once for good measure. Then he spun to face the tunnel entrance and cast his own thought back, amplified with his mindshaping power.

"Indeed. And I have come to solve a problem," Hyrak projected.

In the darkness of the tunnel, three blazing slits of light appeared—the dragon's luminous eyes. She emerged, slowly, her head first, followed by her long white neck and then her body, wings folded carefully in. She was smaller than he expected, but once she was in the open air, and the first of the three suns dipped out of sight below the distant horizon, she swelled to a size more like that of her brother, Ehbor. In fact, Ahmur seemed a bit larger than the reclusive black dragon of Bluetide.

"You come alone to this place? I have warriors racing here even now from a half-dozen encampments. You are skilled, but no man can survive such odds." Ahmur grinned, baring her massive teeth.

"You would not deal with me directly?" Hyrak asked. "I came to prove my might against you, dragon-goddess."

He felt her probe at his thoughts, but he was ready for her. His shields were his finest effort of mindshaping, and he knew that it would take the dragon far longer than the span of a conversation to breach them. He felt her frustration, alien and enticing, as she withdrew from his mind, and in that moment he flashed out with his power, driving a tiny spike of confusion into her serpentine mind.

"I do not sully my talons with the flesh of Chron's children." Ahmur turned as if to leave, her mental words slightly slurred as Hyrak's working wormed its way into her mind. It was a tiny effort, hardly more than a nuisance to the dragon, but it would buy him the brief moment of surprise he required...

"I am no child of Chron," Hyrak said defiantly, drawing his sword back. He charged forward, sprinting fast and carefully, closing the distance between them and driving his sword straight and true into Ahmur's scaled chest.

With a flash of brilliant light, Ahmur attempted to escape. She teleported, carrying herself away from Hyrak, trying to free herself from his impaling blade—but he was too close. Her effort of magic carried Hyrak with her, and the two materialized in a flash of radiance in a wide open plain. It was a grain field that had not yet been put to torch, and Hyrak struggled for a moment to get his bearings. In the distance, the second sun was slipping into its resting place below the horizon.

"You foolish creature," Ahmur spat aloud, thrashing about as Hyrak held to his blade with all his might. "If I die, this world is doomed! Surely Ehbor warned you of this!"

Hyrak shouted up at the dragon, "I know all about your ancient duty. If I cared in the slightest for the fate of this world, I might take that into account. And from what I understand... you don't care about this world either."

Ahmur exhaled a gout of flame, which missed Hyrak utterly but caused the field to catch fire. It spread rapidly, and Hyrak felt the heat of that initial blaze pressing in on him.

"You sought to flee, did you not?" Hyrak shouted over the rising roar of the fire. "When last you battled Ehbor, it was just as you were about to take possession of a Gatemaker and spring free from Murrod."

"Yes," Ahmur shrieked. Hyrak twisted the blade a quarter turn in her chest, and while he knew she was working her best magic to mend the injury, it would not heal while he continued to work his sword beneath her flesh.

"I would see your escape granted," Hyrak projected into the dragon's mind. "For the simplest of favors, I would see you freed from this world. I know the truth of your kind, of your burden and your curse. I will end yours and set you back upon your true path."

"By killing me?" Ahmur inquired.

"By giving you a Gatemaker," Hyrak returned. "All I ask in exchange is a simple price."

"Remove your sword!" Ahmur raged, her words aloud and telepathic in tandem. The force of the pressure against Hyrak's mind was great, and he felt his shields slip. He had to close the deal now, or all would be lost.

With a heaving effort, he ripped the sword back out of Ahmur's breast and slid it securely into the scabbard at his side. He took a few steps back, through low flames, and turned to face the dragon as she clutched at her chest wound with one taloned forelimb. He saw light flicker between her claws as she sealed the wound, and he asked plainly in a voice low and calm, "Do we have a deal?"

"What is the price?" Ahmur asked. In her three unblinking eyes, Hyrak could see murderous intent. The sky was growing darker, but the last of the suns was still several minutes from setting. His rescue was still several minutes from possible. If this soured, he would be at a grave disadvantage.

"I want the violet Bindmetal you keep in your hoard. The block of it that you claimed from Ehbor as prize when you bested him last." Hyrak stomped at a flame as it drew near him.

"That is all?" Ahmur asked suspiciously.

"It is apparently amongst the rarest of the eight variations. I have had my Ellir scouring all of Murrod for it for months, and you have the last of it in any meaningful quantity." Hyrak placed his hand suggestively on the pommel of his blade once more. "Do we have a deal? Or would you care to dance again?"

"I did not expect your boldness before, Hyrak-who-is-not-of-Chron. I will not fall victim to such a ploy again." Ahmur drew herself up, lowering the talons to reveal her scaled chest to be unblemished and whole once more. "But the promise of winning my freedom is enticing. Yet the word of men is rarely kept, in my experience. It is a dilemma."

"Hardly," Hyrak smiled. He had her. "I will give you the Gatemaker when you give me the metal. A fair trade that ensures neither of us has the other at a disadvantage."

"Then I will leave Murrod behind. I cannot say how long it will survive my departure." Ahmur licked at her lips with her great, sinuous tongue.

"I do not care. In one week's time, the Gatemaker will be in your possession. Shall we meet at your lair? I will bring a force of Ellir... to carry the Bindmetal, of course. I have the utmost trust in your word. Dragons are legendarily dependable creatures." Hyrak bowed.

Ahmur replied, "That is quite fair. It has been a pleasure doing business with you."

Hyrak straightened up and inclined his head slightly. "Until then, mighty Ahmur."

Hyrak turned away from the dragon and strode north through the flames. They licked at his skin, but he did not feel it. He held one hand firmly on the grip of his sword, for it was the sword that had earned him the true prize. The Bindmetal was essential to his plan, but the blood of the dragon, captured in the cunningly crafted blade at his side, even more so. He would turn Embrew over to the dragon – poor, useless Embrew – and proceed to the next of his tasks. Goldvast was behind him now... Greendeep lay ahead.

# 9
## Onus

*As hard as it probably is to believe, I have a really hard time connecting with people.* Not in any crazy mystical sense, like what Becky does with those powers Tatyana left her. I mean just like, you know—clicking with people. I think everyone has a few friends, or a significant other, or something like that, that just kind of *gets* them. Well, that's not true—everyone has that except me.

Now hold on a second, I'm not saying I need anyone feeling bad for me. I have friends, damn right I do, but I'm just saying sometimes it's really hard for people to understand where I'm coming from. Becky gets me, most of the time—more since she started being able to literally get inside my head, of course—but it's always been a problem for me.

My life seems awesome on the outside. I have a functional family and I'm a good looking kid who is a little short on modesty, but I count that as an asset. I'm also a guy who's better known for being a pain in the ass than for being someone that people can count on. All through elementary and middle school, I was the typical class clown. If people were laughing with me, or hell, even *at* me, I was happy. There was a way to connect to people in that, in being someone that lightened the mood or brightened a crappy day. I thrived on that. It was a place where my insecurity faded into the background. I was always brave enough to be the fool—even if that was the only kind of brave I could be. It was a safe place for me. It was something I *got*, and a way that I fit into the natural order of things.

When high school started, that's when I started to realize that there was something missing. I didn't have a best friend, and not because I couldn't choose from my many options, but because there was no one that really, genuinely cared about me at the end of the day. I was the kid who handed out a hundred invitations to his birthday party and had three people show up—mom, dad, and grandma. You know what that feels like when you're fourteen? Fifteen? Yeah—that shit happened twice. To have people talking to you and laughing with you all day long, but never a one of them there when it counts?

It blows.

That's why getting swept up in Children of the Line stuff with Adam was so amazing. I mean yeah, I had the chance to overcome my fears and finally make Becky notice me—complete with the shitstorm of consequences that came from the boneheaded decision to solder this magical emotional lobotomy around my neck, but hey, you live, you learn—but what really mattered was I connected with people. I became the kind of friend that matters to a whole bunch of people, and they became the kind of people who mattered to me too.

I miss Mathias though. I shouldn't, really—we have just about nothing in common—but I do. We got tight on Onus, the first time, and stayed tight on Earth. But I think maybe him leaving was just as much my fault as Adam's. Adam's the king of oblivious decision-making (I should know, I'm a charter member of the board of directors of Oblivious, Inc.) but I don't think Mathias left us just because Adam didn't dig him. He left because he needed someone to show up for him, to be connected to him the way that I needed people, before all of this started. He deserved a better friend than I was. He also deserved to not have me try to hit on him while I was blitzed out of my brain in a dark parking lot, but let's cross one guilty ravine at a time.

Everyone deserves to be a part of things and to be important in someone's life. It's what anchors us and keeps us from just kind of floating away, I think. Why didn't I do that for him? He did it for me. They all did.

I have a lot of regrets. A ton.

One day, I'm going to make all of this right.

But nothing I do means anything as long as this damn collar is around my neck. When I apologize to Mathias, it's going to be with the full understanding of what I did, of my guilt and my shame and my fear and my sincere-ass apology right in the front of my brain.

How can anyone be truly real with anyone else while they're letting anything—magic chains or peer pressure or religion or any-damn-thing—edit the way they feel?

Life's too short and too hard for all that bullshit.

¤~¤~¤

"We can leave first thing tomorrow," Adam said. "I know all of the keys for Arctos. We just have to figure out which one will take us closest to the Archive."

"Grandfather can help with that," Jara said. Adam saw how excited she was—it was almost contagious. As much as he had been against this trip, the excitement of getting nearer to knowing the truth, to knowing not just who the others were, but maybe what they were really all meant to accomplish together, was energizing.

Adam looked up at the twin moons, full and bright, in the night sky. The garden outside the guest chambers was cool and pleasant at this time of night, and gathering here had allowed them to give Steven the chance to sleep while they worked out their plan of action.

"We're about the same distance right now from two different Spiralgates here on Onus—Rosgar and Ebugar." Adam eyed the others carefully. "If we can decide that it is safe to chance a crossgate, I can probably make it to either one in two jumps."

"Sounds fine to me," JC said. "Except for the leaving tomorrow morning part. Will Steven be up for it by then?"

Becky nodded. "He's not really hurt too badly, just sort of disoriented. A good night's sleep is probably enough to get him back on track."

"Then allow me to rephrase that with more honesty: I think we need to wait a few days and give my man Yors a chance to bust a few more links on the chain." JC plucked at the red metal chain around his neck. "I know it takes a lot out of him, but this is part of the reason we came."

Adam looked around and realized that Yors had not come out to the garden with them. He must have stayed inside to watch over Steven. "A couple of days won't hurt anything too much," he consented, "and that gives us a chance to figure out what we're getting into when we get to Arctos."

"There's one more complication," Todd added. Todd had knelt down to examine one of the flowers in the garden, a bright yellow plant with a dozen serrated petals overlapping to form a conical shape. "I'm fine with some cautious crossgating to trim the time down on the trip, but caution has to be the watchword here. If things are as messed up down here as the Dukes seem to think, every gate could be opening up in a campsite for mercenaries, necromancers, or whatever else is going on. "

"We can take whatever pops up, bro," JC said with a grin. "I have both booms and you, well—you're kind of scary. Steven has his powers, so long as nobody else tries to kill him with them, and Becky and Adam have their juju. Yors has that sweet crossbow. Seriously—we're a walking factory of ass-kickings."

"I second the motion that we stick around and give Yors a chance to weaken the collar," Becky said pointedly. "Can you even hear the words that come out of your mouth?"

JC shrugged. "History proves my point. We're pretty much undefeated."

"Tatyana and Jonas would probably disagree with you," Adam said.

The garden grew very quiet.

A few minutes later, JC said, "Sorry. I wasn't thinking."

"It's fine," Becky said, leaning against JC and pulling him tight against her. "Everything's just different now that people are gone. We aren't invincible."

"But I can help with some of this," Jara said. "I can help Adam figure out where to put his gates. Hopefully my powers will keep us out of trouble. They're already whispering a little bit of advice. We have to head for the more southern gate, Ebugar. Rosgar is serving as a basecamp for a group of very bad people."

"So we will talk to Moultus and figure out what's up with Arctos. Then in a couple of days, we'll head south to a Spiralgate and get this show on the road. Does anyone else have anything for the good of the cause?" Adam stretched. As excited as he was, he was also tired. The heat of this place, and the excitement of the day with the Council meeting and Steven's attack, were taking their toll.

"You should ask your rulers for their leave," said a sharp, feminine voice from the far side of the garden.

Duchess Ain entered the open space nearest the others, the moonlight illuminating her in her dark gown. Her hair was down instead of pulled back tight, and it made her look quite different—almost lovely. Adam coughed nervously and said, "We didn't know you were out here, your highness."

"The proper term is 'your grace.' There are no 'highnesses' on Onus—only royalty that serves the interest of the people. And the interest of the people is a heavy responsibility." The Duchess continued moving closer to the group, and as she approached Todd she placed a hand on his shoulder.

Adam watched Todd recoil from the touch, as though shocked, but the Duchess did not release him.

"The Children of the Line, and the only living Fatewaker, are precious resources. You have the power to turn the tide of all things amongst you. The people of Onus are in grave peril, and it is your duty to protect them." The Duchess smiled, and it brought no comfort to Adam.

"We will not be allowing you to leave. Not tomorrow, and not in a few days. Until we have quelled the tumult that chokes the life from the southern continent, you are servants of the Council."

Becky shook her fist at the Duchess. "You can't do that," she shouted, "we're not your subjects!"

"You are right. But *she* is," the Duchess pointed at Jara. "And I have already made the necessary arrangements. Fatewaker, your mother and your grandfather are being held in a secure place, for their own safety. While your grandfather has been of great use to the Council over the years, his value is far less to us than yours. Provided you and your friends cooperate, they will be returned to you, unharmed, when we have eliminated the uprisings in the South."

"Are you threatening innocent people?" Todd asked, still gripped at the shoulder by the Duchess.

"No one is innocent, child." The Duchess released Todd and strolled through the center of their gathering, towards the door to the guesthouse from which they had all come.

"If you lay one hand on either of them..." JC shouted.

"I wouldn't dare." Duchess Ain continued walking away. As she reached the doorway she stopped and turned. With a look of poorly feigned innocence on her angular features, she asked, "Jara, I was meaning to ask. Do you know anything about that fascinating bit of jewelry your mother wears? I was thinking what a shame it would be if any of your friends should suddenly go missing and I would have no choice but to take that from her. I imagine that would leave her... quite out of sorts."

Adam watched as though the world was moving in slow motion. Jara sprang towards the Duchess like a wildcat, snarling and spitting, hands flailing and curses spewing from her mouth. Todd caught her—his reflexes never ceased to astound Adam—and held her, but even his wrestler's grip was hard-pressed to contain Jara's fury.

¤~¤~¤

If the guilt gnawing at Shayra was not enough to keep her awake at night, Narred's constant badgering would have been more than equal to the task. Ever since they had returned to the crystal academy of the Mindshapers, Kem Nought, with the two little boys from Founderstone in tow, he had been relentless in his protestations. It was all Shayra could do to shield his thoughts from the others, but she grew tired of having to do so.

The worst thing was that she knew he was right. Each time they allowed a Mindshaper's disembodied consciousness to possess and supplant one of these children's natural personalities, she felt sicker to her stomach. She had agreed to this task, when chosen for it by her peers, but she had not fully realized the toll it would take upon her soul. She felt herself becoming a monster, and Narred felt it too—if anyone was familiar with the monstrous, it was him.

He wanted them to run away, not understanding how impossible that was, but perhaps this would be the step too far that she had been waiting for. Would the investiture of these two little boys finally push her to defy her order and to abandon the post of Collectress?

The others, the eleven Mindshapers already restored to bodies by Shayra's efforts, were upstairs in the Tower of the Flesh helping the boys into the ceremonial silk robes they would wear during the ceremony. Shayra would officiate, of course, and serve as the conduit for placing the minds of two of those trapped in the Tower of the Soul into these new bodies.

The mass of minds in her care had chosen to allow Urellus and Jaes to take possession of these children. It was fitting, in a way, since Urellus and Jaes had been brothers in their original bodies, but they were sullen, quiet minds, unpleasant in the instances that Shayra had forced them to converse with her in preparation for the investiture. It was unlike any of the Kem held within the city's crystal towers to be shy or withdrawn, and Shayra suspected that they were in some way damaged or incomplete. Sometimes a mind faded without a body, in spite of all the magic the Kem had invested in preventing such degradation. If that were the case with either of these two, the promise and potential of the twin children would be lost. A body could not survive a second investiture—it was a strain too great for anyone, no matter their talent or promise.

"Don't they look handsome, Collectress?" called one of the newest Kem as she led the boys down the stairs. The girl looked quite pleased with herself. The boys were suitably attired and their hair had been freshly washed and combed. They were visions, handsome and sweet, and Shayra's stomach churned.

"Show them to the Soul," Shayra said, avoiding eye contact with the boys. She placed her left hand upon her brow and called out with her arts to Narred, who waited outside the boundaries of the Academy. He refused to even be on the grounds during the ceremonies anymore.

"Is it done already? You are getting rather good at your job," Narred replied scornfully. Shayra could feel his love for her, as always, but it was tainted in resentment so often that she began to lose sight of what it had felt like before.

"No. I merely wanted to let you know I love you. And I think... I think this ceremony will be the last for a while. I shall demand of the others that I be granted a time of peace to center myself. They will acquiesce. We will travel far from here for a time—perhaps we shall borrow one of Duke Mendul's cottages on the banks of the Mirrored Sea?" Shayra sent her affection, warm and sure, to Narred's mind.

"And I will spend the entire time we are away begging you to not return," Narred countered wistfully.

"I would expect no less of you, beloved," Shayra whispered.

She allowed the connection to fade into the background of her mind and smoothed her own ceremonial robes. She wore bright blue silk today, sheer in ways that left little to the imagination. So many things that bothered the men and women of the outside world did not bother the Kem. When one had the power to see into the inner mind of those one beheld, the concept of modesty grew pointless.

Shayra crossed the short walk on glass cobbled streets to the soaring tower called Soul. Inside, the boys were seated in a pair of crystal chairs, and the other Mindshapers, both those invested in bodies and those lingering in the air of the tower itself, gathered close at hand. All waited anxiously for Shayra, and now they waited no more.

The Collectress took her place at the altar, raising her hands and beginning the formalized words that signaled the beginning of the ceremony. Magic boiled in her veins at her command, and her arts reached out into the tower to pluck the minds of Urellus and Jaes from the masses, shaping them into tiny bundles, compact and condensed, for insertion into the unshielded minds of the two boys.

She kept her own shields firmly in place, careful to not feel any sympathy for the children. If she grew too close to them, allowed herself to feel what they felt or to understand their memories, she feared she would not have the strength to carry out the gruesome deed. Her shields tightly in place, she slowly pressed the substance of Urellus against one boy's mind, and Jaes against the other's. The process was, as Narred accused, growing easier with time and practice.

A few moments later, a pale glow of azure light worked around the children, their bodies' talents for Mindshaping giving a single, futile effort to repel the invasion of the experienced and powerful pair of Kem. As the glow faded, the investiture was complete.

All around, embodied Mindshapers and disembodied Mindshapers cried out in telepathic unison, rejoicing that two more of their number had been restored.

Shayra knelt down before the seated boys, both now possessed by the minds of men who had been well past their fiftieth summer when they had passed out of their living bodies, and said aloud, "Welcome home, my brothers."

The boy on the left—Jaes, Shayra believed—looked at her with wide, terrified eyes. His brother shared much the same expression, but he summoned the nerve to speak. "We never wished to stand upon the soil of Onus again, Collectress. Why have you done this to us? Why have you forced us back to this pain?"

Shayra was taken aback. Never had an investiture been unwilling! Why would a Kem wish to remain disembodied? She touched the mind of Urellus gently, and sensed then a strange, sickening sensation. His mind was fixed upon a memory, a horrible deed that consumed him. His own shields did not keep her out—they were instead pointed inward, trying desperately to keep himself from thinking of the details.

"What is going on?" she demanded.

"We struck the truth from the minds of all who knew it, and allowed ourselves to die that we might escape the burden of knowing we had done that which was forbidden. But now we are back in flesh. Now we are vulnerable. You must protect us, Collectress. You must keep us safe," Jaes pleaded.

"From who?" Shayra asked, shaking Jaes by the shoulders.

"From everyone. They will hold us to account for what was done. We cloaked the murder of fifty thousand people from the minds of our entire world. One hundred years ago, we did this, and though no man alive today was touched by our working, there will be no forgiveness for what we have done," Jaes sobbed.

Shayra stood slowly, drawing deep, careful breaths. They were right. If the truth of this came to light, it would be the end of these two—a final death, without their minds being absorbed into the Soul of the Kem. And, she surmised, it would be the end of the Kem as well. They would all be held to account for such a crime. Things had become infinitely more complicated.

Shayra shivered at the thought of what Jaes had described, and in the shivering, she felt her shields slip just a fraction of a thought out of alignment. She righted them swiftly and left the tower. She needed to sleep, for the act of investiture was exhausting. But now she had a new worry to haunt her dreams, and this was one she dare not share with Narred. Even her husband could not be trusted with such a horrible truth.

¤~¤~¤

Cambria and the children had made a sort of camp in the strange circular clearing she had discovered, but making camp would not get them to safety any faster. The shallow pool of water at the center of clearing had indeed proven to be a mirage, and Cambria had spent the last of the day fashioning makeshift water bowls from the large nuts of the trees that managed to grow in the sweltering, steaming heat of the Vale.

The older children traveled with her to fill the water bowls and carry them back, carefully, to the others. The clearing was inconvenient in that nothing grew here, but it was also strangely repellent to the wildlife and insects that swarmed through the steamy jungle. They had returned with water just before sunset, and now they merely had to wait for dawn to plot what the next move would be.

Night brought an even more pleasant degree of coolness to them, for which Cambria was thankful, but still she could not get a clear signal out with her powers. Gendric would be able to rescue them, one and all, if she could merely get in touch with him. He would call up that sinister Rak consort of his and her people would slink about in the shadows, carrying these children to the safety of one of the Council cities. Then Cambria would be able to turn her attention towards the truly noble purpose—exacting revenge on Gollus Golluson for his vile assault on Mandor Arn.

But without a way to get a clear signal to Gendric, her plan was merely a flight of fancy. They would rest here for another day or two, and then she would lead her caravan of children to the north. Rura Holc was a long trek for such young ones, but it was the closest place of which she could be certain of safety. They appeared to be rather near the center of the Vale of Steam now, so they still had the bulk of their journey ahead of them.

Cambria nodded in and out of sleep for some time, waking with a start whenever one of the children cried out in their dreams. They were holding up well for little ones that had just lost their parents and homes, and she admired their resilience. Children were not a thing she had ever aspired to have, and this journey had not changed that fact, but she found these to be more on the impressive side than most.

As she struggled to sleep and recapture a measure of her strength for tomorrow's journey, she thought she felt something strange. She sensed a kind of gurgling or shifting in the ground, but she dismissed the feeling as the pangs of an empty stomach and turned over, fighting for rest.

¤~¤~¤

The squall had caught up to the Razormaw yesterday morning, and it had raged for nearly twelve hours. The storm batteries were filled to capacity, and Grell managed, throughout the storm, to finish the rest of the critical smithing required for tonight's attack.

The captain, tired from the work but content with its quality, climbed out of the starboard hold, securing the hatch that led to that most delicate of pieces of the plan as he emerged onto the deck. He touched the hatch carefully, sealing the metal along its seams with his magic. There was no need for any of the others to enter that hold—not yet.

The sun had been set for several hours, and night had reached its darkest. The moons hung full in the sky, but low at this time of night, and it was the best time to do dark deeds.

Vediri ordered the men about by gesture more than words, and they sprang to their tasks in silence. The ship itself moved quietly as well, her sails taught and her chains muffled with cloth. The lanterns were shuttered, and it was by Fendris' keen eyes alone that they navigated within sight of the Bridge City, Igar Holc.

Igar Holc was to be their first target, because it was the most vulnerable to sea assault of all the great cities. It was also of great strategic importance, for there was no way to move from the northern continent to the southern, or in reverse, by land without passing through the city. The sea was a place Grell was already confident of controlling, but to control the land and the shape of all that was to come, he needed to take Igar Holc.

"I've been practicing trusting your word, Captain," Fendris whispered, "but you're putting me to the test tonight. When we set sail, I thought we'd just be looting the old bitch astride the land bridge, but the way Vediri has the men preparing, seems like you have a bit more in mind than looting."

"We are torching the city, Fendris. I'd have told you earlier if I thought you needed to know." Grell adjusted the wheel and shifted course a bit. They were heading directly for the city's single port, a wide affair that could handle a dozen deep-water ships at a time. Presently they sighted only three in dock, and that was good. Grell hated sinking ships without a fair fight—and nothing about tonight's raid on Igar Holc was going to be fair.

"You'll be taking a walled Council city with forty men?" Fendris asked incredulously.

"The ship will be doing most of the work, Fendris." Grell signaled for Vediri to make the next batch of preparations. She vanished below decks, and he could hear the sound of the men in the fore hold moving the heavy machinery into place.

Fendris kept his eyes focused on the city and said nothing more. The ship sailed closer and closer, apparently without drawing attention from anyone on land, as the night grew darker. He lifted his wineskin to his lips and knocked back a swig of the gritty, bitter liquor. All around them, the men still above deck were carefully holding lines and making skilled, minute adjustments to the angles with which the sails caught the wind.

In an hour's time, they were near enough that they could have docked, and still no alarm had been raised.

Without warning, Grell spun the wheel, turning the ship sharply to starboard and sailing away from the docks, parallel to the city walls that overlooked the sea. He reached up high overhead and brought his hand down in a sharp gesture. There was a low, throbbing sound, like the beating of a drum in three laborious strokes. Then, carried by the magic of Bindmetal sheets sewn into the sails only hours before, the Razormaw lifted out of the water.

Fendris nearly toppled overboard with shock, but Grell reached out and caught him, righting the small watchman without a word.

Still the ship moved in silence, though now it was sure to be noticed, if just by chance, by someone in the city. It didn't matter. There was not a weapon in the city that was built to attack upward, save for longbows and crossbows that lacked the penetrating power necessary to breach the armored hull of the Razormaw.

As the ship crested the walls and continued to climb, the alarm rang out. Torches flared all along the walls, and archers scrambled into position. The devastation of the city's siege by the Warlord Hyrak several years ago had not yet been forgotten, but these men were not prepared for the Razormaw—they were not prepared for Grell's vengeance. They fired arrows that bounced off the ship, raining back down on the people below. And still the ship climbed.

It sailed forward as it sailed up, reaching an apex a hundred yards straight over the city and coming to rest in the center of the city, directly overhead the lavish and recently rebuilt palace of Duke Igar. Two flags of the House of Igar flapped in the night breeze above the palace, but not three—the Duke was not in the palace this night.

Grell bit back bitter disappointment, but he steadied himself. They could not hide from him, not forever.

"Is this the part where you explain to me how forty men can take the entire city, captain?" Fendris asked, looking over the railing cautiously. "Because I think they'll be full of arrow holes by the time they get to the bottom of scaling ropes."

Grell called out a sharp command to those below decks, and Vediri replied with a similar, guttural sound.

The ship bobbed, tilting and then righting itself as though it had just lost a great deal of weight, and indeed it had. Vediri ordered the men to push a small, incredibly dense block of Grell's hybridized Bindmetal out of the Razormaw's carved mouth, from the same port that they used to fire the lightning harpoon. The block, perfectly square and three yards across, tumbled down to land with a shuddering crash below, ripping through the roof of the Duke's palace. As it struck the ground below, it discharged its contents, unleashing a violent, surging cascade of lightning and thunder, wind and rain, sleet and more. Amplified and intensified, buoyed by the magic of Metalbreaking and the magnificent, unequalled power of Bindmetal unleashed, the cube spawned a hurricane in one moment, a blizzard in another. The weather climbed high, but not high enough to strike the Razormaw, and it spread wide—wider than the walled city.

The storm raged for one hour, during which even Fendris could see nothing below save for danger and peril. Giant blocks of masonry whirled through the air, occasionally climbing so high upon the ferocious winds that they peeked out of the flashing, roiling mass of clouds that seemed to be devouring the city below. There were surely screams from the men and women, and children, below, but they were drowned in wind and swallowed in thunder.

As the sun rose, the storm faded at last.

Not one bit of Igar Holc remained intact. No wall still stood, and no man, woman, or child still drew breath. The docks were destroyed, the four ships anchored there eradicated. The carnage was complete, and the families of the dead would spend a lifetime digging their corpses out of the perfect chaos of the landscape below.

In the center of it all, gleaming with a ghostly inner light, the Bindmetal cube sat quietly—its work done for now.

"Captain... what have we done?" Fendris asked, trembling.

"We've dropped the first storm anchor, and we've made the first Duke of Onus pay for his crimes," Grell said grimly. While he took no joy in what was done, in the thousands of lives lost, he felt a sense of completion. He was one step closer to fulfilling his Purpose.

Vediri returned to the deck at that point, sweat beading her brow. "We've closed the jaw hatch, Captain. The other nine anchors are secured. We can set the new course at your leisure."

Fendris exclaimed, "Nine!?" The little watchman's face betrayed his horror and dismay at the scope of Grell's work—but Grell said nothing.

Instead, Grell drew his spyglass and looked towards the south, plotting a course, by air, for the next city and the next member of the Council. If the winds held favorable, they would be at Ain Holc in just under three days.

# 10
## Onus

*Word reached Ain Holc by early afternoon the next day.* Becky heard the murmurs in the streets of the city as she and JC walked around, trying to determine how to get out of the mess that the Duchess had put them in. The first time someone had said something, a man in elaborate robes smoking a long, stinking pipe on a street corner while conversing with a similarly ostentatious man, Becky paid it little heed. The second time, when a pair of children, obviously starving, spoke of it as they scurried out from underfoot at a public fountain filled with brackish water, she took note.

"Joe, I'm going to try and dig around for something," Becky said in hushed tones. "Can we find someplace to sit down?"

JC looked around at the squalor in the streets and replied, "Not unless you want to catch something." Their travels had taken them farther and farther from the city's center, and the disrepair and despair of the people of the Ain Protectorate was becoming more evident with each step.

Becky rolled her eyes and grabbed him by the hand, leading him towards a small shop with an awning out front. Inside the shop's open-air window, she could see pipes of many styles and colors. Apparently smoking was all the rage in this town. Given that it suppressed appetite, it made a kind of sense, considering the state of hunger most of the citizens of Ain Holc seemed to be in.

Becky sat down on the smooth sandy stone stoop of the shop and said, forcefully, "Just watch me. This shouldn't take more than a couple of minutes."

The last thing she saw before her eyes rolled back in her head was JC nodding and assuming an aggressive stance at her side.

She allowed the blackness of her mindscape to swallow her, and then she launched herself out of her body, towards the palace, with as much force as she could manage. She drew in a sort of mental breath as she did so, knowing there was a limit to how long she could remain free of her body. She darted through the city at the speed of thought, passing harmlessly, effortlessly, through the walls of the palace and flitting about from person to person, brushing against their minds tentatively, skimming for thoughts of destruction in the North. If there was any truth to the word on the street, someone in the palace would know, and perhaps Becky knowing the details would grant them some kind of way to escape the Duchess' hold over them.

After dozens of empty skims, she chanced upon a mind focused intently upon the topic, and she drove her mental projection into that mind, taking shelter in its presence and gathering strength in that other person's mindscape. She probed cautiously, wary at every step to avoid forging the lasting, permanent mental bond that was the danger at all times for an incautious Mindshaper. This mind was that of a Rak, a Shadowbender named Verton. He had only recently arrived in Ain Holc, sped here by his powers to report to the Council about the...

Becky fled from his mind, lancing back to her own body and awakening with a gasp that startled JC.

"What? What is it? Are you OK?" he asked, dropping to a knee and putting a hand comfortingly on Becky's back.

"Just... just let me catch my breath," she said, struggling for air. She had never gone so far out of her body before—the sensation was violently unpleasant.

"We have to get to the others, now. I'll send word to Adam through my link with him. Igar Holc is gone. Something wiped it off the map last night." Becky felt herself trembling as JC helped her to her feet. "What can even do that? On this world, what can possibly destroy an entire city in a single night? Even Lyda wasn't that strong."

JC looked her in the eyes, and she saw, felt, the confidence in him as he said, "Whatever it is, we'll get it stopped. This is what we do."

Becky wrapped her arms around him and hugged him tight, leaning in against his neck. His necklace was hot against her cheek as it did its work, melting his fear away.

She wished she had a necklace to take away hers.

¤~¤~¤

"We know you're up there," Brennid, leader of Jov Nought, called to the empty mountainside. He knew it was not empty, of course—like any Jov worth his salt he could feel the presence of the Bindmetal that Ambrek's rebels had been hoarding. His rangers had traced one of Ambrek's men to this pass, and Brennid had come himself to see if Ambrek could be made to see reason.

"Fine. Don't come out. So be it," Brennid turned away, back towards the path he had followed to reach here. He was two days hard travel from the new site of Jov Nought, but he had a transportation hob worked into his boot that would carry him home in the blink of an eye—but there was always the small chance that such use would overstrain the metal. The academy was too near completion to squander its treasures recklessly—that was why he had to convince Ambrek to end this squabbling.

As Brennid made his way back down the path, he heard the sound of loose stone tumbling behind him. He spun, ready to activate the hob and leap home, but he saw no need—his old colleague, Ambrek, stood out in the open at the foot of the mountain face. He was looking thin, and for that Brennid felt just the slightest bit guilty.

"We have very specific terms for truce, if that is what you wish," Ambrek said. "If you and the others are ready to go back to living honorable lives, instead of being thieves in the night, we would happily break bread with you."

Brennid could see the weariness in Ambrek's eyes. Life on the run, constantly hiding from the Jov Nought rangers, was taking its toll. None of them were young, after all—not a man among them had seen fewer than thirty-five summers.

"When the last of the things stolen from us is returned to our care, we will once more deal with the world honorably, as you wish," Brennid said simply. "But we will not bind our hands with honor until we have forced the people of Onus to make amends for their treatment of us."

"You sound as though there is a list," Ambrek asked, one eyebrow raised in suspicion. "We had thought you taking all the Bindmetal you could find."

"Should we happen upon any of our works, we will take measures to reclaim them. But there is only one thing left that we truly desire. The chime." Brennid smiled. "You cannot tell me that any among your group would want us to leave that abomination out in the world."

Ambrek appeared to consider Brennid's words for a moment. "Do you know where it is?"

Brennid nodded. "Of course. It is where we left it. They picked the rest of old Jov Nought clean, but even the worst brigands didn't dare take the chime. The symbol of all the wrongs visited upon us. Should we reclaim the chime, we will end our war and start the process of letting go of the past... such as we are able."

Ambrek said softly, "Indeed. Such as we are able." More loudly, he called out behind him, "I go with Brennid to see this thing done. Until it is done, however, there is no truce. Be wary, my brothers. Stay free from harm."

While Brennid could detect no sign of understanding from the empty mountainside, Ambrek seemed to have what he needed. The smith, a finer tinker than Brennid would ever be, but a man without the vision needed to lead the last of the Jovs, walked up to stand next to Brennid.

"I have just enough faith left in you to believe that this is no ruse," Ambrek said carefully.

"I need your skill, Ambrek. The things of music were always best turned at your hand, back in the forge of Imperia." Brennid shrugged his broad shoulders. "For that skill and that skill alone, I entertain the notion that we might again stand as allies."

¤~¤~¤

Duke Rega put one arm around Duke Igar, trying to comfort the man, but there was little sanctuary in such gestures. Word had come only an hour ago, by way of a frantic messenger from the Rak, that Igar Holc was no more. The entire cityhad been laid waste in the space of an hour at the hands of a flying ship and a doomsday weapon.

"My nephews. My sister." Duke Igar had his head in his hands, and he was weeping openly. Igar was a self-centered man on his best days, but Rega could not bring to mind the many tensions that so often stood between the two of them, not now.

"The attack was unprovoked," Duke Norwin explained. "Distat, have your people been aggravating the pirates in the Starlight Islands?"

Duke Distat glowered at Norwin. "My people? My people have barely had time enough to rebuild their homes after Lyda put Distat Holc to the torch. We've scarcely a dozen ships in the Endless Sea this past year, and none have reported any trouble with pirates. It's been rather quiet, and we are certainly in no position to start any troubles. Not now."

"Well if Igar knows nothing of this black ship's master and you know nothing of it, then I am stymied," Norwin said with a sigh. "Most of us don't even maintain a formal port, let alone a fleet of ships."

"He struck at my home, at my people," Duke Igar said, looking up. His face was covered in red blotches as his anger rose. Duke Rega could scarcely imagine what he was feeling. "I don't care what his reasons—the captain of that ship must be stopped. Killed. Tortured."

Duke Rura offered up tentatively, "Then let us use what weapons are now at our disposal."

Rega looked at the small, aging Duke Rura carefully. "What weapons would these be? You were begging for soldiers two days ago."

"Duchess, if you would?" Duke Rura inclined his head towards Duchess Ain.

She sat at the head of the table once more, and she had been quite silent throughout the conversation and examination of the Rak messenger's tidings. More silent than she should have been, in Rega's opinion, considering that the strange sky-bound ship was reported to be heading towards Ain Holc. The Duchess folded her hands in front of her on the table and said simply, "We will defend ourselves using any means necessary. I had planned to spare the rest of you the details of my contingencies, but things are far worse than a rising tide of brigands now. I have retained the services of the Wyr, Jara Abison, and the Children of the Line that she saw fit to bring with her. They will stop this threat."

Duke Herin asked nervously, "You would trust the defense of your city to strangers?"

"You did not see them at Rega Holc, Herin. I did. The Gatemaker felled Lyda. The others helped to lead the defense of the city, and in so doing they stopped an army that had nearly conquered the whole of our world. I have faith that, sufficiently motivated, they can bring this threat, and the others that besiege the South, to an end." Duchess Ain stood. "I should converse with them now, in fact."

"They are not yours to order about, your grace," Duke Rega interjected. "Bring them here, and we will discuss the matter with them as a whole Council."

"The time for discussion is over. I will not cajole children into doing what is their responsibility, Rega—this is not the North, where your soft heads and softer hearts drive your pathetic inaction. They are pawns of the Council, as they were always meant to be. The Wyr set these schemes into motion to find and protect the Children so that they could save Onus. You used them to save your city, as the rest of you should recall," Duchess Ain swept her hand around at the assembled nobles. "I expect no less than the same. You are dismissed. All of you. The Council is no longer in session. Make preparations to flee back to your cities—I know that Mendul and Herin have already packed their traveling chests. Rura and I will be collecting the soldiers you promised us soon."

"It will take months to get those men transported to your aid," Duke Norwin said. "The Rak will refuse to carry such quantities of people."

"Again, you make it sound as if they should have a choice. It sickens me that it was the North that finally put down Hyrak instead of the South. At least here we have the conviction to do what must be done. The Rak should answer to you—to us! Too long have the old orders been left to their own devices. But it does not matter. I have the Gatemaker child now. He will transport the soldiers we require."

"And the food," Duke Rura inserted. "The food is nearly as important as the soldiers."

The Duchess made it clear in her tone and her posture that she had been quite serious about dismissing the others. As the five Dukes of the North filed out of the chamber, Duke Distat lingered at Rega's side and whispered, "This establishes dangerous precedent, Rega. We must speak again, soon—without Rura and Ain."

Duke Rega nodded in agreement as the two left the chamber. Before the door closed behind him, Duke Rega turned back towards the nearly-empty hall and said to Duchess Ain, "Are you certain this is the way you want things to be? Your husband would never have threatened our alliance so."

"My husband?" The ruler of Ain Holc's eyes grew wide with fury, then narrow as she leashed that anger. Her face blanched, and Rega realized he had crossed a terrible boundary. "My husband is dead because of you. Because you, and all of these other pompous fools, demanded we keep the orders locked away in seclusion. While Gatemakers still drew breath at Gar Nought, we could have put every soldier in the ten protectorates in front of Hyrak and crushed his rebellion as it was still forming. But you demanded patience. You advocated negotiation. You enforced weakness! My husband is dead because of you, Duras Rega! As far as I am concerned, there is no Council! The South stands alone! You will aid us now because I give you no choice. We are weak because of you! We are dying because of you!"

Duke Rega tried to say something, but as he opened his mouth, the Duchess screamed, "Be gone! Speak to me again and I will have you mounted on my wall!"

¤~¤~¤

It had been a day and a half since the destruction of Igar Holc. The Razormaw sailed steadily south, covering ground rapidly. The captain was sleeping now—a rarity indeed—and Vediri stood at the helm. The grasslands that spread between Igar Holc and Ain Holc had been her home once, as a child, and she thought that her old village was not far from where they now passed.

"I've been talking with the men," Fendris said as he finished climbing down the mainmast.

"From the crow's nest? That is some feat," Vediri said sardonically. She had little use for the scrawny watchman. His good eyes and keen sense of weather were valuable at sea, but now that the Captain's grand plan was in motion, Fendris felt like a liability.

Fendris stepped up next to Vediri. She was larger than him, and far stronger, but for some reason he didn't cower from her the way he did Captain Grell. She hated that.

"Before my watch started," Fendris explained. He placed one hand on the thick post to which the ship's wheel was mounted. "Seems I wasn't the only one aboard that didn't know the whole plan for this voyage."

"I imagine the captain is the only one aboard who knows the *whole* plan, watchworm," Vediri retorted. "Our job is to follow orders and collect the reward at the end. I'm not sure why you can't seem to understand that."

"I understand it just fine. I've been sighting ships for looting longer than you've been alive, you great ugly cow. But this ain't natural. No sea beneath us, weak booze in our bellies, no loot to be seen. We sacked one of the great cities and didn't so much as stop to sort through the rubble." Fendris pounded his hand on the post. "Does he really mean to do the same to every single city?"

"Aye," Vediri said. "I think he does."

"I've grown accustomed to being called a coward and a cheat. A pirate, a scoundrel—many more things besides. My own mother has more than a few choice epithets she saves just for the rare occasion I go a-visiting. But no one has ever called me a murderer. Not until yesterday." The watchman lowered his hands to his side, his shoulders slumping. "If the captain wanted people willing to kill and die for a cause, he should have drummed up soldiers. We're pirates, and this stopped being piracy at sunrise yesterday."

Vediri heard a slight creaking behind her, and she spun around. Eleven of the ship's crew—men she commanded every day, including all eight of the men she had ordered to lever the storm anchor out of the hold yesterday, had climbed up on to the forecastle of the ship, weapons in hand.

"We're taking the ship back to sea, Vediri," Fendris said. "We'd rather not kill you to do it."

"You think you will overpower Grell? He'll grind the lot of you to paste. He could run this ship with ten men now that we are in the sky. He'll throw every one of you overboard." Vediri grinned savagely. "Well, at least the ones I don't toss out myself."

The men fell upon her. Vediri kicked and spit and bit and punched, drawing blood and blackening eyes, crushing testicles and snapping jaws. But the men fought as though possessed, and in spite of her own strength, there were too many of them. In the space of only a few minutes, they had pressed her down to the rough wood of the deck, and now Fendris knelt over her, a knife in hand.

"You're not a killer, watchworm," Vediri spat.

"I wasn't before," Fendris whispered. He plunged forward with the knife, directly towards her heart...

And the knife liquefied in his hand, splashing harmlessly against Vediri's thick tunic. Fendris looked up, panic in his eyes, and Vediri grinned once more, her tongue feeling a gap where one of her teeth had been knocked out in the scuffle.

The captain was standing at the door to his cabin at the aft of the ship. There was blood on his hands, and she could see that he too had been attacked by damn fool mutineers.

"Let her up," Grell growled.

The men holding Vediri down backed off, and she scrabbled to her feet, trotting indelicately to his side. "What will we do with them?" Vediri asked, wincing as she started to take inventory of her injuries.

"Nothing," Grell said. "It won't happen again."

"What?" Vediri demanded. "They tried to kill us!"

"And now they know that they failed," Grell said. He turned back towards his cabin and shoved the door open. Inside, six men were sprawled about, very, very dead. Their chests appeared to have been torn open from the inside.

From the forecastle, Fendris, trembling, called out, "What did you do to them?"

"Every cask of liquor on this ship is full of metal. Flakes and flecks, yes, but metal. You've been drinking it for more than a week, so it's all over your insides now," the captain said grimly. "If you want those insides to *stay* insides, you'll fall back in line. If you'd like me to take them out, try to take my ship from me again."

Vediri clutched at her own stomach.

"Every cask, captain?" she asked fearfully.

"Yes, Vediri. Even the one you drink from. It's hard to trust people on this ship. It's full of pirates, you know."

¤~¤~¤

Another day passed while they sat around and did nothing. Steven was back to normal now, Yors had managed to strip two more links of JC's collar of their power, but that was really all that had happened, except for the Duchess' proclamation that she would be counting upon them to protect her city against any and all invaders.

JC had gathered everyone atop the city walls.

"Pirate ship that flies and drops bombs," JC said, looking out towards the north. There was nothing to see in the sky, not even any clouds or birds to speak of. "That's what we have to go on."

"He has a name—Grell Dorukast. I told that to the Duchess and the Dukes, but it didn't mean anything to them," Jara supplied. "And this Captain Grell is angry. I can't see much about him in general, mostly because I'm terrible at reading the future for people I haven't met, but I can tell that this is personal for him. He's been planning it for a long time."

"So he's a captain of the Ahab variety," Becky said. "What's his whale?"

Both Adam and JC gave Becky a puzzled look.

Becky rolled her eyes. It felt kind of good to JC to not be the only person she ever did that to. "Moby Dick," she explained, exasperated. "Neither one of you? Honestly?"

Todd said, "He has an airship. That has to give us some clues about his nature, maybe even his motivations."

"They say it's a black ship—could it be that it's some kind of shadowform? One of those rogue Shadowbenders maybe?" Steven offered.

"Could be," Becky speculated. "We just don't know enough."

"Then I'll go find out," Steven said, smiling. "I'll just slip into the shadows and skim north until I see it. Shouldn't be too hard. And if anyone tries to jump me when I shift over, I'll be ready for them this time."

"You can't!" Jara said, grabbing at Steven's hand. "You can't leave. If you leave, the Duchess will hurt my mother."

"Then he won't leave," Becky said. "Or at least nobody will see him leave."

Yors grunted and JC turned to the Metalbreaker. "What's up, big man?"

Yors gestured as subtly as he could to a tower midway down the western segment of the city walls. "We being watched."

JC smiled. "Good eyes! Also, that was a pronoun. We are making progress!"

Yors looked baffled, and JC shook his head. "So we have a tail," he said. "Any good tail-shaking plans?"

Becky put a finger in her mouth and absently chewed at a fingernail. JC found it kind of cute, but he knew it drove Adam crazy. Like clockwork, Adam snapped at her to cut it out, and she pulled it down out of her mouth, looking mildly irritated.

"I can make that guard see Steven. Like an illusion. I think," Becky licked at her lips. "Not something I've done much of before, but it's worth a try."

"Just let me go then. I can gate there and back in a few seconds probably," Adam suggested.

"No offense Adam, but my way is a hell of a lot more subtle," Steven said. "Besides, I need to get back on the horse. After Miss Fingernails tried to choke me with my own shadow, I'm afraid that I'm going to hold back with my powers. I need to get past that, and fast. Let me do this."

"How do you know it was a woman?" JC asked. "Could have been a dude, the way you guys change the shape of your shadows."

"I don't think so. I've had plenty of people's hands around my neck over the years, and that... that was definitely a woman." Steven smiled.

"Fine," Adam said sullenly. "But be careful. The more we figure out, the quicker we can stop this and get back to finding out where they're holding Jara's family so we can all get the hell out of this town."

"Agreed," Steven said. He stepped back, into the large shadow cast by Yors, and closed his eyes. "I'm ready whenever you are, Becky."

JC watched intently as Becky moved her hands in a series of small, precise gestures. Without Jonas to teach her how to handle the mindshaping magic she had inherited, Becky had been busy for the past year inventing her own centering techniques, and JC found them fascinating.

A moment later, he felt a tickle in his mind, and he saw Adam's face scrunch up a bit—he had likely felt the same tickle. Whatever Becky had just done, those people she had a strong mental link with had been touched by it as well.

JC looked back at Steven and saw him fade into shadow and then slip away, darting over and down the wall faster than the eye could easily follow. In his place, exactly where he had been standing, Steven stood.

He was not wearing exactly the same clothes, but close enough. What was interesting to JC was his face. The Steven that stood next to them now had his goatee—but Steven had shaven that off before they left for Onus. Sure he had a stubble thing going on right now, but not the full-on goatee.

"You messed up on the face," JC pointed out helpfully.

"What?" Becky asked, opening her eyes. "Oh."

Adam smiled. "That's OK. He looks better with it than he does without it anyway."

Todd and Jara looked to where Steven had been standing, but it was clear from their expressions that they could not see anything. The target of the working, after all, had been the guard. JC figured he and Adam had just been caught in the effect by accident.

"I don't understand. Every time I try to correct the image, it shifts back to this one," Becky said, sweat starting to glisten on her forehead.

"It's not a big deal," Adam said. "If the guard over there can pick out that level of detail with the sun in his eyes, I'd be stunned."

JC looked at the image of Steven more carefully. It wasn't just the clothes and the facial hair that were different. His hair was a bit longer too, but more importantly, his eyes were different. They were lighter, softer—there were not the dark circles under them that had been a permanent fixture since...

"Oh that's messed up," JC mumbled.

Before he could further elaborate, the image rippled and burst as Steven materialized back in Yors' shadow, shifting back to his physical form and panting for breath.

"Did you find it?" Jara demanded.

"Yeah," Steven said, his breathing slowing back to normal. "It's closer than we thought. It isn't a Shadowbender—it's just a boat in the sky. There's not even very many people onboard the thing."

"You went *onto* the ship?" Todd asked, leaning in. "What else did you see?"

"I was only there for a second—I could feel Miss Fingernails closing in on me. The captain was a big, blonde guy. Kind of reminded me of a Viking. The rest of the crew acted really scared of him. The sails had these kind of shiny patches on them, and the ship itself was big—big enough that I have no idea what is powerful enough to hold it up in the air like that." Steven looked around at the rest of them. "Anyone have a clue?"

Yors said, "Bindmetal."

JC looked up at him. "Bindmetal can make things fly?"

"Yors not know anything Bindmetal can't do."

JC smacked himself in the forehead. "You mean I could have had Jarrek make me able to fly instead of making this stupid thing around my neck?"

Yors did not reply. The Jov instead lifted one hand and pointed into the distance. "There."

Everyone pressed up against the edge of the wall, peering towards the north. JC couldn't see anything at first, but then slowly, he made out a small black speck growing steadily larger.

"It's here," Steven said. "I knew it was closer than we thought. So, what's our plan?"

No one said anything. JC leaned in to Becky and whispered, "You have one, right?"

Becky shook her head. "Not this time."

JC nodded. "Then we do it my way," he said aloud.

"What your way?" Yors asked.

"We make this shit up as we go along."

# 11
## Onus

*One hour.* That was all the time they had to get final defenses into place. The ship and its unknown captain had made incredible time crossing the flatlands between Igar Holc and Ain Holc, and now the Duchess could do little but hope she had sufficiently motivated the Children of the Line to do here what they had done at Rega Holc.

She sat on horseback just outside the east gates. She would ride free of the city, directly towards Rura Holc, when the fighting started. A few moments ago the other Council members had left, slipped away by the Rak back to their homes. Standing beside her was Duke Igar.

"Are you certain I can't convince you to come with me?" The Duchess asked. "Whatever happens here, it is not safe for you."

"Are you throwing me out like you did the others? Am I a Northern Duke to your eyes?" Igar said sullenly. "I never thought of myself as part of the North or the South. I was simply part of the Bridge City... and now that is no more. I will not be going with you. I will stay here and see, firsthand, what that villain did to my people."

"No good can come of that," Duchess Ain tried to explain.

"I would know if my people suffered," Duke Igar said. "You should go. I imagine this will get bad very soon, and if you don't ride away now, who will be left to posture and rant at the others?"

"That was uncalled for," Ain said, spurring her horse to action.

"I am entitled," Igar shouted at her as she rode away from the city.

The Duchess could not argue.

Overhead, to the north, the ship was big enough to see clearly. Its sails billowed, gleaming with patches of metal bright and dark, and its slick black hull glistened. Night would not fall for several hours still. The Children would save her city. They had done it before, for Rega Holc.

She brought her horse to a halt.

This was *her* city. It was her husband's city. Ain Holc had been held by ten Dukes in the era of the Council, three in her husband's bloodline and six in the previous bloodline. To abandon it now would not be right.

She turned the horse around and rode back towards the city. Whatever happened next, she would see it for herself.

¤~¤~¤

Becky and JC were helping Yors move along the walls, explaining the angle of fire to the archers while Yors worked hasty, impermanent metalbreaking magic upon their arrowheads for sharpness and strength. The smith was growing tired already, and they still had many archers to reach.

"All the arrows in the world won't do any good against the hull of the ship. We need to hit the sails, or better yet the men on deck," Becky explained. "So the arc of the shot must be precise. The arrow must rain down upon them, not fly straight into them."

"But the target is so high," one of the city's archers complained. "To arc even higher would cost us dearly in accuracy."

"Which is why we have to shoot a lot of arrows," JC said, holding a bundle of broad-tipped arrows out for Yors to shape with his magic. "The more arrows we get in the air, at the angles Becky is talking about, the better chance we end this thing before the ship gets close enough to do whatever scary thing it plans to do."

The archer nodded, as did the others with him who had not spoken, and the trio moved on, Yors struggling to keep up.

"You doing OK, big guy?" JC asked.

Yors nodded. His eyes though, revealed a redness and a sullen expression that seemed equal parts anger and exhaustion.

"Working on Joe's chain takes a lot out of you, doesn't it?" Becky asked. She had suspected as much, but the Metalbreaker was so quiet most of the time that she didn't ever really get a chance to gauge to what extent he was struggling. Now though, it was clear. And there were still thirty-six active links in the chain around Joe's neck.

Yors said simply, "Worth doing."

They continued on, slowing just a bit to give Yors a chance to catch his breath, and Becky looked down over the outer walls to see how things were going there. Todd and Steven were assisting the ground soldiers—what few there were—in the construction of a catapult out among the rubble-strewn field. Becky looked up at the approaching ship and did some quick calculations in her mind.

She wasn't sure it would even be done in time to make a difference.

Dealing with this ship required exactly the kind of strategy that these people had never had any reason to employ. At least at Rega Holc there had been Boltsenders to rely upon, but there were virtually none in the city. The few Raks in Ain Holc were too busy evacuating the Dukes to lend any help to the city's defense. And so they had a choice—Adam could gate away to gather reinforcements or he could stay here and provide defense.

Becky hoped they had chosen wisely.

¤~¤~¤

"Gendric's people would not help," Jara said calmly. She sat on the balcony of the Duchess' palace, on the topmost floor. This part of the palace was level with the walls of the city, and she had a fine view of the black ship.

It would be close enough soon that people would start shooting arrows at it. She didn't foresee much success in that course of action, but she knew that people had to do something—no one was happy sitting around quietly waiting for the end.

Adam stood just behind her, staring at the ship. "I thought the Vols were on good terms with the Council."

"Oh they are. They would try to help, but it wouldn't *be* any help. The ship swallows lightning," Jara replied. "I'm getting clearer visions about it now. It's called the Razormaw. And its captain... I can't quite picture him yet. But the ship is built to stand up to anything its captain could imagine, and he seems like a pretty imaginative person."

"Razormaw?" Adam mused. "Sounds more like a dinosaur than a pirate ship."

"I don't know what a dinosaur is," Jara confessed. "That's another Core thing, I assume."

"Like a dragon but without the magic powers and hideously overbearing sense of entitlement," Adam said. He tapped his foot nervously on the balcony floor. "I think it's time. If we wait any longer, I won't have room to adjust it."

Jara stood up and took Adam's hand. "I will try to help. I can see where the ship will be, and if you can line things up just right, we should be able to give everyone else a chance."

Jara tried to push her vision, her special kind of magic, through their clasped hands and into Adam. She wasn't sure if it was working, or if it was helping at all, but she did it nonetheless. It was all she could think of to help.

Adam stretched out his free hand, fingers spread wide, and flickering sparks of blue and white light manifested all around that hand. Jara watched in awe as the sparks spread out into the open air before them, shooting through the air. The sparks faded away—still present, but now unseen—as they formed a lattice of invisible energy high in the sky and directly between the Razormaw and Ain Holc.

Adam grunted, "It's done. That... is the biggest intercession I've ever tried."

"It looks like it's in the right place," Jara said.

"It has to be. I can't make it any bigger," Adam muttered. "And this is going to drain me dry if I have to hold it for more than a few minutes." The Gatemaker lurched forward to the railing of the balcony and lowered himself to the floor, propping his chin up on the rail and keeping his eyes, heavy-lidded though they were, focused on the magical barrier he had just erected.

"Stay awake," Jara said, squeezing Adam's shoulder. "And believe in the Purpose."

"Does the Purpose care if this city gets blown to bits?" Adam asked, fighting back a yawn.

"I don't know," Jara confessed. "It keeps a lot of secrets from me."

¤~¤~¤

"Something's wrong." Grell looked up at the crow's nest, where Fendris was stationed. While his trust in the man was now a thing of the past, he knew that Fendris wanted to live, and for that reason alone he could still be counted upon. "What's happening?" he shouted up.

Fendris cupped his hands around his mouth and shouted downward, "I'm not sure. The perspective is all wrong, Captain. Light's behaving funny too."

The ship was pressing full-speed ahead, its sails billowing full of brisk wind, but they had somehow ceased to approach Ain Holc. He could see activity on the ground and on the walls, but again—nothing was coming into clearer focus. This was not right.

Occasionally, arrows would streak down upon them. The men lining the walls of Ain Holc fired their arrows nearly straight up, counting on the wind and the force of gravity to pull them back down upon Grell's head. Most of the men, those not needed to secure the rigging lines, were below decks, awaiting orders. No arrows struck Grell as he kept his arts about him, skewing the metal arrowheads away from the forecastle. Most arrows missed the ship entirely, but they were coming faster and faster, like hailstones.

"Open the maw!" Grell ordered. He heard the men below begin to work the mighty cogs that would slip open the forward compartment of the ship.

Vediri's head appeared from the ladder that led to the fore hold. "We're too far to drop the storm anchor, captain. If we open the compartment while we're moving it'll drive us down fast."

"As soon as you can, fire the harpoon," Grell barked. "Be ready to reel it back in quick."

Vediri disappeared back below deck, and Grell felt the metal substance of the harpoon sliding into position beneath his feet. Every ounce of metal on this ship was a part of him, attuned to the rhythm he had established in its construction. It was a magnificent engine of destruction, and its next target was tantalizingly close. He could see the banners of the house of Ain flapping above the city walls—three flags. The Duchess of Ain was here.

Below him, with a furious twang, the harpoon launched from the massive ballista built into the ship's forward hold. The lance of metal flew forward, and Grell watched as it seemed to hang in the air directly in front of the Razormaw. Its trailing chain clattered and clanked, and Grell could hear the coils of chain below continuing to unspool, but the harpoon wasn't actually getting any farther away from the ship.

"Pull it in!" Grell shouted.

Somehow, Ain Holc had erected a defense in preparation of his coming. Grell couldn't quite understand how it worked, but he could see it now—he could see what it did, and he could see how it would thwart his plan. This could not be allowed.

"Fendris! Drop!" Grell commanded. "Vediri, the helm is yours!"

His first mate leapt up from the hold, ignoring her wounds and injuries as she raced to take the wheel. Fendris was sliding down the main mast, skipping several rungs of the ladder as he dropped. Grell lifted both hands and brought them together in a resonant clap. Then he clapped again. Then a third time. The beat echoed out from him, carried on the magic of metalbreaking, and set about changing the enchantment worked upon the sails.

Concentrating intensely, Grell lifted the ship still higher in the air. If the arrows could get over this barrier, so could he.

¤~¤~¤

"This is bad," Todd said with a grunt as the team he and Steven were assisting secured the heavy pull-rope to the arm of the catapult. The crankshaft was in place already, and Steven imagined the device was ready for action.

Of course he hadn't given catapults much thought since a brief infatuation with the middle ages in seventh grade, so he was open to the possibility of being completely wrong.

"What is it?" he asked.

"The ship is climbing. Adam's going to have to reposition the intercession, or maybe drop it entirely. He's way too out of practice to keep this up." Todd shielded his eyes with his hand as he stared up at the ship.

Beside them, the captain of Ain Holc's city guard ordered the catapult readied for firing, and four men started turning the mighty crank that drew the arm down tight against the weapon's base. Once it was secured in the primed position, other men started to load large stones—the remnants of the city's original walls—into the basket.

"Maybe this will work," Steven mused.

"Not while the intercession is in place. It's stretched low because he expected the ship to drop under it. We didn't think it could go any higher than it already was." Todd turned to the captain. "Don't fire until we get a signal from Jara!" he commanded.

The captain nodded sharply and then directed men at the other two catapult crews to similarly wait.

"Do you think," Todd asked, "that you can get both you and me up there? On the ship?"

Steven squinted up at the ship. "The sun is seriously working against me right now. When I shadowslide, it's usually along something. Moving straight through the air is trickier when it's this bright out. Especially carrying someone."

"Then we can catch a ride," Todd said, gesturing to the loaded catapult.

"This sounds like a Joe plan," Steven said, looking at the basket full of large, heavy stones skeptically.

"We'll be in shadowform, right? If it was a Joe plan, we'd be throwing our bodies up there. That's significantly crazier."

Up above them, from the walls, Steven heard the buzzing whine of JC's energy rifles. Shot after shot rang out, but none made contact with the ship—Adam's intercession was still in place.

"Why hasn't he moved it up yet?" Steven asked, worried.

"I don't know," Todd said. "Get us in the catapult. We have to be ready—we'll only get one chance."

¤~¤~¤

"So much Bindmetal," Yors said, covering his ears as he shouted to Becky. Only a few feet away, JC was firing barrage after barrage of blasts from his rifles, and the sound was hard for Yors to handle.

"In the ship?" Becky shouted back.

"More than Yors ever seen at once. Can feel all of it, even down here." Yors tried to remember the forges on Murrod, or even the mine he had first been stationed at when they had arrived in that horrible jungle for the first time, right after the men in gold robes had taken his daughter from him, right before he heard her death scream echoing in the tunnels. Even in the mines of Murrod, where Bindmetal was more plentiful than anywhere else on any world ever found, there was not so much metal all so close together.

"Can you bring the ship down? With some Jov magic or something?" Becky asked.

Yors shook his head as he unslung his crossbow. "Yors not very good at faraway magic. Sorry." He fit a bolt, a very particular bolt shaped from green Bindmetal, into the crossbow as he wound the weapon to readiness. "But Yors has one good trick."

Yors lined up his shot, but did not take it. He would have only one, so he could afford no mistakes. "When Yors fires, Becky take JC and get far from Yors. Off wall good. Other part of city, better."

"What are you going to do?" Becky asked nervously.

Yors replied with a resigned sigh, "Faraway magic."

¤~¤~¤

Adam cried out as the intercession collapsed. Jara was right beside him, trying to feed him strength through her magic, but it was not helping. He could barely stay conscious, and the effort of moving the intercession, a segment half the size of the city held up better than a hundred yards in the air, was too great.

"I lost it," Adam whispered.

"Can you put it back up? A new one, higher up?" Jara asked.

Adam looked up, watched as the ship started to level out and resume its forward motion, towards them all, and shook his head. "No. I've got barely anything left."

"Then it's up to the others," Jara said. She unfurled the rolled white flag that had been affixed to the railing of the balcony, and the wind caused it to whip and snap at full extension. "That's the signal for the catapults."

Adam watched as Joe's energy blasts started to actually strike the ship, and waited for the catapults to fire. Joe's shots seemed to be having little effect, but they were at least hitting the Razormaw—it was more than he expected the catapults to do. The ranges were all wrong. The angles all bad.

Beyond sight, concealed by the city's walls, the first catapult fired. Adam saw the barrage of rocks fly up, slick with a strange blackness, and felt his heart sink as they flew too wide, missing the ship.

But that blackness did not miss the ship. It leapt from the rocks to the ship, a rapid-flash of shadow, and he realized what it was.

"Steven?" he asked quietly.

"And Todd," Jara said. "Something big is about to happen."

¤~¤~¤

Steven and Todd materialized on the deck of the ship in the shadow of the captain's cabin, and they crouched there in silence getting their bearings. Todd carried a sword borrowed from one of the catapult crewmen, and Steven was planning to rely upon his Rak magic. He wouldn't have been any good with a sword anyway, but he was suddenly missing his gun very much.

Todd pointed towards the forecastle, where the captain stood with his back to them. The stairs that led up to the forecastle were guarded by a large, tough looking woman with short, spiked braids of hair and a wiry little man with narrow shoulders. Both were focused on matters going on ahead of the ship.

"I'll take the two on the stairs," Todd said. "You get to the captain. If you can get him away from the wheel, the ship should start to drift, maybe into a better line of fire for the catapults."

Steven nodded, and a moment later they launched into action.

Steven sprinted in shadowform, his limbs lengthening and his fingers sharpening to points as he slid up the stairs and past, through, the two crewmen that stood between him and the captain.

Todd, who Steven could sense only minimally in his peripheral vision, charged the stairs, sword at the ready, in silence.

Steven pounced upon the captain, raking across the man's back with his shadow-talons. The captain cried out more in a sound of surprise than true pain and turned halfway, keeping one hand on the wheel.

"Rak," the captain spat. "Pet of the Council."

"Steven," Steven corrected him. "Nobody's pet."

The captain drew a short sword from a scabbard at his side and swung rapidly at Steven, always keeping one hand on the wheel. In spite of this handicap, Steven struggled to defend against the attack. His own limbs, granted extra toughness and substantiality by calling upon the shadow, could take several hits from the powerful man, but once he shifted to blocking he found that the captain left him no opportunity for offense. Rage burned in the captain's eyes, and that fury lent him speed and strength well in excess of Steven.

Steven lunged once, seeking to drive his shadow-talons into the captain's meaty thigh, but as his blades plunged into the big blonde man's leg, he realized the opening had been a feint. The captain brought his short sword down in a heavy chopping motion, the sword momentarily blazing with light as it fell, severing Steven's left hand from his wrist.

Steven recoiled, shadow steaming from the stump of his right hand. He screamed with pain and shock, and as he stumbled backwards, he tripped over the unconscious form of the large woman that had been on the stairs. Todd had made it to the top of the stairs, and he grabbed Steven and kept him from falling down the stairs himself. At the wheel, the captain turned his back to them both, as though he was not concerned.

"That looks bad," Todd said, staring at Steven's missing hand.

Steven grunted, "It's fixable. Where's the little guy?"

"He ran," Todd said. "His heart wasn't in the fighting, not like hers."

"He's good," Steven said, glaring at the captain's back. "Probably better than you."

Todd clenched his teeth and released Steven. "Be ready to pull my ass out of here if this goes wrong."

Steven grunted assent.

Todd, sword at the ready, called to the captain. "Turn and face me."

The captain, making no effort to turn, replied, "Not right now. I'm busy."

"I'd rather not kill a man from behind," Todd said firmly. "But I will."

The captain laughed, but still did not turn.

Todd swung the sword in a tightly controlled slash, biting through the already-tattered clothes on the captain's back and drawing a bright red line of blood across the man's muscular shoulders.

With an audible sigh, the Captain turned to face Todd. As before, Steven saw that he did not release the wheel. From this vantage point, Steven could see the man's face more clearly, and he could see that it was not masked with arrogance—it was masked with determination. The rage in him was cold, not hot—this was a man who had thought long and hard about what he was about to do. He was the most dangerous kind of criminal, the kind Steven had always dreaded having to face when he was a cop.

"You are on my ship. You brought a *sword* onto my ship. Your threats are meaningless to me." The captain waved his free hand through the air in a lazy gesture that appeared dismissive until Todd started to scream.

Without waiting to see what was happening, Steven lurched into action. He was still in his own shadowform, unable to return to flesh until he had regenerated the missing hand, and he swallowed Todd in the shadow as well, racing off the edge of the ship and falling like a stone towards the ground below. The landing would be hard, but not fatal. They had done all they could. Several of Joe's energy blasts nearly hit them as they tumbled down.

The ship was directly over the city now.

¤~¤~¤

Yors fired his crossbow. The bolt flew swift and true—he was, after all, an incredible shot. The projectile tore into the ship, burrowing through the thick, reinforced hull and coming to a halt just as its green metal tip broke into the ship's fore hold.

At the top of his lungs, Yors sang a song. It was a simple song, childish in all ways—a song he had learned as a toddler at Jov Nought, many years ago. Its beat was measured and repetitive, and it was this cadence that he used to channel the magic of the Jovs up, up, up into the airship.

With every ounce of power at his command, Yors broke the metal in the ship. The Bindmetal was too hard to work with, too resistant to reshaping at such a range, and too precious to destroy. But the ordinary metal, the nails and the chains, the bolts and the pins, the swords and the hooks, the forks and the flagons... every bit of non-magical metal aboard the ship shattered and then liquefied.

Sound distorted, waves of echoing noise building all around Yors and causing the section of the wall upon which he stood to tremble to its foundations. But none of that mattered, because he had done it.

The ship was coming to pieces.

¤~¤~¤

The enemy Metalbreaker's working slammed into the ship, and into Grell's senses, like a fist. He tried to fight it off, to undo the powerful, sure magic of his foe, but it was no use. He slowed the process, nothing more. Within a minute, the ship would fall apart, its very strength now turned against it.

Grell himself abandoned the wheel—it no longer mattered. He grabbed Vediri's unconscious form and slung her over his shoulder and darted down the stairs to the low mid-deck. He saw Fendris cowering there, in the shadow of the stairs that led to the aft deck, and pointed to the watchman. "Take her there," he said, pointing to the hatch that led to the starboard hold. With a sharp popping sound, his magic split the seams on the hatch, and Fendris scrambled to action even as Grell dropped Vediri unceremoniously on the deck before him. All around them, men swarmed as the masts started to shift and sway.

Without another look back, he charged down into the rear hold. He had one last thing to do. The ship, and her captain, might be going down, but not without first destroying Ain Holc.

"Drop the anchor!" he roared.

At the front of the ship, he heard the men heaving to shove the great Bindmetal cube out of the carved mouth of the Razormaw. Without their pry bars and the metal track in place there, it would be hard work—but they would do it. A second city would fall.

¤~¤~¤

Adam watched the shadowforms of Steven and Todd tumble down from the ship, but Jara convinced him that they would be fine, that Steven had it under control.

Adam watched as the ship above them started to crumble, listing to one side then the other as a mast toppled and bits and pieces of the ship began to rain down upon the panicked city below.

Then Adam watched in horror as a large, metal cube disgorged from the front of the ship.

"That's the weapon!" Jara screamed.

Without any real faith that the magic would respond to his command, Adam reached out his hand and tried, with all the energy left in his veins, to open a crossgate. The bright orange disc appeared, horizontal and wobbling, unstable and unsafe, just below the cube. The portal held steady long enough to swallow the bright metal cube, then it winked closed.

A moment later, the cube appeared again, but this time it was not below the Razormaw—it was on top of it.

The cube slammed into the deck of the ship, tearing through a sail and shattering a mast in the process. As it struck the deck it discharged its magic—the horrible magic that had laid waste to the entire city of Igar Holc. A thousand, thousand storms of every type and description unfolded in that space, in that moment, high above Ain Holc.

Wind roared and spun in tornado funnels as lightning fired again and again. Hail and snow and rain and more, all swirled in the vortex of wind and water and the resonant, staccato bursts of thunder.

For one hour, the storm raged. Its effects spread wide rather than low, creating a ceiling of fury above the city but doing relatively little harm to the city itself. When it calmed, all that remained of the ship—wreckage and cargo and perhaps even bodies, tumbled down out of the sky, crashing into the ground just outside the city's west gates.

Overhead, the storm had calmed, but not entirely ended.

The first sound Adam heard when his ears ceased to ring from an hour of consecutive thunderclaps was Joe shouting exultantly from the walls.

# 12
## Onus

A*in Holc survives because of you,"* Duchess Ain said quietly. "But it is also cursed because of you." She made a show of looking up at the perpetually drizzling cloud that had taken root in the skies above Ain Holc. In the three days since the Razormaw had been destroyed, the cloud had shown no sign of dissipating—although the Bindmetal cube that had caused the weather was nowhere to be found.

"That doesn't matter," Adam said. "We saved you. We did what you wanted. You need to release Jara's family and let us be on our way."

They had gathered beneath a hastily erected fabric pavilion outside the west gates of the city so that the Duchess could survey the efforts that were being made to clean up the wreckage of the Razormaw. They were all there and all relatively whole. Steven's hand, severed by the captain of the ship, had regrown while he was still in shadowform and thus never really been gone from his physical body. And Todd—Adam worried about Todd. Both his hands were bandaged. His palms and fingers had been perforated with scores of holes when the captain—a Metalbreaker—had caused the handle of his sword to sprout dozens of razor-sharp needles. Todd's hands did not properly open or close right now, and Adam feared there might be nerve damage.

The Duchess sighed. "If only it were that simple. But this pirate and his senseless destruction was only one of the many threats we face. And your services are needed now more than ever." She lifted her hand overhead and made a sharp gesture. A moment later, two guards escorted a pale figure to the pavilion, their heavy footsteps in the muddy ground making loud slurping sounds.

"This is Fillip, a Rak sworn to service with Duke Herin. Tell them what happened, Fillip." The Duchess was trying to affect a tone of sympathy as she spoke to the bedraggled Rak, but Adam wasn't buying it.

"We carried the Dukes homeward, three days ago. The journey is far for many of them, and hard on their graces, but it has been done this way many times before." Fillip's voice was low, and Adam strained to hear. The others were also listening intently, although Adam could see something in Jara's face—she already knew some of what he was about to say.

"When we came to the land bridge—to the ruins of Igar Holc—we opted to speed through, staying in the shadow instead of lingering in that blighted place. But as we drew nearer, we discovered that the storm that brought the city to the ground has not yet ended, not truly. When one draws near, it grows in fury once more," Fillip covered his eyes with his hands. "The lightning flashed again and again. It tore at our shadowforms, and those we carried. It grew worse as we traveled closer, and at last we had no choice but to fall back."

"Are the Dukes alright?" Becky asked.

"Yes—they are weak, but we managed to mend their shadows before we returned them to flesh," Fillip said. "The same cannot be said for all of my brother and sister Raks. Two of them died while trying to mend their own forms."

"Wait, so what does this mean?" JC asked.

"It means the land bridge is now impassible," Duchess Ain said. "The northern continent and the southern continent are truly cut off from one another. The sea routes remain open, but slow and fraught with their own peril. If the Dukes are to get home, and if the South is to gain any support against the enemies that already lurk close at hand, we need a Gatemaker." The Duchess smiled at Adam. "Fortunately, here you are."

"And you need a Fatewaker to point you to these enemies. To ferret them out before they do any more harm to innocent people," Jara added glumly.

"You are indeed a wise little Wyr," Duchess Ain remarked.

"Then I want to negotiate the terms of our assistance," Adam said.

"I'm listening," the Duchess replied. With a dismissive gesture, she signaled for her guards to help Fillip back towards the city interior.

"Jara and I will stay, because there are very specific things you need our help with," Adam said, holding up his hand to quiet the others. "But the rest, everyone else, can go."

In his mind, Adam heard Becky begin to protest. "We can't go to Arctos without you, dumbass. You're the guy who opens the Spiralgate."

"I know that. Just let me finish," Adam mumbled in his mind. Becky appeared to back down, pulling out of his thoughts.

"I will take them to the nearest safe Spiralgate and send them on their way, then I will return here. Jara will stay here as ransom for my own return. And once I get back, Jara and I will help you protect your people. Because it's the right thing to do, not because it's what you want us to do." Adam folded his arms in front of his chest.

"I do not care about your semantics, so long as you play your part," Duchess Ain stated. "But this is an arrangement that I can work with."

"And," Jara said, interjecting just as Adam was starting to relax. He had no idea what she was going to say, or if she was about to ruin everything. "As soon as everyone is in position and the enemies of Ain Holc and Rura Holc have been stopped, you will release my mother and grandfather and Adam and I will be free to go. We are not here to clean up every mess in the South—just yours."

The Duchess narrowed her eyes and stared at Jara. "By what measure is an enemy of freedom determined to be mine, or Rura's, or that of any other?"

"We'll help you bring peace to all of the lands north of the Vale of Steam. That's all." Jara now folded her own arms in front of her chest. Adam liked to think that he looked defiant when he did it—she just looked petulant. And yet, she was a Wyr, and there was always a strange kind of weight in her words.

"I accept these terms. You have the remainder of this day to set your friends upon their road, Gatemaker. Tomorrow we begin the redeployment of northern forces." The Duchess started to walk back towards the west gate. As she left the shelter of the pavilion, a guard extended his shield over her head to keep her from getting wet in the rain.

Once she was out of sight, Becky turned to Adam and punched him in the shoulder. "Why did you do that?"

Adam shrugged, rubbing at his shoulder where she had struck him. "None of us can figure out where Moultus and Hessa are being kept, so this seemed like the best way to get everything we wanted."

"Except you gave her what *she* wanted," Todd said. "I never like to see someone that full of themselves win."

"Who goes and who stays?" Steven asked. "I don't like the idea of you two being here with the Wicked Witch of Ain Holc by yourselves."

"I was thinking Todd could stay here with us," Adam said. Todd nodded slightly. Adam couldn't help but look at Todd's bandaged hands. "And maybe we can get one of those Bloodmenders to take a look at your hands?"

"So then the three of us will go to Arctos and find this Archive place?" Becky asked, pointing to herself, JC, and Steven.

"Yors go too," Yors added.

Jara looked up at the Jov and asked, "Don't you want to stay with me? I was hoping you would."

Yors leaned down and gave Jara an uncharacteristic hug. Adam had noticed the smith avoiding making direct, physical contact with her ever since they had arrived in Igar Holc, and even now when he initiated it, there was a stilted awkwardness in the gesture.

"Yors fixing JC," the Metalbreaker said.

"Good," Jara said, smiling as the hug ended. "Someone ought to."

¤~¤~¤

Four large draft horses from the personal collection of Duke Stes, on loan to Duchess Ain to help with the rebuilding of the city walls after Hyrak's men had at last been driven out, strained mightily as they tugged the last of the four large blocks of Bindmetal into the warehouse on the southern edge of the city. It was just after dusk, and still it rained.

The blocks had been recovered from the wreckage of the Razormaw, and the Duchess' advisors had insisted that their existence be kept secret from everyone, especially the other Dukes currently convalescing in the palace. While the blocks appeared to be safe—their magic had been discharged in the storm-explosion that had demolished the ship—they were potential sources of great power or great wealth for Ain Holc.

The small crew of workers, paid handsomely for their discretion, had moved the blocks all in the first night out of sight, and then spent the last two days positioning them in the securely locked warehouse where they would not be stumbled upon by any random travelers or homeless denizens of the city looking for a place to sleep.

As the last of the blocks was slid into place, snug up against the other three, all in a nice row, the workers filed quietly out the double doors of the warehouse, securing the doors with heavy lengths of chain and a complicated, expensive lock.

¤~¤~¤

"Grandfather told me lots of things about Arctos," Jara explained as the traveling party made their last preparations. "I know you have to arrive when it is night here, because it will be day there. Day is very important on Arctos, because it gets very cold at night. Very dangerously cold."

Becky nodded. Jara had explained this all to them once, earlier today—that was why they had waited until nighttime for Adam to take them to the Spiralgate and send them on their way. Rain drizzled down upon the makeshift tarp that had been stretched over the guest house garden.

"When you get there, you want to find an Archivist named Marriq. She was a friend of my grandfather's when he was an apprentice to the Archivists—she will help you if she knows you are there on behalf of his work." Jara double-checked the strap on Becky's backpack.

Everyone was gathered in the garden, bundled up in the thickest coats and cloaks that could be found in the always-warm city. They were sweating through and through, but it wasn't until Steven, Yors, JC, and Becky were suitably bundled that Jara would give her blessing for the journey to begin.

Jara sighed. "Adam will open the portal every day at midnight here, which should be mid-day on Arctos. So you'll never be more than a day away from returning home. You'll be fine. I can feel it."

With that, Jara made her good-byes. She was not permitted, per their agreement with the Duchess, to travel to the Spiralgate with them, and so she said good luck to each of them now, and then she left the garden.

"I wish I had learned how to make chaingates," Adam muttered. He and Jara had plotted the course of the two crossgates it would take for him to carry everyone to the Ebugar Spiralgate, but he remembered Embrew's special talent, the ability to weave crossgates and Spiralgates together seamlessly. If he had that, he wouldn't need to worry about what might be waiting for them at the Ebugar gate—they could bypass the need to deal with its physical surroundings altogether.

He opened the first of the crossgates there in the garden, and a flat disk of golden light appeared, a doorway to a tropical jungle hundreds of miles to the southeast of Ain Holc.

JC stepped through first, then Steven, then Becky. Yors followed, and then Adam found himself standing alone in the garden with Todd.

"I think I should go with them," Todd said. "I know that's not what you want to hear, and you know I'd rather be here with you, but... it's important we find all of the answers we need, and this may be the only chance we get."

Adam bit at his lip. "You aren't worried about me?"

"Never. You can take care of yourself, and really—the Duchess is going to keep you so busy ferrying people from one place to another, I think the only real danger you'll be in is not getting enough sleep." Todd kissed him, and Adam felt himself melt a little into that moment.

"We've never been on different worlds from each other before," Adam said. "I'll miss you."

"Good. That'll keep you out of trouble," Todd said, smiling. He stepped away from Adam and pulled a large bundle from behind one of the trees in the garden. He started to strap on the heavy coat as he slipped the straps of the backpack over his shoulders. "Shall we?"

Adam sighed and escorted his boyfriend through first this crossgate, and then the next. In a little less than ten minutes the entire traveling party was arrayed before the abandoned, and obviously long-disused, Ebugar Spiralgate. Adam selected the geometric key for the Firgar gate on Arctos, the one Jara had insisted was closest to the Archive, and the Spiralgate slowly spun to life.

Adam waved, heartsick, as his boyfriend vanished into the glowing, spherical portal. Then his best friend did the same, and the sensation grew worse. He watched Steven go as well, then JC, then, bringing up the rear, Yors.

As the Spiralgate closed behind them, Adam realized that he was the only person from Core on this entire world now. The thought made him sick to his stomach.

In the dark, with only unfamiliar stars as companions, he started his way back to Ain Holc.

¤~¤~¤

It was deep into the night. The warehouse was silent, save for a persistent rat gnawing at some manner of refuse in the corner. When at last he was certain that he was completely alone, Grell freed himself from his improvised life raft. The second of the four cubes of Bindmetal was, like the other three, one of the few storm anchors that had survived the devastation in the sky, but unlike the others, it had been empty of charge long before it fell.

The surface of the front of the cube slowly flowed open, creating a hole large enough for Grell to crawl through. Once he was out, he set his magic to the task again, sealing the hole and leaving no evidence of his presence.

In his heart, he had always known that the Razormaw would only take him so far, but he had hoped it would be farther than this. There were Dukes, and a Duchess, left unpunished, and so there was work left to do.

¤~¤~¤

# End Act I

¤~¤~¤

# 13
# ARCTOS

*Becky had grown up in the center of Iowa.* She had never been particularly fond of the deep, rapid-onset winter that gripped her home state each year. But in spite of all that, as she emerged from the Spiralgate, with JC, Todd, Yors, and Steven at her side, she found herself utterly unprepared for what true winter was.

The sky was a dark, steely gray, bounded by thick and trundling clouds. As the argent light of the Spiralgate faded, the intensity of the cold that whorled all around them in wind that seemed to blow from every direction at once truly set in. The heavy cloaks and coats they had donned at Jara's insistence meant nothing to this cold, and it was all Becky could do to keep her teeth from immediately starting to chatter.

JC took her hand and helped her down from the slippery, ice-coated platform upon which the gate mechanism rested. The snow, hard-packed and slick, crunched slightly under her foot as she stepped off the dark stone landing.

"Careful," he muttered. "It blows here." As he jumped down into the snow, he hunched over and began to fiddle with something in his pocket.

Becky said nothing, afraid of letting what passed for her body heat escape from between her lips. She looked around, as the others were—seeking a sign of civilization or shelter. At best they had perhaps six hours before sunset, and shelter by then was imperative. Everywhere she looked, she could see nothing but white. Snow and ice piled in dunes all around them, but there was no sign of inhabitation or structure. Not so much as a tree broke the shifting white monotony.

"This is not a good sign," Steven's voice echoed in Becky's mind.

She jumped slightly, startled by his sudden activation of the link between them that she so often kept muted. "Can you search in your shadowform?" Becky asked, regaining her composure. "That has to be faster than whatever progress we make trudging through all of this snow."

Steven nodded and squatted down, pulling his shadow up around him and allowing his body to dissolve into darkness. With the light of the sun diffused by the clouds, his shadow flickered out faster than Becky had ever seen it move. It gave her a small measure of faith.

JC wrapped an arm around her shoulders. "I brought the compass," he whispered into her ear. "But it's acting kind of weird."

Becky arched an eyebrow at him. "What does that mean?"

JC tapped his forehead and then tapped hers.

Becky closed her eyes and allowed their minds to touch. Unlike the connection with Steven, which she fought so often to still, the connection with JC, precise and focused, opened easily at her command.

"So I have been trying to get it to point to the Archive, but it doesn't respond to that. So then I started getting frustrated."

"You do tend to do that," Becky chided.

"Yeah, I know. I'm working on it. Anyway, I kind of bitched it out, for all the good that did, and I told it that all I wanted to find were answers. The truth, you know?" JC's voice seemed to sink lower in tone inside their private mental communication.

"And?" Becky asked, her curiosity aflame.

"Look at the needle," JC replied silently. He had the compass cupped in his hands, hoarded from the sight of the others, and Becky peered down to see the needle pointing unerringly behind her. She looked back over her shoulder to see Todd and Yors huddled talking quietly, much like she and JC were.

"Yors?" Becky asked. "There's plenty that he probably knows. Maybe he can use his metalbreaking to lead us to where we are going?"

"It isn't Yors," JC said sullenly. "It's Todd."

Becky said nothing. She turned to stare at Todd. He had been part of her life for so long now that she had almost forgotten how much about him she did not know—how much about himself he never shared. Perhaps it was finally time to turn her arts upon him and learn what secrets Adam's boyfriend was keeping.

Just as that resolve had started to solidify in the oppressive cold, Steven's shadowy form appeared once more, fading back to flesh and substance. Before he had fully reformed his body he reached out one shadowy hand and placed it upon Yors' shoulder.

"I need you to help me lead them there, big guy," Steven said, gasping for breath. "There's a house, a cabin, kind of, to the west. I'm not sure we can make it by sunset, but maybe. If you can help me cut a trail through this snow."

Yors nodded and, without hesitation, began to press westward, his massive shape crunching the hard-packed snow into the vague semblance of a trail.

Todd followed him promptly, but Becky held back a moment, covering JC's compass with her hand.

"This stays between us. I need time to get into his head." Becky cast her instructions into JC's mind, and he nodded his understanding.

"We have to go now," Steven said, gesturing for Becky and JC to follow him. So they did.

The passage of time was challenging to keep without visible sun, and even with it, Becky would likely have been a poor judge. It felt as though they walked for hours. A persistent tingling numbness suffused her feet, and her face was stiff and raw. No one spoke, and even the silent communication channels she maintained with Steven and JC were left quiet as everyone focused all of their effort into pressing westward. The cabin that Steven had seen was out there, somewhere, but they had seen no sign of life or passage in the intervening hours, and Becky could feel her hope flagging.

She drew in a bitterly cold breath and prepared to cast her thoughts far away—attempting to stir the mental line of communication she maintained with Adam. She had little confidence that it would work, but if they were going to freeze to death on the tundra of an alien world, she at least wanted to say good-bye to her best friend.

"There!" Todd shouted, his voice hoarse and raspy. Becky followed his outstretched, bandaged hand and saw what might have been a cabin, mostly buried in a snowdrift. It might also have been just another snowdrift, but Todd's proclamation was all it took to stir the faint embers of hope again. She found herself possessed of a second wind, pushing forward just behind JC as he surpassed the compressed snow trail Yors was cutting.

They bounded through the snow like children, great leaps and sputtering starts all at once, and as they grew closer, Becky could see the dark shape of a doorway and, more importantly, a tiny square window. The window was aglow—there was light inside, and that meant—that had to mean—warmth. She feared she's never again know what that word meant. They scrambled to the door, carved of stone, not wood, she noted, and JC knocked mightily against it. Behind her, she could hear Steven and the others catching up.

For a few minutes, nothing happened. The five of them stood there in a rough huddle, Joe knocking every few seconds upon a door that did not budge.

"I'm taking the door out," he muttered, fumbling numbly for his energy rifle.

"No," Steven said. "Whoever is in there is moving around. The shadows are shifting."

With a slow, laborious creaking sound, the door pulled inward, and at first Becky could make out nothing but the warm, golden light of the cabin's interior. Then she saw the shadow of a figure, an old woman, hunched low and leaning upon a walking stick. Her skin was a deep bronze color and her hair was the color of steel. It fell long and straight to her shoulders, and it obscured her eyes. She wore light clothing, in no way suited to the weather, and she scowled out at the group with dark eyes.

"What are you doing here?" She asked in her small, sharp voice.

"We're looking for the Archive," JC said from between chattering teeth. "We've come from Onus."

"No one comes from Onus anymore," the woman retorted, half turning away from the doorway. "The gates are closed."

"Not all of them," Becky added. "Not when there is great need."

"And I suppose you have great need?" The old woman shouted back, anger clear in her eyes. "Go away!"

"We'll die in the night," Todd said simply.

"Good," the woman said, shaking her head. "The fewer fools wandering about, the better off we'll all be."

She pushed hard on the heavy door, starting to swing it closed, when Yors shouldered past Becky and planted one large foot in the doorframe, preventing the door from closing. "Yors told to find Marriq. Where she?"

The old woman stopped. "That is not a name spoken of on Arctos anymore," she muttered. "You come from Onus? Did you know one of her students there?"

"Yes," Becky said, nodding briskly. "Moultus."

"Moultus..." the old woman whispered. She stepped back, releasing her grip on the door. "Hurry in. The nightfall is almost upon us, and we would do best to have the door sealed before then."

Yors held the door wide and waited as the others entered. Becky was the second in, behind JC. As she crossed the threshold of the doorway she was suddenly overcome by a wave of nearly oppressive heat. Almost without thinking, she began to strip the great coat and wrappings from around her.

The others followed suit, returning to the casual clothes they had worn at Ain Holc and leaving their coats in a heap near the door.

"You're Marriq, aren't you?" JC asked as they settled onto small stools arranged around the strange metal stove-like structure at the center of the cabin.

"Once, I was Marriq the Archivist, yes. Now, I have little use of names. No one comes all the way out here, and I go nowhere. So it is, and so it has been." The woman rubbed at her hands anxiously. "It is good to be remembered though. Moultus was a fine student. He would have been a finer Archivist."

"He sent us, in a manner of speaking," Becky said carefully. "We were led to believe you could help us navigate the Archive to find the answers we seek."

"Once, his advice would have been quite true. But things have changed a great deal since Moultus' apprenticeship. I'm afraid you've come all this way for nothing, child. The Archive is no more. It was lost to us more than a decade ago."

"Oh," Todd said.

"Seriously?!?" JC shouted. "Can we not catch one goddamned break?"

Becky put out a hand to calm him, but as she tried to do the impossible, it was Steven who spoke up.

"Wait a second, Joe. Marriq, you said it was lost. Not destroyed?"

"No," the old woman said, her expression unreadable. "I do not think it is destroyed. Merely lost. Inaccessible."

"That's something we can work with," Steven said.

JC's expression, only a moment ago one of frustration, suddenly shifted. He grinned widely and started to crack his knuckles. "We get to laser stuff, don't we?"

¤~¤~¤

Arenara watched carefully, crouched low in the shadow of a snow dune. She wore all white and her naturally pale skin and hair only aided in the functional invisibility she affected. The cursed *xallyr* had woken after decades of slumber, and she had to report back to the others. After years of freedom, all of the old memories, the old horrors were once more vibrant in her mind.

At first, nothing emerged from the blue-white fire-sphere that formed from the *xallyr*, and she dared to hope that this was but an echo of the old days, not their return. But then the first of them emerged from the sphere, monstrous and vile. Each of them carried within their breast a beating heart and the weak, watery blood that had nearly brought this world to its ruin. This could not be permitted.

She crouched lower, waiting for the shifting, hungry snow to pile up around and over her, as she watched a total of five figures emerge from the ball of light. She thought of striking them now, catching them unawares and bringing their threat to an early close, but something made her hesitate. If she killed them, would more come? Perhaps she had only to let the magic of Arctos close in around them and let the endless cold swallow them in its dark embrace. Then there would be no one to blame, no retaliation warranted by whoever sent them.

That had been the choice she had made once, very long ago, and it had been the wrong one. One of so very many wrong choices. But she had learned much from one hundred years of dealing with humans. She had learned much from her study of their ways. They all had. Her people would not be victims again, not when they had finally retaken what was rightfully theirs.

Waiting was perhaps a mistake, but striking now was just as easily one as well. She toyed with her options until her keen eyes caught the strangest thing...

One of the invaders had vanished in a bolt of shadow. This was something unexpected—sorcery she had never before encountered. It was not the magic of her people. Were these emissaries of the *onysar*?

There were too many questions. She could not make the decision herself. As the shadow-rider reappeared and the group began to press to the west—nearer a place they could not be allowed to reach—she decided to instead follow them. She had to learn more before she reported back to the others.

She crept behind them, easily obscured from their sight and significantly faster than them. The snow did not break beneath her footfalls, and she found it an easy thing to get ahead of them, lie in concealment, and then wait for them to pass. Thus she moved infrequently, saving her strength for battle should it arise but always watching them. The shadow-rider did not again work his magic, and none of the others exhibited any particular spellcraft that she could see. Her earlier fears were laid to rest, and she began to think it unlikely that agents of the *onysar* would be forced to gouge a path through the ever-falling snow. Whatever these were, they were new to her, but they moved with purpose, unerringly toward the citadel.

She did not fear them, but she grew more and more curious of their intent with each passing hour.

At last, as the sun drew near its final rest and the fall of night was creeping down upon them all, they came to a halt. She peered carefully at what they were doing and then she saw something that her keen eyes had missed a hundred times on her patrols—a cabin. There was a human living there—living this close to the citadel! How was it possible that the creature had evaded her detection for so long?

She sniffed at the air, and then she noticed it—the creature, unlike the five new arrivals, smelled familiar. Whatever it was that lived in the cabin, it was not precisely human, but nor was it Hindra, for she knew the scent of her own kind better than anything.

She felt a tiny tingle of fear in the base of her spine—a cold sensation creeping up on one who did not and could not experience cold. What was happening in that tiny stone home?

The others had to be told—but so often, they did not listen. Perhaps there was a way to convince them of the danger of the strangers, and of this abnormality that lurked in the cabin.

Night fell.

¤~¤~¤

"It would be better if you saw for yourself," Marriq explained patiently. While the feisty old woman had been full of spunk when they had arrived, now that she was answering their questions JC found the best word to describe her was 'instructional.'

"But we cannot leave until morning, so I might as well paint you a picture of how things stand." Marriq stood, leaning heavily on her walking stick, and began to pace around them. They were arranged on low stools surrounding what looked to him like a wood-burning stove, although it produced no smoke and he had not yet seen Marriq feed any logs into the small, squat metal device.

The rest of the cabin was bare. There was a large cupboard on one wall and a pile of thick blankets in one corner, otherwise there was nothing here to mark the place as a home and certainly not as the home of a scholar. There were no books, no scrolls—none of the things that had cluttered up the nooks and crannies of Moultus' home in Igar Holc.

Marriq spoke in a steady, practiced cadence, and JC found it easy to get swept along in her words.

"For as long as there has been life on Arctos, there has been the Archive. A building of glass and stone built to house every word ever written on first this world then the others, when the Gars began to move us between worlds, it was a place of wisdom and knowledge the likes of which cannot be equaled. Those who maintained the Archive were the Archivists, and for a time I was among them. We accepted all who came, regardless of intent, for it was the belief of the Archive that information was free. We even recruited Archivists from other worlds, hoping to add their own knowledge to our great catalog of truths and secrets. But the placement of the Archive here, on Arctos, was not the wisest decision ever made by the scholars." Marriq stopped her pacing and closed her eyes.

"Are you alright?" Becky asked.

"Remembering is a heavy burden," Marriq said sullenly. "But it seems as though I may be the last who can."

"What happened to the Archive?" Todd asked. "Why is it lost to you now?"

"History is as much the study of antecedents as it is events," Marriq resumed, "and to know what befell the Archive you must know that Arctos is not a good place to live. There are places that are habitable, after a fashion, but no place in this land is truly welcoming to man or beast, and this makes for a hard life from birth until death. Most people work their entire lives just to scrounge food and shelter, or to mine enough minerals and metals to trade for food and shelter. The Archive was in many ways an affront to the work ethic of the lands of Arctos—a place of decadence and idleness, they claimed. Why should the farmers work themselves to death to feed the scholars? Why should the miners slave their lives away in the mines to provide the mineral that brings light to libraries? These were not bad questions to ask—I asked them myself, from time to time—but they were a symptom of a greater disease. There were three factions within our people, three ideologies that took root in ancient times and refused to be stamped out by reason or discourse."

"Politics," Steven grumbled. "It's always politics."

"Indeed," Marriq said. "Indeed. In our case, the three voices of the people demanded such different things that there was never a shortage of conflict. The traditionalists were content with how things were. For scores of years, theirs was the most dominant ideology, and it was to that belief system that most of the Archivists subscribed. In the times of traditionalist ascendance, the Archive was well-provided for. But the others grew slowly and steadily, until there came a time, perhaps fifteen years ago, that they each accounted for a third of the population. A stalemate of ideology brought our economy and our very way of life crashing to a halt. The traditionalists were unwilling to raise arms against the others—there are so few of us on Arctos, we are not as populous as the other worlds—and so things grew more and more tense."

"What were the other two ideologies?" Becky asked. JC could tell she was genuinely intrigued. He was doing his best to follow along, but even the best orator could only command his attention for so long.

"The fatalists were the slowest group to gain momentum. They were an accident, truly—a movement born of those who heard of the books of the Wyr that were housed in the Archive. They became obsessed with the idea that fate was already written, that human decision was meaningless. In many ways, their belief sapped them of their free will, but more importantly it sapped them of their desire to help others. They became selfish and introverted, and a particularly popular movement among the outer villages on the Bound, where life was hardest."

"It's an understandable dilemma," Becky said quietly. "I've struggled with it a bit myself, having spent time with a Wyr."

Marriq shook her head. "I'll not debate it with you today, child. There is much to be said of the Wyr, but most of it is false and little of it kind." Marriq looked up at the door and squinted for a moment, then shook her head and resumed her story. "The last faction were the hedonists. When life is hard and often short, there are always those who believe that their best interest is to enjoy it. The hedonists went too far, of course—they believed that their sole purpose was to experience joy. What seemed harmless at first, and often an affectation of the young, slowly grew into a cancer within our society. The traditionalists persevered for a long while, but, as I said, slowly the balance tipped and conflict arose."

"Twelve years ago, after three bloody years of strife, a truce was called. It was truce born out of desperation, and it was the death knell of our society. The fatalists and the hedonists allied, finding a measure of common ground in their selfish ideologies and a common foe in the traditionalists. They rose up as one and drove the traditionalists out of the furnace cities and into the outer regions, what we call the Bounds—permanent exile. Then they marched on the Archive and drove the Archivists into the Bounds as well. Most of them joined with traditionalist forces in the outer villages and took to farming or mining, providing the necessities for the others in the furnace cities, but some, like myself, strove to retake the Archive. We feared what would come of it. The hedonists had no use for its lore, and the fatalists would soon discover that the words of the Wyr were written in a code decipherable only to their own kind."

"So there's the very real chance they burned the library to the ground," Todd said solemnly.

"Hardly," Marriq said, her mouth curling into a thin smile. "You are not aware of the nature of Arctos, are you?"

Todd shook his head.

"Nothing burns here. Nothing. There is no fire—not anymore. That was taken from us even before the truce. And it is, I think, a tale for another time." Marriq had reached her stool once more in her pacing lap around the room and settled herself down upon it. "Those of us who tried to reach the Archive were thwarted not by its destruction, but by its construction."

Yors grunted. "Yors like that. Yors keep those words for later."

Marriq continued, "Someone had taken residence in the Archive in the two years we were away. Whoever, whatever, lives there now, they built a mighty dome of ice over the whole of the Archive. It is smooth and thick and impenetrable. No axe or pick will dent it, and, as I have already told you, there is no fire to melt it."

"But ice is translucent," Becky said. She looked at Steven, and JC saw something strange in her eyes—something hungry. It made him nervous, and he made a special effort to take Becky's hand in his own as she spoke. "Maybe Steven can move through it, emerge from a shadow on the inside of the dome."

Steven nodded. "It's certainly worth a try," he conceded.

"The five of you bring Onus magic with you, and that might be the key to it all," Marriq admitted. "That is the only reason I'm willing to take you there. I have to make sure the Archive is unharmed."

JC stood up and stretched. "Awesome. So we head out first thing tomorrow, Steven sneaks in and raids the place, and we'll be back to the Spiralgate in time to make the first rendezvous with Adam. Cake walk."

Becky sighed. "Has it ever been that easy for us to do anything?"

"Maybe this time will be different." JC smiled.

"Not likely," Becky muttered.

"You speak like a fatalist," Marriq chided.

"You would too if you spent as much time with this guy as I have," Becky said, rolling her eyes.

¤~¤~¤

Venot was an ugly city. While all five of the furnace cities were ugly in their own way, none of them quite lived down to the hideousness of Venot. Hunna walked carefully down a narrow alley between two large taverns, trying his best to not run afoul of the drunken revelers that were even now spilling out of the doors and windows of the place. It was past midnight, and the establishments were closing up as best they could, but the party would go on in the streets and alleys, as it did every night.

Hunna passed a grate in the flagstone street and stopped to bask in the hiss of steam that emerged from the metal grate. Far below the surface of the city, the great furnace belched steam and heat into the maze of pipes that wound like serpents throughout the substructure of Venot, and this was but one of the places where the cracks in the decades-old pipes were showing themselves.

The sky was overcast, as always, but Hunna looked up at the sky anyway. He hoped to see the stars again, one day, but that wasn't likely unless he left Venot, and that wasn't going to happen. Nobody left Venot, or any of the cities. Why would they? Everything one needed to live, to love, to laugh, was here.

But Hunna didn't care all that much for laughing or loving. Not in the sense that the couple he passed, groping and grunting as they worked furiously to remove one another's clothes, did. He had a purpose and he had, he supposed, best be getting to it.

He emerged from the alley and passed the fountainworks, where fresh water, both cold and hot, was collected by those who took the time to carry it in buckets back to their homes. The fountainworks was quiet this time of night, since most folks were drunk or sleeping, and he found the burbling of the fountains soothing.

When the morning sun rose, it would be his distinct honor, as it was every day, to read the roll of births. In a place caught in the perpetual throes of celebration, new life was the one thing that everyone took time out of their celebrating to, well, celebrate. Hunna enjoyed the roar of the appreciative crowd as he read the names of all that had been born since the last sunrise, even though all too often his list was horribly short.

It was what it was, he reminded himself. All things that happened were meant to happen, and there was nothing to be done about it.

He paused for a moment as he stood next to one of the hot water fountains. Something was amiss. He squinted through the gentle cloud of steam that clung to the air around the hot water jets and saw someone emerging from one of the steel grates in the pavement.

Access to the pipe tunnels was forbidden and dangerous, and he shouted at the shadowy figure. The man—it certainly looked like a man—bolted the moment he heard Hunna's voice. Hunna would have tried to catch up to him, but he was a fat man with little patience for the rigors of running.

He scratched at the mop of thick, damp curls atop his head. Who would be down in the pipes? Why? There was nothing to be done for them. They were old and breaking, one by one. One day, the furnace would go out altogether. The heat that protected the city from the cold would fail, the night would creep upon them and freeze each and every one of them to death.

It was what it was, and it would be what it would be.

He looked down at the roll of fabric in his hand, upon which the list of births was written. There were as many names written on this roll as there had been the past week combined, and this was a good omen.

He was suddenly struck by a heavy sense of weariness. He should sleep, he told himself, and he picked his way once more through the streets of the city. He stepped over slumbering men and women as often as he skirted around them, and the general stink had grown quite foul. He carried a single bottle of hot water from the fountainworks with him, and resolved to use some of it to wash up when he got home. These people who had eschewed homes in favor of just sleeping wherever they fell after their day-long festivities made little sense to him.

He passed a blood-letter on the street that was, apparently, still open for business. He considered a small tithe, but thought better of it when he saw the filthy quality of the man's needles. Glass globes filled with blood lined shelves on the man's handcart, and Hunna smiled politely as he declined the man's attempts to land him as a customer. Hunna had given blood yesterday, or perhaps it was the day before—and didn't feel quite up to it just now.

He imagined that once he was out of sight, the blood-letter would get back to his real work anyway at this time of night—stealing blood from the assorted inebriates littering the street. They all had their part to play, after all—the fatalists kept their wits about them and kept the city running with their metaphorical sweat and blood, and the hedonists made their contributions more literally.

It was a night like every other, save for the strange incident at the fountainworks, and Hunna had already mostly forgotten about that by the time he waddled into his ground-level home and splashed a bit of warm water on his grimy neck.

The morning would be here soon, and they would celebrate the first three-name day of the past year.

¤~¤~¤

As the first rays of the sun crept over the distant white horizon, Marriq woke. She had never been much of a sleeper, even in her younger days, but the excitement of her guests had stirred feelings in her, and memories, she had not dealt with in many years.

She worked her way silently around the cabin, pulling on her traveling clothes while the others slept scattered around the hearth. She opened the grate and peered at the hearthstone inside the metal stove, and she could feel that it still burned strong. The day it began to falter would be the beginning of the end for her, she knew, but today was not that day.

Once she was sufficiently bundled up, she started to prod the sleepers with her walking stick, starting first with the large one, Yors, that had so rudely snored throughout the night. Marriq hadn't spent the night in the company of others for well over ten years, and even then she had most certainly not kept company with snoring men. Yors roused quickly, and as he began to silently ready himself, she tasked him to wake the others and produced some trail rations from her pantry cupboard.

The food here was bland, nothing like the sumptuous meats and cheeses of Onus that she recalled from her time there teaching recruits, but it was food, and it was something Marriq had in abundance. She didn't eat much herself, so sharing her stores was no great loss.

Her guests ate groggily and silently, save for the one called JC who insisted on making off-colored jokes, and it was nearly thirty minutes after sunrise by the time they were ready to travel.

"Can you spring one before we go?" JC asked Yors.

Yors shook his great bearded head. "Need strength for travel. Soon, Yors promise."

JC sighed and said no more about the subject, and Marriq simply took it all in. There was something about these travelers that did not ring quite true to her, but she would wait to voice her suspicions when they were better rooted in fact.

"Any advice before we head out?" Todd asked Marriq. "Because if you don't think we have a chance at getting in, this would be a good time to go ahead and break that to us."

Marriq smiled slyly. "I believe that a determined person can do most anything, child. And you do all look quite determined."

She turned away from Todd and put one hand on the latch of the door. She was struck once more by the strange feeling she had experienced last night, during her recounting of history, and she felt the flesh on the back of her neck prickle.

She sighed. Her days of daring adventure were long over—ended by choice and by sacrifice in a mountain cave at the outer edge of the White Bound some forty years ago. The old instincts were dulled by age and disuse, and these days they more often led her astray than aright.

She pulled the door open, and as she did so a gleaming blade of ice, eight inches long and razor sharp all along its length, plunged into her chest and drove her down to the ground, gasping and crying out in pain as blood soaked through her traveling cloak.

Five feet beyond her door was a tall, thin humanoid figure, garbed in white robes with long, flowing white hair. The female figure's skin was the color of fresh frost, and in the hand that had not just hurled the dagger she held a spear of fire.

"It cannot be..." Marriq said.

# 14
# ARCTOS

*The wind roared all around them, shaking even the sturdy stone walls of the cabin.* JC darted out of the cabin door at nearly the same instant that Yors hauled Marriq's stunned and bleeding form back inside. JC's hands had already gone for the energy rifles slung over his shoulders, but as he cleared the doorway he was driven back into the wall of the cabin, hard, by a gust of wind.

Todd and Steven dashed out, but the mysterious woman in white batted both of them about as she had JC, the cold wind answering to her gestures like a trained dog. Every time he tried to regain his feet she blasted him again, and the icy bursts were starting to get to him. His eyes watered and stung, and his face was quickly going numb.

"What do you want?" Steven shouted over the howling wind that kept him pinned down in an awkward pile with Todd.

The woman did not respond though, and the great flickering spear of fire she held seemed to flare. The wind died a bit as it did so, and JC leapt at the opportunity. He hurled himself forward, more concerned with closing the snowy distance between the woman and himself than actually getting to his feet, and he felt the metal links of chain grow hot against his chilled flesh. Courage boiled in his veins as he scrambled across the snow. The woman retreated a half-step, perplexed.

She whirled the spear around, bringing its tip—or at least what appeared to be its tip, given that it was simply a length of animated flame—around to point at JC. She hissed something in words that JC didn't understand, but that didn't stop him from colliding with her.

On four different worlds over the past two years, JC had solved the vast majority of his problems by knocking them over. This was not that kind of problem.

He collided with her thin figure only to find that it was not frail, and it would not topple. She was rigid and unmoving; it was more like smashing into a mountain than a person. He cracked his head against that stony countenance and saw stars in his peripheral vision as she plunged the spear of flame down into his back, pinning him to the frozen ground as white-hot agony lanced through his entire body.

He was dimly aware of what happened next.

While he had nobly distracted the woman, Yors emerged from the cabin, crossbow aimed and drawn. With the resonant twang of tension released, the crossbow fired a simple steel bolt towards the woman. She was fast though—far faster than she ought to have been—and she dropped low to the ground, her head down near JC's, as the bolt sailed over her.

"What are you doing?" JC managed to grunt through the pain of the spear, his teeth gritted.

"Vigilance," the woman replied simply. Then she was on her feet again, the wind rising up around her as she ran towards Yors. She closed the distance rapidly, leaving the Metalbreaker no time to reload his crossbow. As she fell upon him, he swung the great device like a bludgeon, and as it smashed into her frost-white jaw, JC heard the crossbeam of the weapon crack. She remained unfazed.

Steven joined in the melee, and as both he and Yors exchanged blows in hand to hand combat with the woman, JC felt himself beginning to black out. The pain was too much. He wasn't sure if he was bleeding, but either way—it hurt so badly. So bad that he couldn't move, no matter how hard he tried. He caught a glimpse of Todd, trying to crawl towards him unseen by their foe, and JC realized that he must surely be making his way to the rifles. Groaning with the horrible effort of it, he tried to lift one shoulder from the ground. If he could just pick himself up a bit, Todd would be able to slip one of the rifles free. As it was now, the straps crisscrossing his chest would keep them pinned, useless. Or maybe Todd could pull out the damn spear...

"Joe," Becky's voice materialized in his mind. "I'm trying to get into her head, but I can't. I don't know what else to do."

In his mind, in the tiny corner of himself that didn't writhe in agony, he smiled. Becky was asking *him* what to do. There really was a first time for everything. "Can you make this not hurt?" JC asked.

"Pain is with us for a reason, Joe." Becky responded almost automatically.

"Noted. Can you?" JC grunted as he finally stopped trying to lift his shoulder and arm. It wasn't happening. And Todd wasn't going to make it anyway.

The woman knocked Steven back, in spite of the fact that he was mostly transitioned to his shadowform. She had formed a new spear of fire, and with it she had cut a burning gash across both Steven and Yors' chests. Yors was down on a knee panting, Steven was sliding backwards slowly, looking for an opening... and while that was going on, she turned to find Todd trying to escape towards JC. With a fierce downward slashing gesture of her free hand, she brought a blast of wind and fist-sized hailstones raining down on Todd. He instinctively curled into a tight ball, but the hailstones bounced off his body with sickly thudding sounds.

Then, in a rush of relief and exhilaration, JC's pain was gone. Becky had done it—she had channeled away his pain just as the collar channeled away his fear. He forced himself to his feet, and then, his gloved hands scorching, he plucked the length of flame from his back, awkwardly and cast it to the ground where it sizzled and spat in the snow.

"You wanted to start a fight?" JC asked, his eyes narrow. "Let me show how to finish one."

He drew one rifle in a smooth motion, bringing it up before his eye and sighting calmly, steadily. Without hesitation, he aimed for the woman's head and pulled the trigger.

"Joe! No!" Becky roared in his mind, but it was too late.

The energy rifle discharged, and a blazing bolt of energy blasted into the woman, sending her crashing back into the cabin.

JC stomped past the others and into the cabin, where Becky looked at him, horrified, from where she was tending to Marriq. His enemy was lying on the floor of the cabin, knocked all the way into the ring of stools and up against the hearth in the center of the building. She was unmoving and unconscious, but not dead. She drew breath. Her flesh was unmarred by the bolt.

"I don't get it. This thing can blow up buildings." JC looked down at the rifle. "Why isn't she ash?"

"Marriq said nothing burns here," Todd said, appearing in the doorway, rubbing tenderly at one shoulder. "That must apply to whatever kind of energy the rifle fires too."

"Well I know one thing that burns," JC said, pointing to the attacker's second spear that still flickered in the snow outside the door where it had fallen.

"She is a Hindra," Marriq said weakly, sitting up with Becky's help. "They are all dead. They have been dead for ages. This cannot be."

"Are you OK?" Becky asked, examining Marriq's chest.

The old woman coughed and pushed Becky's hands away. "I am fine." She produced, from within her coat, a many-pointed oval of metal. Several of the points were slick with blood. "The dagger struck my Archive key. It bit me deeply, but far less deeply than her blade would have."

Steven helped Yors inside finally, and Marriq hobbled over to her cupboard to draw forth fabric for binding their wounds.

"So what do we do about her?" JC asked, pointing at their comatose assailant.

"Well we don't kill her!" Becky shouted, charging up to him and grabbing his head with both her hands. "You aimed for her head, Joseph! You expected that shot to kill her!"

"And?" JC asked. "She would have killed us."

Becky said nothing else. She looked at JC in a way she hadn't looked at him in a very long time... with disappointment. Then, without saying another word, she let go of his head with her hands and with her mind. As she closed their connection, her working upon his pain failed, and all of the agony of the spear wound returned in blinding, momentous detail.

Screaming, he blacked out.

¤~¤~¤

Something woke Hunna. His globe lamp was faintly glowing from its stand in the corner of the room, and he sat up slowly, rubbing at bleary eyes. The simple window shade was drawn, but he could see from the light trickling in its periphery that day was already upon them.

A sick feeling gripped his broad stomach. The sun was up. He had failed to read the roll of births at sunrise! How was this possible? He hadn't even taken any desix last night!

"Don't worry yourself too much," a soft voice whispered from the far corner of the large, cluttered room. "I had one of my boys read them this morning. You looked so peaceful laying there, I couldn't bring myself to wake you."

Hunna stood, fumbling as he cast his sleeping blanket aside to make sure that he was, in fact, wearing clothes. The voice was female, and he had his modesty to protect. Thankfully, he had never undressed before collapsing into bed last night. He looked to the small table next to his sleeping pallet, and sure enough, the scroll of names was absent.

"It is my responsibility though," he muttered.

"But you overslept. What is it your people say? What will be, will be? Well, you be'd asleep. Is that how it works? Is that how you absolve yourself of guilt?" The voice grew sharper, and its owner emerged into the feeble light of the lamp. She was quite plain looking, with dark skin and short-cropped black hair, but she was a woman, and there had not been a woman in Hunna's home ever. Ever.

"Who are you? You... you look a bit familiar," he said cautiously. He resigned himself to the inevitability of what was about to happen. Even after years of truce, there were always stories of random hedonists who broke into fatalist homes and had their way with them. The urge to satisfy one's desires was all that mattered to those people.

She laughed, but it was a sound without joy. "You don't recognize me? I'm wounded. After all the trouble I took to take care of your indiscretion."

Hunna arched an eyebrow. "What is your meaning?"

"You have one job in this city, Hunna, and you slept through it. If I didn't know any better, I'd think that you indulged in a few drinks last night. Maybe something else more unsavory. What would the others think if they knew you'd resorted to such base habits?" She smiled and he was struck by the brilliant whiteness of her teeth. That was an uncommon thing in Venot.

"I did no such thing! I would never!" Hunna sputtered with mustered conviction. It wasn't entirely true though, was it?

The woman walked up to him and placed one soft, dexterous hand upon his shoulder. She said quietly, "I know. You aren't any fun. Everyone knows that. So tell me then why you went to bed instead of waiting at the Fountainworks to do your duty?"

"I..." Hunna stumbled over the answer. "I'm not quite sure. I went there to wait, and then I... I don't know why I left."

"As I suspected," she whispered, almost purring. "You're not the first man to speak of such things. Tell me something else, Hunna. Did you see anything unusual last night?"

"No, not at all," he replied quickly. But then he caught himself. "Well, actually, I think perhaps I did. I can't quite put my finger on it though. It's just on the tip of my tongue. Does that ever happen to you?"

She shook her head. "No. But I'm not some weak-willed fatalist either. You were drugged, or duped, or something. It's been happening all over town for weeks. And like all of the others, you aren't going to be any use in helping me track the problem down." She turned away from Hunna and moved towards the door.

"Wait! Who are you? Where do I know you from?" Hunna followed her, tripping over the tangle of blankets at his feet and catching himself, just barely, on the side table.

"Karrin. We met last year, but I'll let you figure out the rest." She winked at him—an act which made Hunna severely uncomfortable.

"Why are you investigating this strangeness? Who tasked you with such duty?" Hunna managed to stammer out the words, but they lacked the authority he had been attempting to muster in his tone.

She laughed a true laugh, and the sound was almost musical. "There was a time not so long ago when people did what was right because it was right. Even a hedonist like me can still see that there are things beyond ourselves that sometimes require doing. We have very little time and very few parties interested in helping solve the crisis."

"What crisis?" Hunna asked, his eyes wide.

"Oh, you haven't noticed it yet. Most people haven't. But I can feel it in the air—the chill. The furnace nearly went down last night. Venot is doomed." She smiled again and added, "Which, I suppose, gives all of you fatalists a kind of grim satisfaction." She stepped out of the bedroom and a moment later Hunna heard the front door of his home close behind her.

He felt it, then. The chill in the air. The end of them all was at hand—but what was happening? What could he not remember?

¤~¤~¤

Becky looked around the cabin and felt her insides twisting into knots. They hadn't even been here a full day yet, and already everything had gone horribly wrong. They had found Marriq, but beyond that, every move had been a misstep. Yors and JC were too injured to travel, at least for a few days. And time was, as always, against them.

For the past two hours, Becky, Steven, Todd, and Marriq had tended to JC's wound, which left him delirious with pain, and Yors', which he bore much more stoically. Becky left small workings in both of their minds to ease the discomfort, but only barely—anymore that that she feared would leave them dangerously vulnerable to overexertion or worse.

"We leave them," Steven said solemnly. "I don't like it any more than you do, but we don't have a choice. And from what Marriq was saying, I'm the only one of us with a chance of getting in anyway. So Todd, you come with Marriq and me. Becky, you can stay here and watch over these two. We can be in touch by mindshaping if anything happens on either end."

Yors nodded glumly, and JC was too out of it to voice his opinion, but Becky was not at all OK with this plan. "Every time we split up, something bad happens. Now you want to split us up even further? And what do we do about her?" Becky pointed at the still comatose form of the woman in white.

"She comes with us," Marriq said stiffly. "That creature cannot stay in my home."

"So you're going to drag her dead weight along with you, leave now, and still make it to the Archive and back here before sunset? That won't work!" Becky's voice rose to an almost shrieking pitch. She could feel desperation bubbling up inside her, but she didn't know from where. She suspected though... and that was certainly contributing to that feeling of her guts twisting up.

"There are ways," Marriq said simply.

Becky glowered at the old woman, but the withering glare she received in return caused her to take a step back.

"Do not think for a moment you can intimidate me, child." Marriq turned her back to Becky. "Men, we leave now or we do not leave at all. Which of you is carrying the Hindra?"

Todd sighed and hoisted the white-clad woman unceremoniously over his shoulder. He had stripped the bandages from his hands, and Becky could see that while they still looked like they had been through a great deal of trauma, he seemed to have regained much of their function. Steven pushed open the door, and Marriq, walking stick in hand, marched outside. Todd followed, and Steven turned back to look at Becky. He said, "I'll be back. We'll all be back. Soon."

Becky said nothing. She wasn't sure what she could say.

The door closed behind him, and Becky felt tears spring, unbidden and unwanted, to her eyes. She blinked them back and instead busied herself with making sure JC was comfortable. While he was sleeping he looked so peaceful—innocent. While he slept, he made her think of the times he made her laugh and of how much he loved her, instead of the times he scared her. Like this morning. He'd almost killed that woman. Or creature. Whatever she was, to kill her in cold blood, that wasn't who they were. That wasn't what they stood for—every death they had been responsible for over the last year and a half weighed upon her. But to him, it was nothing.

She touched the metal links around his neck, and they were cool to the touch.

"Yors help," Yors said quietly. The smith had wobbled over to the blanket on which Becky had laid Joe out, and he gingerly lowered himself to one knee. He reached down to wrap his thick fingers around the chain at Joe's throat and began to hum.

The song was unfamiliar to Becky, but its rhythm was infectious, and soon she found herself humming along. This made Yors smile, just a bit, and they hummed together for almost ten minutes. As the song drew to a close there was a soft but audible popping sound and a tiny puff of blue-green smoke burst from between Yors' fingers.

Another of the red links in Joe's chain was now a darker, duller color.

"Thirty-five." Yors said reassuringly.

Becky touched him on the arm and whispered, "Thank you."

¤~¤~¤

Marriq was not a young woman and had not been for some time. But she kept pace with the two young men at her side as they pressed steadily westward. The day was fading fast, and she could tell from the men that they were growing nervous about that fact. She knew that what she was about to do was risky, but there was little she would not dare to retake the Archive. They pressed on until the last possible moment, when the final edges of sunlight were but a rosy glow on the cloudy horizon.

"We stop here," she said, planting her walking stick firmly in the snow.

Without hesitation, Todd dropped the Hindra in a thick drift. Steven, on the other hand, wore his hesitation plainly upon his handsome face.

"There's no shelter here," Steven said.

"Obviously," Marriq replied. She pulled a small, sharp knife from her belt. "What I am about to do will either work, or it will not. If it does not, then... then I imagine you will say unkind things about me when you reach the far halls."

She knelt down in the snow next to the Hindra and carefully drew her blade across the creature's flesh at the upper arm. Todd made a weak effort to stop her, but he was exhausted, and the cold was wearing upon him. Once the creature's blood made contact with the air, the point was moot anyway.

A wave of vibrant heat and a flash of flame burst from the Hindra's body, causing snow near her to melt almost instantly to tiny rushing rivulets of water. Carefully and with skill she had imagined long gone from disuse, Marriq coated the blade of her knife in the slowly trickling blood and then paced a small circle around the walking stick, scattering droplets of blood in a ring of protective warmth.

"What the hell?" Steven asked.

"Hindra blood burns. It will burn for many hours, and it will keep the worst of the night's cold at bay." Marriq finished her circle, once more standing next to the Hindra. Still the Hindra did not move, and for this she was grateful. There was no telling how long it would be until the creature awoke—and from the first signs of its stirring, they would abandon it and flee as fast as they could. It was not a good plan, but it was all she had.

Satisfied that the small wound had not brought the creature any closer to consciousness, Marriq propped herself upright once more with her walking stick and waited for the heat to melt and dry a place sufficient for her to sleep.

"What exactly is she? You called her a Hindra, but that means nothing to us," Steven asked as they made the barest semblance of a camp.

"They are mysteries, even to the Archivists. It is said that they ruled Arctos long before our time, but it was also said that they all perished in the dark ages of our world. I know that many of them did—I have seen their spirits with my own eyes. But apparently, not all of them are gone." She let out a long sigh. Old memories and the barest spark of regret flickered about her mind. She was not accustomed to regret.

"So if nothing burns on your world, except their blood, where does that fireplace thing in your cabin come from?" Todd asked.

"That is a good question. A smart question. Moultus did well choosing this group to seek the Archive." Marriq smiled faintly. "The device that brings heat to my home is a precious, rare thing—a hearthstone. It is magic of the oldest and most important kind, and to have one for a single home, such as mine, is rare and, some would say, wasteful. Usually hearthstones are bigger and they protect and heat whole villages or, in some cases, cities. But the art of making them is lost to us now, and they are not forever. Nothing is."

"But is there a connection?" Steven asked, looking pointedly at the Hindra's still shape.

"Once there was an order among our people, the Circle of Stone. Some called them Hearth Keepers. Their blood had the same power as the Hindras—some say because their blood was mingled with Hindra blood, long ago. Whatever the reason, the Hearth Keepers made and maintained the hearthstones and all was well. But the uprising of the fatalists and the hedonists did not end well for the Hearth Keepers, even as it did not end well for the traditionalists and the Archivists. Always distrusted, they were killed one by one until none remained. And now, our world creeps step by step towards the end of all heat and all life."

Todd shook his head almost angrily. "So these Hearth Keepers were the only ones with the power to save everyone, and they were hunted down for what? Being different?"

Marriq sighed. "Exactly that."

"It makes no sense. Didn't the fatalists and whatever know that they needed them in order to survive?" Steven asked.

Marriq said nothing.

"They don't care though." Todd scowled. "That's their whole thing—why do anything, why get involved in anything, if the outcome is preordained anyway? I've seen people like that before. People who put *everything* in the hands of the Purpose, or God, or whatever. People who use those higher powers to avoid taking responsibility for their own actions. It's the worst kind of stupid."

"It isn't stupidity, child," Marriq interjected. "It is fear."

Todd seemed to have no rejoinder for that remark, and there was no other conversation for the remainder of the night. One by one they drifted off to sleep, with Marriq holding out the longest, always watching the Hindra. They would need her blood once more, on the return journey, and they could not afford for her to wake just yet. Once the boys were both deeply asleep, Marriq stood slowly, old bones creaking, and hobbled over to the body of this creature born of myth.

She placed her hand upon the arm, where the wound she had inflicted had long-since scabbed over, and she felt it—she felt the blood. She whispered to it in quiet words, words she had memorized so laboriously at the Lodge, a lifetime ago. She stilled it and quieted it, singing the blood to sleep and hoping that, in so doing, she was buying them time.

Regret gnawed at her soul once more. The blood that had once burned in her veins was gone—sacrificed for reasons both noble and selfish—but still she had an affinity for it.

Her life had taken such a twisted path to come to this place. It was not the physical fire this creature had brought into her life today that would save them all—it was the fire of hope. If these creatures still lived, there might yet be a way to save the people of Arctos. All she had to do was reason with them, if such a thing were even possible.

¤~¤~¤

In spite of the circle of protective heat that Marriq had fashioned of the Hindra's blood, the sleep that Steven experienced was not restful. When they woke with the rising sun, he was nearly as tired as he had been when he fell asleep, and his back was a mess of pain and knots from sleeping on the uneven, soggy ground. Neither Todd nor the old woman were complaining though, so he bit back his own protestations. Todd had once more slung the Hindra over his shoulder, and they started out for what Marriq assured them was the last leg of their journey to the Archive.

They spent most of the day trudging through snow. Still the Hindra slept, but now Marriq joined her in silence. Steven took the lead, and the walking helped work the kinks out of his back. For a time, Todd kept pace with him, but after the first three hours even his prodigious strength started to wane and he started to fall behind.

"Press on. We grow near!" Marriq said as a form of encouragement. Todd didn't seem to enjoy her encouragement, but he did push harder and was at least able to keep up with the old Archivist.

The wind howled all around them, high in the cloudy sky, but it did not carry snow or ice with it, so Steven took that as a good omen. He had been listening to the sounds of the wind for so long on this journey—it never stopped—that he had not at first noticed all the sounds that could not be heard. The plains and hills of Arctos were barren of all life, not just plants. No birds sang, no predators howled in the distance. If there were creatures out here, they moved soundlessly and he had spotted no trail of them. The rations that Marriq had shared with them in her cabin had included no meat. Perhaps there were no animals on this world?

Now that he had noticed the silence behind the wind, it was all he could think about. Absently, seeking escape from his churning mind and his sore body, he cast a thought at Becky. The connection between their minds sprang to life almost instantly, pulled taught with tension and energy.

"Steven? Is everything alright?" Becky asked, her mind radiating worry.

"Yeah, nothing to report. I was just—my mind was wandering, that's all. We should be there in the next hour or so. How are Yors and JC?" Steven tried to sound professional, but he could not help the warmth that slipped into his tone. This method of communication brought back feelings—strong feelings—of Tatyana, and as much as those feelings haunted him, they also comforted him.

"Yors is an even worse patient than Joe, believe it or not. Just when I think he's truly resting and I take my eyes off him, he gets up, hobbles over to Joe, and strips one of the links on his collar. He's taken out three while you've been gone." Becky sounded both frustrated and relieved.

"That's a lot faster than he was when we were on Onus," Steven mused. "Did he say why he's pushing so hard?"

"I think... I think it's because he saw how scared I was. During the fight," Becky ventured.

"Was that what you look like scared? It looked more like what you look like pissed off to me," Steven said.

"You'd be surprised how similar those two things are for me," Becky snickered. "You should focus on what you're doing. I'm going to knock that big jerk unconscious in a second and then maybe I'll get some sleep too, finally. Be careful, Steven. I love you."

Awkward silence stretched between them—far vaster than the actual distance that separated their bodies.

"I mean, I... you know, I..." Becky stammered.

"I know," Steven answered carefully. "It's not you. Just... keep it together. We'll be back as soon as we can." Steven turned his attention back to his march, deliberately tuning out the connection with Becky. He lacked the power to close it himself, but he knew she felt the change in his mental posture.

Once he was confident she was no longer lingering in his mind, Steven let out a deep, frustrated sigh. "Dammit," he muttered.

"What's that?" Todd called from the rear of their small procession.

"Nothing," Steven said, shooting an angry glance back over his shoulder. The last thing he needed was this. There had been hints throughout the past year, but never anything this overt. The legacy of Tatyana was not solely his burden to bear, and now he and Becky were going to have to have a very real, very serious conversation about it. He had absolutely no idea what that conversation would entail.

"It looks like something to me," Todd said, pointing ahead of them.

Steven squinted his eyes and made out, in the distance, a structure. It was bluish in color, tall and smooth, and the best word he could use to describe it was a dome.

"There it is," Marriq said cautiously. "The Archive lies at the top of the next hill. Now we shall see how mighty the arts of Onus truly are."

They pressed hard, nearly running the last hundred yards. After a few minutes, they were standing up against the dome of ice that had, somehow, been erected to protect and seal off the Archive. It was easily eighty feet tall and hundreds of yards across. The surface was perfectly smooth and incredibly cold to the touch. Light passed through it, but only barely, and it was virtually impossible to make out anything inside.

"Now what?" Todd asked, depositing the Hindra at the base of the dome with a bit more ceremony than yesterday.

"We wait a bit longer," Marriq said. "The sun will draw down behind the dome soon, and that is when its light will be most fully within it and the shadows of the Archive most pronounced."

Steven nodded. "You know a thing or two about shadowbending?"

"I know a thing or two about everything," Marriq said matter-of-factly. "Now help me set up a circle. We'll spend the night here."

"Can't we just," Todd pointed towards the dome, "use her blood to melt a hole in the ice?"

Marriq shook her head. "This is not natural ice. There was no such dome here before the revolution. However the fatalists and hedonists did this, it was a work of magic. I worry that material disruption of the dome will summon its maker." Marriq looked carefully at their Hindra captive. "And I grow more and more fearful that one such as this one is the maker in question."

They made their tiny camp once more, with Marriq setting the circle of burning blood and Todd and Steven scooping out the snow to speed the process of drying and firming the cracked earth that existed below the eternal snow.

As the sun crept lower and lower in the sky, Steven watched. When it was at last completely obscured by the dome, Marriq nodded sharply and Steven stepped into action. He closed his eyes and felt outward, into his own shadow and through it, looking for an opening, an aperture through which he could travel. Of all the things the Rak were known to do, direct transportation like this was the weakest of his arts—he had rarely needed to travel far enough that such a thing was more appropriate than simply transitioning to shadowform and skimming across the distance. But now, this was the only choice. He felt it, slowly, as his powers touched the threads that bound one shadow to another, and then it was a matter of feeling through those threads, pulling and tugging at the right one to guide him out into the real world once more.

With a sickening, disorienting swirl of shadow and motion that twisted at all of his senses, he found himself tumbling out of the shadow. He fell out, then up, then down, landing painfully on the frozen ground outside the Archive.

He could make little out in the shadow, and blood ran freely from his nose. He sopped at it with the cuff of his jacket sleeve, but this new exertion had demanded a heavy toll of him, and he took a moment, leaning back against the shining glass wall of the Archive as he gathered his strength and his bearings. No act of shadowbending had exhausted him so since the defeat of the Obliviates and the retaking of his full measure of power.

The building itself was as Marriq had described it—many stories of glass and stone. There were a few lights within, and there were signs of motion as lights traveled from one room to another. Someone was inside the Archive.

As he felt his strength return, Steven stuck to the shadows as best he could, relying upon natural stealth rather than his arts for fear of squandering the energy they would require to carry him back to the other side of the dome wall.

He reached the doors of the Archive after a few minutes of careful movement through the sculpture-littered grounds. Abstract ice sculptures provided ample cover, but he saw no one moving about the grounds. The light of the sun was fading quickly, and he could feel the cold rising. He would have to flee back to the safety of Marriq's circle soon.

Steven pushed slowly through the double glass doors of the Archive—the only entrance—and they opened without sound or resistance to his touch. He was in a sort of lobby where stairs leading both up and down formed a junction. He heard the sounds of voices coming from behind the stairs that went up to the second floor, and he carefully crept around them, to the great hall of bookcases that made up the main level.

Globes of glass that radiated a faint light hung suspended from silver chains set into the thick glass ceiling, and bookshelves of dark glass stretched on and on for as far as Steven could easily see in their feeble light. The voices were somewhere in the maze of shelves, whispering angrily, and he pushed himself to find them. The chill in the air grew sharper, and he told himself that he would spend only a minute more. He had to know what they were up against, so he could be ready in the morning when he carried all three of them into the Archive.

He came to a bookshelf adjacent to the conversation, and rather than risk being seen he reached out to slide a few books—a series of volumes bound in dark metal—off to the side so he could get a glimpse of who was speaking just beyond the shelf.

Three white-robed figures spoke in angry tones, using words he could not decipher. Their flesh was the white of fresh frost, and their hair, long and unbound, was similarly alabaster. All three were men, and one, the one speaking right now, had a look of pure rage upon his features. Steven didn't need to be able to understand what he was saying to be able to read *how* he was saying it. Hindras. Three of them.

He carefully stepped back away from the shelf, his blood racing, and collided with the rock-solid shape of another Hindra.

The creature grabbed his arm in its incredible grip, and it shouted a single word in its foreign language.

More globes of light suddenly activated in the ceiling, and all around him, Steven saw Hindras emerge from the alleys between bookshelves. There were not three or four Hindras here, there were dozens of them.

The one that most concerned Steven, however, was the one that held him in its vice-like hand.

Steven drew back his free hand to strike the creature, and as he did so, he felt it—the sun. Sunset was here. Cold rolled in upon him, heavy and horrible, choking out the wind in his lungs and smothering the heat of his blood. He felt his heart still.

He felt the night fall.

# 15
## Murrod

*It wasn't especially safe to travel on the main road, but they had little choice.* Mathias and Norrun had been pressing hard towards Hineros for almost two weeks, and the Prince City of the West was now visible on the horizon.

It was midday, thankfully, and their journey had been relatively without incident. Each night that they had slept on the side of the road had been nerve-wracking for fear of Ellir attack, but Greendeep's defenses appeared to be doing a serviceable job of keeping the four-armed creatures at bay.

Along the way, they had little to do but talk, and the conversations had largely avoided the subject of their journey in favor of anecdotes of Norrun's exploits as a young man. With each passing day, Mathias grew fonder of the older man, and as he recounted the tale of the boredom inherent in his original job as a gem cutter in Monarka, Mathias drew to a stop. The slight traffic of men and handcarts on the road continued around them.

"What is it?" Norrun asked, rubbing at his bald head.

"Gem cutter is a fine lot in life," Mathias said pointedly. "And while you were certainly not much of a rule-follower, you've yet to tell me why you left Monarka and came to the gnarlroot fields."

"I have to save some mysteries for another day," Norrun said, grinning. "It's what keeps you coming back for more."

Mathias shook his head. "I suspect that particular story is a bit lacking in humor or adventure. But you are right—I will have to hear it another time. We're close enough now we ought to get ourselves ready."

From the carry-bags slung over their shoulders, they both produced gray hooded, sleeveless smocks and pulled them on. The clothing was common among lower class men in all cities, and if Hineros was anything like Imperia they would be paid very little attention in those clothes. They had prepared their cover story: that of poor workers striking out for Hineros to try and improve their lot before the Ministry of Labor consigned them to the working class for all their lives to come. It was an easy story to sell since it was very much rooted in truth, and they were hardly alone in road-weary travelers spinning that same tale.

Hineros was the frontier of Greendeep. It was a place most often in conflict with Goldvast and also a place where it was said daring men could truly make names for themselves. It also happened to be the place where Mathias hoped to find answers as to what was really going on with Hyrak and with the mysterious behavior of the Chaplains of the major Ministries, but few would suspect him of it in such company.

"Are you absolutely certain this is something we ought to be meddling in?" Norrun asked as they resumed their pace towards the city. "I know you're worried that this Hyrak fellow is some butcher from another world, but we haven't seen a wild Ellir in two solid weeks of plowing through the jungle. Whatever the Ministry of Security is doing to keep the Ellir out is working, so he doesn't seem like a very present danger."

Mathias replied, "I can't argue that. But I have to know what's going on, and if it's something bad, I have to warn my friends."

"The ones that you haven't seen in months? The ones that left you all alone here?" Norrun asked quietly.

"They didn't leave *me*—I left them. But yes, them." Mathias tugged at the rough hood of the smock, pulling it as low as it could go to shield his eyes from the sun and from the inquisitive gaze of the admission knights that would surely be standing watch at the city's boundary.

"You have a way to get ahold of them while they're on a different world?" Norrun asked. "Because that's the trick I've been waiting to see."

Mathias shrugged his shoulders. "I'll find a way. I have an idea, but we have to tackle one problem at a time."

They said little else as they walked the last hour to the outer boundary of Hineros. They found themselves standing in line at a checkpoint for nearly two hours, and the first sun was nearing sunset when they reached the front of the line.

Hineros did not have a wall—unlike Imperia and Monarka it had no easy access to the natural stone reserves of the Greytall Mountains that bristled along the northeastern border between Greendeep and Bluetide. The checkpoints administered by the admissions knights were merely gated arches that had been erected at the city boundaries along both major roads. It would have been an easy feat to circumvent the checkpoints, but without the paperwork that only the admissions knights could grant, access and movement within the city would be a challenge for strangers.

As Mathias stepped forward to explain his name and purpose for visiting to the knight, a commotion rose up behind him and he looked back. A group of executive knights—the enforcement division of the Ministry of Security—carrying a large box-like handcart were coming into the city. They ordered the men in the long, snaking line to stand out of the way. Mathias and Norrun complied, and without slowing or even acknowledging the admissions knights, the executive knights pulled their cart through the archway and into the city. Walking at a brisk pace behind them was a young man near Mathias in age. He was about Mathias' height and spare of frame. He had short-cropped dark hair and a thin line of beard along his jaw that drew attention to his narrow face. He looked at Mathias for a moment but did not slow, and in that look Mathias noted a strange mixture of pride and worry.

"That one was a bit of a looker," Norrun whispered in Mathias' ear. "What do you suppose he does?"

A man behind them in line with long, tangled blonde hair and a mass of half-healed sores and cuts all along his bare arms intruded into their conversation and muttered, "Surveyor. Been seeing more of them about lately, always in a hurry."

"I am not one to admit my ignorance often," Norrun said slyly to the blonde man, "but what in Chron's name is a surveyor?"

"Damned if I know," the stranger replied with a sigh. "But they're high in the chain of things. Better off than you or me."

Norrun nodded. "Who isn't?"

The stranger bowed his head deeply at that and said nothing else.

Mathias answered the admissions knight's questions without incident, and soon he and Norrun were issued passes good for three days in the city. They passed through the arch and for the first time in either of their lives, beheld the Prince City of the Frontier. It was an interesting contrast with the bustle of Imperia. Less of the central work of the bureaucracy happened here, and that was evident. The city was more widely spaced out with many patches of wild greenery. The roads were pressed and packed dirt, and the buildings were more often wood than they were stone. There were many shops and taverns. As they explored the city's east side, Mathias did not notice a single runner.

"Did you know they never kept sunboxes out here?" Norrun asked Mathias as they crossed the wide, low bridge that linked the east and west halves of the city across the sluggish River of Songs. "Men in Hineros were working low labor jobs long before we lost control of the Ellir."

"So no place will be hit as hard as Hineros when they draw the line of demarcation between labor class and everyone else," Mathias speculated. "It's a wonder more people here aren't in an uproar."

"Not so much of a wonder," Norrun said, frowning. "They have their hands full with other problems." As they stepped off the bridge into the western half of the city, its contrast with the east was pronounced. The buildings were falling apart, and the men here moved frantically from place to place.

Mathias grabbed one of the men, middle-aged and limping, and asked, "What is going on?"

"Sightings of a raiding party from the south. Every man able is deploying to push them back." The man twisted out of Mathias' grip and said, "You'd do well to get yourself to the front as well."

As the man limped away, Mathias called to him, "Why isn't the east side worried?"

"What they want is on this side of the river," the man shouted angrily. "Everyone knows that."

Norrun sighed. "Of course everyone knows that. Silly us." He turned to Mathias and whispered, "What have you gotten us into?"

"I believe you said not so long ago that you wouldn't mind dying in a wild Ellir attack," Mathias said, attempting humor. "At least this way we can see what they are up to. Maybe catch a glimpse of this Hyrak person."

"Except it isn't an Ellir raid," Norrun said.

"It's closing in on night time," Mathias said defensively. "Why would the women attack at night?"

The two climbed a low hill on a broad street bordered by ramshackle adjoining homes. As the street crested the hill, it provided a clear view, and they looked out to the south. Men were gathering, under the direction of knights of both the executive and judiciary services. The men appeared well-versed in the procedures they were following, and Mathias imagined such raids were not unfamiliar to the inhabitants of the city. What was unfamiliar was the sight beyond the city boundary. The jungle was sparser here on the southwestern edge, and emerging from it were hundreds of women. They carried brightly burning torches and they wore the carved animal masks that were so often seen by the men of Greendeep as symbols of the women's barbaric civilization.

"That's a little more than a raid," Norrun muttered. "What do you think they're after?"

Mathias turned away from the sight of the slowly advancing women and instead scanned the western part of Hineros. It was possible that the fortunes of the other cities were being poured into the defense of the western part of the city, but not by the looks of the structures here. Many buildings were tumbled or burned, and it appeared that little work was ever done to restore them. Whole blocks were abandoned ruins. As his eyes moved quickly over the many blocks of the city in the failing light of the last sun, they fell upon one thing of note. He felt the hairs on the back of his neck rise.

Near the far western edge of the city, all alone in the center of a block of desolate ruins, was the unmoving metal form of a Spiralgate.

¤~¤~¤

"You promised me his life!" Jarrek roared. The former leader of the Jovs was on his feet, his heavy boots squelching in the damp straw that passed for his bed. Across the cavern from him was Hyrak.

"I traded Embrew for the lynchpin to my plan, Metalbreaker, but we will retake him. You have my word on this." Hyrak turned to face away from Jarrek, focusing on something happening in the adjoining cavern.

Grunting with frustration and rage, Jarrek threw himself forward, charging at the former warlord. Hyrak, without even looking back in his direction, sidestepped easily, causing the smith to collide with the cold stone wall of the cavern.

With preternatural grace, Hyrak took a half step and grabbed Jarrek's reeling form, sliding one powerful arm around his neck in a chokehold and bringing the other into his gut in a thunderous punch. Jarrek went down, sputtering and gasping for breath.

Hyrak squatted down and whispered, "Our bargain is predicated upon your obedience. Are you renegotiating our terms?"

Jarrek shook his head. "No," he managed to force out between gasps.

Hyrak smiled, and Jarrek did not like the way that the expression looked upon his scarred visage. "The Ellir are delivering Bindmetal into the forge chamber now. You will begin immediately."

Slowly regaining his breath, Jarrek looked up and asked, "What shall I be making for you?"

"You will make me the keys of which we spoke." Hyrak stood and stepped away from Jarrek. "When those are finished, you will start the hammer."

Jarrek struggled to his feet. "What of the bells?"

Hyrak's brow furled. "Not yet. I have not yet acquired the source metal for that. Unless you have determined a way to work the enchantment yourself?"

Jarrek shook his head. "The technique was that of Gurse, my father, and there is no way he was not put down when he covered our escape from Imperia."

"Then I will find the original device and I will have it brought to you. You can study it, learn its secrets, and make the bells for me."

"Then?" Jarrek asked, daring to allow hope to seep into his words.

"Then I will turn over the Gatemaker. By then, he will have served what little purpose I require of him." Hyrak gestured towards the cavern entrance. "The smithy awaits you, Jov. Oh—I have need of one other service first."

Hyrak drew his sword in a smooth motion, and it whistled as it cleared the scabbard. He inverted it in his hands and presented it, pommel first, to Jarrek. The smith could see that the warlord did not fear his using the weapon against him—one more sign of how confident Hyrak was of his mastery of the situation. Yet there was little Jarrek could do to turn the tables, and the reward for compliance was so great... he would not try again.

Hyrak tapped the blade of the sword. "I need the reservoir released. While you are making tools of Bindmetal, I will be making tools of another sort. The time is upon us to turn this world on its head."

¤~¤~¤

The sounds of battle were growing louder outside, and once the cart was deposited in its stall, the knights excused themselves to head for the front lines. Tyrick stood alone by the rear of the cart containing the Metalbreaker that he had been using for repairs the past few weeks.

Tyrick had never transferred the Metalbreaker to the pens by himself. Officially, this was well outside the purview of his duties as a surveyor, yet with battle being joined in the outer streets of Hineros, he realized that the detachment of executive knights that worked for him were sorely needed elsewhere. He put one hand on the locking mechanism of the cart, but did not open it.

He could hear the Metalbreaker moving around inside, whimpering. While the young man was strong and possessed of powerful magic, he had been in captivity all his life. He would bow to a forceful command, and Tyrick himself was no weakling. Why then did he struggle to bring himself to open the door?

After a few minutes of indecision, Tyrick noticed the sounds of battle outside were starting to fade. He assumed that meant the battle was moving on to a different part of the city, rather than ending. The force of women Goldvast had set against them was a large one, and Tyrick found himself more worried about the consequences of their travel than of their invasion. They would be driven back—they always were—but in crossing the perimeter, had they damaged it? Surely they had. That meant he would spend every waking moment the next few days repairing that segment of the perimeter. He might even have to take more than one Metalbreaker out into the field, if that was possible. This one needed rest.

Drawing in a steadying breath, he worked the mechanism of the lock on the cart, turning and sliding its four components until it clicked open. He cautiously swung the wooden panel outward, and he saw the Metalbreaker rocking in the corner, his arms wrapped tight around knees drawn up to his chest. The wooden box on his head and the wooden chains binding ankles and wrists to one another were intact.

"Come out here," Tyrick said forcefully.

With only scant reluctance, the captive scampered to the door of the cart. Tyrick helped him down, as he often did out in the jungle, by gripping his upper arm and steadying him as he slid both feet out of the cart to touch the ground. As the smith stood upright outside of the cart, he turned towards Tyrick and reached up with both chained hands, placing his pale, strong hands on Tyrick's shoulders.

Tyrick thought he heard a sound from within the box atop the smith's neck, but he could not make it out. He shoved the Metalbreaker away, uncomfortable from the touch of the smith, and grabbed the smith's upper arm once more, leading him through the workshop and towards the pens.

The rear of the repurposed Surveyor's Guild building was where all of the materials required for the defense of Greendeep from Ellir aggression were kept. He led the smith through the foundry, where great caskets of Bindmetal shavings were kept, with new ones arriving all the time. As the sunboxes of the other two Prince Cities slowly failed, they were ground down to metal dust by a few Metalbreakers housed in Imperia and Monarka, then most of the filings were transported to Hineros, where Tyrick and the other surveyors supervised their use in building and reinforcing the perimeter that stretched along the southern boundary of Greendeep.

They passed out of the foundry and to the long, low tunnel that led to the pens. For reasons that had never been made particularly clear to Tyrick, the pens were underground but not below the main guildhall. They were part of an older structure and had been in use for holding Metalbreakers captive for decades. They walked the long declining tunnel to a chamber carved into the cool stone beneath the River of Songs. A slow, endless trickle of water ran down the leftmost wall of the tunnel, in spite of many efforts to seal the corridor from the water overhead. It made Tyrick nervous, and for that reason he had never been farther than half-way through the tunnel. The knights, acting on orders from the Ministry of Security, handled the rest of the transfers. Tyrick's job was more concerned with quantities and measurements than the handling of captive smiths.

They reached the end of the tunnel, lit by very infrequently placed oil lamps, and Tyrick squeezed the smith tighter still. There was a door here, and it was barred with a heavy beam of metal.

"How does it open?" Tyrick asked aloud. He did not expect the smith to answer—or to even know what he was talking about.

But with a soft grunt of acknowledgement, the smith pulled out of Tyrick's grip and walked cautiously to the door, sliding his bare feet forward slowly until they made contact with the heavy door. Then he reached forward with his chained hands and felt around until they rested upon the metal beam. Sweat glistened on his pale skin as he strained with broad muscles to lift the beam. As he did so, Tyrick heard a gentle sound—a song of some kind. The metal seemed to waver for a moment, undulating as it wrenched free of the supporting metal rods that held it in place, and with a heave and loud grunt, the smith lifted it upwards all the way over his head.

Tyrick pressed the door inward, and it opened soundlessly. As he passed the threshold, he could see what usually happened—the tracks in the dirt on the floor revealed that one knight stood on each side to lift the bracer beam, while the third deposited the smith inside and closed the door. Tyrick could see no way of getting the smith in the door and still being able to lock it once more—one person could not lift it alone, unless he was a Metalbreaker, apparently.

While the smith stood, straining to hold the beam aloft, Tyrick peered into the cell—for that is what it was. It was damp and cool, and while pallets for sleeping were present, they were spotted with mildew. Inside the chamber there was a single lamp suspended from wooden chains, casting faint, smoky light on the four denizens inside. While it was possible that there were other Metalbreakers still out in the jungle working, or detained by the struggles above ground, there seemed to be sleeping accommodations for only eight. Tyrick had known the smiths were a precious resource, but to think they were so rare gave him great worry. They had to be better cared for than this. The safety of all Greendeep depended on these people!

As he looked around, there was no food to be seen, nor water. The smiths were fed by the knights, using that movable panel at the front of the box that enclosed their heads, but he had imagined they were also fed back here while they rested and recovered from theday's work. Some of these smiths looked to be upon death's door. One was quite old, and of the four presently here, only the one he had been working with appeared even remotely healthy.

The grunting of his Metalbreaker brought him back to the task at hand. He couldn't leave his Metalbreaker here. The damage the women had done to the perimeter would be extensive, and he needed the smith well-rested and ready to work hard tomorrow. He had been with this smith all day, and knew that not once had he been fed or granted a drink of water. If he left him down here now, he would not be tended to at all this night.

Tyrick thought carefully about the course of action he was about to take, and then he pulled the door closed. He helped the smith return the beam to its position across the door, snug in the metal brackets that held it there. He took the captive by the arm, more gently this time, and led him back up the tunnel.

He would keep the smith at his flat tonight. He would bring him back to the guildhall first thing tomorrow, ready to head out into the jungle and get to work, and if Tyrick was careful, none of the knights would even know it had happened.

¤~¤~¤

"Considering the prodigious expense of keeping the Surveyor's Guild in operation," Chaplain Voss complained, "it seems ridiculous that we can't keep Ellir out of Imperia!"

Chaplain Reid rubbed at his eyes. He was tired. It was the middle of the night, and these insufferable blowhards were demanding an audience, in person, about matters they simply could not understand.

"There has been one verified Ellir sighting in the city in the past two months, Voss," Reid said, unwilling to mask the exasperation in his voice. "That's an astonishing control rate. That's better than when we had the whole bank of sunboxes operational."

"Are you saying this is acceptable?" Voss questioned, his willowy frame trembling with indignation. "The safety of our people is your job, Reid!"

The others said little, but Reid could see them nodding in silent agreement with the head of the Ministry of Incarnation's tirade. Calmly, Reid lowered his hand from his face and glared at Voss.

"I am saying that our people are a pampered, spoiled lot. If once in a while one of them dies because he was too stupid to stay indoors at night, then he deserves to cycle back to the nursery. Unless what you are really complaining about, my old friend, is the paperwork that your Ministry has to do when such things happen?"

Voss gasped, covering his mouth with his hand in shock. "How dare you say such a thing about me?"

Reid stood. He was several inches taller than Chaplain Voss, and he used that height to very deliberately look down at his colleague. "You will do as you are told." He looked at the others. "All of you will do as you are told. Chron demands we maintain the security of Greendeep, and I am doing that. There will be an occasional breach by the Ellir—it is unavoidable. If you wish me to better protect the streets, then you will find the funding to spare to increase the ranks of my knight orders. Unless you care to put up the money, however, your voice in these matters is meaningless. Security is my domain. Tend to yours!"

The others hurried to flee the office, but Chaplain Voss did not go. He trembled, to be sure, but he did not leave. When the last of the other chaplains had left, Voss found the courage to speak. "You should know where it was."

"Where what was?" Reid asked, turning away and grabbing the case he had carried with him from his home.

"The Ellir. It was prowling around in the museum wing of the Ministry of Words," Voss shook his head. "The executive knights that patrol the grounds drove it off, of course, but still—why would it be there?"

Reid turned back towards Voss, his eyes wide with anger. "Drove it off? They didn't kill it?"

Voss shook his head. "They tried their best, but it was fast and strong."

"They're all fast and strong!" Reid shouted. "What if it got what it came for and you let it get away?"

"It didn't take anything with it," Voss defended.

"Except the one thing you most severely lack: intelligence. Whatever it was here to learn, it learned. That's the only reason for one of those things to flee while the suns are set." Chaplain Reid swung the rectangular wooden case at Voss as if to strike him, and the skinny chaplain squealed as he ducked out of the way.

Reid scowled and said, "Get out of my office. I have things to do."

¤~¤~¤

"I will not," Embrew asserted. The old Gatemaker, freshly bathed and newly clothed in a soft-spun robe like those worn by the domestic women of Goldvast's inner communes, stood before the dragon-god Ahmur. He did not have his staff to lean upon, but he found that simply being free of Hyrak had brought strength to him that he had not known in ages. It did not hurt that Ahmur's servants had also cleaned and dressed his improperly-healed stomach wound, allowing him to rest completely for the first time in ages.

The dragon's voice sounded in his mind, soft and sickly-sweet, "It is imperative that my women be allowed to leave this world. They are not safe here—you have seen the wicked workings of the men of Greendeep. I would have my people safe on another world, far from me, rather than continue to endanger them here."

Embrew could feel the dishonesty in the dragon's honeyed words. He knew exactly what she wanted—for he had been present before, when she had tried to use Becky to coerce young Adam into opening the Spiralgate for her.

"You lack the power to do this yourself?" Embrew asked, incredulous.

"There are certain restrictions upon my ability to work the Spiralgate. Restrictions that in no way affect you," Ahmur explained.

"And what is in it for me?" Embrew asked. He knew he dared much by resisting the creature, but he could not see her, and so she did not inspire as much fear in him as she might otherwise have. He had to know what was really going on here, and why Hyrak would have so willingly traded him away. Had not the warlord kept him alive for a very specific reason?

The dragon could maintain her subterfuge no longer. "You will live!" she roared in his mind. Embrew recoiled, sent sprawling by the force of her mental shout.

"I have no friends, no family—you have no leverage with which to compel me," Embrew replied from the floor. "And you know this."

The dragon said nothing, and after several minutes had passed, Embrew suspected that she had, in fact, left him alone. He chanced a quick look around with his arts, sensing the space and dimensions of the chamber in which he cowered. It was large, and littered with small objects, but there was no dragon here. There was, instead, another humanoid shape, shorter than his own but fuller.

The figure approached him, and then she said in a low voice, "You ought not to have angered her. Our goddess is not forgiving of her enemies."

Embrew nodded weakly. "Few gods are."

The woman helped him to his feet, and then she asked, "Is there anything we can do to convince you to help her? She has sent hundreds of our sisters to die in securing access to one of the gate-places. We would not have those women die in vain."

Embrew sighed. "There are rules that a Gatemaker must not break. I fear that opening the Spiralgate for one of your goddess' kind would be a terrible violation of those laws. And besides... I lack the strength. I have been too tired for too long."

"Do these have something to do with that?" the woman asked, tapping Embrew's Bindmetal manacle cuffs gently with one finger.

Embrew nodded. "Indeed."

The woman wrapped her hands around the two metal bracelets, squeezing tight. Embrew felt the flesh at his wrists grow quite warm, and then a horrible cracking sound echoed throughout the great treasure chamber.

As she removed her hands, the two violet metal cuffs fell from his wrists, shattered into a dozen fragments.

Embrew turned to grab her, joy and hope boiling over in his heart. "How have you done this? Those shackles have been my prison for two decades!"

The woman replied simply, "Sometimes when I touch that kind of metal, it shatters. It always has."

"Who are you?" Embrew asked. "I would know the name of my savior."

"I am called Plyssa," the woman said sheepishly.

"Then I will help you, Plyssa," Embrew said. "Get me to the Spiralgate, and I will open it for your goddess."

Embrew was not often glad that he could not see, but in this moment he was. This way he did not have to see the look of happiness writ large across this amazing woman's face as he lied to her. He would indeed open a Spiralgate, but not for Ahmur or Hyrak or anyone else.

He was going home.

# 16
# ARCTOS

S*o I'm not exactly famous for thinking things through.* Ever since I was little, instant gratification and the quickest solution have been my bread and butter. It probably comes from being the youngest in the family and always wondering why I had to wait so long for things that my older brothers were getting. It's hard to rationalize why you can't drive a car at ten when you see your sixteen year-old brother get his driver's license.

So when I was twelve and my parents wouldn't give in to my whining and pleading and demanding, I stole my dad's truck. Stealing makes it sound malicious or something, but that's not it—I just wanted to drive. I didn't think through it, I just did it. I grabbed the keys off the little plastic hook by the garage door, crept through the dark garage, and popped the door off of the automatic lift thing. I rolled up the door, nice and quiet, and when the moonlight spilled in on that gleaming black crew-cab pickup truck, I was filled with an overwhelming sense of justice.

I was really concerned with justice back then. What was fair. It was only fair that I should get to drive the truck. Brad got to. I was just as good as Brad. See—that was the train of thought I was packing back then. Becky would tell you it isn't that much different today, and I guess she would know, since she now has the super-power to hop on my train of thought.

Anyway, I crawled up into the driver's seat, pressed in the clutch, and let the truck roll back out of the garage and down the driveway. Our house is on a slow street, and it was way after most sensible people hit the sack, so I didn't look around too much—I was more concerned with making sure that Mom and Dad didn't wake up and hear what I was doing.

I spun the wheel and brought the rear of the truck down around, pointing it towards Becky's house, actually, and then, once I was as far as gravity was going to take me, I turned the key. The truck hummed to life, and I shifted into first gear and eased my left foot off the clutch as I ground my right down on the gas. The truck roared as it lurched forward, and I was off.

The street lights kept the roads lit well enough that I never realized I didn't have my headlights on. Details like that didn't seem all that important, considering the fact I was driving my dad's brand new truck. The only reason Dad had said no was because he didn't think I could handle it—I was proving him wrong. I was just as good as everyone else, I deserved everything I wanted. All those shitty little selfish thoughts were bopping around in my head as I cruised down our street and turned onto East Twelfth. There was a stoplight up ahead, turning yellow, and I floored the gas, scooting through the light just before it turned red and taking a hard right onto Forest Avenue. Now Forest is a pretty dark street—it cuts through a wooded stretch between two developments, and the trees crowd the streetlights pretty badly. I didn't think anything of it because *I was driving*! My heart was still racing, and by this point the stupid kiddy cellphone that my parents insisted I have was buzzing in my right hip pocket. That would be Mom. Or Dad.

As much shit as I knew I was in for taking the truck, I knew I'd be in worse shape if I didn't answer that phone, and so I reached down in my pocket and pulled it out. I flipped it open—yes, that's how lame it was. A flip-phone. Seriously, Mom? And there was a new text. I squinted against the bright light of the phone and opened the message.

It was from Mom. It said two words: 'Home. Now.'

I clicked the reply button, and just as I was tapping the 9 button for the third time (because that's how you make a Y on one of those phones. Seriously, Mom?), the world exploded.

I hit a parked car. The truck ground to an almost instant halt, and I flung forward. I wasn't wearing my seatbelt, because seatbelts are not cool, obviously, and the airbag deployed just in time to blunt the force of me flying forward and cracking my head against the shattered windshield. The engine block of the truck mashed backwards, driving the airbag-wrapped steering wheel into my gut. I vomited. I bled. I cried.

The first thing I saw when my vision cleared was my cellphone, pinched between the dashboard and the last remnants of the lower windshield. Its screen was pointed at my face, and all it said was "X." I'd never even made it to the Y.

I don't remember a lot after that. The next couple days are actually a total mess. So was my relationship with my parents, for years. Hell—most of our dysfunction to this day probably stems from that night. Why had I been so stupid?

That was what I had been—stupid. Selfish. Dad never let me forget it. And I never let myself forget it either.

That was the day I let the fear into my heart. I didn't grow less impulsive, just more fearful. I took fewer foolish risks, and withdrew into being the goofball I had always been. But I was a safe goofball.

I still saw that crash in my dreams. Then one day, it went away. One day, in one fell swoop, the dream, the nightmare, the memory was burned away.

That was the day I let Jarrek put this chain around my neck.

Why was I fighting so hard to get that fear back?

Wasn't I just being the man I would have been if the crash had never happened?

¤~¤~¤

Steven shifted to his shadowform. He didn't know if it would help him survive the cold, but it was all he could do. The stony grip of the Hindra passed harmlessly through his body as he converted to black ephemera. The white-robed Hindra shouted something in its strange language, but Steven didn't try to puzzle out its meaning. With an audible grunt of effort, he flung himself away from the Hindra, and the others that rapidly approached him now, and darted for the door of the Archive.

He felt strong in here—the light globes in the ceiling cast long shadows all around the many bookshelves, and his state of wellness while in shadowform was directly related to the proximity of other shadows. Even after the horrific exertion of direct teleportation through shadow that had gotten him through the dome, the presence of all this darkness rejuvenated him. As he dashed towards the door, moving far faster than his legs would ordinarily have carried him, he felt a glimmer of hope. He was faster than they were, at least in this instance, and once outside he would be able to grab one of the shadows around the statues in the courtyard and leap back outside the dome.

A Hindra was barring the door. Unlike so many of the others, this one was wearing sturdy traveling clothes, fur-tufted armor and bleached cloth of some kind. His hair was close cropped but still white, and his eyes were wider-set than the other Hindras inhabiting the Archive. It held a small dagger of gleaming metal in one hand, and the other was extended forward, palm out and fingers splayed. It obviously wanted him to stop.

Steven drove forward, intending to pass through and around the Hindra. Solid objects were only minimally disruptive to his shadowform when he willed it so. As he was about to plow through the Hindra, it squeeze its extended hand into a tight fist and flame blossomed all around it. A curtain of fire swept up around the Hindra, barring the door and catching Steven in a backdraft of heat and light.

He recoiled, screaming, as his shadowform was nearly evaporated in the harsh light of the fire. All around him, he saw books and scrolls begin to combust—the nearest shelves were more than a dozen yards from the curtain of flame, but still they began to smoke and smolder, and within a moment open flame was licking at the closest shelves.

Other Hindras swarmed in, willing wind and cold to action to temper and extinguish the flames, but already incredible damage was done. They looked anguished, but the Hindra at the door did not quell his fire barrier, and Steven, trapped in shadow form until he could regenerate enough mass to convert back to his fleshbody, tried to scamper away into the shadows behind the ascending staircase.

He slid backwards quickly, propelling himself by will more than limbs, and as he fell into the shadow of the staircase he pulled as much of that darkness into himself as he could manage. Then, with a shuddering gasp, he dropped into the shadow altogether, dissolving his form and sending it outward to reincorporate at another shadow—the shadow of the dome outside, where Todd and Marriq waited for him.

Emerging from the shadows outside was agonizing, and Steven feared how much damage this task was doing to him.

As he appeared, barely within the circle of heat that Marriq had created from the blood of their Hindra captive, he saw chaos everywhere. He remained in shadowform by chance, and it was all that saved him as a blast of wind ripped at their tiny campsite, blasting away the packs they had carried with them and causing Marriq to grab her staff, still anchored in the center of the circle, to keep from being blown out of the circle entirely.

Todd was down low, body pressed to the ground, to minimize the impact of the wind, and it howled for almost a full minute, passing harmlessly through Steven.

Outside the circle, their captive had woken. Rage was written large on her face, and Steven could see Todd struggling against the wind to crawl forward to reach the author of their misery.

Marriq noticed Steven and shouted, "She woke a few minutes ago. She can't enter the circle, so she's trying to drive us out of it."

Steven nodded.

The wind began to quiet, and as it stilled Todd launched himself to action, coming up first into a sprinter's squat and then all the way upright and forward, lunging and striking at the Hindra with a pair of rapid jabs. His fists struck her with wet thudding sounds, and Steven watched in amazement as the Hindra gasped and winced from Todd's blows.

"You can hurt her?" he asked, although Todd did not hear him.

Todd continued to slam punch after punch into the Hindra, and just as she went down, gasping for air in the snow, Steven realized... Todd was outside of the circle. And he wasn't freezing to death.

Steven knew that Becky suspected Todd of keeping secrets—her suspicions were carried to him every time they spoke mentally, part of the permanent link between them that he wasn't sure she was even aware of. But now, he could see it, whereas before he had not—there was something strange going on with this young man. But right now, that strangeness was saving their lives.

Suddenly a ripple appeared in the dome—like circles of disturbance in a pond when a stone is dropped into it. Through the ripples, moving through the ice like swimmers breaking through the surface of said pond, two more Hindras appeared. One was like their former captive, robed and long-haired, but male. The other was the warrior from the doorway, and Steven knew they were in deep trouble. He grabbed Marriq by the hand and then the pair of them darted forward to grab Todd as he kicked the gasping Hindra backwards. As the Hindra flew back to strike the dome, the warrior Hindra called out a single word, and Steven knew that it was a name—her name. Arenara.

That was the last thing they heard though. He grabbed Todd by one arm and saw, gleaming and smoking, the blood of the Hindra on Todd's hands.

He had scooped up the burning fluid from the ring around the campsite when he had attacked—that was why he was hurting her, that was why he was surviving the night's cold. The burns from the blood added to the ugly scabs from his injuries fighting Grell to leave his hands a truly hideous sight.

With a single, steadying breath, Steven pulled Marriq and Todd with him, down into the shadows and away from the campsite and the dome. The strain was incredible—he felt as though his entire body was being stretched and torn.

He was trying to carry them back to the shadows inside Marriq's cabin.

They didn't make it.

¤~¤~¤

There was little to do while they waited for Steven, Todd, and Marriq to get back, so Becky had taken to telling Yors everything she could about their adventures on Onus, Murrod, Rettik, and back home on Earth.

"Core same as Earth?" Yors asked, sitting up on his stool. The smith had finally stopped overexerting himself. JC was still sleeping more often than not, with at least a little prompting from Becky's powers, but he was mostly awake right now and occasionally contributing to Becky's stories—especially when he felt misrepresented by her descriptions.

Becky nodded. "Our world doesn't know anything about the other seven worlds, so we just called it 'Earth' and never thought anything else of it," Becky explained.

"Earth... dirt," Yors said simply. "That silly name for world."

"I guess I never thought about it that way," Becky conceded.

"But Core means heart of things. Center. Why your Earth called Core by everyone else?" Yors asked.

"I don't know," Becky said. "It just is. I don't think the names of the worlds mean anything in particular."

"Murrod means 'many pieces' in language of Ellir," Yors added. "That only thing Yors knows about world names."

"More than we knew," JC mumbled from his corner of the room.

"Can Yors tell story?" Yors asked sheepishly.

"Um... yes?" Becky replied, perplexed. The smith had been growing more comfortable talking with her since the others had left, but he was still not prone to sharing.

"When Yors first taken to Murrod, with other Jovs, things not so bad. Yors' wife came with, and small home made in Hineros. Men that ran city very nice, and Yors almost happy. Hard, because family not allowed to leave home or forge—women not welcome in Greendeep. After first year, things started to change. Men running city not the same—first leaders got too old and taken away, new leaders came in and not at all the same. Same time as new leaders take over, Yors and wife had baby. Little girl. Most beautiful thing Yors ever saw. Still. Forever."

Yors was quiet for a while, but Becky knew his story was not yet done, and she let him have the time he needed to collect his thoughts.

"One day, men decided Jovs not working hard enough. Too many distractions, men say. Too much danger. So men in gold robes take away women—Yors' wife. Yors' daughter. Baby girl holding Yors hand as men take her away. Yors fought hard—killed two men. But still baby girl taken away. Killed." Yors' eyes grew cold and hard.

"Yors fail family. Will not happen again. Yors with new family now—Jara. Jara's friends family too. JC. Becky. Everyone. Nothing more important to Yors than family." Yors sighed. "But Yors miss wife and baby-girl. Miss them so much."

He rubbed absently at his arm, in a place where Becky could see the faintest impression of a burn or a scar in a small, circular shape.

She walked across the room and put one hand on Yors' knee. Comforting gestures were not her specialty, but she knew he needed something. Sharing his story had been hard for the smith.

As she made contact with Yors, she felt the flickering edges of his thoughts. She did not fully connect, but the turmoil in his heart and his mind was easy to read at even the surface level, and she let a few details settle into her own mind.

Pieces of a puzzle began to fit together, and she looked at the spot on his arm with new understanding. Carefully she asked, "Who is Toren?"

"Toren Yors' father. Toren good man. Good father. Never let anything bad happen to family." Yors explained, his voice quavering. "Toren who Yors wish to be."

Becky nodded. "So if I understand Onus customs correctly, that means your full name is Yors Torenon, right?"

Yors nodded.

Becky took Yors' hand in her own. "It is a pleasure to meet you, Mr. Torenon."

Yors said nothing. He didn't have to. Becky could feel within him the first flicker of something Yors had not experienced in a very long time. Pride.

¤~¤~¤

Everything was turning upside down in Venot. Hunna stood on the outskirts of the Fountainworks, where that infernal woman, Karrin, was addressing a massive crowd of people. All of them were doing something that was highly unusual in Venot—they were wearing warm clothes.

As Karrin worked them into a fury about the need to take action, Hunna shook his head. These were hedonists she was addressing—since when did they care about anything besides self-gratification? It was senseless and shameless the way they were suddenly galvanized to action. For years beyond counting they had done nothing of consequence, and now they were trying to take command of the city from the fatalists.

All this because they were getting a little cold. Clearly the furnace had not failed utterly—had it done so, they would all have been dead several nights ago. Whatever was happening with that arcane contraption, it was still staving off the worst of the cold. As long as it lasted, they would last—this was the way of things. For the hedonists to rally behind Karrin and try to change this outcome was unthinkable.

Sadly, as the crowd threw out another bellowing cheer at Karrin's call to action, Hunna realized there was practically nothing he could do about it. His fellow fatalists cared little for the comings and goings of their hedonist brothers and sisters, and even this uprising would be dismissed as the natural order of things. But it was not! How could they not see that?

Sighing, Hunna turned away, accidentally bowling over a small girl who had arrived even later to the rally than he. The girl held back a sniffle from a knee that scuffed as she tried to catch herself in the fall, and Hunna extended a greasy hand to help her up. The girl was not yet of age, but Hunna could already see the tell-tale bruises and scars of excessive blood-letting. He hadn't realized that they were harvesting from ones so young.

Once the girl was back on her feet and mesmerized by Karrin's circular rhetoric, Hunna hurried away from the gathering. All of the noise was unsettling to him, and there were surely things to attend to. Perhaps he would check in at the infirmary to see if there would be any names added to the roll of births for tomorrow's pronouncement.

As he scuttled out past one of the hot water fountains—now more of a lukewarm water fountain—he noticed that the security grate next to the fountain was ajar—someone had pried open the leaden seal and left the grate open.

Out of a sense of civic responsibility—something these blasted hedonists had certainly never shown any interest in before Karrin started to stir them up—he knelt down to press the grate closed once more. As he worked the heavy metal back into place, he heard a sound from the bottom of the tunnel beyond the grate.

Behind him, Karrin shouted something that caused the crowd to erupt into a massive cheer once more.

In that moment, Hunna could stand it no longer. If hedonists were suddenly men of action, then perhaps one fatalist could become a man of curiosity. Suppressing a shiver at the foul smell that drifted up from the darkness at the bottom of the shaft, Hunna slid the grate fully aside and backed himself down into the hole, sucking in his vast belly to squeeze through. The ladder rungs set into the stone of the shaft were slightly sticky and wet, and his fingers squelched as he gripped them. Pungent moss squeezed up between his fingers—but there were places on the rungs that were bare of the stuff. He was not the first to make the climb—and recently at that.

He backed down the ladder, one rung at a time, until the light of the gray morning sky was but a small square high above him.

The sounds from below were growing louder—a heavy banging sound, like metal upon metal. And then, after a particularly loud smash of noise, he heard the unmistakable sound of someone cursing.

Some fool was working on the furnace.

¤~¤~¤

Another night had come and gone, and still Steven and the others were not back yet. JC was awake this morning, finally well enough that Becky was not zapping him with her powers to compel him to sleep. Yors and Becky were making breakfast from the rations in Marriq's cupboard, and JC was tired of laying around being useless.

Careful to not draw Becky's attention, he slowly sat up from the folded blanket on which he slept, sliding his back up along the cabin's wall to brace himself. The wound in his back was healing well—he was incredibly lucky that the spear of fire had done as little damage as it had. Breathing hurt. Moving hurt. But he could still do both, so that was a win.

"Any word?" JC asked after he had caught his breath.

Becky spun around, startled, and glared at him. "Why are you sitting up?"

"Because I can," JC said with a weak smile. "Join me in cherishing the victory."

Becky scowled a bit harder, then yielded and smiled, but he could see that it was a forced smile.

"So that's a big hell no on the communication from the guys?" JC asked again.

She nodded.

"Yors sure they back soon," the smith said, shuffling back towards JC. "Yors work on chain now, make Joe better."

JC waved him off. "You've done a ton big guy—more than I was expecting, for sure. Don't push yourself any harder. You were pretty beat up too."

Yors shrugged and gestured to the fresh dressing on his chest. "Becky fixed Yors up good. Hardly hurt at all."

"Who knew that I'd get so much practice with bandages," Becky muttered. "Totally what I expected to do with my life."

"Well, maybe you should use that other thing you're good at and see if you can touch base with them?" JC asked. He made a small move, trying to shift his weight around so that he could give standing a try, but the move clearly aggravated his wound, and the blinding pain that lanced through his body quickly put a stop to the idea of standing.

Becky flashed him a look that nearly stank of guilt and said, "I can't."

JC arched an eyebrow and attempted to connect with Becky by way of their mental link. He felt her defenses bristle at the touch and then the connection sprang to life—but instead of meeting in the non-space of Becky's mind, she joined him in his.

"I love what you've done with the place," she murmured as she looked around the disordered chaos of JC's mind. Normally the landscape of these conversations was featureless—in part because Becky had quickly mastered the creation of a sort of landing-zone in her mind. JC lacked the skill to do it, so they were instead in his front memory, and it was a mess from being in and out of consciousness for the past couple of days.

"What's going on?" JC asked, taking her hands in his. She pulled back slightly from the touch, and he knew something was terribly wrong as surely as he knew that she was about to dismiss his worries.

"It's nothing," she said. "I just can't make contact with Todd right now."

Holding tighter, and thankful that at least in his mind he could move around, JC asked, "What about Steven? You have way better range with him anyway, right?"

"What does that mean?" she asked defensively.

"I mean you have a stronger link with him, like with me and with Adam, right?" JC asked.

"Oh, well, yes—a leftover from Tatyana's time in my head. Yeah. I do. But I don't think it's a good idea to use it right now." Becky looked down at her feet.

JC didn't say anything for a few moments, but he also did not let her go. After a reasonable amount of silence had fallen, he whispered, "I am not an idiot. I know how you feel about him. But I also know that isn't you—it's her. She left more behind than just her super-powers. Anyone can see that. It doesn't bother me—not too much. It's not like before, where she was in control of your body. It's just memories or whatever, bouncing around in you. I get that. It's not like you'd ever act on them."

Becky pulled her hands from his and looked up, her expression unreadable. "How do you know that? *I* don't even know that! These things just rise up in me, out of nowhere!"

"I trust you." JC said simply. "And I know you wouldn't hurt me. Not like that."

Becky took a step away from him and turned her back, facing the flashes of memory that floated around the mindscape. She reached out and touched a memory, and JC smiled. It was one that was probably unfamiliar to her—the hospital, last year, when he had confronted Tatyana about her secret possession of Becky.

"You knew right away," she said softly. "How did you know?"

"She wasn't you. And you'll never be her—no matter what shadow of her is left in you. You're a whole person, Becky. It sucks that she died—it sucks a lot—but at best, what's left of her is just one little piece. The whole person is real, and incredible, and stronger than anyone I know." JC walked up behind her and wrapped his arms around her. "Try to talk to Steven. We have to know what's happening. It will be OK."

"I'm embarrassed," Becky said. "I'm not really used to that feeling. How do you deal with it?"

"What makes you think I've got any background in that?" he asked with a broad smile.

In an annoying moment of serendipity, a memory flew past the pair of them, gleaming brightly—it was JC's near-naked streak through Becky's birthday party, years ago.

Becky looked up at him over her shoulder and said, "Your track record speaks for itself."

JC kissed her gently. "The trick is to just pretend it never happened. When that doesn't work... own it."

Becky nodded.

A moment later they were back in their bodies, and from the look on Yors' face, the conversation had actually taken a minute or two of real time. Becky, still across the room, lowered herself onto a stool and said, "I'm reaching out to Steven now."

Yors and JC watched her closely, quietly, for nearly five minutes of silent anticipation. When the time had elapsed, she opened her eyes and said, "I can feel him, but I can't find him. I'm going to try one more time. He's scared—really scared. I'm going to try to climb the link like a rope, instead of just calling out. I'm not sure what that will do."

Yors walked over to Becky and helped her to one of the folded blankets littering the floor. "Sounds hard. Becky should lay down."

Becky nodded appreciatively as she lay back and closed her eyes. JC watched the whole thing with a nagging feeling of helplessness, but there truly was nothing he could do to help her. This was her thing, her way of contributing to the grand, mysterious quest of the Children of the Line. Everyone had a part to play, and Becky... was playing Tatyana's.

"And doing a damn fine job of it," he whispered under his breath.

Another five minutes stretched out before them, this time more nerve-wracking than before. Becky's breathing had quickened and she was sweating, tossing about on the blanket so much that Yors was holding her hands down so she didn't hurt herself.

JC almost pressed upon their connection, but he feared what the distraction would do to her, and so he held himself back. With a detached sense of wonder, he realized that he had just checked himself from doing something stupid—because he'd been worried. Afraid. Just a little. The work Yors was doing on the chain was working!

His miniature discovery was brushed aside a moment later when Becky sat up, gasping, and a great, ugly shadow splashed up in the far corner of the cabin. The shadow of one of the stools, thrown by the light from the small furnace, elongated and deepened until it discharged three gasping figures. Marriq was first, then Todd, and Steven appeared last, pale and shaking.

"What the hell?" JC shouted.

Todd recovered first and stood up. Even his dark skin was paler than usual, and he was sucking in hungry breaths. "We got stuck in the shadows. For hours," he managed to say. "We don't have much time."

Marriq, her walking stick absent, grabbed the nearest stool and used that to help herself to her feet even as Becky and Yors fell upon Steven, tending to his unconscious body.

"The Hindras will be coming for us. We have to move now," Marriq said. "They know where we are, and they know what we know."

Becky looked up from Steven, towards Marriq, and asked, "How are we supposed to run? Joe can maybe stand, but he certainly can't walk. And Steven looks completely wiped out."

"I don't know," Marriq said sharply. "But we either try, or we die."

# 17
# ARCTOS

*If we run, we can make the trip to Venot in twelve hours.* That gets us there just before sunset," Marriq explained patiently. "If we will be safe anywhere, it is in one of the furnace cities."

"Are you even listening to me?" Becky shouted angrily. "Joe can barely stand, Yors can't push himself right now, and Steven looks..." she shuddered. "We're in bad shape."

Yors watched the exchange between the two women unfold with detached curiosity. Not long ago, he struggled mightily with his interactions with women (and children), but he had come a long way since accompanying Jara into the dungeon of Hyrak Arn last year. Now... now he still didn't understand women, but he was getting closer every day.

"Not run," Yors said calmly. "All walk."

Becky shook her head, "Maybe we can pull that off. Maybe."

Then Marriq added grimly, "If we shuffle along, we won't make it. We haven't a Hindra to bleed for shelter anymore. I imagine the next Hindra we run into will be bleeding *us*."

Yors walked over to the metal-wrapped stove in the center of the room and tapped on it with one sturdy knuckle. "Yors fix. Make heat come with."

Marriq's eyes grew wide and she looked, stricken, at the smith. "You can't! If you tamper with it, it may lose its enchantment. You have no idea how precious that hearthstone is. How impossible it will be to replace."

"Yors is right," Steven said weakly, opening his eyes. "We either carry the heat or we might as well just sit here and wait for those things to catch up to us and kill us."

Marriq closed her eyes. "Very well. I'd rather live to see the inside of the Archive again. The hearthstone is worth the risk, I suppose."

"You want to go back there?" Todd asked incredulously. "The place is swarming with those Hindra things! The Archive is lost to us, just like you said it was. We came here for nothing. The sooner everyone gets settled on that, the sooner we can focus on the important thing—getting back to the Spiralgate and signaling Adam for a ride home."

"The Archive is not lost!" Marriq spat, her old body trembling with strength and rage.

Yors tried to tune the argument out, instead turning his own efforts and attention to the workings of the hearthstone. The stove itself was made of simple metals and would easily bend to his arts. The stone within was, as best he could tell, actually stone, and thus a bit outside the scope of his power. If he reshaped the stove structure and double-walled its containment pocket, the heat would extend in a tighter dome—a necessity once it was no longer shielded inside the four walls of the cabin. He could arrange metal rings in the housing, through which straps could be run. Someone would have to carry it, and it was not light.

As the fight continued around him, Yors realized that the load would surely fall upon him. He was used to it. Yors was the one that got things done while everyone else talked. He'd never had much use for talk.

"The Hindras are not invincible. This is why we must make it to Venot," Marriq explained in a vague approximation of patience.

"I'm listening," JC added from his own bedding. "I'd like to have another crack at those things."

"I have an old friend that still lives in Venot. She should be able to get us in touch with a Hearth Keeper, if any of that old order still survive. Once we have one of the Winterblooded, we can seek the one thing that even Hindras fear." Marriq watched Yors as he started to reshape the stove. He could tell she did not approve of the humming, but without the rhythm, there was no safe way to work the magic. If he was Becky, he would have stopped to explain that to her. But he was Yors, so he kept working.

"That doesn't sound ominous or anything," Becky said sullenly. "But if you really think there's a chance—we did come here for the Archive. And we've already come this far."

From the corner of his eye, Yors saw Todd grimace, but the young man held his tongue.

Yors continued to work. The metal bent and flowed in his hands, easily shaped by his will and the beat of the song he was humming. It would have been easier to work the magic through a forge and hammer, but life since escaping Murrod had not often provided Yors with the easy way of doing anything. He stretched and folded the metal, cupping tightly around the hot hearthstone in its belly. The first wall shaped easily, the second only a bit harder, and then he set to sealing the compartment. The hearthstone was dangerous, and pulling the metal in as tight around it as he was would create a great deal of trapped heat. Bindmetal would have made the work easier and safer, but he had precious little of it with him, and he could not bring himself to part with the enchantments already painstakingly worked into his trinkets. Perhaps when he was finished removing the enchantments from JC's chain, he would use that Bindmetal for a grand working—something of significant purpose. Alas, he was still a long ways away from that.

The portable furnace would be a rushed piece at best, but it would be done to his satisfaction in another ten minutes. Then they would venture once more into the cold.

¤~¤~¤

Hunna had to hunch over to move safely through the tunnels. After only a few feet his back was already killing him, and he regretted climbing down the ladder almost instantly. It was dark down here, and it smelled atrocious. It was warm at least, but beyond that, Hunna could think of little to recommend a vacation into the Fountainworks tunnels.

The voice he had heard ahead had not cursed or spoken again, but the banging sounds continued, and Hunna focused on those sounds. He crept one foot in front of the other in his awkward hunched position towards the sound. After a few minutes, panting and sweating in the heat, he noticed a notable increase in the temperature. He lifted the hem of his over shirt with one hand and soaked up the sweat from his brow. The tunnel, steadily lowering, came to an abrupt halt.

Hunna felt around in the dark, his hands once again squelching in the rampant moss that grew upon the tunnel walls. He nearly gave up, but just as he thought he had searched the whole of the pitch black end of the line, he came across a narrow opening that appeared to give way to a passage leading off to the right.

He squeezed through the opening and was forced to crawl as the ceiling came down even lower. Still the banging sounds persisted ahead of him, and the passage continued to turn inward, to the right. After another twenty yards of slouching about in the muck, the tunnel doubled back on itself. He skirted the wall where the tunnel folded back in, and as his head cleared that barrier, a bright light shattered the darkness and caused him to recoil, bringing a sludge-covered hand up to shield his eyes.

A terribly thin man, middle-aged with the dark copper skin of the old Bound-dwellers, was beating at a broad metal pipe with a rudimentary hammer. His head was shorn to the scalp. He was stripped down to the waist, wearing only a loose-fitting pair of shorts in a style common among hedonists. On the ground next to the stranger was a large hand-saw, and it was obvious the man had been trying to use the saw upon the pipe earlier, for it was marred by dozens of ragged, superficial cuts.

The light in the chamber was coming from a pool of dark red liquid that floated atop the sludge coating the stone floor. Tiny glimmers of a golden mineral danced in the liquid, casting light.

"You shouldn't be down here!" Hunna asserted. It wasn't until after he had spoken that he realized his position on all fours and covered with muck lacked any semblance of authority.

The man looked up from the pipe just long enough to take note of Hunna and then resumed beating on it with the hammer.

Hunna's temper flared. He was not the most important man in all of Venot, to be sure, but he was a member of the civil service. He was entitled to more respect than this! He crawled the rest of the way out of the tunnel and into the chamber and stood, making a rough effort to wipe the slime from his trousers and hands, but truly only making a further mess of himself.

"Make yourself useful," the stranger said once Hunna had stood. "There's another hammer in the bag next to you."

The clerk looked down to his left and saw there was indeed a canvas bag of tools, and he bent down to pluck a small hammer from among its assorted contents.

He marched over to the pipe, his indignation seemingly forgotten, and set to pounding on the pipe with the hammer. The pair of them worked in easy tandem, never hitting at the same time and thus subjecting the thick metal of the pipe housing to a steady rain of blows.

After nearly five minutes of beating on the pipe and being lost in the ringing echoes of the sound, Hunna felt a strange fog slip free of his mind.

He dropped the hammer to the floor with a clatter and grabbed hold of the intruder's arm. "Stop that!" he shouted.

The man looked up at Hunna was a puzzled expression. "Did you just shake me off?" He did not wait for a response, instead taking a slow, deliberate swing with the hand that did not hold the hammer in the direction of Hunna's head.

Hunna released the intruder and skittered back away from the madman, his eyes wide. "You tried to assault an officer of the city! Is there no end to your crimes, hedonist?"

The man smiled. "If I was a hedonist, would I be down here working?"

Hunna squinted. The man had a point. In fact, they were wasting time—the pipe needed to be opened up after all, and the longer they stood here arguing, the longer it would take to...

"Stop! Whatever you are doing, stop it!" Hunna shouted, shaking his head violently. "Why does my head hurt so badly?"

The man's smile disappeared. "You shouldn't be able to do that," he muttered. "I'm sorry, but I haven't time for this."

The man lowered his hammer to the ground next to the saw and turned to face Hunna fully. Without being up next to the pipe, his torso was fully exposed, and Hunna saw a mark graven into the man's skin, on the left side of his mid-section, that he had not seen in many years.

Before he could raise yet another charge about the man's crimes, the figure lifted both hands up, palms out, and pressed them towards Hunna. The heat in the room suddenly intensified, gripping Hunna in a steamy hold that drove him to his knees, head swimming. It became harder and harder to breath. A moment later, everything went black.

¤~¤~¤

Becky helped support Steven, but the inequity in their heights made her efforts feeble at best. They limped along in the snow in the middle of their tightly-packed party as the day began to fade.

At the rear of the party, just behind Becky, Yors carried his traveling hearthstone on a pair of thick ropes slung over his shoulders. The large squarish device stuck out in front of him, casting a sphere of heat all around them that was playing merry havoc with the snow upon the ground.

In front of Becky and Steven, Marriq led the way with Todd at her side, carrying JC. Becky monitored JC's condition carefully with her powers, constantly worried that the jostling would tear open his wounds. Fortunately Todd was doing a great job of keeping him steady, but still she worried.

"We will camp up ahead," Marriq shouted over the ever-present wind.

Becky peered ahead and thought she saw something not far from their location, obscured by the blowing snow. "This is the way we came," she muttered.

"I think so," Steven replied. "But it's hard to say. Everything looks the same. I have no idea how she navigates."

"Stubbornness," Becky retorted.

They pressed on for another twenty minutes when Becky could finally make out the object she had first glimpsed through the whiteout—the Spiralgate they had used to enter Arctos in the first place.

Yors lowered the furnace down onto the ground, letting out an audible sigh of relief once its weight was off his shoulders. He settled down in a nearby snowdrift—which was rapidly dwindling to a pile of slush—and rubbed at his shoulders.

Marriq walked off a circle around the furnace, carving a line in the snow with a fresh walking stick retrieved from her cabin. The line indicated where they would have to remain to stay within the protection of the furnace and out of the fatal night air.

Becky glanced at the cloud-obscured sun that was, even now slipping behind the horizon. "How long do I have before it's too dangerous to be outside of the circle?" she asked.

Marriq eyed the sky carefully and replied, "Ten minutes."

Becky nodded and drew in a deep breath of the warm air. Then she plunged out of the circle, making directly for the Spiralgate. She heard some shouting behind her—she couldn't tell if it was Steven or JC—but forged ahead, reaching the stone platform upon which the Spiralgate rested after only two minutes of effort. She climbed up on the platform and placed one gloved hand on the dark Bindmetal surface of the gate.

Unlike Adam, she had never really stopped to study these things. They were his domain, just as the mind was now hers, and she was content with that division. They were hours past the scheduled time when Adam was to open the gate in case they needed to escape back to Onus, but Becky had to try and make contact. It had now been three days since they arrived on Arctos, and they has surely missed enough rendezvous that Adam was worried.

With her hand gripping the smooth metal of the gate's nearest band tightly, Becky closed her eyes and willed the dormant, still connection between her thoughts and Adam's to life. Nothing happened. She concentrated harder, feeding her power and her will into the metal at her fingertips, trying to tap into whatever strange magic it used to link the worlds of the Spiral together. She floundered at first, and she feared she had spent too long here already, but then she felt the tiniest glimmer of connection—a whisper, faint and hollow, of the bond she shared with her best friend when they were on the same world as one another. Through that flickering bridge of connection she was able to pull a few images—images of rain and tears, of shouting and the clashing of metal upon metal. She tried to pull more information from the link, but it was bottlenecked by the vast distance. In return, she pressed outward a few simple images and sensations, hoping she could effectively communicate their situation in such brief terms. She willed him not to worry, that they were alright and that they were getting close to a solution, but she also tried to hint to him the dangers of this place and to impress upon him how vital it was he not come here himself.

She did not know if her message made contact, and if it did, she did not know if he understood it. But that was all the time she dared spare, and she dashed back through the snow, towards the comforting curtain of heat that Yors' contraption cast around their camp.

She burst across the line of the circle just in time, and she felt bone-chilling frost climb up one foot and leg as she pulled that last trailing body part into the circle.

She suppressed a scream as the pain shot through her body, and before she knew it, Marriq was there, stripping her boot off and rolling up the flash-frozen leg of her pants. The flesh beneath was pale and blue, and Becky feared that it would be lost, but Marriq set to massaging the foot and calf with her hands, working the flesh and the muscle in a way Becky had never before seen.

Slowly, feeling began to return. It did so with cramps and intermittent stabs of pain, but Becky bore it well, grateful that she could feel anything.

"Were you successful?" Marriq asked, when she appeared done with her work.

Becky shrugged. "I did everything I could. We'll see if it worked."

"I did not think such powers could traverse the space between worlds," Marriq added. "You must be very powerful among the Kem."

"The powers I have belonged to a Child of the Line. I think perhaps they are all very powerful. Steven is one too." Becky smiled towards Steven, who was resting but watching her with careful, nervous eyes.

Todd settled down next to Becky and Marriq. "JC's sleeping now. That guy is heavier than he looks," Todd said.

"Thanks for carrying him. I don't know what we would have done if you hadn't been able to haul him with us," Becky replied. "It means a lot."

"He's my friend too," Todd said simply. "I would never have just left him behind. I do have a question though."

Becky smiled. "He's OK, I think. Things are chaotic there, but I was able to touch his mind, so that means he's OK."

Todd breathed a sigh of relief. "I was worried. I've never left him alone like this before. The whole time we've been here, I keep thinking I made a mistake not staying there with him."

"He's a big boy, Todd. Adam can take care of himself."

Todd shook his head. "It's my job to keep him safe. No matter how big or powerful he gets."

"That's what people who love each other do for each other," Becky said. "And I think maybe you came along because you realize that part of keeping Adam safe means helping him get the answers he needs about the Children of the Line."

Todd's eyes grew hard. "He didn't need those answers before you two talked him into it."

"Todd," Becky said, taken aback. "What's wrong?"

"This is a stupid risk, Becky. This whole trip was a stupid risk. Look at Joe. He was speared with a bolt of fire through the back. For some reason that didn't kill him, but by every right it should have. Everything that's happened here, every ounce of blood shed and every cut, scrape, burn, and blister is on you." Todd stood up. "I just hope it all turns out to be worth it."

He turned to go sit with Steven and Yors, and as he did, Becky could not help but look at his bandaged hands. Guilt was not a usual experience for her, but it boiled in her breast now.

¤~¤~¤

"They have seen us!" Arenara pleaded. Her wounded head, damaged by the strange light weapon that the humans had wielded against her, was largely healed now that she was back among her own people, but their maddening tendency to lurk rather than act was stirring within her a massive headache. "If we do not find them and kill them, they could bring more of their kind down upon us."

She sat in a high-backed chair around a shining glass table. There were six others similarly arrayed around the table, and together they were the rulers of the Hindra people. Arenara was not usually a member of the Circle of White, but she sat here now in the stead of her normal representative because of her special knowledge of recent events.

Most of the others were, like her, scholars. The caste system that bound the Hindras together had suffered greatly since the coming of the humans to these lands, and only the reclusive scholars of the *he'dai* caste had survived the great purges in any appreciable number. Of the seven representatives in the Circle of White, four were of the *he'dai*. Of the others, only one was dressed in the black robes and bald head of the *har'toi*—the powerful dreamers that once ruled over all of the Hindra peoples in the times before.

He was silent now, as ever, speaking only when the others seemed to be at an impasse. The final two seats around the table belonged to the warrior caste, fur-wearing huntsmen of the *hahn'du*. They were in agreement with Arenara, of course—the *hahn'du* always favored war with the humans. It had been their influence in the earliest of days that brought the wrath of the first humans down upon the Hindras in force.

It had not been often in her long life that Arenara had agreed with the *hahn'du*, but now they seemed the only ones willing to listen to reason.

"You are teachers and learners, my brothers, my sisters—it was from you that the humans learned the first lessons imprinted in this Archive. Surely you have seen in the histories you have studied the folly of not learning from the past. The humans will stop at nothing to kill us—it is the one cause around which they have always rallied in the past. Please, we must hunt down these intruders and put them to the knife. If we do not, they will not hesitate to bring the Archive down around us." Arenara leaned back in her seat. She had done her best to make her case—now it fell to her fellow *he'dai* to come to their senses.

"The dome is our strongest magic. They lack the power to breach it," one of the others said softly. "You have listened too long to our brothers patrolling the lands beyond the dome. We should never have allowed you to join them, Arenara. Your place is here, studying. We have much to learn of the other worlds if we are to be ready for the coming of the *onysar*."

Arenara said nothing. She knew that Camborianus would not yield to her points—he was far too comfortable here. His only aggressive action in the past century had been the vote to overtake the abandoned Archive.

The other two *he'dai* nodded agreement with Camborianus, and Arenara felt her heart sink. That was that. A split vote, with Shiranduin of the *har'toi* abstaining—as always. They would take no action against the intruders and, before much longer, the armies of men would come back in force. They would come with their numbers and their anger and they would find a way to destroy everything the Hindras had tried to build. Even without magic, they would find a way to destroy. It was the one thing humans could always be counted upon to do.

As she stood to leave, too angry to even listen to the formalities of the casting of votes, the whispering voice of Shiranduin said, "Wait."

She turned to look at the old man in the black robes. She knew his age, but did not see it, except for the worry in his brow. He was, like all of them, made perfectly. Some thought him to be the last of his caste, but Arenara knew better. There were a handful of the *har'toi* left, they just refused to gather at the Archive. Even in the old days it had been rare to see more than one or two of them in any one place. They preferred to be spread widely across Arctos, observing all that unfolded in their home world.

"These men are not like the others. This one wielded the shadow of the world as we wield her breath, blood, and tears. I have seen in dreams the movement of dark forces. The *xallyr* has stirred once more. Arenara is right—we cannot afford to chance doing nothing. We may well face the coming of a new invasion. I side with the *hahn'du* and Arenara. We must act. We must destroy them before they destroy us." Shiranduin closed his eyes, and Arenara could see heavy lines of worry crease his alabaster face.

"So we shall hunt the invaders," Arenara said smugly, looking to her colleagues of the *he'dai* with clear disdain.

"No, child," Shiranduin corrected her. "We shall hunt all men. But if it eases your mind, we shall start with the ones that injured you."

¤~¤~¤

It was well past noon on their second day of traveling when the entourage reached the city of Venot. JC was walking on his own two feet today but leaning heavily on Todd for support. The spear of fire that had run him through had left a great deal of pain behind but, miraculously, very little truly debilitating injury. JC liked to believe that he was healing faster because of heretofore unknown super powers—perhaps he was the Bloodmender Child of the Line, he mused—but the truth was, he suspected that the spear had been more smoke than fire.

He chortled at his inner pun-making.

Venot, as Marriq had explained while JC was half-paying attention and half-trying not to feel like a complete tool for having to be carried by Todd like a sack of potatoes, was one of several cities that were heated and powered by massive hearthstone furnaces deep under the ground. Built long ago when the Circle of Stone was still strong, the cities were now the sole domain of the hedonists and fatalists, for the traditionalists, along within any surviving Archivists, were driven out to the rural areas that Marriq called 'the Bounds.'

The city was nothing like the walled cities of Onus or the endless spires of Rettik. As best JC could tell, the city had no means of defending itself at all, so in that regard it was really more like cities back home. It also had a distinct smell that reminded him of the sweltering heat of Imperia, on Murrod.

The buildings of the city were mostly squarish and low—no more than a story or two. As they entered the city on paved streets, with no one challenging their entry whatsoever, Marriq explained that the heat field of the furnace extended only so high, by design, for fear of the damage that such heat would do to the atmospheric conditions of the region.

"Are you taking a risk being here?" Becky asked.

"Life is risk," Marriq said with a simple shrug. "I prefer the risk of angering a few fatalists to the risk of being slain by Hindras."

JC certainly couldn't find fault with her argument, and as they continued on into the city, he started to feel better. The heat here was different than the heat of Marriq's cabin and Yors' improvised traveling stove—it was pervasive in a way that seemed completely wrong for this world. But it sank into his bones and his skin and he found himself starting to sweat beneath the traveling clothes. It felt good though—like a long trip into a sauna back home. The heat didn't last—it appeared to be radiating from the city streets in an intermittent, unpredictable pattern.

At JC's insistence, Todd lowered him to the ground, and he found he was able to manage walking unaided, so long as he was careful.

Marriq gestured to a rundown looking building a few blocks from the city edge, and they filed into the abandoned building. Todd and JC brought up the rear save for Marriq, who came in last and closed the door behind her.

"The outer edges of the city are usually reserved for hedonists, and they don't often make it home. We should be safe here for a bit. Yors, that hearthstone is precious, but we can't carry it around in the city. It will attract the wrong kind of attention." Marriq explained.

Yors nodded and pointed to the stairs in the back of the largely empty room. "Yors hide upstairs?"

"Yes," Marriq said. "You don't look anything like a city-dwelling man of Arctos. Neither do you," she pointed at Todd. "We have to move quickly and attract the least amount of attention. If we're to find Vanuella before we are found ourselves, you'll have to stay here with the big man."

Todd scowled at the old woman, but said nothing.

"But the rest of us are good to go?" Becky asked.

Marriq eyed Becky, Steven, and JC carefully. "You'll pass for a city-dweller at first glance, I suppose. The trick would be to not get a second glance. We'll split into two groups, one heading into the west districts, one into the eastern half of the city. We are looking for a woman named Vanuella. She's likely in a hedonist part of the city, so start at the outer edges and work your way in. She's probably a blood-letter, or an artificer. Her previous skill set is underappreciated in today's society."

JC's eyes grew wide. "Please tell me this girl is a hooker."

Marriq arched an eyebrow. "I'm not familiar with that term."

Becky, however, was, and before JC knew it, his girlfriend was twisting his ear in her right hand.

He winced as he squirmed and the muscles in his back spasmed. "Just asking," he muttered. "Injured guy here, remember? Be gentle."

Becky sighed and released him. "JC has a point—he's still pretty hurt. Maybe he should stay here, and we can just split up into three single search parties?"

Marriq shook her head. "I will take him with me. You will go with Steven. Can you use your magic to stay in touch with me?"

Becky paused for a second, then said, "Not quite. I can stay in touch with Joe a lot more easily."

"Fine. We go now. There is no time to waste. If you find Vanuella, tell her of me and convince her to return to this place with you. Todd, Yors, you must guard the hearthstone. If we cannot find Vanuella, we will have no choice but take our chances alone and that hearthstone is the only hope we'll have."

Marriq handed her walking stick to JC. "You will need this more than me."

JC took the stick in hand and made a few tentative attempts at walking with part of his weight supported by the long shaft of wood. It was surprisingly helpful.

Becky gave him a hug, carefully avoiding squeezing too hard, and then the four of them filed out of the abandoned building, leaving Todd and Yors, looking grim, behind them.

For nearly two hours, they canvassed the west side of Venot. Fatalists working shops that were largely devoid of customers time and time again knew nothing about anyone named Vanuella, and Marriq's tone was growing more and more desperate with each rejection. JC knew he was slowing Marriq down, but he was pushing himself as hard as he could go.

"There are an awful lot of establishments around here but not very many people to visit them," JC observed as they crossed beneath an arch into a new part of the city. Creeping along the arch were a number of thick, woody vines. The leaves on some of the vines were flecked with frost. JC stopped to pluck one of them, and Marriq took it from his hand.

"One of the shopkeepers told me that the hedonists have been gathering for meetings. That's unusual. I assume we will come across these meetings eventually—or perhaps Becky and Steven already have. Have you had any word from them?"

JC shook his head. "All quiet on Radio Becky. What's with the frost on that leaf?"

Marriq lifted the leaf to her nose and sniffed at it. "The frost is newly formed. That shouldn't happen—the furnace regulates the temperature of the city perfectly. It is a marvel of engineering. If frost is forming here during the daytime, that makes me nervous. We may not be able to continue our search at night."

JC shrugged. "You're the boss. I'm just here to look pretty."

Marriq dropped the leaf on the ground and the pair continued moving from shop to shop, stopping anyone and everyone they met to ask after Vanuella. For a time, while JC's strength was at a bit of a peak, they covered both sides of the road at the same time, with Marriq taking the left and JC taking the right.

He found the fatalists fascinating in an inexplicable sort of way. They were dull, apathetic people, but at the same time there was a passion in them that he could feel more than see. They had conviction, faith, in a way that no one he had ever known had possessed. It was just the fact that what they believed in—that their choices made no difference—was so screwed up... that was what he couldn't get his head wrapped around.

"I know her," a young woman said as she sullenly tapped on the counter of her bread shop. JC's eyes lit up—this was their first lead all day.

"She's a lamp maker on Eleventh. Unusual sort—she buys two good loaves of bread every week. Not many hedonists do much of anything with that kind of dependability." The woman popped a small cube of bread into her own mouth and chewed at it lazily.

JC asked, "So we can find her in her shop then, on Eleventh?"

The woman shook her head. "Doubtful. She's probably at one of those rallies. They have them a few times a day now, and all night long in some parts of the city. Most of the hedonists never miss them."

"What are they rallying for?" JC asked, trying to sound only vaguely interested. This covert spy-stuff was not his strong suit.

"The furnaces are failing. The hedonist leaders are trying to revolt against the fatalist administration to take control of the city's resources. We're only a few days away from open war again, I think." The woman continued to chew her bread, utterly unimpressed by what she was saying.

"Aren't you going to do anything about it?" JC asked.

"Why? What will be, will be. There's nothing we can do about it anyway."

JC said nothing else to the infuriating woman and hobbled back outside, leaning heavily on the walking stick. Marriq was waiting for him there.

"Anything?" she asked.

"Oh, plenty," JC said. "Let me get Becky on the horn so I don't have to repeat the story twice..."

He closed his eyes and reached out to Becky, feeling his way along the permanent link between their minds. The connection was tenuous and wispy, and he ground his teeth as he intensified his concentration—but it did not help.

He couldn't make contact with Becky's mind. Something had gone wrong.

# 18
## Onus

*The destruction of Igar Holc brought out all the worst in people.* Adam and Jara stayed close to one another, and were usually closely followed by guards from the Duchess' personal staff, but each day that had passed since Becky and the others had left for Arctos seemed to be worse than the day before.

Significant portions of the outer city were burning in spite of the endless rain. No fewer than three distinct raids had happened in the past twenty-four hours alone, and there seemed no end to the bandits and mercenaries that felt it was high time to attack Ain Holc.

"Many of them used to raid up in the Igar Protectorate," the guard that had drawn the short straw and been forced to stand watch over Adam and Jara said. "With the city fallen, there are no resources to plunder, so they've had to adjust. And with that storm wall keeping everyone south south, and everyone north north, Ain Holc is the next closest target."

Adam nodded. "How are the new troops settling in?" he asked.

The guard replied, "They've had little time to settle. Those last ones you carried in from Rega Holc have already been deployed to the north wall. Some irregulars from Norwin Holc are laying traps out in the ruin fields to the northwest. We'll get ahead of it soon."

Jara listened to them talk, but her mind was not on the content of their conversation. The Duchess had kept both her and Adam quite busy—Adam ferrying soldiers halfway across the world by crossgate and Jara plumbing the mysteries of fate for insight into when new attacks would come. The problem was that while Adam was dependable and steady, Jara was still an untrained novice. The limits placed upon her power by her mother were gone, as best she could tell, but still the magic wiggled and squirmed as often as it obeyed. She had offered little useful insight to the Duchess, and the increasing desperation of that bitter, vile woman drove Jara to desperation of her own. Her mother and grandfather were still prisoners of the Duchess, held as leverage to force Jara and Adam to cooperate.

And cooperate they had. Aside from the small act of rebellion each night when Jara distracted their baby-sitter guard while Adam snuck off to the Ebugar Spiralgate to open the door for their friends on Arctos, they had been model citizens of Ain Holc. But the fighting continued and Jara knew with absolute certainty that they would never be cooperative enough. The only way she was getting her family back—a family she had spent far too long away from over the past few years—was if she found them herself.

As Adam continued talking to the guard, Jara caught his eye and she saw him wink. That was the signal. As soon as she saw it she slipped quietly away from the pair of them, moving steadily towards the chamber door and then out into the guesthouse hall. They were still "guests" of the Duchess and quartered in the guesthouse, but Jara and Adam had already thoroughly searched the guesthouse. This was not where her family was being kept.

She bolted for the rear door, and once through it she made her way for the warehouse district. There were still many parts of the city they had not investigated, but the warehouse district seemed a good bet—she had a hunch. She was not certain if that hunch was mystical in nature or of the more common variety, but she was willing to take her chances. It would not be long before Adam's distraction was discovered and the Duchess dispatched a cadre of men to round Jara up. It was, by now, nearly a game. The question remained how many times they would be allowed to play it before Duchess Ain grew bored of it and ordered Moultus and Hessa killed.

Her half-run, half-walk through the constant drizzling rain that was to be the final legacy of the flying pirate ship was not particularly pleasant. The warehouse district was separated from the palace grounds by a thick band of manufacturing buildings and the tightly-squeezed peasant district. Like most cities on Onus, all citizens of the city proper lived within its walls—a legacy of Hyrak's rebellion. As Jara understood it, before the wars in the South began, Ain Holc had been surrounded by a massive sprawl of villages and towns. When the survivors of Hyrak's early assaults fled within the city walls, new homes were cobbled together in alleys and unused spaces, creating a near rat warren of homes that blocked whole streets in some places and never appeared particularly safe or cozy. Hyrak's war had changed everything—and it had been here, in the employ of the Duchess' late husband, that her own father had died fighting those men.

Jara wove her way through the residential areas as best she could with little natural light able to pierce the city's new shroud of rain clouds. She felt the tingle of her magic suggesting she was set upon an important path and hoped that it was the path she sought and not just some other destiny arbitrarily assigned importance by the magic of the Wyr. Someday she hoped to find a way to speak to another Wyr. It was said by her grandfather that she and her mother were the last, but neither of them had ever truly studied the old arts. Even if it meant seeking out a Wraithtender to call up the ghost of a Fatewaker, Jara wanted to ask someone to explain to her why her powers were among the most maddeningly useless things ever imagined.

As she slipped past a particularly unstable-looking building, Jara felt her magic whirl to life, bombarding her mind with images. They were tangled and garbled beyond any recognition and she found herself, slightly dazed, approaching the dilapidated doorway of the structure. It was a three-story building, although each story was barely tall enough for Steven or Yors to stand upright in. The sandy-colored bricks of the outer walls were cracked and offset from one another, shearing away from the adjacent building in a pregnant tumble that made the whole thing incredibly dangerous. Jara tried to calm herself, to draw steadying breaths that would help her mind make sense of the onslaught of future impressions, but just as she began to get a handle on the meditation, she felt a heavy, gauntleted hand grip her shoulder.

"The Duchess is tired of chasing you, miss," the guard said grimly.

Jara looked up at him—he was very tall and completely unfamiliar to her. Not one of the babysitter guards that had started to take a shine to her. "I just wanted to go exploring."

"You'll be exploring the dungeons of the palace, I think," the guard said.

Jara sized up the guard, looking over his chain mail and his heavy leather leggings. She thought a well-placed kick might get her free of his grasp, but she was not sure if he was alone or not. In the back of her mind, images continued to dance, slightly askew from one another and still nonsensical. She could almost make them out—but not if she was running away from this oaf.

She held out her hands in surrender. "Take me away," she said meekly.

The guard grabbed her offered hands roughly and proceeded to drag her back to the palace at a quick march. His legs were much longer than hers, and she struggled to keep up. The bouncing and the panting kept her mind from settling, and it wasn't until the guard deposited her back in her guestroom—which she now shared with Adam—that it started to make sense.

"Did you find them?" he asked, hopeful. He was sitting on the bed, legs crossed, when the guard tossed her into the room and slammed the door shut behind her. She heard the key turn in the lock.

She shook her head as the images of her vision started to click together. "No, but I found something else. The captain of the ship—Grell. He's alive. He's in the city." She chewed at her lip nervously. "And I know what he's going to do next."

¤~¤~¤

For the better part of a week, Brennid and Ambrek traveled across the northern continent. They shared the responsibilities of hunting and plotting their destination in silence for most of that days, and they made good time as they pressed across the narrow band of the Borrik Mountains that separated the Green Reaches from the Ullu Woods.

The campfire around which they sat blazed merrily as a brace of rabbits roasted on the spit that Ambrek slowly turned.

"Do you remember hunting in the mountains when we were boys?" Brennid asked.

Ambrek looked up at the leader of the Jovs and he thought he saw a spark of humanity, of decency, in him. "Vaguely. That was a long time ago," Ambrek said.

"I remember the trip we took, our class at the Academy, up here to hunt for mountain bison. Old Gurse brought us, on that wheel-less wagon he loved so much," Brennid reminisced. "I wonder what happened to that contraption."

"Jarrek took a lady friend from Ptorus Holc out in it one night. I believe he also took a cask of very expensive wine from his father's cellar. Not much survived the trip home, if I recall correctly—not the wine, not the wagon, and certainly not Jarrek's pride. That girl was a tough one, and Jarrek was never much of a charmer." Ambrek smiled.

"Did you know that there is no Ptorus Holc anymore?" Brennid asked. "Apparently old Duke Ptorus fought hard when the Council sent us away, and in exchange for his loyalty to us, the other Dukes stripped him of his lands and titles."

Ambrek nodded. "I had heard as much from some of the refugees traveling out of Distat Holc. They returned control of the protectorate to the line of Norwin. Can you imagine, restoring the good name of the only man who ever tried to claim the title of King over Onus?"

"They say the current Duke is a far cry from his ancestor. Some say he is among the easier of the Dukes to reason with," Brennid remarked. "I hope that is the case. I want to talk to him, after we have dealt with the chime. I want to reclaim old Jov Nought."

"Why?" Ambrek asked, lifting the rabbits from the fire and slipping them off on to a pair of camp plates. He handed one to Brennid. "I thought the plan was to establish the new academy at your camp in the Borriks."

"I think perhaps we need two homes, old friend. One for my people, and one for yours." Brennid took the plate and began to devour the rabbit greedily.

"Are we not undertaking this quest as a means of burying the grudges between us?" Ambrek asked from between mouthfuls of rabbit.

"We are undertaking this quest because it is one thing that we can both agree on. Are you really so naïve as to believe there will be enough other things that we can agree on that we can ever truly reconcile our differences?" Brennid spat a small bone into the fire, where it began to sizzle and pop.

Ambrek returned his rabbit to the plate and set it down on his lap. He leaned forward, towards the fire and Brennid on the other side of it. "So you mean to exile those that do not agree with you to the other side of the continent."

"Absolutely," Brennid said. "I'd think you'd be happy with it. It's a far gentler plan than the one I have been entertaining, where I hang you all for treason."

"Like you hung Kassun?" Ambrek asked. He gripped the edges of his plate so hard that his arms began to tremble.

Brennid looked away.

"Nothing to say?" Ambrek asked. "Nothing to say about your object lesson? Nothing to say about how you hung my best friend—your cousin—from your little town square while Houg, his father, watched?"

"I told you both that if you left for Rega Holc, you could never come back," Brennid said. "Why did you let him come back?"

"This is not my fault!" Ambrek roared, throwing his plate down and leaping to his feet. "*You* ordered it done!"

"I had no choice!" Brennid also came to his feet, and now he was making eye contact with Ambrek. His anger was clear, and in his hard eyes Ambrek saw his own anger reflected.

"Of course you had a choice! That's why we came back here, that's why we risked everything to escape from Murrod—so we could all have choices again! Yet the moment your feet touched the sand of the north coast beach, you started inventing ways to take those choices away from our people. You were never meant to lead us, Brennid. Never." Ambrek crossed his arms in front of him. "Jarrek named you his second out of pity."

Ambrek knew he had gone too far—but the thought of Kassun, his loyal friend and the best man he had ever known, murdered by this barbaric fool wounded him deeply. The civil war between the Metalbreakers was deeper and greater than even he, a leader of one side, had known. Until today, until now, he had not allowed himself to truly process what it was they were fighting over. The weight of their history and the span of their differences would never be overcome.

"It is your turn to re-work the hobs," Brennid said coldly. "I will leave you to it. If your work is sound, they will carry us clear of the mountains. The travel should be easier then." He turned away from Ambrek and left the light of the fire.

Ambrek had nothing to add. He had said all he could think of already—and far too much. As much as he wanted to bring the Jovs back together, perhaps Brennid was right. Perhaps they would be better off split in two.

He settled back down on the tree stump he had been using as a seat and drew a set of four Bindmetal ingots from the pouch at his waist. He rubbed them slowly and methodically in his hands, held out before the fire, and sang the magic of transportation into their depleted shapes. Each day they used the hobs to cover many days' worth of miles, and each night they had to be enchanted again, forged anew in the magic of Metalbreaking. Eventually, they would be strained past their limits and they would be rendered lifeless and inert, pure no more.

There was so much that the Jovs had in common with that mysterious metal.

¤~¤~¤

It floated below the surface of the water. A single pane of glass allowed its two occupants to see outside of its tiny cabin, and what they saw gripped them both with terror. The water was dark and endless, stretching as far as they could see in all directions.

Inside, a small sphere seemed to serve as the tiller, and with it they steered the vessel—it controlled direction and also depth. The tiny ship was perhaps twenty feet long and only ten wide, and it cut through the water faster than either of them had ever experienced.

Vediri kept her hands at the tiller-sphere most often, leaving Fendris at the small window to do his best to plot a course. They had a map with them—one of several things that the captain had stored away in this vessel for its eventual use. Weapons. Food. And the map. The map had a course marked in bright red, and they tried their best to follow it, but the map also filled both the first mate and the watchman of the Razormaw with fear.

"We're in a ship that travels below the surface of the sea, Vediri," Fendris bemoaned, "and that isn't even the strangest thing."

Vediri kept her hands on the sphere, finally, after much experimentation, feeling confident in its use. They had awoken in the ship, adrift, five days ago by her reckoning. They had not dared to break the surface of the water to see if their reckoning of the passage of time was correct, but she felt in her bones that it had been about five days. "It's time you accepted it, Fendris. We are playing our part in the captain's plan, and we will follow his orders."

"Did you know about this?" Fendris asked, turning from the window just as a large sea eel slithered past.

"Did I know there was a secret underwater pirate ship in the hold that could magically whisk us away from certain destruction? No, you ass. I did not." Vediri scowled.

"But did you know where we would be going?" he pleaded. "Tell me this doesn't terrify you!" He brandished the map before her.

Vediri shook her head and looked once more at the map in Fendris' hands. The course was clear. The features carefully labeled.

They were in the Silent Sea that stretched east from the coasts of both continents of Onus. No one sailed the Silent Sea. No one. Ever. Some said it was haunted. Some said the weather would crush any ship that touched its waters. Whatever the story, the fact remained—no one ever sailed in the Silent Sea and returned to tell the tale, and here they were. Heading further south still.

"We're going to die," Fendris muttered.

Vediri did not disagree with him.

¤~¤~¤

Narred was a simple man. While some men were born to rule, Narred was born to follow. He followed power as lightning travels from cloud to ground. He followed Tharsica of the Vols until he followed the Warlord Hyrak, and he followed Hyrak until he followed the Gatewitch Lyda. When Lyda was defeated, he'd been on his own for the first time in his adult life, and so, of course, he found someone new to follow—Shayra, Collectress of the Kem.

But a week ago, he left Shayra. He took the mule and he rode far and fast—as fast as a mule could carry him, at any rate. He was tired, for on his trek west he had slept only a little. While awake, he was able to use his power as a Boltsender to keep a thick screen of static in place in his mind, barring his wife from seeing his thoughts. When he was asleep, the effect was weaker, and now that their bond had grown strong over their year together, he feared she would be able to see through the screen and learn the truth of what he was doing.

He made the best time he could for Herin Holc. Mendul Holc was closer, by far, but Duke Mendul was an ally to Shayra and the Kem, and as such he could not be trusted.

Narred followed power, and the secret that he now carried, glimpsed by accident from his wife's mind in a moment of weakness and shock, carried with it dreadful power. There was no saving the Kem, for Narred knew better than most that no power on all of Onus could keep a secret hidden forever. But a wise man, a man accustomed to surviving and thriving and always landing on his feet, could get out ahead of this nightmare. If he brought the truth to the Council, they would forgive him for his part in Hyrak's war. They would be so focused on the eradication of the Kem that he would have the fresh start he so desired.

He would no longer be with Shayra, and for that he grieved. He loved her—more than he had ever loved anything, save perhaps himself. But she was a part of this now. If there was a way to save her, he would find it. But first, he would save himself.

¤~¤~¤

Cambria ran. The children were scattered, screaming, and she knew that she had failed her promise to the warlord of Mandor Arn. These children were not safe, and neither was she.

She darted through the lush, oppressive jungle. The sun was long set, but the heat did not diminish. The foliage blocked sight of the stars and the moons, so she had no means of navigating, save to run as close to a straight line as she could away from the stone clearing.

They had tried to leave the clearing behind. Each of the past six days she had rounded up the children and pressed onward into the jungle, striking towards Rura Holc and away from the heart of the Purpose-forsaken Vale of Steam. But each day, as the sun set, they found themselves broaching a particularly thick patch of jungle only to discover they had somehow turned around and returned to this place.

That was why she had ordered the children to run when the creature attacked.

It was nine feet tall and carved of the same stone as the clearing, dark and accented with thin veins of glinting metal. It lacked a head, but was in other ways bipedal—where a man would have possessed a neck, it had only a lump of polished orange fire opal that gleamed brightly. It had shambled into the clearing, and Cambria had ordered the children to scatter.

Now, as she tore through a lattice of vines before her, she saw that all of her exertion had been for naught. The clearing was somehow before her once more—but at least the creature was not.

She carefully stepped onto the stone, grateful for its strange coolness, and watched with sinking heart as one by one, the children burst from the surrounding jungle, drawn back as she was to this place. The youngest were wailing, with great tears rolling down their cheeks, and the oldest were ill-prepared to calm them. Their ordeal had been too great. Cambria crossed the clearing towards the largest cluster of children opposite her, seeing even more emerging on all sides of the five hundred yard expanse.

As she walked towards them, she could see some of them already beginning to calm down. She was reluctant to call out to them, worried that the sound could draw the creature back. As their crying softened she hoped that the creature, whatever it was, would wander off and leave them be. Then perhaps she would make another attempt at sending out a transmission to Vol Nought and request assistance.

She circled around the slight indentation at the center of the clearing—the crater that was the sole blemish on the surface of the great disc they stood upon—but as she did so she noticed one of the children across from her was pointing directly at her, screaming.

Cambria suddenly tripped, falling to the cool stone with a heavy thud. She looked back behind her to see what she had tripped over and saw that her left foot was trapped—engulfed in some sort of protrusion of the stone clearing. The stone had swept up and around her foot and ankle, squeezing tightly. She kicked at the protrusion with her other foot, but it was unyielding, and she began to panic.

She pointed one index finger at the lump of stone and willed a bolt of lightning into existence. The charge was faint—it was much easier to call lightning down from clouds than it was to generate it internally—but the brilliant bolt of blue-white energy lanced out and struck the stone with a dull, resonant humming sound. It recoiled, peeling away from her foot and flowing like molasses back into the ground.

Cambria scrambled to her feet, fighting off the wave of vertigo that always accompanied significant boltsending, and the children all around her cheered—but none of them came any closer. Their cheers were short lived, quickly fading to whimpers and resumed crying. Cambria started to trot towards the edge of the clearing. Her ankle did not take her weight well, and she feared it may have been sprained. As much as curiosity and growing dread compelled her to turn around and face whatever it was that was frightening the children, she pushed forward, away from the center.

The next thing she knew, she was flying. She was being held over head, high overhead, by two massive hands of stone. She was facing up, towards the sky. The moons were partially obscured by clouds, and she willed all of her arts to action, churning up the power in those clouds and calling it to her. This thing was too strong for her to beat in hand to hand combat—and she lacked even a sword with which to face it. Its grip was as sure as the stone it resembled, and she worried that its hide would be equally armored.

Lightning danced from cloud to cloud, hopping around and growing in intensity as it gathered charge and fury. The creature took a few steps, back towards the center, away from the children, and as Cambria looked around she could already feel the burden of this working—the incredible, unavoidable sense of dizziness—creep upon her senses. This was big—a tri-branch of a size she had never attempted before. Gendric would be proud—and any Boltsender even remotely in the area would know what was happening by the look of the sky. She would reduce this stone thing to ash and the others would come to rescue the children while she recovered.

The creature took another step, and Cambria felt them begin to sink. They had reached the crater in the center of the clearing, and somehow the creature was lowering down into, through, the stone with her in tow. She could wait no longer.

Three bolts of lightning ripped down out of the sky in rapid succession. Cambria tried to arc them around her own body and into the creature's chest, and the first two bent to her will, but the third came straight down, burrowing through her to reach its target. She willed the energy to flow through her, and most of it did, leaving her singed and shocked, but not seriously damaged.

As the light and the thrumming of the energy faded, she could tell they were no longer sinking—but she had not been released by the creature either. It stood firm, strong—unharmed. She closed her eyes, trying to fight off a wave of nausea, but there would be no more boltsending for her, not for a while. She had nothing left in her.

Then she was moving again, suddenly falling.

The creature brought her down, sharply, across its knee. She felt her spine break. She felt her life end.

¤~¤~¤

Grell wore dark clothes, including a head covering that shrouded his blond hair. Stealth was not his greatest skill, but he moved quietly and steadily, as he had since emerging from the safety of his hiding place within one of his depleted storm anchors. For the past week he had studied everything there was to study about Ain Holc, biding time for his other agents to get into place and waiting, always waiting, for the right time to strike. He possessed a map of great importance, the legacy of his mother, that indicated something he was looking for, something very important, was here in Ain Holc, but all of his searching had not yet revealed it, and the thirst for justice, for vengeance, in him grew strong.

The loss of the Razormaw chewed at him, for he had loved that ship more than almost anything. But he had always known it would not survive to see his total victory over the ten members of the Council. He had at least thought it would see him through three, though. Igar Holc was a ruin in his wake, and with its destruction he had crippled the whole of the world, for they now lacked a means of easily transporting goods and, most importantly, soldiers from the North to the South. The people of Ain Holc were still in a panic from his assault a week ago, fearful that another was coming. They had no idea what Grell had planned.

Grell studied the districts of the city, the structure of the walls, and everything else between, above, and below. His plans, careful and detailed, ripe with contingencies, were still in place. He was counting on Vediri and Fendris to do their part and secure the proof he needed that his father had not been spinning fables when he died. While they did that work—the most important part in the plan—he would bring the Council the destruction it so richly deserved. What was more, the people would cheer him on for doing it.

He had hoped to have secured the object his map led to before initiating the next stage of his plan, but he could wait no longer—he was too close to being found.

Grell walked quietly, swiftly, up the small flight of steps that led to the servant's entrance to the palace. His dark clothes were stolen from the clothesline of two servants of the Duchess, and as long as no one actually stopped to speak to him, he would pass as a member of the palace staff. He carried only a pair of daggers with him, but they were fine daggers, made by his own hand and embellished with his own innovations in Bindmetal crafting. They would be weapons enough, particularly since he had now determined that most of the strangers that had been responsible for his defeat were now absent from the city.

Had his ship arrived earlier, he might have had the chance to eliminate the whole of the Council in one murderous swoop. He had learned during his investigations that the Council of Lords was gathered here only a few nights ago, but now the damned Gatemaker had carried most of the northern lords home. How the Duchess Ain had gained control of a Gatemaker was a mystery to Grell—they were all supposed to be dead—but even more of a mystery was the girl, Jara, that had nearly stumbled upon his hiding place earlier in the evening. If she truly was of the Wyr, as the people believed, he had no choice but to act now before her prophetic insights shredded his entire plan.

The palace was quiet, but beginning to stir. Morning was coming, and that meant breakfast was being prepared in the kitchens and other servants, like those whose disguise he now wore, were starting to flit about the grounds, opening windows, readying clothes for the Duchess and her court, and all other manner of frivolity. This was a life Grell could not understand, and it was a life he would be happy to end.

There were guards stationed outside the Duchess' private chambers. Grell walked past the corridor once, eyeing them carefully. They had been on duty all night, but would be relieved by fresh men soon. They wore leather armor and carried spears and short swords—but what struck him most was that they were both young. Untested.

Grell slipped his knives free of their sheaths. In his left hand, he carried Silence, in his right, Shadow. The magic in each was faint and subtle—the type of work in which he was least skilled. But they would do. He spun on his heel and ran down the corridor, towards the two guards and the colorful painted doors of the Duchess' bedchamber.

One of the guards tried to raise an alarm, his mouth open wide as he shouted—but no sound emerged. The entire corridor was draped in soundlessness by the working in Grell's left hand, and then, with a flicker of will and intention, the working in his right hand stripped the light from the hallway.

In the quiet darkness, Grell had every advantage. He had trained in blind fighting for years. He dodged spear tips and sword strokes alike, slipping past the guards as they continued to flail about. He laid his hands upon the doors and considered sneaking past the guards altogether, but they would eventually reach the end of the corridor and summon aid. With an inaudible sigh, he slipped up behind each of the erratic guards and plunged the blades of his knives between their shoulder blades, ending them swiftly.

Then he threw open the painted doors.

The Duchess Ain was standing before a full-length mirror, a stout maid at her side holding two different gowns that likely cost more than the maid would earn in her lifetime. With a start, the Duchess turned to face the door—wearing only a night robe—and scowled at Grell. "One hundred men will fall upon you before you come a step closer," she said with cold finality.

Grell smiled and bowed. "As you say. I am certainly doomed. Whatever was I thinking, sneaking in like a thief in the night?"

"You are no thief," Duchess Ain said. "You are a murderer, I think. But we are ready for you. My Fatewaker warned me you were coming."

"Did she now? Then why was your door so poorly defended?" Grell arched an eyebrow. He hadn't prepared for this particular eventuality, but he saw in her posture something cautious—a lie, perhaps. A bluff.

"Because I wanted the chance to reason with you," Ain said. She made a dismissive gesture, and the maid scurried to a corner by the bed, cowering down nearly out of sight. "My treasury holds more than you can carry without your ship. I would offer you a measure of that gold and command of a fresh ship from Orrus Ain, one of the port villages in my protectorate. You can sail back to the Starlights a rich man."

"A tempting offer," Grell said carefully. "But what makes you think I am here for your gold? Did your Fatewaker tell you that?" He took three measured steps towards the Duchess, but she did not flinch. She was just barely out of the reach of his daggers.

"All men want gold or power. Gold is easier to carry, particularly for a pirate," Ain said with a small smile. "If it is power you prefer, I am sure something can be arranged. It is said that the Igar Protectorate needs a new lord, since Duke Igar failed to defend his city. Perhaps it is time for a change of title. Grell Holc has a certain ring to it, does it not?"

Grell slipped one dagger, Silence, back into its sheath. He took the last step towards the Duchess and extended his now-free right hand. "An offer too rich to refuse," he said, smiling.

The Duchess looked at his hand with momentary disdain then appeared to choke it back and reach forward to accept it.

In that moment, Grell gripped her by the wrist and spun her around, bringing her back up against his chest and the hand with the dagger up across her throat. The Duchess did not scream, but her body grew rigid with fear, and Grell whispered in her ear, "You would never look upon me as an equal, Duchess. Your eyes betray you, as you and the Council have betrayed all the men and women of Onus. I do not want your gold or your thrones. I want your suffering."

"Release her," said the maid.

Grell looked up to see that the maid was now standing, holding a longbow with arrow drawn.

"I thought you looked a bit sturdy to be a proper handmaid," Grell muttered.

"I'm a fine shot with the bow, pirate. I can and will hit you without hitting her," the maid replied. Grell could see that she meant it, and she held the bow like one who was born to it.

"You will gain nothing by killing me," Duchess Ain explained. "The Council will bend all of its powers against you. In a way, I think I would almost welcome death if it meant uniting the Council in the cause of the South at last. You would be doing me a favor." She pressed her throat up against the edge of his knife, drawing blood. "Do it!" she shrieked.

Grell whispered, "I will kill you when I am ready to kill you, your highness. First I will destroy you. First... I will destroy your city."

He willed the magic in Shadow to life once more, and the room was swallowed in blackness. He immediately dropped down to a squat, kicking the Duchess' legs out from under her as the maid's arrow flew past just above his head. In the bottom of his right boot was a tiny stud of Bindmetal, the oldest technique of the Metalbreakers. He tapped that foot sharply upon the ground and the magic in the hob activated, carrying both Grell and his captive away from the palace.

# 19
# ARCTOS

*Do you ever hear music in your head?* Not like the music that gets stuck in your head because you were listening to a song and then you got cut off before you heard the end so it stays in there, playing on repeat, until you do something to dislodge it. And not like one of those summertime pop songs that the radio stations team up to play over and over so that eventually it's just sort of existing in the background of your brain, like the sound of the wind or something. I mean music that gives your life a beat—the cadence of your emotions. If you don't ever hear that, I feel sorry for you—really sorry.

I don't know how old I was when I started hearing the music. Little—definitely little. My mom would say to me, "Joseph! Stop that racket!" more often than just about anything else. I'd grab anything I could find, but her pots and pans worked best, and I would beat out the rhythm in my head for all the world to hear. None of them ever appreciated it, but that's pretty much the story of my life.

When I first started noticing girls, the music became really important. It was like one of those ticking things that piano players use, a metronome, I think... the music in my imagination helped me set the pace. It told me when to speed up, when to slow down, and most of the time, it kept me out of serious trouble.

It didn't keep me out of the accident with the truck. Or lots of other things. It wasn't a super power like everyone else I know seems to have, it was just... I don't know. My dad would call it common sense. For me, it was something a little different. Like Spider-man's spider-sense, it warned me of danger, but not physical danger. Emotional danger. It was JC Stein's very own not-that-super-super-power: emotion sense. I knew when people needed to laugh, or when they needed to be left alone, and most of all I knew when *I* needed those things.

The music in my head pushed me up against Becky, over and over again, until I realized how much I liked her. It helped me get close, keeping my cool. (Shut up. I have cool. I *am* cool. Just not in a conventional way, I suppose.) My inner soundtrack brought me close to friends and close to love and close to the kind of acceptance I had always wanted.

Then I fucked everything up and put this stupid chain around my neck. I haven't heard the music since. Now I'm on my own, trying to figure out my life and how to handle the people in it without that "people sense" I'd come to rely on. I still feel things, I just don't trust my feelings. If a hunk of metal can change the way I feel, how do I know that anything I feel is real? Or that I am making the right moves with Becky?

That's how I knew that it had to come off. When Becky inherited Tatyana's powers and made that connection with me, when I could hear her voice and feel her heartbeat in my mind, I realized how much I missed the sound of my own heart, of my own brain and feelings—my music. For the better part of a year I'd been substituting that music with the sound of Becky in my head, but it wasn't right—it wasn't enough. The collar had to come off right then, right there, so I could be my whole self for her. For me.

But there is something that worries me.

What do I add to this crazy story that we've all been caught up in? Without the chain, I'm just a guy. A guy with laser guns, yes, but a guy. A guy that doesn't remember what it's like to be scared. I've been talking in circles around it for so long now, I... I think it's time to own it.

I put on the chain because I felt like a coward. I wanted to be a hero. If I take it off, will any of that have changed? Will I again be a coward, and no longer be a hero? Has anything I've done since Murrod been me, or has it all been the chain?

Yors hid himself behind another personality when horrible things happened to him. He made a whole 'nother person out of bright red Bindmetal and strapped it to his arm. The old part of him hid out behind the new part, and it didn't grow. It didn't change. It didn't heal.

Didn't I do the exact same thing? What if I'm not even Joe anymore? What if I really am just JC—a made-up person for a scared kid to hide behind?

Damn it. Damn it all to hell. I have no idea what I'm going to do.

¤~¤~¤

Becky and Steven were caught up in the press of bodies—many of them far more naked than she was comfortable with—as they swarmed about some kind of park on Venot's east side, listening to the rallying cries of a lithe man of middle years who stood atop an improvised platform made of heavy barrels stacked on top of one another.

"The furnace is dying! The fatalists knew this day would come!" the man shouted.

Around them, the crowd roared with laughter. In the communal exhalation of breath, Becky smelled the thick reek of alcohol. *Lots* of alcohol.

"But *we* knew it would too! We lived every day like it was our last, and the years have been good to us!" the man continued.

"Except for the needles!" shouted someone from the crowd.

The man replied, "Yes, except for the needles. But now the time has come for the old order to change again! Karrin has a plan, and we will follow! I have loved my life too long, too well, to let it be snuffed out in the night. The furnace may be failing, but it is not the only source of heat!"

The crowd grew quiet.

"The fatalists maintain caravans for trading with the miners and farmers in the Bounds," the speaker began.

"The wagons! The wagons have hearthstones! We can take those!" shouted a woman beside Becky. She glanced over at the woman and noticed that yes, yes indeed, she was not wearing a top.

The crowd roared agreement with the woman's idea.

"But only a few! There is another way, a safer way!" the man continued. The crowd responded well to him, and Becky was amazed that this mob was as well controlled as they were. This had every marking of a riot in the making. Somehow, they listened to the man on the platform. It was curious, but she didn't dare probe into the crowd with her powers. There were too many of them. She grabbed Steven's hand and said, in his mind, "We should get out of here. We won't be able to find anyone in this mess."

Steven nodded agreement and they started to push their way out of the crowd, but it was a task easier said than done. The men, women, and children were so intent upon the speaker that they hardly budged, even when Steven started to shove.

"We will take the caravans and we will send men and women to the villages. We will take *their* hearthstones for ourselves!" The speaker's voice rose considerably. "We will build a new furnace from those stones, and we will live to enjoy many more years of prosperity!"

Steven projected back into Becky's mind, "That plan is stupid. Marriq says the villages provide almost all of the food and the minerals needed to make lamps and forged metal and glass. If they all freeze to death, these idiots will die when the food runs out."

"Say it with me, Steven—not our problem," Becky replied mentally. "We get into so much trouble every time we go anywhere and get involved in local politics. Todd's right this time—we just need to get in to the Archive and get out of this world."

"I won't go to the Bounds!" shouted a man from the far side of the gathering. "It's dangerous!"

A few others murmured agreement with the man as Steven pushed another group of hedonists out of the way. They were almost free.

"We won't be going at all," the speaker said mirthfully. "That is the beauty of Karrin's plan! We shall send our fatalist brothers to do this work! We have bled for them for years, it is high time they bleed for us!"

The crowd erupted into another roar, and the people shifted around, momentarily separating Becky from Steven. A woman of average height was now between them, her back turned to Becky and covered in a long cascade of straight black hair. Becky grabbed the woman by the shoulder and pulled on her to squeeze past her, but as she did so, a brilliant white wave of energy burst from her hand, spreading out in a sphere around her for twenty yards and bowling over nearly a hundred hedonists and Steven. Left standing in the center of the event, Becky still had her hand on the shoulder of the woman, who had turned to face her assailant.

Becky stared at the woman's familiar features in shock. She was... her. She looked exactly like Becky. She was a tangent, Becky's tangent—her exact copy on another world.

Unbidden, her mind lashed out and struck the tangent's mind, connecting and hungrily scouring the other woman's thoughts and memories. The connection struck Becky's mind like a fist, and a second reaction, in some ways more devastating than the physical burst of energy, pressed in upon her mind.

Screaming, Becky released the woman and crumpled to the ground, her mental shields springing up stronger, tighter, than ever before, shutting out everything and everyone—but it was too late. She'd absorbed her tangent's memories, and the feedback in her mind was tearing her apart.

¤~¤~¤

"I still can't make contact with her," JC said sullenly as he followed Marriq to the shop that the bread maker said belonged to Vanuella. "Something is seriously wrong."

"We will figure it out. As soon as I speak with Vanuella, we will head back for the others. Surely if something has happened to her, Steven will get her back there." Marriq patted JC on the shoulder in a gesture that she meant as comforting, but the young man seemed unimpressed. She knew little of offering comfort to people—she had spent far too long with the Archivists to be in any kind of practice with compassion.

She spotted the place on Eleventh to which they had been directed, and she led JC to the doorway. There was a lamp on within, but Marriq found herself unable to put her hand on the door and enter.

"What is it?" JC asked. "Is this the place or not?"

Marriq sighed. "It has been a very long time. Longer than you have been alive. She may not remember me as fondly as I remember her."

JC groaned in obvious frustration and pushed past Marriq, leaning heavily on the walking stick as he opened the door and entered the shop. Marriq remained outside, making some show of examining the lamps on display in the front window. They were well-made, far more intricate than the simple globes that so many people used. Each glass receptacle was filled with blood and suspended within the blood was a faintly twinkling cloud of minerals—sparkdust. The combination of minerals blended to make the sparkdust would determine the color and intensity the lamp glowed. These model lamps did not currently glow, so she knew the catalyst valve at their base was in the off position. With a turn of that single valve, the blood and mineral mixture would make contact with the glandular compound harvested from mondeer herds in the Grey Bound. It was gruesome work that yielded great beauty, and Marriq had no trouble believing that Vanuella had found a fine second calling in the trade.

Inside, she could hear JC speaking with someone, a woman, but she could not make out the words. Gathering her courage, Marriq entered the shop.

"I'll be right with you," explained a beautiful woman, late in years but still vibrant. Her dark hair was threaded with gray and her face carried many wrinkles, but the curves of her figure and the brightness in her eyes marked the woman as Vanuella, Marriq's dearest friend in life and, she had once believed, true love.

Vanuella looked away from JC to smile at Marriq and her expression froze. Her eyes grew wide, and in them Marriq imagined all manner of rejection and disappointment. So she was surprised when the lamp maker rushed over to her and threw her arms around Marriq, squeezing tightly. "Marriq! You're alive!"

Marriq felt tiny tears well in her eyes, but she blinked them back. "Yes, yes. Very alive. And thus in need of breathing."

Vanuella released her grip and smiled the same dazzling smile she had used to such devastating effect all those years they had lived together in the Lodge of the Circle of Stone, during Marriq's studies.

"Where have you been? What brings you to Venot?" Vanuella asked. She seemed to have completely forgotten about JC.

"You," Marriq said softly. "I haven't much time. Horrible things have happened, and I... we," she gestured to JC, "need your help."

"Anything, my sister." Vanuella walked over to the door and closed it, closing a small curtain in the window of the door to indicate that the shop was closed.

"The Hindras live. They live in number and force, and they have taken the Archive as their home. I tried to gain access to the Archive, and they nearly caught me. They will be coming for me now—coming for all of us. They have survived in secret for so long, they will not allow any of us to know that they still live." Marriq could not help the fear that crept into her voice.

"Father never believed your story of the Hindra spirits," Vanuella said. "He thought you just made it up to soften the blow of your leaving the order."

"But you believed," Marriq said softly. "You told me you believed me."

"The Winterblood had to come from somewhere. The Hindras make as much sense as any other the Lodge's old theories. What can I do to help? I am of no use in a fight with mythological beings. I am just a lamp maker." Vanuella motioned towards the workbench, where a lamp was being assembled.

"We both know you are more than that. When the blood did not burn hot enough in you, your father named you Master of Services for the Circle of Stone. You coordinated all of our, all of *their*, works. You knew every Hearth Keeper by name. I am counting on you to know each of them by fate as well.

I need a Hearth Keeper. We have to travel to the White Bound, to the cave where... where it happened." Marriq looked down at the floor of the shop.

"Where you sacrificed the invaluable magic of your birthright? Where you made the choice to live apart from me and my family, the ones who had taken you in when your own family cast you out? You want to go back to the place that brought so much horror to your life?" Vanuella gripped Marriq by the shoulders. "Why?"

"It brought joy as well. Free of the fire in my veins I was able to study in the Archive, as I had always wanted. I have seen things, been to other worlds, and learned secrets of the universe. It was not a bad life," Marriq struggled to explain.

"It was a lonely one though," Vanuella replied.

"Yes. That it was. But I need your help because the key to beating the Hindras and retaking the Archive, and perhaps even saving all of us, was in that cave. The creature that took my powers lived in the far mountains of the White Bound. I must find more of its kind. They alone are powerful enough to kill the Hindras. No other force can do it." Marriq looked up at Vanuella. "Will you help me?"

Vanuella sighed. "Of course I will. There is a Hearth Keeper still living—maybe even two. Only one here in Venot though. I know that he will help you, but there is something you must know first..."

Before Vanuella could elaborate, the door to the shop burst open and a man entered. Sweat gleamed on his shaved head from running, and his shirtless torso was long and covered in hard, flat muscle. He had the tattoo of the Circle of Stone on his side—as Marriq did, even though she was no longer able to stand as a member of the lost order. His bronze skin was still youthful, but in his face Marriq could see the many years he carried with him. He was not young, though two decades younger than she was.

"You'll never believe what happened, 'Ella. Some fatalist wandered down into the steam tunnels. I almost got caught as I was..." the newcomer stopped as he realized Vanuella was not alone, and Marriq glared at him with sudden, painful realization.

"Not him," Marriq said. "Anyone but him."

"Marriq, he is the only one left in the city," Vanuella explained.

"Am I missing something?" JC asked.

Marriq turned to JC, away from the new arrival, and said, "This is Ebram. A long time ago, I gave up my power and my Winterblood so that he could live. And then he forsook everything I, we, ever stood for and sold his power to the highest bidder. He's a deplorable fool and he cannot be trusted to do the right thing in any circumstances, ever." She turned back to Ebram. "Does that capture the spirit of our relationship?"

Ebram's shoulders slumped. "I'm glad you are alive, Marriq."

"I wish the feeling was mutual," she replied sourly.

¤~¤~¤

Hunna woke in the back of an alley. His clothes were drenched with stale sweat and he still had a thick layer of the sludge from the bottom of the tunnels all over him, but he was alive. He felt his arms for puncture marks, but it appeared that he had also been lucky enough to avoid being sucked of blood by an unscrupulous blood-letter.

Hunna's mind was foggy—he couldn't quite recall what had happened in the tunnel. He seemed no worse for the wear, aside from missing several hours, and so he worked his way to his feet and decided to set off for home. Perhaps a nice meal would clear his mind.

The alley he found himself in was not a familiar one to the clerk, but few were—only hedonists too mad with drink or lust to retreat home for a night of sleep or love-making had any reason to frequent such alleys, and Hunna would never be confused for a hedonist. As he waddled out of the alley, feet still making squelching noises as they left a trail of sludge footprints behind him, he noticed that the alley was the space between two rather unsavory places in a part of town he most certainly did not visit. To his left he faced a refinery, and to his right a purification plant.

He shook his head at the grisly necessities of society. Blood was a liquid that did not freeze on Arctos, and blended with the dozens of minerals mined from the four Bounds, it made possible all of their conveniences and contrivances. But no one wanted to think about the hard work required of it. Most of the hedonists did not even properly understand the way a constant stream of blood was fed down feeder tubes to the furnace below as fuel.

The furnace. The idea of the great machine below the city stuck in his mind, sparking a few stray thoughts, but he could make little sense of them and so put them away.

The refinery blended minerals—a dirty, stinking job. The purification plant distilled and filtered the blood collected by blood-letters, sorting out impurities and irregularities to ensure that all the many works accomplished with blood were done correctly. From there blood was sold to artificers or farmers. Before taking the job as the birth clerk for the city, Hunna had briefly been a caravan runner, riding in the mondeer caravan that delivered blood to the farmers in the Red Bound and collected minerals and foodstuffs in return. That job had been torturous, but it brought to mind something he did not often think of—a lady friend.

While he worked the caravan, he had often been in charge of picking up the shipment at this very purification plant. Working there had been a lovely woman named Delya. He had taken quite a fancy to Delya, and she had, in turn, been very kind to him. Hunna had no friends—it was uncommon for a fatalist to care about such things, as everyone was going to die eventually anyway—but he realized that perhaps destiny had brought him to this alley for a reason.

The front door of the purification plant was locked, which was unusual but not unexplainable, so Hunna bustled his way around to the rear entrance, where he had often parked the mondeer sleigh to be loaded with barrels of blood.

The door opened easily as he pressed on the latch, and with a small self-congratulatory smile for his genius, Hunna entered the plant. He felt at one of his pockets, damp from sludge, and was comforted to find that the small pouch he kept there, for times of anxiety, was still in place. The thought of seeing Delya again certainly stirred a bit of the old, debilitating anxiety in him, but he fought it off. He would see her clear-headed, if at all possible.

The steady bubbling of filtration systems was a familiar and almost comforting noise, but he also heard people talking, including a woman, and Hunna thought that it might be Delya. He hurried himself along the elevated walkway towards the main offices of the building and then stopped. Below him, standing between two vast, multi-story glass tanks of purified blood, was Karrin. All around her on the metal-grated ground floor there were barrels and jugs, some of blood, but others sealed and bearing the marks and symbols of minerals, but none of them from the Venot refinery—he knew those signs quite well.

Karrin was speaking to a man that Hunna did not know, but it was her voice he had heard, not Delya's. That explained why it had been familiar, but he could not help but feel disappointed that it was not his old acquaintance.

"The riot will begin any moment now," the man speaking with Karrin said. "Everything is primed and ready. The fatalists will capitulate—they always do."

Karrin put a hand on the man's shoulder and said, "Excellent work, Perrin. By morning, the hedonists will rule the city and the fatalists will be out of the way. Things will finally be as they should be."

"You sound like a fatalist when you say such things," the one called Perrin chided. "Be careful that you not let the others hear it."

Karrin spat at the ground, and Hunna swore he saw the spit spark as it struck the metal-lined floor. "I'll be quite happy to be done with those divisions. Are you sure the hedonists can be trusted to play their part?"

"Absolutely. They're simple-minded as it is, but after your blood-letters have been working on them these past few months, most all of them have a few ounces of the good stuff working around in their veins. They'll do as they're told."

The pair left, both heading to the lower offices and, Hunna surmised, up the stairs to the ground floor front entrance.

Carefully, quietly, he slipped back towards the back door. Whatever was happening, it was not meant to be. Karrin was tampering with the natural order of things, and the others had to be warned.

As he opened the door to the street, Hunna was overcome by the roaring mass of people rushing through the streets. They were heading northward—towards the inner city. Towards the homes of the fatalists.

It was too late for warnings. He had no idea what to do now.

¤~¤~¤

The walk back to the abandoned building where they had left Yors and Todd was awkward. JC was keeping up with everyone, thanks to the walking stick, but other than that, he had little say to recommend the trio of Arctosians as traveling companions. Marriq and Ebram said virtually nothing to each other, and Vanuella spent the hour that they walked trying to convince them to bury the hatchet. Marriq did not strike JC as the type that buried hatchets, but still Vanuella tried.

They entered the building to see Steven and Todd bent over Becky, who was collapsed on the floor in the middle of the big open space. Yors stood at the foot of the stairs, eyes wide.

JC rushed past Marriq into the room and dropped the walking stick, lowering himself to his knees. "What happened? Was she attacked?"

Steven shook his head. "She ran into someone on the street that looked just like her. I know you guys explained that to me, but I can't remember the word for it."

"A tangent," Todd supplied, backing off to give JC room to get closer to Becky.

She was breathing, but each breath was shallow. Her skin was cool to the touch and her forehead was creased as though she was concentrating.

"She touched her, the other her, I mean, and there was a bright flash of energy. Then I felt her mind shut me out, like it was a turtle pulling back into its shell," Steven said. "I'm sorry, Joe. I should have done a better job of keeping her safe."

"She can keep herself safe. We sent her to keep an eye on *you*," JC muttered. "You can come back to me, right baby?"

Becky didn't respond.

JC put a hand on her forehead. He tried again to access her mind through their link, and this time he got an impression—not contact, but a glimmer of thought. "It's all crazy and confused inside her. She must have, I don't know—the tangent must have messed up her powers or something." He looked up at Yors. "Her mind is confused and kind of broken. You can fix that, right?"

Everyone joined JC in looking at Yors, and the big man sighed. "Yors not good at that. Yors had help other times. Jarrek make Yors' coin. No Jarrek, no Bindmetal, no help."

JC looked back down at Becky and then up at Yors. "Can you try?"

Yors came down the stairs, moving cautiously, and then sank to his knees next to Becky. He looked at her carefully, then looked up at JC. He reached forward and wrapped his hand around the chain at JC's neck. "This hurt," he muttered. Then with a sharp twist, and an echoing boom like a massive drumbeat, JC felt the chain crunch up tighter around his neck. Yors' hand came free, and in it was a single, glimmering red link of Bindmetal chain.

JC felt the chain around his neck, and it had indeed gotten tighter—somehow Yors had plucked a single link from the chain. Only thirty-two active links remained.

Yors' hand was smoldering, and JC could see the flesh of the hand beginning to blacken and crack, blood seeping out and sizzling. Yors grunted in pain and then closed the hand into a tight fist around the link. He stood up and started to pace the room, around everyone who watched in stunned silence. His footfalls were a beat, and JC joined him, struggling to his feet and matching the beat. He didn't know if that would help, but he had to do something.

Yors brought his other hand, also balled into a fist, beside his first, then he brought them together into a prayer-like gesture, the metal trapped between his two palms. He stomped louder. JC stomped louder. Some of the others joined in—Todd, Steven, even Vanuella.

With a scream, Yors pulled his hands apart into two fists and extended them both to JC. As he opened those fists, he revealed a pair of small red hoops—earrings. Both his hands were badly burned.

"These keep Becky separate from confusion in mind. Yors not strong enough to pull two things apart, but if others can, Yors can *keep* them apart," he explained in harsh tones. Yors leaned up against a wall, panting for breath.

JC crawled back down on the floor, next to Becky. "How do I clear her head? I just need to do it for a second, right?" He looked at Yors, and the smith nodded.

"I may be able to help," Ebram said. The Hearth Keeper had been quiet since their arrival. He wore a shirt now, obtained from the back room of Vanuella's shop (which had elicited all manner of strange looks from Marriq—JC suspected something more was going on there than he knew). He knelt next to Becky, her head between his knees, and he placed his forefingers on her temples. "I can sometimes cloud people's minds—it is a trick of the Winterblood that many cannot manage. I may be able to do that in reverse for your friend."

Ebram lifted each of his palms to his mouth and bit them, drawing a tiny droplet of blood from each. He rubbed the blood into the soft flesh of his palms and then placed his palms on Becky's temples. He grunted, and his eyes rolled back in his head for a moment.

JC watched the seconds tick by in agony.

"Her mind is shielded—I have never seen anything like it. I can get through it, open it up, but that is all." Ebram's eyes rolled back forward. "Will that help you?"

JC nodded vigorously. "You get me an opening, and I can bring her back. I know it."

Ebram nodded and rolled his eyes back again, pressing firmly on Becky. After a few seconds he grunted, "Now."

JC took Becky's hand in his own and squeezed tight. He grabbed hold of their mental link, feeling it spark with energy now that Ebram had lowered her shield. He poured into that energy his love, his memories of her, his hopes and dreams, like pouring fuel on a bonfire. If he could get it to burn bright enough, she would find her way to him. He knew it. This was what love was—this enduring commitment to one another. Overcoming all obstacles.

For what seemed like an eternity, nothing happened. He poured everything he had, everything he was, into their connection, and still, she did not appear. He visualized the formless black space that they used to talk—his own, since hers was under siege. But she did not appear.

Then something changed. His voice felt louder, amplified somehow, and the connection strained against his mental grip. Something was pulling at it. He tried to reel the metaphorical rope in, and as he did so, Becky slowly appeared before him, faintly lit, in his mental landscape. She was sweating, covered with bruises, but she was there. She was free of the chaos in her mind for a moment... they embraced.

JC opened his eyes as Yors pinned the delicate backs of the earrings through Becky's ears. They glimmered with magic, and Becky opened her eyes.

JC smiled down at her and went to pull her up into a hug, and that was when he noticed that her other hand was being held. By Steven.

JC looked across his girlfriend at Steven and asked, "What just happened?"

Steven shook his head, eyes wide. "I was trying to help."

JC said nothing. He helped Becky sit upright and gave her that hug, but it wasn't the same. As he embraced her, Becky whispered in his ear, "Thank you."

"Earrings short magic," Yors said from across the room. "Magic will fade as damage fixed. Few days and Becky good as new."

Becky glanced at Yors gratefully.

JC turned to face Ebram and offered him a hand to help him stand up. Ebram took his offer, and soon everyone was standing in a loose circle in the center of the room.

"We should leave immediately," Marriq said. "Rioting has begun in the city, and it won't be safe for anyone before much longer. Ebram," she glared at the Hearth Keeper, "will supplement our hearthstone. We make for the White Bound and for the mountains beyond."

"Why?" Todd asked. "What, specifically, is your plan for getting into the Archive?"

"There are beasts that live in those mountains," Ebram explained, "that are the natural enemy of the Hindras. Marriq and I have history with them. She thinks they can be convinced to help us fight off the Hindras and reclaim the Archive."

"And what do you think?" Todd asked.

"I think it's the best plan you have," Ebram said. "And I'm willing to join you in it, so long as my wife stays here."

Vanuella and Marriq both turned to Ebram in shock. Vanuella spoke first. "I will do no such thing. I am coming with you!"

Marriq, however, said only one thing. "Wife?"

# 20
# ARCTOS

*If Steven never saw another snowflake, it would be too soon.* For two days of awkward, horrible silence their group pressed southwest, away from Venot and into something called the White Bound. It was a place familiar to Marriq, and so she took the lead again. Steven was consistently impressed with the drive and strength of the old woman, who seemed to have more energy than any two of the others combined.

Each night they made camp protected by the combined power of the hearthstone heater that Yors carried and Ebram's magical blood. In the two days they traveled, Steven's own strength had largely returned and JC's wound had been healing rapidly. The wound that had grown between them though—that seemed beyond repair.

Becky was especially quiet, and that was a sure sign that something was wrong. Steven wanted to ask her how she was doing, but any time he came even remotely close to her, JC bristled with a muddled combination of hurt and anger. So Steven let them both have their space. Todd had become even more withdrawn, and Steven was growing more and more certain that Todd may have been right all along—they should have left Arctos when they had the chance.

They had left the riots and growing tumult of Venot behind, but they now carried their own special brand of dysfunction into the wilderness of this barren world.

"What have we been eating all this time if nothing grows here?" he asked Ebram as they walked. The Hearth Keeper and his wife had retreated back towards the rear of the group with Steven and Yors after yet another rebuffed attempt at conversation with Marriq.

"Most of our foodstuffs are drawn from fungus cultures that grow in caves. There are many growing caves under the furnace cities, and still more out in the Bounds. There are other vegetables that grow in the Grey Bound, as well as livestock and wildlife that frequent its gentler climate." Ebram pointed forward. "Out here in the White, it's mostly mineral mining and cave growing. The cities have arranged as much trade as possible, but that's been faltering for years."

"So your whole world isn't covered in snow and ice?" Steven asked, intrigued.

Vanuella laughed. "Of course it is."

"You said the Grey Bound was gentler," Steven pointed out to Ebram.

Ebram nodded. "It is. The days are longer there, the nights shorter. It takes significantly less power for a hearthstone to protect a village or a herd shelter, so the old stones last much longer. The loss of the Circle of Stone has not harmed the Grey Bounders nearly as much as it has the White or Black or Red."

Steven considered that for a moment. "You don't happen to have a map, do you?"

Vanuella replied, "No. Maps are drawn on paper, and paper and Hearth Keepers are a dangerous combination." She looked forward at Marriq's back. "It's why they were forbidden from accessing the Archive."

Steven sighed. He was starting to get a picture of what had gone on between these three, even though he'd only heard parts of the stories. Whereas Becky or JC would have just pushed on obliviously and asked for more information, Steven was raised better than that. He did his best to politely change the subject. "Can I ask how you did what you did with Becky's mind back in Venot? I thought I understood what it was a Hearth Keeper can do, but mind magic seems a bit outside the scope of that."

Vanuella touched her husband's cheek fondly. In that gesture, Steven forgot about the age difference between the two of them. They truly were in love—which he imagined made Marriq's pain all the more agonizing.

"Ebram is alone in that gift. Before my father died, he tried for several years to understand why Ebram could stir the Winterblood to touch the minds of others. As best we can tell, it has to do with the... the events that transpired in the mountains when he was young."

The day was drawing to a close, and Marriq stopped, holding up her hand in the familiar gesture that indicated the setting of camp. Yors nestled the hearthstone down in the snow and Ebram automatically set about walking a circle around it and sealing that circle in a shimmering line of his blood.

Marriq approached Vanuella as Ebram was walking off the circle. "They touched him. You know it as well as I do. Your father never truly believed in them, so he could never understand the truth." She sighed. "It's almost enough to make me believe in fatalist doctrine. Ebram is the last Hearth Keeper in Venot. Ebram developed the mind-speaking power of his captors. It is his captors we now seek. I sense the hand of providence in this."

Vanuella smiled, and Steven watched Marriq's face light up, its age lines almost melting away in the expression. Vanuella said, "He will find them. If they still live, he will find them."

"They still live," Marriq said confidently. "That's why they will help us. They want more than anything to die, and we bring them the one way they can do so."

Vanuella's eyes narrow with suspicion. "Why did you need a Hearth Keeper? You have a hearthstone in good repair, so it wasn't to protect you on the journey itself. Why did you need Ebram?"

Marriq looked down at her feet, and Steven found himself holding his breath. What had they gotten themselves into?

Marriq looked up, and her eyes were cold. "Bait."

¤~¤~¤

JC and Todd climbed a hill on day six. The wind had mostly calmed and there was no snow falling at the moment, so JC was hoping they would catch a glimpse of the mountains after days of practically zero visibility. As they crested the hill a full hundred yards ahead of everyone else, they did indeed see the mountains.

JC had never seen anything like the endless wall of stone that stretched across the horizon. There were two ranges, one immediately in front of the other. The front row of mountains were like the Borrik Mountains on Onus—broad and numerous. They were tall but not so tall that *tall* was the first word that sprang to mind to describe them. Behind them though—those were tall mountains. The rear row of mountains were like a giant wall of overlapping white-gray stone, rising so high that they met the clouds. JC suspected that the days would be longer in the White Bound if these mountains did not exist—they swallowed the setting sun faster and more completely than the natural turning of the world would require.

"That's pretty damn cool," JC said, whistling.

"But that's not," Todd said, pointing down the hill before them.

At the foot of the large hill, between them and the mountains, was a village. A full day's travel, or more, separated the village from the mountains, but that was not what Todd was pointing to. Todd was pointing to the scene of carnage below.

There had once been perhaps a dozen standing structures—huts and shacks, by the look of things—in the village. None remained. Their slanted stone walls were tumbled over, and there were bodies barely visible among the snow-covered rubble. In the center of the village, an igloo-shaped dome of large stones had once existed, but it was shattered, pulled apart. From their high vantage point they could look down upon that broken dome and see that something at its center had been ripped up from the earth.

And everything was covered in frost and snow.

The others caught up to JC and Todd and as they looked out, and down, there were several gasps. Becky took JC's hand, and he squeezed her back, his anger about her connection with Steven momentarily forgotten.

"The hearthstone," Ebram said. "It's been taken."

"Then the hedonists were true to their word," Vanuella said solemnly. "They have begun raiding the villages in the Bounds. With a mondeer pulling a caravan wagon, they were probably here a day or two ago."

"If they would have just let me, I could have fixed the furnace!" Ebram said angrily. "I almost had it! This didn't need to happen."

"In endless cold and boundless ice, against the creeping touch of night, the lodge of old and timeless stone stands for the small, weak, and alone." Marriq said softly.

Becky looked at her with an arched eyebrow. "You don't strike me as the poetry type."

"It isn't poetry," Vanuella explained. "It is the oath of the Hearth Keepers." She put an arm around Marriq and pulled her close. "It is your oath no longer, sister. This wasn't your fault."

"No," Ebram said. "It was mine. When I abandoned the old ways, I abandoned the people who depended on us. I spoke the words of the oath with my lips, but never with my heart."

Todd suddenly started down the hill, towards the village. JC slipped out of Becky's hand and stumbled through the snow as he raced to catch up.

"What are you doing?" he asked, panting slightly.

"I'll see if they left any food behind. The packs are getting light, and whatever happens in the mountains, we still have to make it back to a Spiralgate." Todd coughed. "I... we don't have much time."

JC kept pace with his usually stoic friend as they drew nearer the devastated village. "Anything you need to tell me?"

"I've been away from Adam too long. We all have. This was supposed to be easy, and nothing about it has been easy."

They came to the threshold of the village, a two-foot wide band of thick, polished ice. Snow had coated it, but the breeze still swirled the flakes across its surface in places, revealing the gleaming boundary beneath.

"It's like this village. It's here because the people had to band together to survive. There weren't enough resources, enough power, to keep each of them safe alone. Together, they could depend on one another. Apart, scattered, they were all vulnerable," Todd said.

They stepped over the ring of ice. JC felt the currently-welcome warmth of the magic in the chains at his throat rise up. During their six days of travel, Yors had managed to strip the magic from four more links—but still the chain did what it was built to do. He felt no fear. "Staying together didn't save these people though," he said.

"I know," Todd said sullenly. "Being together isn't enough. You also have to be willing to fight. To do horrible things. You have to be willing to do whatever it takes to protect one another. Look around. Does it look to you like these people even fought back?"

JC looked around, and Todd had a point. There were no weapons. There were bodies with their skulls caved in, bodies run through with spears, but no one held even a single weapon. JC shook his head.

"Sticking together is only the first part of surviving," Todd said. "The rest is a lot harder."

¤~¤~¤

Hunna hid in the shadows of the great city he had lived in his whole life. Everywhere he went, he was in danger. He knew too much, and he knew, in his bones, that they would kill him if they caught him.

It had been four days since the last of the caravans was sent out, laden down with fatalist workers. Perhaps a double handful of fatalists remained in Venot, and those that did were being hunted down and executed by Karrin's new regime. The hedonists that had assumed power were not like the others. Just as Karrin had always seemed somehow more alluring than ordinary women, so too did the other men and women of her inner circle. Hunna had not even bothered to learn their names, but he knew that when they spoke, the ordinary hedonists listened.

A cult had grown up amongst the hedonists, a near-worship of Karrin that bordered on sacrilege. Religion was a long-dead habit on Arctos, but somehow Karrin stirred in these people some primal need that Hunna simply did not feel.

There was no escaping the city. As the last of the caravans had left, so too had the last of the hearthstones. The caravans would return, laden down with food and minerals and new hearthstones which Karrin promised to install throughout the city to keep everyone safe and warm, but... Hunna did not believe her.

He did not want to die.

The safest places to hide were the outskirts of the city. These were also the coldest places, as the past few days had seen a marked decline in the amount of heat generated by the furnace. The fountainworks was closed—the hot water fountains were no warmer than the cold water ones. Old loyalties and duties stirred in Hunna for a time, and he wondered how many children had been born that had not had their name read with the dawning of the morning sun.

Hunna's current hiding place was at the very edge of the city, a multi-family home that had a thick caking of permanent frost on the rear wall—the wall that faced away from the city. No one would come here looking for him, and if he was lucky, he would not quite freeze to death in the night.

He climbed the steps to the roof of the building. The work was laborious for one of his impressive girth, but he was in no particular hurry and stopped at the second floor landing to catch his breath. When he reached the top, he peered through the doorway carefully, desperate to remain unseen. But he also had to see what was happening. He had heard only the faintest hint of Karrin's plan, and curiosity burned in him. He knew the right and just thing to do was simply let it happen, to accept that all was as it was meant to be, but somewhere in the past two weeks, Hunna had begun to question his fatalist inclinations. He was no hedonist, of course—but maybe he was a traditionalist. Maybe the balance between resignation and gratification had been right all along?

His caution paid off as he caught sight of a pair of Karrin's enforcers—hedonists loyal to her but in no way particularly skilled at hurting people. They slunk about in the streets, perfunctorily searching homes, but they did not come all the way down the road to this home. After a few minutes they had passed out of sight, and Hunna stepped quietly onto the rooftop. The city was as it had always been, but quieter. He could not even see or hear any of the frequent gatherings and rallies put on by Karrin's lieutenants.

It was what he saw beyond the city that changed everything.

Two dozen men (some of them may well have been women—Hunna's eyes were simply not very good) approached the city from the west, the sun setting promptly at their back. They were pale-skinned, with bright white hair. They wore traveling clothes of fur and hide, mostly—a handful wore long white robes. They marched on the city and were still perhaps half an hour away, but the sun would be set in mere moments. They did not hurry or rush, and as the sun sank out of sight and the bitter cold rose up around Hunna—not quite enough to kill him, thankfully, for even the faltering furnace still deadened the worst of the night—he saw the travelers were completely unaffected.

In his bones, he felt fear. Old stories, childhood tales of monsters coming out of the night, roared unbidden into his mind.

The men who were not, could not be, men walked into the city and past the building in which Hunna took shelter. He fled back indoors and down to the ground floor, watching the dozen strangers through a grimy window. They flowed past and came upon the same group of enforcers that had swept this part of the city earlier. The men, carrying knives openly in each hand, even though Hunna doubted they had ever used a knife to so much as cut a mondeer steak, saw the strangers and then, in unison, fell over. Their skin has the pale blue of one dead of exposure in the night.

Hunna suppressed a shudder. The strangers were monsters, and they had come to a Venot that was half empty and protected by a broken furnace and a madwoman. Panic gripped him.

He fumbled in the pouch at his waist and drew out the small packet of powdered desix. It was a rare pleasure in Venot to have such a treat, and the use of the stuff was strictly limited to occasional ingestion by fatalists like Hunna that sometimes succumbed to anxiety fits. Desix calmed the nerves and mellowed the mind, which was exactly what Hunna needed right now. He knew the risks—too much desix use left a person's wits addled, their will soft, and the mineral was highly addictive. Hunna was a rule follower, and so he took only the smallest amount of powder from the packet and sprinkled it on his tongue to be absorbed into his body.

As the wave of calm washed over him, Hunna experienced a moment of clarity. He remembered, before the calm carried him to a blissful near-sleep, where he had first met Karrin.

Karrin had been the woman from whom he purchased his desix. She was the one from whom everyone he knew that used the stuff purchased it. She was a trader from the Black Bound, he recalled. Her family worked the...

The largest desix mine in the world.

He understood how she had done it, in that moment of clarity. He understood how she had won over the hedonists so completely. But the desix was doing its job in him, now, and he did not care about anything so much as simply sitting still and melting off to sleep.

¤~¤~¤

It was early morning on the eighth day when they reached the mountains. Becky had been uncharacteristically quiet throughout the journey, and now that they were here, she found that they had more important things to worry about than JC's hurt feelings. She touched him on the shoulder and said, aloud, "Do you think this will work?"

He shrugged, and she took comfort in that familiar gesture. "Maybe. Maybe not. They are very impressive mountains, either way. Can you feel any of these things we are looking for out there?" he asked. "If they have mental powers, maybe you can pick up on that?"

Marriq joined the pair of them and smiled. "My thoughts exactly. The Kutak I met spoke in my mind, like you do. It also spoke aloud, but I always felt like it did that only when it must."

Becky sighed and closed her eyes. They didn't realize what they were asking of her, of course—she hadn't talked to them about what happened in Venot. Everyone had been so busy being pissy about who saved her that no one had asked why she'd needed saving in the first place.

Becky's mental shields were in place constantly, even though the earrings that Yors had made for her—and stuck through earlobes she was perfectly happy being earring-free, thank you very much—had washed away the mental impressions she had accidentally absorbed from that other version of herself.

None of them had met their own tangent before, besides Mathias. And none of them, including Mathias, could do what Becky could do. She had, in that momentary contact, soaked in an entire lifetime of memories that were not hers. They fit perfectly into her mind—they were ordered and structured in exactly the same way as hers, after all. She had lost herself, lost the ability to distinguish amongst the two identities, and it had driven her mad. Then there was the strange echo, the building of tension and power in her mind. She had heard from Mathias the stories of how each successive physical contact he had made with his tangent had unleashed more and more destructive energy. The same thing appeared to be true of mental contact, and Becky had instinctively bottled up that energy inside her. The trick that Ebram, JC, Steven, and Yors had pulled off healed the damage done by that other set of memories and thoughts, but the energy was still there, still bottled up in her mind behind her shields.

So now she restructured those shields, segmenting that power off separately. She opened up a bit of her mind and her power to reach out and skim the area around them, probing for minds that might be these Kutaks that Marriq and Ebram spoke of.

The trick seemed to work—except that Becky could feel nothing.

"If they are in these mountains, they are not close enough for me to sense," she said as she opened her eyes. "Do you have a plan B that does not include climbing up those things?"

Marriq sighed. "Ebram, we must do this my way."

Vanuella grabbed at her husband's arm as he took a step towards Marriq. "Don't do this! It is too dangerous!" she pleaded.

Ebram brushed her off. "I made an oath that I have broken. This is my chance to make that right. Let me do what your father taught me. Let me do what *you* taught me," he said. He stopped and turned to her, smiling. "It was not so very long ago that you sent me out on missions into the Bounds to do things just as dangerous."

Vanuella pulled him against her in a tight embrace. "That was before I fell in love with you."

"With your love, I am stronger than I ever was without it—and I survived back then," he said, returning the embrace.

Becky tentatively brushed her thoughts, still situated for probing, against Marriq's. The old Archivist's mind was a whirl of emotion, but it was not as clouded with darkness and jealousy as Becky had expected. She wasn't sure Marriq herself could have described exactly what she was feeling, but there was both love and pride in it.

Ebram disentangled himself from Vanuella even as Becky did the same from Marriq's mind. Then the Hearth Keeper—the last of his kind, perhaps—took a few steps away from the group, nearer the steady rise of the first low mountainous foothills.

He reached into his pocket and drew out a small metal ring, which he slipped in his finger.

"He kept it," Marriq muttered.

Ebram twisted the ring on his finger so that its jeweled setting was pointed inward, and Becky thought she saw that the setting came to a sharp point. Then he drew the ring across his other hand, freeing the blood that boiled in his veins. A wave of heat washed outward from him, followed by a shower of sparks and smoke.

Ebram waved the hand in the air, and Becky felt his mind press outward in a kind of cry or shout. It splashed harmlessly against her shields, and as she looked around at the others, they seemed to not have noticed.

Then she felt Yors put one heavy hand upon her shoulder and whisper in her ear, "We being watched."

Becky looked around, at the nearby crags and lowest peaks, and at first she saw nothing. Then she saw JC tense and unsling one of his rifles, which he handed to Todd. Todd too had tensed, and a moment later they were both holding the weapons.

Becky saw it at that point—a huge white creature, camouflaged in the snow. It was large and furry, hunched over so that it could run on all fours, but its front legs ended in large-knuckled hands with thick, sharp nails. Its head was attached to its hunch-backed body by a short, stumpy neck, and its lower jaw protruded over its upper, revealing large tusks. Its eyes were cold and bright but deep-set behind a heavy brow ridge. It was hard to properly judge its size at this distance, but it looked like, standing on its hind legs, it may have been over ten feet tall.

"I'm not sure we can actually beat that thing if negotiations fail," Becky whispered.

"Things," Yors said, emphasizing the plural. Becky slowly turned her head, and now that she knew what she was looking for, she saw them.

There were probably a dozen of the giant, furry beasts.

And they were all staring at Ebram.

She tried to probe their thoughts, but the power she was holding in check limited her strength. She could detect them only faintly, and only when she was looking right at them. Their surface emotions were a blend of hunger, need, and rage.

One of them reared up on its hind legs and roared, "It is my day to die!"

The others also reared up and roared, calling challenges to one another.

"They're fighting over who gets to die?" JC asked. "That's weird." He lifted his rifle and aimed at one of the Kutaks. "I can help them out," he said.

"No," Ebram said, holding up the hand that wasn't smoldering with shed blood. "Fighting them will not aid our cause."

As Ebram lifted that hand, it was like a starter pistol had been fired. The Kutaks rushed down out of the mountains, roaring, and it was all Becky could to do block out the bloodlust in their minds.

¤~¤~¤

Yors stepped forward. He unstrapped the hearthstone heater from his chest and allowed it to fall to the ground with a heavy thud. He nearly reached for his newly-mended crossbow, but it wasn't going to help. He knew that.

The creatures reminded Yors of the Ellir on Murrod. They were powerful and alien and they made everyone afraid. But Yors was not afraid. Yors was tired. He was tired of being out in the cold. He was tired of carrying heavy things around from place to place. He was tired of this world. He was tired of not being able to get back to Jara and make sure she was safe. He was tired of being tired.

Yors made music when he worked metal. Not always, but often. The music he made centered his mind and made the magic come easier – it helped protect him from the dangerous cost of the magic. Sometimes the music came from him, a hum or a tap or a song, sometimes it came from the metal. Metal did not often sing, but sometimes it did. Ambrek had taught him, back on Murrod, to listen to the song inside the metal, when it could be found.

When he left Murrod for Onus, he noticed something he had never noticed before. There was a song in the world, a rhythm that beat in the sand and soil and stones beneath his feet. He hadn't noticed it when they first left Onus for Murrod, not amidst all the terror of being bartered away like property and the fear of losing his family. But when returning, when stepping from one world to the next, he had felt the change in the song. Then it had faded into the background. A beat heard constantly becomes inaudible, like the beating of one's own heart.

He had felt it again when they stepped from Onus to Arctos. The change reminded him the beat existed, then it faded away again, ever-present.

Yors heard the beat now, at the edge of this world. He heard it in his feet and in his chest and in his head, and it was slow and steady, the rhythm of the beating heart of the world of Arctos.

Metal, be it Bindmetal or ordinary metal, was the skeleton of a world. It was its crust. It was in its soil, its sand, and its stone. Metal was earth. And Yors was a Metalbreaker.

He reached down into the ground, his fingers plunging through first soft snow then hard snow, burrowing down as easily as a hand may be plunged through still water. He fell to his knees, and he reached down into the bones of the world until his arms were sunken up to his elbows.

"Yors, what are you doing?" Becky asked. All around them, Todd and JC started to fire their rifles. The Kutaks were strong and fast, and they raced down the sides of mountains and cliffs in a zig-zag pattern, easily dodging the bolts of cold light fired by the rifles.

Yors felt the song of Arctos spill through his mind, and he did what Ambrek had taught him. He let the music out. Like the arrow he had called back to his hand aboard the Glory more than a year ago, he worked his will through the material instead of upon it. As that arrow had sang out, so too did the ground below them. A thunderous, detonating roar burst from the ground upon which they stood, and giant crevasses opened all around Yors' friends. A perfect circle of chasm yawned first one foot, then three, then ten, then twenty, as the mountains themselves groaned and ground against one another.

The shaking of the earth caused everyone to tumble, except Yors. He was anchored to his elbows in the earth. Steven was on the ground near him and propped himself up on all fours. "What are you doing?" he shouted, as Becky did before.

Yors did not respond. The music of the world was beating in him and he was its conduit as much as its conductor. He unleashed the forces of the world and everything shook.

The Kutaks ceased their advance as they reached the chasm Yors had crafted. With a satisfied grunt, Yors began to pull out of the ground, but his right hand stopped, caught upon something.

He pulled hard, but his hand would not budge. Panic started to stir in him, and the sound of the song of Arctos faded in his ears. "Help," he muttered.

Steven stood up and grabbed at Yors' right arm, adding his own strength to the smith's efforts to pull free. Slowly, the arm started to move. Then, with a sickening popping sound, Yors' hand came free of the earth. In it, clutched tightly in fingers that Yors had not even realized were clenched around something, was a hammer. Its haft was gleaming blue Bindmetal, and its head, fifty pounds in weight, two feet long and a single foot wide, was made of glittering sapphire.

Yors stood, the strange hammer in hand, and surveyed the ground around him. He stood at the center of a small depression in the midst of a perfect circle fifty yards across. The snow and ice on the ground around him were gone, replaced with smooth, dark stone, veined with all manners of metal.

He held up the hammer triumphantly.

All around the chasm that surrounded their new-made island, the Kutaks watched with fearful eyes.

"Creatures listen!" Yors roared. "Or Yors smash!"

The Kutaks took a step backwards.

Yors nodded to Ebram, who was helping Vanuella to her feet.

Ebram spoke to the Kutaks, his voice shaking. "There are Hindras in our lands. Your old enemies. We cannot defeat them without your help."

One of the Kutaks, the one Yors thought had been the first to speak, rose up and said, "Not you. You carry the curse in your veins—you cannot be trusted. You," it pointed its massive, clawed paw at Marriq, "you carry the smell of Borrigak in you. You helped him to receive the blessing."

Marriq stood up straight and tall, her shoulders thrust back proudly. She reminded Yors of his wife.

"I did. And if you will help us, there are Hindras enough at the Archive for each of you to take the blessing. There are dozens of pure Winterblooded at this place. Enough to set all of your people free." Marriq lifted both hands. "You have my word on this. I treated fairly with Borrigak, long ago. I gave my own Winterblood to him freely, and in return he left this world."

There was a great rumbling amongst the Kutaks, and Yors thought they had the look of ones communicating silently, the way Becky sometimes did.

The leader Kutak spoke again after only a few moments, "The tribe will follow you. Should you spin lies, the one called Ebram of Shezra will die so that one of us may receive the blessing. Either way, the Kutak are blessed by this partnership."

Ebram looked stricken. "How do you know where I am from?"

The Kutak glared at Ebram. "You too carry the smell of Borrigak upon you. You are the one he left us to take. But still you carry the blood of the enemy. Marriq of Levla was friend to Borrigak, to Kutaks, but Ebram of Shezra was not. This is known to all Kutaks." The creature grunted. "Where Marriq leads, for now Kutaks follow. But no Kutak will ever follow Ebram."

Marriq spoke. "Then I shall lead. We must leave as soon as possible. The Archive is far from here, and the Hindras will seek retribution upon my people for what I have seen. When can your people be ready to leave?"

The Kutak snorted. "We are ready now. We need no things as your people do. We shall leave at once."

Marriq turned back to the group. She nodded at Ebram, who still looked wounded by the words of the creature. Then she looked directly at Yors. Marriq whispered, "We should go soon. But first, can you explain how you just did that?"

In fact, everyone was staring at Yors. Everyone. He felt nervous all of the sudden, but he saw also that most of them were impressed by what he had done. *He* was certainly impressed by what he had done. Yors had never seen such a thing before—he had simply known instinctively in that moment that it *could* be done. He shrugged in response to Marriq's question.

Only one of his traveling companions looked at him with anything other than awe. Todd looked at him with hate.

# 21
## MURROD

M*agnificent darkness draped across the shoulders of the city.* Clouds hung low in the pitch-black sky, shielding even the light of stars from the streets below. Imperia was silent as the sons of Chron cowered in their homes, restricted by a curfew and safe behind barred doors and windows.

Three days had passed since it had stolen into the museum of the Ministry of Words to confirm the existence of the device that the master desired. The Ellir that now slipped from shadow to shadow, nearly invisible in the darkness, had not properly felt the passage of the time. As the first of the three suns threatened to rise each day, it had returned to its hiding place, a disused tunnel running under one of the alleyways that had once been its home—the long banks of Bindmetal sunboxes. The boxes were gone—carted off to an unknown place for an unknown purpose—and all men avoided those alleys now. There was the fear that the Ellir might return to them one night to exact vengeance for their decades of servitude.

It made the perfect hiding place. While the suns burned, the Ellir slept, and time moved in fits and starts to its keen senses. Only night existed, and each night it had taken careful steps towards its master's goal. It was strange, answering to a master that was not the dragon-god, but it felt no less right to feel the will of Hyrak whisper in its mind than it did mighty Ehbor.

Tonight, it would finally act. A means of escape had been found—a parting in the strange perimeter the men of Greendeep had established to bar the passage of Ellir. It was said that Hyrak himself had traveled to the perimeter nearest Imperia and broken its magical line with his sword. It was a great honor for this particular Ellir to be doing the master's work.

It picked up its pace, running silently down broad, empty streets towards the museum. As it approached the barred rear door, it knew that enemies would be at hand, and it was ready. It gripped the steel bars of the security door with all four hands and wrenched up and back, ripping it easily from its hinges. As quietly as possible it leaned the door against the wall and then knelt to work it blue-skinned fingers under the inner, wooden door. The Ellir had picked these locks the last time it had come here, but they had been changed, and the newer ones were beyond its skill.

Once it had wedged four sets of fingers under the door, palms up, it again exerted its strength—at its peak whenever the suns did not beat down upon it—and tore this door from its hinges as well. Between the two doors it had raised quite a racket, and it heard the sound of shouting from elsewhere in the building.

The museum was a long, low building, a single story in height and built of large stones as most buildings in Imperia were. Each of the twenty rooms in the museum wing had a small window in its ceiling to admit light, but all were too slender for the double-shouldered Ellir. The doors were the only option, and the front door was at the front of the building, at the Ministry of Words itself, and far too heavily guarded. It was from the direction of the front door that its keen senses heard the heavy footfalls of armed and armored executive knights.

The doors no longer in its way, the Ellir ran into the building. The long central corridor was currently empty, and it darted for the seventh room on its right—the exhibit detailing the history of the Jovs. The Ellir felt anger rise in its heart as it entered the room, but the will of its master permeated even its emotions, tamping them down and forcing it to stay focused.

Large displays of both objects and paintings recounted the immigration of Jov metalworkers and the building of the great forges in all three Prince Cities. A collection of artifacts worked by Jov smiths was on display. A large mural depicted the boxing of Ellir at nightfall and the toiling of Ellir servants as men—not smiths, but the ordinary men of Murrod—lounged about idly. It was a portrait of degradation and shame for the Ellir as a people. Young and old, male and female, all Ellir were servants to these monsters before the Jovs escaped.

This particular Ellir touched one hand to its heart. It had been mother to two young ones, several years ago. It had escaped capture by sons of Chron for many years, but one day it had been caught in the jungle while the suns sat high overhead. It had been ordered to return with the men to this place, to Imperia. Its children had followed, and the men, out of sport, had...

The Ellir clutched at the will of the master. Its memories were horrible things that drove it wild with rage. The will of the master, and of Ehbor before him, was sanctuary.

It reached out, into the display of artifacts, and wrapped two arms around a large metal drum, shallow and broad and affixed to a kind of collapsible pedestal. It was heavy, but the Ellir lifted it overhead, separating the pedestal and folding it down with a third hand. The knights would be upon it soon, and it had only one hand with which to defend itself.

Angling the drum slightly so that it could pass through the doorway of the exhibit room, the Ellir made its way back to the rear door. It ran hard and fast, graceful in a way no human could match. It slipped out through the door and then doubled its speed on the open streets of the city. It ran past parks and benches, past squares and flats. For the first time in weeks it did not retreat to its hiding place—it instead ran for the city walls.

A few minutes later it reached the walls. It had lost all pursuers many blocks ago, and it assumed that they would be contacting the gate guards to lock the city down. This was why it approached the wall far from any gate. It placed the drum's pedestal in its mouth, clenched tight between yellow teeth, and bent its elbows back so that the drum was held behind its head, like a large metal-rimmed halo. With its lower arms and its powerful legs, the Ellir scaled the wall as easily as a man would walk across a bridge. Fingers found purchase in the tiny cracks between broad stones, and legs propelled it up over the twenty foot walls in only a few quick bounds.

As it reached the top, it stared out into the untamed jungle that surrounded the city. While men needed roads to travel, Ellir needed no such contrivances. It felt out with its mind for the master and struck upon him. Without sound it leapt from atop the wall to the jungle below and darted into the foliage, aiming straight and true for Hyrak and the opening he had made for it in the perimeter.

¤~¤~¤

It was nearly morning when Hyrak's Ellir servant deposited the drum in the front cavern of his tiny stronghold. With a gesture Hyrak dismissed the Ellir, for its work was done, and he carried the instrument to the forge where Jarrek had been toiling for days on end.

The smith's age was showing, but he was still a master of his craft. His skin was bright red from the heat of the forge-fire, and he was soaked through with sweat. He had stripped off his shirt to reveal a broad chest that was nearly as scarred as Hyrak's own. As sparks flew from each hammer strike upon the metal and Bindmetal that he worked, they showered his body and the smith paid them no heed.

"It is here," Hyrak shouted over the ringing of metal. "Speak to me of your progress."

Jarrek appeared to ignore him, and while this was precisely the sort of thing that men did to him to earn a flaying back on Onus, Hyrak knew that the smith's work was too delicate to casually disrupt. He was working with the precious violet Bindmetal right now, and there was not an ounce to spare to failed workings.

Jarrek set down his hammer and picked up a pair of tongs, which he used to lift the newly-shaped lump of white hot metal. He plunged it into a small bucket of water and a cloud of steam washed up around him. Then he cast the item back onto his anvil, where he cupped it in both hands and whistled softly. As he uncupped his hands, Hyrak saw the device: a large key-like shape made of perfect, shining violet Bindmetal. Jarrek picked up the key and carried it to a low stone bench behind him, where he tucked it into the last pouch on a long sheet of leather. It was the seventh such key, and once it was secured in the pouch, Jarrek rolled the pouch up to form a cylinder, which he bound tightly with a thin strip of leather.

"Your keys," he said, panting. "I've never worked anything that hard in my life."

Hyrak nodded and took the bundle in one hand. He felt the power and the promise in that bundle and he knew his plans were dangerously close to fruition.

He gestured to the corner of the room, where a complicated object appeared to be coming together. "And what of the special project?"

"That one is much easier, as it uses no Bindmetal. I have installed the components you built, I believe. I don't understand what it will do, but it is only a days' work from done. Is it more important than the bells?" Jarrek asked.

Hyrak shook his head. "No. The bells are your highest priority now. I assume the pick is already finished?"

Jarrek bent down and pulled a heavy pickaxe from under the workbench. Its haft was wood, but its blade was bright green Bindmetal. "This is the sort of work I would normally do in blue metal. The green won't hold the enchantment nearly as well. But it is done." He extended it towards Hyrak.

"Oh it must be green," Hyrak said as he took the offered tool in his other hand. It was quite heavy, and he found that even he could not easily swing it with only a single hand. "It will work perfectly. Proceed with the bells, Jarrek."

The smith nodded. "I will need a bit of time to study the workings my father placed upon the drum, but they will be done on time. Is there," Jarrek's voice grew lower and hesitant, "any word on the Gar?"

"Soon. Soon he'll be yours to finish. I told you it would be so, didn't I?" Hyrak turned away from the smith. "Embrew is playing his part just as you are. Soon I will need neither of you any longer."

¤~¤~¤

The defense of Hineros could spare no knights. After three days of strike-and-withdrawal tactics, the massive force of women from Goldvast that had besieged the city's western front showed no sign of yielding, and still they were being reinforced.

For those three days, Tyrick had been unable to take a Metalbreaker out to the perimeter and repair the damage done by the crossing of Ahmur's daughters. Fortunately, there had not been any notable Ellir incursions, so perhaps the conflict was keeping those creatures away. Unfortunately, that meant that after three days, the Metalbreaker that Tyrick had very foolishly taken home was still with him. At his flat.

It was surreal, to say the least. He kept the Metalbreaker in the small guest room of his flat. It was the first time that the Jov had ever been on a real bed—that was evident the first night. It was also likely that Tyrick's cooking—which was nothing to celebrate, he knew—was the best food the poor smith had ever received. Three times a day Tyrick lowered the door-flap on the front of the head box and gently pressed small morsels of food into the hole. The Metalbreaker hungrily devoured them directly from Tyrick's fingers. He also poured water to him, which was much more difficult but far more necessary.

The design of the box, like the design of the chains that bound the Metalbreaker's hands and feet together even now, was cunning. It allowed the feeding and watering of the smith while always keeping him cut off from light.

As the suns rose on the fourth day of fighting, Tyrick entered the guest room with breakfast for the smith. He found the servant laying on the bed, sprawled out face up. He had kicked the light blanket off in the night, and the sunlight was spilling from the window across his body. Aside from the wooden chains and the contraption concealing his head, the smith still wore only a rudimentary loincloth, and that meant that as he lay there his every contour was on display in the bright sunlight.

Tyrick stopped at the door and simply looked at him. His pale skin was perhaps receiving more direct sunlight right now than it ever had in his whole life. He was strong and, in spite of all the hardships he had endured, healthy. He was more sturdily built than Tyrick and there was something about him that the surveyor could not put his finger on—something captivating.

He shook his head. The momentary flight of fancy passed, and he approached the bed and sat down next to the smith. He looked down at one of the Metalbreaker's hands and saw that the wooden manacles had rubbed his wrists raw. He reached down to the nearest hand and lifted it, gently, to slide the manacle up on the arm a bit and gauge the extent of the damage. Open wounds like that would quickly grow infected in the jungle. While he had been able to take better care of the smith here than he would have been left untended in the cell where he belonged, Tyrick did not have the keys to the chains.

As he moved the manacle the smith started awake and drew his hand away, whimpering and scrambling back into the corner of the bed, pulling his knees up tight against his chest.

Tyrick slid a bit closer, setting the plate of food down on the table beside the bed, and placed one hand gently on the smith's strong back. He rubbed there, trying to soothe him. After a few moments, the smith calmed, and Tyrick got ready to feed him.

The smith was so like a child, and yet, from the look of his body, he was not much younger than Tyrick himself. He wondered for a moment what the Metalbreaker's eyes looked like, then shook his head. Again, his mind was getting caught up in impossible things. It did not matter what the eyes of this servant looked like. He was a servant, a tool, and nothing more.

He lowered the feeding door on the front edge of the head box. Before he could insert the first bite of fruit, he heard the smith do something he had not done before—he spoke.

"Thank you," the Metalbreaker mumbled.

There were rules. Everything in Murrod had rules, especially in Greendeep, more especially among the newly-formed Surveyor's Guild. Tyrick knew the rules well. Yet that knowledge did not stop him from breaking one of the most important rules. Without even thinking, Tyrick replied, "You are welcome."

He'd just *acknowledged* the spoken words of a Metalbreaker.

He'd just acknowledged that this was not a tool before him, but a *man*.

He'd just put his entire future in jeopardy.

¤~¤~¤

"I have to admit you've shown uncommonly good sense," Norrun said to Mathias with a wry smile as they hunkered down in the rubble of a building recently toppled by a Goldvast offensive that had since moved on. "Most of the men your age I've known would have been unable to resist rushing up and poking at people with swords by this point."

"It's been four days, Norrun. It has to be nearly over. We keep getting reinforcements from Imperia and Monarka; we'll eventually overwhelm them with numbers." Mathias sighed. He had no interest in engaging in the fighting. He did, however, have a great deal of interest in figuring out why the women were pushing so aggressively towards a Spiralgate that they shouldn't be able to use.

"But they keep getting reinforcements themselves," Norrun added. "If old Chaplain Reid can't see by now that he should be cutting these women off at the border instead of waiting for them to reach the city, this could go on for much, much longer." Norrun closed his eyes and Mathias noticed that the bald man's breathing had quickened considerably.

"Are you well?" Mathias asked, ducking back down with Norrun behind a partially-standing hunk of wall. The Spiralgate was two long blocks away. This was the closest they had been to it since the fighting started in earnest. Anyone who was getting to the gate would have to come down the street they now had a good view of, so this place would be a fine place to catch their breath.

Norrun nodded sluggishly. "Just winded. We've been running awfully hard, and I'm awfully old. Don't have a background like you in dashing about a big, chaotic city either."

"That's right," Mathias said playfully, gently elbowing his friend in the side. "Your background is in gem cutting."

"You don't believe me?" Norrun asked, feigning injury.

"Not even a little," Mathias replied. "And now since we are going to sit tight and wait to see what exactly our masked foes are up to, perhaps we have the time for the truth?"

Norrun closed his eyes again, and Mathias saw the older man's forehead wrinkle in concentration. "The truth is a mess."

"On Core, they say 'the truth shall set you free,'" Mathias offered.

"That's cute," Norrun said, opening his eyes and looking, quite seriously, into Mathias'. "I don't believe it, but it does make a person feel good."

"What drove you from Monarka to the fields?" Mathias asked.

Behind the tiny wall that sheltered them there was the sound of battle. Mathias chanced a quick peek to see a pair of men—not knights of any branch, but ordinary men who had taken up arms to defend the city—clash with a pod of women all wearing brightly colored masks that seemed to represent fish.

He ducked back down and looked at Norrun once more, motioning for him to begin.

Norrun leaned his head back against the wall. "I wasn't a gem cutter. I was contracted to a gem cutter, though—his name was Orius."

Mathias was silent. Norrun had never before mentioned a bindmate. That surely meant that this Orius was gone—dead and returned to the nursery to be born anew. He couldn't imagine how hard that would be to live through. He thought of his own questions about the lives before this one—questions that marked him unusual among his kind. How could Norrun look at anyone, at everyone, and not wonder if they were his beloved reborn?

"What happened to him?" Mathias asked.

"Killed. A judiciary knight tasked to the Ministry of Incarnation hunted him down and slit his throat with one of those fancy blue Bindmetal swords. The ones that kill everything they touch." Norrun's jaw was clenched as he spoke, and Mathias could see in his friend's expression that he had been witness to that death—that it lived in his memory in vivid detail.

"Why?" Mathias asked. "Why would the Ministry of Incarnation order a man killed?" He suspected the answer—it hearkened back to his own youth, before being drawn to Adam and away to other worlds. During a time when he too had feared the Ministry of Incarnation's knights.

Norrun leveled a stern gaze at Mathias. "I know the look that Orius wore better than I know anything. I see the same look in you. The curiosity of the young to know the roads walked before. Orius was one of those—like you, I would dare say—that met with others in dark clubs, deep in the night. He asked questions. He read forbidden histories. He tried every day to learn a little more about the life before this one. He thought it was a secret—that the only ones he told were those he could trust. But he was wrong."

"Someone betrayed him?" Mathias asked. "I... I was one of those men, once. It was always so hard to know who you could trust. Early on, fresh from the nursery, everyone feels that curiosity. But it fades fast for most. That's when the paranoia sets in. I had... very few people I ever felt comfortable sharing my questions with."

"Orius confided in few as well, just a pair of others his age—our age, for he was of the same nursery year as me. And me. He confided in me, in the quiet of our flat. We lay there in silence afterwards, his hand in mine, our contract rings warm against one another." Norrun sighed. "I remember that night so well."

"Did you ever find who had done it? Who turned him in?" Mathias asked.

Norrun closed his eyes again and let out a slow breath. "I found the bastard, yes. And I killed him in the only way I could, because I was too weak to kill him with steel. I killed his future."

Realization dawned upon Mathias. He felt foolish for not seeing it before, for not hearing the words between the words Norrun was saying. Behind them, the battle was done, the victor unimportant.

"You exiled yourself to the fields," Mathias whispered.

"I couldn't be a knight any longer. I couldn't kill the love of anyone else's life," Norrun said.

They sat in silence for a long time.

"If you were a knight for Incarnation," Mathias asked, "can you tell me what happens to me when I die?"

"Without records? No. I didn't lie to you, boy. I've never heard of anyone without records. That was a punishment that even my kind weren't able to dispense. You're special. Congratulations." Norrun forced a smile.

Mathias returned the smile in a gesture of sympathy.

Things had been quite quiet behind them, and he chanced another look around. The fighting, complete with a large amount of smoke that assuredly meant buildings were burning, had shifted towards the western edge of the city again. Regardless of their inability to completely repel the invaders, the men of Hineros were doing a fine job of keeping them from getting to the Spiralgate. It was almost enough to make him wonder if that was where they were truly headed.

He shielded his eyes from the nearly set suns with one hand and peered down the street. He was looking for other buildings that might be of strategic importance in case he was wrong and this was not an attempt on one of Murrod's Spiralgates.

His eyes fell upon a large building that looked familiar to him—partly because it was constructed of more stone than any other building in the whole of the city, but partly because it was built in a similar fashion to a building he had once spent quite a bit of time in.

"Norrun, look at that," he said, tapping his friend on the shoulder.

Norrun joined him in peering over the wall. "What am I looking at?"

"Is that this city's Great Forge?" Mathias asked.

Norrun squinted. "It does look a lot like the one in Monarka. I take it it looks like Imperia's as well?"

Mathias nodded.

Before he could carry the line of thinking any further, a shimmering portal of green light appeared about a half of a block away from their hiding place—a half of a block closer to the Spiralgate.

Mathias felt his heart leap up into his throat. That was a crossgate, a portal that covered vast distances. It was the work of a Gatemaker, and the only

Gatemaker left was Adam. Adam was here! He nearly leapt to his feet. Norrun caught him by the hand and yanked him down—and it was a good thing he did.

The first figure to emerge from the portal was a woman. She wore the carved and painted totem mask of a snake. She carried a sharp spear and leapt through the portal warily, immediately dropping to a crouch and surveying the area, looking for danger. Mathias and Norrun pulled down as low behind the wall as they could while still being able to see.

She was followed by a tall man who walked with a bit of a stoop, leaning on a spear for support. He wore plain clothes, including pants, but as he too turned to take in the area around him, Mathias saw that behind the long gray hair that hung in front of his face, the man had no eyes.

Mathias hissed, "Embrew! He's alive!"

Norrun clamped a hand over his mouth and continued to stare.

The final figure to emerge from the portal was not woman nor man. It was the mighty form of a large, white dragon. Her three eyes glowed balefully as she reared up and then, when she laid eyes upon the Spiralgate, she threw her head back and roared.

¤~¤~¤

Embrew studied the Spiralgate carefully. Behind him, Plyssa stood, spear at the ready, watching his every move. Ahmur leapt to the dusk sky and called out orders to her children, rallying the women that had been making war upon this city for days in order to make it possible for Embrew to safely reach the gate.

He could *almost* see. The shape of things was made clear to him with a simple working, now that his wrists were no longer bound by the Bindmetal manacles that had hobbled his strength for so very long. The fine details of the world around him were lost, but he could see the shape of the Spiralgate in his mind, reflected by his Gar senses. It took him time to get his bearings, but he imagined the hesitance he felt in his bones was born of the disuse of his powers over these past months of captivity.

The dragon was distracted, so this was his best chance to get away. The working would have to be precise—he had to open the Spiralgate just long enough to escape into it and then slam it closed behind him before the dragon could access it.

The gate itself was the familiar shape of all Spiralgates. He could feel the specifics of it, its geometric key, imprinted upon the metal by the same energies that answered to the command of all Gatemakers. This was one of the six remaining gates on Murrod—he had been present when Adam inadvertently destroyed the Mingar Spiralgate.

"Why was this the one we had to use?" Embrew asked quietly, expecting no answer. He had gained a degree of familiarity with the gate nearest

Hyrak's caverns, and it would have been easier to open a portal at that gate, but he had little choice.

"This one is furthest from Monarka," Plyssa said. "My goddess does not wish to tempt confrontation with Chron."

Embrew nodded. He remembered impressions of two great dragons tussling in the sky, right before Jarrek had plunged a dagger into his belly and the two of them had been left to die on the cold sand of Bluetide. Dragons were territorial creatures, powerful and cunning, and now he was going to dare to defy one.

He lifted both hands and focused his mind on the task before him. A cloudy sense of confusion came upon him, but he forced his way through it and instead focused on gathering his power and pouring it into the Spiralgate. The banded hemisphere would amplify his magic and connect it to another gate of his choosing—the Rosgar portal on Onus, far from the painful memories of his old home at Gar Nought—and then he would be free at last.

"Is that what is supposed to happen?" Plyssa asked.

Embrew paid her no heed, for it was unlikely the woman, scarcely half his age, had ever seen a Spiralgate activate before. Images danced through his mind of the gate spinning to life, its brilliant light lifting slowly up out of its platform until it was three-quarters of a globe of translucent blue energy.

But something wasn't right. The images appeared in his mind with clarity, with detail. There should have been no detail. He saw only what his spatial perceptions revealed to him, the compensation of magic for a disability well-earned by his treachery on Onus. The image in his mind was vivid and... false.

He tried to close the portal, to slam it shut, but it was too late—the damage had been done.

He had not opened a Spiralgate as he had intended. He had opened a crossgate—a large one. It was well formed and supported by the full might of his decades of training and expertise as a Gatemaker. Through it flowed dozens and dozens, perhaps nearly a hundred, of the tall, four-armed Ellir. And striding out of the portal amongst them was Hyrak, helmeted and armored in plate mail, with Jarrek at his side carrying a large bag of clanking metal.

Hyrak's voice rang out in Embrew's mind, "You have done the service I required of you, Gatemaker."

Embrew shouted back through that strange mental connection, "What have you done?"

"I have plucked the geometric key to Onus from your mind and I have bent your perception of the working to bring my Ellir army across Greendeep's perimeter. You have been more helpful than I imagined."

Plyssa grabbed Embrew's arm. "Ahmur will not be pleased."

¤~¤~¤

Mathias watched as the momentary hopes that had been born from Embrew's appearance turned to ash. The dragon was one thing—the appearance of a hundred Ellir was another. And there, standing in the middle of them, was Hyrak.

Mathias knew him by sight, even though they had never met. He felt in his bones that the man was Hyrak. The way he stood and carried himself, the way he issued orders to Ellir... he was the man Mathias had feared him to be.

The only thing that kept fear from overtaking his senses entirely was the sight of the white dragon, Ahmur, swooping down to confront Hyrak. The man was a legend on Onus and nearly one here on Murrod, but he was only a man, and she was a dragon-god of Murrod. There was no doubt in his mind that Hyrak had bitten off more than he could chew.

The dragon drew in a deep breath—surely a precursor to a gout of flame. Mathias watched as Hyrak held out one hand and the large man at his side—the smith Jarrek, Mathias realized—handed him a small bell. Hyrak lifted that hand up in a fluid motion and rang the bell...

And Ahmur stopped. She stood there, lungs inflated, but did not move. Mathias felt his jaw drop open as Hyrak continued to ring the bell steadily and walked to the dragon, then around her, and climbed up her back, walking steadily without using his hands to grip anything. He strode up past her shoulders where her wings were unfurled but, like the rest of her, unmoving, and reached the base of her neck. He sheathed his sword in a smooth movement and drew a coil of thick wire from his belt. He unfurled the wire with a cracking motion, like a whip, while his other hand continued to ring the bell. The wire flung out and coiled back up around Ahmur's neck, meeting back at Hyrak's hand. He strung the bell onto the wire and then twisted the two ends together, making a delicate necklace around the dragon's neck.

And Mathias watched the glow in the dragon's eyes dim. She lowered her head to the ground, and Hyrak dismounted. He pointed to Embrew and the woman that stood still at his side and ordered his Ellir to take him away.

Norrun pulled Mathias back down completely behind the wall. "That man just took command of one of the gods," Norrun said in a strangled whisper. His breathing was quickening again. "What are we going to do?"

"We need help," Mathias said. "We can't handle this—no one can."

"Who would be stupid enough to get involved in a war against Ellir and dragons and warrior women?" Norrun asked.

"My friends," Mathias smiled briefly. "We have to get into that building, the Great Forge."

Norrun peered around the corner of the wall for a moment and ducked back down. "Well, it seems that everyone is very busy being in awe of the tame dragon. If we go now, we might just make it."

Mathis shifted into a runner's crouch, and Norrun followed suit. With a sharp nod, Mathias signaled him to follow, and the pair dashed forward as fast as they could, down the street and towards the old stone building. Norrun was not as fast as Mathias, but he kept a steady pace, and even though a few of the Ellir surely noticed them, none of them followed.

Mathias smashed into the front door—which was labeled with a relatively new, painted sign, 'Surveyor's Guild'—and ran for the stairs inside the largely empty frot chamber. What he needed, what he hoped against hope was still here, was a tool of Bindmetal that had been installed in all three Great Forges when the Metalbreakers still called Murrod home. In Imperia, it had been kept on the upper floor.

But as they crested the stairs to the broad common room at the top, Mathias broke out into a grin. Hanging on the wall was a large orange Bindmetal pipe.

"The chime," he said smugly. He ran up to it and struck it as hard as he could with the flat of his hand. It echoed strangely, and he struck it again, and again. Then, once it was reverberating steadily, he leaned down under the tube and said, "Murrod needs help. Hyrak lives."

He collapsed against the wall. "It only carries a few words. Jarrek showed it to me once, at the Forge in Imperia when I was running for Chaplain Reid. They used to use it to communicate with the nobles on Onus for commissions and such." He turned to see if Norrun was impressed by his quick thinking, but it was then that Mathias realized Norrun was not in the room with him.

Panicked, he dashed back down the stairs, and there was the bald man, slumped over at the foot of the stairs. He was gasping for air and his tanned skin had gone bone-white.

Mathias leapt down next to him. "Norrun? What is it?"

Norrun coughed. "My time is up. I thought I felt it coming on, but I was too stubborn to pay attention."

Mathias squeezed his friend's hand. "Are you sure? Maybe you're just out of breath. Tired. You are getting a little long in the tooth." He tried to smile.

"Twenty years from nursery to grave. Who ever thought that would be enough time?" Norrun coughed again. "It wasn't. It wasn't enough time at all."

Mathias felt tears trickling down his cheeks. "I need you. I need your help. Don't leave me alone."

Norrun sighed. "I don't want to. But... nobody asked what I want. Wouldn't have gotten it anyway. That's not... the kind of life I've had."

Mathias leaned over and pressed his lips against Norrun's.

"This is all I had to do to get you to kiss me?" Norrun's mouth curled up at the corners in a tiny smile. "If I'd have known that... I would have..."

Mathias felt the field hand's breathing stop.

He kissed Norrun once more, then whispered in his ear, "I will remember you."

He sat on the stairs, holding Norrun's hand, while the tide of battle outside turned.

There was nothing left that he could do. He was all alone.

# 22
# ARCTOS

B*ack when I was like thirteen, I had this pair of shoes.* They were sweet shoes—bright white with blue piping and that translucent plastic stuff in the heel that would light up when you stepped down. I loved those shoes. I begged my dad for weeks—which never panned out for me, because my dad is a huge opponent of 'frivolous things' which is pretty rich for a football coach, if you ask me. So I turned to my mom, and she was always the one with the soft spot for me, because I was her baby. I guess I still am. Which cramps my style a little, but hey, when you want something bad enough, you take a few kicks to the groin of your pride and you suck it up, because dammit, they were sweet-ass shoes and I wanted them.

So my mom bought me these shoes when I was thirteen, I think. Definitely middle school. It was during my basketball phase (damn, I've had a lot of phases, haven't I?) and I thought they would look pretty badass on the court. My grandma said they were cool, and that woman has amazing taste. She must—I'm her favorite grandchild, so that is proof positive of her good sense. So these shoes were kind of expensive, but not too bad, really, they just weren't normal. They suited me fine, because at the time, I was the only one running around Thomas Middle School with shoes that lit up. And let me tell you, they became my trademark. I wore those shoes every single day. You couldn't pry them off of me! There were days I went to bed wearing those shoes, and I know for a fact that I attended two weddings with them on. And a funeral—I'm pretty sure there was a funeral in there as well.

As time went by, the shoes got old. The rubber in the soles was wearing out and cracking, the eyelets that held the laces were splitting. The lights started dulling and then stopped working altogether. And my feet kept growing. But none of that mattered—I still wouldn't let go of those shoes. I wore them even though they actually hurt my feet, and I wore them even when they had a big gaping hole in the heel that soaked my socks through every time I was dumb enough to step anywhere near a puddle of water. They looked old and tattered and ratty, and they were busted beyond all hope of repair, but as the year went by and my fourteenth year came on hard and fast, I still wouldn't part with those shoes.

Those shoes were comfortable in a way that their appearance, their outsides, couldn't explain to people. If you'd looked at those shoes, you would have seen junk. Garbage. But when I slipped them on my feet, they weren't trash, they were magic. They fit me perfectly, because they had worn out as I had worn in—they were the perfect complement to my feet. A piece of me that couldn't be replaced.

So the winter of ninth grade, towards the end of my fourteenth year hurtling through space on planet Earth, my mom bought me yet another new pair of shoes (she'd been slipping new dress shoes and sneakers into my closet for months, hoping that one day I would just switch over to something new that would embarrass her a little less, especially now that you could see the shape of my big toe deforming the front of the shoes where it pressed out, yearning for escape from its oh-so-comfortable prison). This time though, she waited until I was asleep and then she stole my comfy shoes and threw them away. When I woke up I was furious. For days, I boycotted shoes (which is a pretty stupid stance to take in the winter time, I have to admit) until I finally, begrudgingly, pulled on the new pair of sneakers she bought me. They were OK to look at—black with orange accents and those striped shoelaces that were so big for a while—but they weren't *my* shoes. They felt wrong in a way that I can't explain. My feet hurt when I wore those shoes, but eventually, I got past the hurting. Eventually what I felt like in the new shoes was normal. But I still think back to those old, super-comfy shoes. The way that they slipped on and made me feel *right*. It was a kind of magic that Gatemakers and Mindshapers and all that will never understand, because it's so plain and simple, but it was my kind of magic.

Each time Yors stripped the power from one of the links in my chain, I felt something nagging at me, a familiar sensation that I couldn't quite place. It only lasted a few minutes, then I let it go, because there was always something else going on. After we met up with the Kutaks in the White Bound and Yors got his fancy hammer, he was beat, but on the never-ending hike to the Archive, he did find the strength to take the magic out of three more links in the chain (only twenty-five to go!), and it was at that moment that I recognized that flicker of feeling.

It felt like slipping on those old shoes. Like a part of me that I had grown up with, that was integral to who I was, had been missing and for the briefest of moments, it was back. Slipped on comfortable and familiar and natural. Then it faded, of course, because as long as even one link of that damn chain was working, I was stuck in the new me, the new shoes, but it was at that moment that I stopped being afraid of what I would become when the collar came off. I was going to become *me*, and that was nothing to be afraid of.

¤~¤~¤

It took five days of hard work to reach the Archive from the mountains that the Kutaks called home. Steven was convinced it would have taken them longer had it not been for the amazing prowess of their new companions. The Kutaks were fast and strong, nearly tireless, and seemed to have an instinctive knowledge of the land that made travel far more direct. They took paths Marriq admitted she would never have chosen, and invariably these paths shaved hours from their traveling time. They were aggravated at the need to stop each night, as the Kutaks were one of those rare creatures on Arctos that didn't perish in the night's cold. Steven envied them that, because even with the heating power of the hearthstone and Ebram combined, he feared he would never truly feel warm again.

After those five days of pushing hard, they reached a series of low hills on the opposite side of the Archive from where he, Todd, and Marriq had made camp about two weeks ago. Two weeks. They had been on this world so much longer than any of them expected. Todd looked miserable, having come down with a cold of some kind, and the others simply looked tired. Steven was fairly sure that yesterday was the Fourth of July, back home—the anniversary of Tatyana's death. Each night when he tried to sleep, he felt her in his dreams. But none of that mattered—they were finally ready to finish what they came here for.

The Archive's defensive dome was exactly the same on the back as it was on the front—smooth and blue-white and thick. Light did pass through it faintly, and from this side the light that cast shadows for Steven's use was most prevalent at sunrise. That was not long from now, so they spent this final night of camping in the snow planning for the assault on the Archive.

The party of Kutaks numbered twelve, counting their leader, Vortigar. Combined with Steven's own party of eight, they were a force of twenty. While that didn't give them numerical superiority over the Hindras Steven had seen inside the Archive on his last visit, he could not help but feel better about their odds with the mighty Kutaks on their side.

The plan was a bit more complicated than he would have liked, but that was what made it a Becky plan instead of a Steven plan. The Kutaks seemed to like it, but their single-minded desire for 'the blessing' that they gained by killing Hindras made them amenable to most plans that included battle.

The fine details continued to be debated long into the night and early into the morning. As Steven chewed on the last of the travel rations that Vanuella had supplied when they left Venot, he heard the merits of the plan continue to be debated.

"And you're sure it can handle the damage?" Becky asked Marriq.

"Of course. The glass is made of Pithysian sand. It is far stronger than the dome," the Archivist explained in exasperated tones.

"But do the Hindras know that?" Vanuella asked.

Marriq smiled slyly. "I doubt it."

Steven leaned back and nodded off for a bit. A little rest would do him good.

It was not more than an hour when dawn finally arrived. As the first rays of Arctos' cold sun rippled across the eastern horizon, Steven stood up and approached one of the Kutaks—Urguroch. "It's time," he said. He looked back to the others, still huddled around the hearthstone, and Becky nodded at him encouragingly.

Steven and Urguroch walked steadily down the slope of the hill, towards the base of the ice dome.

"This might be uncomfortable," Steven explained. "Nobody I know really enjoys traveling through the shadow."

The Kutak grunted and replied with a mental whisper, "Life is uncomfortable."

Steven couldn't argue that.

They drew up next to the dome but stopped just shy of actually touching it. Steven feared that physical contact with the dome could somehow alert the Hindras inside, and surprise was critical to Steven's survival. He put one hand on the furry fore-arm (or was more properly a leg?) of Urguroch and closed his eyes. He drew the shadow of the dome up around them, wrapping it tightly about his own form before extending that armored silhouette over the Kutak. Once they were both fully enveloped, Steven willed them to discorporate, dissolving into shadow and emerging, he hoped, in the shadow of the Archive itself, within the dome.

They materialized, painfully, and Steven gasped for breath as he transitioned both himself and his passenger back to flesh-and-blood. The Kutak looked unfazed by the trip, but Steven felt weak. Fortunately, the worst was over for him. The rear of the Archive featured no doors—they would have to come around to the front to gain entrance the same way Steven had before—but also fewer windows, as the glass structure sat upon a stone foundation that climbed nearly fifteen feet high back here. Tucked up tight against that stone, Steven and Urguroch were impossible to see by those inside the building.

Urguroch took the lead and Steven followed as quickly as he could. They circled the building, searching for their designated target—the first Hindra they found. Vortigar believed, and Marriq agreed, that the dome was the work of specific Hindras. If those Hindras fell, the dome's integrity would be weakened, perhaps even collapsing utterly. So Steven and Urguroch were to start beating Hindras senseless.

There was another statue garden on the side of the Archive, and while Steven slipped back to shadowform to better hide in the array of icy sculptures, Urguroch had no recourse but to dash through as quickly as possible. They moved with equal speed while Steven was in this form, alternating flashes of white fur and black shadow. At the edge of the garden, near the corner of the building that separated them from the front entrance of the Archive, was a Hindra in white robes. He faced away from them, staring up at the dome.

Urguroch reached the Hindra first, plowing into it silently from behind, bringing his mighty frame crushing down upon the willow-thin Hindra. For all the impressive strength of the Hindras that Steven had faced, it crumpled easily beneath the weight of the Kutak, and Steven watched as Urguroch easily drove its head into the hard-packed snow on the ground again and again, rendering it unconscious.

Overhead, there was a faint cracking sound, and Steven looked up to see a tiny dusting of ice crystals fall from the dome. It was working, but certainly not fast.

Steven flexed one shadow-hand into a set of talons and pointed to the unconscious Hindra. "Should I finish it off?" he asked reluctantly. "We don't want to risk it getting back up and coming at us from behind."

Urguroch's heavy brow ridge lowered in a deep scowl. "No Hindras die until Kutaks decide they die. We must not waste the blessing."

Steven nodded. Wordlessly, they proceeded to round the corner and make their way for the Archive doors. They saw no other sentries along the way, but Steven kept glancing behind them, making sure that the first Hindra was not active once more. He also watched and listened to the dome. The next stage of the plan would be starting soon.

¤~¤~¤

Hunna didn't know what day it was. He wasn't sure it mattered. For many days now, the dozen white-haired creatures from beyond the city had stalked in slow, deliberate courses of destruction through the streets of Venot. Every man, woman, or child they met they killed, and now half of their number, as best Hunna could tell, had taken up positions around the perimeter of the city.

If any of the caravans were coming back with those promised supplies, they were not making it into the city. Hunna feared the loss of life, food, hearthstones, minerals, and more that was happening outside the city. But he couldn't think about that—it would bring on another attack.

He was down to the last of his desix. That was likely why he couldn't recall which day it was—he'd been using heavily since the creatures arrived. There were no safe places to hide, as the monsters did not rest and seemed set upon killing all Venotians. So Hunna stayed moving. Whenever he was conscious—which was now more common, since he was hoarding his final dose for a true anxiety attack—he was moving, trying to stay ahead of these strange beings and their power to kill with a glance.

He had seen them do it many times. It was always the ones in furs—the two in robes, one male and one female, seemed to stay back from the killing. The fur-wearers would simply look at a human, or sometimes they would point, and then the human would keel over, frozen to death in an instant. To make matters worse, the furnace had all but failed and Hunna and what few other survivors he had seen were forced to draw closer and closer to the innermost parts of the city just to survive the night. He wondered why the creatures didn't simply break into the tunnels and destroy the furnace, ending all of Hunna's people in a single stroke, but he imagined that perhaps the intense heat below would be too much even for these monsters. It had certainly been unpleasant for him.

Hunna was making his way to a new shelter with purpose, although it was the selfish purpose of a hedonist. He wanted escape from the terror of his circumstances, so he was making his way to the blood purification plant. If his suspicions were true, and Karrin had been dosing the inebriated hedonists with desix by way of the blood-letters in order to gain control of them, there would be more desix there. If he took enough of it, he would simply drift off to sleep and not wake up. Suicide was a direct and flagrant violation of fatalist belief, but Hunna could bear this all no longer. Had he been a stronger man, he told himself, he would have simply found something sharp and killed himself in a more traditional way, but Hunna didn't like the idea of pain. A desix overdose would be painless and soothing.

He had been making his way carefully towards the purification plant for hours, and when at last it came into sight he could not take the last few steps. He looked around frantically, stepping over a pair of frozen corpses, certain that the enemy was here and waiting for him.

He didn't know what it would feel like to freeze to death—it certainly looked fast—but he feared the agony. He imagined his eyes freezing to cold, hard stones in his head, his limbs going numb and then lanced through with pain as the nerves died, and he found his anxiety building again.

He dashed for the rear door of the building and, finding it ajar, stepped inside and slammed the door shut behind him, louder than he had meant to. If they had not already known he was here, they would sure know now.

He huffed and puffed out onto the metal walkway over the primary tanks, his stomach rumbling with hunger and anxiousness. As he peered down over the railing he saw Karrin looking directly up at him.

"You are the last person I expected to see," Karrin said, scowling. "Get out of here."

"What are *you* doing here?" Hunna asked, panting for breath. "There's nothing left for you to do. Most of your men are dead."

Karrin tapped the large glass tank of blood. "I can take the bastards out with me. I've dumped a hundred pounds of sparkdust into this tank. I sent one of my troops into the streets, trying to draw those monsters to me, here. When they come in the door, I'll ignite the tank and blow them to ash."

Hunna arched an eyebrow. "Sparkdust makes light, not fire," he said. He felt sorry for this foolish woman and her misguided plans. All of her work to take over the city had been for nothing now.

"You don't know anything," Karrin said. Behind her, from the front offices, a chilling wave of cold rippled through the air. The windows of the offices frosted over and then shattered, and Hunna hunched down, covering his head with his hands.

One of the white creatures, the female robed one, stalked down the steps to the plant floor, a fur-wearing male immediately behind it. It looked at

Karrin, then up to Hunna, and said, "I received your message. My people have nothing to say to you."

With a nod, the robed creature stepped out of the way and the fur-clad one gestured sharply towards Karrin. Hunna could not help but watch, morbid curiosity driving him to peek from between his fingers.

The same chill wind that had killed countless hundreds in the streets of Venot washed over Karrin, but it did nothing. She did not freeze, or falter. She stood there, resolute, and said, "Are you sure about that?"

Hunna saw the one in robes draw up to her full height, eyes wide, mouth contorted in rage, as she roared in anger, "Destroy the Winterblooded!"

¤~¤~¤

"They've taken one of them down," Becky said to the others, opening her eyes. She was in only tenuous contact with Steven, but she had seen clearly his witnessing of the Hindra that fell before his Kutak companion's assault. "It's time to work on the wall."

The Kutaks rushed forward as one, more like a stampeding herd than a fighting force, and they spread wide around the dome, beating on it with their large fists. Each strike echoed marvelously, and Becky found deep satisfaction in the sound.

Todd and JC took up positions about halfway between Becky's vantage point and the dome, opening fire with their energy rifles. They aimed higher on the dome, and while the blasts seemed to have little effect, it was the accumulation of all the stress—from losing the Hindras inside that maintained the dome to being struck by the strength of eleven Kutaks at its base to being peppered with blasts at its top, that would topple the structure.

But the attack continued for nearly three sustained minutes, and not a crack formed. She got no impressions from Steven—no other Hindras had yet fallen to him or Urguroch. It wasn't working.

"I can help," Ebram said from behind Becky. "I can melt ice—let me do it."

"No!" Marriq shouted. "You are too important to risk." She looked back at Vanuella and then turned away abruptly towards Becky and Yors. "Do you have any other ideas?"

Becky looked up at Yors, and the big smith nodded. Resting his sapphire hammer on one shoulder, he turned and padded down the hill, tapping JC on the shoulder. JC handed his rifle to Todd, who took it up smoothly and continued the attack on the dome using both weapons, one in each bandaged hand.

Yors and JC reached the base of the dome, in a spot between two Kutaks, and Becky watched with dread as the third and final stage of her plan came together.

On Arctos, nothing burned except the Winterblood—the blood that ran through the veins of both Hearth Keepers like Ebram and the Hindras that now controlled the Archive. This had been said over and over again, but it wasn't quite true. One other thing burned on Arctos—the metal links around JC's neck. They still burned hot with magic when combatting the rise of fear in JC.

JC backed up against the dome, pressing his body against it, pressing his head and neck back up flush against the featureless ice. Yors took position directly between JC and Becky, blocking him from her sight. He lifted his great hammer high overhead.

Becky grabbed her mental connection to JC and brought it to life, channeling the pent up energy from her encounter with her tangent through that link to power a simple working—she clouded JC's mind. With all that power, the working was graceful and magnificent, perfect in every way. She reached in and captured one of his memories, twisting it and turning it and then setting it free once more.

She stole from him the memory of his role in the plan and replaced it with a conversation too terrible to imagine. In his head, she left memory of being told that he would be making the ultimate sacrifice. The hammer would come down upon his throat, killing him, but driving the blazing hot metal into and through the dome.

Tears welled in her eyes as she finished the memory and cast a simple thought to Yors, signaling that it was done.

Yors moved for but an instant, and Becky saw JC's eyes wide. Hurt. Betrayed.

Yors swung the hammer.

Fear blossomed in JC's mind and was instantly swept away, converted to heat by the red Bindmetal at his neck. The dome behind him sizzled and popped, shimmering.

Yors' blow missed JC, colliding with the dome directly over his head, as close as possible to where JC stood but not hitting him. JC collapsed to the ground.

A crack formed in the dome and began to spread, branching and racing around the ice in time to the shots from Todd and the blows from the Kutaks.

Becky reached out to fix what she had done, to restore JC's memories that he was never in danger, that the plan was always to scare him, not to hurt him.

Below, Yors offered a hand to JC and he took it. As he stood, he turned to face Becky, and she saw upon his face a massive grin.

The dome collapsed.

¤~¤~¤

Steven and Urguroch were inside the Archive when they heard the dome fall. Great chunks of ice rained down on and around the Archive, battering its glass-paned roof. It was chaos, and it was exactly what Becky had hoped for. That didn't make him feel any more comfortable with the idea that tons of ice were raining down on the big glass building he was standing in.

The Hindras swarmed from the places they had been hiding, or researching, or whatever it was they did here. Steven concealed Urguroch and himself in a patch of shadow near the stairs leading to the upper levels, and they watched as Hindras swarmed in panic out from the maze of library shelves on the main floor and both up and down the staircases from the other levels. A full thirty Hindras raced towards the front doors, either to action or out of fear that the Archive would collapse and crush them all. Whichever motive, it didn't particularly matter—they were doing just as they were supposed to.

With a roar, Urguroch launched out of concealment and began swatting aside Hindras. Every last one of these was of the robed variety, and Steven decided to get involved when one of them landed with a loud crack near his hiding place. He flexed his shadowform hand to talons once more and raked those talons across the chest of the Hindra, eliciting a cry of pain and the flickering flash and telltale smoke of Hindra blood exposed to open air.

"Do not kill!" Urguroch shouted over his heavy shoulders.

Steven replied, "Understood."

The Hindras were starting to gather their wits, and most were already backing away from the snarling Kutak, seeking to gain advantage from their powers to make up for their disadvantage in terms of physical prowess. What they did not see as they retreated, casting bolts of fire and summoning blasts of wind, was the onrushing Kutaks behind them.

The sound the Kutaks made as they engaged with their ancestral enemy would haunt Steven for years to come. It was equal parts rage and desperation, and Steven felt that what they expressed was in some strange way like what he had felt when Tatyana died. There was a kind of boundless sorrow in what they did that he could relate to, but never understand.

Vortigar raked his mighty claws across the torso of a male Hindra, who fell to the ground, arms upraised, pleading for mercy.

"There can be no mercy! None!" Vortigar howled.

"So very true," the Hindra said. With a ripple of heat, Steven watched as the Hindra's white robes turned to black, and its long flowing hair disappeared to reveal a bald head. The Hindra brought its wrinkled hand up and plunged that hand into the fur-covered chest of the Kutak leader. With that touch, Vortigar burst into flames, howling and falling back, rolling in the snow and colliding blindly with the massive chunks of ice that littered the front courtyard of the Archive.

The Hindra in black strode after Vortigar calmly, watching with a twisted smile as the Kutak thrashed about and then, as Vortigar grew still, the Hindra knelt down next to him and conjured a blade of jagged ice into his hand. With a quick motion, the Hindra drew the blade across Vortigar's scorched throat and leaned in, lapping up the blood that fountained from the wound.

The other Kutak's roared when they realized what had happened, but each was engaged by two or more Hindras, and there was nothing they could do to save their leader.

Steven leapt towards the Hindra in black, passing Urguroch as he struggled with a Hindra that was, somehow, holding his own in an exchange of physical blows with the mighty hunter.

Steven found no words to shout as he took a ferocious slash at the kneeling back of the Hindra in black. His shadow-claws shredded the robes of the Hindra, revealing a body of nearly skeletal dimension beneath. The spine of the Hindra protruded from its taught, pale skin in a sickening fashion, and his claws splintered upon the spine, causing Steven to pull back, gasping.

The Hindra stood and turned, the dull red blood of Vortigar dribbling down its chin.

"You are the intruder. It is a shame that Arenara and her force did not find you and kill you. Your bravery deserved such a gentle reward." The Hindra lifted a hand, and Steven felt ice creep up around his legs. He was still in shadowform, but somehow the ice was gripping him, holding him tight. "Kutak blood gives us strength. I wonder what your blood will give us."

With a roar, Yors appeared at the edge of Steven's line of sight. As the ice crept up his legs, Steven watched the smith charge at the Hindra from behind, his gleaming sapphire hammer swinging gracefully through the air. Yors' blow collided with the Hindra and sent him flying, the tell-tale crack of shattered bones echoing even over the sound of Kutaks and Hindras mauling each other throughout the courtyard.

Another Hindra rushed towards them, but it was intercepted by Todd, who tripped it and then brought the muzzle of the rifle right up into its face before pulling the trigger and rendering it unconscious with the force of its heatless blast.

Todd coughed, and Steven thought he saw Todd wipe blood produced by that cough from his hand onto the leg of his pants.

JC kicked at the ice that was pinning Steven's legs down and extended a hand, which Steven took as he shifted back to his physical body to conserve strength. Everyone was gathered there with him, all eight of their traveling party excluding the Kutaks.

"We have to help them," Steven said, gesturing to the many skirmishes going on all around them.

"No," Becky said. "We have to get what we came for. This is between the pasty ones and the furry ones, and we are done being involved." She turned to Marriq. "Can you lead us to what we need?"

Marriq nodded. "Follow me."

# 23
# ARCTOS

T*he Winterblooded witch men called Karrin ran as Arenara's partner, Lerrimur, gave chase.* Arenara felt sick just watching that abomination draw breath.

Ages ago, her people had made a grave mistake—they had trusted mankind enough to grow close to them. Some of her kind were foolish enough to fall in love with men and women, to bear children with these lowly, pitiful creatures. The offspring haunted the Hindras even to this day—the Winterblooded. They had other names, names given by men, but what mattered is that the glorious power of the Hindras was within them, and it was not their right. Of all things the Hindras had given up when they retreated to the depths of the Black Bound and hid themselves away from sight and from recollection, they had never stopped hunting these monstrosities. Now there was one—leading men and women in this city in spite of all that the Hindras had done, surreptitiously, to encourage violence against their kind.

Arenara watched Lerrimur pursue Karrin into the maze of blood tanks, and she considered aiding in the hunt but no good would come of it. Lerrimur was a hunter of the *hahn'du*, and his skills were without question. No simple human, even blessed with Hindra blood, could best him. Instead, she surveyed this barbaric operation. As the Hindras had swept through Venot unopposed, they had passed over the industrial parts of the city in favor of finishing the job of eliminating the humans. This city would serve as an example to all those that dared to interfere with the Hindra efforts to reclaim territory.

This repository of blood struck her as strangely humorous. It was blood that made all things as they were on Arctos, and without it even the simplest of chemical processes could not function. Blood was life, of course, but it was also power. Somehow this civilization, in the absence of the Hindras, had developed the art and skill to harvest blood from its citizens and then channel it to industry. It was fascinating—an adaptation that was necessary for human survival and yet would never have crossed the minds of the Hindras. Of course the Hindras had no need for such barbarism, for the blood within the veins of each was sufficient for any task they would ever undertake.

There were tubes of metal and of glass everywhere she looked, and Arenara fancied herself, like all those of her caste, a learner. She traced the tube works up and then caught sight of the walkways of suspended metal that crisscrossed throughout the upper reaches of the massive chamber. It was there, on one such walkway, that she saw the quivering, cowering form of a human.

She shouted, "Come down here. Now."

With a terrified squeak, the portly man (never would it be possible for a Hindra to grow to such girth—this was gluttony at its worst) scrambled to a ladder that led down from the walkways. As he descended, Arenara strolled to the base of the ladder and touched one finger to its metal leg. A bolt of chilling cold ran up the metal, causing the human to shriek in pain as his hand froze to a rung. He peeled the hand away, leaving flesh and blood behind, and finished his descent.

"Why are you in this place?" Arenara demanded. She had no particular power to compel his answer, other than the fear she knew he held in regards to her, but that was often enough, in her experience.

"I wanted something," the portly man murmured.

"What?" she asked. "What was worth risking your life for?"

The human gestured feebly behind Arenara, and she turned. He was pointing to a large canister filled with tiny white crystals.

She walked over to the canister and pulled out a handful. The crystals sifted down quickly between her fingers. It was a mineral of some kind, or perhaps powdered stone. It was inorganic, of that much she was certain.

"And why is this so important? Is it a weapon of some kind?" she asked, turning her attention back to the man.

Before he could answer, Lerrimur returned. He carried the Winterblooded slung over his shoulder. Arenara felt the heat in her body even from across the chamber—she still lived. Good. Her death would be a pleasant reward for Arenara's hard work in Venot. They had been sent by the others to hunt down the intruders, but she had taken it so much further. They would be truly safe when the humans learned to fear them once more, and Venot would be an example of this. It did not matter that they had yet to find the intruders—what mattered is that the Hindras would hide no longer. There was no need for hiding. They were too powerful to stop.

Lerrimur deposited the beaten shape of Karrin on the floor next to the cowering male and turned to Arenara. "I would join my brothers now. What you are about to do is no work for a *hahn'du.*"

Arenara nodded and dismissed the hunter. He fled quickly out the front entrance, treading noiselessly through the shattered glass of the office windows. Once he was gone, she smiled. Her smile seemed to bring new terror to the heavy man, who had helped the barely-conscious Karrin to her feet.

Karrin was bleeding from several cuts, and smoke rose in faint wisps from those abrasions. Arenara felt her anger rising. To think that her kind and theirs had once *lain* together—it sickened her.

The man looked up at her, his eyes wet. "I didn't get to answer your question before," he said firmly. "About the crystals."

Arenara inclined her head. "How obliging. Yes, tell me—what are they?"

"The taste of them," the man said softly, wip[ing sweat away from his shiny forehead. "It grants us power. It makes us powerful. If a person ingests enough, he would be a match even for you." He looked down at the floor, and Arenara could imagine the look of defeat in his eyes. Humans were so soft, so easily preyed upon.

She turned back to the canister and drew out a large handful of the contents, then strolled towards the pair of humans. She extended the handful towards the man. "So you thought to use this to overcome me?" she sneered.

The man made a motion, lurching forward to grab at her hands, but Arenara was faster than the chubby human would ever be, and she ripped her hand away from him, leaving him to sprawl on the ground. Then, smiling, she lifted her hand to her face and poured the handful of mineral into her mouth.

She was almost instantly overcome with a powerful, sedate sense of calm. Her rage melted away, as did her tension and her stress. She felt herself sink down to the ground, relaxed and content. She noticed, only barely, as the man struggled to help Karrin to her feet.

"We should kill it, Hunna," Karrin mumbled. While those words should have concerned Arenara, they did not. Little did.

Hunna shook his head. "I won't be a part of killing. Come on. Let's get you out of here."

The two of them left, leaving Arenara sitting cross-legged on the floor, blissfully unaware of what was happening around her. It was for the best anyway. Yes. Yes indeed.

¤~¤~¤

Marriq led the way and Yors guarded the rear. Becky found herself in the middle, soaking up the incredible sights of the Archive.

Once they entered the front of the Archive, they immediately descended a double staircase made of the same impervious glass that seemed to comprise most of the building. The stairs came to their end at the second sub-level, and the place was only barely lit by a few well-placed globe lamps hanging on chains. There were not bookcases here, but instead racks for scrolls and tomes carved into the stone that served as the foundation of the Archive. Becky had seen the records room of the Council Tower on Onus, and this place, just on this one level, dwarfed that collection's impressive size.

They followed Marriq down a zigzagging path through the bowels of the Archive, and Becky quickly became certain that she would be lost without Marriq as a guide. Unlike libraries back home, whatever organizational system they used here was not visible in the slightest.

"You're wishing you could read all of it, aren't you?" JC whispered.

"If the Kutaks win upstairs, maybe we'll be able to come back sometime. I'd love to know more about—well, everything," Becky replied, also in hushed tones. It was hard to bring oneself to make noise in this place—it was the ultimate library.

They were so close to learning about the Children of the Line, and, if they were lucky, even more. The most highly prized secrets of the Wyr, the only people in all the worlds that could actually see the future, were locked up in this place, somewhere.

Their pace slowed, and Becky stopped looking at the walls and instead took notice of the head of their party, where Todd had collapsed. Vanuella and Ebram were tending to him, but the racking sound of his coughs terrified Becky. It sounded much worse than a cold.

"What's wrong?" she asked.

Ebram looked up. "His blood is running cold. I don't understand."

Todd seemed to get the coughing under control and pulled himself up. "We've been here too long. I'm," he coughed again, "surprised that you haven't all caught something. Let's go."

They continued onward again, but Becky watched Todd more carefully than ever before. He moved sluggishly, the confident stride that so defined him absent now. He needed a Bloodmender, once they returned to Onus. Then again, so did most everyone here. Arctos had been hard on them all.

Marriq held up a hand and they all halted.

Directly in front of them was a bare patch of wall. There was no sign or marking on the gray stone at all, nor was there the carved repository for texts that existed on nearly every other stone surface in the place. Becky watched as Marriq stepped forward and produced the pointed metal device from under her traveling coat—the Archive key that had saved her from the Hindra attack back at her cabin.

She ran the key along the surface of the wall tentatively until, suddenly, it sank into the smooth stone with an audible click. Apparently the wall was not featureless at all, but instead simply enchanted, somehow, to render the keyhole invisible.

Marriq turned the key slowly clockwise, with each distinctive click muttering a word or string of syllables that Becky could not hear clearly. After the fifth click, she pulled her hand back, and the wall split open down the center, its two halves sliding away and back, revealing a small alcove, lit by a floating ball of metal.

Yors grunted approval as he watched from just behind Becky. "Scribe light. Easy Bindmetal working. One of Yors' favorites."

Becky smiled and turned back to Yors, ready to remark how nice it was to hear him sound happy. As she looked towards him though, her eyes met the bright, baleful eyes of a blood-covered Hindra, garbed in black, as it wrapped its slender, powerful hands around Yors' throat.

¤~¤~¤

Hunna held Karrin's hand as they ran. Her injuries made his pace a hard one for her to maintain, but he kept pulling her along. They had no time for plans or anything clever—they had escaped the creature only barely, and there were others.

Hunna regretted that his haste to escape had left no time for grabbing any of the desix, but it wasn't for his own use that he wished he'd pocketed a few pinches, it was for Karrin. She continued to berate him, even as he saved her life, for not killing the white-robe when he'd had the chance.

Killing wasn't in Hunna—he hadn't even been able to follow through on his own suicide. Part of that was his fatalist upbringing, for death was the province of fate, not of the actions of man, but part of it was an inherent abhorrence of the act. Karrin had no trouble ordering death and destruction, but maybe that was because she was a bit of a monster herself. He'd seen her blood burn. At first he hadn't properly thought about what it meant, but now, he knew. She was a Hearth Keeper, and that was the only reason they were running for the edge of the city now. Hunna knew enough about the reviled Circle of Stone to know that their kind could survive, and protect others, in the night. So they would head for the wilderness.

"I'm not going anywhere with you," Karrin shouted, struggling to break Hunna's grip. Desperation made him strong, or strong enough, and he replied, "You have no choice. You'll die if you stay here. They know you exist. They'll do everything they can to kill you."

"So your plan is to run. Run where?" Karrin questioned, easing up on her struggling and now keeping a better match to Hunna's pace.

"Your family estates," Hunna said simply.

"So you do remember me," Karrin replied.

Hunna grunted in the affirmative. His lungs nearly burned from the exertion of their run/walk, but still he persisted. The southern city boundary was not much further.

"We can't go there. Ever since my gifts came to light, my family has disowned me," Karrin added. "So I hope you have a backup plan."

Hunna pulled the pair of them to a stop just outside of sight of the main road that exited the city's southern edge. He turned to Karrin and looked her straight in the eyes. "Then we will head for the Grey Bound. Or perhaps Red. Somewhere far from them. They came at us from the west, so the White is out. We will run and we will tell everyone what happened here."

"Why not another of the cities?" Karrin asked. "You don't have what it takes to make it on the frontier, Hunna."

"Don't worry about me. I'll manage. The cities are no good to us," Hunna explained. "No one there will listen. The hedonists won't act outside of their own gratification, and the fatalists won't intervene in fate. We need the people of the Bounds. We need traditionalists. And maybe a few more of your kind, if they're out there."

"My kind?" Karrin asked. "My kind is your kind. I'm a human, same as you."

Hunna glared at her. "I saw what you did. I understand now what you were trying to do with the blood tank and the sparkdust. You're a Hearth Keeper, right?"

Karrin looked down. "That doesn't make me a monster. I'm still human."

"You're right," Hunna said. "Your power doesn't make you a monster. The fact that you tried to enslave half of Venot, and sent the others out to their death in the cold... that's what makes you a monster."

He pointed towards the city boundary. "We're going there. Now. Come with me and we'll see if there's a chance you can make amends for the things you've done."

"I have done nothing that requires making amends, you oaf," Karrin said, seething. "I saw an opportunity and I took it!"

"As I said. Monster," Hunna said with a stern look.

Karrin's mouth hung open as she searched for a retort, but she appeared to find none.

"Come with me. Please. Show me that there is hope for you—for all of us."

Karrin nodded slowly. Softly, she whispered, "I am not a monster."

Hunna did not reply.

They moved ahead, not running but instead cautious and stealthy. They left the city without incident, and as they traveled south, Hunna took one last look back at Venot. It pained him to leave it, for it had been the only home he'd ever known. But he no longer had a purpose there. There would be no more babies born in Venot, and no longer did the city require him to read the names of the newly-born aloud.

But if he was careful, and lucky, and strong... perhaps one day there would again be need for such a man, somewhere.

¤~¤~¤

On instinct, Yors dropped like a rock, using his weight to rip his neck out of the Hindra's grip. JC watched the big man go down in a tight ball, his heavy hammer thudding to the ground beside him.

With the smooth movement of steady practice, JC brought his rifle up and aimed it at the black-robed Hindra. Judging by the blood covering the creature from nearly head to toe, it had already been through the wringer. As soon as he had the shot lined up, he pulled the trigger.

A burst of brilliant light crossed the half-dozen yards separating JC from the Hindra, but the creature leapt up, somehow sticking to the relatively low ceiling of the sub-level and avoiding the blast as it carried beyond him and struck a stone support beam with a loud crack.

The Hindra skittered across the ceiling towards JC, glistening hooks of ice visible on each of its fingertips and each toe on its bootless feet. JC brought the rifle up and lined up another shot, but Becky knocked the barrel out of line, shouting, "You'll bring the roof down on us!"

JC sighed and tossed the weapon aside, leaping up to grab at the creature's robes and bring it down where it could be given a good, old-fashioned ass-whooping. The first part of his plan worked well, and his hands grabbed huge bunches of the blood-spattered robe. He came down from the jump, dragging on the robe, but the creature's strength and the leverage of its hooked grip left JC hanging from its robes rather than bringing it crashing to the ground.

Becky turned to Steven and shouted, "Get Urguroch!"

Steven took off back towards the steps.

JC swung himself up, pulling his legs in tight and flipping upside down as he drove his legs up and into the chest of the Hindra. He knew they were solidly built people-things, but everything had to breathe.

The impact startled the Hindra and it lost concentration for a moment, which in turn loosened its grip on the ceiling. As Joe's weight fell down once more from the upward strike, his body mass managed to pull the Hindra away from the ceiling, and the two of them tumbled to the cold stone floor.

JC scrambled to his feet as the Hindra did the same. Yors took a swing with the hammer at the creature, but it easily dodged it.

"This place is ours," the Hindra said through what appeared to be a cracked jaw. "You should not have come."

Becky reached out one hand toward the Hindra and replied, "That's too damn bad."

JC felt the power of Becky's magic turned upon the Hindra, unleashing a barrage of thoughts and images against its mind. It recoiled, its eyes wide with what just might have been fear, and JC took the opportunity to scoop up his rifle and swing it like a golf club, bringing the barrel up between the Hindra's legs as hard as he could manage.

The Hindra winced, which was not satisfying enough as far as JC was concerned, and started to visibly shrug off Becky's assault. Sweat beaded on her brow and JC motioned for her to cut it out and back off, but she held on. The Hindra stood fully upright and took two measured steps towards her, its eyes locked upon hers. It was overpowering her—he could feel desperation in her mind.

JC brought the rifle up to fire and let loose. The blast struck the Hindra in the back and brought it down to its knees, but it did not break eye contact with Becky.

He fired again, and this time it spun, its eyes dark and foam flecking at the edges of its mouth. It propelled itself towards him, disregarding the third blast JC fired. Whatever effect the weapon could have, it already had. He threw the weapon at the Hindra and it caught it in both hands, wrenching it apart into fragments and tossing them aside.

Rage boiled in JC's veins. "That was my boom!" he shouted. He lunged forward, slamming his head into the Hindra's head. The collision left them both momentarily stunned, and that was when Steven returned with Urguroch.

The Kutak ran on all fours and pounced upon the both of them, using its hind legs to separate JC out and shove him away as it grabbed the Hindra's arms in its forepaws. It curled its massive, clawed paws around each of the Hindra's upper arms and pulled, its furry shoulders rippling. The Hindra screamed as its arms were wrenched out of their sockets, and then Urguroch bent down and clamped its head in his powerful jaws.

He bit down, severing the head and gorging himself on the blood of the Hindra.

A moment later, the Kutak stumbled back from the dismembered corpse and collapsed on the ground. JC stood up and went to Urguroch, kneeling beside him. He said, "Thank you."

The great, furry creature made no reply. JC watched as his large eyes grew paler and paler, the color fading from them until they were white. Urguroch was not breathing.

"What happened to him?" he demanded, looking around.

Marriq's head was hanging low. "He has received the blessing. It is what he wanted. He is dead."

"That's... what he wanted?" JC asked, confused.

"Yes," came a voice from behind him.

He turned to see Vortigar, the chief of the Kutaks, standing beside Steven as well. His throat had been ripped open but was now covered in a thick, ugly scab. "Kutaks can only die by killing Hindras."

JC said, "So you all wanted to die? You came here so we could help you die?"

The Kutak leader bowed his head in agreement.

JC turned to Becky, who seemed to have recovered her wits. "So when I try to kill someone, I'm a horrible person. But when we all team up to help a bunch of badass yeti-things commit group suicide, that's somehow cool? I don't think I understand the rules you expect me to play by," he shouted.

Becky looked back at him and said, "I didn't know either, Joe."

"Whatever," he replied sullenly.

¤~¤~¤

Becky and Marriq stepped into the secured vault of the Archive together. The others stayed outside. Vortigar returned to the upper levels to aid his brothers in the fighting—his departure felt like a permanent good-bye, and Becky expected he too would soon find a 'blessing' and die.

"This is the vault where we kept all of the materials sent by the Wyr for safe-keeping," Marriq explained. "There are other vaults, but what you want should be stored here."

The single occupied shelf in the vault contained two books and a scroll case. The books were crafted in a way similar to the books Becky and Jara had read at the Council Tower, and that alone was verification enough for Becky. She read the spines on each of the books and found them illegible.

"Can you read that?" she asked, pointing to one of them. "I've never seen that happen before—usually when we travel through the Spiralgate it sort of dumps all of the languages of the new world into our minds. I should be able to read these."

Marriq shook her head. "None of us in the Archive can. They are written in the cypher of the Wyr, so that only a Wyr can read them. We were told it was because of the danger of the truth within these pages getting out."

"Then which one has the answers I need?" Becky asked, exasperated. "Unless we take them all..."

Marriq reached up and took down the scroll case, handing it to Becky. "Open up that bag of yours and start stuffing," Marriq said.

Becky arched an eyebrow. "You aren't going to freak out and tell me I can only take one?"

Marriq shook her head. "You helped me retake the Archive. Without you, my people would have access to none of the lore held here. These books, which I cannot even read, are of no consequence compared to that. If you believe you can take them to someone who can help you read them, so be it."

"How do you know I'm not exactly who the Wyr were trying to keep the books away from?" Becky asked.

Marriq smiled. "Our route here has been a winding one, but the destination was foretold. Open that scroll case."

Becky took the scroll case back out of her bag and slipped the cap off one end, pulling the loosely rolled parchment free. She unrolled it and saw a rough sketch of two women standing in an alcove, surrounded by books, a glowing orb hanging in the air above them.

One of those women was Marriq. There were not many fine details in the charcoal sketch, but the line of her body was a match for the old Archivist. The other woman was a smear of charcoal, as if one image had been drawn then rubbed away to make room for another. The figure resembled Becky, with long straight hair and a fullness of figure, but it also resembled Tatyana, with hoop earrings and long legs.

She could not tell from the parchment which of them had been drawn first and which of them had been drawn second—which had been erased to make room for the other. A chill ran up her spine.

"A few weeks after these books were entrusted to our care, a different Wyr came to the Archive. She brought with her this parchment, drawn by her own hand. She said this picture would help us to know when the time was right to turn over the books. I spoke with her only briefly, but I could tell she was acting against the wishes of her order. There was something familiar about her—something I trusted. I didn't recognize you at first—as you can see, the drawing of you is a bit vague, but I saw it in you, that duality, when you were hurt at Venot. When the boys brought you back to us. That was when I knew." Marriq put one hand gently on Becky's shoulder. "Take them all, with the blessing of what remains of the Archivists."

Becky nodded, still reeling from the shock of the picture, and numbly shoved the two books into her bag.

¤~¤~¤

The Kutaks did not finish off any of the Hindras and allow themselves to die until every last one of their alabaster enemies had been driven off. The Hindras had outnumbered the Kutaks, so Steven imagined their plan had always been to incapacitate enough for them to die from, and to scatter the rest far and wide.

The plan worked.

Once the Archive was secure, they made preparations to leave. Becky had the books but required help from Jara to decipher them. Ebram agreed to shelter them and guide them back to the Spiralgate, while Vanuella and Marriq stayed to start the process of reclaiming the Archive for human use. Before he left to lead them to the gate, and back to Adam and Jara at long last, Ebram restarted the hearthstones that heated the Archive, careful to keep his blood far from any of the precious, flammable tomes within.

Ebram led the way to the Spiralgate, and Steven covered the rear, with Todd occasionally leaning on him for support. Todd had seemed much better—not fully healthy, but certainly rejuvenated, after Becky had claimed the books and proclaimed them unreadable. Steven assumed that, like himself, Todd could see the end of their journey finally approaching.

The three days of travel were quiet. Yors worked once more on JC's chain, rendering two links inert, but he pronounced the shattered energy rifle a lost cause.

When they finally reached the Spiralgate, they did not have to wait long for it to activate—for once, luck was on their side and they arrived just moments before the appointed check-in portal from Adam.

"Thank you," Steven said to Ebram as the blue-white sphere of light materialized. "For everything."

Ebram bowed his head slightly. "If you had not come here, I might still be hiding from my responsibilities. I suppose I should thank you, but a small part of me holds that against you. I enjoyed the life I led before, very much."

JC patted the Hearth Keeper on the back. "Get used to it. We are very, very good at messing up the places we visit."

Ebram smiled. "Will you be back?"

Becky nodded. "Definitely. I don't know how long it will be, but, yes."

Yors lifted up his hammer. "Yors think this belong here," he said sullenly.

"You have earned it," Ebram said. "Besides, I do not know a single man who could easily lift that thing as you do."

Yors stared at the hammer for a few moments then smiled. "Yors bring it back, someday."

"Then we shall eagerly await the return of both yourselves and the hammer," Ebram said with a flourishing bow.

Todd was the first to cross into the Spiralgate, with Becky and JC close behind. Yors was next, hammer in hand. Steven was the last to go through, and as the roaring light of the Spiralgate swallowed his senses, he felt warm for the first time in what seemed like forever.

# 24
## Onus

*You certainly have mastered the art of slow torment,"* Duchess Ain proclaimed. "In fact, I begin to wonder when exactly my suffering is to start?" She was bound snugly at the wrists, as she had been for all of two weeks, and secured to a metal hook upon the wall in a squalid little room that she could only assume was somewhere in her city.

Grell was dozing in a chair not far from her. The fact that he could relax enough to sleep in her presence infuriated the Duchess, but there seemed little she could do but wait. He left her periodically, searching the city for something, but was never gone long, so most of her time waiting had also been time watching the big blonde man scowl and grumble. Something was not going his way.

The pirate captain opened a single eyelid and muttered, "Shut your mouth."

The Duchess considered screaming again—not because it would draw attention, for the magic in the pirate's dagger muffled all sound, apparently, but instead because it would irritate her captor. It seemed that was all she was down to now—needling him into making a mistake.

"When you took me, you said you would destroy my city and make me suffer its loss, as you did Duke Igar and his city. Has my city yet fallen? If so, it was the quietest demolition I have ever heard." The Duchess sneered. Her sneer was a practiced art, a look capable of baiting even the most iron-willed man to hasty action. But Grell was something else entirely, and he did not take the bait.

He did, instead, stand up, both eyes open, and place one hand comfortably on the black-hilted dagger that was sheathed at his side. The other dagger, the one that made screaming useless, was resting on the table next to him. It held down a rolled sheet of parchment that Grell had been consulting constantly for the entire time she had been his captive.

"You can appreciate the suffering of your city without a tongue, your grace," Grell said simply. "It might earn me a commendation from the people of your protectorate, now that I think about it."

Duchess Ain said nothing. She believed that this beast of a man was indeed capable of such a thing.

"I am waiting for the right time," Grell began, "and when the time is right, I will bring your city tumbling down. I thought it was here—the juncture. I have searched everywhere in this city, and it is nowhere to be found. Where have you hidden it?" He stepped up to her and grabbed her chin in his hand.

"I can honestly say I have no idea of what you are speaking," the Duchess replied. "And if it is something you desire, why would I give it to you?"

"Because your kind are all alike. You will sacrifice anything, everything, to save yourselves. I know what you have done. What your husband's father did. The juncture would have been a poetic end to you. It was its last use that ended everything good left in this world." Grell drew back his hand and slapped the Duchess, hard, across the cheek.

She narrowed her eyes and said to him, "Did your mother not love you? Is that why you act out like this against me?"

That did it. For more than fourteen days she had probed every course of action, every potential psychological vulnerability this madman might possess, and against her every effort he had proven immune. But it seemed that perhaps the oldest of tricks was the truest.

Grell drew his dagger and swept it up the side of her face, cutting deeply into her cheek and causing blood to run freely. His eyes were wide and wild, and he moved to make another cut, lower, his anger driving him past his reason.

"It is because of the Council that I will never know my mother!" he roared. He sliced at her stomach—a shallow cut that brought much pain but not a fatal wound. He was still in control to a degree, but he wanted to hurt her directly now. His grand plan was pushed aside by his rage.

It was the best chance that the Duchess would ever have. She lunged forward, the rope binding her wrists passing through the metal hook that held her to the wall as though neither object existed. In fact, her entire body tumbled forward, immaterial as it passed through Grell. When she was clear of him she grabbed the parchment from the table and ran for the door, which also posed no physical barrier to her as she passed harmlessly through its substance.

They were in a cellar of some sort, and she dashed half-way up the stairs before Grell even got through the door. As she burst out into the drizzle-filled air of a crowded afternoon street, her guards were there—dozens of them, weapons at the ready.

Grell charged up the stairs and drew back sharply when he saw them arrayed against him, their armored bodies forming a wall that swallowed up the Duchess.

"I'm not finished with you yet, Duchess. Or your city!" Grell shouted. Then, before any of the soldiers of Ain Holc could lay a hand upon him, he stomped one foot into the ground and vanished.

"I'm sorry," Adam, the Gatemaker, said from behind the Duchess. "I thought I had the area boxed in from teleporting like that, but it's not something I understand very well."

The Duchess said nothing, but she swatted away the Sur that tried to tend to her wounds. "I am fine," she explained in a harsh tone. The Bloodmender backed away.

"Did you learn what he plans?" Jara asked. She was standing next to Adam, and the Duchess was surprised to see what amounted to genuine concern from both of them. They had every reason to hate her. Purpose knew, she so often hated herself.

The Duchess held up the hand that tightly grasped Grell's parchment. "This map was guiding him to something he called the juncture. But either the map is wrong, or he was unable to read it, because he could not find it. He's been searching for it for days."

Jara took the parchment and held it up, studying it carefully. The Duchess also examined it, as her soldiers descended into the cellar to see what other clues Grell had left behind in regards to his mad schemes. The map was drawn in two colors, with a steady line snaking from a dark circle up and to the left, with several smaller circles indicating landmarks or stops. Drawn in red ink, the outline of the southern continent was made.

"The map was drawn twice—the trail first, the outline second," Jara said confidently. "I think the outline was drawn wrong. The distances are incorrect. This circle here is Enbel Igar, a fishing village that used to supply Igar Holc with most of its terril oil. But the distance between that mark and the mark for Igar Holc is too long."

"You're a cartographer now?" Adam asked incredulously.

"Grandfather thinks I need a well-balanced education," Jara muttered. "The point is, I think the two maps are at different scales. Wherever this juncture is, it's west of the city, and south, I think. The curvature of the line is at the wrong angle, a bit."

"Then where is this thing he searches for?" Duchess Ain asked impatiently.

"The Vale of Steam," Jara replied. "Whatever he wants, that's where it is."

"Excellent. I will dispatch soldiers at once," the Duchess stated. "Now, let's return to the palace. I've been in this same dressing gown for two weeks and it's grown positively ripe."

Jara folded her arms across her chest. "I foresaw your capture. Adam traced Grell's route and made it possible for you to escape whenever you wanted. We've gone well beyond our agreement, your grace. Where is my family?"

"Our agreement is that you serve the needs of the Council, as the Wyr and the Gars were always meant to do," Duchess Ain explained. "Why do you struggle so much with the concept?"

"I should have let you die!" Jara hissed, suddenly throwing herself at the Duchess. Fortunately for the child, the Gatemaker caught her and pulled her back, screaming and flailing.

The Duchess was suddenly quite pleased she'd never gotten around to having children.

¤~¤~¤

Narred was lost. His mule had died four days ago, and he had no idea where he was. Usually he had a keen sense of direction, aided by his ability to grab snatches of Vol transmissions to get his bearings, but since fleeing Kem Nought, he had gotten more confused and taken more circular trails and false starts than he would have thought possible. Any transmissions he attempted to intercept were garbled, and he dared not send out any of his own.

He began to suspect, yesterday, that the problem was not natural. His mental defenses kept his wife's prying mind out of his thoughts, but surely she knew why he had left—was she somehow stymieing his efforts to leave? As much as he had wanted to go towards Herin Holc, he thought he...

Yes. There was salt in the air. He was nearing the coast of the Silent Sea—the exact opposite direction of Herin Holc. There could be no doubt—Shayra was keeping him from escaping.

But he was still crossing distance, so even if he was no closer to the safety of Council-controlled lands where he could reveal the horrible secret that the Kem were hiding in their crystal city, he was at least further away from his wife and her maniacal brethren.

He continued to travel towards the sea, with a general southerly angle to his route, as the afternoon faded towards night. He passed the large, meaningless metal shape of a Spiralgate at one point, but he did not stop. The gates were useless and always brought to his mind memories of his brief time working with Lyda. Those were memories best left buried.

When dusk was fully upon him, he caught sight of a fire in the distance—his first sign of other travelers since departing Kem Nought. He quickened his pace as he barreled through the low foothills, hoping to find someone who could aid him. Shayra's powers could extend to him even at this distance because of their bond, but she would have no power over these travelers. They were the key to his salvation.

It was well into evening when he finally reached the location of the camp. Two men had made a camp in the ruins of what looked to be a large village. There were the remnants of low walls and a few stone towers scattered around their campsite, with a single squat tower still standing in the center of the ruins.

Narred pulled his hood low over his forehead, hoping that the dark and the hood would be enough to keep his distinctive profile from being noticed. The odds were anyone this far out in the middle of the wilderness had never seen a drawing of Narred's crooked nose, but he was uncertain how far the Council's bounty on him had spread.

It was a bounty that would be expunged when he traded his newfound knowledge for amnesty. He was certain of it.

"Hello, traveler," one of the men said. As Narred came within the circle of firelight, he found both men more similar than different. One had darker hair, but both were wide shouldered and wore thick beards. Even their dress was similar—well-made and well-worn.

"Good evening," Narred said warmly.

The men looked at him strangely. "You've come to the remains of Jov Nought. Just north of Norwin Holc," the darker haired man said. "You are a long way from anything, coming from the north."

Narred nodded agreement. "I've been fleeing for my life," he explained. "I was a guest of the Kem—Mindshapers. I have seen things that all good people of our world must know!"

The fairer-haired man looked up at Narred, and Narred thought perhaps he had pity in his eyes. "I'm sorry, sir. We do not understand you."

Narred grew angry. "Then you are fools. I demand you take me to Norwin Holc!" He pointed to the south. "I must reach the Duke immediately!"

"Yes, that is the way to the city," the fair-haired one said, speaking to Narred as though he were a child.

"We don't have time for wandering imbeciles, Ambrek," the dark-haired man said to his companion. "Let us dismantle the chime and be done here."

Narred lifted one hand and called upon his power, summoning a bolt of white-hot electricity into his fingers, pulling the power from his body and causing it to crackle wildly. He would show them who was an imbecile! He knew this was more of Shayra's doing—somehow she had scrambled his words.

The men leapt to their feet, backing away from Narred's outstretched fistful of energy, their hands up as they tried to calm him. But Narred lost sight of them as he found his eyes pulled to the short round tower near their camp. Something was there that called to him, to his power—a repeater.

He released the energy back into his body, nullifying the working, and turned to run towards the tower. If there was a repeater in there—a Bindmetal rod like those installed at several of the great cities—he could make contact with other Boltsenders. While he had feared Gendric learning his location before, he now saw Vol transmission as his only means of communication. There was no way Shayra could garble that—it was a vulnerability in Mindshaper magic.

The men chased after Narred, shouting at him to stop, but he ran anyway. The tower's door was hanging by a single hinge, and it easily tumbled to the ground when Narred slammed into it. The tower itself was hollow inside, with only two things of note inside—a ten foot tall rod of yellow Bindmetal suspended vertically on a thin wire, and a massive tube of orange Bindmetal, resting atop ten smaller tubes of similar material. A thin, broad piece of wood was wedged between the large tube and the smaller ones.

Narred grasped the golden rod and felt the transmissions of his Order come to life in his mind. He heard loud ones and faint ones, from all over the world. He heard Gendric ordering troop movements and he heard the faint, final transmission of thoughts from Cambria, still floating in the air because no one had yet listened to them.

He didn't know what to do, what to say. He could contact any Vol in the world from here, for this was perhaps the best-functioning repeater he had ever seen. It was nearly as strong as the central repeater at Vol Nought, but without the background noise of being surrounded by Boltsenders.

"Step away from the Bindmetal," the dark-haired man said. Narred turned, bringing a hand up to launch a warning bolt of lightning, and as he did so the man punched him squarely in the nose, breaking it once more.

Narred went down, blood streaming from his nostrils and pain flaring across his senses.

"I wonder who did that, Brennid," the one called Ambrek said as he entered behind the other. He was looking at the orange tubes.

Ambrek walked up to the piece of wood wedged into the tubes and whispered, "There's still a tone in here."

"That isn't possible. Who would even use that thing?" Brennid said, twisting Narred's hands behind his back and lashing them together with what felt like steel wire.

"I don't know," Ambrek said. He took the wood in both hands and, with a grunt, pulled it out. The upper tube chimed loudly, and Narred thought he heard words in that sound, but they reverberated so much that he could not separate one word from another. The sound carried down into the ten smaller tubes and then, as quickly as it began, it was gone.

¤~¤~¤

A courier burst into the Duchess' audience chamber, gasping for breath. Adam and Jara were there with her, of course, as she presented them with an outline of her expectations for the next day. In an hour Adam would sneak off to the Spiralgate to make contact with the others on Arctos—there had been so many missed rendezvous times that he began to worry that something horrible had happened to them, but Jara insisted that they were fine, so he trusted that. He had to, because otherwise that meant he had abandoned his best friend, his boyfriend, and everyone else to a strange world to die.

"I am busy," the Duchess said dismissively to the courier.

"But your grace, we just received a message," the courier explained, panting.

"About the pirate?" she queried.

"No, ma'am. Not that kind of message."

The Duchess arched an eyebrow. Adam thought it possible that he hated her even more than usual when she did that.

"Tell me then," she said impatiently.

"The Metalbreaker chime in the vault rang, your grace. It carried a message from the forges of the Metalbreakers," the courier had a look of profound awe on his face as he spoke.

"The forges have not sent word to us in twenty years," the Duchess mused.

"And there's no one left manning them," Adam said under his breath.

The Duchess fixed her gaze on Adam for a moment, then turned back to the courier. "And what did this message say?"

"It said 'Murrod needs help. Hyrak lives,'" the courier explained, his eyes even wider. "That isn't possible, is it, your grace?"

The Duchess stood suddenly. "Of course not. You are dismissed. Speak not one word of this, to anyone. Do you understand?"

With a fervent nod and a bow, the courier fled the chamber.

The Duchess turned to Jara. "What do you know of this?"

Jara, however, did not answer. Her eyes had rolled back in her head, and Adam grabbed her, steadying her as she began to tremble. Her body was suffused by a brilliant, pink light. A moment later, she returned to normal, sweat running down her face.

Jara grabbed Adam's hand, squeezing it so hard it hurt. "Mathias. Mathias sent the message. You have to go to him, Adam. Take the others. Hyrak has to be stopped." Then Jara fixed her gaze upon the Duchess. "I know where you are hiding my family. I've finally seen that. Release them and I will stay with you."

"Jara, no!" Adam exclaimed. "You're coming with me, with us!"

Jara shook her head. "I have to stay here. In case you fail. Go, now. Get them to Murrod. To the Sulgar Spiralgate."

Jara shoved Adam, that same pink light flaring in her touch, and Adam felt his powers activate, the familiar crossgate working he had used every night for weeks opening and carrying him to the Ebugar Spiralgate. Jara had woken his powers, had forced him to action—something he'd never seen her do before.

As the crossgate closed behind him, he thought he heard her whisper, "Prove my vision wrong."

¤~¤~¤

# END ACT II

¤~¤~¤

# 25
## Murrod

*The single moon of Murrod, a dusky red color, hung in the cloudless night sky.* Adam's left hand was tightly squeezing Todd's bandaged right, and all around him, in the blazing glow of the Spiralgate, were his dearest friends. They had been separated for nearly three weeks, and now they were back together again.

"I hate this world," Becky grumbled as Adam sealed the Spiralgate behind them, leaving the group alone in the darkness.

"But it's warm," Steven said, stretching his arms overhead. "That counts for an awful lot in my book."

"Too warm," JC muttered, swatting at an insect that buzzed past him. He was already starting to shed the heavy layers of clothing he had accumulated on Arctos, and the others soon followed suit. Adam had no need to do such a thing, as he was still dressed for the warmth of Ain Holc on Onus.

While the rest of them braced for an entirely different climate, Adam surveyed the area. They were in a city, or at least a large town—a couple of blocks away he could make out standing buildings. There was little but ruins close at hand, and there was no light burning in any window that he could make out. There were plenty of bugs all around—a Murrod staple—including the occasional flash of fireflies several hundred yards distant. The place felt deserted—and it shouldn't be. The light of the Spiralgate would have carried for miles in every direction on a night like tonight. He expected a welcoming committee.

"It's strange," Todd whispered in Adam's ear. "It seems like maybe we missed whatever Mathias called to warn you about." Adam had missed that voice and this closeness. He hated that they were on Murrod right now and not back home.

Drawing his thoughts back to the matter at hand, Adam shook his head. "We don't know how long ago the message was sent. I have no idea how long it takes for word to travel from world to world like that."

JC tapped Adam on the shoulder. He had stripped down to just his sleeveless t-shirt and jeans, and he had his one remaining energy rifle slung across his chest on its thick black strap. At his side was the smith, Yors, now once more wearing his simple leather tunic and breeches. The smith carried the huge sapphire hammer that he had not put down since Adam first saw them emerge from the Arctos-Onus Spiralgate, mere moments before he had spun a new portal to Murrod. While the walk through the transit corridor had afforded Adam the chance to explain what was going on, it had not given him a chance to learn the details of what had happened on Arctos.

"Yes?" Adam asked.

"Mind if we go scout around a bit? See what's up?" JC asked.

Adam was shocked. "You... are you asking me for permission?"

JC shrugged.

Adam smiled and looked at Yors. "Whatever you are doing with that chain of his must be working... he's a different person already." Looking back at JC he said, "Sure. But be careful. We will find a place to hole up somewhere here—maybe there?" Adam pointed to one of the nearest intact buildings.

Yors' eyes grew wide as Adam pointed. "Yors know that place."

Todd asked, "You've been here before?"

Yors squeezed the grip on his hammer tightly, and Adam could see beads of sweat forming all along the smith's forehead.

"Great Forge of Hineros. This... this where..."

Becky interjected, touching Yors' hand gently and saying, "We won't stay there." She cast a quick look around and pointed to another structure, not far from the forge. "There. That's where we will crash for now. It certainly looks abandoned."

Adam began to interject—if that building was the Great Forge it was the place where Mathias' message had originated—but he suddenly felt the sharp pressure of Becky's thoughts against his mind. "Shush. I'll explain in a minute. Just let them go look around."

Adam nodded, and JC and Yors took off—moving towards the east rather than to the south where the forge building stood. Steven gestured at the two of them as they departed and said, "I'm going to keep an eye on them."

A moment later, Becky, Adam, and Todd stood alone at the foot of the Spiralgate.

"That's the place Yors worked when he first came to Murrod," Becky explained. "That's where his family was killed by the sons of bitches that run this stupid world."

"Only part of the world," Todd corrected. "Don't forget the crazy girl-cult in zoo masks that tried to burn you at the stake."

Becky scowled.

"Then we won't *stay* in the forge," Adam said. "But we have to check it out. Come on—before they get back."

Adam took a few steps towards the forge, but then stopped suddenly as Todd grabbed him by the shoulder with an iron grip.

"Don't move," Todd said. "Don't take one more step."

Adam spun his head around, trying to see what was happening, but Todd's grip made even twisting his neck a challenge.

Becky's voice echoed in his mind, "We're not alone."

"I don't see anyone," Adam thought back at her.

"Ellir," Todd whispered. "Lots and lots of Ellir."

Then Adam saw them. Or rather, he saw their eyes. Those weren't fireflies in the distance, surrounding the clearing that held the Spiralgate. They were the faintly glowing eyes of the nocturnal, homicidal Ellir.

¤~¤~¤

There were Ellir in the city. Every ounce of training that Tyrick had undergone since being appointed to the Surveyor's Guild screamed out in his mind—he had failed. The smith was still with him, of course, but after the fourth full day of conflict Tyrick finally decided he needed to get rid of the problem he had made for himself.

But there was nothing to be done. While the suns were up, when the fighting in the street was between the men of Greendeep and the women of Goldvast, it was reasonably safe to move around. But there were no knights of any branch to spare in the city, and so the business of surveying the perimeter had been left undone. It was simply too dangerous to go out into the jungle without military support.

They were back once more in Tyrick's flat, and the smith was sitting quietly in the corner. He had been quiet and docile throughout their four days together, and Tyrick found the smith's predicament wearing on him. The heavy wooden box and wooden chains that he had seen as necessary implements before grew reprehensible and deplorable as each day ticked by. As much as it defied his training, Tyrick knew that there was a man inside that box—not a tool.

It turned Tyrick's stomach to think of the other smiths locked up below the Surveyor's Guild building. It was unlikely that anyone had taken care of them at all since the open fighting broke out, and even he had not thought of them until just now... his concerns had been more squarely situated on his own problems. He stood at the window of his flat and watched the streets outside carefully. He had put out the candles in his home, as had every other man with any sense at all on the west side of the river. The fighting had pushed into the east now, and there was no safe place to seek refuge. The Ellir attacks had been savage and thorough the first two nights, but they were nowhere to be seen tonight. Of course there were also no men (or women) in the streets either. He couldn't even imagine how many men had been slain.

Even more troubling, he couldn't figure out how the beasts had made it past the perimeter.

Out of the corner of his eye he caught a flicker of movement down the street. Whatever it was, it was passing on a cross street and was not easily discernible from this vantage point. He moved quietly to the door and pressed it open on silent hinges, leaning out to see what was happening.

A moment later, before whatever was happening came fully into view, he felt a strong, soft hand on his shoulder. The smith had approached him and was gently pulling him back away from the door. Tyrick pushed the hand off roughly and whispered sternly, "Stop."

The smith backed up a step and bowed his head, trembling slightly in the pale moon light that spilled through the open door. Once more Tyrick's guilt over his complicity in the captivity of these smiths boiled over in his heart.

The smith made a soft sound, but if it was a word, Tyrick couldn't make it out through the muffling box of wood surrounding the smith's head.

Tyrick turned back to look outside and saw a curious sight indeed. Five figures were moving past the intersection at the end of the street. Three were Ellir, tall and four-armed and unmistakable by silhouette even if their blue-skinned features were largely invisible against the darkness. In the center of their procession was a tall man, walking with a pronounced stoop and with tangled, dirty gray hair hanging down before his face. The man was old—clearly not of Greendeep—and leaned heavily on the last figure for support. That supporting form was a warrior woman of Goldvast, complete with a large totem mask, painted like a snake, slung across her back. The man and the woman were obviously prisoners of the Ellir—but why? The Ellir, at night, were not customarily the sort of beings to take prisoners.

These Ellir besieging Hineros by night somehow circumvented the perimeter. They took prisoners. They kept their savage instincts in check, keeping the city under control and locked down at night rather than murdering every living man in the city. None of these facts equated with the Ellir he had ever encountered before... and Tyrick felt certain that whatever those two prisoners had done to be worth being captured by the Ellir made them a part of the answers.

"Chron forgive me, but I have to know..." Tyrick muttered under his breath. He looked back at the smith and he resolved to do something else as well. The perimeter had been everything to him a few short days ago, but now... it meant nothing. If he was about to do something stupid, what harm would one more stupid move really do?

"Hold still," Tyrick said firmly. He worked the locking mechanism on the smith's box to open the front panel, as he normally would to provide the smith with food or water, but once he flipped it down he drew the large hunting knife from his boot. With a steady sawing motion, he cut through the seamless wooden structure. It took only a few minutes. Before he sawed through the final few inches along the back, he moved to the smith's wrists and ankles, easily sawing through the wooden chains at their centers. He would take care of the cuffs attached to each limb, and the dangling lengths of dully rattling chain, in a minute.

Then he led the smith outside. The smith moved slowly, as if in shock. Once he closed the door behind him, Tyrick turned back to the smith and pried his fingers into the crack he had formed in the headbox. With a grunt of effort, he pulled the two halves apart, splitting the last few inches of joined wood apart and lowering the two halves away from the smith's head.

The smith had shaggy blonde hair and a patchy growth of golden beard, with a short, round nose and large ears. Behind the unkempt mane of hair, Tyrick could see bright green eyes that were wet with unshed tears.

"You should have a name," Tyrick said softly. "People need names."

The smith, however, seemed to pay Tyrick no heed. His eyes were fixed past, and above, the surveyor. Tyrick turned to see what the smith was looking at and saw the bright disc of the moon hanging overhead.

"Sky," the smith said simply, his words dripping with awe.

"That's as a good a name as any," Tyrick said with a small smile. "Come on, Sky. We have to find out where they're taking the prisoners."

¤~¤~¤

The wind whistled past Jarrek's ears as he sat astride the dragon Ahmur, immediately behind Hyrak. The dragon's great wings beat infrequently, but still they sailed rapidly through the night sky. They traveled east, and had been for a full day and all night. The seemingly endless jungles of Greendeep sped by below them.

"The dragon can travel by magic, can't she?" Jarrek shouted.

Hyrak held up a hand, and Jarrek grew quiet. Clearly the warlord's mind was on something else, or was, perhaps, some*where* else.

A moment later, Hyrak lowered his hand and his reply came in the form of the mental communication the warlord now favored and Jarrek detested.

"There seem to be limitations on which of her powers I am able to compel her to use while the bell is working its magic upon her. A disappointing drawback, I must say."

Jarrek snorted and replied, "So you *just* have a giant, armored flying fire-breathing war machine instead of a giant, armored flying fire-breathing war machine with magic powers. I can see why you're upset."

"I'm glad your anger with me has subsided to the point of sarcasm," Hyrak said. "Your work for me is almost through, but we must deal with the rest of the real powers of this world before you can discharge that duty."

"And Embrew," Jarrek asked, desperation seeping into his tone in spite of his efforts to remain composed, "is being held for me? For my vengeance?"

Hyrak nodded. "I was just checking in with my detachment of Ellir in Hineros. He is safe and awaiting your return."

"They are mighty warriors, but who is watching over him during the day while they are useless?" Jarrek placed a hand upon Hyrak's shoulder.

Without moving a single muscle, Hyrak backhanded Jarrek with his mind, the warlord's mindshaping power conferring the strike with more power than even his impressive physique could accomplish. Jarrek was knocked back and found his fingers compelled to release their grip upon the makeshift saddle Hyrak had affixed to Ahmur's white-scaled back.

A moment later, Jarrek was dangling from the dragon, his mighty arms wrapped around the pistoning shoulder joint where Ahmur's wings met her back. He screamed out, "Pull me up!"

Hyrak turned slowly and narrowed his milky-white eyes into a baleful glare. "You will never touch me again, Jov. Do we have an understanding?"

"Yes!" Jarrek screamed. "Yes!"

"Good." Hyrak turned back to face forward.

"Will you help me up?" Jarrek asked, pleading.

"My benevolence has reached its limit simply in letting you dangle there," Hyrak replied succinctly. "Hold fast, Metalbreaker. We have only a few hours left until we land."

Jarrek said nothing, steeling his resolve to maintain his bear hug on the undulating base of the dragon's wing. But he could feel the Bindmetal in the small bell strung around the dragon's neck and he entertained for a moment the notion of reaching out and shattering it—freeing the dragon to exact her revenge on Hyrak. This warlord deserved no loyalty from him, not after months of captivity and torment. And yet...

He could not. He grew increasingly convinced that he himself was a victim of Hyrak's mental powers, just like Embrew had been, but... he didn't know. Nothing was more maddening than not being able to trust one's own mind.

Except, perhaps, trying to keep hold of a dragon as it barreled towards the soon-to-rise suns and, he could only assume, the domain of the dragon Ehbor.

¤~¤~¤

Chaplain Reid hurled the last remaining object atop his desk, a mostly-unused leather-bound journal, across the room. It struck the wall not far from the courier's head, but the young man did not flinch.

"Get out. Get out now," the Chaplain said with a dismissive gesture. The courier made haste to depart, likely thankful he was still alive considering how few couriers survived the delivery of bad news into this office, and Reid was left alone with his thoughts and the crumpled piece of parchment in his hand.

He collapsed into his chair and cast the paper to the floor, then started to rub at his temples. In the mirror this morning they had looked a bit gray—something almost unheard of among the men of Greendeep. Now, with this news, he felt his age as never before.

"Hineros lost?" he mumbled. "I spent every coin in our coffers building that damned perimeter, and what good did it do us?"

"I take it you've heard the news?" a high-pitched voice asked. Reid looked up to see Chaplain Voss standing in the doorway wearing his heavy black ceremonial robes.

"I don't want to hear it," Reid said. "I will deal with you when I deal with all of the others. Tomorrow."

"I'm actually not here about the siege," Voss explained, stepping into the room but not taking a seat. "Although I thought you might like to know that I overheard men in a tearoom last night referring to it as a *war*."

"It is not a war. I have kept this land out of open warfare for twenty years. This is a blemish—a skirmish. Nothing more." Reid glared at Voss. There was a smugness in the usually cowardly Minister of Incarnation's face that Reid found wholly alarming.

"As you say. Security is your business, and I trust you to it. But as I said, I am here on business of my own. I would like you to meet someone." Voss turned back towards the doorway expectantly.

A few moments later, a young man entered. He wore plain brown clothes that did not fit him particularly well, and his face carried a slightly vacant expression. Reid's eyebrow arched. "Fresh from the nursery?" he asked. The man was little more than a boy, scarcely twenty by Reid's estimation.

"Indeed. This is Sennot. Chron chose him especially for what many consider to be the highest of honors. I wanted you to meet him right away." Voss took a seat now, and he gestured for Sennot to join him in the other vacant chair.

Chaplain Reid inclined his head slightly, and Sennot returned the gesture. "I care little for guessing games, Voss. What will this young man be doing for us?"

"At Chron's request," Chaplain Voss added. "Do not forget that part. Our dragon-god wants this done, and as you well know, there is no being that can change the mind of Chron once it has been set upon a course of action."

Reid drummed his fingers on the desk in front of him impatiently. The look of arrogance on Voss' face was growing, and Reid wished he had slit the smug bastard's throat on any of the dozens of opportunities he had had over the years.

"May I present the new Minister of Security?" Chaplain Voss said, grinning.

Reid exploded across the desk, grabbing Voss by the black robes and hauling him up out of his chair.

"You haven't the power to depose me, you sniveling flower-eater!" Reid shouted. Spittle sprayed across Voss' face, and the smaller man winced... but the smile did not abate.

"No one is deposing anyone," Voss forced out awkwardly.

Reid released his grip on the Minister of Incarnation, and Voss tumbled back into his seat awkwardly. Through this all, Sennot sat quietly, watching.

"Your time has been called," Voss explained, grinning widely. "I know what you did—the bribes to my clerks, the extortion to the underministers. You are a stubborn old fool, Reid, but the end comes for us all in time. Chron has named the time of your end, and it is now. Within the week you will die—

no matter how much you rage against it, no matter how stubbornly you fight it... you will die. You will be reborn, as all must be in time, and you will start a new life."

Reid lowered back into his own chair, shaking his head. "No."

"It's disheartening, I know. I have counselors who can speak with you if you like—some men, weaker men, sometimes have breakdowns when their time is called," Voss added helpfully—but Reid knew it was not sympathy but bitter joy that motivated the chaplain's words.

"And you without a bindmate," he added. "A pity about poor Heracis, but more's the pity that you never found a replacement for him. I can only imagine that your next life will be... difficult. Starting back at the bottom. Or, perhaps..."

Reid looked up, locking eyes with Voss and seeing the exact shape of the scheme boiling in that balding head. The line of demarcation.

"I should kill you right now," Chaplain Reid growled.

"Oh please," Voss said, standing and straightening the front of his robes. "You will do nothing of the sort. I'm your last chance at salvation." He reached into the pocket of his robe and drew out a matched pair of Bindmetal contract rings. "Today you are too angry to consider it. Any day in the past, your hatred of me would have made such a thing unthinkable. But now, every last minute of your life is a grain of sand upon the scales, tilting inexorably in my favor. Our fates will be intertwined, Reid. Not because you love me, and not because I love you—but because neither of us wants to be a member of the abominable worker caste we have created. But it will be my ring upon your finger, not the reverse. It will be known that you bowed to me."

Voss swept out of the door, Sennot close behind him. Reid had nothing to throw at them as they departed.

He pulled open the drawer of his desk and opened the small box within, where his contract rings were kept. There were rules—protocols, set down by Chron in the very beginning of Greendeep. The rings were the key to rebirth, and his was upon no one's finger.

But he would be damned if he would ever wear Voss' ring. His prestige would not be fuel for the fire of Voss' ambition. There had to be another way.

For twenty years, Reid had kept Greendeep out of war. He had done this through innovation, creativity, cruelty, and more. Rules were mere obstacles to him. And, perhaps, the chaos in Hineros was the opening he needed to overcome this newest barrier.

¤~¤~¤

Becky called out mentally to JC and Steven, but they had already noticed what she was warning them of—the area was surrounded by Ellir. There were not that many of them, as far as her surface level sweep of the area could determine—perhaps a dozen. But it was the contents of those thoughts—murderous rage, one and all—that most troubled her.

She was close behind Todd, who in turn had his hand upon Adam's shoulder. She gently spun a mental link into place between the three of them and whispered mentally, "We absolutely cannot beat these things in a physical fight."

"I could take one. Maybe two," Todd replied. "If Joe can get his gun into play, and Yors gets over here with the hammer—we could have a chance. Are you sure they are going to attack?"

"Pretty sure," Becky said, looking around again. The Ellir did not appear to be moving—yet.

"I can drop an intercession all around us—clear us a path to safety," Adam added. "It'll have to be pretty big to keep them all pushed away, but it can't be worse than the flying pirate ship at Ain Holc."

"I'd like to remind you how assed up you were after that," Todd thought sternly.

"Noted," Adam said. To Becky, he sent the thoughts, "Can you give the others the signal when it is time? They'll only have a minute, maybe two, before the intercession comes down."

She nodded. She pointed to the pile of packs and discarded winter clothing all around them. "We can ditch the clothes, but we'll need the bags. Or at least mine—I have the books from the Archive in there." She knelt down and plucked her bag from the pile. "Just this. Everyone else will make do without. Let's go."

Adam turned back to Todd, smiled, and then threw his hands up in the air.

Becky felt a tightness in the air as Adam worked his arts. Intercession was subtle—it didn't conjure streamers of light like many of his other abilities. The working flowed out of him and all around them, expanding the distance between them and the Ellir beyond the normal constraints of physical space. The only hole in the intercession, the only place where distance behaved normally, was directly ahead—towards the forge building.

Adam lowered his hands and Becky hurled the command at the others. Then she ran as hard and as fast as possible towards the forge. Adam and Todd were just behind her, the effort of the working robbing Adam of energy and leaving Todd to half-carry him. Behind them, she heard JC let out a whoop as he, Steven, and Yors barreled towards the forge.

Becky smashed through the door—which was locked but not particularly sturdy—and the others followed suit. As Yors entered, panting, Becky pointed to the door and asked, aloud, "Can you bar this?"

The smith nodded and pushed the door shut, running one large hand over the metal of the knob and lock. His power expanded and reshaped it to compensate for the splintered doorframe where Becky's impact had smashed the door latch clear free of its housing. A moment later, he was done. "Will not hold up to much beating," Yors remarked sadly. "Yors will find way to brace."

Becky smiled and said, "Thank you."

Behind her, Adam let out a sharp breath. "Intercession is down. If the door and the walls will hold a few minutes, I can get something smaller and tighter up around us here. I just need to rest a second."

JC looked around and grunted. Becky also took in the sight of the main room of the forge—it was empty. There were stairs leading up and a double door leading to other chambers beyond, through which Yors had just passed, but here, every stick of furniture was gone except for a large wooden handcart.

"Not exactly what I was expecting for a place called the 'Great Forge'," JC mused. "Must have been picked clean after we smuggled all of their Metalbreakers back to Onus."

A loud smashing sound, and several grunts, came from beyond the double doors. JC darted towards them, but before he made it through, one swung back into the front room and Becky saw Yors standing there with a captive. The young man he had caught was standing in front of Yors, with both arms twisted behind his back in the smith's mighty grip. The captive wore a sleeveless gray smock and a kind of pants covered in thick pockets. The smock had a hood that was drawn up over the captive's head. As Yors pushed through the door the captive shook his head violently, causing the hood to spill back around his shoulders.

"Mathias!" Becky shouted.

# 26
## MURROD

A *dozen Ellir beat against the walls of the Surveyor's Guild – the old Great Forge of Hineros.* They could not enter—Adam's powers had seen to it, but Mathias winced each time a blow landed on the door and each time one of the raving creatures shouted. There had been little time for pleasantries, once Becky had convinced the large Metalbreaker that Mathias was no threat.

And Mathias was indeed no threat. Norrun was dead—his body taken upstairs, out of sight from the others here. Mathias was not properly sure how much time had passed since his friend had died—more than two days, surely. He had eaten only a pittance, from the reserves he found here in the guild hall, and mostly he had slept fitfully, waiting for help to come. He had not expected help to come in the form of Adam and Becky and the others. It made sense of course—other than Embrew, Adam was the last surviving Gatemaker as far as Mathias understood things. But seeing them again brought back more complicated feelings. Compounded with his grief over Norrun, Mathias felt like his insides were boiling over, a whirlwind of confused feelings, regrets, anger, and more.

Adam was sitting in the center of the room, Todd at his side, as always. Becky was also with them, helping to keep Adam focused. The need to repel the Ellir outside would fade soon—Mathias was confident from the hue of the sky outside the windows that the first sun would rise soon. Then perhaps there would be time to truly catch up.

"So, how've you been?" JC asked, sidling up next to where Mathias stood, against a wooden post that supported the upper levels.

Mathias sighed. "Not especially well. You?"

JC shrugged. "I'd complain, but it doesn't help anyway. Glad to see you're alive."

Mathias replied, "It's taken some doing. I'm glad my message made it to you. We have a very serious problem. I suspect we will need more help than just the six of you. Perhaps, in the morning, Adam can open a gate back to Core? We need Jonas' help."

JC's eyes grew wide, and his mouth hung slightly open in an expression Mathias could only assume was shock.

"What? What did I say?" Mathias asked anxiously.

Steven had apparently overheard the direction of the conversation, and he joined them around the heavy wooden column. "Mathias, we didn't have a way to get in touch with you after it happened," he said quietly.

"After *what* happened?" Mathias asked, louder. Becky looked up from Adam, and Mathias thought he saw something in her eyes as well—pity? No. Sorrow.

"Jonas is dead," JC said bluntly. "He never woke up at the hospital."

Mathias said nothing. Outside, the shouting and banging of the Ellir started to still. As the quiet rose up all around them, Mathias felt his heart beating harder and harder in his chest, the sound of it, the crushing weight of it, drowning out everything else around him. Jonas had been his friend, his mentor—the one person on Core that had not brushed him aside after he'd given up everything to join Adam's band of would-be world-saviors. Jonas had been good to him, to everyone—and now he was gone? It wasn't possible.

JC extended a hand towards Mathias' shoulder, but Mathias swatted it away. "What happened? He was healing! When I left, Becky had just gone into his mind and made sure he was fine!"

"He never woke up," Steven repeated, his tone deliberate and calm. "The doctors aren't sure why."

"Did we miss an Obliviate?" Mathias asked. "Did one slip past us, somewhere?"

JC shook his head. "We thought that. But it's been a year, and nothing else has happened. If there was one of those things out there, it would have done something else, made some other move. But nothing's happened. He just died, Matt. People just die, sometimes."

"Not sometimes..." Mathias mumbled. "All the time."

"The first sun is up," Todd said, standing. "It should be safe to relax."

Mathias watched as Todd helped Adam to his feet. How did they do this? How did they keep going? He didn't have the strength. There had been too much death already. And there would be more in the days ahead. Hyrak would see to that.

"Where's Yors?" Becky asked.

Mathias looked around the large room, but the smith was nowhere to be seen. He wasn't sure when he had last seen the Metalbreaker—perhaps not since he had released his grip on Mathias after finding him hiding in the back.

A great clap of thunder sounded, shaking the very floorboards beneath their feet.

"Are those things attacking again?" Steven asked, flexing his hands as shadows started to swirl around his body.

"No," Mathias said softly. "That came from below us—from the tunnels."

¤~¤~¤

Sky followed closely behind Tyrick. Tyrick could feel the proximity of the newly-freed smith as the two of them pressed up tight against the side of the building where the Ellir had taken their prisoners. The first sun had cleared the horizon, and the second would soon follow. This was the safest time to encounter the Ellir, but Tyrick still preferred caution.

The building itself was not familiar to him—but he was not a native of Hineros, and he had found himself with little time to explore the city between tours to the perimeter for maintenance. They were rather far south of the Surveyor's Guild and his own flat, but still on the west side of the River of Songs. It was possible this building was a home, or a block of smaller flats, but the walls were sturdy wood and the corners were inset with stone—whoever had called this structure home before the fighting began, they were wealthier than most that lived on this side of the river.

Sky gestured toward the door, and Tyrick nodded. The smith had grown bold once freed of his shackles, but there was still a deference in his bearing that made Tyrick almost ill. A lifetime spent answering to the commands of the men of Greendeep would not be undone simply by removing a few restraints.

Tyrick slid carefully along the wall, his every sense alert. No one was moving around outdoors, but that wasn't a shock—the Ellir may have retreated during the day, but the other problem became more pronounced while the suns were up: the masked warriors of Goldvast. It was clear from the outset that the women and the Ellir were not working together, but their dual presence left the men of Hineros with no relief. Luckily, there appeared to be no animal-masked marauders patrolling this part of the city right now, but it was impossible to say for how long that would be the case.

They reached the door, and Tyrick gave it a tentative push. It opened easily—not barred or locked in any way. Sky still close behind him, Tyrick squatted down and drew his hunting knife from his boot, then pushed the door all the way open.

Immediately inside the door was a small cloakroom, but beyond that was a larger hall, complete with a long, rectangular dining table. From this vantage point, Tyrick could see only one end of the table and no Ellir. They passed through the cloakroom, Sky closing the door soundlessly behind them. Pegs set into the wall held several cloaks and a large traveling bag, but otherwise this room was unremarkable. They slipped through the open archway into the dining room, and Tyrick drew back quickly. At the far end of the table, tied to a pair of stout wooden chairs, were the two prisoners. The old man looked much the same as when Tyrick had first caught sight of him, but the woman had been divested of her equipment—her elaborate mask and whatever other gear and weapons she had carried were now removed from her. Heavy coils of rope wound round each of them, securing them to the back of the chairs. They sat quietly as two Ellir stood facing them. The tall, blue-skinned warriors each had both sets of arms folded across their chests and lower torsos, respectively, and stared blankly at the prisoners.

This didn't make sense. Tyrick peered carefully around the corner, but he couldn't understand why the prisoners did not simply order the Ellir to release them. Did they not realize the suns were up? The room had only a single wide window, which was covered by a heavy gray shade, but the light of the morning suns was apparent at its edges.

Tyrick sucked in a deep breath and stepped confidently into the dining hall. He walked to the end of the table nearest him and leaned forward, both hands on the smooth wooden surface. "Release them," he said forcefully.

The blank looks on the faces of the two Ellir suddenly fell away, replaced by furrowed brows and snarling sneers. Something was indeed not right. One of the mighty creatures stayed in place, close by the prisoners, but the other leapt up on to the table and lunged forward, all four arms extended towards Tyrick. He saw it then, clipped upon the loose belt of rope around the creature's waist—a sun-shaped talisman of yellow-gold Bindmetal. He had heard rumors of such devices around Imperia. It granted an Ellir its freedom during the day.

Tyrick ducked down and the Ellir sailed past him, colliding with what was immediately behind Tyrick—Sky. The smith held his ground and did not fall when the snarling Ellir fell upon him, instead reaching up and locking hands with the Ellir's upper limbs, engaging in a vicious bout of wrestling. No sooner had the two begun to grunt and strain against each other than did the Ellir's second, lower set of arms begin swinging at Sky's stomach, landing blow after blow. The smith grunted and gasped.

Tyrick came back to his feet, behind the Ellir now, and grabbed the heavy chair from the foot of the table, swinging it with all his might into the Ellir's back. The chair cracked but did not break, and the Ellir was knocked away, colliding with the wall and momentarily dazed.

Sky took the opportunity to suck in several steadying breaths and Tyrick took him by the arm, pulling him along the side of the table away from the gasping Ellir.

Tyrick chanced a quick glance away from the combatant Ellir and towards the one still standing guard, and his eyes grew wide as he watched that Ellir flailing madly about. It was sunk into the floor of the dining hall up to its knees, and it was attempting to brace its lower arms on the floor to push itself out, but those hands too seemed to pass through the insubstantial floor. It howled with rage.

"Beware!" the old man shouted.

Tyrick tore his gaze away from the besieged Ellir and back towards his dazed foe, but Sky had been watching that Ellir, and he took it upon himself to end this. The smith met the Ellir's charge by squatting low and bracing, shoulder out. Their collision came with a sharp crack, but Sky seemed uninjured. He pushed up with his legs, driving the Ellir up into a flip, landing on its back on the table.

Sky clambered up onto the table and gripped one hand in the other, bringing his coupled hands down again and again on the creature's chest like a hammer beating an anvil in slow, measured strokes.

Tyrick heard several of the Ellir's ribs crack.

"Enough!" he shouted. Sky stopped, panting, sweat running down his pale face.

The Ellir did not move.

Tyrick approached the captives, stepping carefully away from the sunken Ellir who was now merely a head protruding from the solid wooden floor of the room. He used his knife to saw through the heavy rope of the old man first. Once the bindings were free of that one, he turned his attention to the woman.

"You aren't going to try to kill me if I let you go, are you?" he asked hesitantly. This was the closest Tyrick had ever been to a woman, but the stories... the stories did not paint them in a beneficent light.

"Hurry up," the woman hissed. "We aren't alone here, and you need my help."

Tyrick arched an eyebrow and then realized what she meant. They had been trailing a party of five, not four. There was one Ellir unaccounted for.

As soon as that thought crystalized in his mind, the creature struck.

It came from beyond the doorway at this end of the dining hall, and it moved quietly, not making nearly the ruckus of its fellows. It grabbed Tyrick's arm and twisted, sending the knife skittering across the floor as Tyrick shouted in pain and went down to his knees.

Sky turned and hopped down from the table, approaching the Ellir cautiously in a careful crouch. The Ellir recognized something of a threat in him, perhaps having seen the prone body of its colleague upon the table, and echoed that fighter's crouch as it released its grip on Tyrick and shoved him aside.

The old man stood from his chair and stretched one hand out towards the Ellir, fingers spread wide. A shimmering haze sprung up between the Ellir and Sky, and as the two crept further and further forward, Tyrick watched in awe as neither appeared to actually be getting any closer to the other.

"Finish the rope," the woman whispered urgently.

Tyrick retrieved his knife and finished sawing through the bonds that held the warrior woman to her chair.

Without a word, the woman leapt to her feet and darted up behind the Ellir, nearly sliding to a stop as she dropped to her knees and reached forward—plucking the sun-shaped talisman from the creature's belt.

She gripped it tightly in both hands, and Tyrick heard an echoing, screeching sound begin to build all around her, bouncing off of every surface in the room.

Sky screamed, "No!"

And then, with a flash of light and an acrid puff of smoke, the talisman shattered into a thousand pieces in her hands.

The Ellir stopped immediately, standing upright as a complacent, dull look settled across its face.

The woman barked, "Leave this place. Travel north without stopping until you can travel no more."

The Ellir nodded sharply and then, without a word, began to run. As it did so, the old man made a small, dismissive gesture with one hand and the hazy field of distortion between Sky and the Ellir faded. The creature passed Sky without a word and left the room, and the home, a moment later.

Sky approached the kneeling woman and offered her a hand up, which she reluctantly accepted. The smith gestured down at the ground, at the blackened fragments of the Bindmetal talisman. There was some kind of shock, or perhaps regret, in his eyes.

The woman simply shrugged. She turned back towards Tyrick and the old man. "My name is Plyssa. And that's Embrew. Thank you."

Tyrick smiled. "The tales they teach us in nursery would have us believe your kind lack even language with which to speak. I am pleased to meet a woman that proves such tales false," he said formally.

"Then you'll be a lot more pleased in a moment. Embrew and I have to leave Hineros, now. We have to get to the communes and spread word to the chieftains. Our goddess has been taken captive, somehow, by that man, Hyrak. The commands she issued to our forces here are no longer hers—she speaks with his voice. We must warn the others before he turns us all into pawns of his dark schemes." She brushed her hands on her tunic, leaving streaks of soot in their wake. "Did either of you see my mask?"

Tyrick shook his head. "You are traveling to deep Goldvast? How? Even leaving the city will require something of a miracle. I... we will help you, if you wish. It is my duty as a Surveyor to keep Greendeep safe from its enemies. If what you say is true, the Ellir and the people of Goldvast may soon be a singular force—a force beyond the power of the Surveyor's Guild to repel. But as I said—that journey will be difficult, day or night, and will take weeks." He noticed that, somehow, Sky had slipped past him, into the rooms beyond the dining hall.

"Months, actually," Plyssa said. "Your people have no idea how large our nation really is."

"Then how...?" Tyrick asked, rubbing at the thin line of beard across his chin.

"I will carry her there," Embrew said softly. "She has yet to ask it, but I have grown accustomed to being ordered around, I suppose. A crossgate for two is no different than a crossgate for four." With that he turned and tapped one hand on the wall of the dining room. Sparks of orange light began to dance across the surface of the wall, spinning and swirling until, a second later, they had formed a shimmering oval of light. A portal.

Tyrick muttered, "By Chron." Only the gods had such power.

Sky returned to the dining room with a large wooden mask, brightly painted in many shades of green, in his hands. He stretched the mask out to Plyssa, and she took it with the slightest nod of what Tyrick imagined might have been appreciation. Then she took the old man by the arm and stepped towards the portal. "Come with, or do not. I don't care."

The pair stepped into the light and vanished.

Tyrick looked to Sky and asked, "What do you think?"

The smith looked perplexed, his eyes wide. Tyrick sighed. Of course the smith didn't have an opinion. For his entire life, he'd been treated like a tool or a beast of burden. Tyrick also noticed the places where the Ellir struck Sky in the stomach and chest were starting to bruise.

Sky replied, after a moment, "Same."

Tyrick arched an eyebrow. "What is the same?"

Sky pointed back behind him, at the still-smoking remnants of the Ellir's talisman. Then he stepped towards the portal and asked, "Go?"

Tyrick nodded. He had questions, and duty, and the only way either would be satisfied is if they followed that strange pair.

¤~¤~¤

Yors stood in the dank tunnel that snaked from its origin beneath the old Great Forge of Hineros all the way to a sickeningly familiar dungeon under the River of Songs. The door that had barred his passage into that dungeon, locked by a heavy rod of metal across its sturdy frame, was now a wreckage of twisted steel and shattered wood. He held his sapphire hammer in one hand, and he breathed laboriously, but not from the effort of demolishing the door—that had been easy. He strained with all of his willpower to rein in the boiling rage and the undulating, chaotic swirl of grief and terror that this place awoke in him.

This had been the place they were kept. When the orders came down from whoever was in charge of such things and all the Jovs in Hineros and their families were rounded up, they had been brought here. He had been inside this cursed place when they...

When they ripped out his soul and murdered the twin lights of his life. The so-called men of this world had done this for no reason, out of nothing more than fear and the need to establish control. He had been in this cell when they hauled his wife and his tiny daughter away. Their screams haunted him, always. They had broken him so utterly that he had become someone else to escape the pain.

Now it was Yors that was in control, of himself... and of this situation.

He stepped across the threshold and was immediately struck by the stench of the dungeon. The mildew-stink of moldy straw and the soft and steady drip of water that seeped through the heavy stones separating the dungeon from the river above hit him first. Slowly, his eyes adjusted to the miniscule amount of light cast by the torch he had wrenched free of the tunnel walls on his way here. He saw a lantern hanging from the ceiling, but its fuel had run out.

The others were coming behind him — the sound of his assault on the door would bring them running. He did not want them to see this place and its horrors, or the effect it had upon him. Yors turned back towards the tunnel, content that he had seen enough, when a soft moaning sound issued forth from the shadows at the far corner of the cell.

Yors stomped in, hammer at the ready. He held the torch out, and in its flickering light he saw a pile of bodies. There were six of them, tangled upon one another in a quiet, mostly nude heap. Each was restrained by chains of heavy wood and each had a head encased in a barbaric wooden cube.

Yors howled in rage and one of them, atop the pile, gasped and whimpered. As it did so, so did the others. They were alive. Huddled together for warmth in the chill dungeon, they were malnourished and in many ways crippled, but they lived!

Yors lifted the topmost figure from the pile, and the man—his age was difficult to discern in this light and without his face visible, but he seemed notably younger than Yors—yelped weakly. Yors helped the man to his feet and said firmly, "No more. Yors free you. All of you."

As he started to examine the wooden box on the man's head, the first of the others arrived. Steven and Todd had run down the corridor—they were short of breath as they entered the cell—and Yors glared at them. "You will help, or stay out of Yors' way," he said.

"What's going on in here?" Steven asked, approaching Yors. The smith watched Steven take in the sight of the prisoners and Yors thought he saw the man's face take on a sickly, greenish hue.

"This is even more fucked up than the things we usually find," Todd said. "Come on Steven, let's get these people out of here."

Steven nodded, and without another word, the three of them established a system. Yors helped each captive up and then Steven and Todd led them carefully, gently, out of the cell and into the tunnel, where the others met them and then led them back towards the surface.

At the bottom of the pile, Yors helped a man of advanced age to his feet. The man's skin hung in loose folds upon his bony frame, as though he had once carried a great deal of weight but had now wasted away to nothing. The man took Yors' hand and gripped it tightly. Once he was on his feet, Yors gestured to the others that he would handle this one, and he carefully led the man past the rotting straw mats towards the remains of the door.

"Did I hear your name?" the old man asked. His words were muffled by the hideous wooden contraption atop his neck, but Yors made the words out well enough.

"Yors," Yors answered simply.

"Why are you here?" the old man asked. "You got away!"

Yors stopped and looked the old man over. His voice was familiar, somehow. "Does Yors know you?"

"Damn right you do," the old man said, breaking out in a rattling, hacking cough that brought him nearly to his knees. Yors caught him and supported him through the spasm of coughing. "I ain't surprised you don't recognize me. Not sure I'd recognize me. It's me, you big oaf. Gurse."

Yors smiled. Gurse was the father of the lost leader of the Jovs, and as fine a teacher as any Metalbreaker had ever had. He had sacrificed his freedom to assure the rest of them the chance to flee to Onus with Adam—he'd stayed behind to beat the drum that would still the terrible dragons of Murrod.

Unable to help himself, Yors threw his arms around the old man and lifted him in an exuberant bear hug.

Old Gurse broke out into a fresh coughing fit, and Yors let him down. Offering a steadying arm, he led his old teacher out of the cell carefully, moving slowly to account for the restricted gait allowed by the wooden chains around the old smith's ankles. They reached the tunnel and continued forward. Only Steven was still here—the others had taken the captives back to the Great Forge, or the Surveyor's Guild, or whatever the monstrous men of Murrod called it now.

"I can take him," Steven said, extending a hand.

"I can take myself," Gurse said angrily. "But it ain't time to go anywhere yet."

Steven looked at Yors, perplexed.

Yors nodded and asked, "Gurse knows?"

"I felt it when you carried it into the room. I'm probably the last man on this Purpose-forsaken world that even knows what real, true Metalbreaking feels like. The others are all young ones—whelps with only an inkling of the arts. But I felt it like I can feel my own heartbeat when you smashed in the door. It isn't from here, is it? The pulse of it ain't quite right."

"No. From Arctos." Yors replied, lifting the hammer up and extending the gleaming sapphire head towards Gurse. He knew so little of the hammer, and the power it granted him. He welcomed Gurse's insight. The old man reached towards it awkwardly, but when his outstretched hand touched the smooth stone, he stood up a bit straighter.

"Not as good as having the Hammer of Murrod, but it'll do. It'll do." Gurse said. "Bring it down, boy."

Yors nodded and pulled the hammer back, then turned to look Steven directly in the eyes. "Take Gurse up. Tell everyone to stay out of tunnel. Yors be back soon."

Steven whispered, "Be safe, big guy."

Yors turned away as Steven and Gurse made their way up the shallow incline. Once they were out of sight, Yors set about his work. He held the hammer tightly in one hand and, with the other, started to feel along the stone walls of the tunnel. This was all very new to him, the type of metalbreaking unlocked by the hammer, but it came with a set of strange instincts, and he followed them now as he sought the right spot in the tunnel's structure. As with the rending of the earth that had accompanied his summoning of the hammer in the mountains of Arctos, he felt the stone as though it were metal, and it sang to him as any other metal would. It whispered its secrets in meter and verse and rhythm and he followed the beating heart of the world to the right place.

He wrapped both hands around the shining haft of the hammer and brought it up over his head. Without even meaning to, he began to hum the old, simple song he had sung as he rocked his little girl to sleep so many years ago. As the music rose up in him, he struck with the hammer.

The stone splintered and cracked, a gaping wound opening and then racing both up and down, spreading outward like a lightning flash of spider webs, shattering the tunnel and spreading towards the cell, where decades-old pillars and carefully fitted stonework exploded into dust.

The River of Songs rushed down to fill the void beneath it, reclaiming territory it had ceded in the distant past of this city. Steadily, unafraid, Yors turned and strode up the tunnel, back to the others. The water raced behind him, lapping at his heels, but he did not run.

There was no longer anything in this place worth running from.

¤~¤~¤

"But what are we going to do with them?" Becky whispered sharply. She was looking at the sickly sextet of prisoners from the cell below, though she needn't have whispered. The roar of the collapsing tunnel underneath them made it hard for even regular speaking voices to be heard. Nonetheless, JC leaned in close to hear what Adam's response would be.

Steven, Todd, and Mathias were doing their best to break away the shackles and headgear of the prisoners, using tools that Mathias had scavenged from the building during his time hiding in the back rooms. This left Adam, Becky, and JC standing near the back door, waiting for Yors to emerge when he had suitably worked out his anger on the passageways below.

"Most of them are barely functional, but the older one that Steven brought up last—he's a leader to them. He can take care of them while we..." Adam's voice trailed off. He spoke in a louder whisper, but the noise coming from below still drowned out the sounds of his words more than a few feet away.

"Do what?" Becky asked. "We came to save Mathias, right? Well, here he is. Saved. So what is our next play here, exactly?"

Adam shrugged angrily. "Don't look at me! If I was calling the shots we'd still be back home! Do you have any idea how royally screwed we are when we get back? We've been away for more than a month!"

JC groaned in exasperation, rolling his eyes. "Get over it. We're here. And if Mathias is right and Hyrak is here, then it's our job to stop him. Period." JC pointed his thumb back over his shoulder, towards the prisoners. "And you have a job to finish with them, too."

"What the hell are you talking about?" Adam asked incredulously. "I've never seen these people before in my life."

"They're Jovs, dumbass. The same Jovs you promised to get off of Murrod the last time we were here. So why can't we do that? Why can't we get them to Onus?" JC stared at Adam.

Adam said nothing for a moment, and JC counted that as a personal victory. The ambient noise of Yors' demolition below had come to a gradual halt.

"I guess we could. If we can get them to the Spiralgate, and you guys can provide cover of some kind, then I can open a corridor back to Onus. If I send them to the Weigar gate, that puts them close to both Ambrek and Brennid's factions—they can have their choice of who to join up with," Adam speculated.

"Might be the first time in a long time some of these people have had choices at all," Becky murmured.

"Then they will be safe and we will get down to the business of finding Hyrak. This time, when we kick his ass, it will stay kicked," JC said emphatically.

A deep cough startled the three of them, and JC realized that Yors had rejoined them in the main room. He was filthy, covered in both thick dust and the sloppy mud of such dust soaked in river water. The smith said, in a voice choked equal parts dirt and emotion, "This is good. Send them far from Murrod. Send them home."

Adam nodded. He gestured for Mathias to join them, and the former courier quickly did so. "We've just about got everyone released from the chains and boxes," Mathias reported.

"We're going to try to ferry them to Onus," Adam explained. "Do we have a chance of getting to the gate without a fight?"

JC couldn't help but scoff audibly at that. "I'm not worried about a fight. It's daytime, right? Ellir are no trouble."

Mathias began to argue. "But the warriors from Goldvast may be a problem. If we move quickly, we can get everyone out and move on ourselves before they realize what we are up to, but your powers may draw their attention, Adam. With Embrew among their number, there's—"

Adam and Becky interrupted in perfect unison, "Wait, what?"

Mathias drew in a sharp breath. "I haven't told you this yet?"

"Told us what?" Becky demanded.

"Embrew is alive. I didn't believe it at first, when I saw him, but he was among the party Hyrak brought with him when he besieged the city. He helped Hyrak bring in the Ellir, though it didn't seem like he was doing so by choice," Mathias explained.

"That's nice. Is there any food here?" JC asked.

Becky glared at him and he caught the slightest impression of her thoughts through their mental link. She thought he was being random, and while that perhaps was one of his more charming characteristics on a good day, she wasn't having any of it today.

Mathias nodded with a puzzled look on his face. "Well... Yes? I can show you where."

"Great," JC said. "I think you have a really fricking huge amount of catching us up to do. That goes better on a full stomach."

Mathias sighed. "I suppose I do. So much has happened so quickly, we ought to all get our bearings before we take any other rash actions."

Mathias looked towards the stairs leading up to the second level and then back towards Adam. "There are some food stores up there. Adam, can you help me get some things, and we can feed everyone? I'd say the prisoners haven't eaten in days." JC almost thought he saw a little blush of color rise up in Mathias' cheeks as he looked at Adam, and he groaned a bit inwardly. This again.

As Adam was agreeing, Todd stepped up and placed a hand on Mathias's shoulder. "I'd say they haven't eaten well in a hell of a lot longer than that. I'll help too."

JC moved to offer to help—he loathed standing around—but Yors grabbed his arm and said, "JC stay. Yors need help."

Without another word, the little knot of people split up. Becky followed Mathias, Adam, and Todd upstairs, and JC noticed Steven was attempting to keep the prisoners calm, with the help of the older man—Gurse. That left JC alone with Yors, who led him back through the doors to the rear room, where the great bins of metal shavings lined the walls leading to the opening to the tunnel that was now little more than a wall made of uneven stones.

Yors gestured for JC to sit on a bench in front of one of the bins of metal remnants, and JC did so heavily. "What's up?" he asked.

Yors sat down next to JC and laid his hammer gently at his feet. Then he turned himself so that he was mostly facing JC and reached up with both dirty, meaty hands and touched them gently to the collar of Bindmetal links around JC's throat.

"Yors hear what JC said. About taking Jovs home. Yors not believe anyone else have thought of this. Jovs owe JC great debt. Yors... Yors will pay. But JC must keep secret for Yors." Yors spoke quietly.

JC replied, "Of course. I'm down with secrets. What's the deal?"

"Metalbreakers strong on Murrod," the smith explained. "Very strong. With hammer, even stronger. Yors not want others to treat him different. But Yors must use magic for right reasons. Freeing Jovs, helping JC... these right reasons."

"OK," JC said. He was unsure where this was going.

"One other reason right also. Greendeep horrible place. Yors must stop Greendeep, men, from ever doing to others what happened to Jovs. Yors must avenge Yors' family... families of all Metalbreakers." The smith was almost shaking.

"What are you going to do?" JC asked in a whisper.

"Yors going to destroy nursery. No more men in Greendeep, no more danger. Vengeance for all Yors' friends. For wife. For daughter."

"You want to destroy their nursery? Like, where they keep babies and stuff? You can't!" JC replied, nearly shouting. "The others will never go for that!"

Yors squeezed the metal at JC's throat tightly, saying nothing. JC felt it begin to vibrate with a pulsing beat that started, exploded to riotous loudness, than dissipated all in the span of a few seconds. As it did so, he felt sensations flood into his mind. For almost thirty seconds, his life replayed before him, particularly events of the past two years. He watched the battle for Rega Holc in grim detail. He fought to free himself from the collision of negspacer and low-walker forces on the moon of Rettik. He witnessed his late night visits to Becky's bedroom window. For thirty seconds, he felt all that the chain had robbed him of since it had been forged into place around his neck. Then its magic reasserted itself, and the fear was gone, wiped away as though it had never been, leaving him with many questions, but no answers.

"How many?" he asked, blinking small tears away from his eyes. "How many did you just turn off?"

Yors, sweat beading on his brow and leaving little trails in the dust there, replied, "Eight. Still fifteen left. Less than half to go."

JC whispered, "I'll keep your secret. We have to finish this."

Yors stood and said, "Yors appreciates JC's understanding."

¤~¤~¤

"I have given you all we agreed upon! I will give no more!" roared the dragon-god Ehbor. The sleek black scales of the god of the Ellir gleamed with water as the creature reared up on the beach with the light of the third sunrise at its back.

Hyrak watched the dragon carefully. He had left Ahmur with Jarrek, some distance back in the sparse jungle, and stood unarmed before Ehbor. He carried the second bell, strung on its tight coil of wire, but aside from that, he wielded no weapon or talisman that might give Ehbor reason to suspect his plans. His mental shields were, of course, in place. He wanted this to end peacefully, but he was prepared for it to go otherwise. He only regretted that the bell's effects would not take hold before it was around the beast's neck. Ahmur had proven particularly vulnerable to the magic of the bells—Ehbor had no such characteristic.

"I need the rest of them, Ehbor," Hyrak explained in a forced, patient tone. "If I am to crush the rest of your siblings' forces, I will need more soldiers under my command."

"I have ceded nearly a hundred to your control already," Ehbor growled. The dragon blinked its three luminous eyes and narrowed them in concentration as it glared at Hyrak. "And what have you accomplished? Trading trinkets with my sister? Starting skirmishes in Chron's least precious city? You promised me victory, and you have brought only contrivance. Nuisance. I could have accomplished your year's worth of progress in a single day, had such accomplishments been of any value to me."

Hyrak bowed deeply, feigning obeisance. He had grown to loathe this great black dragon more with each passing day of his time on Murrod. "Then perhaps we could renegotiate the loan of Ellir that you so generously provided?" Hyrak asked. "What if, instead of giving me more of your precious children, you gave me less? I could return this last contingent to your control, if you could give me a different kind of aid."

The water behind Ehbor began to bubble and churn, and Hyrak tried to focus his eyes, and his mental magic, upon the surface of the icy ocean. Whatever stirred there did not think, at least not at any appreciable level of sophistication, but he thought he saw something dark and swift moving beneath the waves. The dragon appeared unperturbed.

"What aid would you require?" Ehbor asked, leaning in, intrigued. The dragon-god swatted at the water with his left wingtip, and suddenly the disturbance was gone.

"I need your knowledge of the Greytall Mountains, great one. I seek a place of power there, and I haven't the time to study them myself. But no one has dwelt more closely to those mountains than you—I believe that you have seen that which I seek in your journeys over the years." Hyrak fought back a smile. The dragon would never allow Hyrak into its mind, past its defenses—the creature was too naturally distrustful. But if Ehbor thought he was getting the best end of a bargain, his satisfaction might undermine the strength of his defenses.

"Chron once called those mountains home, warlord. They lurk closer to Monarka than Bluetide by a whole day's travel. Your flattery betrays your foolishness. But I will aid you, in exchange for the end of the previous agreement. The bond I have granted you with my Ellir will be broken—leaving you with only the original twenty—and I will deal no longer with your mad schemes. Is this amenable?" Ehbor leaned in close, and Hyrak smelled the stench of fish on the dragon's breath.

Hyrak bowed again, even lower than before. "The place I seek is spelled out in my mind, great one."

He felt the dragon reach into his mind and pluck the thought—carefully arranged outside of his mindshaping shields—with its own prodigious power.

"Easy enough," Ehbor scoffed in Hyrak's mind. "Why is this place of importance to you?"

Hyrak visibly tensed as the force of the dragon's mind collided with his shields like a battering ram, splintering them and bringing a tidal wave of pain crashing upon his consciousness.

"Stop!" Hyrak shouted.

Ehbor did not listen. The dragon struck again, its mental force increased tenfold, and Hyrak fell to his knees, choking back a scream.

"What are you hiding, human?" Ehbor roared aloud.

Hyrak could bear it no longer. His shields were little more than pebbles of magic strung together with his grim determination, and another strike from the beast would end them, revealing his plans to the dragon and assuring his defeat. He had to trust that enough time had passed. Wincing as he forced himself to see past the pain, Hyrak grasped the coil of wire from his belt and snapped it towards Ehbor, causing it to lash out and unspool like the crack of a whip.

Ehbor saw it coming. The dragon reared back out of range of the whip and beat its wings furiously, rising up into the air. Hyrak changed tactics, pouring his strength instead into a quick working of mindshaping, casting his thoughts at the dragon like a fisherman's net, skimming the surface of the creature's ancient, alien mindscape. He caught what glimmering thoughts he could before Ehbor roared and vanished in a flash of violet light.

He'd missed his chance to claim Ehbor. The plan would require adjustment now.

But Hyrak was many things—warlord of Onus, scientist of Rettik, and more—and he would adapt. He allowed his mind to sort through the fragments of thought he had snared from the dragon before its escape, and he felt a smile creep across his scarred face. There it was—the place in the mountains he needed. Ehbor had thought of it, before his assault—he had recognized it instantly from the description Hyrak had prepared for him.

And now Hyrak knew where it was. He may only have had one dragon... but one dragon would be enough.

# 27
## Onus

*Sleep came fitfully to Jara Abison.* It had not even been a day since she had forced Adam to leave, abusing her power as a Fatewaker to compel him to act. It had been the first time she'd really done anything like that deliberately—it felt wrong. It reminded her of how her mother's fatewaking talents had been abused at Hyrak Arn.

She tried to sleep, to let the terrible vision that had struck her in Duchess Ain's great hall fall away under the weight of simpler things, but sleep did not come. The vision did not fade. She could make no sense of it, and was not particularly certain she wanted to.

Jara had faith that the future could be changed by those determined enough to do so—she believed, in her heart, that was what made the Children of the Line so important. But she had not yet seen proof to support her belief. Her every vision had, in its own fashion, come to pass. And this one portended chaos, change, destruction—all the things that she had been led to believe the gathering of the Children of the Line would forestall. So JC was right to bring everyone back out into the Spiral of Worlds once more, it seemed. Dark times were nearly upon them all, and only a united front, all six Children, could turn it back.

Or so the Wyr would have everyone believe. Had her fellow Fatewakers seen what she had seen in that crushing wave of pink light, would their faith have been shaken? Hers was.

A knock at the door disrupted what little rest Jara had managed to eke out in her sparsely appointed guest room. She was expecting no one at such a late hour, but she had grown accustomed to the idea that her magic—which haunted her dreams, this night—would forewarn her of any true danger. She slipped from beneath the light sheet of the bed and padded on bare feet to the door, moving soundlessly. As she passed the small table next to the door she saw the collection of glass figurines that she had received from Jort—the amryw that had started this particular journey. She had carried them with her, in her pack, from Igar Holc, and now they were the last thing she had of that place—perhaps the last glasswork that Jort would ever do. Survivors of the massacre of the bridge city had been few and far between in the weeks since its fall.

Jara pulled the door open to reveal one of the Duchess' household guards standing there, his wicked looking spear held firmly in one hand while the other hung in the air, about to knock once more. He wore the slightly conical helmet that held a sash across his lower face—the ceremonial garb that most of the guards assigned to duty watching over Jara did not bother to wear. He was here on important business, it would seem.

"The Duchess requests your presence," the guard explained abruptly.

"The Duchess has no power over me," Jara replied coldly.

"She expects you to accompany me to the garden," the guard said, somewhat befuddled by Jara's defiance. "She wishes me to tell you that she is taking you at your word, Fatewaker."

Now it was Jara who was befuddled. Curious, and a bit angry, Jara gestured towards the hallway behind the guard. "Then let's be on our way."

"Don't you want to put on some proper clothes for an audience with her grace?" the guard asked, indicating Jara's simple nightgown.

Jara glared at him.

With a sharp nod, the guard spun on one heel and led Jara to the side door of the guest house, to the secluded garden where the Duchess Ain had first told Jara of her heinous kidnapping of Jara's mother and grandfather. It was not a place that held good memories, obviously.

The guard held the door open for Jara, and she passed him, stomping out into the garden angrily. A great sheet of oilcloth had been strung up above the garden, keeping the rain out. "What do you want?" she demanded, seeing the Duchess standing there, her back to the doorway.

Slowly, Duchess Ain turned towards Jara. Her face was the cool mask of indifference it so often was, but there was also something else in her expression—something almost foreign.

"I wanted to prove that I trust you, Jara. I... Perhaps that would have been the right thing to do from the start. But what has passed cannot be undone. I return them to you," the Duchess explained.

Jara heard shuffling footsteps behind her and turned to see two other figures join her and the Duchess in the garden. Moultus walked first, slowly, with Jara's mother close behind.

Jara raced to the both of them, hugging them mightily in a way she was certain was not at all lady-like. The three of them talked quickly in hushed tones, Jara filling her family in as much as she could on what had been happening, and Moultus and Hessa telling Jara of their boredom during their incarceration at the Duchess' rural estate.

After a few minutes, Jara realized that Duchess Ain was still standing there in the garden, silently watching them.

"Thank you," Jara said softly. "But you are right. You should have just trusted me."

The Duchess inclined her head slightly, but said nothing else. She reached down and plucked a single golden flower from one of the garden beds and, tucking it behind one ear, walked past Jara's family. As she came nearer, Jara said, "We'll talk in the morning. I have some thoughts about the Vale of Steam."

The Duchess said nothing by way of acknowledgment, and a moment later, she was gone—back inside the palace.

"That woman is horrible," Hessa said, drawing Jara into a hug once more.

"Yes," Jara said under her breath. "But maybe not for much longer. I've seen some things. Please, listen carefully..."

¤~¤~¤

The air was growing stale. Vediri didn't understand how this underwater boat functioned—aside from a rudimentary skill at steering its strange spherical tiller—but she did know that its many layered enchantments did not undo the basic human need to breath. Breathing was, in fact, one of the few things that she and Fendris had been doing at all over the last ten days.

At least she thought it was ten days. It was a guess, at best. She had slept ten times, trusting Fendris to man the controls during those intervals. Beyond that, she did not know. Without sun and stars to guide her, all she could do were trust her instincts. The problem was that, like Fendris', her instincts screamed constantly for her to turn back.

Their destination, marked so clearly on the map in Grell's steady script, could not be. They were in the forbidden Silent Sea in pursuit of a port that could not exist in a vehicle that ought not to exist... and now she feared they had spent too long below the water.

"All I taste in the air is the stink of you," Fendris muttered as he roused from his slumber. Aside from his short spurts relieving Vediri of the controls, the watchman had done little on their voyage. To be fair, he was a watchman with nothing to watch, for the view outside their tiny glass porthole was uniform blackness, broken only intermittently by fish.

"And I, you," Vediri muttered. "I think we have no choice, watchworm—we will surface soon. Perhaps the vessel is rigged in such a way to take on new air when it surfaces?"

"Or perhaps we shall be struck dead by the curse of the Silent Sea," Fendris hissed irritably. "But at this point, even that would be preferable to this ceaseless wandering. Whatever the captain wants us to find—he's wrong this time. There's nothing out here. At the rate we've been traveling, by my estimation, we should be dangerously close to coast near Sur Nought by now. Much further, and we'll be near the remnant camps—the bottom of the world."

Vediri sighed. She knew he was right. The captain's directions clearly indicated that if they reached the bottom of the world—the tumultuous southern sea that linked the familiar Endless Sea to this malefic body through with they now traveled—they will have missed their mark. The thought of making this same nerve-wracking, guess-and-check trip in reverse chilled her.

"I'm taking us to the surface. Make whatever preparations you can," she commanded. "Perhaps we can put those eyes of yours to some good use and get our bearings."

Fendris nodded and began to rummage through the small chest of equipment the captain had left aboard the vessel. He emerged with a spyglass in one hand and a small, single-hand crossbow in the other.

He offered the weapon to Vediri, but she declined. "If there's anything up there when we come up for air, I doubt that will do much good. I have my sword and two daggers. I'd rather stick to what I know best."

Fendris muttered something under his breath that Vediri could not make out, then returned the weapon to the chest. He offered her something she did take—a strip of the dried meat that constituted the bulk of the vessel's food stores. While their air was growing thin, their food larder would likely outlast the journey. Vediri wondered if the food and drink aboard this little ship was laced with metal fragments like the food aboard the Razormaw. She shuddered at the thought.

Without another word, Vediri drew back the control sphere, and the ship responded, slowing in forward speed and instead beginning to rise. This was their first significant adjustment to depth since waking in the vessel after the destruction of the Razormaw, and almost immediately Vediri—who had spent so much of her life at sea, felt seasickness rising in her belly. From the look on Fendris' face, she was not alone.

"Slow down!" he shouted nauseously.

Vediri did, easing up on the sphere and slowing the rate of ascent. The ship itself began to groan, its metal skin shifting in the lessening pressure. Fanciful images of the ship splitting like an overripe fruit and the black water of the Silent Sea rushing in to drown them danced through her mind.

Fendris leaned up against the porthole, nearly blocking the view, but Vediri could make out the brightening of the water from around his head. Sunlight was reaching into the sea at this depth. They were nearing the surface.

With a sudden lurch, the ship came to a stop, and brilliant daylight poured in the glass window, causing Fendris to recoil, covering his eyes as they adjusted to the sudden radiance. The light inside the ship—feeble light cast by a glowing orb of simple metal, one of the oldest techniques of Metalbreaking, was nothing compared to the true light of the sun, pouring in as it climbed above the horizon.

"Well, at least we have been heading the right direction," Vediri said. The porthole was on the port side of the ship, and their allegedly southerly bearing was confirmed by the sight of the rising sun framed in that round aperture.

"I'm going out!" Fendris said, scrambling to the back of the cramped compartment. A short set of ladder rungs set into the rear wall of the ship led up to a square hatch, secured by a round locking wheel. The watchman climbed the ladder easily and began working at the wheel, but his strength was not equal to the task.

Vediri pulled the equipment chest away from the starboard wall a bit and climbed onto it to help Fendris. Together, they wrenched the wheel widdershins. The seal between the hatch and the outer skin of the ship cracked audibly, followed by a rushing hiss of fresh air. For a moment, they stood there, breathing the glorious salt air.

Then Fendris completed the unlocking of the wheel and pushed upward, hard, causing the stiff hinges of the hatch to creak. He finished his climb and vanished from Vediri's sight. She followed quickly, and the two of them stood atop the ship, taking in the daylight with hands shading their eyes.

"Do you think there's something out there?" Vediri asked. "Beyond the horizon? No one has ever been, they say. It... it would be a better bounty than vengeance."

Fendris chuckled. "I thought you had already bought all that the captain was selling."

"I believe in Grell. I always have. But there's something incredible here. We're part of something incredible." Vediri sighed and turned, slowly, to face the west. The top of the vessel was relatively flat, and her boots found easy footing, but she feared falling into the water. Perhaps the Captain's Metalbreaker magic was saving the ship from the curse of the sea, but a lowly pirate such as she had no such protection.

As she turned her back to the sun, she strained to see the coast of the southern continent, but she could not. All she saw was sea—more and more sea.

Fendris, however, squinted and stared beside her, and she allowed him to make several annoying noises of confirmation and puzzlement before she finally asked, her temper fraying, "What is it? What do you see?"

"The Horn of Ros, I think. We're not nearly as far south as I figured us to be. And what's more..." the scrawny watchman's voice trailed off.

Vediri slapped him promptly across the back of the head. The little man started and slipped—tumbling off the edge of their tiny vessel and splashing down in the water.

Fendris began to scream, but Vediri could not help but laugh, at least a bit. Fendris was alive—he had not been struck dead by the sea, or any of the other rumors and myths that the pirates in the Starlight Islands told about this place. And here, so far from the coast, if such a curse was real, it would surely happen swiftly.

She reached down, kneeling and gripping the edge of the hatch with one hand to balance herself, and plucked Fendris easily from the water with the other, pulling the sopping wet sailor onto the surface of the ship.

"You are a cold bitch," Fendris said, sulking, as he wrung seawater from his tunic.

Vediri smiled and pushed a hand up through her spiked braids. "I was thinking of a quick dip myself—thought you'd appreciate going first."

"It isn't funny," Fendris muttered. "I could've died."

"But you didn't. The Purpose must be watching out for you, watchworm!" Vediri laughed.

A crack of thunder and a brilliant flash of lightning brought her mirth to a close. The sky was clear—or had been, just a moment before. Suddenly dark clouds were starting to form above them, spread all along the sky in all directions. They undulated and flickered, and Vediri did not like the look of them at all.

"Get down below," she instructed.

"Do you think," Fendris whispered, nearly whimpering, "it's the curse?"

"I don't believe in curses," Vediri lied. "But I do believe in storms. We need to dive before this one hits."

¤~¤~¤

Brennid and Ambrek sat quietly facing the likely author of every misery ever inflicted upon the Jovs—the great orange Bindmetal chime in the center tower of the ruins of Jov Nought.

Their Boltsender prisoner was tied securely outside, sleeping off the effects of the rather serious blow to the head that had brought him to heel. Ambrek was not sure what to do with the man, but he had clearly seemed somehow deranged last night.

"Shall we do it together?" Brennid asked, staring at the chime.

Ambrek did not reply. He looked at the tube of metal resting atop the ten smaller tubes. He saw himself reflected in its gleaming surface, even in the sparse light that crept in from the narrow windows high up in the tower walls. He could almost imagine their forbearers polishing the metal, shaping it as a true wonder—a device that could easily communicate with other worlds.

"In the beginning, it was a marvel," Ambrek mused. "Before the exile, it allowed us to barter for Bindmetal with the people of Murrod. When the earliest of our order made it, they couldn't have known what it would become, could they?"

Brennid shook his head. There were dark circles under his eyes, and a barely contained anger evident in his breathing, if not his words. "It does not matter what it was—it only matters what it is. This was the whip that cracked to command us to action, slaving away in the forges of Greendeep to build tools for those who abandoned us there. When we break it, we put behind us all of that—we send a message to the Council that we are no longer their pawns."

"But what of the message we released from its chambers last night?" Ambrek asked carefully. There was much to consider before he allowed his former friend to destroy the chime. What had seemed like an easy decision in the Borrik Mountains now weighed upon him heavily.

"The message can have come only from Murrod, and I do not care what happens on Murrod. And neither should you. That place was our prison, and it is behind us now. Join with me in putting it behind us forever. Then, as we discussed, we can forge a new future for our brothers. The Jov Order needs this." Brennid slowly stood. He stepped closer to the chime and placed one hand upon it. "Do this with me. My anger will sully the working if not tempered by your patience."

Ambrek also stood, but he held back from placing his hand upon the upper chamber of the chime. "You said something very wise a moment ago, Brennid."

"I say wise things as a matter of course," Brennid said grimly.

"I imagine you believe so," Ambrek said, smiling softly. "But you said it matters not what the chime was, only what it is. But its time as the cracking whip, as the voice of injustice—is that not behind us now? Truly, what is the chime, now? Symbol, yes, but of what? Of how far we have come, perhaps? Of how we should remember what we have endured, always, lest it happen again?"

"Put your Purpose-damned hand on the chime, Ambrek," Brennid growled.

Ambrek sighed. "There is no harmony in you anymore, is there?"

"Hand. Now." Brennid commanded.

Ambrek reached out and placed his hand gently, almost lovingly, on the surface of the chime—as far from Brennid's hand as he could manage. The cost of Metalbreaking was this—what he saw before him, in Brennid's eyes. It was clear to him now—even more so than it had been upon the road—that the price had claimed the self-proclaimed leader of the Jovs... and it was unlikely he would ever recover from its debt.

The two of them drew in deep breaths and began their working. Magic buzzed about the room, a steady drumbeat of power echoing from Ambrek—the sound of his heartbeat, amplified by magic and skill—and an erratic, jangling discordance rising up around Brennid. Together, their two workings plied the metal of the chime and, in a matter of three minutes' time, it split in two, the smaller chime tubes below it warping and cracking as the magic that bound it all together faded away in a plume of smoke and a flash of lost power. Most of its substance was Bindmetal no more—the ultimate act of destruction, wrought with arts designed for creation.

"We accept your offer," Ambrek said softly, leaning down and claiming a piece of the dormant orange Bindmetal from one of the lower tubes for himself. So much of it was destroyed, but this piece remained viable. In this piece, there was still potential.

"What offer?" Brennid asked.

"Jov Nought. This Jov Nought, our original academy—my band of Metalbreakers will make our homes here." Ambrek looked around him. The place was a ruin, with only the walls of this tower still standing. Relocating the others and then rebuilding this place—it would take years.

"I thought you'd at least spend the rest of the journey back north trying to talk me into abdicating my post and reuniting the camps," Brennid said, smiling slyly. "Why change your mind?"

"I see now what I refused to see before. You were right—we are too different to ever be forged back into a single shape. But perhaps something new can rise from the remnants of what was?" Ambrek tucked the Bindmetal fragment into his belt pouch, along with the traveling hobs they would need for their journey.

"Then should we be off?" Brennid asked. He looked up, at the yellow Bindmetal repeater mounted high in the tower. "Or perhaps you would help me get up there and claim that for our people?"

Ambrek shook his head. "I agreed to dismantle the chime. I will not help you start a war with the Vols as well. If you were in your right mind, you would want no such thing either."

Brennid scowled. "It is possible that you have some wisdom in you as well. Back to the road then?"

"I would like to take our strange captive to Norwin Holc before we leave," Ambrek said. "It wouldn't feel right leaving him tied up out here—but I am not certain he can be trusted if left behind us unbound. Something about him is strange indeed. I cannot quite put my finger upon it."

"I can," Brennid said. He walked side by side with Ambrek towards the door. "It's the way he speaks. That language he uses. I can't understand a word of it."

"There are many languages out there besides the Council tongue," Ambrek said. "They are not common, but they are not so very rare that they would strike me as odd."

"But you're missing something vital, Ambrek. Since we returned to Onus, have you heard anyone speak in a language you can't understand?" Brennid asked.

Ambrek drew to a stop. "No. I don't believe I have."

"The Spiralgate does something to a man when he passes through its rings. It touches his mind, they say. So whatever that Boltsender was speaking out there, it wasn't a language—it was gibberish. And a man doesn't get to be a Boltsender, certainly not a middle-aged Boltsender, if he's a gibbering idiot." Brennid pointed north. "Kem Nought is that way. I think our friend here ran afoul of some of the Mindshapers. No love lost between them and us, that's for sure, but... I admit I'm curious what he's done to bring this kind of torment down on himself."

Ambrek touched a finger to the bridge of his nose in thought. Then he stopped and pulled his hand back, realization dawning. "That nose!"

It was Brennid's turn to look puzzled.

"Did you see his nose before you broke it? I recognize the nose—the features. And he's a Boltsender! Of course—curse me for a fool, I should have seen it right away!" Ambrek grabbed at Brennid's arm. "We must take him to Norwin Holc, immediately. I need you to do this with me—it helps us both, I swear it. The Duke will offer us the reward, I know he will, but that is not what matters—we will be the Order that finally brought the last of Hyrak's lieutenants to justice. The Jovs will be lauded as heroes, Brennid—as we should have been all along—all of us."

"Hyrak's lieutenant? Who is this man, Ambrek? I did not travel with you and the others to Rega Holc; the war there is only whispers to me." Brennid's agitation was becoming visible again, but Ambrek could not contain his excitement.

Ambrek replied, "We've captured Narred, Brennid—I'm sure of it!"

¤~¤~¤

Grell slit the throat of the honor guardsman in perfect silence. He had pulled the guard into a seamstress' shop, abandoned at this early hour, and he sopped at the blood quickly with a half-finished gown plucked from the mending table. He needed the uniform unbloodied.

All night, men had been scrambling about Ain Holc following the Duchess' orders to assemble a small team of her best men for a task of delicate importance. Grell had no doubt this task was related to his map—foolishly left behind in his haste to escape capture after the Duchess freed herself from his captivity.

But it seemed as though perhaps the leaving of the map was not so foolish after all. Clearly the Wyr girl had seen something in the map that Grell himself had not, for once it had fallen into her hands, the Duchess' men had begun their preparations.

Efficiently, Grell stripped the ceremonial armor from the guard and began to slip into it himself. It was not a perfect fit, but the straps could be loosened, and he worked simple magic upon the breastplate to shape it better around his solid frame. He tucked his blonde braid up snugly under the ugly helmet and then pulled the sash across his mouth that would render him almost impossible to distinguish from the others. His features didn't look at all Ainish, but if he just kept the helmet on, he would be fine.

In truth, he didn't need to stay concealed within the party for the entirety of their journey—just long enough to learn where they were going and what they were planning to do. He would be able to travel faster than these soldiers anyway—he was a Metalbreaker with plenty of trinkets left up his sleeves.

Once suitably attired, he pulled the guardsman's corpse back out of sight—he didn't need the seamstress raising the alarm too early when she opened her shop—and stepped out into the perpetually rainy morning, openly walking the street for the first time since he arrived in this horrid city.

He traveled the four blocks to the staging grounds and merged easily into the last batch of guards reporting to the leader of the expedition—a man not much older than Grell but notable for his prodigious size—he was easily over seven feet tall.

"I shall choose a dozen of you to head south with me as soon as her grace bids us go," the commander shouted over the steady drizzle. "Word comes that she approaches now. Be ready men—this is a task of vital importance to her grace."

Grell sneered beneath his face cloth. Even if the Wyr-child had deciphered the map, it was unlikely she knew exactly what was waiting at their destination. Duchess Ain certainly had no idea. If she did—she would do everything in her power to bury this secret, not bring it to light.

No more than ten minutes later, as the men stood about talking quietly, the Duchess arrived in a small procession but without the pomp Grell had expected. She had a few guards of course, and several street people traveled in close proximity—an old man, a woman, and a child in ragged traveling clothes, hoods raised. Perhaps her abduction and treatment at his hands had taught the vile royal some manners? He doubted it.

"Men—you embark upon a journey to solve a mystery," Duchess Ain explained as the guardsmen grew quiet. "We know the route you must take and the general nature of your destination, but not what you might find there. Perhaps the greatest enemy our people have ever faced desires what lies hidden at your quest's end, and it is imperative that we do not let him have it."

Grell could not help but smile. They were playing right into his hands. He would find the juncture, and with its power, truth. Vengeance would be his at last.

The Duchess continued to speak empty platitudes and encouragements, but Grell paid them little heed as he entertained thoughts of his victory. Somewhere, far to the east of here, the rest of his plan was coming together, hopefully. Things were at a delicate stage, but even without the proof that Vediri and Fendris were gathering, he would have the power. Proof without power would be meaningless—power without proof was at least a start.

He felt a persistent tug at the short cloak of his stolen guard uniform, and the pirate captain turned and snapped angrily, "What?"

"He's right here," Jara shouted, smiling up at him. "Like I told you."

Grell reached down on instinct, grabbing for his belt and the transportation hob concealed there, but the guards were upon him too fast, drawing his arms back and pinning him tight.

"Take him to the dungeon," Duchess Ain said as the guards not holding Grell back parted to allow her to draw nearer to him. "And have someone with a knife cut at him for a bit. He wants vengeance so badly, let's see how he handles a bit of mine."

Grell said nothing. He seethed. He strained against the strength of his captors. But he said nothing.

The Duchess turned to the tall commander and said, "Make haste for the Vale of Steam, Essindir. I fear you may get there, learn the secret, and return before this one talks."

The commander bowed with a flourish, and then a sack of dark cloth was thrown over Grell's head. This did not diminish his seething.

¤~¤~¤

Shayra had sequestered herself in the Source tower and erected every mental shield she had ever studied, and yet still she could not find peace. Everything was falling apart around her, and every embodied Mindshaper looked to her for answers and guidance. For leadership.

But Shayra was no leader.

She sat on the floor at the top of the tower, cradling her shaved head in her hands. Tears would not flow, but they had yesterday. Her mind was a tangle of pain and fear and loss and panic.

Narred was gone. She had exploited the permanent bond between them—the sacred testament of their love—to level a pair of horrific workings upon his mind, ensuring that he could not reveal the secrets of the Kem, but she was besieged by her regret over these actions, particularly in light of the fact that even she was now convinced that her order was not a force for good on Onus at all.

The twins had brought something worse than doubt to her—they had brought truth. The past was filled with a terrible deed that she had not wished to know about, but now she did, and she could not un-know it.

When she was chosen as Collectress as a young woman, nearly twenty years ago when the Council ordered the orders to withdraw from the affairs of Onus, she had seen it as an honor. She had never expected to be a leader among the Kem, and she was ill-prepared for the responsibilities that came with leadership. But when the others had withered in the isolation, she had remained strong—in part because of Narred. And now...

She wanted to vomit. She wanted to die. She wanted to scream.

"We all had a part to play," whispered a thought in her mind.

Shayra looked up, but could see nothing aside from the spray of shifting colors cast by the crystal column at the center of the Source. The minds of the oldest of the Mindshapers called the Source home—consigned to serve as part of the Source rather than awaiting new host bodies like those in the Soul. Shayra spoke rarely with these elders, for they were often uninterested in the affairs of those walking about in flesh and blood. She had, in fact, not even been in this tower since Narred had stolen his way to the top and called out to his former master, Hyrak, across the Spiral of Worlds using the power of these same ancient minds.

In a way, she had hoped that the climb up the stairs, and the defensive onslaught of mental energies, would have killed her, as it nearly had Narred. But she had climbed the crystal stairs unmolested, and now—after an entire night of misery—one of them deigned to speak to her.

"I do not care what the reason was," Shayra said sullenly. "We have always been taught there was only one truly sacred thing in all the worlds—the sanctity of thought, the power of creation inherent in every human being. You—all of you—helped Jaes violate that tenant. We are all unworthy of our gifts because of this—all of us, forever."

"There are things no man or woman should know," the voice whispered in reply.

"Who are we to decide that?" Shayra asked. She knew it would be easier, more succinct, to communicate in thought—but she refused. The magic felt dirty to her now.

"You do not understand. You are a first generation Mindshaper, Shayra. All Collectresses are—must be. But having never lost your body and existed as this, as pure thought, you cannot appreciate our responsibilities. Thought is our domain, and we are the only ones equipped to decide when a thought must be eradicated." The ancient mind did not lose its patience with Shayra, but she could feel a strange, disquieting desperation in its tone.

"Then decide it again," Shayra said, suddenly seizing upon a solution to her misery. "Strike it from my mind! I will command the twins to not share it with me again, to bury it in their deepest shields. Take it from me, so that I may continue to serve the Kem in good faith."

The thought of the elder did not make contact with her. Instead, the lights emanating from the crystal column intensified and began to scintillate, shifting across the spectrum rapidly. Dozens of thoughts began to whisper at the edges of Shayra's mental perception, and then, there was quiet. Calm.

The same elder's thoughts returned to her mind. "We could do this. But there are consequences. A mind is a tapestry, if it is any one thing. Perfectly made, it will endure for centuries. But should you snip a thread from the tapestry, you risk unraveling it. Not all at once—our snip shall be precise. But over time, when stress is applied to the tapestry, one never knows when another thread will come undone, then another. Perhaps a century from now. Perhaps a decade. Perhaps tomorrow. But eventually, it will come undone."

Shayra hissed back, mentally, "You did it to everyone on this world!"

"The minds of the Kem endure for generations. The minds of the others... do not. The risk was deemed acceptable," the elder replied matter-of-factly. "If we are to do this to you, we will need a corporeal Mindshaper to aid us. Will you submit to Andoria serving in this capacity?"

"Yes," Shayra said. "Do it now, please. Make me who I was before the secret. Make me innocent of this horrible deed."

"As you wish, Collectress."

# 28
## Murrod

*From time to time, I've been accused of a few fairly rotten things.* Some people think I'm shallow, others think I'm stupid. The case could have been made, once upon a time, that I was a coward. Becky would say impulsive, Adam would say foolish. Steven would say—well, I don't know what Steven would say. We're not really that close. Todd... Todd would say I was confused. He saw me at maybe my lowest—him and Mathias.

Right before things got the worst they'd ever been for me, I was all of those things. No, not stupid. But the rest—that was me. Painting with a set of watercolors of negative character traits, you could have painted a pretty accurate picture of JC Stein.

But there are things about me that all of these people—friends and girlfriends and casual acquaintances alike, don't see. Seriously—I'm amazing, in my own special ways. I'm loyal and I'm passionate and I'm perceptive.

Yes, I am.

I know it doesn't seem like it, from the way I'm always rushing head-long into things, but I see things clearly, most of the time—more clearly than the others, bound up in their own messes.

When we got back from Rettik, I was the one that noticed that Becky wasn't acting like Becky—that Tatyana had somehow taken control of her. It wasn't obvious—not at first. But I knew from the little things, and like my mom always says, little things add up to big things.

That's possibly why things are bad between Steven and me. It isn't that I don't trust him (although I've never had a particularly warm spot in my heart for cops), it's that I don't trust *her*. Tatyana. She used to be awesome (and smoking hot), but after she died, when she became whatever she became after that, she got desperate. Desperate people do stupid, foolish, confused, impulsive, shallow things.

Oh. Well shit. Is that irony? I never paid enough attention in English class.

I guess that about sums it up, doesn't it?

I notice things—especially things that other people miss. I noticed things happening between Becky and Steven, even when they dismissed them. It was tearing me up, and I didn't know what to do. How do you even have a rational conversation with your girlfriend about this? I don't think there's a non-insane way to say, "Hey, I think the leftover brain patterns of our dead friend who gave you your super powers are making you hot for this semi-buff semi-attractive cop instead of your semi-hyper semi-charming boyfriend." It doesn't really roll of the tongue, right?

All I could think of was that if I just got rid of the collar, it would all be better.

So yes, I notice things... but sometimes I can be a big dumbass, too.

¤~¤~¤

Mathias joined Becky in helping to lead the malnourished Metalbreakers towards the Spiralgate. Todd, Steven, JC, and Yors had all taken up defensive positions along the short route from the Surveyor's Guild to the gate, but there appeared to be no need. In the broad daylight, there were no Ellir to attack them, and the sounds of conflict between the knights defending Hineros and the Goldvast warriors had veered both south and east—across the river.

Adam reached the metal bands of the Spiralgate a full minute before Mathias with the first half of the prisoners. Mathias watched as Adam spun his hands in intricate gestures that seemed almost second nature—so different from the halting, nervous young man that had first come to this world, back when Mathias had lived a far simpler life. Adam was a year older than when Mathias had last seen him—and even after all that Mathias had endured in that year, his throat caught when he looked upon him. But as was always the case when it came to Mathias' desires, it mattered not. He tried to put the thought out of his mind.

The bands spun to life, glowing brilliantly blue as they coalesced into a sphere of light.

Of all the assembled Metalbreaker prisoners, only the one called Gurse was older than Mathias, and only Gurse appeared to have any particular skill with language. The old man took the lead, and together he, Mathias, and Becky ushered the Metalbreakers into the sphere of light.

When only Gurse remained, Adam reached out and grabbed Gurse by the hand.

"If you head directly south, you will find yourself in the Borrik Mountains," Adam explained.

"I know of them," Gurse said. "Wouldn't imagine mountains have changed all that much in the thirty years we've been gone."

"Probably not. If you head for the Underpass, Ambrek's scouts should find you. They'll take good care of you. I'm sorry we can't come with you," Adam said.

Gurse shrugged his bony shoulders. "I can manage this lot. Take care, Gatemaker. This world is a cesspool. Don't let it ruin you."

Adam nodded. Gurse turned to the others and smiled fiercely, waving briefly towards where Yors was standing watch, near the street leading north from the Spiralgate clearing. Yors inclined his head sharply.

Gurse turned and crossed the threshold into the Spiralgate, and then with an audible popping sound, the gate snapped closed.

"Now, you guys!" Adam shouted. Right in front of the gate, Adam whipped one hand around in a large oval, the fingers on the other hand curling into a tight, precise gesture. A flat disc of gold light appeared there, and everyone bolted for the portal, as planned.

Mathias was the first inside the crossgate, and he walked several yards inward, away from the opening. Within a few minutes, everyone was assembled.

Adam entered the portal last and closed it behind him, sealing them in what appeared to be an endless corridor of gold light.

"Safest place I can find to have a conversation," Adam said, smiling. "I can hold it without opening the other end for a while—so where are we heading? Anyone? Mathias?"

Mathias paced a few steps, gathering his thoughts.

"I came to Hineros trying to find out what was happening. I'd heard rumors of Hyrak working with the Ellir, and this made me uncomfortable," Mathias began.

"Understandably so," Steven said. "I've never met the man, but his reputation is certainly detailed."

"Well Norrun and I found out that Chaplain Reid was diverting a vast portion of the treasury of most ministries to Hineros. I just assumed that whatever that lunatic was doing was bad for Greendeep. But I had to know beyond a doubt, so we worked our way across the country to find out for ourselves." Mathias continued pacing. "The trouble is, I didn't get much for answers here—aside from seeing Hyrak in person taming a dragon-god, tricking Embrew into opening a portal to bring a small army of Ellir into the city, and being a general terror."

"Answers in Surveyor's Guild," Yors supplied. "Crates of Bindmetal dust—many fortunes' worth. Gurse explain—Jovs used to work dust into barrier, keeping Ellir out of Greendeep."

"That makes sense, I suppose. But I'm not sure where that points us next. Hyrak flew east when he left Hineros, but Chron only knows where he went." Mathias sighed.

"Then let's ask him," JC said.

"Ask who?" Becky inquired.

"Chron. That's the dragon that oversees Greendeep right?" JC asked.

"No dragons," Adam said emphatically. "They do not solve problems. Have you noticed this? I have! Every problem we have is made *worse* by applying dragon to it, not better."

Steven arched an eyebrow, but said nothing. Mathias imagined the former police officer had not yet had the chance to encounter one of the mighty dragons that appeared to be a common fixture of many worlds in person.

"Then we can leave this crossgate and I will use my compass to find Hyrak," JC said impatiently. "It'll find him as well as it found us Metalbreakers, or Becky, way back when."

Yors grunted, "Not work."

JC started to argue, but a withering look from the smith suddenly cowed the young man—something Mathias found curious if not outright suspicious.

"It was only an expression, but I *suppose* we could ask Chron for help," Mathias muttered. "It isn't the craziest thing we have ever tried. But there are rules—protocols. Even regular men of Greendeep can't get an audience with the dragon-god, and I am hardly regular, since my records were shredded. And the rest of you aren't even his subjects. We'd be run through a hundred times before we got close. Chron is notoriously strict."

"So who can get such an audience?" Becky asked.

"A Chaplain of one of the ministries. As far as I know, they are the only ones that can meet with his eminence in person," Mathias explained. "But my people detest outsiders. None of the chaplains are going to help us of their own free will."

Becky smiled, and then JC smiled an almost mirror image of that smile.

Adam put his head in his hands and groaned. "What part of 'no dragons' did you people not understand?"

Todd walked over next to Adam and put his arm around him, pulling him in close. "No one deserves it more," he said. "Come on. You know it."

Mathias asked cautiously, "What are you thinking?"

"I think we're heading for Imperia," Becky said. "I'm going to go mindshape your old buddy Chaplain Reid into getting us an audience with a dragon."

¤~¤~¤

Jarrek watched Hyrak stroking the white dragon gently on its neck as he issued specific instructions to her. The dragon's three eyes were glowing faintly, but otherwise the dragon stayed perfectly still as Hyrak outlined a complex list of tasks.

Then the warlord turned back to Jarrek. They were back once more at the caves that Hyrak, Jarrek, and Embrew had called home for so long.

"She knows what she must do. She will continue to send word to the leaders among her people, and they will begin marshalling for the next stage of my plan," Hyrak said. The warlord sounded very satisfied with himself.

"How many stages does your plan have?" Jarrek asked, exasperated. "And at which stage, precisely, do you take me back to Hineros to retrieve Embrew so I can finish him off? We had a deal, and I have honored my end."

"I have not yet fully tested the tools you have wrought for me, Jov," Hyrak said icily. "I would have thought your adventure on our flight back to Bluetide would have taught you to still your tongue."

"I'm tired, Hyrak. That is all. Tired of smithing, yes, but mostly of not knowing what is going on. I accept that you will not trust me with your whole plan—I am perhaps happiest not knowing what you plan to do with those items I have crafted for you. But what new torment will you be putting me through next? I wager it has something to do with the thoughts you plundered from Ehbor's mind?" Jarrek found himself looking not at Hyrak as he spoke, but at Ahmur. The dragon had reared up her head and now appeared to be whispering—the light of her eyes flickered in time to the syllables that hissed from between the great beast's teeth.

"You are catching on," Hyrak said. "We travel for the Greytall Mountains as soon as I am content that Ahmur has fully roused her nation's warriors. We will travel with speed and stealth, for I am not particularly comfortable with the idea that there are still two dragons potentially between us and our goal that are not yet under my control." Hyrak gestured to the pair of coiled wires on his belt and the tiny red Bindmetal bells hanging from each. "You do good work, Jarrek, but I am not so confident as to take unnecessary risk. We shall travel only at night."

"On your bright white dragon?" Jarrek asked, smirking. He expected to be struck by Hyrak's gauntleted hand, but Hyrak smiled instead.

"We will not be seen. Rest now, if you are able. Tonight we fly. The journey in the mountains will not be easy, even on dragon back. We seek a very particular place, and I will need your help finding it." Hyrak knelt down and began to carefully rummage through the pack of wonders Jarrek had forged at his behest.

"I have never been to those mountains, Hyrak. I doubt I will be of any help to you."

"But you are a Metalbreaker, Jarrek. I am told that your people have a particular affinity for finding junctures." Hyrak pulled the green Bindmetal pickaxe from the pack.

Jarrek's flesh grew cold. His stomach twisted into knots. "That... that is what you wanted the pick for? How do you know of such things? Even among my people this is rare knowledge."

Hyrak smiled, his scarred, burned lips peeling back away from his teeth in a most disgusting grin. "There is almost nothing I do not know, Jov. Now get some sleep. We have wonders to perform."

¤~¤~¤

JC was the first to emerge from Adam's redirected crossgate. He found himself in a large living space filled with overstuffed furnishings. The windows were draped in heavy red cloth that permitted only a fraction of the sunlight from outside to brighten the dark wood floors or the large, cold fireplace that dominated the longest wall in the room.

Steven was close behind him, and the two of them fanned out to check the room and its immediate surroundings for unwanted guests. Mathias had assured them this was a safe place, but Steven's overcautious police mentality had won out over JC's preference to simply jump in and bust heads.

JC strode confidently into the foyer, his energy rifle primed and ready with its persistent whining hum, but the small entry way was empty. He checked the door and found it locked, and then clicked it open, pulled it open just a crack, and peered around the street outside.

Imperia was much as he remembered it—crowded with people who, largely, didn't do very much. The streets were wider and the structures more evenly spaced from one another in this part of town—a notable change from the flat where Mathias had been living on their first visit. He noticed a sheet of parchment tacked to the door and ripped it down. He read the bold heading across the top of the sheet—Notice of Incarnation-Related Vacancy. The remaining information on the sheet referred to the date of some manner of auction for the contents of the home and the home itself.

"Clear!" shouted Steven from wherever the other exit from the living room had taken him.

JC returned to the main room to find Adam sitting, and nearly dozing, in one of the plush armchairs. Todd was sitting next to him, while Mathias and Yors paced—likely for different reasons—near the fireplace. Steven stood in the doorframe leading to the rest of the house.

JC handed the parchment to Mathias. "Is this why you knew it was safe to come here?"

Mathias scanned the document quickly and JC watched his shoulders slump. "Not quite. I was hoping he had held out a bit longer—Kemer would have been a great help to us. But he's gone now. So many people are gone now." Mathias sighed. "But we have three days before the auction, so the place should be safe for us."

Becky emerged from behind Steven, a glass of water in each hand. She handed one to Adam, but Todd took it with a dismissive gesture—apparently not wanting them to disturb Adam as he recovered from his frequent gatemaking efforts over the past few hours.

Becky took a long drink from her own glass and then asked, "People don't loot places like this?"

Mathias shook his head, a look of horror on his face. "Murrod isn't like Core. There's a much healthier respect for the laws here." Then he looked up at Steven, blushed slightly, and added, "No offense."

Steven smiled and said, "I'm not a cop anymore, Mathias. And I know how messed up the system is back home, sometimes. Most people are good—but some people are not. That's the same on every world, I refuse to believe otherwise."

"But in Greendeep, violating the law comes with heavy penalty. The Ministry of Incarnation oversees the property rights of those called for reincarnation, and their judiciary knights slay looters on the spot," Mathias explained.

"Well, people on Earth would follow the law a lot more religiously if every infraction ended in death," Steven mused. "But if all of your people reincarnate anyway, wouldn't that take some of the sting out of a death penalty?"

"If a man is in a position to be looking forward to his next incarnation, he likely has no need of anything that could be gained by successfully looting," Mathias said. "If you don't contract with someone of advantageous social standing before death, you return assigned to a lower station than your previous life. And any day now, that will get worse. A new and lowest station, from which there can be no escape, is to be implemented soon—this week, I believe. It has sent many of my people into a frenzy."

"That's fucked up," JC said sympathetically. "I'm glad you're free of that all."

Steven arched an eyebrow. "How's that?"

"One of the reasons I left Murrod originally was because Chaplain Reid and Chaplain Voss destroyed my incarnation records. Not only does that mean I will never know who I was in previous lives, but I will never again be issued a new life," Mathias said.

"So you are not stuck in this assed up system anymore. Which is a big win, if you ask me," JC said.

"I was going to live forever," Mathias said softly. "I was going to have an unlimited number of chances to find happiness. Forgive me if I do not always see the victory in this."

"Oh, dude—I didn't mean..." JC tried to explain, but the look in Mathias' eyes told him he ought not to bother. The damage was done.

"I will be in Kemer's study. He often took his work home, particularly scheduling books. If we are lucky, he may have record of Chaplain Reid's itinerary. I'd hate for us to break into the Ministry of Security if he isn't there." Mathias walked purposefully past Steven towards the rear rooms of the house.

"I can just find him with the compass," JC muttered. "But whatever."

Becky handed JC the glass of water, now only half full, and said, "Have a drink. Sit down for a minute. Let Mathias work through his issues, and Adam catch his breath. Then we'll be back to plunging into trouble."

JC took the glass and gulped down the cool water. It had a faintly metallic taste, but he didn't mind—it was better than the stale, musty taste of water on Arctos. He turned to hand the empty glass to Becky, but noticed that she was rubbing at her temples fiercely.

"What is it?" he asked. "Mindshaper stuff?"

"No, just a migraine, I think," Becky muttered. "It's been building for a while."

JC helped her to the last remaining chair in the room, looking up at Yors, who was now leaning against the mantle above the fireplace. He worried that the Metalbreaker's solution to Becky's tangent encounter in Venot was coming undone, but Yors shook his head gently. Whatever this was, it was something else, as far as the smith was concerned. Still, JC eyed Becky's therapeutic Bindmetal earrings suspiciously.

"I'm fine," Becky said. "Just, maybe I could have some more water?"

JC nodded vigorously and darted out of the room and into a long hallway. The first room to the right was where Mathias was digging through the drawers of a large desk, but across the hallway was what Mathias assumed was the kitchen in this place. A long counter ran along one wall, with a small stone well in its center. A metal bucket had already been hauled up from the well, still partly full of water. He tipped the bucket to pour more of the clear water into the glass and then returned to the living room.

Steven continued to stand more or less in the center of the doorway between the hall and the living room, and JC gave him a gentle shove as he muttered, "Excuse me."

Steven didn't respond, or move, and JC slipped past him and approached Becky. Her eyes were closed, and he touched her hand and said, "Here's that water."

She did not respond.

JC narrowed his eyes and looked back over his shoulder towards Steven—who was standing stock-still, his eyes closed.

A tangle of emotions started to build up in JC's chest, making it hard to catch his breath. He felt heat rise up in the fifteen links of Bindmetal that remained active around his throat, but even the ghost of the fear they were banishing was enough to drive him nearly wild.

He slammed the glass of water on the small table beside the chair and then closed his own eyes, dragging in deep, deliberate breaths to try and calm himself as he groped about in his own mindscape for the tether that connected his mind to Becky's. It was not the ugly mental fusion of a botched mindshaping, but a carefully built bridge that made it possible for them to easily connect whenever they needed. It was special—something she had only with him, and with Adam (which didn't make him particularly jealous for obvious reasons) and... with Steven. That was the one that rankled.

He crept along that tether until he found himself in Becky's mind, in the formless black landing where their communication always took place. And she was there already—but she was not alone. He was there—Steven.

JC drew just near enough to overhear what they were saying, but not so close that his presence would be easily discernible—he knew Becky would find him if she was looking for him, but she seemed quite caught up in the conversation.

"Ever since Venot," Becky said, her voice quavering, "it's been getting worse. This pressure inside of me. I don't know how to stop it."

"Do you..." Steven began hesitantly. "Do you think it's her?"

"She's gone," Becky said, shaking her head. "I know you wish that wasn't so, but it is. If she was here, I'd know about it. All that is left of her is the power."

"But then why was I able to help pull you out of that mess in your mind?" Steven asked. "If there was still a sliver of Tatyana in here, that makes sense—you know how she and I were connected. But if she's not here, then why did it take me to save you?"

"I..." Becky whispered. JC strained to make out what she said next. "I think I *wanted* you to save me," Becky finished.

"Not JC?" Steven asked.

Becky wrapped her arms around Steven and pulled him close. "I'm confused," she sobbed. "I don't know him, not always. Sometimes he's the boy that I love, and sometimes he's this other thing that I don't understand—but I feel like I know you so well. And I... I love you too, Steven. I don't know when it started, but I feel it, all of the time. Constant."

"Becky..." Steven replied softly.

JC felt his fists clench tightly, not just here in thoughtspace, but also in his body—squeezing tightly, tiny ragged fingernails biting into calloused palms.

"The migraine was me denying the connection between us," Becky said, regaining her composure. "Once I opened it again... all of that pain went away. And you were here. And here we are. And... I feel better. Safer. Whole."

JC couldn't handle it anymore. He spun and ran, retreating back to his own mind. He tried to will that connection between him and Becky to close, to shatter into a million pieces and blow away in the wind—but he could not. He had not the power. He had no powers at all except the stupid chain—the chain that made him, what had she said? That she didn't know him. Well he could take care of that.

He opened his eyes and turned to Yors. "Come with me," he said from between clenched teeth.

Yors followed as they pushed past Steven's infuriatingly still shape and down the hall to a bedroom. JC sat down on the edge of the bed and leaned forward, head down. "Take more of them. Now," he instructed.

"Yors not ready to do more," Yors explained. "Magic needs time to rebuild."

"Now!" JC shouted. He felt tears starting to trickle down his cheeks, so he refused to look up.

He would be himself again. It wasn't too late to fix all of this.

Yors knelt down in front of JC and placed one hand on each side of his head, humming softly a tune that JC had not heard him use to center his magic before. It had a quick, sharp beat to it, and by the third repetition of the main through line, he felt several of the links around his throat begin to hop and vibrate erratically.

After nearly ten minutes of humming, JC felt the first link go dead. It was followed quickly by another, then another... until seven in all were newly bled dry of their magic.

He looked up to see Yors, white as a ghost, sweat soaking his face, his hair, and his beard. The smith's eyes were hard and dark, and he glared at JC with dark intent.

"Thank you," JC said carefully.

"Eight left," Yors said savagely. "Thank you for making Yors feel like a servant again."

"I didn't..." JC said. Again, he realized he had crossed a line. Like with Mathias a few minutes ago, like with everyone in his life, at one time or another, he had gone too far.

"Is fine," Yors said, standing shakily. "JC owes Yors. Remember this."

¤~¤~¤

Under Plyssa's direction, Embrew crafted an interlocking series of four crossgates, each pushing to the greatest distance Embrew could manage. While others of the Order of Gar had greater range than Embrew, none could so seamlessly connect one gate to another, and to his passengers he was certain it seemed as though they simply walked a long, single corridor of light.

But Embrew could feel the weight of the working on his shoulders. He was tired, nearly exhausted, but he also sensed in the instinctive geometry of his kind that the distance they had traveled was immense. They had, in the space of perhaps an hour, traversed a huge portion of the world. They were near Spiralgates, which surprised him—he could feel at least two gates within a single crossgate from their final destination. Why had it been so important for Ahmur to lead her forces to Hineros, to that particular Spiralgate, if her people controlled several in their own territories?

"When we come out, if Embrew is as precise as he claims, there will be some confusion. I've brought us all the way to the Circle of the Heavens. No man has ever been within the Circle, and my sisters will not take kindly to the three of you. I probably won't be able to stop you from going to the dungeons—but I can keep them from killing you on sight," Plyssa explained as she fastened her large mask over her face. "So don't do anything stupid."

Embrew's senses, augmented by his arts to detect the shapes and distances all around him, but not things such as color, felt one of their companions, the mostly silent one called Sky, tense.

"Shhh," Tyrick said, patting Sky on the back. "I will be with you."

Embrew had puzzled together things about Tyrick and Sky, and about Plyssa, but he kept mostly quiet. Once he had deposited them here, he would recoup his strength and then make for one of the nearby Spiralgates. He would return to Onus and warn all who would listen of what little he knew of Hyrak's scheme. For some reason, the warlord had been pleased to learn one of the geometric keys to Onus from Embrew's mind, and that could only bode ill for Embrew's home world.

Embrew drew himself up to his full height and spread his arms wide in front of him. His arts, like his senses, were stronger now that Plyssa had freed him from the shackles that had hobbled his powers for nearly twenty years—and as tired as he was from the day's exertions, he had enough strength left for a show of power.

"We arrive," Embrew said dramatically. "I shall make our presence known."

He opened the crossgate in a bright violet hue—a color requiring a great deal of strength to maintain. He flushed the pattern of the crossgate threshold with additional power, creating a more spectacular lightshow than was necessary. Partly he did this to ensure that anyone in the area stood clear and avoided the unfortunate consequences of being present when a person materialized through the gate, but mostly he wanted to clearly display his power. The violet hue of the portal would provide a localized intercession field for as much as a full minute, protecting them all from attack as they emerged.

"Let me go first," Plyssa cautioned. She passed by Embrew and stepped across the threshold out of the corridor of light and into the so-called Circle of the Heavens, her hands raised up to show she was unarmed.

Tyrick and Sky followed, side by side, making the same gesture, even though Embrew could sense the shape of Tyrick's knife secured inside his boot. And Embrew himself followed last, gathering a halo of the spare energy from the portal around himself in a trick that his old teacher, Corudain, had once called "remarkably ostentatious."

As he emerged, his senses were almost overwhelmed by the sheer quantity of shapes all around him. They were under the open sky, atop a highly elevated platform of some kind—and there were hundreds of figures arrayed all around them. Women, all, he could not easily count them, even with his arts, and nearly all of them was armed with a spear and masked in another of the large rectangular masks that marked them as warriors in Goldvast's army.

"Stand down!" Plyssa shouted. "We bring important tidings from the battlefront!"

"You bring men to this sacred place!" one of the figures shouted. "This is against Ahmur's commandments!"

"They are my prisoners!" Plyssa shouted back. "They are a source of great knowledge and great power. Take them below, to the Circle of the Darkness. They will cause us no troubles, you have my word!"

The many women arrayed around them murmured to one another, a sound tinged more with anger than acquiescence, until one voice arose, louder than the others, and stilled the buzzing whispers.

"You are of the House of the Snake. Secrets are your trade. What is your clan and your assignment?" the woman demanded.

Plyssa knelt down and bowed low, replying, "The Chieftain honors me with her question. I am Plyssa of the Rolling Fields North of Sayr. I am assigned to the Duty of the Temple, as I have been for the past two years."

Now the murmur rose up again, but this time its tone was quite different. Embrew did not understand the hierarchy that governed the women of Goldvast, but it appeared that Plyssa's station as a member of Ahmur's honor guard afforded her a great deal of prestige among these women whose home was quite far indeed from the dragon's lair.

"Then the words of Plyssa will be heard," the chieftain replied. "Take her prisoners below. On my authority, place them in the third wedge."

Women swarmed around them now, jabbing at Embrew and the others roughly with spears but not doing any true injury. Tyrick, Sky, and Embrew were led down a long spiral stair that seemed to wrap around the outside of the great column they had first appeared atop of. There was no outer wall, and a misstep upon the stairs would send any one of them tumbling hundreds of feet to their death.

They walked many loops around the structure, which felt to be nearly one hundred yards across to Embrew's spatial perceptions. They moved in silence, although Embrew occasionally heard a soft whimpering come from Sky.

Eventually, they reached the ground and were then shown into a doorway at the base of the column. Inside, another spiral stair gorged deep into the earth, and they traveled down fifty feet to a round room surrounded by five large, circular doors placed equidistantly around the perimeter of the chamber.

A guard opened a door and they were shoved inside, Embrew tripping over the lip of the doorframe where it curled up to match the circular door. Tyrick caught him and kept him from sprawling on the floor, but by the time this was done, the round door had already been secured behind them.

"There is no light here," Tyrick said, likely for Embrew's benefit. "But I hear noises in the distance."

Embrew's senses flashed outward, feeling the shape of the room—a great wedge, forty-five yards to a side, comprising seventy degrees of a circle. Inside the wedge there were dozens of figures—all of them smaller than Embrew. Child-sized. And all of them male.

Embrew held up one hand and sent a tiny whisper of magic into the crooked gesture of three fingers. A small disc of gold light spun into being parallel to the floor, just above his hand—a tiny crossgate operating on minimal energy, spanning only a fraction of an in inch from opening to exit. It was an adequate source of light for the others, if a sorely inappropriate abuse of gatemaking.

"What is this?" Tyrick asked in awe.

"Are they children?" Embrew asked.

"Male children," Tyrick replied. "Is this the nursery of Goldvast? Why... why are there young boys here?"

"Why wouldn't there be?" Embrew asked. He noticed Sky creeping slowly towards where the children were huddled together, just beyond the ring of light cast by Embrew's working.

"The nursery of Greendeep has only males," Tyrick said. "Just the reincarnations of those who have passed out of their lives. There are no women raised there—there never could be."

"Then I would imagine Goldvast does things differently. Perhaps more traditionally." Embrew said, with a slight smile.

"You mean through rutting?" Tyrick asked, his expression drawn in disgust. "Like animals?"

"Hello," Sky said suddenly. The quiet young man walked slowly to the edge of the light and extended one hand towards a child—perhaps ten summers in age, Embrew thought, from his size—that had crept closer than the others.

The boy stepped into the light fully and then recoiled, throwing his hands up over his eyes to shield them from the light.

"How barbaric," Embrew muttered. "To keep them in the dark like this."

Tyrick said nothing, but his head hung a bit lower.

Sky followed the recoiled child into the darkness and Embrew sensed him reaching out to touch one hand softly to the boy's cheek.

"Friend," Sky said.

The boy opened his mouth as if to speak, and Embrew sensed then that the boy had no tongue. Quickly he probed about the room with his arts and discovered this was not a unique attribute to this boy—none of them did. The twenty-seven young boys in the room, all between ten and fifteen summers by Embrew's estimation, had had their tongues cut out as surely as Embrew's eyes had been struck from his head.

"They cannot speak. They are herded here, like animals. What is the meaning of this place?" Embrew asked.

"They are breeding stock," said a voice from outside the door. "Still too young to be of service, but not for much longer."

Embrew turned back towards the door and realized there was a small aperture in it—a tiny slot that had been closed before but was now open. It was crafted in such a way that it could allow objects, likely food, to be placed through the slot without allowing any light to follow.

Tyrick knelt down against the door, his face close to the slot, and asked, "Where do they come from?"

"Nearly half the children born in the communes are male. Some are put to death, of course, but others are brought here to raise until they are old enough to help us conceive a new generation," the voice answered.

Embrew asked sharply, "Why tell us this?"

"My totem is the owl. I spread truth," the voice replied. "I am to watch you to ensure you do not hurt any of the stock."

"People," Tyrick shouted empathically. "Not stock. They are people. Children."

The voice chuckled. "Your indignation ought best be saved for someone that does not know your kind as well as I do, man. I have seen the likes of your companion before—I know what he is. And I know what you are... surveyor. Hypocrite."

Tyrick stood up and paced away from the door. "I freed him," he muttered.

"Yes, yes. Very noble of you. Did you free them all?" the voice asked.

"What is she going on about?" Embrew asked.

Tyrick shook his head. "I did not. I should have, but I did not."

"So you picked a calf from the herd and decided that instead of working it to death in the fields, you would pamper it in the palace. So what is it now... a pet?" the voice asked. "I walked the perimeter, many months ago. I hid in the underbrush as I watched you work—I am certain it was you, though so many of your kind look the same to me. And I would say, by the look of him, that your friend there, your pet, was the one toiling in the dirt that day under your command."

Tyrick said nothing.

"Enjoy your stay. I am sure the chieftains will wish to interrogate you soon enough."

Embrew spoke once more, asking, "Why say any of this? Why antagonize him?"

The voice replied, slow and quiet. "They think themselves superior to us, the men of the jungle nation. But I have seen them at their worst, in my long years. I have been a spy for longer than most have been alive. They are all the same, eventually. Monsters. What we do seems harsh, but the boychildren live. It is more than I can say for what I have seen his kind do. And you, Gatemaker of Onus... you would do well to realize that your people chose the wrong side in this conflict. You chose men with which to bargain, and more's the pity for that."

¤~¤~¤

They waited until nightfall, which Mathias assured them was a safe proposition in Imperia. According to the documents Mathias had found in Kemer's desk, the chaplain had been staying at his offices almost non-stop over the past few weeks, so their attack on him would have to happen there.

Steven had some healthy reservations about breaking into a place proclaimed the "Ministry of Security," but the others didn't seem particularly worried. That likely had something to do with the fact that it was Steven who would actually be going in and scouting around. His powers as a

Shadowbender made him the logical choice for it, but his efforts at breaking and entering had not been historically successful ventures.

They were, right now, in one of the many open park spaces that surrounded the large, walled ministry building. The streets were quiet this time of night, with large lamps casting steady and regular illumination around the edges of the manicured park.

Yors had remained behind, exhausted from working on JC's chain. JC was here but in rare form as a sour mood had overtaken him. Becky was here by necessity—Steven would have been just as happy to have left her back at the house. Things between them were now immeasurably awkward. She had confessed feelings for him that he simply did not feel in return—not in any genuine way. His affection for her was nothing more romantic than that—care, but not love. But he had found it impossible to rebuff her advances... the words had simply been unwilling to come to his tongue.

He wanted to talk to her more about it, but privacy was hard to come by, and he feared that if they had the conversation in their mindscapes again, he would be similarly tongue-tied. While he was there, old emotions, and the lingering trace of Tatyana's love for him, overwhelmed his judgment. Only in the world of flesh and blood could he keep all his wits about him.

"I can slide in, grab this Reid person, and then pull him back out here so Becky can do her thing," Steven said. "No reason to complicate things with a huge insertion team."

"Except you don't even know what Chaplain Reid looks like," JC muttered.

"That's a fair point," Becky said. "How many of you even do?"

Todd coughed. "It was dark and I was kind of busy threatening to club him to death the only time I ever saw him. I'm not sure I could pick him out of a lineup."

Mathias sighed. "So I will be going in. And Becky—you can be ready right away when we get back out here? One shout from Reid, even out here in this park, will raise the entire ministry's executive knight team. That's a bigger fight than we can easily handle."

Adam cracked his knuckles loudly. "No one will hear anything out of him. The minute Steven pulls him out of the shadow, I'll wrap him up so tight in intercessions that the sound of his voice takes a week to reach anyone's ears."

Todd smiled. "That's the least butch threat I've ever heard. You know that, right?"

JC had cupped his two hands together and now pulled them apart to reveal his small Bindmetal compass resting on his adjacent palms. "The asshat is in his office, on the third floor, in the corner. He's moving a little—the needle wags back and forth pretty steadily—but he must just be pacing or something. Maybe giving one of those supervillain monologues. But he's definitely in that room right now."

"Then we might as well go now. Mathias, are you ready?" Steven asked, holding out one hand.

Mathias gulped and asked, "Does it hurt?"

"A little," Steven admitted. "But it hurts less if you are ready for it."

Mathias reached out and clasped hands with Steven. With an effort of will, Steven reached out the shadows of the park's benches and shrubs and called them to him, pulling them up around him and Mathias like a sheer blanket and spinning them around until the pair of them were completely enveloped in the shadow. Once this was done, his working carried into the second step, dissolving their substance into that shadow so they could slip from shadow to shadow. He felt Mathias' grip on his hand tighten and then he too grimaced as their physical bodies adjusted to the transition.

He willed them into motion, and as bolts of shadow, they darted across the park and into the building, gliding up the stone walls and into the window of a room adjacent to where Joe had pinpointed Reid's location. The sights around them were a blur as they moved quickly, taking in only enough of the surroundings to get their bearings. Mathias followed easily, without resistance, and Steven guided them through the office adjacent to Reid's chambers and then under the door into that corner room.

With a sharp exertion of will, Steven returned them both to their physical, three-dimensional bodies just inside the door to Reid's office... where the Chaplain was indeed pacing back and forth in front of the crackling fire. His desk was littered with scraps of parchment, many of which were crumpled up. The chaplain's back was to them as they soundlessly appeared, and Mathias released Steven's hand, tensing up as he braced to charge the Minister of Security.

"Chaplain Reid," Mathias said. "We've come to settle a score with you."

Steven froze. The plan had been one of stealth—to grab the minister unawares and slide him through the shadows to Becky's waiting magic. Now they were engaging him in conversation?

The minister turned slowly, and Steven was taken aback at the man's face. Everyone they had seen as they had traveled across Imperia today had been young—men in their twenties and thirties. Chaplain Reid was older—in his early forties according to Mathias—but he looked far older than that. Wrinkles were piling up in his flesh, and age spots were forming along his forehead, where his dark hair was receding. The man was still fit, but his shoulders were bowed and his knuckles, clutching a small glass of what Steven dared to say was some kind of liquor, were large and knobby.

"Get in line," Reid said, his voice cracking.

Mathias drew back. "What happened to you?"

Reid replied, "The price for refusing Chron's call. I thought you'd come to see me, eventually. My agents saw you at the courier hub, a month ago. Then you got away from us, and we lost track of you. I assumed you were making some kind of trouble over the line of demarcation." Reid took a sip of his drink. "You never did know your place in this world."

"You don't understand what's happening here, Chaplain. You never have," Mathias hissed.

"You stole away the Metalbreakers and tried to upend our civilization, you petulant child," Reid said. "And now you return to, what? Finish me off? I assure you, time will do that more efficiently than you ever could. Who's this? Did you find some poor fool stupid enough to contract with you?" He looked to Steven.

"We need your help, sir," Steven said cautiously. "And we're not going to take no for an answer."

"Of what use can I be to you? My plans are undone. My every effort to save this nation has been for naught." Reid downed the last of his drink.

Mathias answered, "You're going to get us an audience with Chron."

"Boy, Chron has no affection for me just now!" Chaplain Reid gestured towards his face with his free hand. "Can't you see that? I have angered the dragon-god."

"We need him to help us find, and stop, Hyrak," Mathias said. "I know you care about that—I know you've done everything in your power to protect us all from the Ellir—and Hyrak controls the Ellir, at least in part. But now he controls more than that—he has Goldvast under his boot as well."

Chaplain Reid stared at Mathias for a moment and then threw back his head and laughed.

Steven looked at Mathias. This wasn't going quite the way he had expected.

"Perhaps it is best that I did not kill you on the rack in my dungeon, Mathias," Chaplain Reid said. "I will happily help you in this."

"You'll what?" Steven asked.

Mathias glared at the chaplain. "This is some kind of trick."

"No trick at all. I have resolved to accomplish one last thing before I die, and that is to find that mysterious man. My expensive Surveyor's Guild project could not keep him and his forces from attacking us, but perhaps, in person, I can make a more decisive stroke." The chaplain strode over to his desk. Steven tensed, one hand flexing as shadow talons grew from his fingertips.

The minister took a small box from inside the desk drawer, tucked it into his pocket, and turned back to Mathias and Steven. With a rather alarming smile he said, "I'm ready—and there is no time to waste. Shall we be on our way?"

# 29

## MURROD

P*lyssa was not prone to nerves.* She was a warrior of Goldvast, chosen by the totem of the snake, and she had defied expectations (and rules) for as long as she could remember. But to stand at the center of the Circle of the Heavens with the fifteen chieftains arrayed all around her, one and all standing in judgment over her every word, she found her confidence shaken.

The more questions they asked—for of all of them, only one chieftain had ever even met her before—the more she felt that her answers were insufficient. Everything their civilization was built upon depended on her convincing the assembled leaders of Goldvast that their dragon-goddess had been compromised, but such a thought was difficult to accept from even the wisest advisors, and Plyssa was very much an unknown.

"I beg you to let me explain," Plyssa implored. She was standing, thankfully, but with her interrogators spread all around her, it was difficult to know whom to face as she spoke. She chose the chieftain who had allowed her to be heard in the first place, thinking that perhaps hers was a sympathetic ear. Each chieftain sat on a low cube of stone, save her savior, who sat instead on a small pedestal of white Bindmetal.

"You appear before us in the company of an otherworld magician and two men of Greendeep," one of the chieftains behind her accused, "and now expect us to believe that we are all in danger? The only danger we see before us is you!"

Plyssa scowled, but did not turn. "I found the fastest way to travel to you; that is all. And those men aided in my escape from Ellir forces so that I could bring this warning to you. Ahmur—"

"You will not speak of the goddess!" shouted the chieftain before Plyssa. So much for the sympathetic ear she had been hoping for.

"Then that will make this conversation difficult to have," Plyssa asserted. "I stood in the honor guard of the goddess—that gives me the right to speak of her. You can't deny me that."

"But not the right to abandon your reverence for her greatness," said a chieftain from off to the left.

Plyssa fought back the urge to roll her eyes. "Of course. What I meant to say was that I needed the help of those I traveled with to escape the Ellir so that I could bring tidings of what has befallen our goddess."

"The Ellir do not count the women of Goldvast as foes," one chieftain said.

Plyssa turned and glared at the speaker. "They burned how many fields, raided how many villages, in the past few weeks, and you dare say such a thing?"

"That was not the Ellir," said another chieftain. "That was the man called Hyrak. And he was placated in treaty with our goddess. Our peace with the Ellir remains intact."

"If you insist. Then I was held prisoner by Hyrak, by way of his Ellir. Let me get to the meat of the matter!" Plyssa shouted. For once, no one questioned her when she stopped to draw a breath. "Hyrak's treaty with our goddess was a ruse. Somehow, he has taken control of our goddess and she now answers to his will."

As expected, there was an uproar from the chieftains and their assembled entourages beyond the inner circle. It took quite some time for the group to calm, but they did at last as each of the chieftains turned to face the one on the white pedestal. When silence was restored, it was she who said, "Secrets are not the only trade of those who wear the mask of the snake."

Plyssa sucked in a sharp breath. This was not going well.

"Lies slip from the tongue of the serpent," the chieftain said, "and more so is this true when one considers the origins of the messenger."

Plyssa scowled. "I am a sister of Goldvast, as I have always been. I speak the truth now, as I always have. The snake chose me, not I it."

"Always is forever, from beginnings to endings," the chieftain said.

"What does that mean?" Plyssa asked.

"If you have no proof to support your word, we cannot take the word of a single woman over that of the goddess. The word of Ahmur is law, always. And the last word of Ahmur, delivered by her very will to our very hearts, just hours ago, stands against your assertions." A different chieftain spoke now, standing from her cube at Plyssa's left periphery.

"What law is this?" Plyssa asked, her heart sinking.

"We are to make ready for full mobilization. And any who retreat from the siege of Hineros are to be put to death," this chieftain continued.

"You mean any who bore witness to her subjugation by Hyrak?" Plyssa asked, drawing up to her full height. She locked eyes with the speaking chieftain. "That is very convenient."

The chieftain upon the white pedestal said firmly, "Then present us your proof."

"How? All I know is what I saw with my own two eyes," Plyssa said. "How can I make you see what I have seen?" Her anger started to flare in her heart—anger at having no means of convincing these people to listen to her. She took for granted the freedom of argument and discussion on the frontier and even, to an extent, in the company of Ahmur. Here, in the secluded heart of Goldvast, everything was structured and rigid—inflexible. Cold.

She felt her hands, clenched into fists, begin to shake, and a sound echoed in her mind—a tone of rich resonance. In front of her, she eyed the pedestal of white Bindmetal upon which the one chieftain sat, and she fought the urge to unleash her anger upon that object, shattering it. It was her special gift, the one thing she had kept always secret, but it always brought peace to her. She needed peace now. There was no way she was not about to end up dead. What good were secrets if one was dead?

Then she thought of something, something she knew was possible, but she alone could not do. She lacked the skill, but perhaps not the talent. She needed help.

"Allow me to fetch one of the prisoners from below, and I will show you my proof," she said. She was grateful for her mask, for it hid from them her fear.

¤~¤~¤

Becky and Adam stood next to each other, jumping at every shadow. They waited for Steven, Mathias, and Chaplain Reid to appear, each ready to spring into action.

"Seems like maybe it's taking too long," Adam mumbled.

"They're fine. If anything bad happened, I'd feel it through my link with Steven," Becky replied. She reached out, tentatively, to verify that the link was still present, and it was. "They should be out soon."

"Head's up!" Todd called, pointing to a spot on the ground beside a large bush where stray shadows had started to flow and pool together.

Adam held up his hands and started his working, and Becky did the same.

The shadows swelled and rose up from the ground, disgorging three figures in rapid succession. A moment later, those figures were no longer masses of shadow but instead the separate forms of Steven, Mathias, and the Minister of Security.

"I've got him held!" Adam shouted as the air around the minister began to waver.

Becky arched an eyebrow. Reid was, for some reason, smiling.

"You can let him go, Adam," Steven said. "He came willingly."

Adam hesitated for a moment and then lowered his hands. The wavering in the air vanished abruptly.

Mathias looked at Becky and said, "Can you find out what he's up to?"

The minister continued to smile. "Your lack of trust is quite disappointing, Mathias. I assure you, my motives are genuine. I will help you find Hyrak—even if that means getting you an audience with Chron."

Becky replied, "I hope you don't mind, but I think I'll take a look around. I don't have much trust for people who torture my friends."

JC grabbed her hand. "Be careful."

Becky turned back to him and felt a smile play across her features. "You're worried about me," she said. Then she planted a quick kiss on his cheek. "You've come a long way on this trip already. But no reason to be afraid... I've got this well in hand."

Then she turned towards Reid and closed her eyes.

She launched her mind into his like a dart, fast and direct. He had no appreciable mental defenses—most people didn't—and she cut easily into his mind. Before she could even begin accessing memories, she was assaulted by his base emotions. The undercurrent of Reid's mental landscape was one of desperation. There was an almost unassailable sense of pride underpinning everything else, but the roiling tide of desperation beat against the tower of that ego in unpredictable bursts.

She tried to lift herself up out of the desperation, but it was like a storm-tossed sea, and in spite of her power she was little more than a sailboat upon those waters. The memories, the thoughts she was here to scan, were inside the lighthouse that was Reid's pride, but to reach it was a perilous journey.

She willed the desperation to calm, shaping the substance of his emotions and thoughts into a calm patch of that metaphorical sea, but the moment she shifted her focus away from that working, the desperation reasserted itself, fiercer than before.

She threw herself upward, trying to rise up out of the turmoil and land like a caped superhero atop the tower, but the waters splashed up in the vague impression of tentacles, ensnaring her legs and ripping her back down once more.

Becky began to panic.

She lashed out with her power in every way she could think of, but still the power of Reid's desperation pulled her down, burying her and drowning her in equal measure beneath its weight. She reached into the deepest reserves of her magic, bringing every ounce of it to bear at once. Then she stopped. All of the sudden, a bubble of brilliant golden light had formed up around her, protecting her from the savage storm of Reid's thoughts.

It lifted her up slowly, steadily, until she reached the summit of Reid's pride, and then it popped, leaving no trace of its passage in the air around her.

"What the hell?" she asked, but there was no one to answer her.

She lifted up her hands and Reid's memories swirled up around her, rectangular images like windows onto each of his thoughts, whirling at rapid speeds as she combed through them to find the answer to why he was willing to help them—what he was after.

She found the answer, and she could not help but laugh.

She slipped easily back into her own body, realizing that no more than a minute had passed during her struggle. Reid was staring at her, clearly unaware of what she was doing.

"When does my interrogation begin?" he asked, rubbing at one temple.

"It's done," Becky said, smiling. "We can trust him, I think. At least as far as this goes. He really does need to find Hyrak. I'd say he's desperate to do so."

Reid narrowed his eyes. "What did you do, witch?"

"I dug around in that big self-centered brain of yours," Becky answered. "And I figured out what it is you really want. It's kind of cute, in a sick, sadistic sort of way."

"Well?" Todd asked.

"Mathias, how does someone at the top of the food chain like the minister here reincarnate? How does he find mister right to help him move up in station on the next life?" Becky asked.

Mathias shook his head. "Those at the highest echelons of our society are given the ability to contract twice—if they can bind themselves to two individuals whose station sums to that of their own, they can reincarnate at an equivalent level in the next life. Otherwise, they have to travel to the bottom and start over again, climbing one life at a time."

"I don't see any rings on any of those fingers," Becky said, chiding.

Reid grew livid. "You people killed my bindmate!"

Becky watched Adam go pale. And she whispered in his mind, "Stop. It was an accident. Don't give him the satisfaction."

Then, aloud, she continued, "So the minister here has a plan to come out ahead in the reincarnation game. A way to keep hold of his station in life with one ring, instead of two, since he's waited too long to find two suckers to take him. He has too many enemies who would rather see him banished to the bottom of the heap—and he has standards. Pride."

"Is there a point in here?" JC asked.

"He wants Hyrak as his *venai*," Mathias said, eyes wide. "He's powerful, he's connected, he has at least one army, maybe two... he's higher in station."

Todd laughed. Adam chuckled. Reid fumed.

Becky said, "You want to convince the most evil son of a bitch to ever walk on any world, ever, to join you in a sham wedding so you can avoid having to get dirt under your fingernails in your next life. I wish the two of you all the best. If you get us to Chron, and to Hyrak, you can have him. I, personally, just want to see the look on his face when you get down on that knee and pop the question."

¤~¤~¤

Hyrak had been mostly occupied on their flight to the northwest. Jarrek watched the warlord balance perfectly on the dragon's back even while clearly engaged in his strange mindshaping that masked them from the sight of those below, and he did all he could to keep from entertaining the thought of shoving Hyrak off the dragon to die on the ground below.

Such thoughts would get Jarrek killed, if Hyrak should happen to catch them in the sweep of his powers.

The mountains were growing nearer—Ahmur flew with great speed. True to his word, Hyrak had them traveling only at night. Hyrak and Ahmur rested during the day while Jarrek worked. There were adjustments to be made to the largest, and most esoteric, apparatus that Hyrak had instructed Jarrek to build. It was unlike any device Jarrek had ever seen before, but he followed Hyrak's orders to the letter, even crafting its smallest components by way of mental images impressed upon his mind by Hyrak's magic.

Whatever the device would do, it could be no more terrifying than what Jarrek knew, for certain, awaited them in the Greytall Mountains. The juncture was an old piece of Metalbreaker mythology—a story told to him by his father long ago, when Jarrek was named leader of the Jovs on Murrod. It had seemed a fairy story at the time, meant to inspire awe in those who heard it, but if it was just a tall tale, why was it kept secret, known only to those who held the highest ranks in the Order of Jov?

Jarrek looked at the handle of the green Bindmetal pickaxe he had crafted at Hyrak's insistence, with its power so carefully described and invested into the metal. He had imagined it would bring down walls when used. How foolish he had been.

Everything he had done was foolish, he supposed. All compromises made as a means to an end—towards finally punishing Embrew for what had been done to the Jovs. Corudain was the worse culprit, but the leader of the Gars was long dead, surely. Embrew would do—he had played a part in their exile. And Jarrek had been willing to stay behind while all his brethren escaped, just to put paid to that debt of vengeance.

But it eclipsed his reason then, and it did so more profoundly now. Each working of his magic brought him more and more into discordance with the world around him—Ambrek had warned him of this, once. He had paid no heed, of course.

This moment of clarity that crept upon him in the night would do no good. When the suns rose, he would be put to work with more modifications to the contraption in Hyrak's pack, and the thirst for vengeance would boil up in him again.

All of the sudden, Hyrak started, his eyes snapping open. "Fascinating," he muttered.

"What? What has happened?" Jarrek probed.

"I felt a working of mindshaping—a powerful one. Just a moment ago, south of here—towards Imperia. That is surely not Ehbor's work, and not Ahmur's. Chron lairs near our destination, not behind us... so who could have done it?" Hyrak mused.

Jarrek had no thoughts to contribute. To his knowledge, there were no mystic practitioners on Murrod. The only magic native to this place, aside from the three dragons, was what was contained in the Bindmetal, and such workings, even though similar to mindshaping, would feel quite different to senses like Hyrak's.

"I have no time to deal with the curiosity," Hyrak said finally. "But I hate to leave unassessed dangers at my back."

The warlord lifted one hand high overhead and a faint swirl of bright white light whipped through the air.

Hyrak stated plainly, "With Ehbor in retreat, he will not dare contest me if I steal control of another score of Ellir. I have directed them through our breach in the Greendeep perimeter, to the location of this unknown Mindshaper. I shall see through their eyes, and we will end this threat before it begins."

¤~¤~¤

JC walked with Becky as they returned to their makeshift base at Mathias' old boss' home. Traveling to the temple of Chron at night meant running the risk of an Ellir attack, so they planned to rest until the first sunrise, then Adam would prepare the crossgate to Monarka, the only remaining Prince City of Greendeep that JC had not had the pleasure of visiting.

He did everything in his power to not let Becky know of his eavesdropping on her conversation with Steven, but it was obvious that she could tell something was going on with him.

"Hold up a second," Becky said, taking his hand. The others, including Chaplain Reid, were moving at a brisk pace, and their destination was now in sight about three blocks away.

JC slowed down as Todd and Adam, the members of the group closest to them, continued on, talking quietly. "What's up?" JC asked.

"I just wanted to tell you that I am proud of you," Becky said. "I've always been proud of you, but seeing how far you've come in the past few days, especially—I know that Yors has worked a lot on the collar, but it isn't him that has to deal with how you must be feeling, it's you. And you've handled it so well. I see more and more of the old you coming through, and that's amazing."

"Every version of me is amazing," JC said simply. "I actually am afraid of running into one of my tangents somewhere, because then you'd all be falling over yourselves to hook up with him."

Becky smiled. "This is almost over. You know that?"

"Oh yeah. Eight links left," JC said, plucking at the chain around his neck.

"No, not that—although that is spectacular. I mean, this wall between us. Which is all about me, you know—I'm working through my issues." Becky squeezed his hand tighter.

JC thought of a handful of smartassed things to say, several of them hurtful, but bit his tongue. He wanted to ask how Steven fit into their relationship, or if this wall between them had a name that could be spelled using any of the letters from 'Tatyana.' But before he could decide the best way to tackle his retort, he saw something moving in the shadows between two houses off to their left. Something tall... with four arms.

"Run!" he shouted, reaching back over his shoulder for the energy rifle. Becky stared at him, dumbstruck, as he slipped the rifle off his shoulder and lined up a shot, pulling the trigger as soon as the stock was braced against his shoulder. A buzzing filled the air as brilliant light flared out in a coruscating beam that blasted through the space between the two houses, missing whatever was there.

"What is going on?" Becky asked. Up ahead of them, the others had stopped and spun around. Around them, candles lit in several houses.

"What are you doing?" Steven whisper-shouted.

"Ellir!" JC yelled. He squinted his eyes, trying to catch sight of the four-armed figure again through the small sighting brackets atop his rifle.

"I don't see any—" Steven said, and then it was upon him. An Ellir threw itself down from the rooftop of the nearest house, driving Steven down with a sickening thud.

Becky screamed and raised one hand, sparks of blue light blazing as she shoved at the creature with her mind. The Ellir stood, shaking its head, and took a step towards her.

JC pulled the trigger on his rifle as he spun it around, the muzzle only a few feet from the creature's head as the beam lanced out and vaporized its skull.

More of them leapt from the rooftops—more than JC could easily count. They were hard to see in the dark, and what seemed like ample light from the street lamps was not enough to cancel that advantage. JC grabbed Becky with the hand that wasn't gripping the trigger of his rifle and he pulled her in close to him. He felt the frosty grip of fear at the base of his spine, swiftly washed away by the remaining magic in his collar, and he whispered to Becky, "You'll be safe. I've got you."

Todd barreled through an Ellir on his way to Steven. The creature was knocked off balance but not over by Todd's forward shoulder rush, and Todd came to a skidding halt next to Steven, shaking him to wakefulness. "You need to get up and do something that involves shadows and ass-kicking," Todd barked at the semi-conscious Shadowbender.

Adam had gotten his wits about him now as well, and he was moving his hands in a quick pattern that ended in a sharp gesture towards Todd and Steven. A moment later the Ellir that Todd had bum rushed darted up to the pair, but its four arms could find no purchase on Todd or Steven as it tried to grab hold of them—they passed harmlessly through one another in the wake of Adam's transposition.

Mathias was ushering Reid to safety inside the house, and as he threw the door open, JC caught the sight of Yors, gleaming blue hammer raised overhead, storming out into the street.

"Less little stuff," JC shouted to Adam as he fired again towards a pack of three Ellir that were now racing towards the Gatemaker, "more getting-us-the-hell-out-of-here!"

JC's shots missed – the same arm that was protecting Becky was making him unable to properly line up a shot. Becky snaked out of his grip and said, "Focus. Let me help too."

She closed her eyes, and suddenly JC could feel the thoughts of the others – Adam, Todd, Yors, Mathias, Reid, Becky – even the groggy thoughts of Steven. They were in a kind of rapid communication, a link brought on by Becky's magic.

"I'm trying to weave a confusion working around them," Becky said through the link, "but they are pretty resistant to my powers. It's like some other working is already affecting them."

"Keep trying," Todd said as he left Steven's side for a moment to run up behind the three Ellir approaching Adam. "Drop the transposition when I tell you to, Adam!"

Todd ran up behind the Ellir and plunged his hands harmlessly through the chest of each of them. Then he mentally shouted, "Now!"

The transposition came crashing down, and suddenly the physical space occupied by Todd and the physical space occupied by the two Ellir had to reconcile. Todd won out, as the recipient of the gatemaking magic, and the chests of both Ellir burst open.

"Oh my god," Adam said, shaking his head. "You just killed them."

"They were going to kill us," Todd said, sweeping out his leg to knock over the third Ellir, "so get over it for right now."

Steven, starting to come around, swiped half-heartedly at another Ellir, one charging towards Yors' onrushing form. The shadows that so effectively hid the Ellir piled up at his insistence, and the Ellir was suddenly tangled in fibrous shadow, leaving it vulnerable to the downward smash of Yors' hammer.

JC steadied the barrel of his rifle in his left hand and fired two more rapid shots, each time striking an Ellir.

But for all that they killed or knocked away, there were still easily a dozen more running out of alleys and leaping down from rooftops all around them.

"We're at least an hour from sun up," Mathias added mentally, returning to the fray without Reid at his side. He was carrying a pair of plain metal swords. He ran towards Adam and Todd, tossing the second sword to Todd, which Todd promptly used to run through the Ellir he had knocked down a moment earlier.

"I'm trying to wrap my head around whatever working is gripping them all," Becky said. "There's more coming, by the way. The working is like a thread stretching from Ellir to Ellir – and there are a bunch more on the way."

JC fired another shot that missed. Yors swung his hammer at an Ellir that used three hands to catch the crushing weight of the sapphire weapon, its elbows cracking loudly but not giving. The two wrestled for a moment before Steven came up behind the Ellir and raked his shadowclaws across its back, causing it to cry out and slip. Yors' hammer crushed its collarbone, and it collapsed, howling in pain.

"They can't control themselves," Todd said sullenly.

"I thought they were actually themselves at night," Adam asked. He gestured towards an oncoming Ellir and a rapid flash of light engulfed it. "Holy shit! I just teleported it!" he cried aloud. "I have no idea where I sent it, but I did it!"

"Party later," Todd said, swinging the sword skillfully at one Ellir while Mathias, more clumsily, engaged another.

"I have it!" Becky shouted. "The working—I think I can unravel it. But if I do that, the person who made it will know what I can do—and I don't think we want that."

"Who made it?" Mathias asked, grunting.

JC fired again, this time clipping two different Ellir.

"Hyrak," Becky said aloud.

"Hyrak can mindshape?" Adam asked.

"Apparently," Becky replied.

"Awesome," Todd said, running through his opponent. JC saw the sword's point emerge from the back of the creature, but it did not fall, instead lashing out with one blue fist to punch Todd squarely in the face. Blood fountained from his nose.

"If you can do that flash teleport thing," Steven said, panting as he wrestled with an Ellir using his shadow-enhanced strength, "maybe you should do it now on us."

"Can't," Adam said. "No clue how to control where it outputs." He ducked under an Ellir's swipe and punched the creature ineffectually in the gut. "JC, can you get this one off me?" he called.

JC lined up the shot carefully and fired, and the Ellir went down with a thud. "Any other requests?" he asked.

"Clear a path for Reid," Adam replied. "I'll get a crossgate open. Monarka." Adam began to spin a green disc of light into being.

JC set to work firing on the Ellir that stood between the house and the portal Adam was constructing.

Becky suddenly shouted exultantly. "Found it! I hijacked the working for a second..."

The Ellir all, in unison, stopped. Not for long—just for a few seconds—but they all paused, and Mathias, Todd, Steven, and Yors made quick work of the ones they were tangling with. In that moment, JC fired again and again, mowing Ellir down like fish in a barrel while the collar burned hot against his neck. He was thankful for its presence—thankful that, for him at least, guilt was bound up in fear.

Mathias ran for the house and fetched both Reid and Becky's backpack, and they filed quickly through the portal as Becky's redirection of the Ellir came to an end and a fresh wave of the blue creatures flooded into the area.

"I don't think he knows exactly what I just did," Becky said as Yors brought up the rear and Adam closed the portal behind them all, "but we have problems anyway. The working was two-way, I think. Hyrak saw what they saw. He knows we're here, and he knows an awful lot of what we can do."

"So?" JC asked, wiping sweat from his brow and stowing his rifle across his back. "Sure, the dude is scary, but seriously—he's one guy. We are a whole team of badasses. And this minister dude. Let him know what's coming. Maybe for once, the bad guys will be afraid of us!"

It was an attempt at a pep-talk, which JC had never been nearly as good at giving as his father was, but he thought it went over fairly well. It was all bullshit, of course, but... weren't all pep-talks?

¤~¤~¤

"You are in grave danger," Aniess said as Plyssa reached the bottom of the stairs with her escort. The old woman was recognizable to Plyssa even behind her elaborate owl mask—or perhaps because of it. Aniess was the only follower of the owl-totem that Plyssa had ever met, and the old woman had been like a mother to Plyssa her entire life.

"I have to show them the truth—I would think you would appreciate that," Plyssa said, embracing Aniess tightly. "What are you doing here?"

"I have been here a few days now—I was called to offer wisdom in the crop rotation debates, they say. I think a few of the chieftains wanted to know more of my observations of the border, but were unwilling to ask openly," the old woman replied. "You look well, aside from this foolishness you've involved yourself in."

"They granted permission for me to take one of the prisoners up to the Circle of the Heavens with me. I need his help to show them what I saw," Plyssa explained. "Will you open the door for me?"

Aniess nodded, and a moment later she had unbarred the door. It swung open soundlessly and Plyssa peered into the dark. Standing immediately inside the door were Tyrick and Embrew.

"I need his help," Plyssa said, looking past the two of them.

"Whose?" Tyrick asked.

"What did you call him? Sky?" she asked.

"The pet," Aniess said with a soft 'tut-tut' sound.

"Why?" Tyrick asked defensively.

"I have no time for this. Sky! Come here!" she shouted.

The shy young man stepped into the small circle of light at the doorframe, and Plyssa reached out and grabbed his hand, pulling him along. "The rest of you must remain here. If this succeeds, you will be out soon. If not, I trust Embrew can make arrangements for your... care."

Both Tyrick and Embrew stared at her with looks of puzzlement, but Plyssa had no time for lengthy explanations. She gestured to Aniess, and the woman swung the door closed and slipped the bars securely into place.

"Sky, you can feel the magic metal, right?" Plyssa asked in a low voice that she hoped was calming.

Sky nodded.

"I... I can too. But I am very bad with it. When I try to work with it, it breaks. That is essentially all I have ever been able to do with it. But not you, yes? You can do more than break it?" Plyssa continued.

Sky nodded more vigorously. He took Plyssa's hand and pulled it up against his bare chest, placing it over his heart. "Feel," he said.

Plyssa yanked her hand back. "Yes, I'm sure. I need your help, or we are both dead." She led Sky up the stairs, and her escort followed.

Before she climbed the last stairs to leave the chamber, Aniess called up to her, "You make your mother proud today."

Plyssa tried not to think about that. She didn't know her mother—she had been killed in a raid by Greendeep knights when Plyssa was very young. Ever since then, under Aniess' tutelage, Plyssa had been trying to fit in, to be worthy of a mother she had never known.

Today, perhaps Aniess was right—today she would save all of Goldvast from Hyrak. Or die trying.

They traveled the outer stair up to the Circle of the Heavens, and there was again a shocked murmuring as she brought Sky by the hand into the center of the circle.

"Calm yourselves," she shouted. The chieftains looked at her with a mix of shock and anger, but Plyssa didn't care. She took off her mask and set it on the ground beside her—she wanted them to see her clearly. "This is Sky—a prisoner of the Princes of Greendeep. He is a shaper of metals, like those brought to this world by the Gatemakers in decades past. He will help me show you the truth."

She walked over to the chieftain upon the white pedestal, Sky close behind her. "We will need your seat, chieftain."

The chieftain stood, proudly, and stepped aside. "This is unusual, Plyssa. We anger the goddess by offering you this opportunity. Do not bring shame upon us all with further deceit," she said.

Plyssa did not respond. Instead, she knelt down next to the pedestal and gestured for Sky to do the same. She placed both hands on the white Bindmetal, and Sky mirrored her movements.

She whispered, "I have no idea what I am doing. I can shape it a little, but then... it breaks. Every time. Can you help?"

Sky stroked the metal softly, purring in a low tone, then reached out and took Plyssa's hand in his once more, pulling it to his chest and repeating, "Feel."

Plyssa looked around uncomfortably. Such interactions between men and women were unseemly at best, especially in this sacred place. But she looked into Sky's bright eyes and she put thoughts of the others aside. She felt his chest thrumming with the purring sound he was making, in time to his heartbeat. Then she realized that, through her other hand, she was feeling the same rhythm in the pedestal of Bindmetal.

"Same," Sky said. "Now."

Plyssa nodded. "I feel it."

"Try," Sky said.

Plyssa poured the strange magic of her gifts into the metal. She felt it begin to respond to her command, flowing and shaping—but she had felt this before. It was what came next, the setting of the metal into its new shape and purpose, that always went awry.

But then she started to hum. It was a song she had heard long ago—she fancied it had been sung to her by her mother. The song matched the cadence of Sky's song, and the song of the metal, and she poured her will into the working.

The pedestal stretched and elongated, crafted by thought and by song rather than by hammer and fire. It flowed up into a tall oval, gleaming and polished—a full-length mirror of Bindmetal. As she willed the working, the magic of her intent, to finish, she heard a loud, resonant chiming sound that clearly was heard by all assembled, judging by their collective gasp.

She touched Sky on the forehead and said, "Thank you."

Sky smiled.

Then she stood and turned to the chieftains and said, "Behold! This mirror shows the memories of whoever touches it. It cannot lie, and you may test it in any way you wish. But here, now, see the truth of what has befallen our goddess!"

Plyssa laid one hand upon the edge of the mirror, and her vivid memories of Hyrak's abduction and command of Ahmur played out in glorious color upon the shining surface of the object.

# 30

## Onus

*Nothing would brighten the spirits of the people of Ain Holc quite like a public trial.* Had the Gatemaker still been in her possession, Duchess Ain would have even dispatched him to gather up the rest of the Council so they could be present. With the pirate Grell in custody—in a cell secured without metal, which was no easy feat—there could be leveled some measure of justice for the massacre of Igar Holc.

The Duchess sat in her throne room, listening to the steady drizzle of rain beat against the stained glass windows. The rain would never sound right to her—not in this incessant state since the destruction of Grell's ship. Some of her brightest advisors could not even begin to guess how long the effect would persist—weather control was an art unknown to the people of Onus, after all, so Grell's devious weapons of storm and thunder were particularly challenging to understand.

She imagined that perhaps she would ask the girl, Jara, if her vaunted precognition could see an end to the dreary overcast sky. It seemed a small thing, compared to all else that plagued Ain Holc, but she cared about her people, even if few believed that.

A young man dressed in her colors entered silently through the far door of the audience chamber. She did not know his name, but she recognized his face as one of her pages—the son of a mayor in one of the outlying villages of the protectorate, she thought. He waited patiently to be acknowledged by her, and she allowed him to wait perhaps longer than she should have. It had been so rare she had the chance to simply think, in silence, of late. Her extended time as a captive to Grell had thrown off all manner of important governance, and she had been trying to catch up ever since her return.

"Yes?" she asked impatiently.

"Word has come in from Vol Nought, you grace. You had asked to be alerted if Porza received any updates," the page explained.

"There is no need to remind me of my commands," Duchess Ain snapped. "Send her in."

The page bowed deeply and then darted out the door only to be replaced a few moments later by Porza Rinnelon, a middle-aged Vol with waist-length auburn hair, a full figure, and a single leg. Porza walked with the aid of an elaborate crutch, but she moved faster and more surely than most two-legged people in the Duchess' employ. Porza had been stationed at Ain Holc for nearly two years now, ever since she lost that leg in the Battle of Borrik Fuir.

"What word from your people?" Duchess Ain asked.

"Gendric is stretched thin, your grace. Forces from Gollus Arn have swelled with what appears to be remnants of some of the mercenary bands formerly under Hyrak's command. They have taken Mandor Arn and done serious damage to Jerrit Arn. Reinforcements to the remaining citizens under Warlord Jerrit's protection have been slow in coming from Weldaf Holc, and it has only been the aid of a few roving bands of Sand Dwellers that has provided any true relief to the Vol forces attempting to keep the peace." Porza sighed and took a few steps closer to the throne, her crutch striking the stone floor loudly. "Gendric calls the assault on Mandor Arn a slaughter. As far as we have been able to tell, there were no survivors. We lost one of our best Vols there as well."

"The Mandor line was loyal to the Council," the Duchess said solemnly. "They will be avenged. Please message back to Vol Nought that we will be dispatching forces soon to support their efforts." She touched one finger to her lips and mused, "Why is Weldaf being so difficult?"

"Forces dispatched from Ain Holc tomorrow will take weeks, if not months, to reach a place where they can do any good, your grace. There are a few Rak left in the city—do you want me to start gathering them to transport your soldiers?" Porza grinned.

Ain had not seen the Boltsender this excited since she had come to Ain Holc. The prospect of helping her people, even in this small way, appeared to be bringing purpose back to a life that had been upended by tragedy. She wondered why Porza had refused, repeatedly, to have one of the Sur Bloodmenders restore her leg.

The Duchess shook her head. "No—I have a different plan. Something quite delicate. Just send the word—help will be on the way soon."

Porza bowed awkwardly and turned, showing herself quickly out the door. As soon as the Boltsender was gone, the Duchess stood and saw herself out the side door, to the private antechamber she had ordered her steward to prepare.

Sitting comfortably in one of the two chairs in the room was a special guest, sipping at a small glass of spiced wine. The Duchess took the other seat and poured herself a generous serving of the wine.

"I've been wondering all day why you could possibly want to speak with me," her guest, Hessa Moultuson, asked. "But I admit, I much prefer interacting with you in this way, rather than being abducted in the night."

"In less civilized times, before the construction of the Council, abduction in the night was common across Onus—frequently, daughters of nobles were abducted for ransom or, in less savory circumstances, for dowry and marriage. In a matter of speaking, you could be honored that you were worth such trouble," the Duchess said with a forced smile. She had no love for Hessa—no love for anyone with whom she was forced to bargain. But it seemed this unassuming woman had something Duchess Ain wanted—needed—very much.

"You should skip the pleasantries, your grace—you have no talent for them," Hessa said, taking another sip of the wine.

"Very well. It occurs to me, after a night of serious contemplation, that I had perhaps gone about my dealings with your family all backwards," Ain explained.

"Whatever gave you that impression?" Hessa asked sourly.

"I thought that what I needed most was your daughter's ability to see the future. I thought you and the scribe were simply the leverage I needed to assure that Jara did as she was told. But then the strangest thing happened. Yesterday, while we were baiting our trap for that lunatic pirate, you were seen by a criminal on his way to my dungeons," the Duchess set her glass, half-empty now, upon the small table that sat between them. "An ersatz Boltsender from Hyrak's so-called Lightning Legion was apprehended almost a week ago just east of the city, and as he was being transfered to my dungeon, he saw you. He volunteered the most fascinating information to my jailor."

She watched Hessa's face, looking for a reaction, but the woman was inscrutable—the Duchess found herself nearly admiring that. "What do you imagine this criminal had to say that I found so compelling, Hessa?"

Hessa took a tiny sip of her wine and then set her cup upon the table as well. "I honestly can't say." She rubbed absently at the Bindmetal coin lashed around her arm, and the Duchess could not help but smile. It was true. She knew it.

"It appears that these unexplained magicians wreaking havoc throughout Onus all have some stories in common. They were mercenaries in the employ of Hyrak—that we all know, of course—who found themselves summoned to the dungeons of Hyrak Arn. Then, the next time anyone saw these people, they were skilled mystics—without an ounce of formal training. Isn't that fascinating?" The Duchess felt her smile widen. "I want to keep your secret, Hessa. I truly do. It is hard to say how the Dukes would react if they knew that you had betrayed the oaths of the Wyr and used your magic—passed to you from your sainted mother, I believe?—to empower such dark forces."

"I very much doubt that you have my best interests at heart," Hessa replied in a cold near-whisper.

"You wound me," Ain said.

Hessa's eyes said, quite plainly, that she wished that were truth and not hyperbole.

The Duchess waved a hand dismissively. "The truth is, I think the easiest way to put that all behind us, and to keep from rousing the ire of the rest of the Council, is if you just do whatever you did to those mercenaries to some of my soldiers. Some of my bravest and noblest and, of course, most loyal men and women would serve the Ain Protectorate well, don't you think? In particular, I want something I am not so certain you ever provided for Hyrak. I want Gatemakers."

Hessa's eyes narrowed. "What makes you think I would do this for you?"

The Duchess threw back her head and laughed. "Didn't you hear me before? I said I went about things all backwards before. I used you as leverage and Jara as my weapon. Now, it is you who are the weapon I need. And Jara... Jara is my leverage. The minute I sat down in this room, my household guard seized your daughter. If you ever want to see her again, you will do exactly as I say."

"Did they now?" Hessa asked, her eyes twinkling. "Are you certain about that?"

The Duchess leapt to her feet, shoving the table aside and spilling the wine. One of the glasses tipped and rolled to the floor, shattering loudly. "Where is she?" she demanded.

Hessa crossed her arms in front of her chest and leaned back in her chair. "Are you ready to negotiate with me like an honest, decent person?"

"I'll have you thrown in the dungeon! I'll have your cooperation pulled from you on the rack!" the Duchess shouted. She felt her anger boiling in her veins, and she fought back the rampant urge to claw at the infuriating woman sitting before her. She eyed that red coin—if she plucked it away, she would do irreparable harm to Hessa, she knew it. But would that also harm her ability to give the Duchess what she wanted?

"Do you honestly believe I'm afraid of your dungeons? That there is anything you can do to me that I have not already endured? Give up, your grace. You've lost. All you have left to work with is compromise."

The Duchess hated that word.

¤~¤~¤

Ambrek and Brennid traveled the road to Norwin Holc with the prisoner securely bound behind them, strapped down to a makeshift cart that Brennid had cobbled together from some of the remnants of the former structures of Jov Nought.

"The Council's reward for his capture will be used for the establishment of the new settlement," Ambrek said as they walked. Norwin Holc was visible up ahead, and he wanted matters settled squarely before they turned Narred over to Duke Norwin.

"Not even a share for your brothers in the north?" Brennid asked, smiling. Ever since their discovery of who Narred was, Brennid had somehow mellowed in demeanor. Ambrek didn't properly know why such a change had come over his companion, but he was grateful to not be at one another's throats.

Ambrek smiled back. "Perhaps a token of esteem. Your crafting of these shackles was ingenious," he added, nodding deliberately at the manacles of lead adorning Narred's wrists. Brennid had forged them swiftly and efficiently, using the ordinary metal to cut off Narred's access to his prodigious abilities as a Boltsender.

"It's hardly the first set of shackles I have made." Brennid inclined his head as a pair of travelers passed them by on the road, making better time towards the city than the Metalbreakers.

It was midday, and while there was not a tremendous amount of traffic on the road, Ambrek found it peaceful to watch the merchants and traders flowing steadily into the city from the outlying communities. He and Brennid had grown up around the area, of course, and as much as had changed for them all, some things were very much the same.

Norwin Holc was a city that prospered largely from farming. Situated in the gentle hills where the Edgewalls blended with the Green Reaches, much of the city had been rebuilt since the war with Hyrak. Thankfully, the bulk of its original structure and character remained. Ambrek remembered it as Ptorus Holc, but before that it had also been known as Norwin Holc, and the return to its original name suited the place.

The gates were wide open, and the sounds of the people that called the broad, low city home were intoxicating. So much of the time that the Jovs had spent since coming home to Onus had been spent in isolation in the Borrik Mountains, it was nice to be out amongst people again.

An amiable gate warden called out to them as they approached the double-wide archway leading into the city and asked, "What brings you to Norwin Holc this day?"

"A gift for the Duke," Brennid said, gesturing towards Narred. "A war criminal found wandering just north of here."

The warden arched an eyebrow and peered down from his slightly elevated vantage point. His eyes grew wide as he took in the sight of the bound and gagged man strapped down to the cart that Ambrek and Brennid pulled. "Is that...?"

"It is," Ambrek said. "Can you help us get him to a safe place?"

"And an audience with the Duke, of course," Brennid added with a stiff, awkward little bow.

Ambrek watched his old friend carefully. Brennid was up to something. The mysterious jocularity of the smith was one thing, but this formality, this deference and respect for the nobility—this was not like Brennid. Like many of the Jovs, Brennid did not hold the royalty of Onus in respect, but rather contempt.

Cautiously, Ambrek followed a few steps behind as the warden appointed another guard to watch over the traveler's entrance to the city and personally led them to the palace. Brennid took both handles of the makeshift cart without a word, making small talk with the warden.

Ambrek reached into his belt pouch and pulled out the small lump of Bindmetal he had used just this morning to speed their journey to Norwin Holc. It was spent, of course. He rubbed at it carefully, as subtly as he was able, and tried to whisper some measure of magic back into the thing. To do this without attracting Brennid's attention was difficult but not impossible, and he continued at it over the course of the twenty minutes it took for them to wind their way to the open-air courtyard where Duke Norwin took audience with the citizens of the protectorate.

The warden went ahead of Brennid and Ambrek, explaining in hushed, hurried tones what good fortune had befallen them. Ambrek, his working as complete as it could be, squeezed the hob tightly in one hand and stood next to Brennid. The citizens who had gathered in the courtyard were gently pushed back by Norwin's guards, leaving just the Duke, the warden, the two Metalbreakers, and the prisoner in a large, open span of thick lawn.

"The Council owes you a great debt, my friends," Duke Norwin said, his eyes bright and a smile beaming from ear to ear. "This monster has been sought by some of the finest trackers and huntsmen in all of Onus. How did you come to capture him?"

"We are men of extraordinary talent," Brennid said softly.

"Of that there can be no doubt," the Duke said. "Tell me, what are your names?"

"Our names would mean little to you, your grace," Ambrek said, stepping deliberately in front of Brennid. "We are merely visitors, reliving past glories near our family home to the north. We happened upon Narred while he slept, and we recognized him at once."

Brennid reached out and put a hand on Ambrek's shoulder. In a cold, almost imperceptible whisper, he said, "Be still. I will handle this."

Ambrek shook his shoulder to free himself of Brennid's touch and continued speaking to the Duke. "We had heard there was a reward for his capture?"

"Of course—a handsome one at that. More coin than my treasury can easily spare, I'm afraid—I will have to send word to Rega Holc to request the balance you shall be owed sent here. But I can reward you quite well in an immediate sense." Duke Norwin looked around at the murmuring crowd. "If nothing else, a fine celebration of your feat is in order!"

"What we really want," Brennid said, stepping past Ambrek with a hard shove, "is to shake the hand of a true Duke. I have been waiting for such a chance."

Ambrek heard the sharp rhythm of Jov magic suddenly swell up, masked at first by the sounds of the people all around them. Brennid was doing something.

The Duke extended a hand and took a few steps, closing the gap between himself and Brennid. Brennid did the same. Ambrek heard the song of the magic, discordant with the cost that weighed upon Brennid—the thirst for vengeance that claimed those who pushed the magic too far.

"No!" Ambrek shouted as he watched rivulets of metal liquefy and spin through the air, tiny droplets plucked from jewelry and clothing all around the square, coalescing in a split second into a single, gleaming dagger in

Brennid's hand. Brennid lunged with the dagger towards the heart of the Duke.

Ambrek was not fast with his magic—he was patient. Slow workings were his specialty. He could not bend or blunt the knife, not in time. All he could do was whip his hand forward, sending the transportation hob he had been holding sailing forward to strike Brennid in the back of the head—activating in a flash of light.

Brennid disappeared, carried miles northwest by the magic.

"What is the meaning of this?" the Duke demanded.

Ambrek sighed and lowered himself to the ground in a gesture of submission. "I did not know what he was planning, your grace. You must believe me—I would never have brought him here had I known it. He has gone mad. He... I assume he blames you for what happened to our people."

"Your people?" Duke Norwin asked. "Jovs? You are Jovs? Is this..." the Duke's flesh grew pale, his eyes wide, "Are you connected to the pirate, Grell Dorukast?"

Ambrek looked up. That wasn't possible. She had a son? "What did you say?"

"A Metalbreaker named Grell destroyed Igar Holc a few weeks ago—rumor is that he has sworn to destroy every Council city. Was that man one of his agents?" Duke Norwin gestured to his guards to draw up around him.

"No. Not precisely. Doruka was one of the most powerful Jovs this world has ever known—a living legend among our order. Around the same time that the decision came down from the Council that all Jovs were to be exiled to Murrod, she vanished. It was rumored that she was killed by... by agents of the Council," Ambrek explained. He could feel something rising up in him—something unfamiliar and dark. The jangling, burning sensation of rage and vengeance stirred in his heart. He had spent a lifetime working the magic slowly, taking every precaution to avoid the toll of Metalbreaker magic. But this all made too much sense to ignore—and it was so much harder to fight back the urge for revenge when it was justified.

"If this Grell has even half his mother's power, and he has sworn vengeance upon all the cities of the Council, then perhaps the rumors were true. And there will be no stopping him." Ambrek stood up, and the guards surrounding Norwin drew their swords.

"Please—I mean you no ill will, your grace. But I must go now, for all our sakes. Narred is yours—a gift from your new neighbors. The only reward I ask, the only reward I will accept, is the return of land that is rightfully ours to us. Old Jov Nought belongs to the Jovs once more. Is this acceptable to you?" Ambrek glared at the Duke.

Norwin considered for a moment, then nodded. "For what it is worth, I cannot believe that the Council had anything to do with the assassination of this Doruka person. I was not a member at the time you speak of, but—that is simply not how things are done."

"It is worth very little," Ambrek said. He started to walk away from the courtyard and then stopped, turning back to say, "Be wary. I do not know if Brennid will try to come back, or if the urges that plagued him just now will pass. If he does come... make a great deal of noise. When a Metalbreaker succumbs to the rage, he lacks the centering to tune out sound. It tampers with the magic greatly. It may be all that saves you."

Then he walked directly for the open gates of the city. He did not look back again, and he did not, honestly, care what happened next to this place. And that frightened him.

¤~¤~¤

Fendris issued several prayers to the Great Purpose that were highly out of character for the wiry watchman, but he felt they were necessary, considering the circumstances. The storms that had started to swell when he and Vediri had come up for air had grown more intense with each hour, and Vediri had now proclaimed the weather so dangerous that, until the storms abated, they could not dare to surface. They would have several days before the air grew as stale as it had been, but still, Fendris felt trapped. He'd never been fond of tight spaces.

Unable to surface, they had little choice but to continue on course to the captain's marked destination. The tiny underwater craft drifted aimlessly through the space marked on the captain's map. Vediri swept the vessel in a steady pattern fifty yards below the surface, and Fendris kept watch out of the viewing window.

"Perhaps the issue is one of depth?" Fendris asked nervously. None of this voyage made him comfortable, of course, but he had found his curiosity over what they were here to find growing. The captain had put a great deal of energy, resources, and planning into getting them to this place, and yet... there appeared to be nothing here.

What little light would have normally made it down from the surface to this depth was muted by the storms raging above them. If the turmoil on the surface of the allegedly calm Silent Sea made Vediri uncomfortable, the watchman could not tell. She was cool and collected, as ever, and he tried to follow her lead.

"We can barely tell what's out there around us now—if I go much lower, will you be able to see anything at all?" Vediri asked.

"Perhaps the captain left something of use in with the supplies?" Fendris asked. He started to rummage through their food stores and the chest that had contained the map that led them here, but there was nothing else of consequence. Whatever tricks Grell had possessed, they were invested in this vessel, not in its contents.

Fendris looked back out the window and saw something—a glimmer of what appeared to be light. It emanated from below them, rather than above—and it was moving rather swiftly away from them.

"Wait—I see something!" Fendris shouted. He called bearings to Vediri, and she followed them, tilting the sphere that controlled the vessel's movement with a now-practiced hand. They dove deeper—how deep Fendris could not say—and veered off the course of the map just enough to keep the tiny light in Fendris' field of vision. Vediri accelerated, causing whatever sorcery propelled the tiny ship to zip forward, and Fendris was at last able to make out the source of the light—a fish with a single, luminescent eye. He nearly cursed under his breath and told Vediri to relent in her pursuit of the creature, but then he saw that it was not alone.

There were many other fish—perhaps even a hundred or more, although few glowed as brightly as the one they trailed. The fish had swarmed around several outcroppings of stone that were now visible in the gentle ambient light of their eyes. Vediri had piloted the ship into the space between two of these structures—there were perhaps six in all. They were tall, cylindrical in shape, and appeared to reach all the way up to the surface or higher.

Vediri locked the controls in position and joined Fendris at the window. "What are they?" she asked.

"I've no clue," Fendris said. "In all my years at sea, ain't ever seen something like this. Dare we go down?"

"I'd have thought you'd want to climb to the top," Vediri asked with a grin. "You want to see this as bad as I do, don't you?"

"Whatever was worth all this trouble? Aye, I'm interested to know more of it. If there's treasure marked by these great stone posts, I'm happy to claim my share." Fendris returned the grin.

Vediri returned to the controls, and the vessel started to descend once more—slowly, but surely.

¤~¤~¤

Shayra opened her eyes. The Collectress of the Kem found herself sitting upright, legs folded in a meditation pose, in the crystal tower the Kem called Soul. She was a bit unclear on how she had come to be in this exact place at this exact moment, but she took several calming breaths. She noticed that she was alone, surrounded only by the scintillating lights of the crystal structure all around her. She was also naked, but this was not of particular concern to her, since she saw her pale blue robes folded neatly by the door to the small chamber.

She stood and slipped into the robes, the two layers of sheer material fitting comfortably around her spare frame. She then closed her eyes and ordered her thoughts. She tried to trace them back, to see what had brought her here and why she might be so out of sorts. Perhaps she had been drinking wine? That seemed unlikely, as Shayra rarely allowed herself such indulgences.

In her mind, she found nothing to reveal what had happened—her most recent memory, only a few minutes old, danced back into her mind's eye, and she saw herself arguing with Narred over the investiture of the twins.

The twins! She must have somehow gotten lost on her way to the ceremony. The discovery of twin Mindshapers was so rare—she had picked out the perfect elder Kem minds to place into the young boys.

She hurried out of the chamber, and out of the tower altogether once she realized it was empty. In the courtyard of Kem Nought, milling about and speaking in the language of the mind to one another, she found the majority of her young charges. They were all old minds in young bodies, the first important steps in Shayra's discharging of her duties as Collectress. And there, before her, was one of the twins.

She knelt down before him and said aloud, "I'm sorry to keep you waiting. Where is your brother, so we can get started?"

The boy arched an eyebrow at her and then replied, in her mind, "What are you talking about?"

Shayra stood up and stared down at the boy. Telepathically, she said, "You should not have mastered such communication yet. Your gifts were only just emerging."

"Collectress, your mind is confused," the boy said, his thoughts flickering against Shayra's preliminary shields. "I am Urellus. You invested me into this body many days ago."

"That... that is not possible," Shayra stammered aloud. Only she had the power to do such a thing—how could she not remember it happening?

Her efforts to untangle the mystery were interrupted by a piercing female scream from the Flesh, the dormitory tower of the academy.

Shayra dashed towards the tower, fearful that something had befallen one of her charges, or that her beloved Narred was somehow involved. Urellus followed her, as did several of the other reborn Kem. She threw the door of the Flesh open wide, and she saw Andoria, one of the children invested with the mind of perhaps the eldest Kem currently embodied, standing just inside the door, aghast at the sight before her.

The other twin, the one that she assumed had been invested with the mind of Jaes, dangled from the stairs. He had lashed a braided length of cloth around the railing of the stairs and then around his own neck and thrown himself off the edge.

He was dead.

The other Mindshapers began to wail in grief, but Shayra moved immediately to action. She ran up the stairs and pulled the body up, laying the small boy on the landing midway up the flight and putting her hands to his temples. She willed her magic to action, trying to coax the flickering remnants of his mind out of this body to be returned to her care until a new body could be found.

But Jaes' mind was nowhere to be found. She was too late, somehow—he was truly dead. Lost to them all.

Urellus, down below, shook his head as Shayra looked down at him. "I was afraid this would happen."

"What is going on here?" Shayra demanded, rage and sorrow building up within her.

The others, still in shock over Jaes' death, said nothing.

"Narred!" Shayra called aloud. He did not answer. She turned her efforts inward, focused instead on calling to him with her mind through the link they shared. She found him after a moment's effort—far from here, somewhere in Norwin Holc. She attempted to make contact with him, but suddenly a screen of mental static sprung up between them—as though he had used his boltsending abilities to block her out.

Shayra stroked one hand gently on the faintly blue cheek of the boy lying dead beside her on the stairs. She did not know what was happening. Narred was gone. One Mindshaper was dead. She had invested two Kem minds into bodies and yet had no recollection of the events. There was only one possible explanation: someone had tampered with her memory. Someone had done the unthinkable, the forbidden, and she would have answers.

"We warned you," Andoria said, shaking her head. "But you insisted."

"Insisted upon what?" Shayra demanded, standing up once more and striding angrily down the stairs.

"You were heartbroken, and you didn't wish to know the truth any longer," Andoria said solemnly.

"Tell me what has happened!" Shayra shouted, aloud and with her mind in resonant tandem.

"Narred betrayed us. He betrayed you, and all of us—he murdered three new children you had brought to us for investiture. Then he fled. You were devastated, and you demanded that the memory of what he had done be erased from your mind. We tried to argue with you, but you would hear no reason," Andoria explained.

"But before he left, he..." Urellus pitched in hesitantly. "He attacked my brother with his horrible boltsending magic. He did damage to his brain, left him irrational and dangerous. That... that must be why he finally killed himself."

Andoria looked at Urellus and gave a slight nod.

"How much of my memory is gone?" Shayra asked in a choked whisper.

"Several months," Andoria answered. "It was what you wanted, Collectress."

"What... what happens now?" Urellus asked.

Shayra narrowed her eyes. "I will have Narred's head for this!"

¤~¤~¤

"There is no point to this," Grell replied. The pirate was in the smallest cell in all of Ain Holc, a five foot by five foot by five foot cube of solid stone construction, marred only by the heavy wooden door and its small circular window, buried sixty feet below an old stone building. The big man could barely fit in that chamber—he could not stand fully upright without his head striking the ceiling. But he tried to do so—every few minutes standing and stretching, rapping his upraised fists against the stone ceiling in a gesture Moultus found reminiscent of a rat trying to escape a cage.

Moultus sat on a wooden stool just outside the cell. He wore nothing made of metal—a precaution insisted upon by the Duchess even after Moultus had assured her that it was a known fact that there was a rather short range at which a Metalbreaker could accomplish any working of note on unfamiliar metals. Of course the Duchess had not listened to him, though—she didn't listen to anyone.

Moultus had been down here for hours, attempting to learn something from Grell. The Duchess threatened torture, but she had been too busy since Grell's capture attending to whatever other matters occupied her time to set about beginning whatever manner of torment she was devising that would not rely upon sharpened metal instruments.

Moultus asked a different question. "Why are you doing this?"

"You would not understand," Grell said. He stretched again. Again, he inadvertently struck the ceiling.

"I understand vengeance was once an all-too frequent obsession amongst the Metalbreakers. But the Jovs learned to control such impulses a long time ago. But you... you never studied under a Jov, did you?" Moultus asked. He was frantically scouring his memory, trying to scrounge up everything he could remember about the Jovs from his studies. His time with the oft-silent Yors had not brought any new insights to him, but during his apprenticeship with Marriq, back when he had still believed himself destined to become an Archivist, he had learned much of many things, and his memory was still sharp, in spite of his ever advancing age. He recalled the tales of mad Metalbreakers, and the particulars of the arts they practiced. He wished he had studied these things more carefully, but for so long the Jovs had been a non-existent part of Onus, a footnote in history after they were bartered away to Murrod.

Grell laughed coldly. "You think to get inside my head—to figure me out, old man? There is no great complexity to my design. And I am not some fool Jov that pressed himself too hard and lost control. I am in perfect control of myself and my circumstances."

"You are in prison," Moultus replied with a small smile. "I fail to see how you are in control here."

"Give it time," Grell replied. He stretched again, colliding with the stones overhead.

"You'll injure yourself if you keep that up," Moultus chided. "Perhaps a different question will be of more interest to you. What will the Duchess' people find when they reach the Vale of Steam? To what treasure does your map lead?"

"There is no treasure—but it doesn't matter. They won't find it. The map will draw them near, if it has indeed been deciphered, but the thing I seek, the instrument of my retribution, will not be found by ordinary men." Grell pressed his face up into the open window of the door. "If one could simply happen upon it, it would not have lain hidden for so long."

"It's fortunate that my granddaughter has joined the search for it then," Moultus added. He tried to exude confidence in the claim, but he was worried—not just about Jara, who always inspired worry in him, but also about himself and Hessa. They played a dangerous bluffing game with the Duchess right now, but Jara had demanded they trust her plan, and he was trying. Failing, perhaps, but trying nonetheless.

"Then perhaps they will find it," Grell said. "A pity. She seemed like a nice girl."

He pulled back from the door and stood upright again, striking the ceiling.

"Why do you keep doing that?" Moultus demanded.

Grell did not reply.

Moultus scratched at his head, running one hand through his thin white hair. He was missing something. To calm his mind, he started counting slowly—an exercise that he had practiced many times when dealing with exasperation as a young parent to Hessa, many years ago.

The silence stretched between them for a forty count, and then Grell obnoxiously struck the ceiling of his cell again. Moultus continued to think about what he was not seeing, or inferring, from Grell's words and actions. As his internal count reached eighty, Grell again raised his momentary racket.

It was steady. It was predictable, it was... rhythmic.

"There's no metal in range," Moultus said, standing up hurriedly. "Whatever you are trying to do, it won't work."

"Range," Grell said with a contemptuous snort, "is relative."

Moultus heard, faintly, the sounds of shouting outside—above ground. "What are you doing?" he demanded.

"That trollop of a Duchess brought every scrap of Bindmetal she could salvage from my ship inside her city. That is *my* Bindmetal. Worked by *my* hands for more than a decade," he struck the ceiling again, "and I know it better than I know my own face. It hears me. It heeds me."

A loud screeching sound burst from somewhere behind Moultus—at the top of the long flight of cut stone stairs that led down to this dank prison hole.

"What are you doing?" Moultus repeated, trying his best to not sound afraid.

"Leaving," Grell said. "And if you want your granddaughter to live, you'll get out of the way. My quarrel is with the Council, not with their pawns."

The door atop the stairs burst open, and Moultus watched as a ragged jumble of different colors of Bindmetal bounced down the stairs. It was roughly spherical, a yard across at its widest places, and it bristled with sharp edges and ill-fitting angles.

Moultus backed up against a wall, pressing tightly, and the ball rolled awkwardly past him, drawn towards Grell. It smashed into the door of the cell and then started to unfold, a sort of articulated arm of metal segments scrabbling up the door loudly. Grell reached one brawny arm through the small window, not able to clear his elbow through the space, and when his extended hand touched the unfolding contraption, there was a flash of light... and both Grell and his Bindmetal savior were gone.

Moultus charged up the stairs, into the dimly lit stone barn above the cell. There had been a dozen guards placed here, men who had families and futures. They had allowed Moultus to speak with the prisoner, leaving him in peace for these few hours while they milled about up here... and they were dead. All of them. Their bodies were scattered about, scarred by massive wounds from, he could only assume, that Bindmetal contraption whirling about.

Somehow, Grell had built that thing from Bindmetal scraps, sight unseen, from blocks away. His power was unfathomable... but his next step was not. He was heading for the Vale of Steam. And for all he had said about not having any quarrel with Jara, Moultus did not believe him. He looked around once more, at the pointless death Grell had unleashed, and he feared that Jara would not be spared by that lunatic's hand.

# 31

## Murrod

*Religion never made a whole lot of sense to me.* My mom and dad are pretty religious, and so are my brothers (depending on who they're dating at the time). But for me, religion was always that place where you had to go and sit still in uncomfortable clothes for a long time while someone in silly clothes lectured at you from the front of the room. And listening, sitting still—neither of these really falls in my wheelhouse.

You see, I was always mixing up *religion* with *church*. Church is the things I don't like, really—religion is something else altogether. It's faith, if nothing else, and over time, especially once Jara came into our lives, faith started to make sense to me—just not in the way that church wanted it to.

My mom used to watch this show on television about these angels who would travel the countryside, restoring people's faith in God and in each other. I didn't really get into it too much (almost nothing ever blew up on that show), but it practically always included a moment where one of those angels would say to some distraught person, "God has a plan."

Getting mixed up in the troubles of other worlds brought a new name for the plan to my mind—a new name for God, even—the Purpose. Can you imagine how strange that is, to know that there is this all-powerful destiny out there, guiding events in the direction of its choosing? I mean, maybe you can—if you are religious, if you are a person of faith, then that makes perfect sense to you. But I didn't believe in God, not really, and so this idea was sort of... awe-inspiring. All of the sudden, after meeting Jara and hearing her predict the future time and again, I was a believer—but I believed without the *need* for faith.

I think I have faith in people, mostly—the jury is still out on that. But faith in God, or destiny, or the Purpose, or whatever? I don't need to have faith in that, because I actually know it is real.

That kind of freaks me out.

You see... some people have purpose, and some people have Purpose. Note the capital letter. Adam? He's got Purpose. Last of the Gatemakers, only person able to bend Spiralgates off course after they are created, etc. The universe has big plans for him. It also has big plans for the other five Children of the Line. But then there are the rest of us—the hangers-on and the bystanders. I got swept up in this, same as Becky—because we were with Adam when a nutjob shadow demon thing attacked us in a parking lot on a cold January night. Becky... she inherited a role in the Purpose, because of Tatyana. But me, this guy, JC Stein... my purpose has no big P. It can't, can it? I'm a footnote in the story of big, important people doing big, important things. And the only thing that makes me awesome (other than my sense of humor) is this artificial bravery around my neck.

But as we traveled across Murrod in pursuit of an alliance with the dragon Chron and the defeat of the warlord Hyrak, I was getting closer and closer to pissing away the closest thing I had to a super power. I knew, as we arrived in Monarka, that my role in the Spiral of Worlds was coming to an end. I could feel it in my bones. If I didn't figure out what my new niche was, what new role I was to play as background extra in the continuing saga of Adam, Becky, Steven, and the three people whose names we *still* hadn't learned even after everything we went through on Arctos... I was going to be forgotten. Left behind.

Becky was already thinking about leaving. She didn't know that I knew what had gone between her and Steven, but I did—and it swallowed me whole, when I let it. Yors was doing his job too well... fear was starting to seep in, a bit at a time. Maybe this was how it was supposed to be—the Shadowbender and the Mindshaper were always supposed to be together, and when Tatyana died, Becky assumed her job in the big cosmic tapestry that only Jara could see.

Fuck it. Fuck Purpose. Fuck any damn system or rule or cosmic entity that thinks it gets to decide who should be what, or who should be with who. I have faith in something more important than any of that crap—me. I'm bigger than destiny—I'm JC. And I don't know how... but I know for damn sure I still fit into this story somehow.

¤~¤~¤

Yors had little to say as Adam's double crossgate deposited them in the building that Chaplain Reid directed him to and then vanished. They were closer to his ultimate destination, and that made him pleased, but he was struggling with his emotions and he couldn't bring himself to let the others see. So he stood amidst them all, arms folded across his chest, hammer slung over his back, and listened.

"This is a Ministry of Security safe house in Monarka. I use it as a residence when business demands I operate here," Reid explained. "I have no affection for this city—its denizens are pretentious and the proximity to Chron gives them a sense of superiority that I find absolutely disgusting."

"Have you ever seen yourself in a mirror?" JC asked. The room was lined with wooden panels, featured a door at each end of its rectangular shape, and had no furniture or ornamentation to speak of.

Reid scowled at JC and continued, "I will need to make arrangements through official channels to gain an audience with Chron. The initial request will take several hours, but you should be safe here. The pantry is fully stocked, there are four full guest suites upstairs, and the pool is through there," he gestured towards the door nearest to him.

"I know I'm not supposed to like this guy," Becky said wryly, "but he's certainly got good taste in secret hideouts."

"You are not leaving my sight," Mathias said.

"You don't trust me?" Reid asked, his eyes gleaming. Yors found it difficult to resist striking the insufferable bureaucrat. He took a few breaths and thought of calming techniques taught to him in his youth at long-gone Jov Nought, but... they did little to quell the turmoil in his heart.

"Not for a moment," Mathias said.

"Why don't we come with you?" Steven said to Reid. "A few of us, anyway. Just to make sure everything is on the up and up?"

Reid shrugged, and Yors noticed how much the chaplain's shoulders sagged. "If you insist. The Ministry's offices here will be easily convinced that you are knights in my employ."

Steven looked around at the others and asked, "Anyone up for joining us?"

No one leapt to volunteer, and Steven sighed. He patted Mathias on the shoulder and said, "Guess it's just you and me babysitting the despot this morning."

"Afternoon," Chaplain Reid corrected. "It's far too early for me to believably turn up at the Ministry. I'll make arrangements for breakfast, and a midday meal... we will head out in the afternoon. In the meantime, please—avail yourself of the amenities. Knowing that death comes for me any moment now, I find myself less concerned about the budgetary implications of guests."

Reluctantly, and with open suspicion clear on his face in the case of Mathias, the group started to disperse—most through the far door, with Reid, to the guest rooms, although JC went to investigate the pool first. Before long, Yors was standing there alone, standing silent watch over the empty room.

JC returned to the room, smiling. "The pool is kind of awesome. Do you swim?"

Yors shook his head. He pointed to JC's throat and said, "Yors ready for more."

JC's eyes lit up, and he stepped next to Yors. "It's funny—back on Onus you were so careful to work slow and steady. Why is it different here? Are your powers really that much better on Murrod?"

Yors shook his head. He wanted to say many things to JC—this boy was the closest thing he had to a friend right now—but as always, he lacked the words, or the confidence in his words, to express himself. He wanted to explain to JC that while the magic came easier, it was more that Yors had changed than it was the power. He cared less about maintaining his center, and he had begun to slide into the emotional chaos that was the price of his arts. But instead, he said, "Many things different here."

JC shrugged and closed his eyes as Yors began to work the chain in his hands. Yors tapped one foot irregularly on the wood-slatted floor to establish the rhythm of the work, and after a moment, JC asked, "Why not the lullaby? I mean, I know it's kind of silly, but... I like when you hum that as you work."

Yors stopped his tapping and closed his eyes. This place was bringing back so many memories, memories that caused him to abandon reason and succumb to vengeance and rage. Even the music of his work had changed, and JC had pointed it out now, brought it to the attention of a mind that was half-wild with barely restrained anger.

Yors didn't want to be a monster. He wanted to be a hero and a friend. He wanted to be a husband... he wanted to be a father. But these people on this horrible world had taken those things from him, and now...

He tried to hum the lullaby that he had sung to his daughter on the first nights on Murrod, but the music didn't ring true. With a frustrated, angry sigh he resumed his beating on the floor, stomping more than tapping, and wrung his hands about the chain. Magic flowed through him and into the chain, and his emotions clouded and boiled inside him.

With a shuddering effort, Yors managed to complete the working. The magic in the red Bindmetal around JC's neck was stilled, its enchantment removed. Five more links were now dead—only three remained.

He heard JC gasp—the impact of fears delayed suddenly swirling back through his mind. Yors knew that sensation, in many ways—it was like his own transition back and forth between himself and his protective personality, Toren, had once been.

"Three left," Yors said. "Three that JC must remove himself."

"Wait, what?" JC asked, his eyes snapping open.

"Mind magic dangerous," Yors tried to explain. "Requires slow changes. This why Yors not just destroy chain in first place. JC go mad. Last links ready to break—JC can do this."

"I'm not a Metalbreaker," JC stammered. "How am I supposed to do that?"

"Magic weak now. Slows fear down, not stop it. JC must rise to challenge—must confront fear and accept, embrace. This will break remaining links."

Yors wanted to be alone now. The magic sang in his blood, demanding him to act, to rage, and he wanted to fight against that. JC had reminded him of the calm he had known before embarking on this journey, before utterly submitting to the magic in the tunnels under Hineros. He wanted to try, somehow, to hold on to that peace. Yors stepped away from JC and towards the door that led to the rest of the house. As he left the young man lost in confused thought, he said simply, "Yors has faith in you."

¤~¤~¤

In spite of Hyrak's promise to fly only at night, it was midafternoon and Jarrek found himself once more riding on the back of the white dragon,

Ahmur. The three suns beat down on them and Jarrek was doing something he had been quite certain he would never attempt to do in life—he was forging Bindmetal while sitting atop a dragon.

"Are you done yet?" Hyrak demanded.

The warlord had grown impossibly impatient since his failed assault on the enemy Mindshaper late last night. He had snapped out of his shared perceptions with the distant strike team of Ellir and immediately started strategizing for how to deal with his enemies, and Jarrek was fascinated to discover that those who had freed his people had, for some reason, returned to Murrod. He remembered well the three young men that had met him and his father in their home in Imperia the night that the possibility of escaping this world had become real.

"Of course," Jarrek said, putting the finishing touches on the small padlock of red Bindmetal. It was crafted of the last spare scraps of the material Jarrek had in his possession. Whatever Hyrak's plans consisted of, they would no longer be able to shift and adjust by simply directing Jarrek to make him something new. Between the pick, the keys, the contraption in the bag, this new padlock, and the bells, Hyrak had everything he was going to get from Jarrek.

Which meant that Jarrek was now more expendable than ever before. He wanted, of course, to demand answers from the warlord about when he would be given his opportunity to kill Embrew, but he knew better than to ask such a thing while Hyrak was in this mood. The thirst for vengeance—justice, he told himself—was one thing, but the desire to survive outweighed it in these present circumstances.

"It is a small thing, but one I feel may yet prove of use," Hyrak said. Then he pointed with his gauntleted hand. The warlord's armor—ordinary plate mail, but a work of art that was a testament to Jarrek's skill as a smith of even simple metals—gleamed in the light of the suns. Jarrek followed the line of the outstretched finger and saw, nestled in the point of intersection between two vast mountains, a small level plateau. "That is it, is it not?" Hyrak questioned.

Jarrek replied reluctantly, "Yes."

The juncture—the single point of the world where all of the forces that bound it together converged—was an almost legendary thing. There were tales that, in the oldest of times, Metalbreakers could command the very substance of a world itself, the earth and stone upon which all was built—if they possessed the anchor stone of a world. These anchor stones, each unique to its world, were found buried beneath the junctures. Ancient Metalbreakers retrieved the anchor stones, tales said, and crafted them into hammers that could change the very shape of the world.

The juncture was recognizable by its smooth surface and the dark stone of its construction. It was mottled by ribbons and swirls of precious metals and glinting gleaming fragments of gemstones. It was everything Jarrek had heard of in the old stories, and he felt the gentle pull of it upon his magic. Here, the beating heart of Murrod could be felt—this was a place where the pulse of a world could be taken.

Ahmur glided to a landing upon the surface of the juncture, which was perhaps five hundred yards across, and Jarrek slipped down from the dragon's back excitedly. Hyrak moved more slowly—Jarrek could tell he was instructing the compliant dragon with his powers. The anger inside that beast, should it ever get free, terrified him, but he worried now more about the chance that *he* had to get free.

The Jovs of old crafted the anchor stone hammers, but they feared the power of such artifacts in the wrong hands. So, as the legends went, they buried them once more in the place of their birth—beneath the junctures of each world. Jarrek could reach down and call out to the hammer, calling it to him and putting an end to Hyrak once and for all.

He ran for the center of the juncture and skidded to a halt, panic and desperation driving him to incredible speed. He placed one hand on the smooth stone and concentrated on that surreal connection that he could feel between himself and this place. He called out to the beating heart of Murrod, to the gleaming emerald anchor stone that was buried here... but nothing would come.

"I wouldn't have brought you here if I thought for a moment you could access it," Hyrak said as he walked, nonchalantly, towards Jarrek. "The harmony that your power depends on, and robs you of, is the key to these places, as I understand it. And there is no harmony in your bitter, vengeful heart."

Jarrek looked up, frustration scrabbling at his insides. "How do you know these things? The junctures, the anchor stones, even the source and cost of our power—these are closely held mysteries of my order. It makes no sense to me."

Hyrak sneered. "I kept you chained in my cave for more than a year. Do you truly believe I did not take that opportunity to pilfer every stray thought and secret from your mind?"

With a sigh, Jarrek stood. "I imagine you have much to do," he said. "I don't know the shape of your desire, but I am at least bright enough to have put the pieces together. Even the smallest shift will take hours with such an imperfect tool—you know this?"

Hyrak nodded. He lowered the pack he carried to the ground and from inside, drew the green Bindmetal pickaxe Jarrek had made for him. For a second, Jarrek caught sight of the white metallic device that took up most of the space inside Hyrak's pack of wonders... and he thought he saw some of the glass nodules on the device flashing.

"I intend for what I do to be anything but small, Jov. Attend to the dragon—and be wary. This working will take more than a day, by my estimation. In that time, you will do everything in your power to protect me, as will she. And if you cross me—she will destroy you. Have we an understanding?" Hyrak asked coldly.

"Yes," Jarrek muttered, walking slowly towards the dragon, whose sinuous neck was extended as she probed the skies with her three bright eyes.

More than a day? The pickaxe was a simulation, a fragment of the power one might expect from the true anchor stone hammer of this world. Its ability to bend, break, and shape the earth and stone beneath their feet was ponderous—but genuine. A working of such time would act upon a magnitude that beggared the imagination.

He turned to watch Hyrak work. The warlord was kneeling upon the stone, tapping on it with the blunt end of the pickaxe. Green sparks erupted all around him with each tap. Jarrek could feel the change already—slow, but noticeable. The pulse of the world, so near the surface here, was quickening. In time, it would be racing. And then... none could say.

¤~¤~¤

It was strangely quiet in the Ministry of Security's safe house. Mathias, Steven, and Yors (the last a quite unexpected addition) had gone with Chaplain Reid to make the necessary arrangements for them to travel to the lair of Chron tomorrow. Todd and JC had taken advantage of the pool, JC with a wide grin and Todd with a kind of stoic dread.

"What do you think they talk about, when it's just the two of them?" Becky asked. She sat on one end of the long, low couch in the sitting room—Adam sat on the other end.

"They actually get along way better than you'd expect," Adam suggested. "And even if they didn't, you couldn't keep Todd away from the pool. He loves the water."

"It's been a long time since we did this," Becky mused.

"What do you mean?" Adam asked.

"It's just that, for the longest time, we've pretty much never been alone together. JC is with me, or Todd is with you, or we're saving the world from Obliviates or whatever. I miss you. I miss us—and when we get back, you'll be gone, off to Michigan for school." Becky looked down and picked at a fraying hole in the knee of her Onus-made pants.

"Assuming my mother ever lets me out of her sight again. We've been away so long, Becky. I've told her as much as I possibly can about stuff—she did see Mathias kind of blow up a prison, as I understand it—but still. She worries. She's a mom like that. And your mom and dad, and... And I don't want to talk about this anymore. It's making me sick to my stomach." Adam sighed. "Besides—we talk all the time. We do the telepathy thing now. That's like, way more private conversation than we ever had before!"

Becky smiled and looked up. She whispered, "But some things feel really weird to talk about that way."

"Like what?" he asked.

"Well, when we are in our minds like that, sometimes—and I swore I was never going to tell you this—when we are talking about things, certain strong thoughts and feelings kind of pop up—like pop-up windows on the internet. I mean, only I can see them, but still. Like... when you lie, or exaggerate... I can usually feel this flash of uneasiness from you. So I know. And if you talk about something heavy, or personal—memories come with it, sometimes." Becky tapped her forehead with one finger. "I don't know how to filter that stuff out."

"Well," Adam shifted awkwardly on his end of the couch, "that is a good thing, right? It just means I've been more honest with you than I've ever been with anyone, I suppose. But now you've got me thinking really hard about pretty much every conversation we've ever had in the mindscape though..."

Becky smirked. "Nothing to worry about. If you'd flashed anything crazy at me, I'd have teased you about it by now."

Adam laughed. "That's a relief."

They sat in silence for a few minutes, Becky continuing to work at the hole in her pants. Finally, Adam asked, "So what do you really want to talk about?"

"It's kind of personal," Becky said haltingly. "You don't want to hear it."

"We've dated. We've shared a weird mental link. We've toppled enemy regimes on other worlds. There is nothing you can say that I won't listen to," Adam said with his best reassuring smile.

"Fine. I... I want to ask you a question. And you cannot judge me, in any way, because of this question, or I will never, ever forgive you for it." Becky said, her eyes fixed on the floor.

"Sure thing," Adam said.

Becky coughed a few times then, in a low voice, asked, "I have a couple of questions about sex."

Adam sucked in a sharp breath. He hadn't expected that.

Sheepishly, he replied, "Then you're probably talking to the wrong guy."

"What?" Becky asked, suddenly looking at him with wide eyes.

"Are you judging me now? It kind of feels like you are," Adam said in a rapid mumble.

"I mean, I know that stuff is different between two guys—that's almost why I wanted to ask you, besides you being pretty much the only person I could even come close to asking, anyway..." Becky rambled.

"It's not that, Becky. It's... Todd and I, we've never... you know." Adam blushed. He blushed so hard he could feel it in his toes.

"Never?" Becky asked incredulously. "But... never? Not even prom?"

"We've come close, but... never. I mean, we've fooled around. We kiss—we kiss a lot—and we've... done some stuff. But no, like, actual sex. Oh god. I am talking about sex with you. This is a new place for our relationship. I don't like this place." Adam said nervously.

"You two... you must be the most boring gay people in the world!" Becky said, suddenly smiling.

"It's just that... I wanted to... we... we wanted to wait for..." Adam tried to explain, but for some reason the words wouldn't come out in the right order. That was probably the mortification talking.

"I think it's sweet," Becky said. "Really. And it makes me feel way, way better."

"Because you and Joe haven't either?" Adam asked. "Right?"

Becky nodded. "But I think... I think that's going to change. Soon."

"Why?" Adam asked. "Wait—scratch that. Not certain I want the answer."

"He's different, Adam. The closer he gets to having that collar off, the more he grows up, and... and I really like him. I really love him." Becky smiled.

"That doesn't mean you have to sleep with him," Adam said. "That can still wait. You've waited this long, right? Why now?"

Becky shook her head. "What if we find Hyrak tomorrow? What if the dragon isn't strong enough to stop him, and we have to do it ourselves? What if we fail? This could be my only chance, you know?"

"For sex?" Adam arched an eyebrow. "You've had plenty of chances."

"No, you dumbass—to be with Joe. The real Joe. Not the collar and the bravado and the recklessness, but the guy who loved me first. That's the guy I've been waiting all this time to finally ask me out, you know." She stood up.

Adam thought of something. "Hey, wait a minute—before the collar, you were dating me. Are you saying you would have rather been with him than with me, back then?"

Becky grinned—a very JC-like expression, Adam thought—and answered, "Adam, I knew you were gay from the minute you walked into that school. I may not have wanted to admit it—but hell yes, I would have left you for him. Hell, for all I knew, *you* would have left *me* for him!"

Adam feigned shock. "What we had was special! And besides... Joe is not my type. Ew."

"Good night, Adam," Becky said, leaving the room.

"Good night, Becky," Adam said, pushing his thought to her through their link. "And whatever you do, if you decide to do... stuff... please, please, please turn this link off before you do. Promise me."

He waited a few minutes with no reply.

"Becky! Promise me!" he thought again, somewhat frantic.

"Good night, Adam," Becky said... and the link went silent.

¤~¤~¤

Wind rustled through the branches of the grove where the chieftains of Goldvast marshalled their forces. While many had not been completely swayed by Plyssa's Bindmetal-enhanced testimony, some had. They had reconvened away from the Circle of the Heavens, downwind of the great structure. Here, amidst the shadows of the fruit groves, more than two hundred warriors of many totems were gathered. Plyssa watched the chieftains explaining the task before them to the assembled women, and she did not envy them the task. How did you convince people that their god was fallible? At the core of the thing, what had stopped so many of the chieftains from agreeing to act was the refusal to believe that a *man*, even one as powerful as Hyrak, could somehow best Ahmur.

But Plyssa had spent enough time with Ahmur to know that the dragon-goddess was indeed fallible—perhaps even vulnerable. The arrogance and the pride of the dragon-goddess was without peer, and Hyrak had exploited these things to draw her out into the open and use his strange talismans to take command of her. In a way, Plyssa thought the women of Goldvast better off without their dictatorial goddess, but she also knew that Ahmur was a fundamental part of their society. That was why the assemblage of warriors was not here to plan for defeating Ahmur—they were here to plan for rescuing her.

Word had been sent to retrieve Tyrick and Embrew from the rearing pens in the Circle of the Darkness—they would stand no chance of liberating Ahmur if not for Embrew's abilities. A vast distance separated the safety of the commune-filled heartlands of Goldvast from the embattled north where Ahmur was serving as a pawn in Hyrak's plans. They would be here soon, and she would be happy to turn Sky back over to Tyrick. The oddly insightful, and alarmingly simple-minded, smith had not left her side since their joint working of magic upon the Bindmetal in the Circle of Heavens, and she could not abide the way that the other women looked at her as this man followed her dutifully about. Men were a rare sight, if not a subject of campfire stories, and Plyssa had spent enough of her life already being looked at with sidelong glances and spoken of in whispers by her peers. This was a step too far, as far as she was concerned.

As if on cue, she saw a small procession of warriors—all of them in masks depicting cats of various colors and sizes—leading Embrew, Tyrick, and a few other Goldvast warriors, bound in chains and without the adornment of their masks, towards the marshalling grounds. "Who are they?" she asked of the chieftain closest to her—a leader of one of the far southern regions, whose name she could not recall. Like all chieftains, she had forsaken her mask and totem, and her features were broad and flat—unattractive but open.

"The task we undertake is one that requires a touch of madness—of fury. These women dared to push too far against the wishes of their chieftains, and they were consigned to prison for this. We have asked them if, in exchange for their release, they would undertake this perilous mission. All of them accepted," the chieftain replied. The corners of her mouth turned up, ever so slightly. "They are largely considered mad... but so are all of us who believed you."

"The vote of confidence is overwhelming," Plyssa muttered. She turned to the ever-present Sky and said, "There is your friend. Go to him and tell Embrew to report to me here."

Sky nodded once in acknowledgement of the command and then jogged towards the oncoming procession, his eyes hard with focused determination. She watched him move, and she realized that what she had done—ordering him about—was no better than what the men of Greendeep had done to him, time and again. And yet it was so much easier to treat him as such, as a tool, than as a man. What did she know of treating men as men? She was a warrior of Goldvast, and they had no use for men outside of those they captured for mating.

She turned her attention to other things, watching the chieftains ordering their warriors to readiness. This was a massive force, especially for the often-disjointed legions of Goldvast, but the real trouble continued to be what it had been in the back of Plyssa's mind from the beginning—they did not know exactly where to go. Word from the goddess had been slow in coming, and never with any indication of from where she sent it. Embrew could open a doorway to almost anywhere, but where was he to point that ability? Where would Hyrak, and thus Ahmur, be, that would make any degree of sense? What did the madman need a dragon for... if not to battle other dragons? That meant Chron or Ehbor.

Embrew, Tyrick, and Sky reached her, and her accompanying chieftain stepped away—unwilling to spend time in the company of so many men. Old prejudices were hard to break, and for all her revelations, Plyssa had given these women no reason to trust these men. "Where are we going next?" Embrew asked.

"What makes you think we are going anywhere?" Plyssa asked, her tone bordering on mockery.

"I assumed I would be left to cool in the dungeons until I was needed, so this must now be the time for such work as only I can do. You have convinced them to disregard their goddess? That is no mean feat." Embrew shook his head. "This is a fine force assembled—more than two hundred, I count. More women answer to your cause than Ellir answer to Hyrak's. This bodes well."

"But the war to come will cost more lives than this. If he has both a goddess and the Ellir at his command," Tyrick questioned, "we are unequal to the task."

Sky touched Tyrick on the elbow and said, "Break."

"Break what?" Tyrick asked. Plyssa saw a strange flurry of emotion in the surveyor's expression—there was guilt as he spoke to Sky, but also other, more complicated notions. Affection, concern... there was depth to whatever relationship they possessed. She wondered, not for the first time, how much of the propaganda about the single-minded, conquest-obsessed men of Greendeep was the construction of Goldvast leadership rather than truth.

Sky pointed to Plyssa and smiled as he said again, "Break."

Plyssa looked at the blonde Metalbreaker carefully. "I thought you didn't like it when I did that?"

"Metal. Bad." Sky explained.

"That we can agree on," Plyssa said. Then she turned to Embrew. "We'll need a portal to the north—as close to the home of Hyrak as you can get us. You were with him, so... I assume you know where he lairs?"

"He will not be there," Embrew said. "He is a man of ambition, and such men rarely stand still once their plans are in motion."

"We have trackers. We will find his trail, I am sure of it. But we must start somewhere on this quest, and the longer we stand around here, the more likely some of these women are to realize what in incredibly foolish errand they have agreed to do. Let's get them ready for the march."

Embrew walked at her side, and Tyrick and Sky stayed behind in the smaller clearing. Before long, they would be half-way across the world, committed to battle.

In a way Plyssa could not properly describe, this felt *right*. As unlikely as it seemed, she had the undeniable sensation that she was embarking upon the right work. If she believed in destiny... this was it.

¤~¤~¤

Becky was lying in bed when Joe came in. She knew that Chaplain Reid and the others had returned about an hour ago, but people needed to sleep, and whatever had been decided upon would wait for morning.

JC was still a bit wet, his short dirty-blonde hair spiked up and the scent of water—but not chlorine, she noted—in the air as he moved in as quietly as possible. The red metal links around his throat tinkled as he moved, but he wore only a pair of shorts, and he slipped into bed beside her, snuggling up against her and whispering, "Beds are awesome."

She rolled over to face him, startling him.

"You're awake?" he asked.

"I was waiting for you," she whispered.

"Am I in trouble?" he asked, his eyes bright in the moonlight that came through the sheer curtains across the windows of the room.

"I thought... I wanted to..." she began. Becky was a woman of many words, but these words did not want to come out. As she stammered and struggled, she opted to instead flash a tiny image of her intent to JC along their mental link... and she saw him blush briefly before his lips curled up into the widest grin she had ever seen on a face accustomed to grinning.

"Are you sure?" he asked. "I don't want you to do anything you don't want to do." His face suddenly scrunched up, and Becky saw a tiny, rapid flash of light and smelled the sudden acrid whiff of ozone. JC rubbed at his collar and his eyes lit up, but he said nothing.

"I never do," Becky said, pulling him close against her and pressing against him in a writhing, probing kiss. His body responded easily, readily to her touch, and they were suddenly grinding against one another, the space between them vanishing into the undulating mass of two bodies unrestrained around one another, at last, after what felt like an eternity of control and resistance.

It took little time for JC to divest her of her clothes, and for her to push his shorts down over his knees and free of his feet with her own feet. They were naked, for the first time together, and then, in the pale light of the moon of Murrod, they made love. It was not perfect, but it was intimate, and it was... it was hard for Becky to describe. Which was how it should be, she thought.

Sometime later—longer than Becky had thought possible—she lay there, awake, as he lay, entangled with her, sleeping. She closed her eyes, and she felt contentment, peace, and pleasure. As sleep began to overtake her, she felt a presence in the back of her mind. It was tiny—a glimmer of mist and smoke, a dream born just before sleep, like a sensation of falling that starts you awake, and it whispered to her, "What have you done?"

Against reason, she replied, "What I wanted to do."

"But this... this is not what I wanted. What about Steven?"

Becky frowned, in her sleepy, dream-like state, and replied, "I don't love Steven. I love Joseph."

"It... it will do." the dream voice whispered.

And sleep fell upon her then—sleep full of joy, and contentment, and happiness, and many, many things that had never been a part of the daily vocabulary of Rebecca Hanson. The dream faded, and like so many dreams, it did not remain with her when the morning came.

# 32
## MURROD

*"This is definitely the best breakfast I have ever eaten,"* JC said between mouthfuls. He was sitting next to Becky, and he was doing everything in his power to keep from telling everyone what had happened last night. In the back of his mind, Becky was whispering threats—veiled and otherwise—demanding he exercise some discretion.

But he knew better than to run his mouth. He chewed on what appeared to be ham (he wasn't truly certain if Murrod had pigs, and he wasn't about to ask for clarification in case the answer was less appetizing) and let the conversations of the others go on around him.

"I know that time is critical," Chaplain Reid said as he dismissed the chef who had brought this sumptuous feast to the table, "but there are things that are simply not done. Demanding an immediate audience with our dragon-god is one of them."

"But the longer we wait, the more intricate his plans could become," Becky argued. JC was amazed at how adeptly she was having this verbal conversation while also bouncing the occasional admonishments into his mind.

"He won't help us if we piss him off," Todd said, pushing his plate away from himself, scraped clean of even crumbs.

Reid leaned back in his chair. "There is something else you may want to consider. As you have no doubt surmised, I am rather powerful in this city," he began.

"For now," Mathias reminded the minister coldly.

"Oh good, I see we are to resume posturing emptily first thing this morning," Reid muttered. "As I was saying, I have many connections. While I was filing the appropriate paperwork to gain access to Chron, I also asked some of my information agents to gather what news they could that might be helpful to our mutual cause. Those efforts may have borne fruit."

Yors reached for a biscuit and, in the process, managed to spill a goblet of some kind of juice. JC contributed his napkin to the cleanup efforts, and he noticed that Yors' hand was shaking.

"Hey—are you OK?" he asked.

Yors grunted in the affirmative and settled back into his chair, but JC thought the Jov looked a bit green, almost ill. That wasn't good. He looked down at his own plate and felt his appetite fading. Was there something in the food? Had Reid decided to kill them all with poisoned breakfast?

In his mind, Becky whispered, "Stop that. Please—we need to know what Reid's people have turned up."

JC shrugged, keeping one eye on Yors, and folded his arms across his chest as Reid continued.

"Yesterday afternoon, a group of masons quarrying building stone in the Greytall Mountains a few hours northeast of Monarka reported seeing a white dragon carrying two riders," Reid said.

"So they passed through this area," Adam said. "We need to know where they are going!"

"We appear to know that," Chaplain Reid continued. "They didn't just fly through—they landed. Assuming they chose that spot for a reason, they may well still be there."

"You could have told us this last night when you returned!" Adam said. He looked towards Steven. "Did you know about this?"

"No—we didn't hear anything like this while we are at the ministry building last night," Steven said.

"My informants approached me this morning, of course," Reid said smugly. "While the rest of you were lying in bed sleeping, I was collecting and sorting reports. There is certainly a reason I have been Minister of Security for nearly twenty years and the rest of you have, as best I can tell, amounted to very little."

Mathias stood up from the table. "Can we investigate this? The plan to seek audience with Chron was built around needing help finding Hyrak. If we know where he is, we have to take the chance and go after him. And besides... the sooner we can end this alliance, the happier we will all be."

"I don't know," Adam said.

"If we have the chance to take him out, by surprise, I think Mathias has a point," JC said.

"When you say 'take him out' are you suggesting we're going to kill this man in cold blood, Joe?" Steven asked. "Because I agreed to help stop Hyrak, I never agreed to kill him. We've seen too much death already on this trip."

"It's a euphemism, Steve-o. You can decide what it's euphemistic for." JC said with a shrug.

"It will be dangerous," Todd said. "And we'll need Adam to stay back in case we need our asses pulled out of the fire... but we should do it."

And that was that. They spent the next twenty minutes making preparations. JC had his energy rifle ready to go, and Yors his hammer. Todd and Mathias still had the swords they had acquired in Imperia, and Chaplain Reid produced a blue Bindmetal short sword for his own defense. Becky insisted that she didn't need any conventional weaponry, tapping her forehead as though that explained everything. Steven took a sword offered by Reid, but it was plain that he had little experience using such a thing.

"You... you want my Boom?" JC asked hesitantly. He was standing with Steven as they waited for the others to gather in the changing room off of the pool—where they had first arrived in Monarka.

"What? Why do you ask that?" Steven questioned.

JC slipped the strap of the weapon from over his head and held it out. "You've got more like, formal training with guns and stuff. I've probably swung a sword more than you, so... maybe this is smarter?"

Steven took the offered rifle and handed his sword to JC. JC took it firmly in one hand and swung several quick practice slashes through the air.

"Thank you," Steven said. "I promise to take good care of it."

"Her. It's a she. Well, it's actually probably a he, because it is made of... well... I don't think this is the time for that conversation. But anyway—I like to call it a she." JC smiled. "And if you take care of her, she'll take care of you."

The others trickled into the room, Becky and Reid coming last with Reid walking with a noticeable limp. JC arched an eyebrow and thought at Becky, "What happened?"

"He is literally falling apart here," Becky replied in JC's mind. "The man has maybe a few days left before he's too brittle to even move around. It's sick. But his mind—Joe, it's crazy how determined he is. I've never felt anything like it."

Adam, taking position at the front of the group, spread his arms wide and started to open the crossgate to the location Chaplain Reid's operatives had identified. "Everyone has a part to play. Let's do this," he said as the portal of green light appeared. "Let's catch us an evil warlord."

Almost in unison, Steven and Reid both said, "Without killing him."

¤~¤~¤

Tyrick struggled to free himself from the vice-like grip of the serpent that coiled around his chest. The sea snake was twenty feet long and it had struck swiftly, pinning his arms to his side and causing him to topple in the cold sand of the Bluetide beach.

He called for help, but the sound of the crashing waves dampened his cries, and most of the others were spread far and wide, searching for clues as to where Hyrak had taken their precious goddess.

Tyrick could feel his ribs cracking—nothing was broken yet, but it was only a matter of time. His knife was impossibly far from his hand, and even if he had it in his grip, he had no way to move his arms as the snake wrapped itself around him in yet another coil.

"Ty!" came a shout from somewhere up the beach—behind Tyrick.

A moment later, Sky was there, down on his knees in the sand, wrestling with the snake. Sky had the creature's broad, triangular head in one hand and was fighting to unwind it from around Tyrick's body.

A wave of frigid sea water rolled in, crashing down upon both of them, and the snake, and Tyrick started sputtering, trying to clear the salt water from his lungs.

Sky didn't miss a beat. He continued to fight with the snake, straining to overpower its incredible strength with his own—and he was succeeding. As Tyrick coughed the water clear of his lungs, he realized that he could, in fact, breathe. A few seconds later, he could slip one arm free of the constraints of the snake and, once that arm was free, the other. He bent back his foot and pulled the dagger from his boot, but as he was about to plunge it into the snake's scaly side, Sky said sharply, "No!"

Tyrick paused and allowed Sky to continue pulling the snake free. Holding its hissing, snapping jaws thrust out away from his body, Sky carried the creature a few steps away and then threw it out into the water, where it immediately slithered away.

"You saved me again," Tyrick said, sitting upright on the beach and brushing sand from his hair and beard.

Sky smiled. Tyrick saw the innocence in that face—in spite of the horror it had witnessed. He was drawn to this smith, powerfully so, but as he yearned to reach out and touch him, so too did he see in those bright eyes his own complicity in the treatment of the smiths of the Surveyor's Guild reflected.

Sky extended a hand to help Tyrick up, and he took it. As they stood there, looking out over the foaming sea, Tyrick felt Sky's arm reach out and draw him close. "Friend," Sky said confidently.

Tyrick felt his stomach lurch—not from the word, although it too had been like a punch to him, striking right in the hard lump of guilt that gathered in his gut—but from what he saw in the distance upon the water.

"We have to get to the others, now," he said to Sky, turning from the sea and starting to run through the sand towards the rocky expanse and the low stones that concealed the many caves of Bluetide.

Sky followed close behind, and Tyrick prayed to Chron that they would be fast enough.

They scrambled through the stone-strewn plain and he caught sight of a few of the cat-masked women that had spread all throughout the region, combing every stone and cavern for hints as to Hyrak's plans. He shouted to them, and as they turned to face him, their masks concealed what he imagined to be looks of fear upon their faces.

The black dragon, Ehbor, was behind him. He could feel the wind whipped to life by the beating of the dragon's great wings.

Then that wind intensified, and they were bowled over by it—Tyrick, Sky, and the four women. Tyrick rolled on the stones and backpedalled in a crab-walk, scraping his palms upon the sharp stones.

The dragon's three eyes glowed balefully as it touched down, scattering rocks everywhere, and bellowed in their minds, "Why have you come to this place?"

The women said nothing in reply, and Tyrick saw that Sky was awestruck, although not particularly afraid, so it fell to him. Hesitantly, he answered, aloud, "We would free the goddess Ahmur from the clutches of the man called Hyrak."

"My sister deserves whatever captivity she has fallen into," Ehbor replied, also aloud, his voice deep and rumbling. "And you are trespassing."

"Yes," shouted a voice emerging from one of the caverns. "Tell us where we should go next, and we will be on our way." Tyrick saw Embrew emerge from the cavern, leaning on a staff of dark, twisted metal. The cave he came from was the one they had first arrived at with Plyssa's people—the place Embrew had been held captive.

"Gatemaker," Ehbor said, turning. "I had thought you discarded by Hyrak. You now work against him?"

"I help those who would see him stopped," Embrew replied, picking his way closer to the dragon slowly. "This we cannot do without your help, mighty one."

"He tried to capture me, as he did my sister," Ehbor said in a hissing whisper.

Tyrick watched the dragon's eyes narrow in anger.

"He seeks to take us all—he carries three bells, made from a drum he forced my children to steal from Greendeep for him. They are potent weapons indeed, if they can claim the will of a dragon." Ehbor stretched his neck out to its full length, and Tyrick heard the bones of that neck crack and pop loudly as the dragon worked out its stiff joints.

"Congratulations on your escape," Embrew said, drawing to a stop ten paces from the dragon. "Your mind is as quick as your talons are sharp."

"He will hunt my brother," Ehbor said. "When last the three of us engaged in open conflict, it was Chron that emerged victorious. It was Chron that barred the Spiralgates in all other lands, making it so that when the men of your world came, they would treat only with his children. He is clever and strong, but he is also prideful. Arrogant."

"I had wondered why Ahmur sought always to move on the gates of Greendeep," Embrew said. "Your insight already helps us greatly."

"You are a flatterer. My own children lack the capacity to flatter me. It is perhaps a shortcoming I had not properly appreciated. But if you seek Hyrak, I would seek him in the lair of Chron, near the city men call Monarka." Ehbor looked down, directly at Tyrick. "I have no quarrel with Ahmur's daughters, but this one... this one is a son of Chron. And this one," he turned to Sky, "I have not seen one of these before—it is unlike any who stand now or ever in my lands. Born of both worlds. Fascinating. These two I will take for myself, as recompense for your trespass."

"I think not," Tyrick said, leaping to his feet. He brandished his dagger—a gesture of abject impotence, he knew, but all he could think to do—and took a step nearer the dragon, placing himself between Ehbor and Sky. "Take me if you wish, but this one stays free."

"I am not taking prisoners," Ehbor growled, eyes narrow and a low rumbling beginning to echo in his throat, "I am taking dinner."

"Then I am even more certain you shall not take him," Tyrick said.

The dragon lowered its head and brought it close to Tyrick—so close that he could feel the hot breath of each exhalation from the dragon's great nostrils. "You have courage."

Tyrick could think of no retort that would not betray how afraid he was, but he managed to keep from collapsing in terror—barely.

The dragon drew its head back up, away from Tyrick, and looked back at Embrew. "I sense the horde of women you have brought to my land. Gather them. Gatemaker, can your portals accommodate one of my size?"

"Not easily, your greatness," Embrew said, "Can you not travel by your own power?"

The dragon opened its jaw slightly and Tyrick almost thought the expression on its reptilian face resembled a smirk.

"Not if I am busy masking the presence of all of you from my brother and sister's senses. If you can get us there, I shall lead you all, and as many of my Ellir as I can quickly summon, to Chron's doorstep. Perhaps together we shall put that impertinent Hyrak in his place at last." The dragon started to beat its wings and lift from the ground. "I will return in two hours. Be ready for me."

As the dragon took to the sky, many other women, all wearing their masks, started to race towards where Tyrick and Embrew were standing. Tyrick helped Sky to his feet and said, "Now we are a bit closer to even, my friend."

Sky nodded, but his face was creased into a frown. "Both? What?" he asked.

"I don't know," Tyrick said. "Perhaps he spoke of your nature as a Metalbreaker?" He could see that the dragon's few words had affected Sky deeply, but he did not know how to help.

Plyssa was one of the women who reached the three of them first, and she slipped her snake mask off of her face and asked, "What in the name of Ahmur did you just do?"

Embrew smiled slyly and said, "I believe I just gained you an ally."

"The dragon-gods are blood enemies of one another! He cannot be trusted!" Plyssa whispered, scanning the sky to be sure Ehbor was not near enough to hear her.

"If there is one thing Hyrak is truly gifted with, it is the ability to unite disparate factions against a common foe," Embrew said. "I have witnessed this on my own world, and I believe I am witnessing it here, now, on yours. We dare not trust that creature, but we can, I think, count upon it to help us get to Hyrak. Then it falls to you to free your goddess."

"Ty," Sky said.

Tyrick asked, "What is it?"

Sky placed one hand on Plyssa's shoulder, than one on his own chest. "Not same. Dragon. Not same," he struggled to explain.

Tyrick thought he understood what Sky was trying to say. Whatever the dragon had noticed in Sky, he had said that no one ever entering Bluetide had been like him. But somehow, Plyssa was a Metalbreaker too. So that wasn't it.

Tears welled in Sky's eyes as he repeated once more, "Not same." With a deep, shuddering sigh, the Jov said, "Alone."

¤~¤~¤

Steven held tightly to JC's energy rifle as he emerged from the crossgate. Adam's portal opened at the edge of a broad, flat plain surrounded by upswept mountains, and the suns were high overhead on a clear, bright day.

Steven immediately stepped off to the side from the portal and dropped to a firing crouch, bracing the rifle for a shot as he covered those still emerging and took stock of the situation.

In the center of the wide disc of flat, dark stone on which they stood, a man in black metal armor knelt, striking a green pickaxe upon the ground in a steady pattern of blows, each blow causing emerald sparks to erupt all around him.

Between the portal and the man (who Steven assumed to be Hyrak) was a dragon. While the others talked somewhat casually about dragons, this great white lizard was Steven's first encounter. She was on the ground, on all four limbs with her wings tucked up along her back, facing away from the portal. Sitting on a saddle-like contraption on her back was a large, barrel-chested man with a thick beard who very much reminded Steven of Yors.

Other than that, there was little else to see—no obstacles, no cover, and no army of soldiers or henchmen. The dragon was in the way and the others were just starting to exit the portal, but Steven dared to take a shot at Hyrak. He sighted carefully, training from the army and the police coming to him like second nature. He pulled the trigger and the weapon flared, firing a brilliant bolt of blue-white energy towards Hyrak, only to have it suddenly engulfed and nullified in one of the intermittent sprays of green sparks bursting from the stone platform all around the warlord.

With that shot, the element of surprise was lost and the dragon spun towards the portal just as the last of the group emerged and Adam willed the shimmering disc of light out of existence.

"You had a better chance of hitting Ahmur!" JC shouted as the dragon roared and took one menacing step towards the group.

Everyone scattered, running in all directions. Steven held his ground, readying to take a shot at the oncoming beast. A moment later, Yors was standing next to him, his face pale and glistening with sweat. "This not right," Yors said. He slammed his own sapphire hammer down onto the platform, and suddenly a low wall-like ridge of stone burst up from the ground about ten feet from the edge of the plateau on this side, creating a measure of protection for everyone.

Steven popped up over the ridge and fired twice at the dragon. The first shot flew wide, but the second struck her and she immediately recoiled, hopping backwards, unfurling her wings, and retreating a dozen yards as she let loose a blast of flame from her lungs that washed up against Yors' protective ridge with little effect.

Steven looked around. The group had paired off when they scattered, with Reid and Mathias closest to Steven and Yors. He could barely see Todd and Adam, who were partially obscured by the curvature of the stone defensive wall, but he could see Becky and JC. They were up to something.

¤~¤~¤

"Can you make me invisible?" JC questioned in his mind.

Becky replied mentally, "I think so. I don't know how well it works on a dragon, but... I think so."

"Then do it," JC said. He could feel the fear brewing inside him, and he knew that the collar wouldn't sweep it away—with only two links left, it didn't have the power to overcome this. But he did—he was strong enough. He squeezed the sword tightly in his hand and he looked clear past the dragon—other people would deal with the dragon. He would stop Hyrak.

"It will take a minute," Becky said aloud. "Just promise me you will sit tight for a second while I weave it all together. Please."

JC grabbed her hand and squeezed it tightly. "Say the word. We're in this together." Then he leaned in and kissed her, hard. "As promised, I'm going to kick his ass so hard it *stays* kicked."

He felt the sudden flash of heat and smelled the metallic tang in the air as another link in the chain at his throat failed. Yors had been right. He could do this. He could conquer his fear himself.

Becky, blushing, slid down as low as she could against the stone wall. Another blast of flame from the dragon brought intense heat to the air all around them, and she started to chew on her lower lip. "It's... not as easy you'd think."

"You can do it," JC said, grinning. "I have faith in you. In all of us. We've got this."

¤~¤~¤

"The dragon is not the problem," Todd said, ducking back down to report to Adam. Adam didn't have the nerve to look over the sheltering wall.

"I'd say it's a big ass part of the problem," Adam grumbled.

"We have no useful plan here. I wasn't expecting to pop out in the middle of a firefight," Todd said. "If I can get to the others, can you build us a crossgate to get us around the dragon and right up in Hyrak's face?"

Adam nodded. "Easily."

"Then get ready. When I shout, open it over there," he pointed, "next to Yors."

Adam sucked in a deep breath and started the calculations in his mind that would bend space in the shape of the crossgate Todd required. As he did so, Todd skittered around the curve of the wall in a low crouch, ostensibly gathering the others for a surprise attack.

¤~¤~¤

Steven continued to exchange shots with the dragon. His energy blasts and her gouts of fire breath were evenly matched, in that neither could properly target the other in the gaps allowed between shots of the other. He was able to keep Ahmur's flight advantage suppressed by aiming high routinely, but she kept any of them from being able to mount a reasonable offense for fear of being roasted.

"This wrong," Yors said again, hunched down beside Steven. "Yors stop this. This place not meant to be used this way!"

Steven fired again, but this time, as he stood to fire, Yors followed. The smith vaulted over the wall with surprising agility, landing in a loping gait as he charged towards the dragon. Steven watched, awestruck.

The dragon's rider shouted, "Toren? Is that you?" but Yors did not acknowledge the man. The dragon reared up on her hind legs, her eyes flaring brightly, and she swung the razor-sharp talons on her forelimbs wildly as Yors charged into her reach. The smith swung his hammer up with one hand, shattering one of Ahmur's talons in the process and causing the dragon to cry out in rage. She belted a gout of flame into the sky, and Steven caught a glimpse of Todd darting behind him towards Mathias and Reid.

Steven spared them little attention, instead firing twice at the dragon as it reared up, managing to land one of the two shots in one of Ahmur's unfurled wings, tearing a hole in its scaled flesh. Again the dragon howled, and Yors continued past her, towards Hyrak.

¤~¤~¤

"Your informants appear to have left out some details," Mathias hissed at Chaplain Reid as the fighting beyond the wall intensified.

"No matter—I have seen the people you travel with do some impressive things. It makes one wonder what they need you for," Reid countered. "This venue is interesting to me. The Ministry files were very clear that we were never to allow any of the Jovs near this place—it was of great concern for those operating out of Monarka in particular, given the proximity. What do you think this place is?"

"I don't know," Mathias confessed. "Why don't you go ask Hyrak?"

Todd came near them, JC in tow, and said, "We're hitting Hyrak now, while he's distracted by Yors and the dragon."

Mathias readied his sword as Todd and JC both shouted, "Now!"

A swirling portal of gold light opened up beside them and JC promptly disappeared from view.

"What?" Mathias asked.

"Mindshaper thing. Go!" Todd said. They rushed through the portal, Chaplain Reid lagging noticeably behind.

¤~¤~¤

As Yors barreled towards the recoiling, shrieking dragon, he offered a quick one-handed swing of the hammer at the back of her rear right leg, which caused her to topple and catch another shot from Steven squarely in the chest. Yors heard Jarrek—he recognized his former leader—cry out as the dragon rolled onto her side, pinning him. He had no time to deal with this. The dragon could mend her own wounds, and surely would—there were mere moments that Hyrak was undefended.

He could feel in his bones what was happening. Somehow, Hyrak was using that Bindmetal pickaxe in his hands to replicate the effects of a hammer like what Yors now possessed. His conversation with Gurse came back to mind, and he realized how familiar this place was to him—how like the clearing in the mountains of Arctos this was... where he had found the hammer he now carried.

If Hyrak was trying to shape the earth with that pick, Yors would show him how it was truly done—he would call the hammer of Murrod from its resting place beneath this field of stone and undo whatever working Hyrak was in the midst of. Yors didn't know much about the old secrets of the Metalbreakers, but he knew this in the same bones that vibrated with the power, and the wrongness, of what Hyrak was now doing.

He felt the center of the space—right where Hyrak now knelt—and charged up to the warlord, hammer swinging. Green sparks exploded up around him, but Yors ignored the burning pain of the sparks. Hyrak looked up and opened his milky white eyes to see Yors swinging the hammer, in both hands, directly at his head.

Hyrak replied swiftly, bringing his own smaller green Bindmetal pickaxe up to block the blow. As the two implements of unequal power struck, a shockwave rippled out, crumbling Yors' stone wall to pebbles and suddenly leaving Steven, Becky, and Adam exposed. Yors' hammer vibrated, but Hyrak's pickaxe exploded into fragments of shattered, twisted metal, pushing Hyrak and Yors away from one another.

Yors saw a glimmering disc of gold light appear a few feet from Hyrak, and Todd and Mathias rushed out, swords flashing. Hyrak drew his own sword in a fluid motion, fending the two of them off with minimal effort, but he was distracted. He did not see Chaplain Reid emerge from the portal—for what good that was worth—nor did he see Yors take up the position he had formerly occupied in the center of the plateau. Yors knelt down and pressed his hand to the stone, calling out with his magic to the hammer below. He listened to the beating of the world, and he tried to align his own rhythm to it—but he could not. No amount of humming or breathing could calm the jangling discordance of the vengeance he craved—and he understood what was happening. He could not summon this hammer, because he had lost his way.

He felt the ground beneath him begin to shake, and he looked up to see Hyrak, still engaged in rapid stroke and counterstroke with his large sword, laughing.

"You are too late, Jov. The working has come to pass. Watch! Watch your end unfold!" Hyrak shouted. With a powerful slash of his sword he cut across Mathias' chest, causing blood to rush out. Yors heard Adam shout from behind him, and a sudden crossgate swallowed Mathias, pulling him to safety.

Todd struggled with Hyrak. Behind Yors, the dragon roared and fire flashed as Steven and the dragon resumed their battle. Steven had erected a shield of shadow that offered far less defense than the wall Yors had allowed to fail.

Yors lifted his sapphire hammer parallel to the ground in both hands, feeling through its magic the shape of what Hyrak had done. He tried to undo it, to counter it, but the hammer he held was not of this world—it could do only rudimentary, crude work upon the stone and earth of Murrod. It lacked the connection to this world required to reach deep and stir it to action in a place like this.

There was nothing he could do.

¤~¤~¤

Becky was next to Adam now, treating Mathias as best she could while maintaining the shield of invisibility around JC. She watched him—she could see him, even if no one else could—and she worried.

Hyrak was a better swordsman than Todd, of course, and he was steadily driving Todd back, towards the edge of the plateau and a long, lethal fall below.

She whispered to JC telepathically, "Hit him now, Joe! Now!"

JC struck the warlord from behind, his sword slashing across the back of Hyrak's legs, where the armor was weakest. Hyrak cried out—surprised—and fell to his knees. Todd scrambled away, and JC grabbed Hyrak's head, pulling off the warlord's helmet and bringing his blade up across Hyrak's scarred throat from behind.

"You are done," JC said. "Done hurting people. Done ruining lives and worlds."

"You are the poor little child that fears his fear," Hyrak said, mocking. "I know of you. I know of all of you. You are soft. There is no mettle in you, no conviction to do what must be done."

"Bullshit," JC said as he pulled back his sword, slicing open Hyrak's throat.

"Joe!" Becky shouted, aloud. He'd killed him! He'd murdered Hyrak in cold blood. Why?

Hyrak toppled over and rolled, landing on his back as blood spurted up from the gaping wound in his throat. Becky pressed herself into JC's mind, trying to reason with him, to calm him, to scream at him—she didn't know. But she saw what he saw and heard what he heard as he stood watching over the fallen warlord's blood-choked breaths.

"Come," Hyrak mumbled, crooking one gauntleted finger towards JC. "Must tell you... why..."

JC leaned in, bending over Hyrak—his curiosity burning as brightly as ever, in spite of the horror of what had just occurred.

And Hyrak reached up, revealing what was cupped in that hand that had beckoned JC closer. It contained a gleaming red Bindmetal padlock—open. With a swift movement, Hyrak snapped the lock into one of the links of chain around JC's neck and Becky felt her connection to him blink out—terminated suddenly, painfully, and utterly.

"Joe?" she asked aloud. Adam looked up at her, but she could not tear her eyes away from what was happening.

JC extended his hand and helped Hyrak back to his feet. Hyrak was wiping at the blood around his throat, but it was clear that it had ceased bleeding. Everything else had stopped—the dragon was still, Steven was still—everyone stood watching what was happening in frightening slow motion.

Hyrak shouted, "I cannot die. Have you not been told the tales?"

Of all of them, it was Chaplain Reid that regained his composure first. The minster of security charged towards Hyrak, bright blue sword in hand.

Hyrak pointed towards the minister and said, "Kill him."

JC moved to intercept Reid, his sword swinging up and matching the chaplain blow for blow until, after a few such exchanges, JC's strength was too great a match for Reid, and the minister fell to the ground.

JC stood above him, sword pointed at Reid's throat.

"No," Becky shouted. She didn't understand. She didn't understand what was happening, why this was happening. "No, Joe! Don't!"

But it was too late. JC leaned in, driving the tip of his blade through the throat of Chaplain Reid, then pulled it out and wiped the blood on Reid's tunic.

Hyrak strode confidently towards Ahmur, JC at his heel. No one moved to stop him—Becky found that she couldn't move, no matter how hard she wanted to. A powerful mindshaping was thrown upon them like a heavy blanket, slowing their reflexes.

Hyrak climbed on the dragon, taking the seat in front of the Jov who sat there, head hung low in shame. JC scrambled up and gripped tightly to rear of the Metalbreaker's saddle. And with the beating of wings that were, even as they watched, healing, Ahmur took to the sky.

Hyrak's mindshaping ended, and there was a flurry of activity. Becky watched it all with hollow, empty detachment.

Steven rushed to tend to Mathias' wound, but it turned out to be more surface than it at first appeared. Yors struggled to his feet, tears shining in his big, dark eyes. Todd stood next to Chaplain Reid's body, shaking his head. Adam watched the sky—Becky could feel him trying to plot a trajectory for where the dragon would head next.

Steven helped Mathias to his feet, and they all slowly, sluggishly, gathered around the center of the plateau.

"What happened?" Adam asked.

Mathias knelt over Chaplain Reid's body for a moment, then joined the rest of them.

"He didn't die," Steven said. "What is he?"

"I mean what happened to Joe?" Adam asked.

"Magic," Yors said. "Jarrek greatest worker of red Bindmetal Yors ever know. Made lock to turn working around. JC trapped inside new person now. Like Yors and Toren." He looked to Becky. "Becky understand?"

"We're going to find him," Becky said grimly. "And you are going to break that collar off of him." She grabbed Yors by the beard. "Do you understand me?"

"It... not that simple," Yors said. "Only one link left in chain. JC must break it."

"How the hell can he do that if he isn't himself anymore?" Adam asked.

Yors looked at Becky. "Becky must reach him inside new person."

No one said anything for a few seconds, until Todd asked, "Does anyone else feel that?"

Becky cared about almost nothing at this moment—she was wrestling with Yors' words, with what it would mean, what it would take, to 'reach him' inside whatever monster Hyrak had made him. But she could feel what Todd was noticing—a trembling in the stone beneath her feet.

"We're leaving," Adam said. "Now."

¤~¤~¤

They returned to Monarka by crossgate just in time for Mathias to see a sight that would haunt his dreams for the rest of his life.

They emerged in the street outside of Reid's residence in the city, and in the distance the Greytall Mountains were clearly visible. That was why it was so easy to see as five of them, in perfect synchronicity, detonated. Their peaks exploded as massive jet-like plumes of smoke and ash and soot blasted up into the sky. Lava burst and boiled out of the now missing peaks of these mountains, but not in any way proportionate to the rushing clouds of black ash that billowed up and out into the upper atmosphere.

Mathias reached into his pocket and gripped tightly to the pair of contract rings he had stolen from Reid's body, trying to take some measure of comfort in them – but they did not help.

The sky was growing dark. Men were screaming with fear all around them in the city.

"Oh shit," Adam said. "That was his plan all along?"

"He's going to destroy the city with erupting volcanoes?" Steven asked. "It's not the most efficient way I could think of with his kind of power."

"The suns," Mathias whispered. "He's blocking the suns."

In the distance, a band of Ellir howled in mad, murderous fury.

"How long will this last?" Steven asked.

"How long will those things keep churning that ash into the sky?" Becky ellaborated.

"Forever," Yors said sullenly. "That is working Hyrak made. That is working Yors failed to stop."

# 33
## Onus

*It seemed as though Jara had spent most of her life on the road.* After her father's death, she and her mother had traveled far from their home and made a new place for themselves with the monks at Gar Nought. After the fall of Gar Nought she had traveled to other worlds—first Core, then Murrod, before returning to Onus at Rega Holc. Then she had spent nearly half a year traveling south from Rega Holc, by land and by sea, to Hyrak Arn to rescue her mother. A short jaunt north to Igar Holc brought her perhaps one of the longer stretches of sedentary living she had recently known, but then events had driven her south to Ain Holc and now she was walking, painfully, into a dense, hot jungle.

"I have a friend that is a Gatemaker," Jara said to no one in particular. The Duchess' soldiers had been easily fooled into believing that her grace had ordered Jara to accompany their group, but they were not conversationalists of any great renown. The entire arduous journey, by foot, then by uncomfortable horseback, and now by foot again, had been one of quiet movement, quiet meals, and quiet evenings. She hated it.

But she could feel the pull of their destination, growing stronger with each hour, and knew that this misery was worthwhile. There was a moment of incredible importance lurking somewhere in the Vale of Steam, and now that the stinging insects and shimmering haze of the jungle's natural heat were upon them, she could scarcely contain the curiosity gnawing at her.

She'd had only glimpses of future sights during the journey, and each was more cryptic than the last. She saw a vibrant, green world swept in darkness, and she saw a flashing, burning arc of blue-white energy burst from the darkness, curving towards her. As interesting, and fascinating, as that vision was, it seemed to have little to do with what was looming in the jungle, and yet that was the vision, in varied forms and from many angles, that came when she opened her arts to the vagaries of the future.

"I hear something ahead," one of the men reported to Essindir. Jara was close by the tall captain, for it seemed to be the only way she learned anything at all.

"Scouts!" Essindir ordered sharply. Two men darted forward, into the thick underbrush, and everyone else waited, alert and ready for whatever lurked unseen as twilight began and what little sunlight reached the jungle floor faded.

Three minutes later, one of the scouts returned, panting. He lifted his conical helmet from his head and wiped at the sweat glistening on his forehead with one sleeve of his uniform tunic. "There is a clearing ahead," he explained, "and it appears to be occupied by children, sir."

Essindir nodded and, for the first time on their uneventful journey, turned to Jara. "Have you any insight, little Wyr?"

Jara snorted angrily at the diminutive title, then closed her eyes and opened herself to her magic. The now familiar image of the green world going dark and the lance of blue-white energy emerging from it resumed, and she shook her head to clear the meaningless image. It would have meaning soon—of that she was certain. But it did not help matters now. She tried again—pushing forward, trying to hone the focus to her wishes—but something, somehow, resisted. Fate did not accumulate in this place—just like when she had tried to see the names of the Children of the Line. This strange blankness was not new to her... she had seen one other such instance of this...

"No," she said cautiously. "Something here blocks my vision—it distracts me with other images. I think it's been doing so since we started. That makes me very worried, sir. Be careful, please."

With a curt nod, Essindir began directing his small force of men. There were a dozen in total, not counting Jara, and he ordered them to spread out so that they could approach the perimeter of the clearing from as many vantage points as possible. Then he held up one hand and asked, "Where is the other scout?"

Jara looked around, suddenly frantic—but she couldn't see the other man. A horrible, agonized scream tore through the air from ahead of them, and at that moment Jara caught a flicker of vision, a moment of insight that somehow slipped through whatever obfuscation was in effect in this place. "Grell," she murmured. "Grell is free. He's on his way here."

"Or perhaps he is *already* here!" the captain exclaimed. "Advance!"

The men charged forward, hacking at the jungle vegetation with their swords. Jara chose to stay close to Essindir and followed tightly behind him, just out of reach of the backswing of his mighty sword strokes. They needed less than a minute to press through the thriving green underbrush here, and then they emerged onto a smooth circle of cool dark stone, swirled with ribbons of metals and sparkling with flecks of gemstones.

Jara felt her stomach lurch as she set foot onto the stone, and she looked around to see the rest of Essindir's men breaching the jungle and finding themselves in the clearing. Towards the center, some distance away, a group of what appeared to be more then twenty children—most far younger than Jara—were gathered, facing inward in a tight circle.

Essindir motioned for the men to continue their advance, and from eleven lines of origination, they stalked inward, one cautious step at a time, towards intersection.

The men moved with relative silence, but Jara heard every jingling bit of metal on their persons as the sounds of the Vale of Steam faded away in this place, leaving eerie, silent calm. The children up ahead were murmuring, some even crying, but Jara could not yet make out what they were doing.

When at last the soldiers of Ain Holc reached the children, Essindir reached out and placed one gloved hand upon the shoulder of the tallest child, a girl, and demanded, "What is going on here?"

The girl stepped back, away from the others. Through the space she vacated, Jara could see the corpse of the missing scout. Blood still seeped from where the man's two arms had been ripped from their sockets.

"What is this?" Essindir asked, bringing his sword up to readiness. "Who did this?"

The girl replied softly, "You shouldn't have come here. It doesn't like adults. It takes care of us, but it... it won't like you."

Jara's senses screamed at her, and instinct drove her to leap aside just as a hand of dark stone emerged from the ground, passing as easily through the stone of the clearing floor as a man moves through water. The creature to which the hand was attached emerged quickly. It was nearly nine feet tall, and it was carved entirely from the same dark, metal-and-gem-studded stone as the clearing. Instead of a head it had a gleaming prism of polished fire opal, and there was blood upon its massive hands.

Essindir's men were amongst the best Ain Holc had to offer, and they reacted swiftly to the creature's presence. Essindir himself was the first to engage it, spinning and slashing at its torso with his blade, but the sword was met with a dull clang as it struck the impervious stone of the creature. Others began to hack at the monster from behind, but again and again their swords had no effect.

It became increasingly clear to Jara that the creature was not interested in the soldiers. They were like gnats to it—it backhanded one, sending him sprawling, and it took several steps forward—towards Jara. Then it was busy with the guards again, until it knocked two more away and took another step towards Jara. This time one of the men—the scout that had originally sighted this place—planted himself firmly in the creature's path. He stabbed forward with his blade, striking at the gemstone head of the thing. The sword struck and, for a moment, Jara suspected the blow had yielded some effect. Then the creature, with speed that seemed impossible from something made of living stone, reached out with both hands and wrapped them around the scout's unhelmeted head. In the same smooth motion, it squeezed its two massive hands together and crushed the scout's skull. Then it stepped towards Jara, who backpedalled, unable to look away but no longer unable to move.

Fear, and realization, had given her strength. "It isn't after the adults," she muttered. "It's after me."

¤~¤~¤

Shayra strode down the streets of Norwin Holc as though she owned the place. Her journey from Kem Nought to Norwin Holc had been swift and marred only by an unfortunate encounter with roadside brigands that she had easily dispatched with her arts. Her mind was bent upon one task—finding Narred and making him pay for his betrayal of her and the Kem.

It was early evening, and the thoughts of the man watching over the entrance to the city easily revealed to her that the Duke would be found in his humble palace, but she had no concern with formality. The same guard's thoughts had also been quite helpful in providing her the location of the jail where Narred was being kept.

The streets of Norwin Holc were quieting down for the night. Many of the farmers that filled the city by day traveled home after a day of hawking their produce and goods in the large, open-air markets, and Shayra easily navigated her way into the city's heart as the men and their mules and carts bustled their way out of the city to farmsteads and villages not far from here.

Following the route that her helpful guard had taken many times, Shayra was drawn to the large, elaborate jail of the city. This was no dungeon, nor the simple, nondescript building that comprised the above-ground prison in Mendul Holc. Norwin Holc's jail was an elaborate structure, three stories in height—the tallest building in the city, as best she could tell—and decked out in waving flags and ornate carved stonework along artfully designed ledges at each level of elevation.

She came to the wide double doors of the jail and saw a single guard resting comfortably on a stool, barring her way. He wore much the same simple uniform as the guard at the outer edge of the city, and he smiled warmly as Shayra approached.

"Can I help you, my lady?" he asked, standing and bowing.

"I would visit with one of your prisoners," she explained. "This is a fine prison. I have never seen its like."

The guard smiled proudly. "Only the finest for Duke Ptorus," he explained.

Shayra arched an eyebrow. She could sense at the surface of the guard's thoughts his desire to share the story of this place, and she braced herself to collect the answers she truly sought while his mind was busied with the tale.

"Up until about thirty years ago, this was Ptorus Holc, and our lord was a kind, fair man, beloved by all. He crossed the Council on a matter of great importance—or so they say—and he was ordered deposed. Thus we became Norwin Holc once more, though that's a story for another day," the guard began to ramble, "and Duke Ptorus and his family were ordered imprisoned for life. Now the Duke, he'd never done anything to hurt the people of Ptorus Holc, and so it was decided that he would not be made to suffer as he lived out his last days. This prison was built, more magnificent even than the Duke's palace, as a gift from the people that loved him in spite of the Council's decree. While the Duke and Duchess have since passed from this world, the gift of the people remains."

While the man spoke, Shayra plucked the location of Narred's cell, on the third level, from his mind. She smiled graciously and said, "Thank you for your story. Most fascinating." Then, with a simple gesture, she placed a working of her arts upon his mind and murmured, "Sleep."

The guard collapsed back onto his stool and fell back against the left door, suddenly snoring loudly.

Shayra lifted the simple key ring at his belt from him, unlocked the door on the right, and slipped into the beautiful prison where her husband awaited her justice.

Each level consisted of three hallways, lined with cells on either side, with the stairs placed at alternating ends of the building. She strode down the center aisle of the ground floor, pulling a simple working about her to mask her presence from the guards and prisoners. She noticed many of these cells were full, but always of people whose minds screamed out their guilt of minor crimes. The stairs at the end of the hall were watched over by a guard that could obviously not see her, and she walked past him and up the stairs, her slippered feet silent on the broad steps.

The second floor was less occupied, with only perhaps half of the cells along the main aisle full, and rarely more than two people in a cell. These prisoners had thoughts she found unpleasant, so she accessed few of them as she marched along. They had recently been fed their evening dinner, and most were occupied with eating. Shayra caught an impression of power from one man, a middle-aged fellow with the dark features of a Dweller in the Sands. She paused for a moment in front of his cell, and the man looked up from his meal.

He pushed his braided hair away from his face and squinted his eyes, then asked, "Who are you?"

"You can see me?" Shayra asked, checking to assure that her invisibility working was still in place—and it was.

"Of course," the man said. With that, he returned to hungrily devouring his meal.

Shayra made a note of the man's thoughts—they were slightly guarded, protected by rudimentary shields of magic. He was indeed a Mindshaper—a candidate to serve as host to one of her charges back at Kem Nought. And this was a body she would not mind coopting with another person's mind, for he was a criminal, incarcerated here on this level because of the severity of his crimes.

But she was not here at this moment in her capacity as Collectress.

Another guard watched over the final flight of stairs leading to the top floor, and Shayra's working masked her from his sight as easily as it had the others. At the top of the stairs she could see that the highest level consisted of only nine cells, each large and square and spaced equidistantly from one another and from the outer walls of the building.

Only one was occupied.

She approached the transparent crystal cell, admiring the construction of the structure. It was made of faintly blue crystal, and she could feel working through the material a faint, but enduring working of Kem magic.

"This is a Boltsender cage," she said as she approached. "I didn't know such a thing existed. Perhaps, had Kem Nought possessed such a thing, we would not be standing here today."

Inside, she saw Narred, his hands clapped together in lead shackles. His crooked nose was swollen and crusted with blood—it had been broken again, recently. She nearly felt sorry for him, sitting there.

She tapped the crystal with one long fingernail. "The crystal stops the transmissions. The shackles, I assume, make gathering energy for a bolt difficult."

Narred did not reply, but he stared at her with wide, wild eyes. She was reluctant to reach out to him, to his thoughts—she feared that her anger over what the others had revealed to her about Narred's actions would drive her to do something unforgiveable. The idea of coring out his mind, of erasing all that made him who he was and leaving him nothing more than a vegetable, was appealing. Betrayal was one thing that Shayra could not countenance.

"Have you nothing to say for yourself?" she demanded, her anger evident in her tone.

Narred stood up, his heavy chains rattling. He shouted at her—but the words made no sense. They were gibberish.

"What?" she asked. She reached out with her arts, touching his mind and finding her first efforts repulsed by the same screen of static that had been keeping her out since she had come to her senses at Kem Nought.

"Let me in," she demanded, "and I will undo what has been done to you."

Narred's eyes narrowed in suspicion, but she felt the screen of static in his mind retract, pulling away and allowing her access to at least the forefront of his thoughts. Once there, she easily laid her hands upon the working that was scrambling his language, and she felt the familiar signature of her own arts upon it.

"I... I did this?" she asked, suddenly confused. The others had said nothing of this. Perhaps they had not known? But she would gain no satisfaction from this confrontation if she could not hear the weak, flimsy excuses he would parade before her for his actions, and so she unwound the working.

"Have you come to finish me off?" Narred shouted the moment his words were returned to some semblance of order.

"I have come to learn why you have turned against me," Shayra said. "I gave my heart and soul to you, and you murdered my people. I do not understand, and I wish to... before I kill you."

Narred asked, "What are you talking about? I haven't hurt any of your people. I left because I could no longer bear to be a part of what you do, of the secrets and the possession and the abduction. And then you reached out and punished me for this—it is I who have been betrayed. I thought I wed a woman who would set my feet upon the road to redemption, not one that would make me party to further tragedy."

"What... what drove you to leave?" Shayra asked. Her emotions were a confusing tangle as her powers sensed the sincerity of not just his words, but his thoughts. Something was off in all of this—something was false. But it was not Narred.

"The twins. I warned you that I could watch your precious investiture happen no longer, and I made ready to leave. That is all!" Narred exclaimed.

Shayra felt his static shield tense—he was keeping something from her.

"Tell me the whole truth," she demanded coldly. She had to keep control of her emotions—she had no choice.

"You... you don't know?" Narred asked, confused. "What happened? What did they do to you?"

"Tell me the whole truth," Shayra repeated.

"The brothers, Jaes and Urellus. They were part of a cover-up, of a massive destruction of memories that affected thousands of people. The thing you swore was against everything your people believed in—they did it on a grand, horrible scale. You honestly don't remember this?" Narred pushed up against the crystal wall of his cell, separated from Shayra by only an inch of the blue-tinged material. "They did it to you too, didn't they?"

"I..." Shayra began. She could not find words. Narred's explanation rang true, to his mind but also to hers. Thoughts careened about inside her head, her orderly mind suddenly thrust into disorder. The gaps and spaces in her memory, places that had been imperfectly filled with explanations from the Kem, stood revealed for what they were. Narred's truth better fit those holes, but in the piecing of these fragments together, something broke. She felt it within her, a gnawing, wild scrambling. Her sanity was a tapestry, and this conversation had yanked at a broken threat in its edge. The more she pulled upon the thread, the more everything came unraveled around her.

"Let me out. Let me help you," Narred said. "Please, my love."

Shayra, still reeling, reached for the door of the cell and fitted several keys from the ring to the door before she found one that fit. With a sharp click, the lock came undone, and Narred pulled the door open. He rushed out and took Shayra in a tight embrace, and she felt comforted by him—but only barely. Her mind was a thing of chaos, and she did not know how to quiet it.

"I promise to get us help," Narred said. As he held her tightly with one arm, his other lifted up into the air, fingers splayed wide, and Shayra felt the electric tingle in the air of Vol transmissions being sent. "If they were willing to tamper with your mind, to distort your memories and fill your head with lies, they'll stop at nothing to protect their secrets. We have to run."

¤~¤~¤

Gendric collapsed into the cot he had set up in the back of the commissary building of Vol Nought. He was exhausted, could barely see straight, and wanted nothing more than a few hours of uninterrupted sleep.

The past weeks had not gone well, and every hour brought new crises to his attention. This secret hiding place was juvenile—he had in fact once hidden here as a child after running away from home following a fight with his mother—but it afforded him the chance to collect himself.

The south was far worse off than anyone could understand. It wasn't just the depredations of the warlord Gollus—it was the horrible events unfolding even now in Weldaf Holc. But things were happening so quickly, there was no opportunity to gather with the Council and pass on anything more than snippets of intelligence. His Vol forces stationed at the other Council cities were kept busy by the Dukes, coordinating communications as the world reeled from the destruction of Igar Holc.

Gendric closed his eyes.

In that brief, tenuous moment of calm, a transmission radiated across his senses, not because of its power but because of its specificity. This was a signal from someone he had been hunting for for quite some time, and it was addressed directly to Gendric in its coding.

Without bothering to move, he lifted one hand and caught the signal with his boltsending arts. As the words translated into his mind, he could scarcely believe what he was hearing.

"Gendric Tharsicast, Leader of the Vols, you know who this is. I wish to surrender myself to you—in person. I have information you will desire, and I wish to be taken into your personal custody."

Gendric sat upright despite his body's protests. That was a transmission from Narred—Narred who had been in hiding for nearly two years since Gendric bested him in single combat in the streets of Rega Holc.

He called upon the most delicate of his arts and disassembled the signal, peeling it apart layer by layer, tracing its course through the world by feeling the unique echo of each Bindmetal repeater that the signal traveled through. It took nearly four minutes, but he found it—the signal had originated from Norwin Holc.

Now the real problem began. How was he to get there? Norwin Holc was more than half a world away, and Nenasha, like most of the Raks, was trapped north of the ruins of Igar Holc by the perpetual storm still raging across the land bridge.

He had to sleep. As much as his mind was racing, he could do nothing more tonight. In the morning, he would set a plan into motion. Even if he had to walk the entire way by himself, he would capture the man who betrayed his mother. Gendric found it hard to believe that Narred had any information that would matter—this was surely a ploy to try and save his own traitorous neck. It wouldn't work.

¤~¤~¤

Duchess Ain had regained her composure, although the amount of time it took would have greatly disappointed her mother, who had stressed propriety above all else when she was a girl. She sat on a new bench she had ordered delivered to the guest house garden, wearing peasant's clothes. She was doing her best to project humility, but all she felt was humiliation.

She had been outsmarted by a child, a housewife, and a librarian. But in spite of everything, she knew that the dangers presenting themselves in this world, dangers that threatened not just her people, but all the people of Onus, required sacrifice. She had been ready and willing to sacrifice the lives of her soldiers and her subjects, or the lives of her hostages. She sacrificed the coins in her coffers and the treasures in her vaults. Why was it so much harder for her to elect to sacrifice her pride?

Hessa and Moultus entered the garden, unaccompanied by guards, and the duchess gestured to the bench sitting opposite of her. It was a nicer bench than her own, larger, more ornate, and it was placed upon stone blocks in such a way that it was raised a few inches taller than hers. The positioning was deliberate—calculated to send the message she knew her tongue would not easily convey. She was admitting defeat in what small ways she could stomach.

"I expected to be brought here in irons," Moultus said as he and his daughter approached the bench.

"That would serve none of us well," Duchess Ain replied. She gestured to the bench and asked, "Would you care to have a seat?"

Hessa eyes both the bench and the duchess suspiciously, but she took a seat and her father soon joined her. They stared at the duchess.

"Grell has escaped," Ain said. "You... were there when it happened, were you not, Moultus?"

The old man nodded.

"I find it difficult to believe that he is still in Ain Holc, even though my guard captains assure me they would have caught him if he tried to leave. He has means of travel they cannot detect, as you both know. And, surely, he is now traveling the same course that my men, and Jara, follow." The Duchess folded her hands in her lap slowly, deliberately.

"I sense a threat coming," Hessa replied.

"No threats. You were right to push back upon my behavior. I... I do not often ask for things. Perhaps it is a consequence of my upbringing, or my title. But I should have. I should have asked for your help instead of attempting to extort it. You are owed that much, and more, as a citizen of Council lands." Ain felt these bitter words upon her tongue, but she forced them out.

Moultus coughed to clear his throat and asked, "What are you asking us for, then?"

"I want to save Jara, and my men. I want to stop Grell, once and for all—and to learn what this is all about. To do these things, I need to get to the Vale of Steam, and I need to do so with a sizable force of men. The few Raks still in my service are unable to move so many people. I need a Gar." The duchess leaned forward, wringing her hands now. "Can you help me, Hessa? Can you make a Gatemaker of one of my men?"

Hessa shook her head. "I'm sorry, but I can't."

"Your daughter's life hangs in the balance!" Duchess Ain said, her composure faltering. "You would choose to do nothing to help her?"

"I do not *choose* this," Hessa said, her words quiet and laden with emotion. "I chose none of this. And I no longer possess the power."

"What?" the duchess demanded. "But, I know of your abilities. As I told you, I have witnesses that..."

"I'm not that woman anymore," Hessa said. "And I can't become her again. Those powers are bound up in the trauma I experienced at the hands of Hyrak's torturers, and those pieces of me have been swept away. I can... I can suppress magic, though not perfectly. But I can no longer write new magic into a person's destiny."

"The coin," the duchess said, leaning against the back of her bench. "Can you not simply remove it?"

"No!" Moultus said. "I do not believe you would survive the change, my dear. The damage done to you, the scars the coin protects you from, are deeper than anyone should ever be expected to survive."

Duchess Ain stood, taking momentary comfort in once more being positioned above these people. "Is there nothing you can do? You are a Wyr, can you at least offer me some snippet of prophecy to point me in the right direction? Is it too late, or may I still find a way to stop the pirate?"

Hessa held up both hands, frustration writ large across her face. "I cannot. That was never a gift of mine."

"It is the birthright of all Fatewakers! You truly are defective, you foolish woman. And as much as I need her, I hope... I hope that your daughter does perish at that lunatic's hands. I would have your dreams haunted by your utter uselessness for the rest of your pitiful, homeless days!" The duchess spun on her heel to storm out. This had all been a great waste of time.

But the scrawny scribe stood up, grabbing hold of her wrist as though she were some common woman, and he pulled her to a halt, waving the index finger of his other finger in her face. "Now you listen! I have had my fill of you! You are no noble! I have served in the courts of Rega and Distat, of Herin and Igar, and I assure you, you are not one-tenth the man they are!"

"I am not a man, you oaf," the duchess shrieked.

"Nor are you much of a woman, your grace," Moultus continued. "I have known the duchesses of the north to be intelligent and wise, scholars and defenders in equal measure. I would not list you in the company of such great women simply because you married a man with a palace. You have ruled here long enough to have learned the truths written in Council law, but you show time and time again signs that you think that even learning is beneath you. It is not!"

Moultus gave the duchess a shove and she found herself pushed back onto her bench. "Not all Wyr have the power to see the threads of the Purpose alone. They are Fatewakers, not Fortune Tellers! Most command the gifts my Hessa once possessed, but you are right, many do see beyond the moment, and often do so better when they work in concert with one another. It is a subtle art, secretive and capricious, and yet you seem to think it something to be drawn upon like water from a well. My granddaughter sees the secrets between worlds more clearly than my beloved wife saw the moments beyond tomorrow, and you squandered that gift with demands about military movements and battle strategies. If only the Purpose would save me from foolish, ignorant monarchs!"

Moultus turned to Hessa and extended his hand to her. "Come, my daughter, whom I have loved when we believed no magic stirred in you as much as I love you now that only its embers remain. We are leaving this city to the fate its mistress has so richly earned it. It takes no mystic insight to foresee the future for this deplorable woman."

¤~¤~¤

Grell pushed harder than ever before as he raced between the thick trunks of trees in the Vale of Steam. He was close—everything he had ever known and every dream he had ever dreamt pointed him to this destiny. The place on the map was close by, and the answers he had longed for his entire life would be found.

As he hacked at the tangled vines that barred his way with a heavy hand axe, Grell remembered his father's tales. His mother, Doruka, had been a mighty Jov and a ferocious warrior. While she carried Grell in her womb, she had been ordered by the Council to carry out some dark deed. They had forced her to come to this place, threatening the life of her husband and her unborn child, but Doruka was clever. She did as they asked, but not precisely *how* they asked. She knew they would never allow her to live, knowing what she knew, so she found a way to defy them. They ran her through when the deed was done—unknowing that she had somehow tricked them—and with her last breaths she used a transportation hob, like those Grell had used to make it to the Vale, to return to her husband, hidden away on a boat in the Endless Sea.

As she died, Grell's father listened to her tell this tale—empty of details so that he would not become a target of Council retribution—and then Grell's father cut Grell's tiny form from his mother's dying body...

That was when the dragon Candara discovered their boat drifting into her territory. And the dragon had taken one look at the mewling baby and said to Grell's father, "I will allow you to live. I... would see this one grow to manhood. I would see what wonders this one brings into the world. Bring him back to me each year, on this day, so that I may see if this bargain remains wise."

Grell hacked at another tightly snarled patch of vines. He had seen the dragon every year, even after his father had died. Never had the dragon spoken to him, of course—in all these years, it had only spoken the once, to his father... and there were days that Grell doubted that his father had told him the truth. Grell had asked his father often for more, but he knew little. He believed that the secret involved the southern stretch of the Silent Sea—and that was all he would ever say.

Even if he did not always believe his father, Grell knew that he did indeed have a special destiny, and a Purpose—and that Purpose lay just ahead.

The last barrier between him and his quarry fell, and Grell stepped into a massive clearing of cool, polished stone to see a gigantic stone monster rearing back to strike at the Fatewaker girl—Jara.

As Grell's foot touched the clearing, he felt a ripple of energy burst from his body, a shockwave of sound that flowed out of him and through the stone until it reached the rock creature. The creature seemed to freeze, unmoving and no longer bearing down upon the girl.

All around the battle he could see the scattered, and often broken, forms of the soldiers from Ain Holc that had accompanied the girl. And there were children, huddled together, a hundred yards from the center, whimpering.

Grell strolled towards the creature, but before he engaged with it, he offered a hand to the girl. "I owe you a debt, Wyr. Without you, I may have not found this place."

Jara took his hand reluctantly, and Grell hauled her easily to her feet. He looked around and the few soldiers still drawing breath. "I will offer you my protection, child. I am about to learn a secret, and I would think the presence of a Wyr will lend veracity to my claims when I lay them before the people of Onus and reveal the evil of their so-called nobility."

"Get on with it," Jara said.

Grell turned to the creature, and as he looked carefully upon it, he knew what it was called—it was a golem, a construct of animated stone given life by the magic of...

Of his mother.

He reached towards it, and the creature lowered itself to the ground, prostrating itself before him. Grell extended both hands and laid them on either side of the elongated, rectangular fire opal that served as the creature's head. As his hands gripped hold, his heart began to race. He could hear sounds, feel the beating rhythm of the very world below his feet. And he could feel the echoes of magic wrought in this place in years past, back to his mother, standing in this place...

Grell could feel the truth.

# 34

## Murrod

Becky sat on the rooftop of the Monarka safe house. She clutched her knees tightly to her chest and rocked, very slowly, as she watched the impenetrable cloud of ash overhead shift and spread and churn. It was an apt metaphor for how she felt inside.

"You up for some company?" Steven asked, pulling himself out of the window to join Becky on the ledge overlooking the city below. There was panic in the streets—men running, screaming, everywhere. She heard an Ellir howl and, almost immediately, another round of screaming.

"I'll take that as a yes," Steven said, sliding up close to Becky. "How are you doing?"

"My boyfriend was just abducted and brainwashed by the single most evil bastard we have ever met," Becky said, her tone dripping acid.

"I was there," Steven said.

"That sure did a lot of good, didn't it?" Becky asked.

"Hey," Steven said, holding up his hands defensively, "I'm trying to help. You know that if there was anything I could have done to stop that, I would have. Everything happened so fast."

Becky sighed, barely holding back a sob. She didn't want to cry. She wanted to fix this, not to bemoan it. But here they were, holed up in this stupid house, sitting around, doing nothing. "Have the others decided what we're going to do next to get him back?"

Steven nodded. "Two teams. Mathias, Todd, and Adam are going to get us the meeting Reid was setting up with this Chron dragon thing. Yors and I are going to stay here with you."

"Because I need a babysitter now?" Becky asked, her anger spiking again.

"No," Steven said. "Because we understand what it's like to lose the people we are closest to." He reached out and wrapped his arm around Becky, pulling her into a side hug.

For more than a year, she had thrilled at the touch, at the closeness of Steven. It was a secret joy, a kind of spiritual fire that was stoked just by being near him. They had even, in their thoughts, grown closer. But now, sitting here with the gaping wound of her severed connection to JC still yawning wide and ugly in her mind, the gesture left her cold.

She pushed Steven away. "Don't. I don't... I don't want that."

"It's a hug," Steven said, hurt. "Friends do that for each other."

Becky closed her eyes. "I know. I do. I just... I don't have it together right now. He's gone. I... I love him, Steven. I can't let this happen to him. I have to save him. No matter what."

"We will," Steven said. "This isn't over yet. Yors is working, right now, on what our options are, as far as the Bindmetal that they used to do this to JC. But you have to promise me that, whatever we do, we do it together. You cannot run off on your own to save him."

"That's what he would do, for me. It's what he *did* do, when I was taken hostage by Ahmur. He saved me, all by himself. He... he went and got that damn fool collar around his neck and then he ran into the woods and jumped on a burning pile of logs and saved me. He..." she put one hand over her mouth as thoughts connected and collided in her mind. "He only ever got the collar for me. And now, because of that thing—because of me—he's gone. Lost."

"JC is more than just a guy who loves you, Becky. And you are more than just a girl, a young woman, who loves him. Don't simplify people like that. People are complicated. His feelings for you, yours for him, and all of the things you have done to, and for, and because of each other... they are not so easy to boil down to causes and effects. Love makes us greater than the sum of our parts, I think." Steven patted her on the knee. "Somewhere, deep inside of him, behind the magic metal junk, he's still himself. When the time comes, that will be what saves him—he'll save himself. And if I had to guess, I'd say that the reason he'll save himself is you. Think of yourself that way, Becky. You aren't the reason he's lost—you're the reason he'll be found."

¤~¤~¤

Todd and Mathias took the lead while Adam brought up the rear of their tightly-spaced group. They pushed through the city and already the impact of Hyrak's scheme was apparent. The streets were crowded with men, whereas before, nighttime brought a degree of peace to the city. There were few lights on—candles were kept low or extinguished by those indoors, hoping to hide from what they feared would be outside.

The noise was the worst—every few moments, someone would shout or scream. Adam was confident it was not yet as bad as it would soon be. It was truly night time now, not just the darkness brought on by the ash cloud, and people would retire to bed eventually.

But there was little time to waste if he and his friends were to put a stop to whatever Hyrak's next move was. They had to get to Chron, and Mathias insisted the best way to do that was through the channels that Reid had already established upon their initial arrival. So they pressed through the busy, chaotic streets on their way to the Joint Ministry Complex.

Adam thought of several ways to jumpstart a conversation as they walked briskly down the streets, but nothing felt appropriate. Joe was gone, the course of this world had been irrevocably shifted, and now... now he questioned if stopping Hyrak was even within their power.

"There," Mathias said, pointing at a massive building, larger than any palace Adam had seen on Onus, with a number of large towers, each emblazoned with a banner representing the ministry contained therein. "One of Reid's aides should have the information we need about the time and location of the meeting with Chron."

If there had been any security stationed around the building, it was long gone—either put to work quelling the riots in the city or, more likely, suddenly out patrolling for the imminent Ellir incursion.

Todd shoved open the doors atop the short flight of steps leading to entrance of the Ministry of Security tower, and inside, candles were lit in abundance. Mathias took the lead again, up a curving flight of stairs to a complex of offices where people still bustled about. "Underministers," Mathias said by way of explanation. Adam nodded. If there was one thing he was sure Greendeep had no shortage of, it was bureaucracy.

They approached Reid's personal office, and as Mathias and Todd pushed open the double doors, they saw someone sitting at his desk, feet up on the surface and a large, half-full bottle of wine in hand.

"What is the meaning of this?" he said, sitting upright and sputtering. The man was thin and almost sickly looking, with a balding head and a weak chin. He wore dark robes.

"Chaplain Voss," Mathias said. "How... unexpected."

"Do I know you?" the man asked. He squinted at Mathias, then at Adam, then stopped and took a long, hard—almost hungry—look at Todd.

"Yes," Mathias said. He turned to Todd and asked, "Can you hold the doors?"

Todd nodded and smiled, and that was all the cue Mathias needed as he charged towards the desk, drawing his sword in a smooth motion and placing it up against Voss' throat.

"My name is Mathias of Imperia. Does that name sound familiar?" he demanded.

"No," the minister stammered. "Not particularly. But I work with a lot of names. I am the Minister of Incarnation, you know."

"I know who you are!" Mathias shouted, pressing closer with the sword and drawing a narrow line of blood from the minister's pale flesh. "The last time we saw each other, Chaplain Reid had me on a rack. Torturing me. And then you—"

"Your papers!" Chaplain Voss exclaimed. "You were the one we destroyed the documents on!"

"Glad to know I made an impression," Mathias said sourly.

"Mathias," Adam said cautiously. They had little time to deal with the consequences that would follow if the minister raised an alarm.

"We were working with Chaplain Reid to arrange a meeting with Chron," Mathias explained. "Did you happen to hear anything of that while you were making yourself at home in this office?"

Chaplain Voss smiled nervously. "That, er... that meeting was canceled. Chaplain Reid perished a few hours ago, and so his departmental rights were transferred to the new Minister of Security. He and I are, um... we are close, you could say."

"How did you know Reid died?" Todd asked from beside the doors.

"I know when everyone dies," Voss said, a trace of confidence winning out over his quavering fear. "It's one of my jobs. I get reports from Chron himself every hour."

"That must be a lot to keep straight," Mathias said. "Lots of paperwork."

"It isn't so bad," Voss said. "I have a wonderful memory—it is one of the requirements of my post. Almost anything I hear or read stays up in my head, somewhere."

"Aren't you special," Adam said, drawing closer to where Mathias had the minister pinned to his chair. "We need to see Chron, right away. Can you make that happen? Are you *that* special?"

"Think carefully before you answer that question," Mathias said, leaning in closer and causing his sword to bite even deeper into the minster's throat.

Heavy pounding started at the door. "Go away," Todd muttered as he braced himself against both doors.

"Yes," Chaplain Voss said. "I can get you in to see his greatness. If it prevents my death, I am happy to oblige."

"That's all I need to know," Adam said. He pointed to the wall of the office and wove a tight green crossgate. Mathias ushered Voss up and through the gate, and then Todd darted away from the doors. As he ran into the portal, Adam turned back to see the doors burst inward and a trio of the knights of Murrod—he had no knowledge of how one told the different branches apart—run inside, weapons ready. Adam stepped through the portal and slammed it closed behind him.

¤~¤~¤

Adam's next crossgate opened exactly where Chaplain Voss told him to go. As the gate disappeared behind them, Yors took stock of their surroundings. They were outside of Monarka—he could see the lamplights of the city boundaries to the east, barely. To the west, amid a series of low foothills, he could see a Spiralgate—but that was not their destination.

They were on a large plain out front of a low hill of solid stone—a foothill to the nearby Greytall Mountains. There was little vegetation here, as the dense forests and jungles of Greendeep were all more to the south of their location.

Cautiously the group pressed towards the hill and the large round doorway of iron bars that sat squarely in its lower center. Mathias escorted their new guest, Voss, at the front of the party, and Yors brought up the rear. He could not bear to look Becky in the eye as they walked, and he was quite sure he had said nothing in hours. He was shamed—not just of his failure, which was grievous enough, but of what he had become. He had lost his way, as so many other Jovs had over the years... but after all he had endured, for it to come now, for him to lose the harmonious balance required for the true pinnacle of Jov magic, was an utter failure of his people, himself... and those he had lost, whose memories were, at times, all that kept him going.

He felt unworthy to carry the hammer of Arctos, especially since the hammer of Murrod had outright refused his call. His feelings of inadequacy were not merely suspicions, they were facts. He had failed.

He sullenly turned back towards where the crossgate had opened and noticed something curious. They had crossed nearly fifty yards and were nearly to the threshold of the hill gate, but the course they had taken was haphazard—their tracks were a messy tangle of zigzags and sidesteps. Why was that?

Yors grunted, "Becky."

She stopped and turned back to him, her gaze icy and no less than he deserved. "What?"

"Yors thinks something wrong here." He pointed to the tracks.

Becky sighed and took a few steps back to stand next to Yors, kneeling down to examine what he was pointing at. "They're footprints. What's the big deal?" Then she muttered, "Wait. Something is... out here."

She held up both hands, and a faint nimbus of blue light played across the air between them. Yors heard her draw in a sharp breath and then she brought her hands down in a sharp chopping motion.

In that instant, the plain before the hill was suddenly crawling with enemy forces. There were dozens of Ellir by Yors' quick estimation, all standing in even, orderly rows. Well over a hundred women in the ornamental masks of Goldvast were interspersed among the Ellir, their numbers much harder to discern. In the midst of this small but potent army was a black dragon, coiled and resting on the ground. A few others, including a handful of men, were near the dragon's head as it lay upon the grassy plain.

Before Yors could say a single word, the dragon's eyes lit with brilliant white light and its head reared up. "We are discovered!" it's voice called out in the minds of all before it... including Yors, Becky, and the others, who were just now turning to see what the commotion was about.

"That was a really big invisibility shield," Becky said. "I... should probably not have pulled it down."

"You have got to be kidding me," Adam said. He looked at Yors and asked, "Can you bring up another one of those defensive walls, Yors?"

Yors shook his head. He didn't know if he could. He didn't know if the hammer would even respond to him at all anymore.

"Then we'll do it my way. Mathias, get the Minister of Incarnation's ass in gear and get that door open!" Adam called. He lifted both his hands and started to move them through the air in intricate patterns. Yors could feel a tightening in the space around them and knew Adam must be creating another of his barriers. Yors couldn't remember precisely what they were called—it was one more thing at which he was proving to be a failure.

"Wait!" called a voice, deep and loud, from near the dragon.

The initial mobilization of the Ellir and women mustered around the dragon came to an abrupt halt, then the forces began to pull back, parting to make room for one man. An old man walked, leaning heavily upon a staff. His long gray hair was combed back straight down his back, leaving his face clearly visible, and it was a face hard to forget. He had no eyes, and Yors remembered his name from the Metalbreaker escape from Murrod—this was Embrew.

Adam's reaction was more pronounced. With a dismissive gesture, the barrier he had been constructing with his magic came down and the Gatemaker ran towards the old man. In turn, the old man quickened his pace and his lips curled into a warm smile. They met close enough to Yors and Becky that their words could be heard.

"Embrew!" Adam shouted, embracing the elder Gar.

"Adam," Embrew said. "I did not expect to find you here."

"You... Mathias said you were alive, but I didn't know where to look for you," Adam explained. "How did you come to be here, and with all of these people? And the dragon?"

"It is not a short tale," Embrew said. "But we are here to help. We have been waiting to head Hyrak off, by surprise... but that may no longer be an option."

"Sorry!" Becky shouted, still standing beside Yors.

Embrew bowed his head and said, "Much has changed since last we met. I will tell you all I know. But let us draw nearer the nursery. Ehbor does not enjoy the company of strangers, and it is best not to aggravate the dragon that controls the majority of the Ellir on this world."

They walked a bit closer to the gate, where Voss was exchanging passwords with a guard on the other side of the metal bars, and Yors did not follow. He cared little for whatever else was being said—he had heard all he needed to. This place was the nursery. This was where he would claim his vengeance for the murder of his family and the thirty years of torment the Jovs endured.

His regrets and his fears and his worries melted away in the heat of his rage. But he kept it inside, concealed. This was not the moment. Soon. Very soon.

¤~¤~¤

Adam and Becky were still meeting with Embrew outside when Chaplain Voss showed the rest into the antechamber inside where they would wait for

Chron to see them. Yors sat quietly in the corner, and Steven paced anxiously, but Mathias could not bring himself to wait quietly in this place.

The nursery of Greendeep was the place he had been born—it was the place they had all been born; every single man on this world could trace his roots to this massive complex. But he remembered virtually nothing of his time here. Flashes of memory, of learning and playing, occasionally surfaced, but never a coherent string of events.

And this was the place where the dead were reborn, reincarnated into new lives and raised away from the world until their twentieth year, when they were returned to the outside world and given twenty years as adults to make their way in the world and better their station before the cycle began anew.

"I'm going to walk around," Mathias said.

Chaplain Voss stood from where he had been sitting, quite quietly, next to the door. "No! That is not permitted. Only the highest ranking officials of the Ministry of Incarnation are permitted inside the nursery."

Before Mathias could retort, Todd slammed the minister back down into his seat. "My friend is taking a walk. You will shut up and let him do that," he stated.

Voss sputtered a bit, but said no more, and Mathias slipped out of the room. Todd followed him a moment later. "Can I join you?" he asked.

Mathias shrugged. "We're not likely to see anything very exciting, but I welcome the company."

They walked down the hallway, following its curves and twists deeper into the ground. There were only occasional rooms, and always they were configured like the waiting room—small offices or other holding areas. The real work of the nursery surely happened lower in the complex.

"I wanted to tell you, personally, how sorry I am about Jonas," Todd said after ten minutes of walking in silence—never once running into another person.

"Thank you," Mathias said. "But you have nothing to apologize for. It's not your fault he's dead."

Todd replied hastily, "I meant I am sorry that you weren't told. I can take some blame for that. Adam's been pretty distracted for quite some time, and I think we both know that I have an awful lot to do with that. I owed you better than that."

"You forgot me," Mathias said. "It's why I left in the first place. I never belonged in your world. Or his."

"Jonas'?" Todd asked, arching an eyebrow.

"You know damn well what I mean," Mathias said. "We're adults. But I came back here, back home, because I thought it was best. I stand by that. But I wish I had been able to properly say good-bye to Jonas. That... that I regret very much."

They walked a bit further in silence, and then came to the end of the corridor. It ended abruptly, in a smooth, flat wall. Mathias walked up to the wall and ran one hand along its surface. "This is strange."

"If this place is some kind of nursery, it's very short on babies," Todd said.

"Exactly," Mathias said. He continued to probe the wall, and after a few seconds he found a place where the surface of the wall was not quite flush with the rest of the structure. He pressed on that small section and it yielded to his touch with a soft click. "Help me push," he said. Todd joined him, and they pushed the heavy wall, now freed from its locking mechanism, as it pivoted on an unseen central axis, leaving room for the two of them to slip past it.

They stood in a massive chamber, mostly dark, filled with glass tubs. There were thousands of the tubs, packed tightly in long rows stretching as far as he could see, and each filled with a faintly luminous yellow liquid. "What in Chron's name?" Mathias asked. He crept up to the nearest tub. It was covered by a glass lid, and the whole container was fogged over. He wiped away the condensation on the side of the tub and saw, floating in the liquid, a man.

"There are no other doors out of here," Todd observed, looking around as Mathias peered into a few other tubs. "This is the whole nursery, Mathias."

Mathias said nothing, growing more frantic as he looked through the tubs, trying to find some manner of organization, some system of indexing, that he could use to find who he was looking for. If this was where the reborn were reborn, then he would be here—Norrun would be here, somewhere.

"You are not supposed to be here," a voice rumbled from above them.

Mathias looked up and saw, clinging to the ceiling of the huge room, the mighty golden form of the dragon-god Chron.

"I just want to see my friend," Mathias said reverently. He was actually in the presence of Chron. The enormity of that had not sunk in when they had been making these arrangements, but now, here he was. Mathias had been raised to believe Chron was the creator of all mankind—the most important being in the universe. While at least some of that was a lie... there was no shaking the ingrained sense of deference that Mathias felt towards the giant dragon above him.

Seemingly at home upside down on the ceiling, Chron replied in his deep, rumbling voice, "Who do you seek?"

"He was called Norrun in his most recent life," Mathias said.

"Seventy-third row, sixty-sixth position," the dragon stated. "Your companion is not from this world. Are you the ones who wished to speak to me about the man called Hyrak?"

Todd touched Mathias on the shoulder and whispered, "I've got this. Go find your friend."

Mathias nodded gratefully and took off at a run, counting rows and positions as he ran. He could hear the sound of Todd and Chron's conversation carrying clearly through the chamber as he ran.

"You are perceptive. I am not from Murrod. I travel with a group that seeks to stop Hyrak, great one," Todd explained.

"I am not my brother or my sister," Chron said sharply, "I require no flattery. Speak plainly. I have much to do."

Mathias reached the right position—as best as he could tell, for nothing was labeled or marked in any way—and wiped away the fog on the tank. He drew in a deep breath before looking, afraid of what he would see. With equal parts fear and hope, he peered in and saw... Chaplain Voss.

"Voss? But... Voss is alive..." Mathias muttered.

"You are in the wrong row, Mathias," the dragon roared. "Details matter."

Struggling with what he had seen, Mathias slid over one row and looked through the thick glass and glowing liquid to see the tall, flatly-muscled shape of his friend Norrun. He was younger than Mathias remembered him—barely twenty years of age. He was sleeping, as had been everyone in the tanks Mathias had examined, and he looked to be at peace.

"He's not a child," Mathias said. Then, more loudly, he shouted, "None of them are children!"

"Of course not," Chron said with a note of amusement.

"If men are reborn fully grown, why do we wait so long to go back out into the world?" Mathias asked. "And why do I remember being a child?"

"Do you? Do you really?" the dragon asked. Chron shifted a bit and then, in a burst of movement, dropped from the ceiling, spreading his great golden wings out to catch him and slow his descent as he rippled and shifted, his body shrinking until it landed on two feet upon the ground next to Mathias. Chron had assumed the form of a man—a perfect man with golden skin and white-gold hair; a man who Mathias' heart ached simply to look upon.

Somewhere behind him, he heard Todd running towards him, but Mathias felt no fear.

"I give everyone pleasant dreams to pass the time," Chron said, tapping on Norrun's tub.

"Does... does he dream of me?" Mathias asked.

"No," Chron replied. The dragon-god's human features betrayed a sort of confusion. "Why would he?"

"He had affection for me in his previous life," Mathias said. "I thought maybe that stayed with him..."

"That is not possible," Chron said. "This Norrun never knew you."

Mathias tried to wrap his head around that as Todd caught up to them. Mathias held a hand up to Todd, indicating that everything was alright, and Todd remained a few yards away, watching Chron like a hawk.

"Why the delay?" Mathias asked.

"So that those who knew him before will forget. It is easier this way." Chron said.

"How is it possible that Chaplain Voss is here, in one of these tanks, and also out there with my friends?" Mathias asked.

"You ask many questions," Chron said. "I grow tired of answering them."

"Please!" Mathias asked. "I have to know!"

"You already know," Chron said. "Do not waste my time demanding answers you have already deduced for yourself."

The dragon was right. Mathias had the sick feeling that he did understand—that everything he had been told of the cycle of life and rebirth in Greendeep was both true and very, very false.

"The Voss out there is copy, isn't he?" Mathias asked. "A copy of the one here, the... the original?"

Chron nodded. "An elegant solution to the reproductive problems of your civilization, but a taxing one. I spend the vast majority of my time, and my power, in crafting these copies. They are imperfect—they last only two short decades."

"That's why Reid was falling apart so quickly," Todd said.

"One more question," Mathias said. "Just one more, and I will stop."

"Very well," Chron said. "But if you ask it, you must live with its answer."

"Can I see me?" Mathias asked. "The... the original of me. Can I see him?"

Chron shook his head. "No."

"Why not?" Mathias asked. He knew why. But he couldn't accept it. The dragon was right. Now that the question was asked, he had to live with knowing the answer.

"Your original was ordered destroyed by Chaplains Reid and Voss. They believed you to be unstable—a danger to all of Greendeep. It is rare that such a thing is done, but I trust my ministers to make such determinations. Men must live governed by their own kind, if they are to live at all. This is, I suppose, the reason I differ so much from my siblings. When we were first brought to this world, we... could not agree on that matter. And now here we are." Chron cocked his head. "It is time to meet with your friends, Mathias of Imperia. Shall we go?"

Mathias nodded numbly and followed Chron towards the chamber door. In his mind's eye, he saw a single event happening over and over again, a memory trapped in some kind of perpetual state of repetition. He saw his incarnation records being shredded in the torture chamber beneath the Ministry of Security in Imperia. He saw, what he now knew to be, the order being given to destroy his body here in the nursery.

"I've only twenty years," Mathias said. "And everyone else has forever."

"Not at all true," Chron said. "You have only twelve remaining."

Todd, from behind him, said, "But Mathias is like twenty-three. Maybe twenty-four?"

"Mathias does not have a full twenty years. This last process of copying him from the original was flawed—some imperfection arose in the process that I have not yet discerned. Trust me—I am never wrong about such things." The dragon did not even look back at Mathias as it pronounced his death sentence.

"What kind of imperfection?" Mathias asked. "What does that mean?"

"It is curious," Chron said. "I have never had such a problem before."

They continued walking in silence. Mathias could think of nothing to say. What was he supposed to say to his creator after receiving such news? Twelve years. It was no time at all.

"Go on, your greatness," Mathias said as they entered the main tunnel through the pivoting secret door. "I will... I will catch up."

Chron continued on without comment, but Todd did not. Once the dragon passed beyond the curve of the hallway, Mathias turned to the wall and began to beat his fists upon it. He struck again and again and tears flowed down his cheeks. His stomach churned. His lungs tightened, as though there was not enough air in all the world to fill them up again.

"It isn't fair!" he wailed.

Todd took him in an awkward embrace, whispering, "I know. I know."

¤~¤~¤

The war council met outside of the nursery gates. Steven was surprised he made the cut to be invited—he had been waiting with Chaplain Voss and Yors inside when suddenly Becky's voice called into his mind to get outside.

And immediately in front of the gate, there stood not one but two dragons.

"Ehbor is the black one," Becky explained in his mind as he took position near her and Adam. "Chron is the gold one. The other people by Ehbor, with Embrew, are Plyssa and Tyrick and Sky—they're the ones that convinced those women down there to turn against Ahmur."

"That's the white dragon?" Steven asked.

Becky nodded and her mental explanations stopped, so Steven turned his attention back to the conversation happening in front of him.

"The fool has made my work easy," Ehbor said. "His blotting out of the suns will give my Ellir their fullest strength. He has stolen command of at most one hundred of them, while thousands answer to my command."

"But he possesses our sister," Chron said. "You are certain of this?"

"We've seen it," Becky said. Both dragons turned to look at her, and Steven was surprised to see that neither looked especially perturbed. Becky was apparently semi-accustomed to chatting up these kinds of creatures, which Steven definitely did find perturbing, himself. "Ahmur was not herself—she was defending Hyrak."

"Perhaps it was a willing alliance? Our sister is a clever schemer," Chron offered.

"She didn't talk," Becky said. "She loves the sound of her own voice, and she didn't say one word the entire time Steven fought with her."

The woman in the snake mask next to Embrew said, "She's right. Our goddess does indeed like the sound of her own voice."

Chron seemed to chew on that for a moment and then replied, "It would take clever sorcery to command one of our kind."

"And it is sorcery he possesses in supply enough to take us both!" Ehbor said. "He attempted to take me, but I was too quick for him. He will be coming for you—for us—I am certain of it. Men like him do not settle for an incomplete collection."

"And I will be trophy to no man," Chron said grimly. "I will send word to my new Minister of Security in Monarka. I will have every knight in Greendeep rushed here to aid in my defense. You, my brother, call for your Ellir. With the help of these outsiders, and the daughters of Ahmur that have seen the truth of things, we will be a match for Hyrak, our sister, and whatever meager forces they possess."

"About that," Adam said nervously. Steven was relieved to see that at least one of them wasn't a seasoned dragon negotiator. "One of the forces he possesses is a friend of ours—a friend that we very much want to see rescued. He's been captured much like Ahmur, I think—his mind is not his own right now. I just need to know that your forces won't hurt him."

Ehbor looked down at Adam and snarled, "One human is not worth the shifting of our stratagems."

"He is to us," Becky said, stepping forward with her hands balled into fists.

"Very well," Chron said. "Ehbor, you have never learned how to properly deal with the humans."

"You coddle them," Ehbor hissed. "I eat them. That you think your way more appetizing than mine is why we have never gotten along."

Steven summoned his courage to calm his nerves and asked, "Do we have any weapons that can take down the dragon? Nothing we have was particularly effective yesterday."

"We will face our sister," Chron said. "She must be subdued without being slain, and only we have the best chance of that."

"She could die," Ehbor said. "I have weighed the consequences many times over the years, and I once again lean towards favoring the implications of her death."

Chron suddenly spun, bringing his mighty tail around like a whip and cracking it across his slightly smaller brother's snout. Ehbor roared and scrambled back a few steps as the humans all around him scattered.

"That is not your decision to make!" Chron roared. "She lives. You live. I live. Had I been present when last you attempted to kill one another, I would have put a stop to this blasphemous line of thought then, but I shall make amends for my mistake now!"

"Guys," Becky said.

"You hold no sway over me, brother!" Ehbor roared.

"GUYS!" Becky shouted.

Both dragons swung their three-eyed heads towards Becky and snarled in verbal and telepathic unison, "What?"

"He's here," Becky said. "I can feel him. Hyrak is here. We're out of time."

# 35
## Murrod

*Chaos erupted all around them.* Tyrick watched as Hyrak flew overhead, standing upright astride his great white dragon. Clutched in the goddess of Goldvast's talons were several dozen Ellir, and they started to leap from her grasp, landing amidst the forces that Tyrick had helped to bring to this place. He could see no difference between the Ellir loyal to Ehbor and those loyal to Hyrak—they were all four-armed blue monsters to him—but Hyrak's Ellir seemed more focused upon engaging with the Goldvast warriors than their fellow Ellir.

One other figure leapt down from the dragon's back as it flew overhead—a young man carrying two swords and swinging them wildly as he careened towards the earth. He came down in the midst of a pack of the fierce warrior women that had been released from the prisons of Goldvast just for this occasion, but, miraculously, he appeared to be besting them.

Tyrick was not a warrior—he was a hunter on his best days, but mostly he was a surveyor—a watcher and a planner. There was no opportunity for planning here, though. Sky was beside him, fear and worry clear on his innocent features. Embrew was also close at hand, beside Plyssa, and Embrew's friends were springing to action. The dark-skinned young man and the handsome one with the red-gold hair had drawn swords and rushed to engage with the handful of Hyrak's Ellir that were approaching the dragons and the nursery gate, while the three that had been conversing with the dragon-gods remained nearby and still.

"Protect the dragons," the one called Adam shouted.

Tyrick thought the idea that he was somehow capable of defending a god from attack laughable, but he drew his hunting knife and kept his eyes overhead on the white dragon as it flew in wide circles.

"Do not go up there," the girl, Becky, demanded of the dragons. "He's trying to lure you out!"

"Together we are more than a match for her," Ehbor rumbled.

"Yes," Chron said.

"Wait," the tall man, whom Tyrick had not heard the name of, said. "There's something not quite right up there."

"There's no Bindmetal up there," Plyssa said. "I should be able to sense the bell around Ahmur's neck!"

Tyrick felt a stirring in the air, a blast of fetid breath upon his neck, and then he spun. His instincts drove him to action and he darted forward, knife ready. He plunged it up into the air above him. An instant later he was splashed by a fountain of bright red blood—blood issuing from a dagger wound in the sensitive underbelly of the dragon, Ahmur, who suddenly appeared before them, charging towards Chron.

"God damned mother fucking mindshaping bullshit!" Becky screamed.

Tyrick was knocked to the ground by the dragon's tail and felt himself suddenly being pulled away, sucked into the shadows upon the ground by the strong hands of the tall man as he whispered reassurances that the sickening feeling of discorporation Tyrick was experiencing was normal.

As the shadow swallowed him, Tyrick saw Hyrak stand and run up Ahmur's back and neck, leaping over her head and towards Chron. As he flew through the air, he slashed outward with his hand, unspooling a fine wire whip of metal that struck Chron and snaked around his neck with lightning speed. Strung along that wire was a tiny red Bindmetal bell.

A moment later Tyrick felt himself reappearing, several yards distant, behind a shimmering wall of distorted air that reacted to Adam and Embrew's uniform, side-by-side movements. On the other side of the wall two dragons stood, one on either side of Hyrak, both with eyes dulled from their usual glow and bells strung around their necks.

"We need to shut down those bells," the tall man said from beside Tyrick. "Where the hell is Yors?"

¤~¤~¤

Yors could hear the roaring of dragons and the sounds of battle outside. He knew that he belonged out there, helping—but he could not. He could not turn away from this birthplace of all his misery. The thirst for vengeance that writhed within him demanded action.

He walked farther down the sloped, spiraling corridor, hammer in hand. Even if the magic of the hammer would no longer answer his command, he would destroy this place. He would pull it apart one stone at a time with his bare hands if that was what the task required.

Then he paused. Something... something familiar was happening outside. He listened more closely, fighting against the rage in him for a moment of calm just sizable enough to allow him to make out the sounds of what was happening at the mouth of this corridor outside.

He heard singing.

He knew the song.

It wasn't possible—but it was true.

He turned away from the nursery and ran, his heart racing, towards the gate.

¤~¤~¤

The dragons were turning their back on Ehbor, blowing out gouts of flame upon the hundreds of figures fighting in the wide open space before them. Hyrak climbed back once more on Ahmur's back, and Plyssa couldn't bear to see her goddess used in such a way. It wasn't right.

Not far from her, Adam shouted, "Todd!"

She thought she saw the one called Todd in the path of the fire. She also saw many of her people blasted and burning, or besieged by savage Ellir, and she knew she had to do something.

She lifted her hands and tried to reach out to the metal in the bells that commanded these two proud, majestic creatures to bow to that madman. She could feel the bells, tiny though they were, and she willed them to break, to shatter at her command—but they did not. They were too far away, perhaps, or too well-made. So she would have to do things the other way—the way Sky had helped show her atop the Circle of the Heavens.

She started to hum, but the sound was insufficient amid the din of the battle and the roars of the dragons. So she, instead, started to sing her mother's lullaby. She had not sung it aloud in a very long time—but it brought her calm and peace... it brought her to her center. She reached out to the metal in the bells once more—but her working was blocked. Then she saw, huddled down tightly in the saddle atop Ahmur's back was a second passenger—a Metalbreaker. And no matter how talented Plyssa was, he was better.

"Damn it!" she shouted, cutting off the song. It was no use. She turned around to see what the others were doing, but as turned she saw a single figure standing in the open gate to the nursery. He was a large man with a bushy beard and a broad, muscular frame—she had seen him only in passing upon the arrival of Adam and Becky earlier.

His eyes were wide and wet with unshed tears, and his mouth hung open. "Yors... No, *I*... I thought you were dead," he said.

Before she could ask him what he was going on about, she heard Adam call out, "Becky, no!"

¤~¤~¤

Becky ran around the edge of Adam's intercession. She knew he would have to keep up the effect and that, even with Embrew's help, it was too important to keep Ehbor out of reach from Hyrak. He couldn't stop her.

She also knew she had promised Steven that she wouldn't do anything stupid, but that wasn't an option right now. JC was as close to her as he had been since leaping down from the dragon's back a few minutes ago, and he was fighting two warriors of Goldvast at the same time. He moved with power and grace, not the frantic energy that she knew so well. He didn't see her, and she whipped a quick working of mindshaping around her to discourage the few Ellir loyal to Hyrak that were nearby from coming after her as well.

She came within a dozen yards of JC just as he ran his swords through both of the women he was fighting. There was no mercy, no remorse—nothing recognizable in his face, or his eyes, as he slid his blades free of those two bodies and turned towards Becky.

"JC," she said, lifting her hand up as though that would stop him. "Joe. It's me. It's Becky."

"Who?" he asked. His voice was deeper. Not much, but... deeper.

Becky replied, "Your girlfriend."

JC turned his head sideways a bit and then said, "Oh." And then he lunged towards her, swords extended.

Becky dropped to the ground and rolled away, the books in her backpack gouging into her back as she tumbled. JC slashed at the ground where she had been a moment before, and then again as she came up in an awkward, off-balanced crouch.

"Stop! Stop this!" she shouted. "This isn't you, Joe!"

He swung again, and Becky knew she couldn't get out of the way in time. But then someone smashed into her, shoving her out of the way. She heard the straps on her backpack rip and then she tumbled, tangled with whoever had knocked her out of the path of Joe's downward swing. She came up from the tumble to see pages of dry, brittle paper flying through the air. He had slashed through her backpack and destroyed the books from the Archive. JC seemed to lose interest in her then, turning to engage with a pair of Ellir that, Becky assumed, answered to Ehbor.

She looked down to see that it was Todd who had saved her. "Why did you do that?" she demanded, shaking.

"I saved your ass. Get back to Adam. Now." Then he turned and retrieved his own sword from where he had dropped it when they had rolled away from JC's blow.

"We just lost everything we went to Arctos to learn," Becky said as she snatched up the one page still fluttering through the air. "And he didn't listen to me." Then she turned to stare at JC's back as he waded into the fray once more. "Of course he didn't listen to me. Why start now? Well," she raised her voice towards him, "I'm not done with you, Joseph!"

¤~¤~¤

"I need you to get that infernal wall of Gatemaker magic down," Hyrak said to Jarrek. He had returned to the white dragon's back to retrieve his equipment.

"I've no tricks left up my sleeves," Jarrek shouted. "You are the one with all of the contingency plans."

"Do this for me, and I free you. If that intercession comes down, you will be released from service to me, and you will have your final revenge on Embrew. The wall separates you from your vengeance as surely as it separates me from the last dragon." Hyrak turned, made a sharp gesture, and then jumped from Ahmur's back, carrying the bag that held his secret contraption, only to land with grace upon Chron's. "I will even loan you the dragon."

Jarrek crawled forward onto the proper seat of the saddle and nudged Ahmur to turn from her position attempting to flame-char the enemy back towards Embrew.

It was finally time for the Gar to pay for his crimes.

¤~¤~¤

Embrew felt the dragon turn and charge towards the intercession with his mystic senses, and he leaned hard upon his staff as he braced himself for the strain this would place upon the working. "Adam, hold fast," he said.

Beside him, the young Gatemaker was doing amazing work. In the absence of proper training for so long, his style and his techniques had evolved differently than Embrew was familiar with, but there was no denying the raw power at his disposal. On a typical day, Adam would likely be able to hold this intercession in place himself against even something as powerful as a dragon. But this was no typical day.

He could sense the fractures in will, in confidence, and in strength at play in Adam's half of the working. Gar magic was a heavy burden, and it was not meant to be wielded as a weapon, or even properly as a defense. It was traveling magic, meant for grand gestures at infrequent times, but Adam's companions had clearly come to rely upon him for it.

And Embrew's own strength, even unfettered at long last from the shackles that had bound him for nearly twenty years, was but a shadow of its former might.

The dragon, with Jarrek upon its back, charged headlong into the field of the intercession, leaping up and taking flight. Each beat of its wings was powerful enough to carry it hundreds and hundreds of yards, but to all outside observers it appeared to hang in mid-air, not advancing. But the strain on the working as it attempted to stretch the distance before the dragon and compensate for its rate of travel was immense.

Behind them, the dragon-god of the Ellir roared, "I need no humans to protect me!"

"Embrew," Adam muttered, "why is this so hard?"

"Dragons are creatures of magic—fluid and enduring at the same time," Embrew found himself suddenly at a loss for breath. "We can't hold much longer."

"Then drop it now!" Ehbor roared, unleashing a fiery blast.

Both Adam and Embrew grunted. Now the magic was adapting to intrusion from both sides. It was only a matter of time. "Run, Adam!" Embrew said. With a sigh of relief, he dropped his half of the working, and

Adam did the same. Adam scrambled off to the left, and Embrew to the right, towards the nursery gate, where Tyrick, Sky, Plyssa, Steven, and the Jov that had traveled with Adam were gathered, watching the carnage beyond unfold.

The two dragons collided in a tangled mass of writhing, snarling claws and teeth, but before Embrew could properly assess the scene, he was struck across the jaw by a powerful fist.

Jarrek had jumped down from the dragon's back and stood over Embrew now, seething.

"I thought I had you on the beach that day," Jarrek shouted. "But you had the audacity to live!"

Embrew said nothing, and Jarrek punched him again.

"How many of my people died on this cursed world after your kind abandoned us here?" Jarrek demanded.

Again, Embrew remained silent. He could no longer sense anything happening more than a few feet away—he was close to blacking out. Blood ran freely from his nose and from cuts along his cheekbones.

"I will end you at last! For all those lost!" Jarrek brought both hands overhead and clasped them together, ready to bring a hammer-like blow down upon Embrew's frail body—and Embrew could not bring himself to stop it. He lacked the strength, but also the drive. Everything Jarrek believed was true. It was telling, he mused in those moments, how this sin that meant so much to Jarrek was amongst Embrew's lesser ones.

But the blow never came. Someone had intercepted the blow, catching the large smith's hands in their own. Embrew's magic probed the dimensions of his savior and discerned it to be Sky.

"No," Sky said, grunting as he struggled to hold Jarrek's cupped fist overhead.

"Out of my way, boy!" Jarrek shrieked.

"Not us," Sky insisted.

"What are you going on about?" Jarrek shouted.

"Not us," Sky repeated.

"Not who?" Jarrek asked, his voice calming even as he continued to struggle to overpower Sky.

The younger smith replied, "Jov. Har... Harmony." Sky said, stammering over the longer word.

Embrew sensed a change come over Jarrek—a tension that he had always, always known to be there, through more than a year in captivity together, vanished. Then he felt a displacement of space as a thin, sharp object suddenly emerged from inside Jarrek's chest.

Embrew pushed his range of sensing out just enough to see that another figure had crept up behind Jarrek—Tyrick. It was Tyrick's long-bladed hunting knife that now protruded from Jarrek's chest.

Blood bubbling from his mouth, the elder smith collapsed to the ground, and Sky fell upon him, holding him tight.

"I... I thought he was about to kill you both," Tyrick explained.

Sky looked up at Tyrick, but Embrew's senses could not tell what expression those eyes must have conveyed.

¤~¤~¤

Becky tried to wait until Joe was being beaten by one of his Ellir opponents, but that never happened. This new personality that Hyrak had inflicted upon him was tireless and skilled, and it seemed there was little that could stop him. All around her, things were starting to calm down. Most of the Ellir Hyrak had brought with him were down or dead, even though that action had come at great price to the Ellir belonging to Ehbor and the warriors of Goldvast that fought harder and with more skill than any warrior Becky had seen on five different worlds.

Hyrak, astride Chron, had taken to the air to firebomb the area, though Adam, Embrew, and Steven were doing their parts to get people to safety, even evacuating the wounded inside the nursery.

Ehbor and Ahmur still fought. She thought she caught stray thoughts of Yors and the female Metalbreaker, Plyssa, bending towards trying to break the bells around Ahmur and Chron's necks once more, but that didn't seem to be working—neither could focus on the task as emotions surged inside of them. Todd and Mathias were... she didn't know. She'd lost sight of them, and she couldn't help but feel angry with Todd for allowing her pack and the books from the Archive to be destroyed.

Becky brought her attention back to JC. She saw the trail of blood and death that he left as he carved his way across the battlefield, and she knew that, free of this enchantment and free of his chain, he would never forgive himself for his part in this. But he couldn't experience that guilt until she freed him, and this was her chance.

He dispatched his Ellir foe and turned to find his next opponent. As he saw Becky, she made eye contact with him and dove into his mind. It wasn't his mind, not exactly—it was foreign and strange, familiar enough to seem right but filled with contradictions and false impressions.

She tried to rummage through his mind, to access the memories and thoughts of the real Joe, but the padlock Hyrak had affixed to the chain blocked all of it—it was a wall she could not break or scale. But she was here, inside this not-Joe, and it was her best chance at reasoning with him. She summoned his mind to her, bringing him into the formless black non-space where they could converse without interruption at the speed of thought.

But he said nothing. He thought nothing. He was not a complete person—he was instincts and obedience and power and skill, but he was a shadow. A fragment.

There was no reasoning with him, she saw. He was more automaton than man, right now, and it broke her heart to see him so.

"Joe, I love you. I know I haven't always shown you that—I haven't even always known it. But I know now, more than anything, how true that is. I love the boy you have always been, and the man you have become. I love your compassion and your joy. I love that you never, ever stop doing what you believe in. I love the courage you show, every day."

"It's that courage I need now, Joe. I need you to show it to me once more. I need you to be brave and strong, like I know you are, and I need you to fight past this thing that has been done to you. The padlock works on the collar, Joe, but the collar only works while you let it. Yors told me you had only one link left, and that the link was yours to break. Break it, Joe. Break it now. Break it for me. For you. I know you can do it. I believe in you. I always have. I... I always will."

Becky slipped out of his mind and back into her body just in time to see JC pause. She thought, just for a moment, that she might have done it.

Then all hell broke loose.

¤~¤~¤

Ahmur tore away from Ehbor with a sudden, furious beating of her now-tattered wings, and as she scrambled away, Hyrak and Chron dove from the air.

Yors watched it happen. Everything that was unfolding all around them was happening in slow motion as he looked upon this woman, Plyssa, and saw his wife's eyes. His own chin. His daughter was alive, and standing before him, and that brought him back to center, to harmony—but it dulled him as well. It swallowed his heart as much as it set it to racing. She... she recognized him, on some instinctive level. They had said little since making eye contact—in the twenty minutes that the battle had raged all around them, they had simply existed alongside each other... for the first time in almost thirty years.

But Hyrak could not be allowed to win. Yors tore himself away from beside Plyssa and ran towards where Chron and Hyrak plunged towards the wounded Ehbor. Just before Chron struck Ehbor, Yors skidded to a halt and slammed the sapphire hammer of Arctos into the ground. A powerful ramming column of stone burst from the earth, colliding with the downward rushing Chron and sending the dragon reeling back, dazed.

But Hyrak threw himself clear of the dragon even as it rebounded from the blow, and as he tumbled through the air, the warlord lashed out one hand—exactly as he had done before. The whipcord of steel wire snapped out and struck Ehbor, spiraling around the black dragon's neck and then fusing with itself. The bell was in place.

Plyssa ran to Yors' side and pointed both hands towards Ehbor and the bell. "I can destroy it!" she said, grunting.

"No," Yors said, knocking her hands down. "That worse than Hyrak controlling them."

"How can it be worse?" Plyssa demanded.

"Red metal changes mind. Break it too fast, mind breaks too. Evil dragon not as bad as insane dragon," Yors said.

All around them, in the instant of Ehbor's capture, the battle turned. Every Ellir that had, moments ago, fought at their side suddenly turned, in tandem, towards the gates of the nursery.

"Retreat!" Adam shouted from the field of battle. Yors had seen the Gatemaker go out there, protecting their allies from Chron's fiery breath. Now he saw Adam creating a gate of red light to carry them away—to run, like cowards.

The other Gatemaker must have been doing the same thing, because a similar light was radiating from inside the nursery entrance.

Yors grabbed Plyssa by the hand and charged towards Adam's gate. As they ran, he saw Becky shouting at JC to stop—but he was running towards Hyrak and his assembled trio of dragons.

Without a word, Yors scooped Becky up, kicking and screaming with anger, and charged into the portal right behind Adam. His only comfort was that his daughter was right behind him.

¤~¤~¤

Adam and Embrew's escape route had been hastily planned, but they emerged from their crossgates far enough away from the field of battle that they would be unseen without being too far away to see what was going on.

The wounded had been left behind. Embrew and Adam, Becky and Steven, Yors and Plyssa, Sky and Tyrick, Mathias and Todd were all here, none in good shape. All of them looked how Adam felt—defeated.

"What will he do next?" Mathias asked. "He has a world in permanent darkness, an army of relentless killing machines, three dragons, and whatever resources the men of Greendeep and the women of Goldvast will give him out of loyalty to their gods."

"He won," Steven said. "Won't that be enough?"

"No. Look," Adam said, pointing.

Hyrak and his forces had begun a march towards the west.

Becky, nearly shaking with anger, said, "He's mindshaping—sending out thoughts and commands. I can hear them. I... I think he knows that. He doesn't care."

"Well?" Todd prompted.

"He's directing Ehbor to call the Ellir. Not all of them, but most of them. And he has Chron and Ahmur sending word to their people. You were right,

Mathias. He's counting on most people to do exactly what the dragons tell them to." Becky relayed.

"And they will," Tyrick said. "To defy the dragon-god is unthinkable."

"It's not as hard as you might think," Mathias muttered.

"Wait—he's doing something else. Here—let me show you..." Becky said. She made a few gestures with her hands and then Adam felt a simple, temporary bond connect all of them in one dark thoughtspace—illuminated by a large rectangular projection, like a movie theater screen, that Becky willed into existence. "I grabbed the senses of one of the Ellir. We're seeing and hearing what it does."

The destination of Hyrak's march was clear from this vantage point—they were approaching the Spiralgate.

"Please tell me he isn't also a Gatemaker," Adam muttered.

"No," Embrew said. "He lacks that power—and no Bindmetal can be enchanted to open a Spiralgate."

Yors nodded his agreement.

Hyrak approached the stone platform upon which the Spiralgate was erected. The warlord carried the large sack that had been with him, or slung across one dragon or another's back, throughout the battle. He set the bag down on the ground and opened its drawstring, pushing it down to reveal its contents.

Inside was a shining white steel device, shaped like a large egg, perhaps the size of a toddler in a car seat. It was studded with small glass nodules that blinked intermittently.

"Is that a Node?" Adam asked incredulously.

"Where the hell did he get a Node?" Becky demanded. "How does he even know what a Node is?"

Hyrak knelt down and tapped the top of the device. The pattern of blinking lights increased considerably, and then a voice issued forth from the machine, saying, "Uu2.0 ready to assist you, citizen Hyrak."

Hyrak, a rare trace of warmth in his voice, replied, "Uu, run my wave acceleration experiment. Input coordinates from con-x memory."

Becky scowled. "Uu is the name of Gallan's brother's Node. The one she made the Obliviator out of. That's... Son of a bitch. Hyrak is Gallan's brother?"

"The one who figured out how to open a Spiralgate with a Node," Todd said. "But they had no control over where they opened it. Gallan only got us home by opening the gate with the coordinates you gave her, Adam—right?"

Embrew hung his head low. "He has a geometric key to Onus. I... I gave it to him. I didn't realize it, at the time."

"He's going back to Onus to finish what he started," Becky said.

The Spiralgate slowly started to spin and twist, glowing brilliantly as it accelerated. A few moments later, sparks began to shoot from Hyrak's Node.

"Citizen Hyrak, this unit is failing. This unit's Node material core is impure. Error. Apologies," the module said in its melodic voice.

Hyrak patted the device gently. "I know, my friend. A little dragon's blood and my con-x clip was never a permanent solution."

"He can't open it again!" Adam said exultantly. "And if he doesn't move fast, he won't get anyone through it before the Node crashes and the gate closes!"

Then Hyrak started walking towards the Spiralgate. He reached to his belt and pulled out a tightly rolled bundle of leather. As he walked, he untied the strip of leather that held the roll closed and slipped something out from inside it—a small violet Bindmetal key.

Hyrak walked right up to the threshold of the Spiralgate transit corridor and then casually tossed the key into the blue-white sphere of light.

Adam felt the entire world groan and twist, and he collapsed to the ground, his body wracked by dry heaves. Todd was immediately there to help him, but Adam noticed that Embrew was experiencing the same effect.

"What the hell is happening?" Becky demanded.

"Space," Adam said. "He just broke space."

"That's incredibly vague," Steven said.

Embrew struggled to his feet, with Sky's help, and explained, "Hyrak just made that Spiralgate connection permanent. The Weigar Gate on Murrod and the Rosgar gate on Onus are now connected, forever—open perpetually. The fabric of the Spiral of Worlds was just ripped apart and sewn back together by a madman."

"A madman with an entire world's resources at his command, now," Steven said.

# 36
## Onus

*While the rock monster bowed before Grell, Jara crept closer to him.* She could feel the strange force that muted her powers giving way, like a curtain torn away to reveal the light. When she stood next to Grell, as he held his hands against the creature's head, she whispered, "Tell me what you see."

Grell began to speak in a quiet, distant tone, and Jara could feel the truth of the words as surely as she could feel the stone beneath her feet.

"My mother defied the Council, as I knew she had. They ordered her to destroy a prison full of the Council's enemies, and she refused. But they threatened the lives of her family, and so she finally relented. They brought her to this place, this juncture, and she..." Grell licked at his lips. "She worked her magic upon the very bones of the world. With this."

Grell lifted his hands upward, not releasing his grip on the fire opal head of the creature, and the head separated from the stone body, sliding easily free. As it detached, a shining rod of orange metal—a handle—emerged from within the creature's body. Its head was a giant hammer.

"They forced her to sink the prison, on an island in the Silent Sea. But she did not—she was no murderer. She hid it away, instead—burying the inmates alive on the floor of the sea." Grell shifted the hammer, taking its handle in one hand and then tapping it upon the creature's headless body. Soundlessly, it dissolved into a pile of dark sand.

Some of the children whimpered nearby, and Jara looked at them. "What was the monster?"

"She left it to keep the hammer out of the wrong hands. But she crafted it as she was dying, and her thoughts were of me—of her child. It cares for children as she did. And it hates the tools of the Council as she did." Grell looked down at Jara. "She believed she was saving the people in that prison. She believed they were worth saving and worth sacrificing her life for."

"I think they were," Jara said. The faintest impressions of destiny were starting to swirl around her, but truthfully she spoke solely from a hunch. "What will you do now?"

"I had planned to use the power of this juncture to destroy the remaining cities of the Council," Grell said solemnly.

Jara stared at him in horror. She had, for the briefest moment, forgotten who this man was and what he was capable of. But Igar Holc was gone because of him—thousands of people were dead.

"But perhaps that is not the way," Grell said. "When I felt the imprint of my mother's magic in this hammer, it brought me clarity. I do not hunger for vengeance. But I am not finished with my quest."

"To make the Council pay for your mother's death?" Jara asked. "Haven't enough people paid with their lives already?"

"Yes," Grell said. "I thought to punish everyone for the sins of a select few. Now I see how I can punish only those who deserve retribution. I will release the prisoners that my mother saved. I will bring them before the people of Onus and reveal to all the dark deeds of their nobility."

"That's surprisingly reasonable," Jara said. "But they will want to make you pay for what you have done, too. I lost friends in Igar Holc."

Grell looked down at Jara and said sternly, "I fear I have not shed the last innocent blood required to make this right. But I will try to avoid doing so unnecessarily"

"Thank you," Jara said.

"It is not for you," Grell said as he swung the hammer up and laid it over his shoulder. "I fear I have dishonored my mother. That was never my intent, but she... she was a better person than I am."

He gestured towards the children with his free hand. "Gather them up. I will get you safely back to Ain Holc before I make my way to the sea."

Jara looked at the pirate incredulously. "Why?"

"Someone must tell the Council the tale of my Purpose. It wouldn't be much of an adventure to unleash the truth of their sins if they didn't try to stop me."

¤~¤~¤

It was daylight on Onus when Hyrak's army marched through the Rosgar Spiralgate on the shores of the Silent Sea. It had been nearly a year and a half since Hyrak had last set foot upon the soil of Onus, and he had missed it. On Rettik he had been an unappreciated scientist, but it had been here on Onus that he had cultivated the reputation, and the skills, that made him the master of Murrod and, soon, this world as well.

It took only a few minutes for his Ellir to lay waste to the disorganized camp of brigands that had made their home in the shadow of the gate. He even recognized some of them as soldiers once part of his army, but they had thrown their lot in with new leadership, and Hyrak had no need for disloyal, fickle men. He commanded the Ellir now.

As soon as the battle was finished, he ordered the forces to march up the coast, snaking northward towards his former stronghold at Hyrak Arn. He was certain that some fool had claimed it by now, but he would make short work of whoever had dared take a seat upon his throne.

He watched as eight hundred Ellir marched in orderly rows up the coast. They were obedient and loyal while the sun burned in the sky, which was perfect for marching them into position. Their master was now Hyrak—Ehbor's will had been subverted and was unable to reach through the Spiralgate anyway.

The Ellir that remained active on Murrod, along with the dragons, were rounding up able-bodied soldiers from amongst the citizens of Goldvast and Greendeep and moving them towards the Spiralgate. Hyrak would need to marshal his own forces, raising once more the black and red banner that had once waved over his mighty legions, to establish a stronghold here at the permanent gate to Murrod.

He was disappointed that Jarrek was lost to him, but not surprised—the smith had exhausted his utility either way. Onus had other wonders to offer, and Bindmetal was only one means to Hyrak's end.

He looked to his left and saw that JC stood at attention there, unmoving. This was now the closest thing he had to a lieutenant. The boy was loyal and fierce—programed as such by Jarrek's final act of Bindmetal smithing. He would make a fine agent for Hyrak.

"Come," he instructed the boy. With JC walking a half step behind him, Hyrak marched behind his army, breathing in the sea air.

He had lost too much time on Murrod. He had much to make up for, if everything was to be ready for the arrival of his benefactors.

¤~¤~¤

It was three days after Hyrak's victory at the nursery when a swirling portal of blue-white light materialized in the market square of Ain Holc. Adam watched the structure of the portal carefully from the inside as Embrew ushered everyone out into the city. Adam was the last to exit, and Embrew closed it behind him.

"I'm not sure I can do that," Adam said. He had watched Embrew build the chaingate, routing a Spiralgate from Murrod (the same one Adam had once used to evacuate the Jovs) to the Ebugar Spiralgate on Onus and then seamlessly transitioning the travelers into a crossgate. It was a technique unique to Embrew, as he understood it, and Adam desperately wanted to know how to do it. But learning it would not be easy.

The group that had returned to Onus was much smaller than the one that had tried to stop Hyrak at the nursery. Adam, Todd, Becky, Steven, and Embrew were the only ones here. Mathias, Sky, and Tyrick had stayed behind to do what they could to protect the people of Murrod from their new Hyrak-controlled overlords. Yors had stayed behind with Plyssa, eager to get to know his daughter after decades apart.

"I was starting to think you'd never show up," a voice said from behind them. Adam turned to see Jara standing there, arms crossed.

Adam replied, "We got caught up in some things."

Jara approached and examined each of them in turn, her face grimly serious, until she came to Embrew. She hugged Embrew briefly and Adam heard her whisper, "Welcome home."

When she came to Becky she reached out and took one of Becky's hands in her own. "I know," she said. "I saw what happened. I'm sorry. But... it isn't over yet. There's still hope."

Becky nodded, then said, "That's what I was hoping you would say. That's why I have an announcement. Adam, Steven, Todd—you can go home if you want to. I know that people there are worried, that everyone has lives to get back to, whatever—but I am staying here. I am not going home without Joe. Period. Not while there's still hope of getting him back."

Steven's mouth hung open slightly. "You actually think we would leave without him?"

Adam scowled. "He's one of us, Becky. We're not leaving him in Hyrak's hands. No way. Home... home will have to wait. That's all there is to it."

"I'm glad you all feel that way," Jara said. "We don't have much time. We're evacuating as many people as possible to Stes Holc. The Council is attempting to convene there—those of them that are not trapped north of the Storm Wall—and that will be where we coordinate the defense of the South."

"What? Why?" Adam asked. "There's still time to gather forces here and at Rura Holc."

Jara shook her head. "I've seen it already—Hyrak attacks Rura Holc tonight. I can't foresee a way of stopping him from taking the city. Ain Holc will be next—we're just too close to Hyrak Arn. We're easy targets. My family has already left for Stes Holc. We should follow. Now."

"He's only been here for three days," Steven muttered. "How is he moving so fast?"

"He has an army that doesn't sleep," Todd replied. "They don't get tired, they hardly eat anything—they're perfectly built for this. That bastard knows what he's doing."

¤~¤~¤

Hyrak was disappointed at the pathetic resistance Rura Holc mounted as he marched three hundred Ellir up to their low, feeble walls. His soldiers climbed the walls without ropes, scaling them with the aid of their extra arms and dropping into the city. It took some concentration from Hyrak to keep the Ellir from killing anyone needlessly, but the impressions coming to him from his forces seemed to indicate that the city was barely half full.

No banner flew over the palace of the duke—he was not home.

"They knew we were coming," Hyrak said. "They think they can run? Did they learn nothing from the last time?"

He turned to JC and said, "Instruct the Ellir to kill any children they find. If the Duke had time to organize his own escape, he should have had sufficient time to evacuate the children as well. Any that die tonight are blood upon his hands."

JC bowed and ran towards the city, where the Ellir had torn the gates from their hinges.

Hyrak sighed. During his first campaign, Rura Holc had withstood him in siege for months. They had not rebuilt in his absence, not like they should have. It was pitiful. He hoped Ain Holc would mount sterner resistance, but he doubted it. They were, somehow, aware of his plans.

"The girl," he said, remembering the young Fatewaker that Embrew had escaped with to Core, right before Lyda's attempt to murder him inside of a Spiralgate and Hyrak's subsequent bout of amnesia. "I'll deal with her soon enough."

¤~¤~¤

Grell had overstressed much of his supply of Bindmetal in getting the children from the Vale of Steam to safety at Ain Holc. That meant that he had been forced to travel much more slowly towards the eastern coast than he had expected. It was five days after his retrieval of his mother's legacy when he finally reached the sea. He had traveled stealthily to avoid many conflicts along the way—the ubiquitous brigands that plagued the southern continent were being drawn north and thus into his path of travel.

The sight of the Silent Sea filled him with both dread and hope. There was hope that he could finish what his mother had started, but also dread—a pirate's dread, born of the horror stories told of this sea. Vediri and Fendris had been given ample opportunity to explore the sea while he sought the juncture, and now it was time for them to compare notes. If they had located the sunken prison, this leg of his quest was nearly done.

He strode along the beach, watching the calm, quiet sea for some time before he worked up the nerve to set to work. He waded out a few feet into the warm water and pushed both hands down into the surf. He called slowly and surely to the Bindmetal shape of his submersible ship—a ship he had never even had the chance to name before it was pressed into service.

He could feel it—distantly—and he summoned it to him. It would take some time to make the journey, he knew, so he set about creating shelter for himself on the beach using the hammer and its newfound ability to manipulate earth and stone.

His first attempts were ugly and crude, but he was a quick study, and by the end of the day he had fashioned a sophisticated series of caverns. He had no need of such a place, but the practice both soothed his mind and passed the time.

It was nightfall when the ship arrived. It floated up to the surface silently, only alerting Grell to its presence by the gleaming of its metal skin in the light of Onus' two moons.

He approached the ship cautiously, not wanting to startle the occupants. He imagined they were both mightily perplexed at why they had suddenly lost control of the ship. He was particularly eager to see Vediri and tell her what he had learned – that all of their struggles had been worth it.

He climbed up onto the top of the vessel and tapped on the hatch. No one inside made a move to open it, so Grell worked his arts again, coaxing the locking wheel on the underside of the hatch to turn until it opened with a loud hiss.

Grell opened the hatch and peered down into the ship – but it was empty. Vediri and Fendris were gone.

¤~¤~¤

The accommodations in Stes Holc were nowhere near as elegant as those in Ain Holc, and the entire city smelled of livestock, but Jara found she rather enjoyed the place. They had been there for three days in a huge diplomatic complex that bordered on being described as a campground.

"Adam and Embrew are bringing in Dukes Rega and Distat," Todd said as he joined the extended family around the low table where they shared meals. Jara, Moultus, and Hessa dined tonight with Becky and Steven.

"You didn't go with Adam?" Steven asked.

"I've seen Rega before," Todd said, shrugging. "And it's probably safer to be up there rounding up Council members to discuss war plans than it is down here."

"It seems we are right back where we started," Moultus said. "A gathering of the Council to discuss turmoil in the South."

Jara did not want to talk about the war that was now upon them. Her visions of each conflict were clear and heavy, and the less they talked about what was happening, the easier she could keep them from intruding upon her every moment. Since her encounter with Grell in the Vale of Steam, her magic had been keener than ever before – even things that had been hazy and indistinct in previous visions were clearer now. There were still exceptions, of course. She could not see Todd's fate, for example – just as always.

"I haven't asked," Jara said, looking at Becky. "But did you find what you were looking for at the Archive? I know that rescuing Joseph is more important, but perhaps I could take a look?"

Becky scowled and dug into her pocket, retrieving a single crumpled piece of paper. "This is all I have left. The genius there," she pointed angrily at Todd, "let my bag with the books get torn to shreds."

Todd sighed. "Would you rather I had let *you* get torn to shreds?"

"Knock it off," Steven said. "It wasn't anyone's fault. What's done is done. Unless that page happens to be the one that had the answers on it?"

Becky handed the page to Jara. Jara laid it flat on the table and smoothed it with her hand several times, peering carefully at the Wyr symbols inscribed there in heavy ink. They unfolded before her, but revealed little. "This is the cypher index. It tells what the prophecy contains, but not its details."

"So we only managed to save the table of contents. Typical," Becky said. Exasperated, she added, "I took one flip through each of the books, and now they're gone forever."

"Are they?" Jara asked, perking up. "You saw them once—can you remember what the pages said?"

"I can't read that language," Becky replied.

"Well, do you remember what it looked like?" Jara asked.

"I guess. I mean, it's up here," Becky tapped her forehead with her index finger. "I can go in and retrieve it, sure. But I still can't read it, so what good..." Becky's eyes grew wide. "I can share the memory with you. Then you can read it!"

Jara nodded smugly.

Becky closed her eyes and her forehead furrowed with thought.

As she did so, Todd stood back up from the table. "This doesn't seem like a very good idea to me," he said. Jara thought he looked somewhat panicked.

"Just sit down," Hessa said. "There is no harm in what they are trying."

Todd shook his head and started to pace. "Adam wouldn't like this."

Becky whispered, "Got it. Here it comes."

And Jara was suddenly pulled up and out of her body, deposited in a vast black void, lit only by a faint glow issuing from her own body. A moment later, Becky was there, beside her. Becky held out one hand, and a swirl of blue light erupted from it, resolving after a moment into a series of images—memories of the pages of the two books that Becky had retrieved from Arctos.

Jara watched the language of the Wyr unfold before her, and she soaked in the contents of each book. As facts and details accumulated in her mind, she fought to keep from betraying any hint of emotion to Becky.

"I have it," Jara said. "Take me back now, please."

In a whirl of light, Jara was back in her body.

"Well?" Steven asked.

"It was hard to read," Jara said. "The originals would have been clearer."

"So there's the possibility that you read parts of it wrong?" Todd asked, stopping and placing both hands on the table, leaning in close to Jara.

"Not wrong—just incomplete. But I know the names of the remaining Children of the Line. For sure," Jara said. "Should we wait for Adam to get back?"

"No!" Becky said. "They're just names—but we fought hard to get them. Who are they?"

Jara closed her eyes and read the names from within her newly-minted memory of deciphering the texts. "Colton Taylor. Celia Walsh. Cruz Moreno," she said. She felt the weight of Purpose in those names.

"They all start with 'C'. Is that significant?" Becky asked.

"A name is a name," Steven said.

"And now we have them," Todd said, releasing a breath he had been holding since he had leaned upon the table. "I'm beat. I'll see you all in the morning." With that, he left the dining area, retreating to the tent that he shared with Adam.

"Do any of those names mean anything to you?" Becky asked Steven.

Steven shrugged. "Not really. But when we get back—after we save JC—Nathaniel will be able to find them. There's no one his connections can't turn up."

Conversation shifted into trivial topics for the rest of the meal, and before long, both Becky and Steven had excused themselves from the table. Hessa also left, kissing Jara on the forehead as she left.

"What did you hold back?" Moultus asked his granddaughter, leaning close conspiratorially.

"What do you mean?" Jara countered nervously.

Jara counted herself a fair liar, but her grandfather was not fooled. "You saw more than you are saying," Moultus whispered. "A secret shared is a lighter burden."

"Also, not much of a secret anymore," Jara argued. "But grandfather—I do need to tell someone. But I can't tell them—I can't. I don't want to be the one to bring that kind of truth into their lives."

"What is it?" Moultus asked, wrapping one arm around her.

"The Children of the Line weren't *discovered* on Core," Jara said in the quietest whisper she could manage. "They were *hidden* there. They were born here, on Onus."

¤~¤~¤

I don't think Hyrak ever sleeps. The Ellir don't, and he keeps them moving constantly—but he seems to at least accept that I still need sleep. It is only the few hours each day that he lets me rest that I can risk even thinking about what is going on.

The first thing I remember is Becky telling me "I believe in you. I always have. I always will" while dragons fought behind us. I heard those words, through the fog that had choked me out and stopped me from being me anymore—and something inside me started to fight again. I was scared—more scared than I had ever been—but her words made me brave. And when I found that courage, the last link on the collar went dead—royally screwing up Hyrak's stupid ass padlock of brainwashing. Its extra personality—whoever the hell I was for the hours that it was working—is weak now, barely working. The rest of it, how it locks my mind off from the outside, from Becky but also from Hyrak—that remains. Thank God.

So here I am, in camp with a few hundred Ellir, putting villages to the torch if they don't swear allegiance to Hyrak. Why? Why am I doing this? I only get to ask myself that question when I am alone.

When Hyrak calls me again, it will be to tell me to do something horrible. And I'll find a way to do it—I'll try as hard as I can to forget who I am for a little bit, to become who I was when that padlock was put on my collar. I'll stop being me and I'll start being *him*. Most of the time, it's easy to set that other me aside and get back to myself. It depends on how horrible things are around me. But I'll find a way.

Because if I keep playing along, I'll figure him out. I'll find out why he can't die, and I'll find out how to get around that. I'll figure out every secret this asshat has. I'm scared shitless, but I keep going. Because even if they don't know it, the others are counting on me. Becky is counting on me. Maybe every world in the whole Spiral is counting on me.

I found my frickin' Purpose. Capital P. I'm going to get in close to Hyrak, closer than anyone ever has, or ever will...

I thought my part in all of this would be over when I broke the last link of the chain around my neck, but I was wrong. I have one more thing to break. Hyrak.

My name is Joseph Christopher Stein. Please... Don't let me forget that.

## About the Author

A teacher and enthusiastic nerd, Jeremiah L. Schwennen grew up on a dairy goat farm in a small town in Iowa. After an exciting childhood and the acquisition of a hard-fought degree in English Education from Iowa State University he now finds himself happily married to an amazing man. By day Jeremiah teaches English and reading in various capacities in central Iowa, and by night he reads comic books, watches science fiction TV shows, and both writes and plays as many board and role-playing games as he possibly can.

Metalbreaker is his third novel.

Connect Online!
Visit www.spiralchain.net
Like *Spiralchain Series* on Facebook
Follow @spiralchain on Twitter

Cover design by Andrew Jason Aguirre

Print publishing by Createspace

## Acknowledgements

*Without the people listed below, this book would not be in your hands right now. Their passion for this project, faith in me and my story, and generous funding through Kickstarter made it possible to bring Metalbreaker into the world.*

**Graphic Design / Cover Art**
Andrew J. Aguirre

**Metalbreaker Advance Readers**
Justin Kolehart
Vincent O'Brien

**Kickstarter Special Mention – Extraordinary Contributors**
Jeremy and Natasha Cue
Jukibu
Markus "Mark" Bomke

**Kickstarter Backers**
Jeff Sorensen
Melissa Spencer
Jason Roth
Josh Parrish
Tyson Hood
Brian Peterson
Tara Schwennen
Joe Van Haecke
Christi Donald
Jamie Cole
Karen Brinkley
Scott O'Neil
Robert Derifield
Stacy Frelund
Shyann Bohling
Kas Kelly
Jeremy Bonefas
Swordfire
Ellen Power
Cullen Denison
Derek "Pineapple Steak" Swoyer

Made in the USA
Charleston, SC
28 January 2017